Falling Leaves and Mou

C000056822

About the

Born in South Africa, Brenda George grew up in the small mining town of Luanshya in Northern Rhodesia/Zambia with her parents and three sisters. She married Edward George there and later moved with him to Pietermaritzburg, in South Africa. They had no children and were later divorced. She has been a freelance editor, a literary agent and a teacher of novel writing. She edited the international best-selling novel, *A Man Cannot Cry*, and the three books of *The Josiah's Kingdom/Broken Wings Trilogy,* all of which were written by her sister, Gloria Keverne. The sisters share a unique writing /editing relationship, as Brenda started writing novels herself in 1982 and now devotes all of her time to this much-loved pursuit. Brenda, a prodigious researcher, has been deeply interested in American history and politics since she was a young girl and has visited the United States on several occasions, during which times she did extensive research for her novels. *Falling Leaves and Mountain Ashes*, which is the first of a five-book series. *Song of the Shenandoah* is the second.

The author: Brenda George

Falling Leaves and Mountain Ashes

The Story of a Mountain

A NOVEL

Brenda George

E-mail: brendag@mjvn.co.za

First Edition 2007

Second Edition 2010

ISBN: Softcover   978-1-4691-2511-4

Ebook   978-1-4691-2520-6

To order additional copies of this book, contact:
Xlibris Corporation
0-800-644-6988
www.Xlibrispublishing.co.uk
orders@xlibrispublishing

Xlibris Corporation (USA) Office
Toll Free: + 1-888-795-4274
Fax:1-610-9150294
orders@xlibris.com

Dedication

I dedicate this book to the following persons, precious blessings all:

*M*y blessed late mother, Dorothy Gwendoline Keverne. So sweet. So giving. Her family meant everything to her. It was a great privilege to look after her for the last four years of her life when she suffered so much in her silent world! *I miss you so much, Mommy darling! With much love and gratitude, for all you were – and are – to me. Thank you for what you taught me about unconditional love and inner strength.*

*M*y wonderful eldest sister, Barbara, who has had to carry so many heavy burdens in her life. Yet, for all her many struggles and heartache and disappointments, she remains a caring nurturer, with a ready smile and an ever-attentive ear, for loved one and stranger alike. She has such a big and generous heart, full of love! *Thank you for always being there for me, my sweet Big Sister, Barbie.*

*M*y beloved sister, Gloria, for her extraordinary writing talent! From her I learned so much of what I know about the craft of writing! I discovered, not only my ability to edit (I had the rare privilege of editing her two published novels, the major international bestseller *A Man Cannot Cry* and the *Josiah's Kingdom/ Broklen Wings Trilogy),* but to write myself. *I learned from the Master!* The consummate dreamer of Big Dreams, she gave me the belief that mine could also come true! *Thank you, darling Glory, for the riches you have bestowed upon me!*

*M*y daft and divine youngest sister, June. Dear, humorous Junie, my Sunshine Sister, who has been such a solid rock in my life, always giving sound advice and a helping hand. We've had such fun together! *May you swiftly be granted the spiritual wonders you are seeking, darling Pathfinder!*

*M*y grateful thanks go to my highly talented niece, Brigette Johnson, for all the brilliant work she did on the cover of *Falling Leaves and Mountain Ashes* and its sequel, *Song of the Shenandoah* . She may be quiet and modest, but, with the eye of the true artist, she's a genius in her work, which covers so many art forms. *You're absolutely amazing, Briggie!*

*M*arcel Talbot deserves special mention for his caring and support, and for being such a wonderful helpmate to me. A writer's dream to have around, I don't know what I'd have done without him! I thank him for his encouragement, whole-hearted support and absolute belief in my work. *Love you, Babes!!!*

And lastly:

*T*o the memory of the colorful visionary, the late George Freeman Pollock, of Skyland fame and the displaced mountain people of the Blue Ridge Mountains of Virginia, who inspired the writing of this book . . .

Extracts from Reviews ## "*Falling Leaves and Mountain Ashes*"

I am so mesmerized by your writing, your evocation of the Blue Mtn. ambiance, the unbelievable characters. I have a lot of projects at the moment but yours is so inspiring. . . the characters still stay with me. What a story. Congratulations on a terrific novel.
Stan Corwin – Hollywood literary agent, book packager, writer.

'*...Brenda George weaves an elaborate tapestry of rich, compelling characters, and a passionate story of love, courage, violence, heartache and humor. Her writing is lyrical and visual – a movie in the making! Don't miss this compelling, page-turning read!*'
Annette Handley-Chandler – ex-literary agent, Hollywood screenplay agent, Emmy Award winning producer, writer.

'Any and all readers will enjoy this manuscript ... I loved this story ... The author has an excellent way with words. It is so nice to read a manuscript where so much thought, time, and work were put into the material.'
Cynthia Sherman – Writers' Literary

'Highly detailed description promotes accessible imagery for the reader, and the inclusion of emotive historical facts sets the scene for a story told in a wild but picturesque landscape. A simple and rustic way of life is slowly revealed to the reader, reinforced by accented speech and a meticulously described lifestyle .... This story is told in a highly convincing manner, and the relationships between characters are starkly and realistically portrayed ... compelling reading, Excellent writing ...'
Editorial Committee

'In my younger years, I would read a novel that interested me nonstop until I had finished it. This hasn't happened for me for many, many years – until I started reading Brenda George's "Falling Leaves and Mountain Ashes"... The characters are indelible – so alive, so real, her background so precisely drawn that I was there, with them, where it was all happening, transported to a place and an era that was new to me, yet it was all as vivid as if I had been living in the early 1900's in the Blue Ridge Mountains...An incredible writer and great story teller . . . What a great movie this book will make!'
Felicity Keats – publisher, right-brain facilitator, writer

Beautifully constructed, this book tells the tale of the formation of the Shenandoah National Park, the mountain folk that lived there, the inter-clan feuding, the fierce family loyalties ... The descriptions of the forests take the reader out of this world and into theirs where eagles soar and leaves changed colour with the seasons.
Lesley Thomson – The Lazy Lizard Book Traders

'Brenda George brings us a riveting tale of the hardships with which the mountain folk of Virginia had to contend intermingled with the breathtaking beauty of the area ... Feuds, lawlessness, illegal trade of moonshine and more ... I guarantee that once you begin reading you will not want to put it down.'
The Zululand Observer

'Falling Leaves and Mountain Ashes ... is beautifully written and a compelling read. The reader is transported into the forests and shares the magnificent views from the mountain. It is a love story, an adventure, includes the history of the

setting up the now-famous Shenandoah National Park, the Senedo Indians and a fascinating portrayal of interesting characters'
The Meander Chronicle

"*Brenda George's novel is quite beautifully written (and reminded me of EAST OF EDEN).*
Editor, Mainstream Publisher, New York

Selected praise for "Falling Leaves and Mountain Ashes"

'I'm speechless. I've just finished reading your book and I have never read anything like it! Your choice of words! What a spectacular three-hour movie it would make!' It's just wonderful. This is the best book I have ever read.'
Dave Robertson

'I really loved this book. I've read a lot of books in black and white, but reading this one was like reading in color because of the vivid descriptions!'
Craig Short

'I couldn't put it down. I haven't enjoyed a book like that for years and years. It was beautiful, absolutely stunning. Characters just too much! I could not put the book down!' **Lorraine Herbert**

'I love this book. it's absolutely fantastic, fantastic!!...It's amazing. It is the most awesome book .Wonderful. I loved the characters...it's one I want to keep on my bookshelf forever.' **Bea Wallis**

'I am in love with the book. Totally loving it! I'm obsessed! I am even in sympathy with Eli. I read it everywhere I go.' **Vasti Downs**

'... we are blown away!! It is an amazing piece of work... Jim said it's in the league of James A Mitchener. Wow!!! What an amazing author you are – the book is riveting...' **Rosemary Schreiner**

'... thoroughly enthralled...very different background...characters were very vivid. Excellent, heartwarming, with lots of suspense. Eli was horrible, but such a sad character. I loved it. Brilliant.' **Laureen Grebe**

'I was so sorry to say goodbye to the family' **Celeste al Lamaletle.**

'I loved it, loved it, loved it! I did not want it to end! The characters came alive and I felt like I knew them all personally. Fantastic read!' **Sheena Seymour**

'Thank you for your wonderful book – It is, indeed an epic tale...made all the more poignant by knowing that it was based on fact. Your characters are so vibrant and believable and the story line is so gripping, I could not wait to pick it up again to find out what happened next. It must have been a wonderful experience to create such a rich saga, and you must have lived with those people inside your head for such a long time in order to finish writing that book! **Linda Barlow**

'I can't praise it enough. I started it on a Saturday at 1.30pm, and read it in one sitting! I just couldn't stop reading it... It was beautiful, absolutely fantastic! The characters were also absolutely fantastic. Real live characters – magnificent! I hated Eli and then later got to understand why he was the way he was, and he gained my sympathy. Have you ever read a book where you don't want it to end? I really and truly loved it. The schools should take it to learn how to write good character studies.' **Carol Claaasen**

'You are an AMAZING writer. I bought the book about a year ago, and when it was seen on the bookshelf by my friends, **Monica** *and* **Roger Ashe***, they insisted I must read it NOW, saying it is a fantastic book! I cannot put it down, but find myself wanting to go slow because I don't want it to end. The setting is so beautiful and real and the characters jump out the pages at you. We three friends discuss all the episodes and characters, and ROGER said that 'It gets even better' to which I replied, 'I don't see HOW it can get any better!' ROGER then said, "Read on then you'll know what I mean."'* **Ronel Wood**

'Your book is wonderful. I can't put it down. Your descriptions are so beautiful. And your characters are incredible...it was so beautiful, and I absolutely loved it. And the characters were incredible. She said Jed is a beautiful character .It's the best book I've ever read.' **Rita Dixon**

'I've read it three times and my friend, **Lois Watt-Pringle,** *has read it three times. It's divine, absolutely divine. The story is so good, and ended off beautifully. Loved the characters.'* **Anne Harper**
(Continued at the back)

Falling Leaves and Mountain Ashes

'Before the mountains were
Brought forth,
or ever Thou hads't Formed
the earth and the world,
From everlasting to everlasting,
Thou art God.'

The Bible Psalms 90.2

Foreword

Put your hand in the hand of this truly gifted storyteller; follow her along a poetry-paved path into the beautiful environment and dilapidated homesteads of an extraordinary lost culture that will never again be seen in Virginia's Blue Ridge Mountains. As the story unfolds, experience the tragedy, hardships, violence and strains of the mountain folk. Through Brenda George's wonderful word-pictures, eavesdrop on the intriguing lives of a rustic community of characters uniquely carved by poverty, ignorance, and raw Nature. Share their yearning hillbilly dreams, shy awkward loves and brutal dysfunctional relationships; sense their crucifying secrets and sinister demons; sweat under their toil and suffering.

As two neighbouring clans engage in a vicious feud and the mountain people ward off Nature's elements simply to survive, accompany the gentle Mary Harley on her brave spiritual quest to spread love and light into the terrifying ranks of the lawless Buckos – a tragically flawed, fractured clan. Learn of adult innocence, childlike joy and deathless love mixed with cynical cruelty, brutal domination and loveless death. Watch helplessly as uncaring bureaucracy threatens devastated mountain families. Weep with them as heroic hope is shattered by heartbreak.

This novel, charged with love over the seven long years of its writing, is based upon scrupulously researched fact over many more years. Brenda George is an immensely talented writer whose haunting work begs to be read. No one should deny themselves the experience of *Falling Leaves and Mountain Ashes*. All readers will be sorry to leave its enthralling world . . .

Glory Keverne, international bestselling author of *"A Man Cannot Cry"* and *"The Joshia's Kingdom/ Broken Wings Trilogy"*.

Prologue

*K*nown to be the most lawless region in the northern Blue Ridge Mountains of Virginia, Claw Mountain, situated in the northern highlands, was well over 4,000 feet in elevation at its tableland summit. It was forested with hardwoods and northern conifers: amongst others, chestnuts, giant white oaks, shagbark hickories, tulip poplars, birches, red oaks, beeches, yellow poplars and maples extensively hugged the slopes, with an under-story including mountain laurel, dogwood, wild hydrangea and rhododendrons, while spruces, pines, cedars, hemlocks and balsam firs loftily graced the higher regions. Unlike most of the other mountains of the range, which have crests that are narrow, Claw Mountain had a sizable 15-square-mile plateau, comparable only to Big Meadows with its rather meager five-square-mile plateau. The entire thickly forested tableland was supported by an almost impenetrable fortress of great windswept weathered gray granite boulders, interspersed with foliage, spindly fragile trees that clung precariously to tiny patches of windblown sand, and dripping vines. From it, promontories and knolls dropped steeply into an intricate network of hollows. Indeed, the whole south side of the mountain was exceedingly steep and wild, its sheer granite cliffs and escarpments entangled with vines and thick undergrowth, making it impossible to be settled. The north side of the mountain, on which the notorious Buchanan clan was settled, was only slightly more hospitable, with all valleys and streams dropping into the magnificent uninhabited Wilderness Valley below. The great sweeping valley was blissfully endowed with a scenic rocky river the mountain people called Wilson Run, and a vast unspoiled tract of primeval forest, and across from it, could be seen an unending range of rugged backbone mountains and peaks.

Majestic and forbidding, Claw Mountain branched outward from its tableland in three directions: Buck Knob Mountain, which lay to the west and went deep into the highlands of the range, stretching all the way up to The Sag, was the home of the Buchanan's bitter enemies, the Galtrey clan. The picturesque Beacon Mountain, with its high rock walls on its west-facing side, lay to the south. Bear Rock Mountain lay to the north and east. The giant, lofty "Rock," for which it was named, had once been the privileged view site of the Indians, whose gentle stewardship of the mountains had lasted for 12,000 years. Wildlife had abounded then – wolves roved in packs, and there were elk and mountain lion, while great herds of buffalo grazed in the lush bluegrass valley below.

Once, a war-party Indian trace had run along the topmost peaks of the Blue Ridge, affording them an unrestricted view of the Shenandoah Valley below, while a second peacetime trace ran the entire length of the valley, leading to the great Indian winter hunting grounds of the two Carolinas and Georgia. The Shenandoah Valley beyond the Blue Ridge, known to the Indians as "Valley of the Daughter of the Stars", was a well-traversed migratory trail and a hunting-ground stopover for all the major Indian tribes, including the fierce and warlike Iroquois, from Canada to Georgia, who wished to escape the bitter winter snows of upstate New York and Canada. There were many tribes resident in the valley that shared the same hunting grounds: the Delawares, the Tupelo, the Tuscaroras, the Piscataways, the Shawnees, the Mohicans, the Catawbas – and a little-known ancient tribe, the Senedoes. Though the tribes were mainly peaceable, the valley trace had been the scene of some bloody intertribal battles.

Hugely decimated by British guns, introduced diseases like smallpox, and internal wars, the Indians were finally driven out of Virginia by the devastating French and Indian Wars of 1754-1763, after they had forged an alliance with the French to permanently drive out from the Shenandoah Valley, their land-pillaging common enemies, the British and Dutch, whose settlers had driven the Redman's game from the Shenandoah Valley, and forced the Indians themselves into the mountains, away from their ancestral hunting grounds.

The last remaining Indians pulled out of the "Great Mountains" after the arrival of feisty frontiersmen, who had by now acquired fighting skills similar to those of the Indians. So now it was the turn of the hardy folk who had settled in the mountains to stand on the "Rock" and wallow in the breathtaking views of the Wilderness Valley below. These folk had turned to the Indian crafts of trapping, hunting, gathering and home crafts to survive, but isolation often caused them to become a law unto themselves. Drinking 100-proof moonshine whiskey and toting guns and knives had become a way of life, even for young children, often resulting in fights, feuds and killings.

In some of the more remote hollows, steeped in ignorance and superstition, mountain men taught their boys to shoot when they were as young as six and still in knee breeches. Killing was even considered a boy's rite of passage into adulthood, providing them with much diversion, excitement and entertainment. Those without guns or knives resorted to throwing jagged, skull-crushing rocks, which often lethal sport was known as "rocking". Alas, killing had become a nasty habit of generations. Few murders were reported to the authorities, however. Feeling themselves to be outside the law, they had their own kind of rough "frontier" justice.

Unfortunately, unlike the Indians, who lived in harmony with their fellow earth creatures, killing only what they needed to ensure their survival, by the end of the 18th century, the large-scale market hunting and trapping of the mountaineers had a powerful impact on the wildlife. The buffalo, once so important to the Indians, had long ago been slaughtered to a point of near extinction by the settlers, and by the army as a measure to deny the native inhabitants a major source of food and warmth. Wolves, elk, and mountain lion also had been eradicated, the bear population, badly decimated, and many lesser creatures, endangered. Indeed a bounty had been placed on wolves by the white authorities, which was received when the head of a wolf was presented. As a result, there were hundreds of wolf-killers out in the wilds, some using muskets, and others using cruel metal traps to destroy these mighty, but ferocious, beasts (which were greatly feared by the white settlers). Sadly, many thousands of wolf heads were presented to county officers, each one of them in return for a single "wolf's note", a paper note with a wolf's head on it. A wolf's note was not worth much, but could be used to exchange for goods at trading posts, which encouraged the wolf-killers to kill large numbers of the predatory canines.

Claw Mountain had acquired its name from a strange land formation jutting out from the tableland on its north side, which provided the only access to the plateau. This seeming aberration of Nature was shaped like a giant eagle's claw, being curved in a huge wide loop at its outer protuberance, while a half-mile strip of land connected it to the tableland. It was aptly known as Eagle Spur, for besides its uniquely claw-like shape, a great many eagles could always be seen circling the skies above it. Sometimes these soaring sentinels would swoop down on those who dared to tackle the arduous climb to the top with loud, angry cries and outstretched talons. Some said they were just protecting their nests, while others whispered that they seemed to have assumed a strange guardianship role of the mist-hugging, mysterious plateau, already fortressed by an almost impenetrable granite face and a plethora of giant boulders . . .

Falling Leaves and Mountain Ashes

Book I

'From the Blessed to the Damned'

'Alas, innocence knows not
The evil that exists upon
The glorious mountain
Slopes ...'

Brenda George

1

July, 1899

Eighteen-year-old Mary Harley woke up with a start as she lay on her pallet in the loft. Outside, a rooster's strident crowing jarred against the more melodious twitters and chatters of scores of awakening wild birds. She could hear quails calling 'Bob-white, Bob-white' and the pecking of a pileated woodpecker on the tree right outside the cabin.

Although it was early still, the rising mid-summer sun had pierced the gray dawn and sent insidious little shafts of light through tiny cracks and holes in the shingles, dazzling their crude beds and the floorboards with fine intricate designs. The wooden rafters of the roof sloped upwards to a peak in the middle, further confining the limited space where she and her three sisters slept. The trapdoor was open to allow some air to circulate in the cloistered atmosphere, and she could hear her mother already moving about downstairs, and water boiling on the wood-burning stove below for the daily breakfast fare of corn meal mush. A few minutes later came the distinctive sound of her grinding the coffee beans, the fulsome, tantalizing aroma of which wafted up through the floor-opening.

Mary, lying on her straw-tick pallet in her thin sleeveless cotton nightgown, felt a stirring of excitement when she remembered what day it was. She sat bolt upright, pushing aside the colorful goose-feather tick blanket that her mother had made her. She looked over at the rag-covered blonde heads of her younger sisters, Laura and Nellie, who were aged fifteen and fourteen respectively. They were still snuggled up in deep slumber on the pallets opposite her. Even in the gloom, she could see the perspiration gleaming on their faces and dampening their hair.

"Laura! Nellie!" she whispered, so as not to awaken sixteen-year-old Lona, who was also still fast asleep. Poor Lona wouldn't be going to the store today. "Time to rise and shine!"

Her two youngest sisters stirred on their pillows, moaning a little before stretching languidly and rubbing their sleepy eyes. But remembrance of what day it was soon took hold, and opening their eyes wide, they sat up, smiling and wrinkling their noses at her. After all, going to the store was a special occasion and one they all looked forward to!

Mary got up and lifted the top of a decrepit old suitcase stored in one corner. It didn't contain much, just her three dresses, one for special occasions, and the other two for everyday use, and two pairs of bloomers. There was also a pair of shoes near the bottom, but, of course, she only wore those in winter when it was too cold to walk around barefoot like God intended.

She carefully drew out her best dress, which she had pressed last night with a heavy, heated coal-iron. She always wore it to the store, to corn-huskings (such enjoyable occasions, especially for the men folk – if they found a red ear they were rewarded with a swig of brandy), and to apple-boiling parties, and whenever Reverend Hubbly, the circuit-preacher, came around to give one of his rare, intermittent services. Maw was particular about cleanliness, and Mary had taken her monthly bath in the big washtub in front of the fire just yesterday afternoon.

Laura and Nellie scrambled out of their thin bedding, and lifted the lid off an old box crate in which they kept their few clothes. The three of them chattered excitedly in subdued tones, as they quickly dressed. Though they tried hard to contain their youthful enthusiasm, their giggles soon succeeded in waking up Lona, as they removed the white rag-strips from each other's hair. Mary never bothered to put rags in her hair. It was straight and heavy and black as a Red Indian's, and simply refused to take a curl. Lona opened her eyes and slowly sat up, watching them with a sulky little pout on her pretty heart-shaped face, her blonde hair too, a mess of white rags, despite the fact that she wasn't going anywhere.

Mary couldn't help feeling sorry for her. It was awful to be the *only* girl to be left behind. Usually, Paw allowed two of his girls to accompany him to the store to collect provisions, but last night he had felt in a generous mood because his harvest for "due bills" of exchange at the store was particularly bountiful. Of course, both she and Lona had clamored to be the extra "chosen" one, but Paw said that in all fairness, it had to be the next one on Maw's "store-cloth" list. It had soon been discovered after a frantic racing to get the cloth which Maw kept in a chest in a corner, that Mary would be the lucky one allowed to accompany her father and two youngest sisters to the store.

There often used to be a squabble amongst the girls about whose turn it was to go, since, depending on the state of Paw's pocket (which admittedly was usually somewhat strained), he could sometimes be prevailed upon to buy little play-pretties like hair-grips and ribbons. It got so bad that Maw started keeping a record of whose turn it was to go. Like most mountain women, she couldn't write, but was most accomplished with her needle, so she sewed different colors of embroidery cotton onto a special cloth each time they went, each child being represented by a different color.

Fortunately, Maw was quite content to stay home to cope with the extra load. Indeed, she had already done the milking today, a chore assigned to the girls on a weekly rotational basis (it was considered "womanish" for a male to milk a cow, so Paw, Joe and Percy were excused this chore). And Joe, who had taken over the responsibility of running the small farm since Paw's accident at the mill, considered visits to the store a waste of valuable time, since Paw had a habit of making a social occasion out of it. Paw had been forced to retire from the Elderberry Hope Logging Camp a few years ago, after a pile of logs had become dislodged and rolled down onto him, crushing his one leg, so that he now walked with a severe limp. The loss of his job at the logging camp had hit the family hard for it was robbed of a cash income. The privileged outings were usually sneered at by young Percy, too, for though he would normally do anything to get out of doing his chores, he was simply too lazy to walk that far. So providing he got his supply of gumballs at the end of it all, he was happy to give it a miss.

Mary knew that though they would not admit it, the main reason her sisters fought so hard to go to the store, was that other than at the brush tabernacle and at apple-butter boilings, which were always heavily chaperoned, it was the only place they could catch a glimpse of not only mountain boys who lived in other hollows, but of valley boys too. They were at an age when boys were on their minds a whole lot! Never was this more obvious than when they attended apple-butter boilings. The custom was that a couple would stir the apple butter in a huge kettle. If the paddle accidentally touched the side, the girl would get a kiss. Well, all she knew was that her sisters were awful good at getting the paddle to touch the side.

Lona sat cross-legged on her straw-tick pallet, her elbows planted on her slim knees and her hands cupping her frowning face, with her cotton nightgown ridden up to her pale thighs, looking so downcast, Mary felt tempted to say that she could go to the store in her place. But visits to the store were rare because of the time and distance involved, and generally only undertaken two or three times a year, and her own eagerness to accompany Paw soon overcame her noble impulse.

She gave her sister a wan apologetic smile as she pulled a hasty brush through her waist-long hair, vowing to herself that she would make it up to her by asking her father to bring her back something extra special from the store. She climbed down the ladder to the darkened room below, closely followed by Laura, and then Nellie. Such was Laura's eagerness that one of her tough bare feet caught Mary's fingers on a rung, squashing them.

"*Ouch!*" Mary complained, barely having time to move out of the way before Laura landed on the wooden floor beside her. Nellie was in even more of a hurry. When she was only halfway down, she turned on the ladder and jumped down, landing heavily on the floor boards, on bare feet with a loud ungainly thump, her calf-length skirt billowing up around her like a balloon being blown up. At fourteen, there was still a lot of the child in her.

A single candle kerosene lamp burned on the mantel, but it was turned down low and so did not give off much light, but the sunshine struggled valiantly through a window on one side. Though most of it went up the black metal chimney, smoke from the wood-burner was visible in the air. The smell of it was acrid and stung their eyes. Their blonde-haired mother was busy cooking breakfast, but she turned and smiled tenderly at each of them as they went up to kiss her cheek.

Paw sat at the head of the long wooden table, which just yesterday had been laid out with thousands of dried beans, so that they could separate the white ones from the others. Paw was small of stature, had a full head of curly dark hair, and brown beady eyes that were full of humor and warmth. Despite the constant pain he suffered from his leg, nothing dampened the spirits of William H. Harley for very long. His three arisen daughters lined up to hug him in turn, before taking their seats. Laura compensated for her earlier lack of decorum by taking her seat in a most ladylike manner. Paw beamed at his daughter's paradoxical ways as he did her childlike impatience.

"Jest as soon as we're a'finished eatin', we kin be on our way," he informed his daughters, who nodded eagerly.

Just then the front door opened and in came Joe and Percy, who slept in a small shack that had been built onto the main four-room cabin. Lanky and loose-limbed with adolescence, Joe was a year older than Mary, and a good-looking boy, with a short forehead and solemn brown eyes, topped by heavy black eyebrows. He was dressed in his work clothes, but eight-year-old Percy wore his long white nightgown, his mouth still pursed with the fierce heavy stupor of sleep, his dark hair unruly and dark freckles spread over his cheeks and nose like a rug of peppercorns.

Lona, too, had put on her work clothes and come slowly down the stepladder from the loft. She took her place at the table next to Paw with a heavy exaggerated sigh, sitting with her head lowered. But if she was hoping that Paw would relent and allow her to come too, she was soon to be disappointed. Instead of the sympathy she hoped to achieve with her martyred demeanor, he roared with laughter and tickled her roughly under the chin, a typical teasing that she thoroughly detested.

"Aw, Paw," she said crossly, turning her head away sharply. *"Don't!"*

"Oh, don't take on so, child. That thar store will still be standin' th' next time I'm ready to git provisions. Now yer Maw needs you here and here is whar ye'll stay!"

Mary saw Lona clamp her mouth on a hot retort. What Paw said was law and they all knew better than to bad-mouth him. Lona lapsed into a stony silence as their mother dished out steaming corn meal mush into their metal plates with a ladle. When she reached Lona, she murmured something to her and Lona nodded. Two jugs stood on the table, one with milk, the other with cream. Mary felt her appetite rising as she poured milk over her porridge and spooned a liberal helping of thick cream over it, while the others also helped themselves. Then Paw called

24

for silence with a grating of his throat, bowed his head and gave thanks to the Lord for providing their sustenance. Maw had cooked them all a special treat for after the mush because of the long journey that faced them – buckwheat fritter-bread pancakes, mouth-wateringly hot, which they ate covered in butter and homemade sorghum. Percy consumed his so fast that he gave a big belch afterwards. This earned him a quiet rebuke from Maw, but it had all the others in fits of irrepressible laughter.

After the scrumptious treat, they all followed Paw, slowly dragging his bad leg behind him, outside to the barn, where Sarah, the mule, was stabled. Paw and Joe strapped the sacks of dried beans, chestnuts, walnuts, dried apples, and live chickens in coots, to the saddle. Joe led the mule out, and helped his father climb astride her. Maw gave Mary two baskets, one containing lumps of cheese, thick slices of "journey bread" made from corn mush and smothered with butter and sorghum molasses, and honey-dew cookies, for nibbling on the way, and the other, eggs, for exchange at the store. Laura and Nellie also were given baskets of eggs to carry.

As they set off, Mary turned to look at those remaining behind, who had assembled on the porch to wave them goodbye. Maw stood with her hands on the shoulders of Lona and Percy, while Joe hovered protectively, slightly behind his mother. Maw's washtub of pink and white petunias stood beside the front door, and to the side of it, there was a profusion of small pink climbing roses trailing up several of the supporting porch poles, while honeysuckle crept up one end pole, and sweet peas climbed up a light-wire fencing tacked to the side of the cabin wall in multi-colored profusion. A crab-apple tree stood beside it.

It was seven miles to the nearest store at Fletcher, and they left the sturdy log cabin at Harley Hollow, and went down part of their four-acre truck plot, which ran down alongside the Elderberry Hope Logging Camp, close to Devil's Ditch. As they approached the camp the smell of woodchips, sawdust, oil and pine met their nostrils. Work at the camp started early, and already pairs of lumberjacks were manually sawing giant logs, while others were loading logs onto wagons to be pulled by a team of horses, which already stood in harness, impatiently stamping their hoofs and whishing their tails. The loggers, mainly healthy strong young mountain men, worked in pitch-blackened overalls, and wore hats or large caps. Although it was so early in the day, it was hot and a few of them had removed their shirts, their bare sweaty upper chests and arms tanned and muscular from the manual labor they performed. (Most mountain folk were lean from all the climbing they did.)

The lumberjacks, along with a kitchen crew, lived in a long bunkhouse next to a mess hall, and there were stables for about forty horses behind the camp. The timbering crew were divided into four teams: one team to cut trees up the side of the mountain, another team to drive a team of horses pulling the trunks down to the camp, another team sawed the logs and the last team loaded them onto the wagons, to be sent to the sawmill at Fletcher to be sawed into lumber. Paw had been part of the loading crew.

Some of the loggers doffed their hats or caps at them, while others more audacious of nature, wolf-whistled and waved as they went by. Mary sneaked a sidelong glance in their direction, but she did not have the same friendly spontaneity of her sisters, who responded with smiles and cheerful waves. In fact, she hated going past the logging camp, except for being able to see the horses. She adored horses, even the somewhat runty specimens that comprised most of the company horses at the logging camp. She always made sure she walked with the mule shielding her from the lumberjacks' unwanted attention. Though he guarded over the honor of his daughters with a sharp eye, Paw didn't mind the whistles and the waves too much, because he still knew the majority of the men who worked there.

Bar the logging trails, mountain roads were practically non-existent, and the journey down the steep, winding, often treacherous paths had to be taken on foot or on horseback or, as in Paw's case, on a mule. As they left the logging camp behind, they met logging wagons drawn by a team of horses piled with cut timber and bark, moving slowly up the narrow mountain trail to the logging camp, while wagons drawn by teams of horses piled with logs traveled down the trail to the sawmill at Fletcher, to be cut into lumber. They also came across wagons drawn by four sturdy well-kept mules loaded with bark, traveling up the trail on the long trek to the tannery at Elkton. Each spring, when the sap of the chestnuts began to rise, the barking season, which lasted six weeks, would begin. The barks would be peeled off with a spud bar by about sixty men. Such was the bounty that it entailed taking two wagon-loads of bark a week to the tannery for a full year. This provided mountain men with a good cash income, but Mary hated the barking season. It was so sad to see the mighty chestnuts stripped of their bark. They looked so undignified somehow; as if they'd been robbed of their attire and now stood rudely naked.

As the Harleys moved down the narrow footpath, Mary luxuriated in the feel of earth beneath her feet and the early-morning sun that was already warm on her body. Everywhere there was the calls of wild birds, the busy humming of bees, and the distant sound of cowbells, as cows were set to grazing. The chickens had settled down in their coops and clucked away contentedly, fluffing out their feathers every now and then. The slopes were tinged palest pink with mountain laurel, wild flowers of every color and hue waved in the breeze-blown bluegrass, and soft, puffy clouds hung in the deep azure sky. There were beautiful vistas of the pristine valley below, while behind them, a series of forested smoky-blue ridges swelled in the distance.

To help pass the time, Paw told stories, all of which they had heard many times before, but never tired of hearing, and when he was done, they sang mountain songs as they wended their way slowly down the slopes.

"Over, yonder by the valley, the valley so blue,
Over yonder by the valley, you'll find your love so true . . ."

The journey of some seven miles lasted several hours, and they were foot-sore and weary by the time the Fletcher store came into sight. The small clapboard building was raised about two feet off the ground on stilts, and was fronted by a porch on which were several chairs and benches where the old-timer regulars would sit and bide their time, next to a big water barrel.

As their little party approached, Mary could see several horses and mules tied to the hitching post in front. A Penny-Farthing bicycle was leant against the side of the porch, and some small boys were crowded around a horseless carriage parked some way away. One daring little boy in dungarees stood on tip-toe on a running board, peering alternatively into the interior of the automobile and over his shoulder at the store. He had good reason to be nervous for the spoke-wheeled vehicle belonged to Hannibal Hanford, the owner of a large tobacco plantation in the Upper Graves Valley. Hannibal was the area's most eligible bachelor and posed a splendid upright figure. However, he was stern, bumptious and opinionated, and was not well-liked by the mountain folk, who were usually good judges of character.

His manner was rude and obnoxious, as if he thought wealth gave him the excuse to have bad manners. Like a peacock forever showing off its fine plumage, he loved to display all the trappings of wealth; he owned the finest horses, the most expensive and stylish clothes – indeed, he wore a splendid full-length sable coat well into the warmer months – as well as having the ultimate possession of the impressive gleaming Cambrio automobile.

At first nothing seemed remiss. Several children played hopscotch on the dusty road that led past the store and little Johnny Houston skillfully rolled his hoop around one corner. But when they were about a hundred yards away, Mary suddenly became aware of a harsh unfamiliar repetitive sound emanating from the store. She cocked her head in earnest listening, frowning with concentration to hear above the chatter and laughter of their little group. She was at a loss to identify it. Each loud, lashing sound was followed by chants, whistles and roars of derisive laughter. Obviously alerted by her sudden lapse into silence and the questing expression on her face, her sisters also became aware of it and their words trailed and the laughter died in their throats.

"Paw, what's that strange noise?" asked Nellie, her dainty nose wrinkling in a thoughtful frown. Though her feet were dusty, she looked very pretty in her long yellow dress, with her budding breasts beginning to becomingly strain the bodice, her blonde curls tied back with a matching yellow ribbon.

Paw was a bit deaf, and consequently, he was always the last one to hear anything. But as they drew nearer, he couldn't fail to understand what she was talking about.

"Cain't rightly tell, child," he muttered, his merry, twinkling eyes losing luster for a moment, for the laughter that reached their ears was not happy laughter. Indeed, the barrage of coarse crude cackles and snorting whinnies was cruel, mocking and malicious and as unfamiliar as the sound of artillery fire might be from a place that usually swelled with merriment and the strains of fiddles and banjoes. Furthermore, it suddenly struck Mary that the old-timers, who usually sat sunning themselves on the porch, were not there.

She knew her father had noticed this too, warning him that all was not well, for he added, "Mebbe I ought to go on ahead and find out what's a'goin' on in thar…"

But by now, the curiosity of the two younger girls could not stop their headlong rushing ahead to see what the matter was for themselves. Even as Paw climbed awkwardly off the mule and tied her to the hitching post, patting her fly-pestered shuddering dark-brown flanks (for which he was rewarded with a yellow-toothed nip on the shoulder as he walked past), Laura and Nellie, young and spirited, full of youthful recklessness, disregarded his urgently called cautionary entreaties, and whipped ahead of him and Mary, up the porch steps. She and Paw followed after them as quickly as his dragging leg would allow, but as they entered the store, they were stopped dead in their tracks, as much by the sheer tension in the air, as the unexpected sight that met their eyes.

2

Dressed around the sides of the store were agitated little groups of regulars, who were whispering furtively amongst themselves. The women, some from the valley in their neat black button-up boots and handsome dresses and fancy hats, others, obviously highlanders in their simple homemade cotton dresses, frilly cloth bonnets and bare feet, had gathered their children about their skirts like anxious hens fussing with their chicks. Duke Colby, in his gray-and-blue Confederate uniform, a figure almost as familiar at the store as that of Harold

Fox, the proprietor, watched the proceedings with a look of incredulous bewilderment on his face. Duke, an old Indian-fighter and adventurer, had never married, and owed his devout allegiance to the lost cause of a free and independent Old South below the Mason Dixon line, and was acting stiff sentry over a little group of mountain women, who peeped anxiously over his shoulder.

The four old-timers, who usually spent their days sunning themselves out on the porch, were noticeable by their apoplectic outrage, which they scarcely managed to contain. Amos Peachey, his gray hair all awry, sucked furiously on an unlit pipe, his cheeks hollowing repeatedly over toothless gums, as he watched the intruders with bulging, faded blue eyes and unmistakable pique. Ernie Waits and Lon Peabody stood with their legs bowed and trembling as they, too, were unwilling witnesses to the unhealthy sport taking place before them. For standing in the middle of the store, in front of the counter, was none other than Hannibal Hanford himself, and gathered menacingly in a loose circle around him was a large group of disagreeable-looking, sour-smelling mountain crackers, with revolvers or Owl's Head pistols, stuck in the front of their pants, and their belts hung with knives.

Barefoot and shabbily dressed, they looked a rough bunch indeed, and it was obvious that they were drunk by their loud uncouth laughter and the foul language that escaped their mouths. Mary got the overwhelming impression of imbecilic grins and rotten teeth. They were not from around these parts, so no doubt they were squatters from some lonely distant hollow, perhaps even the dreaded Claw Mountain area itself.

Anxious to protect his three daughters, Paw made nervous little gestures with his hands, in order to try to hurry them outside again, but teased with curiosity, they stood their ground and stared, open-mouthed. The focal point of the deep consternation that fairly bristled in the crowded store, was one of the crackers, a sun-licked, sullen, good-looking youth with bright-yellow hair. A deep, jagged scar ran the full length of his left cheek, lending him such a dangerous presentiment that Mary felt the hairs rise on the back of her neck the moment her eyes riveted upon him. He stood holding a long leather bullwhip, and even as she watched, he lashed it harshly down on the floorboards just beside Mr. Hanford. Mr. Hanford jumped, blinking his eyes rapidly. It was obvious that the mischief had been going on for some time, for sweat beaded the wealthy lowlander's brow and upper lip. Then at the taunting of the other crackers, who were whistling and chanting and clapping, there began a series of whip lashes which threatened to rain down directly upon his person, but were in actual fact clever feints, which missed him by a hair's breath and had the crowd alternately audibly sucking in their breaths, then sighing with collective relief.

Then the young whip-handler began to show off his finer accomplishments. Now the whip whistled and snapped, darted and cracked, with such speed and skill, it was as if it had a life and volition of its own. It darted back and forth like a serpent's tongue, and caught in the madness of its blur, Mary felt it to be a rightful extension of its handler. For the yellow-haired youth reminded her exactly of a striking snake; except for the rampant whip, he seemed as cold, unmoving and unemotional as a reptile. Indeed, evil seemed to emanate from him, tightening the taut stringy muscles of his bare arm that wielded its fury. The whistling whip snatched the red handkerchief right out of Mr. Hanford's top suit pocket, sent his straw boater flying through the air and spinning like a top across the floorboards. Miraculously, it somehow managed to uncurl his bowtie and whip it from around his neck before it ripped off each of the buttons of his shirt in turn. Then it licked around Mr. Hanford's left earlobe, splitting it and drawing a little bubble of blood, producing a little howl of outrage from the store onlookers.

Mary was amazed at the transformation in Mr. Hanford. Though his tormentor could not be much older than her brother, Joe, the landowner was held as effectively at bay as a cat of prey by a lion-tamer, as much, Mary was convinced, by the cracker's formidable presence as for fear of an actual lashing. His frame was bent, shoulders hunched and his eyes blinked repeatedly. His mouth lolled open and the spittle dribbled, so that he presented a figure so pathetic, so devoid of nobility, that Mary felt a cringing shame for him. This formerly pompous, strutting man, usually so full of his own smug self-importance, had been reduced to a pitiful, cowering creature. As much as she disliked the man, she hated to see this systematic, dreadful humiliation of him. It was quite painful to watch. And as he begged for mercy, sobbing with terror, even though the whip had yet not actually touched him but for that pathetic little nick on his earlobe, something inside Mary snapped.

"Oh, Mr. Hanford, why don't you do somethung?" she burst out, without thinking. "Don't jest stand thar!" Then turning to the yellow-haired youth, she said crossly, "And you, Mister, why don't you go on back to whar you came from? We don't want no bullies around here."

There was an immediate lull in the uproarious laughter. Ominously, the snarling whip slowed and then stilled completely. The yellow-haired cracker turned slowly to face her, staring at her with malignant pale-yellow eyes that were queerly lighted. Mary felt a little thrall of fear. The atmosphere was thick with jeopardy and she felt unable to breathe. Her father edged closer to her, his face creased with worry. But everyone else was frozen with inertia. For an unbearably long while there wasn't a sound to be heard, except the distant chatter and laughter of the children playing outside.

"You!" he said softly, with deceptive gentleness. "What's yer name?"

"I . . . I am Mary Louella Harley!" Mary felt her face redden as the entire store turned astounded eyes on her. "And who might you be?"

"It don't matter none who I am. What matters is you tried to int'fere with

Buchanan justice. Now I don't take kindly t'that."

Buchanan justice! Mary felt a stirring of alarm. Why, these were those awful Buchanan boys from Claw Mountain, the ones they called the Buckos! Everybody was scared silly of them. Indeed, their reputation for meanness, drunkenness and lawlessness had swept through the mountains like a blast of odious bad breath. She was scared silly too, now that she knew who they were, but she couldn't possibly let them see that. "Well, Mister . . . uh, I am sorry if'n I interfered with yer . . . er . . . justice, but if'n you got some quarrel with Mr. Hanford, why don't you settle it in a decent manner instead of humiliatin' th' poor man so?"

The cracker stared at her incredulously as if he could not believe her temerity, while Mr. Hanford, his hair awry, looked at her with a strange mingling of gratitude and shame. Disheveled and thoroughly humiliated, his cowardice exposed before the very people he had previously treated with such lofty disdain, it seemed he could not prevent the tears that rolled down his cheeks at this unexpected new blow to his dignity. Mary guessed that to have a young mountain woman stand up for him must be hard for him to take, especially since it was well-known that he despised the mountain folk, whom he insisted cut down his timber. He had sent the sheriff to arrest many a suspected culprit. He had never even condescended to greet any of them in the past. Nevertheless, he clearly could not hide the relief that he felt now that there had been a lull in the commotion. But he stood there rooted to the floor, as if afraid to move in case the spotlight should move back to him.

"Well," the yellow-haired cracker said shortly. "It jest so happens I ain't about to waste no more time with this gutless piece of shit, anyhow."

Only the good Lord knew what would have happened then if the cracker hadn't spotted Laura and Nellie, who were watching him in mesmerized fascination. Immediately, his attention switched from Mary and the unfortunate Mr. Hanford, as his chilling gaze took in their youthful loveliness. Suddenly, as the other crackers followed his gaze, there was a howl, followed by whistles and shouts. Then they started whooping and hollering crude remarks.

"Hey, reckon I'd sure like to git me some a'that!" chortled one of them, a gaunt-looking fellow with brown hair, hitching up his patched brown pants by the suspenders.

"Yeah," leered another, taking off his slouch hat and holding it against his heart. "I'd like t'lick them all over like them is lollipops!"

Despite her sisters pretended disinterest, Mary could tell they were flattered by the little furor they had caused. Indeed, they seemed disappointed when the crackers turned their attention to the store's merchandise. Puffing at newly-lit cigars nicked from a box from the counter, they tried on ladies' hats, juggled gumballs scooped from a large open jar on the counter, filched licorice sticks and brazenly stuffed cans of beans and beef into their vests, under the worried eye of Mr. Fox, who stood behind the counter, looking nervous as a cat having to cross a puddle, wringing his hands in distress. One of the crackers, however, didn't join in their silly antics and stood leaning against the counter, watching them. He seemed the oldest and of a much more sober bent. Out of the corner of her eye, for she didn't want to invite his attention, Mary saw that the man was barefoot, clearly marking him as a mountaineer and, unlike the others, who were slight of build, he was big and tall, and strong-looking as an ox, with black hair and a handsome black mustache.

At last the crackers, tiring of their sport, barged out of the door, to another collective sigh of relief from the onlookers. While her paw went to join a group of old cronies around the pot-bellied stove, Mary, feeling quite shaken by the nerve-wracking experience, pretended to busy herself by looking at the bales of cloth stacked up at the end of the counter till she gained some equilibrium. After a few minutes, she looked up to see, to her considerable disconcertion, that the big man with the mustache was still leaning against the counter and was staring avidly at her. Their eyes met and riveted for what seemed like an eternity, but was probably only for a few breathless seconds. Mary felt flustered and con-fused. His eyes were the most unusual she ever had seen; a striking turquoise-green, and of such burning luminosity, they seemed to strafe her to cinders right where she stood.

At first she thought she must be mistaken, and that it must be her two sisters he seemed so interested in, for they were so much prettier than her, and younger too, with any number of ardnt suitors, while she, just a week off turning nineteen, was practically an old maid. After all, most mountain girls were wed between the ages of fourteen and sixteen. The only man who'd been interested in her up to now was Wiley Holbrook, who was old enough to be her father, smelled of hogs and was constantly sniffing or wiping his nose on his sleeve. Though her mother was always trying to point out Wiley's good points to her, Mary was unconvinced and horrified when Paw gave him permission to call on her. After a few strained visits, however, he had thankfully lost confidence for she had practically ignored the poor man, not wanting to encourage him.

But no, the big mountain cracker was definitely staring straight at her. Still filled with consternation over the ugly encounter, she glared hotly at him, but as the staring between them seemed to endlessly stretch, it seemed to melt away like butter left in the sun, leaving her feeling as limp as a wet rag inside. Finally, she managed to snatch her eyes away, growing flustered as she felt his eyes still upon her, as heavy as boulders. She felt herself blush and quickly turned away, pretending to be interested in the antics of a pair of small boisterous boys dressed in identical knickerbockers suits and matching golf caps, who were dodging around a barrel of flour, accidentally dropping her drawstring purse. It landed on the floor-boards, which had all too recently resounded to the hateful tyranny of the whip, with barely a sound. She immediately bent down to retrieve it but, at the same time, the handsome stranger strode over to pick it up. He reached the purse seconds before she did and, as he stood up, their hands touched briefly in passing. The contact was electrifying.

"You dropped this," the huge mountain man said gruffly, with a twisted little smile on his face, as if to hide his own disconcertion.

"Thank you," she murmured, laying her eyes low. With that, she turned and hurried over to join her sisters who were talking to some girls their own age. They had acted like a bunch of beheaded chickens, running around in demented circles, before settling down and gathering together in a huddle, putting shocked hands over their mouths and dramatically clasping their breasts, as they breath-lessly recounted the incident.

"Oh, Mary," said the Aldershot girl as Mary approached them, still feeling highly unsettled by her encounter with the stranger. "You are soo-o-o brave! That one with the whip is *Eli Buchanan* and you must have heard about him a'fore. He's scary ... but real handsome, don't you thunk?"

Mary was disgusted with her. Betty Aldershot liked anything that wore pants! All the customers were still talking about the rude impact that the Buckos had made on their somewhat boring lives and the whole place was seething with antagonism against them. It was obvious to Mary that they had not observed the handsome stranger still standing at one end of the counter and believed that he must have gone outside with the other crackers – if he was with them at all, that was. Then as Mary glanced at him again, he suddenly seemed filled with a bloody-minded antagonism, for after giving her a baleful glare, he strode angrily towards the entrance to the horrified gasps of those who had caught sudden sight of him. Mary watched him go with a sense of dismay. As he went out onto the porch she saw him pull out a bottle of moonshine that was hooked into the back of his pants. Opening the lid, he drank deeply from it, before disappearing from view. His departure was the signal for all those still crowded inside the store to stampede to the door to see for themselves what would happen next. A few got wedged in the doorway such was their eagerness to get out on the porch. They were followed by Mary. She was joined by Hannibal Hanford, who couldn't meet her steadfast gaze or bring himself to thank her. *Cowardly fellow!* When she got out on the porch Mary wriggled her way through the crowd to the front and was shocked at the spectacle that met her eyes.

The crackers were insolently lolling all over the lowlander's automobile, three of them sitting squashed up inside it at the back and another two on the front seats. Some of them stood on the running boards, giggling dementedly, rocking the carriage from side to side, so it creaked and complained like a wheezing old man, while others viciously kicked at the bodywork, the solid rubber tires and the spoke wheels. Eli, gloriously unrepentant, lay indolently in the sun on the hood of the automobile, with his back against the windshield and his eyes closed. With all his former menace gone, he might have looked as innocently mischievous as a child had it not been for the pair of Owl's Head pistols tucked in his waistband and that incongruous jagged knife scar that ran right the way down his left cheek. The cracker in the driver's seat was swinging the steering wheel from side to side with a leering grin on his face, while a youngster in the passenger seat, periodically honked the rubber ball of the horn fixed to one side of the windshield, with an astounded look on his slack-jawed face.

Mary's eyes anxiously searched for the giant one among them and she was relieved to see that he hadn't joined the others. He stood on one side with his arms folded, watching them with a disgusted look on his face. She was glad, because the others looked so idiotic, so lacking in wits, that she felt a moment of intense shame for them. It *was* a shameful thing, after all, grown men behaving like unruly children, defiantly daring anyone to stop them from indulging in their careless, malicious play.

Hannibal Hanford appeared at Mary's side and stood watching them too, nervously, trembling, too afraid to even attempt a rescue of his once-shiny automobile now covered in dust and dirt and ruined by the dents caused by scores of well-aimed hard bare heels. She saw his face and couldn't help feeling sorry for the man. What a blow to his pride all this must have been. Mary wondered if he'd ever dare show his face around here again. Nobody she knew liked him and he'd likely be a laughing stock from now on. Oh well, she supposed pride did cometh before a fall, as the saying went!

Then urging the others to follow him with an impatient whip of his arm, the big handsome stranger glared scornfully at three children fearfully peering out at him from under the stilted porch and kicked a child's hoop out of his path, before hitting out towards the mountains that reared up in the far distance. The others, one by one, climbed reluctantly out and off the automobile and followed meekly after him. As a final parting insult, however, a few of them picked up rocks and lobbed them back at the ravaged vehicle, grinning, as they struck the windshield, smashing it, and bounced off the already dented chrome- and body-work, before they rambled aimlessly after the big one across the field of waving bluegrass and wildflowers, all fifteen of them . . .

O n the long walk back to Claw Mountain that rose up in the far distance, while his brothers reeled drunkenly around him, roughhousing and giggling like naughty children, Zachary Thomas strode for home troubled by his thoughts and the unfamiliar emotions churning inside him. He could not get the unknown young mountain girl at the store out of his mind. He had found himself totally fascinated by her, struck by the spunky way she had stood up to Eli when nobody else had dared to. *Nobody* messed with Eli! He had this chilling meanness about him that made everybody, even complete strangers, instantly wary of him. Of course, Eli's anger had been somewhat justified for once. The wealthy lowlander had pulled up in his horseless carriage all high and mighty and looking down his nose at them, and had rudely pushed young Jamie out of the way to enter the store as if he were a piece of crud. Jamie had been a long time getting born and as a result was dimwitted. The boy evoked a staunch protectiveness in Eli, especially when he suffered ridicule or contempt from others. Was it stupidity, ignorance or bravery that had made the girl stand up to Eli that way? Her quiet dignity and straight back as she stared at the cloth bales had been almost a relief to him compared to the behavior of the other girls in the store, who had carried on so anyone would think they'd been accosted.

He wondered why the black-haired girl was lingering on in his thoughts so. Some might even consider her plain when, in fact, she was anything but that. She was beguilingly different. Oh, she was not real pretty like the two younger girls who had caught the attention of his brothers, but there was something real compelling about her calm hazel eyes, her clear high forehead and the thick curtain of her straight, shiny black hair that escaped her cloth bonnet. He found her dusky skin and the fine sprinkling of dark freckles on her nose and cheeks appealing too – he thought the milky complexion usually favored by the fairer sex made them seem wishy-washy and weak. Certainly, he had not expected to feel so moved by her.

He shook his head to rid himself of the memory of her turning to look at him and their eyes meeting and holding for much longer than he had intended. Her mouth was clamped with her pent-up indignation, but as the staring between them stretched, it slackened to a soft, bewildered pout. It was then that he felt a churning in his gut, which had refused to go away, despite the fact that they'd left the store, and her, long behind. He raised his eyes to the heavens and gave a huge, tortured sigh, feeling oddly tormented inside. He tried to snap himself out of his present state of sappiness and determinedly stepped up his pace, urging his lagging brothers to keep up with him. They still had a long way to go and it would be dark by the time they finally got home.

3

A few days after the incident at the Fletcher General Store, Mary was in the barn milking Martha, the family Jersey cow. It was just after dawn and gloomy in the barn still, even with the sallow light from the single lighted kerosene lantern which hung from a hook. She sat on a stool, the comforting smells of straw and warm cow dung permeating the air, as she expertly pulled at the speckled udders. Mary liked the feeling of her head leaning against Martha's big warm faw-colored body as she squirted tepid jets of milk into the pail below.

Cows wandered all over the mountain with their clanging bells and, like most mountain children, she had driven the cow home as a girl (a job now regulated to young Percy). Oft'times in the late fall, she would go and look for Martha and would find her among a whole lot of cows belonging to other mountain families. She would leap from one warm patch to the next where the cows had been lying on the ground, to spare her bare feet from the icy chill of the frost.

Sarah, the mule, was in the next enclosure and she could hear her chomping on the oats that she had put in her feeding trough earlier. The handsome rooster, so fine of plumage, had already signaled the break of dawn and was strutting around her, pecking in the straw, while the contented clucks of red fowls came from all around her in the barn, some from above her in the rafters, others in the straw. It was always quite a business collecting eggs, since not all the fowls were kept in the hen-house, which was not large enough to accommodate them all. There were always plenty of them strutting around the yard. One of Joe's main aims when he took over the running of the farm had been to build a much bigger hen-house, but with so much else to attend to, he hadn't yet found the time. Those not accommodated in the henhouse were housed in the barn at night, to protect them from predators.

Mary heard a sound behind her. She looked around and saw the silhouette of a man against the opened doorway, much too big to be either her father or Joe. She leapt up, overturning the milk pail. She stared into the gloom for a few moments before she was able to distinguish who it was. Then her eyes widened in shock. *It was the handsome stranger from the store!* She was so stunned by his sudden, unexpected appearance that her mouth dropped open and she started trembling. What was he doing here? She'd overheard somebody at the store say that he was probably the oldest Bucko, since he'd left with them. In that case had he come to visit her from faraway Claw Mountain?

He stood and stared at her compellingly, the way he had that day. The air between them seemed to crackle with energy, the attraction between them so great it was a powerful and dangerous thing. Surely he wasn't here to ask her father's permission to call on her? Or one of her sisters perhaps? Not that Paw would grant him permission to call on *any* of his daughters if he knew he was kith and kin to those awful Buckos! Oh, how she wished she had her best dress on instead of this awful shapeless brown work one and that her hair was loose like he'd seen it the last time, instead of in a tight unflattering bun.

When he spoke at last, his unflinching words came as an even bigger shock than his sudden appearance had been.

"I came to fetch you, girl, 'cuz I want to make you my wife."

"What?" Her eyes widened in stunned disbelief.

"I want to marry you," he insisted softly.

"Who are you exactly?"

"I'm Zachary Thomas Buchanan from Claw Mountain and th' minute I set eyes on you, I knew you were th' wimmin fer me."

Mary felt her heart soar and sink at the same time. While his words sent a piquant thrill down her spine, the confirmation that he was one of those awful Buckos, after all, came as a sobering shock.

"From Claw Mountain," she repeated hollowly, her chest constricting with the rude reality of it.

"That's right," he said unflinchingly. "Claw Mountain."

Mary swallowed hard. She liked the way he said that and hadn't tried to fool her into thinking he was from someplace else. Still, he must be plain feeble-minded! How could she possibly marry a Bucko? Maw and Paw would never allow it! But what alternative was there for her in life? Until today, it had sure begun to look as if she was destined to become an old maid. Years seemed to yawn emptily in front of her, hopeless and without womanly purpose. *Wiley Holbrook and his runny nose? Never!* But why should she become a spinster when this handsome stranger was standing right in front of her asking her to be his bride? Of course, he was quite a bit older than her too, but not nearly as old as Wiley Holbrook, she was sure. It stunned her to realize that she was actually considering Zachary Thomas's bizarre proposal.

"You wish to marry me, you say?" she asked weakly, overwhelmed by the import of it.

"Damned right I do! And you want it too, I kin tell."

Mary shook her head to clear it. Behind her, Martha lowed and crossly tossed her head so that the bell around her neck clanged, as she complained about the interrupted milking. Mary stared at the huge cracker in dismay. What about her family, her responsibilities here? They would be gathering for breakfast soon, expecting her to bring in the milk and cheese from the spring house. "I cain't possibly…"

"Come away with me, now, and we'll git married tomorrer," he urged.

"Tomorrer?" she echoed hollowly. Then something struck her. "Don't I got to git my parent's permission since I'm underage?"

"How old are you, girl?"

"Near nineteen," she admitted shyly.

"Then that's old enough," he said knowledgeably.

"But I cain't jest leave here without a'tellin' them."

"You do that, girl, and it'll be over a'fore it's even begun."

"Yes," she whispered in acknowledgment.

"Y'kin tell yer parents when it's done. In fact, we kin come back here and tell them together."

Mary could not believe the excitement that was beginning to stir inside her. *Elopement!* Her heart began to pound so loudly she was sure he must hear it.

"Well, then, are you a'comin' or not?" he demanded.

In order to collect her chaotic thoughts, she murmured. "How did you git here?"

"On a horse. Left it tied up down th' mountain and came up in th' night. Slept right here in th' barn."

"Why *me?*" she couldn't resist asking. *The Plain One!*

"'Cuz so help me, girl, try as I might, I ain't bin able to git you out of my mind since I saw you at th' store th' other day!"

Lord knew she hadn't been able to get him out of her mind either. Indeed, she had walked around in a daze ever since and only Paw's sharp enquiry about why she was neglecting her chores, had prompted her to snap out of it momentarily. Later, she overheard her mother chiding him. She'd told him to go easy on her, and that her apparent preoccupation was probably because she was still in shock about the incident at the store. Well, that was true enough, but not the incident Maw was referring to! Yet never in her wildest dreams had she imagined that this man would actually seek her out and want to marry her, no less!

"Will you marry me, Mary Louella Harley?" he persisted. "Will you become my wife?"

There was a long silence, during which time he continued to stare at her with his burning hypnotic gaze. Even in the gloom she could see his striking turquoise-green eyes. How could she have made such an impression on this man? How could she feel so much for him already? *Love at first sight?* That's what it was! How could anyone deny that there was such a thing when that was the bold truth of the matter! Dare she follow her heart? If she didn't and sent him away, she might regret it for the rest of a lonely life!

"Yes," she whispered, unable to believe what she had just said. They would come back to let her parents know, of course, or send word so they wouldn't worry. She knew they would not believe it of her when she had always been so sensible and dependable. She had helped Maw with the younger children when they were little, and with the cooking. Yet she had just agreed to elope with a complete stranger, possibly even a dangerous one! But he hadn't seemed at all like the other Buckos that day, she hastily consoled herself. He'd stood apart from them, seeming ashamed of their behavior at times. And he hadn't messed with or stolen any of Mr. Fox's merchandise either, so he didn't have long fingers. Indeed, he'd been a real gentleman in picking up her dropped purse. And he was so terribly handsome. How often she had dreamed of being swept off her feet by a handsome stranger?

"Yes, I'll marry you, Zachary Thomas Buchanan," she said again, surprised at how loud and clear her words were, while inside her chest, her heart was fairly pounding.

A slow smile spread over Zachary Thomas's face. "Jest knew ye'd come with me! Knew you felt it strong as me!"

With that, he grabbed her hand and they slipped out of the barn, running alongside it. They flew down the mountain together, sticking to the forest rather than risking the open blue grassed slopes, barefoot and holding hands, like she and Joe used to do when they were children, laughing softly, and filled with a strange exhilaration. Such was their headlong flight that by the time they got to the bottom where he'd tied up a big, handsome brown saddled horse to a sapling, they were both panting heavily. Zachary Thomas climbed onto the saddle then reached down and pulled her up in front of him. Then he surprised her by loosening her long black hair from her bun. He buried his face in it, whispering, "Don't reckon I've seen anythung so doggoned purty in my whole life!"

Mary felt a surge of happiness. Filled with a sense of daring and *rightness,* she hung onto the saddle in front of her with both hands, feeling his hugeness and strength envelop her as he took the reins, smelling the masculine scent of sweat and tobacco coming from him. Mary couldn't believe that this handsome, mysterious stranger would soon be her wedded husband . . .

4

In the frail early morning sunshine, they rode through the valley at a leisurely pace, scarcely talking, with just the jingling sound of the livery and the squeaking of the fine leather saddle audible above the sounds of brooks and wild birds, passing the familiar Bearface Mountain with its large half-mile-long outcrop of rocks, fifty feet high or more, which towered above the trees on the crest of the mountain, and heading north, into unfamiliar turf for Mary, since she had never been further than the general store at Fletcher in the valley before. Zachary Thomas pointed out Claw Mountain to her, way in the distance, in the next county. The rugged heights of the mountain loomed up in the west above all the other jagged backbone peaks, its massive boulder-supported plateau so high it was raised above a collar of white cloud. Mary felt a moment of spine-tingling fear as she took in this legendary abode.

As the sun climbed rapidly up the sky and flooded the earth with blazing summer sunshine, Mary, unused to riding, felt increasingly hot and saddle-sore, and to take her mind off it, tried to concentrate on the surroundings. She wished they could take a break, but Zachary Thomas didn't suggest one and she didn't have the gumption to ask him to stop a while. She felt inordinately shy of him now they were away on their own, very aware of his nearness, the coarseness of his clothing, his strong arms around her and his huge rough hands hanging onto the reins. A captive to him, she realized with a quaking heart that she knew absolutely nothing about him bar the fact that he wanted her for a wife – and his name, of course – *Zachary Thomas Buchanan*. 'Tis a fine name, she thought dreamily. Strong and handsome, just like the man himself.

At last, ahead of them across the Conway River rose the rugged, picturesque, 3,000-foot summit of Beacon Mountain. They splashed through the shallow waters, passing from Greene County into Madison County, and headed north-west on a wagon road to the start of Booten's Gap, to the left of which towered the mighty Claw Mountain itself, while Beacon Mountain was to the right. Up-close like this, Mary saw that Claw Mountain was densely forested and wild-looking, seeming infinitely less kindly, somehow, than any of the surrounding hazy blue ridges that melted into the azure of the sky. A large number of eagles soared above the tableland with wild, lonely cries. The sheer rugged granite cliffs, spilling with hanging vines and with tiny trees clinging to the rocks with their exposed roots, made the southern slopes totally inaccessible. Zachary Thomas had already told her that they would have to join up with the horseback trail to Buck Knob in the Wilderness Valley, in order to climb its more accessible northern slopes. As they moved steadily through the pass, Mary felt quite intimidated by the huge, inhospitable mountain looming ominously beside them, and suddenly realized the extent of her own daring. What would she find on the mountain? Where would they live? With Zachary Thomas's father, his wicked brothers, or on their own someplace?

At last they reached the horseback trail of which Zachary Thomas had spoken. When they eventually arrived at the northern foothills of Claw Mountain, it was late afternoon and the splendor of the Wilderness Valley lay spread before them, at the bottom of which flowed a river called Wilson Run. The wildness and loneliness of the area unnerved Mary, for there was no sign of human habitation anywhere – no mountain cabins with smoke puffing out of their chimneys, no chestnut split-pole fences, no bell-hung cows or rooting domestic hogs. They stopped at the narrow pathway that ascended the mountain, which rose steeply above them, a terrifying sight. Zachary Thomas dismounted, grunting as he lifted Mary down.

"This is whar we leave off from th' horse," he said gruffly.

"Whar you goin' to leave it?" she asked curiously as she landed on her bare feet. "Don't you barn it at night?"

"I'm leavin' it whar I done stole hit from."

Mary felt herself go cold with mortification. "You done *stole* him?"

So much for him not having long fingers!

"Yeah. It's a mighty long haul to your'n place. "'Sides, it ain't stealin' proper-like, 'cuz I'm takin' this here horse right back to Beacon Mountain whar I done found it."

Mary had no answer to his logic and said nothing. She couldn't help thinking that it wasn't very likely that he'd just *come upon* the horse all saddled up like that. Still, only *half-long fingers*, she supposed, which wasn't nearly as bad as she'd thought at first.

He mounted up again, and muttered, "Wait fer me here."

Zachary Thomas was gone about two hours, during which time Mary fretted about being come upon by any of his kin, especially the mean, whip-wielding one with the scarred cheek – the one they called Eli. After the Buckos left the store that day, folks had told her how terribly foolish she had been to challenge him like that, hinting that people had actually *died* for doing less. She had tried to tell herself that it was probably just wild rumor, but she kept remembering the strange eerie look in Eli's pale-yellow eyes and way he had reduced Mr. Hanford to a gibbering idiot, and she had a sickening feeling in the pit of her stomach that he might well be capable of doing such awful things.

She sat on a rock gazing across at Fork Mountain directly opposite her on the other side of the great valley and at the beautiful dense vegetation of the Wilderness which stretched towards The Sag, feeling dreadfully alone and vulnerable, and suddenly homesick and bereft now that she was all on her own and able to take stock of what she had done. Who would believe she would be where she was right now? How alarmed her family must have been when they found her gone, the milk pail upended. They must think she was taken by force and no doubt her father had already climbed on his mule and gone down the valley to report her disappearance to the sheriff at Standardsville. Certainly nobody would dream that she had left voluntarily. Maw must be beside herself with anxiety. She didn't think that folks would connect her up with Zachary Thomas for she very much doubted that anybody had noticed their intense exchange at the general store a few days ago. But they might very well suspect his whip-wielding brother had abducted her, since she had stood up to him that day. What if Joe followed her here and got himself shot by one of these infamously hot-tempered Buckos? She wouldn't be able to live with herself if anyone got hurt because of her rashness.

But she mustn't think like that else she'd go mad. Besides, she was sure glad she was about to marry Zachary Thomas instead of Wiley Holbrook, even if he did happen to be a Bucko. She was infinitely relieved when her giant of a husband-to-be, eyes narrowed, came striding along the trail. She had begun to worry in case the owner of the horse had got him arrested. Who knew what might have happened then! She had to admit that while he had been quiet and taciturn during the long ride, there had been great strength in his presence. Without a word, he grabbed her hand. They ducked beneath some low-hanging red osier dogwoods and began the climb up the steep slopes.

"Whar we goin' exactly," Mary asked him breathlessly after a while.

"Homestead of my paw, Obediah. We'll stay thar, an' I'll send word fer th' preacher to marry us tomorrer."

Mary felt a pang of disquiet. *So they'd be living with his father!* She'd soon be meeting the legendary formidable patriarch of the unruly bunch! They moved steadily upwards beneath the canopy of trees, through vine-entangled stands of giant white oaks, chestnuts, maples, shagbark hickories and tulip poplars. Despite the fact that they were both mountain-born, the going was extremely tough and they were soon breathing hard. Occasionally, one of them would lose their footing on the slippery humus. Mary thought how Claw Mountain was so different from Lewis Mountain in that it had none of the wide open spaces she was used to. There was no bluegrass fields like on her home mountain, which meant there was no good grazing for cows.

It seemed as if no trees had been felled on this huge mountain as the forest was toweringly tall and extremely dense and the canopy overhead, thick. Indeed, she couldn't hear a single cowbell. Instead, the mountainside was alive with the bubbling of streams, which trickled everywhere. Springing from nowhere, they spilled and splashed over ledges and down bubbling cascades, mingling with the incessant cries and twitters of multitudinous birds. Veeries and yellow-shafted flickers flitted busily through the canopy overhead, while ravens cried and blackburnian warblers gave their throaty sound. But despite the un-spoiled beauty and naturalness, Mary could sense an air of unease, a vague undefined mood, as if the ancient mountain had somehow absorbed into itself, bad things done by evil men, on its hostile slopes. The higher up they went, the more the feeling persisted.

About two hours later, Mary spotted the first sign of human habitation on the mountain and it alarmed her for it was a shotgun-toting cracker up a tree! The cracker spotted them, too, for he gave a blood-curdling yell and fired two deafening shots. Mary had to stifle a scream.

"What's he doin' up thar?" she breathed, her heart pounding.

"Oh, makin' real sure them Galtrey boys don't pay us no surprise visit."

Mary's eyes widened. "They do that often?"

"Often enough."

"Why?"

"Don't remember exactly," replied Zachary Thomas gruffly. "Bin at it since I was a bitty young'un."

Lord, her future husband didn't even know why they were feuding with the Galtreys, even though it had been going on for some thirty-odd years, if mountain gossip was to be believed! Just then Mary heard yelling in the distance. The cacophony of sound grew steadily louder. At last, they came to the edge of a large clearing on which a cabin had been built on stilts of chestnut logs about halfway up the mountain. She realized that they must have reached the heart of Claw Mountain, Obediah's homestead, Horseshoe Hollow.

To her disgust, it was a pathetic, rundown place that spoke of unkemptness, squalor and neglect. The porch steps had caved in. The barn looked a sorry sight with unpainted doors that were hanging on their hinges. Mangy mongrels groveled for scraps and threadbare Leghorns strutted desultorily around the yard, pecking at unseen tidbits on the ground. An unhitched buckboard stood beside the cabin and a large tin bathtub containing dirty rainwater stood in the dusty yard. Barrels, some stripped of their bands and coming apart, were scattered around the yard, along with broken wagon wheels, rolls of wire and rusted and broken farm implements. There were bottles and jars of all descriptions amidst mounds of broken glass, which suggested they'd been used as target practice. Dotted around the yard, atop small piles of bricks, were several old sofas with broken springs bulging through holes. Mary swallowed hard. It was a deeply depressing sight. She had expected something much grander, despite the shabby appearance of the Buckos themselves (they seemed poor even by mountain standards), since rumor had it that the patriarch, Obediah Buchanan, was a rich man. Well, if he was, a body would never guess it to look at this dreadful place!

And if Mary thought she would only have to contend with the clan's patriarch, she was soon disappointed. It seemed the entire, shabbily dressed Buchanan clan had gathered at their father's abode, for she instantly recognized the sullen faces of the crackers who had so recently terrorized everybody at the store. They were everywhere, out on the front porch, up trees with muzzle-loading squirrel guns, draped over the old sofas, beside sniggering, skinny women, and in the big dusty yard, pitching horseshoes, playing marbles, or cards. Dirty, snotty-nosed children roughed and tumbled with blood-curdling yells. Nearly all of the adults had moonshine jugs hooked on their fingers and kept taking swigs, in between cussing and yelling. Mary quailed at the sight of them, a shiver of foreboding shivering her spine. *What had she gotten herself into?*

5

Mary clung to Zachary Thomas's hand at the edge of the clearing at Horseshoe Hollow, staring at his assembled kin, and whispered, "Did they know we were a'comin' here?"

"Naw."

"Then how come they're all here a'waitin' like this?"

"Paw likes them to be here everyday."

"You maw and paw here too?"

"Maw died ten years back and Paw ain't here."

Mary felt a wave of relief at his words. "Whar's he at?"

"He's taken some barrels of moonshine to Stony Man Camp to sell. That's how come I got to borrow me th' horse. Paw done took all four of th' mules."

Mary had heard of Stony man Camp before at the store. It was a summer vacation camp for rich folk. Well, she couldn't help feeling glad that the Buchanan patriarch had taken all the mules and Zachary Thomas had "borrowed" the horse. Lord knew there was nothing romantic about being swept away by a handsome stranger on a *mule!* As much as she loved old Sarah, folks sometimes took to staring and whistling at somebody who rode a mule! It did not greatly perturb Mary to hear that it was true about his father being a moonshiner, either. After all, stills had been operated in the Blue Ridge Mountains for centuries and were an accepted part of mountain life. While Mary's father did not operate a still because of her mother's strong objections, she did allow him to keep a jug of moonshine on the mantel over the hearth for his own consumption and that of his guests, providing none of them overindulged in it. Of course, every now and then Paw did take too much. Then he'd act playful and like a naughty boy, soon cajoling Maw out of her strenuous objections.

"Ain't yer paw a'feared of a'gittin' caught by them Revenue Men?" Mary asked.

Zachary Thomas shook his head. "Naw, Paw's too far canny fer 'em Revenue fellas. He hates them almost as much as he hates them Galtreys. He travels by mule on switchback trails over th' hills 'til he gits to Stony Man whar he sells it to George Pollock without them gettin' a sniff of what he's bin up to."

Just then, to her alarm, Zachary Thomas dragged her, reluctant and shy, into the center of the dirt yard. One of the crones spotted her and yelled, "Hey, Toad, see yer brother up and done what he said. He's done brung hisself back a bride!"

So he had told them something! That was the signal for everybody to crowd around them. Even those acting as lookouts in the trees climbed down and came to join them. They surrounded the pair in a grinning, imbecilic circle, raw mountain crackers, lean and brown, smelling sour from a mixture of unwashed bodies, ripe sweat and sour-mash moonshine. Many of them were holding double-barreled shotguns or squirrel rifles, with one or two Owl's Head pistols tucked in the front of their pants, or in belts hauling in denim overalls.

Zachary Thomas introduced her to a bewildering number of them in a blur of names. She was relieved that the scar-faced, whip-wielding one was not among them. She felt a moment of panic, however, when a skinny, mousy-haired, toothless hag, of indeterminate age, tugged at her hair and her dress.

"So Zack's got himself a wimmin at last!" she shrilled. "Offer'd to bed him m'self, only I'm too much wimmin f'him!"

"Darn and tarnation, Cora, leave her be!" Zachary Thomas said sternly, glaring at her. "Clem, I want you to go fetch th' preacher, 'cuz me and her is a'gittin' hitched tomorrer."

"Preacher? What preacher?" asked Clem, looking clueless.

"Why, Horace Cleats, of course. Th' *Reverend* Horace Cleats!"

Recognition dawned in Clem's pale-blue eyes, and he grinned. "Oh, sure, I'll go git Preacher Cleats fer you, big brother."

With that, he took off down the mountain at a barefoot trot, casually toting his shotgun over his one skinny shoulder. Another of Zachary Thomas's brothers handed him a moonshine jug and Zachary Thomas took it, hauled it over his shoulder and drank greedily from it. Then he wiped his mouth and handed the jug to Mary. She stared at it in dismay.

"Uh, no, thank you," she muttered.

"Take some," Zachary Thomas insisted. "You gotta be real thirsty by now."

"No ... uh ... I don't drink that stuff," she admitted, to roars of coarse disbelieving laughter.

"You don't drunk moonshine?" Zachary Thomas repeated hollowly, as if the very idea was foreign to him. "How come?"

"Maw says it ain't ladylike," she said, before taking stock of her words. Since it was obvious that all of these women imbibed, they were likely to take offense. And indeed, they did. There were snorts of indignation and derision.

"Oh, so it's ladylike, ye are, is it?" spat out a freckled specimen, with flaming red hair that looked like a tangled bird's nest.

"No, I ain't meant that like it sounded. Maw don't drink, is all. Paw drinks some, though," she added, in an attempt to placate. "Sometimes even more than a little."

The hag eyed her with sullen, slit eyes. "Ye don't say, *Missy?*"

Mary was infinitely relieved as the members of the clan began to drift off to their individual homesites on the mountain as the shadows of dusk began to gather, leaving only the unmarried Buchanan brothers who still lived here at the old main homestead. Besides Zachary Thomas, there were Cletus, Otis and Jamie, a handsome youth, aged about fourteen or fifteen. She had noticed him in the one-horse carriage at the store and that he seemed to have difficulty in focusing his eyes and appeared backward. There was still no sign of the whip-wielder, and Mary began to hope that he didn't live on the mountain with the others.

They went up the broken-down steps to the elevated porch and entered the big cabin. It was dim inside and Zachary Thomas lit several kerosene lamps and hung them on hooks. The main room was huge, sparsely furnished and a real mess – untidy and dusty. Pots and metal plates were piled on a cabinet, near a long home-made wooden table and at least a dozen chairs. Beside a wood-fire stove was a pile of logs. Dusty faded rugs and a few tilted pictures of flowers hung haphazardly on the walls were all that suggested a woman had ever lived in the place.

The brothers sat down at the table and looked at Mary expectantly. By now she was exhausted from the day's journey and the steep climb up the mountain. What's more, she was quite weak from hunger herself, as she hadn't eaten all day. Zachary Thomas had chewed on a cold shank of venison he had taken out of a saddle-bag while they were riding, and had offered it to her. But one look at the half-eaten, half-raw specimen made her want to throw up. Maw always said she was too squeamish for her own good.

"Um, what is thar fer me to cook fer supper," she said wearily, to snorts of satisfaction from the younger men. It seemed they were just waiting for her to offer.

Cletus, a thin lanky fellow, who looked in his mid-twenties, eagerly jumped up and said, "Why, I shot us supper jest a'fore you came."

He went outside, returning proudly holding up a large male hare by its hind legs. It had evidently been shot with a shotgun at close range as its head and front legs had been blown clean off. It had not been skinned, gutted or cleaned, and dripped blood onto the floorboards. Mary had to struggle to hold onto her stomach.

"You expect me to cook it without it bein' skinned?"

Cletus frowned. "Maw always skinned everythung herself," he said coldly.

"Well, I reckon since yer maw's bin gone some long while now, she sure as heck won't be doin' it," she retorted hotly. "Now who has bin doin' it since then?"

Clem looked slightly shamed. "Jest put th' whole danged thing in th' pot and skin it after, when it's cooked! It's mighty easy then. Jest hook most of it out."

Mary almost gagged right then. "That … that's th' most *disgustin'* thung I ever heard of in all my born days! All them hairs! *Ugh!* Everybody knows you got to *skin* a thung *a'fore* you cook it!"

Cletus looked dumbstruck, blinking his eyes rapidly, looking almost as if he were about to cry, before he gave her a glare of pure hatred. Zachary Thomas's look was equally thunderous. Oh dear, it was clear that this clan did not take kindly to censure! She had embarrassed and offended them both. But she couldn't help it. She softened her tone somewhat. "Well, in my paw's household, th' one who does th' huntin' always got to do th' skinnin' and cleanin'. Nobody ever brung anything in for th' table that ain't bin cleaned proper-like!"

Cletus looked at her with his mouth askew. "Well, *excuse* me," he declared with a sneer. "Ain't we a Miss Fancy-britches!"

"Skin it!" Zachary Thomas said scathingly, his eyes narrowed into slits.

Mary blinked and stared at him, nonplussed. Did he want *her* to skin it or his brother?

"I said *skin it!"* Zachary Thomas roared, turning furiously on his younger brother and banging the top of the table with his one fist, making Mary start with fright. Suddenly tension was rife in the air as the two brothers glared balefully at each other. After a moment of fierce eyeball-to-eyeball contention, Cletus backed down with a scowl on his face. He swung around and took the blood-dripping hare outside. He returned with it ten minutes later, gutted, but cleaned so badly there were still patches of fur all over it.

Seeing it made Mary get all riled up again. "Don't you know *anythung* at all about skinnin'? Go back and do it agin!" she demanded before she could stop herself. "And don't you dare brung it back in here till it don't got a single scrap of fur on it, y'hear me?"

Cletus' narrow-eyed, hostile look was enough to send chills down Mary's spine, but she raised a determined chin to show she brooked no nonsense. Shooting a look at his elder brother, he said sourly, "I hear ye."

While he was gone, she lit the logs in the wood-fire stove and put on a big black pot of water to boil. "What vegetables d'you got?"

"Vegetables?"

"You cain't have vittles with no vegetables," she quailed.

"Well, we got us some store-bought groceries!" Zachary Thomas said grimly. Cans of beans an' sech. Otherwise, jest cook it by itself. Meat is all a man needs."

47

Mary stared at him in consternation. How could a family so poor afford store-bought groceries? And how was she supposed to make a hare stew with no vegetables? Then an idea struck her. "Do you at least got flour?"

"Sure, thar's a sack in th' cupboard. Salt and lard too."

"Good, then I'll make some dumplings to go with th' stew. Maybe put some canned beans in it too."

Mary fetched the metal dishes and eating utensils from a cupboard and set the table.

About two hours later, Zachary Thomas impatiently lifted the big heavy black pot onto the table by its handles. She watched the brothers ladle huge piles of the steaming stew and dumplings onto their plates. Without even saying grace, they tucked in, slurping and grunting like hogs at feed, periodically belching with satisfaction, then helping themselves to second and third helpings. Steeling herself against showing her distaste, Mary dished herself out a much daintier portion, nibbling at her food, her appetite suddenly gone.

At last, Otis pushed back his chair, patted his bloated belly and declared, "Well, Zack, she ain't that much of a looker, but leastways, she'll sure feed you right!"

Mary blushed at the backhanded compliment. Young Jamie regarded her with shining eyes that seemed to focus all at once. "Well, if'n you ask me, I thunk she's real purty!" he declared staunchly.

Mary felt a spurt of warmth towards the backward youth. She smiled at him and said, "Why, thank you, Jamie."

By the time they'd finished eating, the stew pot had been scraped bare. Mary made Otis and Zachary Thomas fetch some water which she boiled to wash the pot, the dishes and the eating utensils.

Later, when she had finished, Zachary Thomas said shortly, "You kin take Paw's bed. Me an' m'brothers will sleep up in th' loft."

Mary was relieved to hear about the sleeping arrangements. She'd been worried in case Zachary Thomas expected to sleep with her even though they weren't yet married. "Thank you, but what will I wear?"

"Come." Taking Mary's hand he led her into his father's large bedroom. The room was such a contrast to the rest of the cabin, Mary felt she'd stepped into another world. She was somewhat daunted by the luxury of it all.

On top of walnut chest of drawers was an exquisite parlor lamp, the likes of which Mary had never seen before. Both the outer globe and the base were made of finest translucent porcelain and richly tinted in brown shading to dark orange. They were elegantly embossed with clusters of grapes and leaves in their natural colors, with a bottom base of gold-plated heavy solid brass in open-work filigree design. This exquisite oil-fuelled lamp gave off a brilliant light that cast an enchanting glow in the room.

In the center of the room against the back wall was a handsome, elaborately designed four-poster brass bedstead, with high multi-curved chills and gilt décoration at the head and the foot. There was an enormous walnut wardrobe and a huge, intricately carved, wooden chest with gold metal hinges and ornamentation, and ball-and-claw feet. An Acme Corona hard-coal base burner stood in one corner, the most beautiful, elaborate and ornamental coal burner she had ever seen. Although it was not being used now, the reflectors above the fire-view doors with their mirror polished surfaces reflected the glow of the parlor lamp and made it look alive with coals. An elaborate rug of roses of many different colors lay on the floor. A long Cheval mirror stood in one corner.

On a small dark oak table supported by filigreed wooden legs sat a wind-up Harvard Disc talking machine with a golden oak base on which sat the turn-table and a large flower horn ornamented with gold stripes. A highly ornamental swinging arm and bracket supported the horn and reproducer. A needle attached to the bracket was resting on a cylindrical record. Seeing the direction of her eyes, Zachary Thomas dropped her hand and crossed to it, wound it up by its handle and set the needle to the beginning of the disc record. To Mary's surprise, a tinny-sounding man's operatic voice sounded in the room. She'd seen a talking machine once at the general store, but it was nowhere near as fancy as this one and she'd certainly never *heard* one before.

Without a word, Zachary Thomas went to the chest. He opened it and dug around in it, finally drawing out a voluminous white nightgown that glowed pale-orange in the glow of the lamp. Made of cambric with a V-neck finished with wide embroidery beading and ribbon, its round yoke of tucks and lace insertions was finished with herring-bone braid and hem-stitched lawn ruffle trimmed with lace, with the full sleeves trimmed in the same manner. It was the most beautiful night garment Mary had ever seen, or was ever likely to.

"It b'longed to Maw. Reckon you kin keep it, seein' as she don't got no use fer it no more."

"Thank you, Zachary Thomas," murmured Mary, as she clutched it shyly to her bosom. "It's beautiful." She looked up at him breathlessly, seeing how big and handsome he was and feeling a stirring of attraction for him. Caught up in the misty romantic atmosphere the glow of lamp-light gave the room and hearing the music he had specially put on for her benefit, she longed for him to put his arms around her and kiss her.

But Zachary Thomas merely grunted then turned and stalked out the room without saying another word. Mary bit her lower lip. Oh dear, he must be angry at her for causing trouble between him and his brother, for he had not even bothered to kiss his bride-to-be goodnight.

6

Mary woke up early the next morning, as was her habit, and she lay for a moment with her eyes closed. Then she realized the air in the loft wasn't as hot and stuffy as it usually was in summer and there was a peculiar smell in the room. Her eyes blinked open. She stared through the dimness at the roof. *Where were the sloping rafters?* She felt a twinge of foreboding. Then she felt the rare comfort of the first bed she had ever slept on beneath her, and remembrance hit her like a fork of lightning. She sat bolt upright. *Of course!* Yesterday she had eloped with a stranger and today was to be her wedding day!

Last night, totally worn out by the long journey and the dramatic events of the day, she had slept the deep dreamless sleep of the exhausted as soon as her head hit the pillow, but now, in this cool dark fancy bedroom in the cabin of a notorious moonshiner who was head of this feared clan and, wearing the nightgown of a dead woman, she suddenly felt intensely disturbed and began to realize the full extent of her folly. *She must be mad!* She couldn't possibly marry Zachary Thomas no matter how attracted she was to him! She couldn't marry a total stranger – *a Bucko!* – and be kin to all those awful, loud-mouthed, filthy crackers he had introduced her to yesterday. She couldn't possibly live among them for *the rest of her life!* Why, the only one she had taken to was young Jamie, who was clearly feeble-minded, if real sweet of nature. No, she would just have to talk to Zachary Thomas and tell him that she had changed her mind. Then she would have to ask him to take her back to her parents today. Of course, there would be a lot of talk and unkind gossip on Lewis Mountain, even the entire Blue Ridge, since word got around so quickly through the general stores, but she would have to put up with it. *Small price to pay to get away from this liquor-ridden, lawless lot who clearly had no respect for anyone, least of all themselves!* Why, they were a disgrace to all decent mountain folk!

All was quiet in the cabin and she got up and opened the wooden shutters across the open window, feeling the bracing early-morning air brushing her face. Outside, the creeping dawn was slowly lighting up the dense surrounding forest, which was coming alive with the sound of awakening wild birds. Wisps of mist sailed through the trees like wraiths. Mary pulled the huge white nightgown over her head and changed back into her brown work dress, before looking around the room What had seemed so beautiful and romantic at night looked mighty different in the light of day. She noticed dust everywhere, including a thick layer of it on the flower horn of the talking machine and the coal burner. The mattress drooped in the middle and the bedclothes were tatty and worn, the coverlet a drab dark maroon, the white sheets and the pillows so dirty and gray-looking that Lord knew when they had last seen the washtub. She felt a twinge of repulsion, for she suddenly realized it was the *bed linen* that had smelt so peculiar on her waking – a mingling of stale sweat and the putrid pong of a long-unwashed body. She'd been so tired last night she hadn't even noticed it. The rug was dreadfully faded and threadbare too. Such woeful lack of pride gave her even more resolve to leave.

After hurriedly straightening the bedclothes, she washed her face and hands with the icy water in a cracked and chipped white ceramic bowl with tiny pink rosebuds on it that was on the walnut chest-of-drawers. She wiped them dry on the nightgown because she couldn't find a towel. She turned and, with her face and hands still damp, she inhaled deeply, trying to fill herself with courage. She went to the door and timidly opened it, staring into the large main room of the cabin.

To her surprise, she saw that a fire was already burning in the huge stone fireplace and a pot of coffee was brewing on the top of the wood-fire stove. Zachary Thomas was sitting stretched out on a wooden chair at the large wooden table, drinking a mug of the strong-smelling brew. He looked weary and morose as a bad-tempered bear just out of hibernation. Yet just seeing the handsome black-haired giant she had just yesterday agreed to betroth, set her heart galloping with an odd mixture of attraction, repulsion and terror. She was relieved to find him on his own, because she had to talk to him before she completely lost her nerve.

"Mornin', Zachary Thomas," she murmured, anxiously wringing her hands.

He lifted his head, with a surprised look on his face, as if he had failed to hear her enter, flashing those brilliant turquoise-green eyes at her. "You sleep alright?"

"Jest fine, thank you, Zachary Thomas." She waited for him to talk again, but a slight, awkward silence stretched ominously. Just to dent it, she muttered, "Whar are th' others?"

"Oh, they won't be up a'fore noon, I reckon. Them rascals had a sight too many jugs of moonshine last night, what with Paw out of th' way and all."

"Noon!" Surely he didn't mean that. Then she heard loud drunken snores coming from the loft above them and realized he *did* mean it. "But ...," she spluttered, "who will do all th' chores?"

"What chores?"

"Well, cuttin' wood, fetchin' water, feedin' th' livestock and sech."

"Oh, we buy cut wood from th' Ficks and the Addis clans."

Mary's heart sank. With all the trees hereabouts at their disposal, this bunch was so lazy and good-for-nothing they didn't even do their own wood-chopping! No wonder so few trees had been felled on this mountain. She didn't voice her disgust, however. Instead, she asked, "Who're them folk?"

"Some squatter and tenant folk live on Beacon and Bear Rock Mountains."

"Oh, and th' rest of th' chores?"

"Well, heck, they do what they got to do!" he said sharply, clearly sensing her disdain. "They got plenty hard work on thar hands tendin' to th' moonshine crops and th' stills!"

With that, he lapsed into a morose silence. Mary tried to gather up her courage to give him the news. "Zachary Thomas," she managed at last.

"Ummph?"

"Zachary Thomas, I don't reckon I kin marry you, after all," she said in a rush of soft words.

Zachary Thomas looked up at her sharply, startling turquoise-green eyes blazing. *"Why not?"*

"Jest changed my mind, is all. I don't know you at all. Ye're jest a stranger to me. Will you please take me back to Lewis Mountain today? Maw an' Paw will be frettin' somethung fierce over me."

Zachary Thomas's eyes narrowed. He stared at her for a moment in transfixed silence before he muttered, "Cain't do that."

"Well, if not today, then when kin you?"

"I cain't at all. The preacher's a'comin' a long way today to hitch us up."

Mary stared at him in disbelief. "I know that, Zachary Thomas, but I've jest told you that I've done changed my mind. You'll jest got to tell him when he comes, is all."

"Reckon not."

Mary stared at him in shocked disbelief. "You can't *force* me to marry you," she said quietly, but firmly.

"I ain't a'forcin' you!" he said indignantly. "I asked you to marry me, and you said 'yes' real smart like! Reckon ye're jest sufferin' from what folks call them 'weddin' jitters'. My own maw told me all about 'em. Said she had 'em real bad a'fore she wed my paw."

Mary felt she could hardly breathe. "So you're aimin' on *forcin'* me to marry you, even tho' you know full well I don't want to no more?" she asked, aghast.

"Like I said, I ain't a'forcin' you. It's what you want. It's jest them jitters o'your'n. You'll be jest fine once it's all over, you'll see."

Mary felt a surge of anger. *The stupid man!* How dare he try to force her to do something against her will! *"Mercy be!* I don't believe this!" she said heatedly,

52

her voice rising." Everythung folks say about you lot is true!"

"Be quiet, girl!" Zachary Thomas thundered. "All I'm a'doin' is like my own paw done. Now fix me some breakfast, girl."

Mary stared at him in bald astonishment. "I'll do no sech thung!" she snarled. "Do it yerself!"

"You sure are a stubborn one, ain't ya? Reckon I'm gonna have to learn you to obey yer husband when he talks."

"You ain't my husband and never will be!" she snapped, her hazel eyes flashing.

Zachary Thomas looked at her, shaking his head. "Lawdee be, them jitters sure take hold of a wimmin!"

"Aaaargh!" Mary screamed in outrage. She flew into the bedroom, slamming the door behind her before flinging herself onto the bed, pounding the mattress with her fists and sobbing with rage and frustration. Oh, how could she have been so simple-minded as to believe he was any different from the other Buckos? If the truth be told, he was the worst of the lot! Well, she wasn't going to go ahead with it! She'd rather die first! Her sobs gradually died down and she tried to make sense of everything she had got herself into. There had to be *something* she could do! *Of course!* She'd run away! It was too far for her to go to Lewis Mountain on foot, but maybe she could seek refuge on Beacon Mountain, and they could get word to her father to come fetch her by mule. She knew there were some respectable folk on Beacon Mountain. After all, at least one of them owned a fine horse!

Filled with resolve, Mary got up and tiptoed to the door. She pressed an ear against it to hear if she could locate the whereabouts of Zachary Thomas. There was no sound coming from the other side. She crossed quickly to the opened window. She stuck her head out and looked around. Sunlight was streaming through the tall, towering trees. *The coast was clear!* The cabin had been built on stilts in the front to accommodate the slope, and from this front left-side bedroom, there was quite a drop to the ground. Without a moment's hesitation, she scrambled out of the window and leapt the ten-odd feet onto the hard ground, landing with a thump and going over slightly on one ankle.

Fortunately, it didn't hurt too much. But she was starkly terrified, however, and her heart was pounding inside her breast. She had better not risk running across the yard in case Zachary Thomas walked out on the porch and saw her. She'd have to head for the forest, where the undergrowth was thick, and keep as well away from the clearing as possible. She ran into the forest at its closest point and circled cautiously around the homestead through the dense forest. There was no danger of her getting lost! She just had to keep heading down the slopes and she would eventually get off the mountain.

53

Fortunately, going down would be a lot easier than climbing up it had been. The only danger would be if she unexpectedly came upon some of the homesites of the rest of the clan. Even if the elders were also sleeping off the effects of too much moonshine like those at Horseshoe Hollow, some young'uns might spot her and sound the alarm. Or their coon dogs might set up a racket and somebody might come to investigate, especially since they were so jumpy about the Galtreys.

The steepness of the mountain meant that sheer momentum sent Mary flying headlong down the mountain. She ducked around the trunks of trees, skirted around thickets of bushes, ran over rocky terrain and splashed through streams with sharp stones in them that stabbed at her mountain-tough feet. But she daren't slow down. Any minute now Zachary Thomas might discover she was gone and come after her. What's more, he would probably alert his kinfolk and they would chase after her with their shotguns and pistols and coon dogs, as if they were chasing after a hapless raccoon! Then they may decide that she had committed the ultimate insult in trying to escape and shoot her instead! Lord knew, if rumor were to be believed, they were capable of almost anything and she definitely wouldn't be the first to befall such an ugly fate!

Flocks of wild birds flew up at her passing. Her breath was coming harsh and rasping now, such was the intensity of her downward flight. The sound seemed hugely magnified, since the forest was engulfed in a great eerie silence, but for the monotonous humming of a katydid. The silence seemed to lurch after her like a ghoul, dogging her footsteps and clutching at her with long ghostly fingers, because it held so much hidden menace. It drove her to greater effort.

She suddenly saw a homesite looming in the distance and veered sharply to the left, keeping such a sharp eye on it, she didn't see a root sticking out of the undergrowth. She tripped over it and went crashing to the forest floor with terrible force. She held her hands splayed out in front of her in an effort to protect herself. The ground here was muddy, steep and rocky and she slid down the slope some fifteen feet, scraping the heels of her hands till they were raw and bleeding and brushing past brambles that scratched her face and arms. Mary felt she might never have stopped until she reached the bottom of Claw Mountain, if her one shoulder hadn't slammed against the dark-brown, straight ridged trunk of a towering chestnut tree, which stopped her dead in her tracks.

She had badly hurt herself and she bit hard on her bottom lip in an effort not to cry out. Her hands were burning with pain, she was grazed all over, her shoulder ached so much, it felt as if it had been knocked out of its socket, and her dress was torn and muddy from top to bottom. She could not stop herself from sobbing. *Well, it's no good feeling sorry for myself!* she mentally remonstrated with herself. She just had to keep going. She rose shakily to her feet and, whimpering, started off again, going much slower this time, and hobbling.

54

As she reached the lower slopes, she decided it would be safe to use the pathway, which would be far easier to traverse than the dense terrain that was presently hampering her passage. She managed to reach the path and was able to pick up her speed considerably, despite her injuries. She was just catapulting around a bend edged by thick bushes when she was flung headlong into the arms of someone coming up the path! She got such a shock she gave a loud involuntary scream. The person grunted when she hit him and held onto her tightly to steady her.

"What in hell's name …?"

The young man held her at arms' length and stared at her with pale-yellow eyes that were wide with surprise. Mary recognized his bright-yellow hair and scarred face instantly and almost fainted with terror. *For it was none other than Eli, the whip-wielder!*

In her muddied state, it took the cracker a moment longer for him to recognize her.

"Well, well, well, if'n it ain't th' little bitch from th' store! You don't look so uppity now, do ya? You look like you jest bathed yerself in mud! What in hell's name you doin' here on Claw Mountain?"

Mary could not answer him. She was still panting hoarsely and frozen with fright. She stared helplessly at him.

"Well, Mary Louella Harley, seein' as th' good Lord has seen fit to deliver you right into my arms, I reckon that's a sure sign He wants me to teach you a little lesson for interferin' in my business th' other day."

"Oh, please," Mary begged. "I weren't interferin', I swar …"

"Well, see now, I cain't says I agree with you. And nobody gits away with interferin' with Buchanan justice! Fact is, I was askin' about you at th' store an' was about to pay you a little visit on Lewis Mountain. Seems somebody saved me th' trouble of goin' to look fer you. Now fancy that! Wonder who it could be?"

Mary kept quiet. Surely he didn't mean that! The last thing she wanted to admit was that she was running away from his eldest brother, to whom she was supposed to get married in a few hours' time. Who knew what umbrage he would take at that!

"Never mind, I got me other thungs on my mind, right now!" Eli said mildly.

To Mary's horror, she saw that he had removed his twin pearl-handled Owl's Head pistols from the belt that hauled in his dirty denim dungarees, laid them on the ground and was busy unbuckling his belt, dropping it to the ground. Then he casually fiddled with the galluses on the straps of his blue denim dungarees. The dungarees dropped to his knees. He had no underwear on except a holey vest, and his angry swollen private parts were exposed to her shocked eyes. Mary began sobbing with fear. She didn't know too much about anything that happened between a man and woman, since Maw's careful euphemisms were beyond her, but she had warned her that some nasty men took women "by force", whatever that meant! And right now Mary didn't need anyone to tell her that this young man was the kind about whom she had been talking! *He was going to hurt her!*

"DON'T YOU DARE TOUCH ME!" she screamed.

He regarded her with his scary yellow eyes. "I kin do anythung I want," he sneered. *"And right now, this here is what I want!"*

Drawing her roughly to him, he kissed her harshly, forcing his tongue into her mouth. Mary pulled back in repulsion, pressing hard against his chest with her hands. He smelled vile. He grabbed her, threw her on the ground and pulled up her skirt. Before she could stop him, he ripped her baggy white bloomers down to her knees. Then grinning evilly down at her, he dropped down on her like a sack of grain. Mary felt a surge of outrage. *She'd rather die than submit to this monster!* She bucked against him like an unbroken filly. When she couldn't heave him off her, she began screaming and hitting out at him for all she was worth. He responded by punching her viciously on her face, stunning and silencing her for a dizzying moment. He was busy trying to force himself inside her between her legs with the unspeakable part of himself, when quite suddenly, without warning, he wasn't there anymore!

"YOU STINKIN' SON-OF-A-BITCH, ELI! How dare you defile th' wimmin I'm about to wed!"

Breathing harshly, Mary saw that Zachary Thomas had yanked his younger brother off her by the back of his vest and his face was contorted with rage. Mary didn't know whether to be relieved to see him or not, but she was mighty glad to be rid of her foul-mouthed attacker. She hastily yanked up her bloomers and pulled down her mud-sodden dress, her face red and smarting with humiliation as she shakily stood up.

Taken by surprise, Eli shook himself out of his brother's hold, his face wearing a dark scowl. "You gotta be joshin' me."

"Hell, no, I ain't!"

"If'n what you say is true then how come she was runnin' away?"

"We had us a little squabble, is all, but you kin be sure that we's gittin' ourselves hitched this afternoon. If you don't believe me, ask th' others. Don't thunk Paw would take too kindly to hear 'bout this, neither. Y'know he's bin after me to git m'self hitched a good long while now."

At the mention of their father, something flared briefly in Eli's eyes, before they shut down. He held up his hands in mock surrender.

"Sure thung, Zack. You know I never would have touched her if I'd a'known she b'longed to you. Well, dog m'skin, my long-single brother has found hisself a bride at last!" He gave them a slow, lazy smile that smacked of benign boyish impudence, but he sure didn't fool Mary any — his eyes were queerly lighted like they had been at the store that day! He was mad as a snake to be disturbed in his mischief in so rude a manner! "Sure hope I'm invited to th' weddin'," he added, as he casually pulled up his dungarees and fixed the galluses.

Zachary Thomas's face cleared. "Sure you are, Eli. All my kinfolk are invited."

"Why this afternoon, big brother?" Eli asked solemnly. "Paw won't be back fer a few days yet. Reckon he'll be mighty peeved to miss out on sech an important occasion."

"Mebbe, but I promised Mary we'd git hitched today and I aim on keepin' my promise to her."

Mary felt she was living in the middle of a nightmare as Zachary Thomas turned and grabbed her by the arm, the one with the injured shoulder. His fingers were digging into her flesh as he began dragging her up the slope behind him, with Eli trailing after them. It took all of Mary's willpower not to cry out. Furthermore, she could feel Eli's devilish eyes drilling into her back, giving her the shudders. Well, the oldest Bucko may have saved her from getting forcefully ravaged by him, but he was just as bad. He was going to force her to marry him, and then he was going to do what Eli had failed to do just minutes ago! She vowed to herself that she would not submit willingly to him, no matter what!

When they got to Obediah's cabin, Zachary Thomas pulled her up the partially caved-in steps and into the cabin. "Go git yerself cleaned up a'fore th' preacher man gits here," he ordered gruffly, giving her an angry shove towards his father's bedroom. Then he addressed his brother. "Let's go git ourselves a jug to celebrate!"

Mary returned to the bedroom she had so recently escaped from, smarting with outrage and humiliation, and closed the door behind her. Trembling, aching all over and very close to tears, she pressed her back against it and slid down it to the floorboards. She leaned her forehead against her knees and began to silently sob. *What was she going to do now?*

She thought about telling the preacher when he arrived that she was refusing to marry Zachary Thomas, but soon realized that she had no choice but to go along with it. Zachary Thomas would punish her for it and, even if he didn't, his brother, Eli, surely would! Zachary Thomas would probably beat her as it was, for trying to escape. After all, this was a clan whose capacity for violence was legend in these parts. *Oh, how did I manage to get myself into this awful mess?*

7

Sitting on the floor, Mary sobbed till she had no more tears left, then she sniffed and looked up miserably. How could she have been so stupid as to get involved with a Bucko? What would become of her now? Then suddenly her eyes were drawn irresistibly to the open window. Had Zachary Thomas forgotten that she had already tried to escape by jumping out of the window? Dare she make a second attempt with both him and Eli on the other side of the door? She had sensed some deep, underlying tension between the two, but maybe that would be forgotten if they undertook a search for her. And what if Eli was the one to find her? Mary felt a chill slide down her spine. She would never forget how he had tried to take her by force earlier. If she was forced to stay, would she be in danger of him forcing himself on her whenever she was alone? She didn't think that her being married to his brother would make a jot of difference to him somehow. She cringed inwardly at the thought. She couldn't bear the thought of him touching her again. She had no choice. She had to try and leave this accursed mountain once more!

Her mind made up, Mary quickly crossed to the window. It was still long before noon when she might expect Zachary Thomas's other brothers to arise and, fortunately, the coast was as clear as it had been earlier! With her heart in her mouth, she was busy scrambling out of the window when she heard the unmistakable sound of the hammer of a shotgun being drawn back. She stopped dead and cringingly looked around to see where the sound had come from. There along the leafy branch of a tree growing alongside the cabin, she saw the double barrels of a sawn-off shotgun aimed straight at her.

She gasped with shock. With her eyes fixed rigidly on the lethal weapon being aimed at her, it took Mary a little while to realize who was actually holding it. When she looked up to see, she froze with surprise for it was a filthy little scrap of a girl, with dirty, knotted, straight, fair hair and pale-blue eyes which peeped out of a sharp little face covered in dirt. Not more than ten or eleven years old, wearing dungarees and a tatty filthy vest, she sat matter of factly at the crook of a branch, knees raised on the branch with the big shotgun balanced on them, aiming the thing straight at her.

"Stay right whar ye are!" the girl scathingly commanded, her eyes narrowing into slits. "You git back inside right this here minute, or I'll blow ye clean in half!"

There was no doubt that the girl meant business, for she had real mean look on her hatchet-narrow face.

58

"Who *are* you?" Mary managed at last.

"I'm Emma, an' my Unc' Zack done tole me t'make real sure you don't take it in yer head t'escape."

"I see, Emma. D'you *know* how to use that thar thung?"

"Sure do!" she said indignantly. "I'm th' best shot on Claw Mountain! Even better than Unc' Zack an' he done learn'd me how t'shoot. He sawed 'bout six inches off of th' barrel to make it lighter fer me, and shoot truer. An' this here 12-gauge breech loader takes slug shots, not jest plain old shot or buckshot fer birds an' squirrels an' stuff! I've shot plenty of deer with it. And Unc' Zack's shot a *baar* or two with it in his time too, so ye'd be easy meat to down, that's fer sure!"

Mary felt a qualm of fear. She had no doubt the girl meant what she said. "That so?" she said weakly.

"You marryin' my Unc' Zack like he said?"

Duly warned about the weapon's efficiency, Mary considered how she should answer the child's question. If she told her no, she was likely to blow her in half just like she had threatened to.

"Sure looks that way, Emma," she answered with an exaggerated sigh.

"Why's yer face all swell'd up that way?"

"El . . . I mean, I hurt it when I fell."

"Git back inside," the girl demanded. "A'fore I git tired of a'waitin'."

With the girl's fingers itching on the two triggers, Mary, filled with frustration, hastily backed inside. Safely back in the fancy, but neglected, bedroom of the Claw Mountain patriarch, she sat on the big brass bed with its mattress that drooped in the middle, offended by its rancid smell, trying to figure out what to do. Effectively kept a prisoner against her wishes by a shotgun-toting urchin and the two highly disreputable men on the other side of the door, she realized she had no choice but to go ahead with this charade of a marriage. Well, she would go ahead with the wedding, but one thing was for sure, she would escape from the mountain the very first opportunity that she got!

A short while later Mary stuck her head out the window. "Emma, I need fer you to go fetch me some water to wash with some lye soap and a washrag too."

Emma raised her shotgun and pointed it straight at Mary's head. Clearly suspecting a ruse, she narrowed her eyes and shook her head. "Git Unc' Zack t'go fetch it!"

"I thought of that, too, but I don't want to bother him none. He an' yer Uncle Eli are a'doin' some hard drinkin'."

"Oh!" Emma said. This was clearly something she understood. But she wouldn't abandon her perch for anything. Instead, she put two fingers in her mouth and gave a loud piercing whistle. Immediately, a thin little spike-haired boy wearing just a pair of rolled-up dungarees came running up. He was every bit as filthy as Emma was. Indeed, his face was so covered in dirt she could hardly make out his eyes.

"What y'want, Emm?" the small boy asked anxiously.

Emma shifted on her perch. The shotgun was still unwaveringly trained on Mary despite the fact that it probably weighed as much as she did.

"Beaufort, y'go fetch some water an' soap and a washrag," she ordered her small lackey below. "Then take it in to Unc' Zack's bride."

"Hokay," said Beaufort, before speeding off.

It wasn't too long before there was a soft, hesitant knock at the door. Mary opened it to find the filthy little ragamuffin standing outside holding a wooden bucket of water with a washrag and a bar of lye soap lying on the bottom of it. He was straining with the weight of it.

"Thank you, Beaufort."

Mary took the bucket from him and, closing the door with her one foot, she carried it across the room, the movement slurping water over the edge of the bucket onto the rug, and placed it on top of the chest of drawers. Then she started to clean up, first lowering her bloody hands in the water, making them burn, as she gently ran the lye soap over them. Pressing them against the back of her ruined brown skirt to dry, she crossed to the long Cheval mirror. She carefully studied her face in it. *It was almost as bad as the faces of the two young'uns!* Streaked with dirt, scratched and red and swollen from Eli's blow, her face felt tender to the touch. She washed it carefully using the faded old washrag, before drawing her muddy dress over her head. Standing in just her baggy white bloomers, she gave herself a good all-over wash, noticing a rude dark-red graze on her right shoulder where it had hit the chestnut tree.

Zachary Thomas had told her to clean up, but her brown dress was torn and drenched in mud. She eyed the big wooden chest and quickly crossed over to it. She removed the bucket, placing it on the floor and opened the lid of the chest to a host of treasures. She drew out neatly folded, musty-smelling dresses, wrapped in cloth, one by one. They were exquisite and made of expensive fabrics like velvet, satin, silk and Chantilly lace. Several taffeta silk Heatherbloom flounced petticoats, some trimmed with tucks and double ruffles, others beautifully embroidered, in black, royal blue, or green, looked like some of those she had seen in Sears, Roebuck catalogues. She found an unopened packet of six Burson fine lisle black stockings and a number of elegant drawers. Never had Mary seen such magnificent finery.

Scratching around in the chest some more, she found a silver brush-and-comb set with a matching looking glass, which she took out too. She brushed the leaves, grass and other bits of debris out of her hair using the silver brush. She remembered hearing somebody say after the incident at the store that it was rumored that the matriarch of the Buckos had been a wealthy young woman, once. Now, seeing all these beautiful garments and fancy city-store things, Mary did not doubt it. She wondered how her sons had turned out such rabble. She sighed. So many things in this family did not add up!

To Mary's disconcertion, it gradually got noisier and noisier outside the door as the clan gathered in the patriarch's cabin for the wedding. She was dreading what was going to happen next. The full reality and enormity of being forced to marry into this iniquitous clan swept through her being, filling her with terror and dread. Finally, after she was dressed and ready, there was another knock on the door and Zachary Thomas called out, "Mary, c'mon out. Th' preacher man is here."

As she opened the door with her heart pounding wildly inside her breast, the noise and stench of the unwashed bodies of the gathered clan, hit her like a slap in the face. While Zachary Thomas and most of the others were standing, Eli and an elderly stranger, wearing a slouch hat, were sitting at the table. Emma slipped through the door still holding her double-barreled shotgun, but all the other children appeared to be outside from the sound of their raised voices, since despite its large size, the room was too small to contain the whole clan. As she stepped into the room, everybody turned to her and there were shocked and astonished gasps, before silence fell like a dropped hatchet on a log. Zachary Thomas's look was almost one of wide-eyed panic before it turned decidedly grim.

Mary had not expected this sort of reaction from the clan at all. Clearly, they were strongly reminded of their dead mother by virtue of the fact that she was wearing her clothes. She had found inside the chest, a beautiful, dusky-pink satin shirtwaister gown with a high ruche neck edged in cream lace, the bodice of which had several wide pleats which fell to the belted waist, and sleeves which were buttoned from the wrist to the elbow with tiny pearl buttons and edged with the same cream lace. On her bosom, she wore a diamante brooch in the shape of a bird. On feet that were habitually bare in summer, she now wore a pair of the black lisle stockings and elegant black soft-kid button-up boots that peeped from beneath the hem. She had forsaken her baggy bloomers for a pair of umbrella-shaped lace-trimmed and pink, ribbon-bedecked, finest lisle white drawers. Fortunately, the dress and boots fitted her perfectly and her black hair hung shiny and loose almost to her waist.

She had never before dressed in such elegance, but with Zachary Thomas's odd reaction and the way the assembled Buckos were ogling her like she was a bearded lady in a carnival, she began to wish she'd stuck to her muddied, torn dress, after all. After the initial dazed reaction from the womenfolk, their eyes narrowed in envy and spite and they began to mutter darkly amongst themselves.

Eli slowly stood up, the wooden chair scraping backwards, his eyes glued on Mary's face, his gaze as cold as ice. Even surrounded by a whole bunch of unsavory strangers, she felt the pervasive chill of his presence and quickly averted her eyes back to the man who was soon to be her husband. He was still staring at her with an odd expression on his face. He was clearly angry at her because she was wearing his departed mother's things without permission? *Was he going to chastise her for it in front of everybody?* But he didn't say a word. Just then, to her relief, the elderly stranger at the table stood up and strutted forward.

Zachary Thomas introduced him to her, mumbling, "This here is Preacher Cleats, Mary. He's here to wed us."

The preacher took off his hat and left it on the table. He was a short, rotund man with red hair, a freckled face, a ruddy nose and red-rimmed, rheumy green eyes. Unlike the rest of the company, he wore shoes as befitted his calling. Although dressed a trifle better than the mountain crackers, who had not bothered to dress up or wash for the occasion and still smelled like sour corn-mash whiskey and ripe, stale sweat, his white shirt was somewhat soiled. The funny little man took her hand and raised it to his lips, giving her a smarmy grin. "Well, you do look fine, child. I'd say Zack here is a real lucky fella!"

"Thank you, Preacher Cleats," murmured Mary, feeling her cheeks flaming. She felt terribly conspicuous and out of place. What on earth had possessed her to dress up like a queen to impress this white cracker trash? Even while she was changing into such finery, she had been aware that she wanted to show these disgraceful reprobates how true mountain folk behaved – with a deal of dignity to be sure!

"'Tis a shame yer face be so marked, tho'," the preacher continued. "How did ye hurt yerself, girl?"

Mary felt her stomach drop and she gave Eli a brief, fearful look, wondering what would happen if she were to tell the preacher that *he* was responsible for the condition of her face. But she daren't. "A fall, Preacher Cleats."

"Well, it's across to th' fireplace with ye," he announced with a loud uncouth hiccup.

Mary did as she was bid, striving to maintain her dignity and her balance in the unfamiliar button-up boots, her black taffeta silk petticoat rustling, before she stood next to the giant, barefoot cracker, who, in a very short while would her *husband*. It was only then that she noticed, with some relief, that Zachary Thomas, standing huge on his big bare feet, had washed up, shaved, combed his long hair, greased his mustache and had on a clean white shirt, a black string bowtie and neat gray trousers. He smelled of a mixture of lye soap and tobacco. His immense shoulders were packed with muscles, which were presently moving in bunches beneath the material of the shirt, as if he was nervous.

Despite this, he seemed to dominate the whole room with his quiet intensity and narrow-eyed gauging expression, and Mary felt decidedly intimidated by him, sensing a menace inside him that was carefully contained. The preacher stood in front of the fireplace, rocking importantly on his heels, ready to start the proceedings.

Far from missing having her family here on the most important day of her life, Mary was infinitely relieved that they weren't, for Zachary Thomas's kinfolk kept making lewd comments that flamed the blush on Mary's cheeks as if they had been scalded. They cackled, nipped from moonshine jugs, spat and blew noses on the floor. Then, suddenly, she thought of something! It came to her out of the blue like a gift on the wind. *The marriage license!* They hadn't been to get a marriage license! They couldn't possibly get married without one! Even if it just delayed matters a short while, she might get the chance to escape, or give the sheriff enough time to find her here! Hope and joy soared in her breast!

"WAIT!" she cried. "We cain't git married."

"WHY NOT?" Zachary Thomas roared.

"'Cuz we don't got no *license*," she said urgently. "Everybody knows you got to have a license to be wed! Ain't that right, Preacher Cleats?"

The preacher gave another loud hiccup. "Well, um . . . uh, well, it's like this, see . . ."

"I got us a license!" said Zachary Thomas curtly. "Fetched it a'fore I came to fetch you yesterday!"

Mary looked at him in dismay. He had been that sure of winning her over, he'd collected a marriage license on the way over to Lewis Mountain. She didn't know whether to be flattered, or infuriated, by such over-confidence. She swallowed hard, unable to bear the bitter disappointment of being foiled in this manner.

"You did?" she asked hollowly.

"Sure did!"

"Well, whar is it then?" she demanded to know.

"Gave it to Preacher Cleats the moment he got here. Ain't that right, Preacher Cleats?"

Preacher Cleats puffed up his narrow chest with importance. "That's right! Got it right here in my pocket." He patted his shirt pocket with one orange-freckled hand. "Will register it on my way back. Now, kin we please git on with it?"

Mary was dying to ask to see the license, but that would indicate to the clan that she doubted the word of a preacher. Of course, she *was* silly to doubt the word of a man of the cloth. Zachary Thomas had got a license for them and given it to the preacher to register, as he had said. *She was doomed!* She nodded to the preacher to begin the ceremony. The preacher wasted no time in getting down to business.

"Zack, d'ye take th' hand of this here wimmin?"

"I do."

"Well, then, whar's th' ring?"

There was a stunned silence. Zachary Thomas looked at the preacher in bewildered consternation. It was one detail he had clearly overlooked. He croaked, "Don't got me one."

Mary looked at the preacher hopefully. Could a body still get married without a ring? she wondered. Could it possibly cause the hoped-for delay?

Zachary Thomas frowned as he tried to figure out what to do. Then his face cleared. "Ellie Mae, let me have your'n. I'll give it back to you right after."

The flame-haired Ellie Mae gave him a wicked grin and obligingly wriggled the plain gold band off her thin, freckled finger, handing it over to her huge brother-in-law.

"You got to pay me in kind fer this, y'hear, Zack?' she said, giving him a meaningful wink. "Borrowin' my ring means I git th' same privileges as th' bride!"

Zachary Thomas took the ring from her with a look of glaring distaste.

"Put it on," Preacher Cleats commanded Zachary Thomas, amid a blast of fumes that was unmistakably laced with alcohol. Mary wrinkled her nose with involuntary distaste. *The preacher had been drinking!* Zachary Thomas took Mary's hand. She had to steel herself against snatching it away as he struggled get the ring past her knuckle. Finally, he succeeded, straightened and faced the preacher once more.

To Mary's surprise, the preacher declared, "I now pronounce thee man an' wife," and hiccupped again. He took a tin mug of water off the mantel, hiccupped again and commanded her and Zachary Thomas to bow their heads. Using his fingers, he proceeded to liberally sprinkle the liquid from the tumbler over their heads. Then Mary sniffed a powerful, familiar scent and realized that it wasn't what she had assumed. She and Zachary Thomas had just been anointed with raw moonshine! *What a peculiar ceremony!*

"Blessin's be upon thee, my young'uns!" Preacher Cleats intoned solemnly, to sniggers from Zachary Thomas's kinfolk. "Well, now, be off with you!" he added, chasing them expansively away with his hands.

Mary felt cold inside. Was that it? Was she now *married?* It was the strangest wedding ceremony she had ever encountered. Still, she supposed the preacher could be from a lesser-known religion. Perhaps he was a Primitive Baptist, the religion that was said to rule the southern highlands for, according to their Lewis Mountain circuit-preacher, Reverend Hubbly, they believed in hooch as an integral part of their religion, as well as mass river baptisms, and ignorance, which was considered a *virtue*. They called themselves "Hardshells" or "Iron-sides" and everybody, even the preacher, would come to church thoroughly soused, for they believed that even the most fainthearted person could become a worthy thumper for the Lord after he'd been at the moonshine jug for a good while! But coming to think of it, Reverend Hubbly had also said that Primitive Baptist services went on all day, while this strange wedding ceremony had been so quick, it was almost over before it had begun! Even the clan seemed disappointed that it was over so soon. They stood grumbling amongst themselves.

Thankfully, since the inside of the cabin had grown so stuffy and foul with all the bodies crammed in it, the wedding "celebration" moved outside. Zachary Thomas motioned her to sit on a bench on the porch, while the rest of the clan spilled like flotsam in dirty wash-water down into the yard. The preacher left them almost immediately. Zachary Thomas escorted him down the steps with a hand on the preacher's shoulder. Mary saw him talking to the inebriated little red-haired man down in the yard before pressing something into his outstretched hand. Then he gave him a moonshine jug. The preacher turned and merrily waved, shouting, "GOD'S BLESSIN'S BE UPON YE, MY YOUNG'UNS," and went on his merry little way.

The "celebration", such as it was, stretched well into the afternoon. With a sinking heart, Mary watched the moonshine-ridden revelry of the clan. The Buckos pitched horse-shoes, danced jigs and fired their weapons at glass jars, which exploded with regularity, causing glass splinters to fly in every direction. Any number of fistfights broke out. They were so touchy that more than once Zachary Thomas had to roar at them to stop their quarrels from becoming too violent. Once, he was even forced to go down into the dirt yard and yank two of his brothers apart by the scruffs of their necks. Even so, every now and then, one of them would draw a pistol or two tucked in his belt and shoot wildly into the air. But the worst part came when two of the hags got stuck into each other and were rolling around on the ground, screeching like banshees, while punching and kicking one another, and pulling each other's hair. Mary had never seen such a shocking display.

Taking example from their parents, the children also screamed and yelled and fought with fury. They gouged at each others' eyes, pushed, punched, kicked and pulled hair – but nobody bothered to separate or censure them. Mountain children were generally real well-behaved and respected their elders. Indeed, the mountain children of Mary's acquaintance were so shy and nervous of strangers they would peep at them from behind a bush.

During the entire melee, she and Zachary Thomas sat stonily apart from the others on the bench on the porch, the tension between them unbearable, as they overlooked the disgraceful scene in the yard. They never spoke to each other, staring straight ahead. By stealing occasional sideways glances at her new husband, Mary saw that his face was as dark as a summer thundercloud. After a couple more excruciating hours, Zachary Thomas stood up and said gruffly, "Go inside an' git out of that fancy dress and them boots. Be sure to put 'em back right exactly whar you found 'em. We're leavin'."

"Leavin'?"

"Yeah, we're goin' up to my cabin now."

"You mean . . . you mean y'all don't live here?"

"No, course not. Got me my own place up on Eagle Spur right on top of th' mountain."

"Oh." Mary didn't know whether to be relieved or not. Well, for sure, she'd be real glad to get away from his kinfolk! They were a fearsome strain on her nerves and she felt such a complete outsider among them that she knew if she were forced to live in their midst for any length of time, she would go quite mad! By now they were bleary-eyed and staggering with the effects of excessive moonshine.

After she had changed and returned the beautiful dress, stockings and boots neatly to the big chest as instructed, Mary, clutching the bundle of the nightgown to her bosom, went outside again. Such was the manic self-absorption of her husband's kin that she was sure that nobody noticed her and Zachary Thomas slipping off the front porch, creeping around the cabin and into the forest at the back. She had been worrying more and more about being forced to spend her wedding night with Zachary Thomas and wasn't at all sure what awaited her.

Following a steep path up the mountain, as they reached the higher elevations of the mountain, the natural woodland forest became interspersed with towering red spruces, balsam fir, hung with flimsy strands of grandfather lichen, white birch and pine, below which, a thick cushion of dead pine-needles lay on loamy soil. A fresh, tangy scent of pine pervaded the clean air. Mary was breathing hard with the exertion of scaling the steep upper slopes. Chilly mist swirled thinly around them and Mary shivered, clutching at her bare arms. Once again the ruggedness and inhospitality of the mountain made her feel decidedly intimidated. Then a strange thing happened. Huge eagles began flying directly above them. They swiftly increased in number, so much so, that it boggled the mind, for never had Mary seen so many gathered in one place. Of course, eagles were a common enough sight in the mountains, but they usually never flew in numbers of more than two or three. *Not like this!* There were literally dozens of them. Their wingspans, some easy ten feet across, were magnificent in soaring flight, their broad white tail feathers spread like fans. In an awesome aerial display, they performed in a most odd, un-eagle-like fashion, circling the skies and swooping and soaring, somehow miraculously avoiding collision with each other.

It was a strange, thrilling, awe-inspiring sight, even more so since their cries, as wild and lonely as a symphony of flutes, fill the air with spine-tingling sound.

It stopped Mary and Zachary Thomas dead in their tracks. Mary had always loved eagles, the ancient symbols of power and courage and, as children, she and Joe used to go hunting for their nests, huge bulky structures made of sticks, and lined with grass or moss. Whenever Mary and Joe had gone anywhere near an aerie on some rocky ledge, both parent eagles would swoop, screeching so loudly, it would chase them away.

Well, Mary surmised, one would swear there were dozens of their nests around the tableland with this extraordinary number of birds, yet she knew that they had their own territories and did not nest anywhere near another nest. Besides, if they were merely trying to protect their nests now, they certainly weren't creating the raucous din she associated with that. It was a much more elegant sound somehow, like a celestial salute to the heavens. She and Zachary Thomas stood squinting above them in the gathering gloom, dumbstruck and awed. Mary suddenly saw a large white-tipped black feather floating gently down on currents of air, swaying this way and that, till it dropped, almost ceremoniously, on her right bare foot, delicately balancing just above her toes. To Mary, it seemed like a gift from the gods and she quickly snatched it up, clutching it to her bosom, before returning her attention to the sky. At last, at Zachary Thomas's insistence, they started to move again. He led the way as they climbed in a stunned silence, still keeping a keen eye overhead.

Then another, even stranger, thing happened. Some of the predatory birds, with an elegant sweep of wings, came and landed on boulders or branches along the upward pathway, standing on stout legs, gripping their perches with strong feathered feet and great talons. More and more eagles came to join them, landing on different branches and boulders, before settling down to stare unflinchingly at the human pair with their fierce yellow eyes. The eagles, their hooked beaks almost as long as their heads, their necks craning upward, were the picture of arrogant nobility. Mary had never seen them at such close quarters before. They were great, magnificent, fearsome-looking birds. She noted that the overwhelming majority of them were adult eagles since they had blackish bodies, rather than brown, with a telltale golden wash at the back of their necks, and white at the base of their tails and their wingtips – a much bigger type of golden eagle than she had ever seen before.

As she and Zachary Thomas cautiously climbed past them, they barely stirred. They perched in haughty regality, totally unafraid, even though the two cowed humans sometimes passed only a few feet away from them. One after the other, the eagles landed until it seemed they had all left the sky. They were everywhere that Mary looked. To the left and right and ahead of them, branches and boulders were loaded with the eagles, so they were accosted by arrogant eagle eyes wherever they turned. It was eerie and highly unnerving to say the least! She felt burned by their fierce, unyielding stares. Zachary Thomas also seemed intimidated and disturbed by the wild birds' unusual behavior for he muttered hoarsely under his breath, "Ain't never seen th' like."

Now the mountain face was walled with huge granite boulders. Loose boulders were strewn liberally along the way, some moss-covered, others exposed and gray and craggy. The massive boulders, some four times her husband's height, comprised a giant barrier that seemed impenetrable. It was only Zachary Thomas's familiarity with the mountain that allowed them passage through the rocky maze. It was almost as if this last rocky precipice was deliberately thrown out by the mountain to discourage trespassers from gaining access to the tableland.

Finally, watched by the silent, bizarre guard of honor, Zachary Thomas reached for her hand and helped her up a narrow path between great overhanging boulders. Thankfully, they were nearly at the top for by now Mary's legs were aching and she was trembling with the effort, her whole body still sore from the earlier fall. Zachary Thomas made her go ahead of him and as he pushed her from behind, she finally hauled herself over the craggy ridge. Some red squirrels close to the edge took panic and fled. As if by signal, the eagles beneath them suddenly took off as one. Mary gave a gasp of fright and amazement as the sound and rush of scores of beating wings enveloped her like a whirlwind. Then the eagles soared over the edge of the cliff up into the sky, like a feathered volcano which erupted with wild, tortured cries, filling the air with spectacular sight and spine-tingling sound, as they dispersed in all directions. It was the most incredible thing she had ever experienced, and Mary felt very close to tears. She knew she had witnessed something very unique and very special, and she felt profoundly privileged and awed and inspired. *No wonder they called this place Eagle Spur!*

After watching for several spellbound moments, Mary at last turned her attention to the scene in front of her, as Zachary Thomas clambered up over the ridge and stood up beside her. On a large cleared patch of land, a fair way back from the edge of the ridge stood a chestnut log cabin, chinked with mud, with a stone chimney and a porch in front supported by wooden poles. Big rain-barrels were on either side of the porch. Some way to the right behind the cabin was a makeshift wooden barn. On the other side of the cabin was the most glorious chestnut tree that Mary had ever seen. At least eighty-feet tall, with branches spreading over a huge area, it was full of summer leaves and hanging spikes of small creamy-white blossoms. Its trunk was arrow-straight with a girth of at least fifteen feet. Far beyond it, towards where the spur connected to the tableland, were some giant brooding hemlocks, their thick trunks encrusted with Canadian mayflower, red spruces and Frazer firs, which acted as a buffer to the thick tableland forest beyond it.

The mighty hemlock giants, with their long sweeping branches, stood like proud sentinels as if they were guarding a sacred spot. The sky above, cloudless and immense, seemed to surround them, so close, Mary felt that she could reach out a hand and touch it. The homesite was surrounded on the edge of the ridge by masses of boulders she said heatedly, her voice rising.and thick forest, the trees nearest the edge all disfigured by the wind. *Why, this place looked like something out of a storybook!* It was absolutely beautiful!

Two coon dogs came bounding up to them, a black tick and a redbone, and after curiously sniffing Mary, they went to Zachary Thomas, and excitedly licked at his hands. "Rufus, Red," he muttered. He crouched down and petted them, before chasing them away. Well-trained, they went to lay down a few feet away. Mary turned then to look back down below and quickly drew in her breath, for the view from up here was quite spectacular, a scene of breath-taking grandeur. The ridge dropped steeply away from the giant buttresses of craggy granite rock into the magnificent tree-shrouded valley, sweeping down to the gleaming rocky Wilson Run thousands of feet below. At one point, the river churned in wild, roaring cascades that could be faintly heard even from up here before pitching headlong over a waterfall, throwing up high clouds of spray. Beyond the river rose a series of rugged back-bone blue-hued mountains, whose forests were so full of chestnut trees, the peaks looked snow-capped with their creamy-white blossoms.

The isolated homesites of the Buchanan cracker clan were swallowed up by the towering trees, many of them chestnuts, the dominant tree of the Appalachian forests, and topped by the creamy-colored abundance of their blossoms, with only a few gray plumes of smoke, giving clue to human occupation on the immense mountain. Even the unsightly specter of the main homestead they'd just left, a mere bowl-like indentation, was completely camouflaged from up here by its thick surrounding dense forest.

"Eagle Spur . . . ," she breathed.

8

Mary's feelings of wonder and awe at the magnificent scene visible from the top of Claw Mountain, however, were soon to be rudely dented. Urging her towards the cabin, Zachary Thomas, lighting a kerosene lantern left on the porch, led her inside to a scene of unbelievable chaos and filth! For if Obediah Buchanan's cabin had been untidy and dusty, it was nothing compared to that of his eldest son! Her first reaction to it, after Zachary Thomas had lit up several strategically placed kerosene lamps, was of stunned repulsion, for he shared his living quarters with spiders and squeaking mice, which darted across the floorboards towards their nests – she saw *three* of them!

The floor had obviously never felt the sweep of a broom, for thick powdery gray dust had settled in layers on every conceivable surface and enormous springy-looking gray cobwebs stretched across corners and brushed the rafters. Dirty long underwear and clothes were strewn everywhere, including the floor. There was a rudimentary homemade wooden table and several oak-split chairs, but the table was piled with all sorts of junk, ranging from a pair of mud-caked boots that had likely sat there since winter, to a pile of lead-ball ammunition and a curved gunpowder horn that had a strap attached to it.

Old food fermented on precarious piles of tin plates and a strong putrid smell permeated the cabin! Opened empty food cans were everywhere, on the table and chucked into piles in the corners. A puncheon bench beside the fireplace was similarly covered in junk. A bearskin rug lay in front of the fireplace, its head, huge, eyes glassy, and its mouth open wide to show its fearsome fangs. Above the fireplace, a slender flintlock rifle was mounted, with the longest barrel that Mary had ever seen. The state of chaos in the cabin did not extend to this proud weapon, however. The wooden stock was beautifully decorated with metal ornamentation and had been lovingly polished to achieve a glistening patina.

She felt her skin crawl as she looked about her. Zachary Thomas hadn't married her to gain a wife at all. He had married her to gain a *servant!* Her heart sank with the sudden painful realization and she fought back humiliated tears. Besides being in such a deplorable state, the cabin did not even possess a wood-fire stove. In its place was a black three-legged pot, which hung from a trestle in the fireplace. She would simply have to escape as soon as she could! She didn't want to live for a second longer than she had to on this awful mountain, with its primitive amenities and its filth, and its white-trash inhabitants. In an attempt to mask her dismay, Mary muttered that she had to go outside to do her "business", and Zachary Thomas obligingly tore a couple of pages out of an unearthed Sears, Roebuck catalogue and, unhooking a lighted kerosene lantern at the door, solemnly handed them to her, his eyes narrowed. "Be sure t'mind yerself out thar, y'hear?" he said shortly.

Mary went outside into the night, suddenly feeling full of nervousness, unreasonably wondering what he meant by that little remark. Despite the full moon that hung like an enormous pearl orb in the sky, almost making the use of the lantern unnecessary, all of the tales about Claw Mountain fed to her during childhood came clamoring back on the wings of fright and fanciful imagination. The old mountain seemed so dark, brooding and ominous at this hour, the silence so complete, that she, who could not ever remember being afraid of anything in her whole life, was like a small child threatened with bogeys and witches.

Then all of a sudden, the incident with the eagles, so wildly extraordinary, took on a distinctly sinister tone. Perhaps the boogers had wanted to chase her away, though in their strange, forbidding way the eagles had been more welcoming than hostile. They had even given her the feather, which she had put in a bottle on the mantelpiece before coming out here and which she intended keeping as a good-luck charm. She hesitantly ventured towards the grove of hemlocks,and finally squatted behind a rhododendron bush in full flower, the moonlight ghostly illuminating everything around her. She listened above the quick, trickling sound of her urine, and jumped when she heard the hooting of a gray owl close by. Spooked by it, without even taking the time to wipe herself, she hastily pulled up her bloomers and raced back to the cabin with her heart pounding.

She was dreading what would happen next. Her husband was going to try to finish what his brother, Eli, had started this afternoon! Her determination not to give in to him had weakened considerably. His size was such that she suspected she wouldn't have too much option but to submit to him! She began to fear the act of union itself. She suffered terrible ignorance about it for her mother had only once referred to it in the broadest of terms. 'It be the duty of every good wife, Mary, but a joyful act with someone you love,' was all she had to say about the matter, but Mary had seen rutting animals before and thought she understood more about it after the terrifying incident with Eli earlier today. There was no doubt that that evil man had tried to penetrate her between her legs, with a big, unmentionable and unsightly part of him, and that being so, she wondered if being penetrated by the "unmentionable part" of such a huge man as Zachary Thomas was likely to cause her to suffer terrible pain.

She entered the cabin sick with apprehension. She placed the kerosene lantern back on its hook and gazed fearfully at her husband who stood in front of the fireplace. Zachary Thomas had started a fire and it crackled and hissed as the kindling caught. In the lamplight, he stood tall and forbidding as an executioner, his heavy black brows making him looked threatening and cruel. Without a word, he inclined his head slightly towards the bedroom. There was no mistaking his meaning. He was going to claim his right as a husband without even bothering to feed her first. She hadn't eaten a thing the whole day long, although a tin mug of coffee and some chunks of half-raw cooked meat on a tin plate had been set inside the door of Obediah's bedroom by someone! She had not eaten it out of sheer pique, but now she wished she hadn't bitten off her nose to spite her face, as the saying went!

Mary had left the bundle of Hedina Buchanan's exquisite nightgown on the laden puncheon bench before she went outside. Silently, she picked it up, holding it tightly against her chest as she went through to the bedroom door and closed it behind her. Zachary Thomas had lit only a single kerosene lamp in here, but she was glad of the gloom. Her heart sank when she saw the big double pallet that was to be their nuptial bed in an otherwise starkly empty room.

The sight of it rang with terrifying implication. She hurriedly disrobed from her plain brown work dress, from which she had brushed off the dried mud and worn to get up here, and put on the white nightgown. It fell in voluminous folds about her, to her feet. She climbed beneath the scratchy blanket on the pallet and lay there shivering spasmodically while she waited for her new husband to come and claim his husbandly right. How different things were from the way she had imagined they would be when she had eloped with Zachary Thomas yesterday morning – *a whole lifetime ago!* Yesterday, she had been so naive that she had believed in love at first sight. Now, she was awaiting her passage into womanhood, not with joy as she had fancied, but with terror and with loathing.

It was at least a half-hour later that Zachary Thomas entered the room, by which time Mary was consumed with fear and dread. He sat down at the edge of the pallet and started undressing, stripping to his long underwear and a vest then he extinguished the kerosene lamp and climbed under the blanket beside her. Mary's heart was pounding and she could smell the masculine combination of sweat, tobacco and moonshine on him. He turned towards her and, without a word, ran a massive rough hand over her body. Then he clumsily tried to kiss her. She met his advances with a stiff, unresponsive body and a head turned coldly aside. But if she'd been hoping this would deter him, she was sorely mistaken. He forced her to turn her face back towards him, digging harsh fingers into her cheeks, but she clamped her teeth tightly together when he kissed her and tried to stick his tongue into her mouth. He pulled up the nightgown, though she tried to stop him, frantically pushing away his hands. Then terrified by what would happen next, she struggled dementedly, using all her strength against him like she had his brother earlier, shrieking with all the fervor of her pent-up emotions.

As her fists pounded against his huge chest, he bellowed in outrage and tried to hold her to him, seeming surprised and incensed by her reaction. Then as she continued to fight him off, screaming her aversion, to her shock, he silenced her by smashing an elbow in her face. Stunned by the unexpected blow, she immediately stopped struggling, dimly aware that he was the second Bucko to hit her in the face that day to satisfy his manly lust. He finally managed to get himself a little way inside her. Then he thrust himself forward cruelly, forcing his way through the resistance of her virgin flesh, against the useless defiance of her weak flailing arms. It was so excruciating, it felt as if her body was being ripped apart, and she screamed once more, a loud and demented cry. He proceeded to mindlessly relieve the lustful cry of his manhood, causing pain to wrack her body in endless waves. Tears rolled down the sides of her swollen face and she felt revolted and violated as she lay beneath him, suffering untold agonies. When at last he had finished using her and rolled over to go to sleep, she remained rigid and trembling beside him, unable to stop whimpering, such was her keen distress. How could she have been so taken in by him? She knew she would never forget the excruciating pain and humiliation of this terrible night . . .

9

The next morning, Mary moved around in a daze of acute embarrassment and shame, her head hung low, her face swollen from the blows of two Bucko brothers, her shoulder still aching and her hands stinging. The tension between her and Zachary Thomas was once again unbearable. Neither of them spoke and she could not look him in the eye. Unable to walk properly, she limped back into the forest behind the cabin's clearing (so much less intimidating in the light of day) taking a spade with her. She discovered she had bled between her legs and she felt swollen and raw inside. The pain was still so bad she was almost doubled over with it. She was full of fear when she thought of the implications. What if he wanted her again tonight? In her condition, the pain would surely be even more excruciating than it had been last night. How would she be able to stand it? She wiped the dried blood away as best she could with the Sears, Roebuck catalogue page, filled with an immensity of dismay at a woman's lot. Cold, hard reality was so different from her honey-coated dreams.

After throwing a spade of dirt over her business, she limped back to the cabin, leaving the spade propped up against the porch. When she got back inside, she discovered that all the junk on the table had been unceremoniously swept onto the floor, with the exception of the gunpowder horn and piles of lead balls, which had been placed on the mantelpiece. To her surprise, Zachary Thomas had made coffee for her in a tin mug. In all her days spent with her parents, Mary had never known her father to make her mother coffee. Such actions were classed as those of a "hen-husband" and generally spurned by mountain men. Mary decided it must surely stem from Zachary Thomas's guilt.

Indeed, he did seem morose and silent and shamed this morning. He sat at the end of the table with a tin mug in front of him, his face set in granite, staring through the opened door with brilliant turquoise-green eyes. The table top was caked with grease and grime and dark streaks, which Mary suspected were traces of long-dried blood. Had he used this table as a butchering block? A *slaughter* block even? Mary sat down gingerly at the table without a word and sipped at the welcome steaming-hot, strong coffee, which scalded her tongue.

After about ten minutes of strained silence, her new husband stood up, scraping his chair back. Walking over to the big stone fireplace, he lifted his old Kentucky flintlock rifle off its perch, took the gunpowder horn off the mantelpiece, clipping it onto his belt, then he scooped up a handful of the lead balls, putting them in his one pocket, before turning and striding across the room, ducking under the opened door without a word. She watched numbly as he disappeared over the edge of the precipice.

Infinitely relieved to be on her own, Mary took lonely stock of her situation. Though she wished she could flee the mountain today and never come back, after a long, sleepless and pain-wracked night, she simply lacked the strength to attempt anything as strenuous as that. She also lacked the courage to face any of his family, or indeed, her own, after what she had been through.

After all, she had brought it all upon herself! How could she possibly cause them more anguish by letting them know what she had suffered yesterday at the hands of two Buckos. Suddenly, she realized what a child the old Mary had been. With her romantic notions of love that had no basis in reality, she had allowed herself to be wooed into a demonic world that truly matched the stuff of dark legend. *Well, she was a child no more!* She would have to build up her strength and plan her escape carefully, but only when she was sure of what she was doing. But until then she would act the dutiful wife so that he would suspect nothing, and then, just when he least expected it . . . but right now, her main concern was for her stomach; she was so hungry she felt dizzy with it.

She started a frantic search for food. She crossed first to the three-legged pot in the fireplace. There was nothing in it but thick, rancid-smelling grease. She found lots of unopened food cans, but nothing to open them with. Then she spotted a small tin of store-bought cookies and pounced on it. She sat on the dusty pine floorboards, pulling the tight lid open with frantic fingers. She devoured the entire contents of the tin, spilling crumbs on the grimy, dust-engrained floor. She felt a little better after that, not quite as shaky as she had been. Then she had looked about her in disgust. After all, Maw always said cleanliness was next to godliness! If that was true then this must be Lucifer's kingdom itself!

Weak and in pain though she was, she could not stand the filth and disarray. She had to clean it up. Besides, keeping busy would stop her from thinking of other things – things she would rather not think about right now. She tried to find a broom, even looking in the barn next the house, but she could not find a single one, not even a yard broom. Neither could she find any soap or other cleaning materials, no scrubbing brushes or pails. Indeed, there wasn't much of anything in the barn, besides a few rusty farm implements, piles of empty moonshine jugs and some moldy hides. There was no livestock. No domestic animals or poultry at all, besides the two coon dogs which Zachary Thomas had taken with him. He had told her gruffly on the way up yesterday that he had lived on the top of this formidable mountain for ten years. She was convinced that in all that time, nothing had ever been cleaned and it was *ten years* of accumulated dirt and grime that she was now conspiring to get rid of. It was a daunting thought.

She resolved to tell her husband that he had to go down to the store again and buy a whole bunch of things. She limped back inside the cabin and using a pair of her husband's filthy old long-johns, she tackled the spider webs by swiping repeatedly at them before trying to get rid of as much surface dust as she could by flicking, mopping and pushing it towards the door. Soon the dust was flying and she was in fits of coughing and sneezing. Then she tackled all the rubbish piled haphazardly on the floor. She separated the clothes from the pile, folding them up neatly, ready to be washed. Those cans that were unopened, she stacked in neat rows on the floor. She took all the open stinking tin cans outside in the bowl of her long skirt and put them in a big pile, next to the porch. She would tell Zachary Thomas that he must dig a deep hole and bury them and to make shelves and cupboards to keep things in. So much to be done, so much . . .

Many hours later, her husband came back from hunting. She knew he had been hunting because he had his long rifle over one shoulder secured by one hand, while he was carrying a dead raccoon by its hind legs in the other. The two coon dogs were bounding around him joyfully and barking as if mighty pleased with themselves.

"Quiet, Rufus! Quiet, Red!" Zachary Thomas commanded and the black tick and redbone instantly obeyed, lying below the porch, with their heads resting on their outstretched front legs, tails slowly wagging.

Mary had wrapped her hair in a big cloth she had found and had tucked her dress into the elastic of her bloomers, so that her legs were bare up to her pale slim thighs and she was covered in dust and dirt. Hugely embarrassed to be caught in such an unseemly state, she hastily pulled her skirt out of her bloomers and ripped the make-shift kerchief from around her head. But if she had thought Zachary Thomas would be pleased that his new wife had been so industrious, she soon got rid of the idea. He stood in the opened doorway and, after glancing about the place, his face grew even more thunderous than had been before he had gone out.

"C'mon outside," he muttered to Mary.

She hesitantly followed him outside and around the back of the cabin to the barn. Once inside the barn, with sunlight streaming through the open doorway, he turned on her with his eyes narrowed. "Now let's git one thing straight, right off, girl. If'n you want anythung skinned a'fore you cook it, you've got to do th' skinnin' yerself. So either you'll got to learn real quick else I reckon ye'll starve!"

Mary stared from his grim face to the slain raccoon in a quandary of dismay. He had stood up for her against his brother, Cletus, last night, but now she knew for sure that her stand on the matter had, indeed, deeply angered him. She quailed at the thought and swallowed hard. She was particularly fond of raccoons, with their mischievous black face-masks and handsome bushy tails, and she didn't think she would be able to eat one she'd skinned herself. Without awaiting her comments, Zachary Thomas turned his attention back to the matter at hand.

"I cut th' jugular an' bled th' coon best I could, soon as I kilt it." He laid the unfortunate coon on top of a wooden trestle table next to the door. It had a large unsightly bullet wound through the chest and an exit wound out its back. "I don't usually go to this trouble when it's fer th' pot, only when it's fer th' pelt, but seein' as ye're so darned pernickety, I guess I'll show you how it's done. First thing y'gotta do is skin it by ringin' th' legs and th' feet."

He did this with a knife as Mary watched with a pounding heart, sickened by the sight and smell of exposed flesh and warm blood.

"Now you split th' pelt on th' inside middle of th' hind legs from th' ring to th' crotch. Do th' same on th' front legs, splittin' to th' middle of th' chest, like this." He worked quickly and ably with his knife, like a skilled surgeon. "Then you split th' pelt up to th' middle of th' underside from th' crotch, thru' th' split from th' front legs, and up to th' end of th' bottom jaw, like this." He stopped and looked up at her with his startling turquoise-green eyes. "Now take special note here. You cut around th' tail on th' underside only. You connect th' split like this, see? Now, you skin out both hind legs." He did this quickly, then continued, "Then you make a slit 'tween th' bone and th' tendon and insert a gamblin' stick like this so you kin hang th' critter up." He walked over to the shed wall next to the door and nailed the gambling stick supporting the coon carcass to it. "Now you take th' small sticks like this, so th' base of th' tail is between 'em. Pull it real careful like so th' tail jest slides off th' tail bone. If you wanna keep th' pelt, be sure never to pull off th' tail itself."

Mary watched the procedure in morbid fascination, inwardly closing her nose and scarcely breathing as he worked the pelt off the front legs, slicing the mesentery between skin and muscle when necessary, slicing up the front legs and then skinning them out. He continued his commentary as he worked. "Now, th' thung you gotta remember is this. If'n you want to eat this here coon, you got to remove these two musk glands right here. Them's bitter as gall."

Mary watched as he removed two pear-shaped glands from beneath the coon's forearms. He skinned the coon around the neck until he came to the head, cutting the ears off even with the head. "This is real important," he informed her. "If'n you make a bad ear hole, th' pelt's value drops by a quarter. 'Cuz to sell a whole pelt, th' coon must be trapped an' not shot fir vittles. Kin only trade or sell a tail fer a quarter, sometimes fifty cents if'n it be an especially fine 'un, which this one ain't, so I'll likely only git a quarter fer it."

He skinned right around the eyes, leaving only the eyeballs then he went right down the snout, cutting off the end, so that the nose button was still attached to the pelt. Carefully, he worked the damaged pelt off over the coon's head. He put the removed pelt on the trestle table, leaving the pathetically denuded carcass, pink and sketchy with a thin layer of fatty skin, still hanging obscenely from the gambling stick. Then lifting the carcass, he took the knife and split the flesh down the middle from throat to crotch, removing the intestines and organs, with scraping fingers, and dropping them into a dirt-grimed bowl at his feet. He then skillfully cut off the head, tail and feet.

It was a perfectly executed job. Not a patch of fur remained on the pathetic carcass; it looked like an unborn fetus, like the poor little thing Maw miscarried and had to bury, only one violated by the obscene bullet wound. "Now you soak it in cold water fer a few hours to git all th' blood out. Should be overnight, but I don't reckon we got anythung else to eat fer tonight, so a few hours will got to do. C'mon, I'll show you whar you go t'collect clean water. Fer most other thungs you kin use th' rainwater in th' barrels next to th' porch."

After they had both taken up empty moonshine jars from those piled up in the barn, Mary dutifully followed after her huge, taciturn husband. As she neared the precipice, she was stunned anew by the magnificent scene that lay below in a haze of heat and sunshine -- a vast tree-filled panoramic amphitheater, the river a gilded mirror of the cloudless azure sky above. She swallowed hard. *It was utterly breathtaking!* But Zachary Thomas was in no mood to cater for her moved sensibilities. He disappeared over the edge in a trice and, shivering a little with the chill in the air at such an elevation, she had to hurry after him for fear she would lose sight of him.

After a few minutes of following him down a tricky footpath through the giant boulders and towering trees, they came to a rocky pool, surrounded by ferns, where water bubbled joyously out of the ground and spilled and splashed its windy way down the steep mountainside. Dragonflies and mayflies darted above the surface. Mountain folk considered streams the voice and the laughter of the mountains and, as she heard its tinkling, gurgling chuckles, she dropped thankfully to her knees amongst moss-covered rocks, pine needles and leafy humus, washing her hands thoroughly, but carefully, making them sting again, before scooping water up in her cupped hands and splashing it over her grimy face several times, the icy-cold liquid reviving and refreshing her. She rinsed the moonshine jars out before refilling them, while the yellow eyes of a black-chinned red salamander eyed her curiously.

Later, after they had returned to the cabin, she put the coon carcass to soak in cold, clear water, in an empty pot she'd found amongst the pile of paraphernalia on the floor. She removed the three-legged pot suspended in the fireplace and dragged it out onto the porch. She cleaned it out as best she could by using some suspect cloth she had found to remove the thick coating of grease that had accumulated in it, rinsing it out repeatedly with water from one of the big barrels of rain-water next to the porch. Several hours later, after Zachary Thomas had made the fire, Mary put the coon carcass into the pot with some salted water and boiled it for several hours with the lid on it until the meat was tender. Her mother always baked coon in the oven after boiling it, surrounding it with delicious sweet potatoes, but alas, she didn't have an oven, let alone any sweet potatoes.

Mary removed the coon and struggling with the heavy pot outside, she tipped the remaining water in it over the edge of the porch. She returned inside with the pot, putting it back over the fire, rolled the cooked pieces of coon in flour, having discovered that Zachary Thomas had a supply of lard and flour stored in the barn. Ruing the lack of fresh vegetables to add to the meal, she put lard in the pot and fried the floured coon pieces in it till they were golden brown. She hadn't been sure if she would be able to face eating the coon after she had witnessed it being skinned, but hunger got the better of her. Steeped in a strange and forbidding silence, she and Zachary Thomas supped that night on coon stew enriched with store-bought beans, the can of which had been opened with his knife.

10

The next few days passed in a nightmare blur. Mercifully, Mary's biggest concern had not come about. *Zachary Thomas had not touched her again!* Finding some planks in the shed, she had got him to put up shelves and make cupboards. He had immediately set to it knocking them up and installing them within a few hours, proving to be a surprisingly neat and accomplished carpenter. Once he had finished that task, she got up the courage to ask him to go down to the nearest store to buy them much-needed supplies. No doubt suspecting that she wanted the coast clear to try to escape again, he refused, saying dryly that he'd just recently been, but quickly added he would send some of his brothers instead. He frowned when she started rattling off what was needed, reminding her that it all had to be memorized. Mary replied that she'd write a list and that the person taking it could give it to the storekeeper to fill.

"Y'mean you kin write?" he asked in amazement.

"Yes," replied Mary, meeting her tall husband's incredulous gaze with a cool upraised chin. She understood his surprise. Few mountain children, let alone *girls,* could read and write, but she had been taught to do so by her city cousin, Emily, years ago. "An' cipher, too," she added archly.

Assuming the Buchanan clan had plenty of credit or due bills at the store, since they reputedly had plenty of moonshine to barter with and could afford the luxury of store-bought groceries like canned goods, despite their extremely shabby appearance, Mary proceeded to write an order so large that Zachary Thomas visibly quailed when she handed it to him.

"Jest lucky I happen to got plenty of credit at th' store from my trappin' and my own needs are so few!" her husband grunted caustically, turquoise-green eyes narrowed. Before he left for Horseshoe Hollow, he told her very pointedly to stay put and that he had instructed the Bucko lookouts to keep a sharp eye out for her. Mary knew it would be a mistake to try to escape anytime soon.

After he returned from Horseshoe Hollow to deliver the list to his brothers, he told her that he had advised them to take the mules to fetch all the supplies as their paw had reportedly returned from Stony Man Camp with the beasts, although Zachary Thomas had not yet seen him. But he mentioned Otis had warned him that the clan's patriarch was real sore at having missed the wedding, and he had not come up to congratulate them because of it. Mary vaguely wondered why Zachary Thomas didn't suggest they go there instead, but perhaps he was giving his paw time to cool down. Well, whatever the reason, it suited her just fine. She was definitely in no hurry to meet the man.

Late that same afternoon, several of her husband's brothers delivered the supplies to Eagle Spur. The mules were tethered some way below and the goods carried up the last steep part on the shoulders of Zachary Thomas, Toad, Otis and Clancy. By the time they were finished it was dark and they looked exceedingly weary, their skin shiny with sweat. Mary had nothing but coffee to offer them in the way of refreshments. Well, from tomorrow, things would be different! Among other necessities, there was a cast-iron black kettle for boiling laundry, making soap or rendering lard, clothes pegs, crocks, two washtubs, (a larger one for bathing, the other, to wash the dishes in), a coal iron, coal, two-quart mason jars for food storage and canning. Two brooms, one for the cabin and the other, a yard-broom, two buckets, two scrubbing brushes, an apron, dishcloths, floor cloths and washcloths, disinfectant, borax to wash her hair with once a month, lye soap and soluble lye to make her own in future, a sack of corn meal, another of salt, a smoked ham, sugar, assorted vegetables, apples, eggs, butter, powdered milk, spices, sorghum molasses, soda shortening, yeast, a dozen Leghorn chicks and a rooster, to supply them with eggs, feed for them, a pick, a hoe, a shovel, a scythe, petunia seeds, and seed potatoes and vegetable seeds, including turnips, beets, beans and cabbages for planting, since she intended to start a vegetable garden. 'We've got to git some fresh vegetables in fer th' winter,' she had coolly informed her husband.

Later, without her even asking him to, her husband knocked up a hock in the yard with planks and wire fencing, by lantern-light, for the young Leghorns and the handsome young rooster, while she was busy putting away the supplies. However, this was mainly for them to shelter in at night and for their protection from predators, since the door of the hock would be left open during the day, so they could wander freely about the yard. Zachary Thomas had his hounds so well-trained that while they showed curiosity about these strange critters by sniffing them and watching them with sharp fascinated eyes, they didn't menace them any.

The next day she insisted he make a wooden johnny house with a shored-up pit under it to contain any stench by throwing in carbolic acid disinfectant. Paw had been th' first person to erect one on Lewis Mountain, at Maw's behest. Their neighbors thought it a big joke, however, and lined up to watch Paw come out to use the pretentious thing when he'd finished it, while they continued to squat behind a rock or bush, depending on the rain taking care of any odor problems. Zachary Thomas was as derisive of the idea of a johnny house as their neighbors had been, scowling at his new wife and looking at her as if she'd lost her mind, muttering about how unclean it was (laughable, all things considered!), and complaining that she was "puttin' on airs". Nevertheless, after she'd described how he must construct it, he set to it at once, a good long way behind the cabin, however.

She spent the next few days getting more order out of the chaos that existed in the cabin, working doggedly, scrubbing every conceivable surface in the cabin. She had practically worn out a scrubbing brush on the table alone. She even cleaned out and scrubbed the fireplace! By the time she had finished that particular chore she was covered in black soot and had been forced to take an unscheduled bath in the tin washtub when Zachary Thomas had taken his coon dogs and gone tracking.

Every day, besides scrubbing and cleaning, she boiled clothes outside in the black kettle over a fire. Zachary Thomas's clothes had not been washed for so long that the water was black by the time she finished stirring each load with a stout stick. He had rigged her up a clothes line in the back yard, at her behest, and she hung the washing up there. When it was dry, she ironed them with the coal iron and placed them neatly on a shelf she had got Zachary to put up in the bedroom.

She was also getting the hang of using the three-legged pot. It was a very different method of cooking from using Maw's wood-fire stove, and much more restrictive, being much slower since only one pot could be used at a time, but she had got a little more organized and adept and had cooked up several delicious meals with the new supplies. With most of the filth and grime removed and the added storage space, the place was starting to look half-way decent! She felt a tiny spurt of pride thinking even Maw would be pleased with her efforts.

* * *

Mary's 19th birthday, on the 13th July, came and went without her even telling her husband it was her special day, which would have warranted a huge, fun-filled shindig in the Harley barn on Lewis Mountain, that's for sure. On Claw Mountain, all it meant was bone-wearying work!

Mary had served her husband a midday meal of slices of the ham on hot corn-pone cakes thick with butter, followed by apple fritters dusted with sugar. She had packed the tin plates, mugs and cutlery into the smaller of the tin washtubs to be washed, when she heard a blood-curdling yell, loud angry shouts and a terrible sound of screeching. It sent both her and Zachary Thomas rushing out onto the porch. Hastily wiping her wet hands on her new white apron, her eyes went to the source of the fracas. What she saw halted her in her tracks. She put a shocked hand to her throat. A stranger in a suit was attempting to pull a mule by the reins up over the edge of the ridge and eight or nine eagles were busy attacking him with screeching cries, outspread wings and outstretched talons. Mary had got used to seeing an extraordinary number of the birds gathering over the skies of Eagle Spur in most un-eagle-like fashion every day, but *this!* It was a frightening sight to see such naked aggression from these wild winged predators that had so recently treated her to the most unusual and thrilling experience of her life. It sent Zachary Thomas catapulting down the porch steps, closely followed by Mary.

They ran to the edge of the boulder-engulfed cliff to help the unfortunate fellow, who was obviously some wandering tinker, judging by the big bundle strapped to the mule's saddle. She wondered how he could have made his way all up here unchallenged by the clan's lookouts.

The poor mule was wild-eyed with fear and neighing piteously, obviously badly spooked not only by the impossible feat being asked of it, but by the birds' ferocious and noisy attack. The maddened eagles repeatedly dived and bombarded the man, their huge magnificent wings flapping as they attempted to clutch at him with their fearsome claws, while he desperately tried to ward them off with his hat and yelled curses. Amidst terrible screeching noises and evilly glinting yellow eyes, one eagle swooped down and, wings flapping, had the man by his longish black hair. Another had its cruel hooked beak latched onto his jacket sleeve and was fiercely tugging, while yet another had his talons latched onto his shoulder and was flapping its wings madly as if determined to whisk him away, while the others continued to generally harass him. The man's face was red, his eyes were popping out and he was screaming in terror. He dropped his hat and the reins and hit the winged predator that was clutching his hair with both fists.

Mary ran forward to grab the reins, afraid the mule, encumbered by such a heavy load, would fall backwards and badly injure itself or be killed. She clung to the reins with all her might, skidding as the animal's immense weight was pitted against her comparative frailty. "C'MON, BOY! C'MON!" she yelled, encouraging the mule to greater effort. As the mule struggled to get its hind legs over the ridge, Mary pulled so hard she felt as if her arms were being wrenched out of their sockets.

By wildly waving his hands and shouting, Zachary Thomas at last managed to chase the marauding eagles away. In the meanwhile, despite the mule's valiant efforts to scramble up, it was now losing the battle and sliding backwards, the reins slipping through Mary's hands and stinging her still-healing palms. She yelled at her husband to help her as the eagles let go of their victim and were taking off and flying away with angry, indignant cries, as if highly disgruntled.

Seeing her dilemma, her harried-looking husband hastily clambered down the steep slope off the ridge and, with super-human strength, started pushing the squealing, terrified mule up by the rump from behind, till it finally managed to scramble over on its shod hind hoofs, a feat Mary never would have believed possible.

Trembling with the supreme effort and breathing harshly, Mary petted the poor fretting mule, which stood shuddering with fright, while the disheveled man picked up his dusty hat, bashing it furiously against his leg. He smoothed down his wildly awry hair with one hand and straightened his clothing, clearly shocked by his nerve-wracking experience with the famed eagles of Eagle Spur. With a furious look on his face, he yelled angrily at Zachary Thomas, "Goddamn those loathsome creatures! Every time I try to visit you, they come at me, but never like this. Next time I'll bring my rifle and shoot the whole damned lot of them!"

"Aw, Paw, they're only tryin' to protect thar nests," Zachary Thomas placated.

"What nests? I have not seen a single one of them up here!" he cried indignantly. "Don't know where they come from or what the attraction is!"

PAW! Only then did Mary realize, with a surge of alarm, who the man was – *Obediah Buchanan!* What she had assumed to be a tinker's bundle was, in fact, the big wooden chest from the man's bedroom, strapped, along with some moonshine jugs, to the mule's saddle. Up close, the patriarch of the Buchanan clan seemed to fit all the preconceived notions she had of him. He was a vigorous-looking man in his fifties, who like his eldest son, was huge, though shorter than Zachary Thomas, with powerful shoulders. His longish black hair was streaked with silver and he had a luxuriant black mustache which curved in long defiant bows down his cheeks, giving him a handsome and somewhat cavalier look. But his firm, arrogant jaw and icy, pale-blue eyes told her he was not a man to be trifled with. His navy-blue suit had broad red stripes and an enormous collar, with a red handkerchief stuffed in the top pocket, and he wore a red plaid tie and fancy black-and-white rubber-soled shoes – altogether, a handsome, if somewhat flamboyant get-up, no doubt purchased with moonshine profits from Stony Man Camp.

Mary felt her palms go clammy and her heart begin to pound, for the man she was about to meet had fathered the dreadful Buckos. Thankfully, he seemed to have calmed down considerably after the disturbing and bizarre incident with the eagles – one, she'd never seen or heard the likes of before. He even managed a dry, humorless smile as he noticed her standing beside the mule. Still winded by her ordeal and gasping to get her breath back, Mary was suddenly acutely conscious of how awful she must look. She'd been working hard all morning and her dress, which she had been wearing for days for want of a change of clothing, was stained and grubby, her hair in a stern unflattering bun. She would have liked to be more presentable when she met her new father-in-law, especially as he seemed dressed to impress her.

"Well, now, who have we got here?" he said mockingly in a surprisingly cultured, lowlander voice. "Seems I owe you a thank you for saving the mule." He was as overpowering as his moonshine-laden breath as he crossed over to Mary and slapped a perfunctory wet kiss on her cheek. "Guess you must be my son's new wife?"

"Yes, sir, I'm Mary Harley Buchanan," she said with a little unwarranted curtsy. "Pleased to meet you, Paw Buchanan," Mary said breathlessly, sticking out her hand to him.

He squeezed it so hard she could not stop herself from flinching. He peered at her critically through blood-shot pale-blue eyes, his face so close she could see the open pores on his nose and cheeks, which were bruised with the burst veins of a heavy drinker.

"Well, Zack, me boy, she's obviously a strong one. Could be she'll bear you sons in the fine tradition of the Buchanans."

Mary colored in embarrassment at both his words and his close irreverent scrutiny. However, since he had fathered so many sons of his own, she supposed it could be a sign of approval, however slight. But his demeanor quickly grew stern as he turned on Zachary Thomas with eyes that lacked even a hint of warmth.

"Was real surprised to hear you tied the knot while I was away at Skyland," he said cuttingly.

"*Skyland?*" Zachary Thomas looked puzzled. "I thought you went to Stony Man Camp."

"I did. That's what Stony Man Camp has been called some three years past now! Still call it by the old name most of the time. Habit. But be that as it may, I wondered how come I didn't get an invite to the wedding?"

While his voice was deceptively light, he looked decidedly annoyed, and Mary shot a nervous glance at her husband. The tension was suddenly so marked it seemed to quiver through the air.

"Sorry, Paw," said Zachary Thomas quickly, wiping the back of one hand over his mouth nervously. "My fault. I couldn't wait."

"*Not even a couple of days?*" his father sneered. "I find it insulting to think that my eldest son could not have waited such a short while to have his own father at his wedding! Especially when you've waited so long to be wed."

Zachary Thomas stared at his father helplessly, remaining silent, clearly ill-at-ease. Mary noticed that he was trembling slightly. Was it possible that her great big giant of a husband was actually afraid of this man?

Without ceremony, Obediah suddenly turned on Mary with flashing eyes and said coldly, "The chest used to belong to my good late wife, but I gather you already know that since you had the *audacity* to wear her things at your wedding."

Mary felt a surge of shock and guilt at his words. She did not doubt who had reported her misdeed to her father-in-law. She had seen the envy in the eyes of the womenfolk that day. No doubt they couldn't wait to tell him! Knowing how angry he was over missing the wedding in the first place, Mary was alarmed by his pointed disapproval. Indeed, right now, he was fairly bristling with belligerence. So he had brought the chest here to shame her with its presence while he chastised her about wearing some of its contents without permission! *What could she tell him?* That she was running away from his eldest son when she fell and ruined her only dress? He was not likely to look kindly on the truth either! Her cheeks aflame, she was forced to think quickly.

She raised her chin and looked him straight in the eye. "That is quite true, sir. I was indeed mighty grateful to your departed wife fer providin' my weddin' gown. Seemed so fittin', somehow, when my groom was her eldest, don't you thunk? I guess it were jest my way of honorin' her and includin' her in the proc-eedin's even tho' she be long gone. Fact is, my only regret was that you weren't thar too. And Zachary Thomas *wasn't* th' one who insisted on gittin' wed soon as th' preacher could make it, it was *me*. You see, thar weren't no chaperone at yer place. It jest weren't seemly that I stay another night with all them unmarried males under yer roof. I not only had my reputation to consider, I feared to do so would have bin disrespectful not only to you, but to yer late wife's memory."

Zachary Thomas eyed her in bald astonishment. There was a long testy silence during which Obediah seemed to consider all this. To her immense relief, he broke into a grin and chuckled. "Well, all things considered, I reckon Heddie would have appreciated that! She was old-fashioned like that too. Guess we ought to go inside and drink to the health of the both of you. Zack, take the chest up to the cabin."

Zachary Thomas tensed visibly at his words, his face grim. There was a deathly silence before he finally obeyed. Slowly, he unstrapped the big chest and carried it effortlessly into the cabin on his huge broad shoulders, while Obediah untied the jugs of moonshine strapped to the saddle of the mule then he and Mary walked stiffly over to the cabin, Mary leading the mule by the reins. She fetched a pail of water from one of the rainwater barrels and gave it to the beast to drink, patting it reassuringly before ushering Obediah inside. Father and son sat down on either side of the table with a row of the moonshine jugs between them. Obediah looked around the place, his eyes widening with amazement.

"Hell, son, thought I was in the wrong cabin for a moment! What a *transformation!* It's so clean, reckon I could eat straight off the floor! My Heddie swore by cleanliness too. But I declare even she would have been outshone by this place!"

Obediah gave Mary an appreciative, acknowledging nod, before taking off his suit jacket and hooking it over the back of his chair. His braces were hitched over a stained red shirt and there were dark patches of sweat beneath his armpits. He ordered Mary to sit with them and, too nervous to decline, she sat rigidly at the head of the table. He demanded that Zachary Thomas bring three tin mugs, but his son fetched only two.

At Obediah's enquiring raised eyebrows, Zachary Thomas grunted, "She don't drink moonshine."

Obediah looked at her approvingly again. "My Hedina didn't drink it either."

Mary watched warily as the two men steadily drank together. She noticed that the more moonshine Zachary Thomas imbibed, the more morose and withdrawn he became. It hadn't taken Mary long to find that out about her husband of just days; he was a man of very few words. But she soon discovered that his father was a different sort altogether. The more Obediah drank, the more gregarious he became and the more he liked to talk. His smile got broader and he beamed with a bonhomie she had not expected to find in a man whose reputation was so fearsome. And despite Obediah's uncouthness (he kept aiming strong streams of spittle towards the fireplace), he spoke far better and more eloquently than any mountain man she had ever met, and he had a spellbinding way of telling a tale.

He started to talk about his life with adamant thumps on the table and roars of ironic laughter and, to her surprise, Mary found herself listening with riveted, if sometimes shocked, interest. Some of the background of the notorious clan's story emerged from Obediah, the rest she had heard from mountain gossip, but all in all, she was managing to piece it all together.

* * *

*T*o hear the great man tell it, Obediah Buchanan was the black sheep of a wealthy aristocratic family who had lived in the Graves Mill area and owned vast tobacco plantations and several distilleries. Although he managed one of the distilleries, Obediah had been given to drinking and gambling and his father, angry with him for his unsavory ways and for not joining the Confederate army during the Civil War like his brothers, cut him off from his inheritance. While his brothers, all fine horsemen, volunteered to join the 7th Virginia Cavalry, Obediah managed to evade the conscriptors who, empowered by the passage of the new Conscription Act by the Confederate Government to draft men to the Confederate Army for the duration the war, thrice came to his parent's plantation looking for young men of draft age.

Once Obediah took refuge in a huge chimney, his back against the outer structure and legs raised and feet pushing hard against the opposite wall, above the fireplace, from whence he emerged blackened with soot. Another time he hid under a haystack in the barn and, the third time, he hid in the middle of a cornfield for several hours after they left, knowing they sometimes doubled back to catch many a reluctant conscript.

It was not cowardice that caused Obediah to avoid conscription. He did not wish to join the army because he considered war a waste of time best spent enjoying oneself and because he simply refused to be dictated to by anyone! Nevertheless, condemned as a wastrel and a coward by his father, Obediah rebelled, moving to Richmond, where he continued his wayward ways in the bars and brothels of the war-plagued city.

A few years later, he heard that in the fall of 1864, his parents had fallen foul of "scorched earth" policy of Major-General Sheridan, who was under instruction from General Ulysses S Grant, to render the valley 'so barren that even a crow flying over it would have to carry their own provender,' in order to deny Confederate forces their abundant supply of wheat, corn, meat and draft animals. Sheridan's soldiers had slaughtered thousands of sheep, hogs, cattle, burned crops, barns, mills and factories, and public buildings, as well as destroying hundreds of miles of railroad, leaving the Shenandoah Valley in smoldering ruin, in what became known as "The Burning".

A bunch of disorderly Union soldiers looted the plantation house. Though they had been instructed not to fire dwellings, it had been burned to the ground, after which they killed both his parents, known Confederate sympathizers, for their stubborn resistance. They freed the slaves and set alight the tobacco plantations, driving off the livestock, and took all the horses. But the war and such shocking losses did not serve to tame Obediah any, except to further instill in him a deep resentment towards authority.

In 1870, after the war was over, Yankee carpetbaggers flooded into Virginia, and Reconstruction was begun. Odebiah killed a man over a game of poker and fled to the Blue Ridge Mountains, becoming a fugitive from the law. Before leaving Richmond, however, he hastily married an attractive, intelligent, refined young woman with striking turquoise eyes. ("Yes, Zack inherited her eyes," Obediah told Mary.) Her name was Hedina Charlemaine. Her family was of French extraction, originally from New Orleans, and even wealthier and more cultured than Obediah's. Fortunately for him, after he left Richmond, no serious attempts were made to search for him in the aftermath of the bloody Civil War. Obediah brought Hedina to live on this wild, remote, uninhabited mountain, known as Claw Mountain. The mountain was largely owned by a wealthy valley farmer called Devon Ansley, whose holding exceeded 7,000 acres of Blue Ridge mountain land. He did not abide squatters on his land. But Obediah defiantly built his homesite in a hollow midway up the mountain, west of Eagle Spur.

Soon after the birth of his first-born son, Zachary Thomas, who had been delivered by a midwife from Bear Rock Mountain, Odediah was arrested for felling trees that belonged to Ansley and spent six months in jail, during which time, leaving Hedina, with her infant son, struggling to survive in a harsh unfamiliar environment.

Fortunately for Obediah, his former crime was connected to him. He, nevertheless, emerged from prison a deeply embittered man. Not only had jail been an uncouth experience for one of his aristocratic ilk, a man of great sexual appetite, he had deeply resented being separated from his beautiful young wife all that time. After his release from the Madison County Jail, he swore to get even with Devon Ansley as well as Dean Galtrey, the patriarch of the Galtrey clan, whose clan resided on a neighboring mountain, who he believed had reported his crime to Ansley in the first place, having seen the two of them together shortly before the arrest.

His stay in prison had also deepened his hatred for authority and, from then on, his arrogance knew no bounds. Angry and bloody-minded, he blazed every tree outlining "his land" on the mountain with an axe, and named and renamed hollows and ridges, declaring that none but a Buchanan could set foot on them, boldly proclaiming himself the "King of Claw Mountain". Any stranger who dared set foot on the mountain was driven off by a barrage of shotgun fire.

This brazen behavior could not fail to reach the ears of Devon Ansley and there were whispers about how the landowner would handle such willful provocation. Obediah pre-empted this by paying the man a visit at his three-storied home in the valley and, in an inexplicable turn of events, Ansley moved out to California shortly afterwards, giving Obediah the freedom to continue to run riot over his land and the ammunition for folks to say that the man had been so afraid of Obediah, he had run like a scared rabbit. Rumors abounded about what had actually driven Ansley out West, everything from Obediah winning the mountain land in a hand of poker, to threatening to chop down all his timber, to threatening to kill off him and his entire family, one by one.

Nobody save the two parties themselves knew for sure what had transpired between them and, certainly, Obediah wasn't about to tell his new daughter-in-law, either. But one thing was for certain, whatever had actually happened between the landowner and the squatter, Obediah's reputation as a man not to be trifled with had grown considerably. It was true that the Buchanan clan was not bothered by Devon Ansley ever again. The man died in ignominy in California and no heirs ever came forward to claim his land. Thus Obediah declared that the whole of Claw Mountain was his by "divine right" and he was by then so universally feared, nobody dared challenge this unprecedented so-called "divine" benevolence.

However, the rapidly expanding clan soon became impoverished through having no income. In common with most mountain men, Obediah turned to moonshining. With knowledge gained from running the distillery owned by his family, Obediah soon produced some of the finest whiskey and apple brandy to come from the Blue Ridge. In all, Obediah had sired an awesome tribe of twenty sons (three having died in infancy and one in childhood). The Buckos, as they became known, soon became greatly feared. Mean-spirited and wild, they drank 100-proof whiskey produced from their father's hidden still-site and roamed the mountains, rocking shacks and cabins and folk with impunity, and using their guns and knives at the least provocation, a fact of which Obediah seemed inordinately proud.

*B*y the sounds of it, the Ficks and Addis clans of Beacon Mountain and Bear Rock Mountain were often the victims of the clan's malicious mischief-making. Indeed, by all accounts, these unfortunate clans were subjected to much tyranny and devilment by their more powerful and predatory neighbors. Buck Knob Mountain, on the other hand, was the home of an equally wild and hostile mountain clan, the Galtreys. After Obediah blamed his incarceration on Dean Galtrey, an ugly, violence-ridden feud had developed between the two clans, hatred and bitterness running between them like hemlock. Between their two mountains ran a deep chasm which had carved its way beneath a 2000-foot overhang joining the two mountains, before broadening out on the northern side. The healthy stream that ran through the length of this rock-lined chasm was known as Devil's Creek and was considered "no-man's land" by the two warring factions.*

Should either clan cross this divide, it was considered an act of sorest provocation. Raids were frequently carried out by both clans and there were many casualties among them, including several deaths, all on the Galtrey side, except for one Bucko wife, who had died in a fire when the family's clapboard shack was set alight by some marauding Galtreys, though the Galtrey clan had inflicted many bullet and knife injuries on their enemies. However, a frontier-style justice had long prevailed in the mountains. No murder was ever investigated unless a charge was laid with the county sheriff and mountain people, considering themselves outside the law, preferred to settle their own scores ...

Mary had listened to Obediah, shocked, but utterly mesmerized. After he went to relieve himself out back, she sat thinking back on the fascinating tale. She hoped that the tales of killings had been exaggerated by the patriarch. She knew that mountain men loved to tell tales of gunfights and knife fights around the pot-bellied stoves in the general store, repeating them with great embellishment and relish, as if killing was something to be proud of. She doubted that few, if any of them, had actually killed a single soul in their whole lives. It was obvious to Mary that Obediah encouraged his clan to such lawlessness as a way of snubbing his nose at a society on which he had turned his back and the rejection of any authority over him. To him, Claw Mountain was his inviolate kingdom and his mode of rule, both on and off the mountain, was undoubtedly *fear*.

One thing was for sure, though. By the admiring way he spoke about her, with a reverent tone and a moist eye, he had fiercely loved his departed wife. Such was the power of his oration that she had actually felt his anger and pain at being forced to leave his new wife and infant son to battle life and the elements while he was in jail. *Poor Hedina!* Yet, she and her baby had survived. She, who had come from a wealthy family and no doubt having slaves tending to her every whim, had survived in these extremely harsh and unfamiliar conditions. Mary could not help but feel a wave of admiration for the dead woman.

When Obediah came back and sat down again, he continued in a more serious vein. "Lost Hedina to pneumonia. No doctor would come to see her," he said bitterly. "Had to fetch a doctor myself at gunpoint with some of my boys. But it was too late to save her by then. She died a few hours after we got him there. Felt like I could kill that quack with my bare hands. Only thing stopped me was I knew Heddie wouldn't have wanted it that way. Never knew another woman like her ..."

Mary also found out that Obediah Buchanan was a mess of contradictions. Though he clearly liked to think of himself as a mountain man, his armor easily slipped into the mold of the aristocratic gentleman he professed to be at one time. Then his coarseness would magically leave him and he would seem every inch a man of quality. He would get up and pace the floor, spouting erudite verses of poetry in his lusty baritone, his voice eloquent and cultured-sounding. It was clear that Obediah had also grown to love his place of self-exile a lot more than he had initially bargained for, for when Mary asked if he missed living in a city, he shook his head adamantly. "Hell, no! Heddie always wanted to move back to the city, but it gets so a man never wants to leave these hills. Here a man doesn't have to live by anybody's rules but his own, just the way it ought to be."

Mary nodded in understanding. For hours now, she had sat silently next to her father-in-law, bludgeoned to a rapt listening by the sheer magnitude of the man's presence. This seemed to greatly impress the man.

"I like a woman who doesn't talk too much," he told her, as he took snuff out of a leather pouch and sniffed it noisily up one nostril. "You remind me of my Hedina. She listened good too. Reckon she would have approved of your getting that chest of hers. Zack always was her favorite."

Mary looked at him in surprise. "You mean . . .?"

"Yes, the chest is my wedding gift to you, young lady, and all that's in it! Looking around this place and seeing the fine job you've done here, I'd say you surely deserve it."

"I . . . thank you, Paw Buchanan. It is right kind of you," she murmured. She quickly rose to take another look at the huge chest, examining it closely for the first time. It was made of delicately carved oak with heavy brass overlapping hinges in the shape of leaves, and had ball-and-claw feet. She returned to the table overwhelmed to think that such a fine stately piece (and all the beautiful garments inside) was now hers. Since she had been wearing the same dowdy old work dress every day since the wedding, she fervently hoped she would also find more practical wear in the chest for a change of clothing.

"Well, what you think?" Obediah demanded to know when she returned to her seat.

"It's very beautiful," she said softly.

And it was.

Declining to take supper with them, Obediah left in the late afternoon amid the terror-stricken neighs of the poor mule, which had to descend the narrow path through perilous, granite boulders, pulled by the reins by its impatient owner, while the whole risky operation was overseen by Zachary Thomas.

When her husband returned to the cabin, he eyed Mary suspiciously. "How'd you do it?" he thundered.

"Do what?" she asked, puzzled by his vehemence.

"Twist him around yer little finger like that! Ain't never seen th' like! Never heard him open up that way neither. Told you thungs I ain't even know'd m'self!

And damn, wimmin, when Willie's wife, Pearl, took a dress out of that chest a'Maw's without askin', he took th' chest to their cabin, jest like he done here today, and he make her try on evrry garment in it, right in front of th' whole damn clan. Even made her put on th' underwear with everybody gawkin'. Now Pearl's as skinny as a string bean, all ribs, with skin so white, you kin see clean through it like it were tracin' paper. Believe me, it weren't no purty sight. And all th' while, Paw pointed his finger at her and cackled like a loon. Don't got me much time fer Pearl, but even I felt sorry fer her that day th' way that mean old goat humiliated her in front of everybody."

Mary heard the story with a shocked, sinking heart. Now she knew why his kin had all looked so stunned when she had appeared wearing Hedina Buchanan's dress and boots. It wasn't because she had reminded them of their mother at all, but because they were all remembering what had happened the last time somebody had dared to be so presumptuous. She had an uncomfortable feeling that Pearl's unhappy fate may well have been her own had she not somehow managed to reach Obediah first. Indeed, remembering his initial belligerence, she was sure that his declaring that the chest was a wedding gift for her had, in fact, been an after-thought rather than his original intention and she quailed at the narrowness of her escape.

Was this the reason Zachary Thomas had seemed so afraid of his father earlier? Had he feared that his father would try to humiliate her the way he had poor Pearl? And if that were so, why had her husband given her his mother's nightgown in the first place? Was it simply because it was hardly likely that such a garment would be seen by anyone else other than himself, or missed by his father? It was hard to believe that Obediah Buchanan could be so cruel when he had displayed such charm and gregariousness today. Or was that just a veneer, hiding a much more sinister side of him?

Mary shrugged her slim shoulders at Zachary Thomas. "If'n yer paw seems taken with me at all, it's jest 'cuz I remind him of his dead wife, is all," she replied dully.

11

After supper that night, Mary viewed the contents of the big stately chest Obediah Buchanan had given her as a wedding present. As she went about it, she wondered anew at what had prompted the man to do it, especially after the shameful way he had treated poor Pearl, for it contained a host of what must surely represent precious memories to him. Personal stuff: clothes belonging to his dead wife, a gold locket, with separate miniature photographs of her and Obediah in it, a quill pen and ink-well, well-wrapped in shammy leather to prevent leakage and a locked old leather-covered diary that was rotting with mildew. The locked diary intrigued Mary and she hugged it wonderingly to her chest. *What was written it in?* She felt a burning need to know. After all, it could tell her many things about this strange family. But to read it, she needed the key. What might Hedina have done with it? As it turned out, Mary found the missing key after an amazingly brief search revealed that she had hidden it on the underside of the chest by hammering two nails into the wood and securing it tightly between them – so tightly, in fact, that Mary had trouble wriggling it out. Why had the poor woman gone to such trouble? Was it to prevent her husband from reading what she had written? If so, had she too been afraid of him?

In the months to come, Mary was to read the spidery writing that filled the pages of Hedina Buchanan's diary with faded black ink many times over. She was so grateful that her cousin, Emily, had taught her to read and write all those years ago. Indeed, Mary was the only member of her own family who was literate. There were very few schools in the Blue Ridge and most mountain folk were illiterate and felt no shame in it. After all, there was little time or use for book-learning in their hard, work-worn lives.

Her cousin, Emily Tuttle, had been the daughter of her father's sister, Clara. Clara was a beautiful raven-haired mountain girl, who had married Earl Tuttle, the city-bred owner of a logging camp, at the age of fifteen. Her husband had sold the logging camp for a good profit and bought a gents' outfitting business in Richmond. With the resourcefulness common to mountain folk, Clara encouraged Earl to expand his business by opening up a complementing ladies' outfitter, which she personally ran, showing a flair for fashion that belied her mountain upbringing. Tuttles Department Stores soon came to be associated with quality, flair and service. More branches were opened in other cities and towns. The Tuttles had prospered greatly and, when they had children all four of them, including their only daughter, Emily, were sent to private schools.

Clara had never forgotten her mountain roots, however, and after Emily suffered consumption, a serious lung disease, she sent her to live with her mountain relatives to recover. She felt that the rarified air of the mountains was exactly what was needed to perk up her ailing child. And indeed, the change did seem to agree with the pretty twelve-year-old child with long blonde hair and solemn brown eyes, bringing pink to the wan cheeks of the girl before a month was up. Mary and Emily were much of an age and fast become devoted friends.

Spared the physical duty of performing chores due to her weakened condition, Emily sometimes managed to go for short walks and explore the forests with Mary, before being reduced to gasping for breath. She soon came to love everything about mountain life, while Mary loved to hear all about her cousin's exciting life in the big city. She was awed to learn that Emily – *a girl!* – went to school and begged Emily to teach her to read and write and cipher. This, her cousin readily agreed to do.

Emily had fortuitously brought a good supply of paper, pencils, quill pens, chalk and books with her for her own use, since she had desired to start writing a book while she was recuperating. The crowded, noisy lifestyle in the Harley household and her own listlessness, however, did not lend itself to such a pastime. Nevertheless, after that, her cousin began to tutor Mary, in Mary's special refuge in the forest, and the writing aids were put to good use. They had to be careful not to tell anyone about their activities, however, for Mary's father scoffed at book-learning, considering it a waste of time, especially for a girl. Right now, only Mary's mother knew of her unique achievement in the family. She was very proud of her eldest daughter. After four months of patient, quickly learned lessons, one fine fall morning, a few days before her family was due to fetch Emily to take her back to Richmond, Emily unexpectedly passed away. Mary felt indescribably sad after she came upon her cousin lying on her pallet in the loft; her eyes closed and not breathing. She had earlier complained of being tired and had gone to rest.

Totally devastated after hearing the terrible news sent to them by telegraph from the Fletcher Store by the owner, Mr. Fox, Emily's bewildered family had rushed up the poor roads to Lewis Mountain from the city in a handsome buggy and pair, to be with their deceased daughter. She was buried on Lewis Mountain, for Emily had intimated in her letters to them how much she had grown to love the mountains. Emily's parents gave Mary their daughter's large treasure trove of writing materials, and her books, which Mary had devoured from cover to cover many times over, since. Now, because of this precious gift she had been given, Mary was able to enter into the strange world of Hedina Charlemaine Buchanan.

Mary wondered at the terrible hardships the poor woman had been forced to endure. As one who had been born and raised in the mountains herself, Mary knew that mountain life, though it had its undeniable pleasures, could never be considered easy. And with a boorish insatiable husband, a large brood of loutish sons and the never-ending work that they must have entailed, Mary fancied life on this hostile isolated mountain must have been extremely tough for Hedina. But Mary had known instinctively even before she had seen the miniature photograph of the woman in the inside of the gold locket that Hedina had been a strong woman. The photograph merely confirmed it. The narrow angular features of her unsmiling but very beautiful face, had more than hinted of her indomitable spirit, and, in her worst moments of despair, Mary found herself talking out loud to the deceased woman, sensing that she was invisibly near and could understand.

Hedina's diary, indeed, provided many insights into the Buchanan family and, through it all, ran her deep disappointment in her husband and sons. And though she had lived on Claw Mountain for many long, hard years, Mary sensed that she had always felt like an outsider on this accursed mountain, just the way Mary did right now. Though Hedina had once written of Zachary Thomas that he was a quiet sensitive boy, with a deep love of Nature, Mary fancied that his sensitivity must have been knocked out of him by an overbearing father who sought only to toughen his sons, making them as manly and strong as was he. Though both Hedina and Obediah were well-educated and literate, their off-spring, in common with most mountain folk living in the isolated hollows of the Blue Ridge, had received no schooling whatsoever. Obediah did not seem to share Hedina's concern for their sons and her greatest frustration was that he had deliberately spurned her attempts to teach them manners or even the rudiments of literacy, saying that while social graces and book-learning might have their place in city life, out here in the mountains, it was strictly for sissies and a complete waste of time.

Thinking about the woman's sons' unruly behavior, Mary considered Hedina's concerns about them were well-founded. Hedina abhorred her menfolk's free indulgence and trade in moonshine, bitterly blaming it for their steady slide into poverty and degradation. But Obediah, it seemed, bolstered by moonshine, had carved himself a small kingdom on this accursed mountain and he cared less that his sons were educated, even to a small degree, than he did that he held their strict obedience. In a cryptic way, Hedina had hinted that she could not abide with the way he treated his sons, especially those with a tendency to weakness. Once, she wrote in a bout of despair about not being able to stand the brutality much longer, though she did not elaborate. But she had stayed, poor woman, trapped by a devoted mother love. Mary sighed with sympathy, thinking about her own situation.

Indeed, Mary could well understand the woman's frustration about her sons, for Toad was the first in a never-ending procession of them who came by the cabin to visit and "pay their respects" to the newly wedded couple, usually heralded by a flying circle of angry, screeching eagles, though, thankfully, they did not attack them the way they had Obediah. Mary had the feeling that these scruffily dressed, ill-mannered, leering brothers to her husband, their grinning, imbecilic wives and hordes of filthy, snotty-nosed children, had in fact come to view her again because, for some reason, she held a deep fascination for them, for they giggled and whinnied at her, without pretension or shame. Just the sight of them made Mary's skin crawl. Their way of life, centered in indolence and sloth, so vastly different to her own, made her feel it would be impossible to ever get close to any of them, to say nothing of Zachary Thomas.

Even Eli came to visit, to a much vociferous objection from the eagles; they swooped down on him repeatedly, screeching their outrage. He came on his own when Zachary Thomas was off with his long Kentucky rifle and coon dogs someplace. He stood on the porch, his yellow hair falling over his pale-yellow eyes, with a boyish guileless smile arranged on his handsome face, belying the ugly jagged scar down his one cheek. Her heart pounded fearfully at the sight of him. She did not want to let him in, but she did not want him to think she was afraid of him either. So she reluctantly invited him inside, feeling like she was admitting a wolf into the sheep-pen. He sprawled indolently on a chair and his sun-darkened face, fractured by the tortured whiteness of the scar, wore a look of simmering gloating, as if he well knew the unsettling effect he had on her. His cold pale eyes followed her around as she nervously prepared some coffee for him. Not much older than herself, he was so in command of himself, so unbelievably sure, that she felt as helpless as a small child in his presence. She wondered how he was able to wield so much intimidation through the mere strength of his presence and those eerie pale-yellow eyes, that terrible scar. She was beginning to wonder what he might do when, fortunately, Zachary Thomas returned. Naturally, the moonshine jar came out after that and she went back to scrubbing the cabin floor, trying to ignore the feel of Eli's troublesome gaze on her back as best she could.

Mary had already started her vegetable garden, and what a lot of hard, back-breaking work had gone into that tiny patch of cleared land. The surrounding forest encroached on it thickly, as if sullen and unforgiving at having to yield that much. And Lord knew this mountain land was as spotted with rocks as a man spotted with the pox. First she had to get Zachary Thomas to cut the big trees down in the area she had marked out then, once he had done that with his axe and a handsaw, she had cleared the dense undergrowth and saplings away with scythe and shovel herself, before moving the surface rocks on a slide. Then she had to hand-plow it, breaking up clods of earth by cross-plowing it before she could plant the seeds. Fortunately, though rocky, the soil was rich. After carefully watering the patch of earth with pails full of rain-water from the two barrels whenever it didn't rain, already the greenery of sprouted seedlings was two inches high, from the seed potatoes and cabbage, turnip, bean, beet and onion seeds she had planted.

Every evening, she went out there after she had finished her other chores, because as she removed fast-growing weeds from the trenches, she felt herself becoming connected to the earth, and a strange sense of peace would steal over her. Then she would go and stand at the edge of the precipice and watch the sun set, wallowing in the magnificence of the view as she had that first day with Zachary Thomas. It had become a mesmerizing daily ritual, without which she feared she would go mad for she had nobody to talk to, or with whom she could share things. The flurry of visitors had thankfully all but trickled to a halt, being put off, she strong suspected, by the arduousness of the climb and the threatening eagles. And God knows her husband could not be considered company. He was big and morose and silent as a tree-trunk! Though the tension between them, so intense at first, had lessened somewhat, mainly due to the fact that he had not tried to touch her again after that first nightmare night, they barely spoke except when she had to ask him to do something that she was physically incapable of tackling herself.

Every morning after breakfast, before her husband went tracking, he would spend hours lovingly cleaning his muzzle-loading flintlock rifle, of which he seemed inordinately proud. He would carefully clean the long barrel with a patch and a long iron rod, to remove the gunpowder residue, before oiling it and then polishing the wooden stock and outer barrel, buffing up the brass ornamental inlays and the hinged brass patch box, till the whole thing glinted and gleamed. Indeed, except for the time he spent mollycoddling his rifle (though even she had to admit it was a handsome one!), she got the feeling he couldn't stand to be around her for he would clip the gunpowder horn to his belt and, taking his old Kentucky with him, would disappear for most of the day, leaving her to lonely solitude. He would no doubt visit his father's homesite to revel in moonshine and poker and tossing horseshoes, or perhaps engage in target-shooting with his bone-idle brothers, while she did all the work!

At night, he would go hunting for many hours, invariably returning with something for the table, allowing time for the game to be soaked in salt water for two days to get rid of excess blood, after she had dutifully done the necessary skinning, a task she deplored, but which she was rapidly getting used to. Thankfully, what had made her physically ill in the beginning, was now carried out with increasing skill and a good measure of enforced detachment. Dispensing with the wood-cutting services of the Ficks and the Addis clans (for which she was sure by now the Buchanans never paid, despite her husband's claims), he kept them in firewood, sometimes even making the fires in the fireplace, too. Thankfully, except for those cleared to accommodate her garden which he was leaving to dry out some, he rarely felled live trees, sticking to those already dead from disease, or struck by lightning, which meant the wood was dry and burnt more readily. Though tree-felling had not bothered Mary much in the past, since it was essential for survival in the mountains, after seeing the magnificence of the mountain forests on Claw Mountain from the heady heights of Eagle Spur, she suddenly couldn't bear the thought of living trees being felled. He always made their first mug of coffee for the day, too. Altogether, a strange, uneasy, unspoken alliance rather than a marriage.

Hunting and carpentry weren't Zachary Thomas's only talents. He kept an apothecary of herbs and such in an old satchel, which he used to treat various ailments. Mary discovered early on about the existence of the satchel. The pallet that served as their nuptial bed was riddled with fleas and Mary woke up every morning with lumps all over her body and covered in reddened streaks where she had scratched them with her finger-nails. Amazingly, the fleas never seemed bother her husband. *He* never scratched! When she complained bitterly about them, he fetched the old satchel from the loft, opened it, spread the contents over the pallet. There were all sorts of leaves and bark and oils, amidst more recognizable home remedies such as tincture of lobelia for snakebites, castor oil, and oil of cloves for toothache. He gave her some penny royal leaves, telling her to grind them up with the coffee grinder and scatter the bits over the bedclothes every night. Sure enough, it did the trick! He muttered to her that penny royal was also good to sweat a body.

Occasionally, one of his clan would come up to seek his advice on some affliction or other. He recommended turpentine swabbed on with a feather to ease a sore throat, boneset tea or a tea made from birch bark, or horsemint, to reduce fever, a poultice of cornmeal and onion to relieve a tight chest. Grease from a boiled polecat to get the phlegm up and help ease asthma too. Boneset tea to clear a body out. Whey poured off butter-milk to help with stomach ache. Liquor from red-stemmed ivy to help with the itch. Cherry bark boiled in glycerin for a nasty cough and wintergreen tea to soothe the aches and pains of arthritic limbs. Parched beet leaves to draw a boil to a core. To ease toothache, a red flannel rag dipped on lamp oil was given to the sufferer to bite on. Stump water was good for warts and dew cracks demanded that you pull a yarn through mutton tallow and tie it to the toe.

She once asked Zachary Thomas how he had come by his knowledge and he mumbled that he had learned a lot from Jenny Addis, the "granny-woman" from Bear Rock Mountain, who was the daughter of Ada Addis, the mountain mid-wife who had delivered him, and the rest had come from experience, or his own intuitive remedies he'd simply developed over the years. Although he told her that most mountain folk knew of these home remedies, Mary fancied he had become something of an expert for he spoke most knowledgably about the different herbs and oils and their medicinal uses. But she noticed that Zachary Thomas entirely lacked the dedication of a true healer for he would grouse and grumble under his breath whenever anybody came up to Eagle Spur and chanced to bother him about their ailments and afflictions. Mary soon realized that this was because being around people too much made her husband downright uncomfortable.

A couple of weeks after she and Zachary Thomas were wed, Mary had settled into a kind of numbed routine, when she didn't allow herself to think of anything but the work that needed to be done and her escape from the mountain at the end of it all. To look back became the thing she most dreaded. Whenever she felt homesickness crowding in on her as it often did, she would increase the tempo of her work – which was endless – and she would tell herself she mustn't think of her family, else she'd go clean mad!

Then something happened that brought everything back to her with the snap of a lightning bolt! Zachary Thomas's sister-in-law, Agnes, who was married to his brother, Ebenezer, came to tell Mary that the Sheriff Coley had visited the homesite of the Buchanan patriarch and had enquired if he or any of his kin knew anything about her whereabouts.

According to a gleeful, marble-eyed Agnes, the belligerent patriarch had flatly denied knowing anything about where she was. She scoffed that the sheriff, who had come alone, had been too 'a'skeer'd' to undertake a search. On hearing that, it came home to Mary once more how much her unexplained disappearance must be grieving her parents. How awful it must be for them to have no idea where she was, or what had befallen her. She realized that her frenetic hard work had been to stop such disturbing thoughts from tormenting her.

Now Agnes had broken through that protective barrier and the knowledge bludgeoned her anew. The way that spiteful old hag, with her gap-toothed grin and bulging eyes, had told it, Mary could see she had only relayed the information to gauge what her reaction might be. Though Mary managed to hold a straight back and a calm, passive council, the incident, and the thought of how hard her rash, heedless actions must be affecting her loved ones, upset her so much that, racked with soul-deep guilt and grief, she wept the whole night long. Thereafter, the knowledge sat inside her chest, causing actual physical pain that spread over her chest and went down both her arms, never going away, no matter how hard she slaved.

12

It seemed to Mary that even the weather conspired against her on Eagle Spur.

Sometimes the wind blew so fiercely around it that she feared being blown straight off it if she ventured anywhere near the edge of the high curved giant rock-clinging ridge. Fortunately, the forest, though disfigured from the wind around the edges, grew thickly around the homesite, providing it with some protection. The five-mile-wide thickly forested tableland acted as a great natural buffer from the rear, but there were times when it came in at the cabin face-on with such bruising force that it was impossible to go outdoors. Summer brought rain and thunderstorms to the mountains and, as if the wind was not punishing enough, a summer storm on the top of Claw Mountain could be so frightening as to evoke actual terror in her breast.

At Eagle Spur many explosive lightning bolts set fire to trees and bounced off granite boulders spraying the cabin with fair-sized shattered stones. Once the sky had turned a queer greenish color and the clouds had unleashed a torrent of hailstone the size of a man's fist, which stripped the trees of their foliage, broke shutters, dislodged shingles on the roof and left a deep white carpet of hailstones, resembling snow, in its terrifying aftermath.

Once, she had even experienced a "Jack-a-ma-lantern" lightning ball that was fascinating, if frightening, to witness. It landed from the sky in the middle of the clearing in front of the cabin, a bright, bluish-white, spectacular ball of light with sparks shooting from it. It raced, four feet off the ground, towards the edge of the ridge, bouncing from boulder to boulder before disappearing. She and Zachary Thomas had run to the edge of the ridge and watched it travel in a westerly direction towards Buck Knob, several feet above the tree-tops. Mary had never seen anything so weird, and it badly unsettled her! She stood at the edge staring down long after it had disappeared from view. It was the third such lightning ball that Zachary Thomas had seen, however, and he assured her that they were harmless and didn't start fires like ordinary lightning. But to Mary, to be at the mercy of such extreme weather and strange phenomena was altogether too spooky for her liking.

The weather wasn't her only concern either; she had encountered more snakes in her short time on Eagle Spur than she had in her whole life before that. Though snakes were generally a menace in the mountains and many a doughty mountaineer had died from snakebite, she was forever hearing the ominous rattles of some disturbed rattlesnake, or catching glimpses of deadly copperhead slithering away. It got so bad, she didn't even dare to enter and explore the table-land forest. The one time she tried, a copperhead the length of a man crossed the path immediately in front of her, disappearing into the undergrowth. The forest behind the homesite thus had taken on a deep brooding quality for Mary. Even in daylight it seemed to exude foreboding and, in the darkness of night, she sometimes fancied she saw mysterious lights and heard strange noises in it, making relieving herself at night in the johnny house, a terrifying prospect. It made her thankful she no longer had to use the edges of the forest to relieve herself.

She had once come across a large black rattlesnake sunning itself on a boulder, when she went to collect water from the spring. It had immediately started up the rattles in its tail and reared up into striking position, opening its mouth and showing its venomous fangs and black flickering tongue. It had been a terrifying heart-stopping moment. Then before she could react, it had inexplicably lowered its head, turned, and slid away from her, dropping off the other side of the boulder with a great plopping sound. Zachary Thomas told her that there was a "kettle" of rattlesnakes in the rocks immediately below Eagle Spur, but that the snakes were far more afraid of her than she was of them; it was sparse comfort to her. Superstition ran deep in mountain people, especially when it came to snakes, and she was no exception. They featured largely in her nightmares at night.

Then there were the fabulous eagles of Eagle Spur. Larger than any others she had ever seen, their behavior was highly unusual and scary to say the least. Though they had shown no aggression towards her, these great spectacular guardians of Eagle Spur, the gateway to the tableland forest beyond, were ferocious in attack. It was highly unnerving and menacing to have them gliding the skies as if on the lookout for some unsuspecting victim, while below Eagle Spur sulked the murderous Buchanan clan. All things considered, Mary felt as if dark, mysterious forces were at work on this huge awesome mountain.

*　*　*

A few months after her arrival on the mountain, Mary had another surprise visitor. This time it was her shotgun-toting erstwhile jail-guard, Emma, who barged through the open doorway wearing dirty dungarees and a thunderous expression on her filthy narrow face.

Mary, busy scrubbing the floor, looked up at the thin little girl in surprise.

"Whar's Unc' Zack?" the fair-haired, narrow-eyed slip of a thing demanded to know, her voice low and scathing. At first Mary thought she was just being downright ornery but then she noticed that there were tear-trails running through the dirt on her face and beneath the dark expression, she looked pretty upset.

Mary stood up slowly. "Ain't he at Obed . . . I mean, at yer grandpaw's place?"

"Heck no, he ain't hardly ever thar. We ain't see'd him in a long time. But he's gotta come real quick. Them Galtreys done ambushed Unc' Alvin and Unc' Samuel down by Devil's Creek and shoot'd 'em both!"

"Oh, my." Mary swallowed hard. It seemed that she'd been plunged right into the middle of the decades-long feud between the Buchanans and the Galtreys! "Are they alright?"

"No, them's bleedin' real bad." Emma sniffed loudly.

"Why don't y'all take them down on th' buckboard to a valley doctor fer fixin?"

Emma shook her head despairingly, "Naw, Grandpaw hates all them quacks an' has forbidd'd my uncles t'take 'em! But Unc' Eli says if'n they don't get tharselves fixed real quick, they's gonna *die!"* The tough little spitfire gave a heart-rending sob, before she snarled, "Gonna kill all them Galtreys m'self!"

With the unnerving feeling that the girl meant it and might be tempted to try, Mary was horrified. Though she appreciated the fact that she was very upset, she couldn't bring herself to let it pass. "No, Emma, I know how you must feel right now, but you cain't do that! Killin's wrong, don't you know that? It's real bad! Them that kill go straight to hell."

Emma gave her a hard questing look. "What's hell?"

Mary stared at the child in bald surprise. She'd never heard about *hell!*

"Why, hell is whar th' bad folk go when they die. It's an awful place whar th' bad 'uns git all burned up in flames."

"You mean they gotta die *two* times?" the child cried, aghast.

"Well, no. When they go to hell, they jest burn like . . . well . . . er ... all th' time, I guess."

"Cain't see how that is," said Emma skeptically. "When folks burn in fire they turn into ashes – see'd it fer myself when th' Galtreys set fire to Clancy's cabin and Cecelia was inside. She look'd jest like a log of burned wood."

"Who's Cecelia?"

"Unc' Clancy's first wife. She was jest cinders after."

"Well, these here flames of hell ain't like *mortal* flames," explained Mary. She could see Emma struggling with this and she wasn't at all surprised. It didn't make much sense to her either.

"Whar do all th' good folks go then?" Emma muttered finally.

"Heaven. It's beautiful in heaven. Paradise."

"What's paradise?"

"Well, paradise is whar everythung is perfect. It's someplace in th' sky and very beautiful. Nuthin' bad kin happen to you in heaven. So you see, it don't make no sense at all to be bad and git sent to hell."

Suddenly seeming hugely impatient with her, Emma screwed up her eyes and said furiously, "I ain't come fer no preachin' from no fancy-britches like you! I want Unc' Zack! Jes' tell me whar I kin find him."

"Well, if'n he ain't at your grandpaw's place then I guess he must have gone trackin'. He did take his coon dogs with him."

"Oh shi-it!" cried the spitfire despairingly. "Means he'll be down in th' Wilderness then! I'll never find him in thar!"

"Guess so. How come he don't go to your grandpaw's with th' others, Emma?"

"Guess it's 'cuz Unc' Zack always likes to be by hisself. He ain't one to meet up with his kin much. I'm th' *only* one that ever gits to visit him up here – a'fore he up an' married you, that is!' she said scornfully. Considering her vehemence, Mary was left in no doubt that her marriage to her favorite uncle definitely did not please this fiery little Miss. "That's when he learn'd me to shoot! Gave me this here shotgun when he got that Kentucky rifle a'his. Says nuthin' will make him part with that. It is a mighty purty 'un tho'."

"I see."

It surprised Mary to learn from his ragamuffin niece that her husband was such a loner, having virtually separated himself from the rest of his family. She had assumed he was very much a part of their daily lives, especially since he'd been with them at the store that fateful day.

"Anyways," said Emma huffily, "you tell Unc' Zack soon's he comes home that Grandpaw wants him down at Horseshoe Hollow so's he kin remove them bullets like he done a'fore with Unc' Toad and Unc' Johnny, and then they kin plot after what t'do t'them Galtrey boys fer re-venge."

Biting her tongue on a remark about revenge being ungodly, Mary nodded. "Sure, Emma, I'll tell him, I promise."

When Zachary Thomas came home several hours later, looking grim-faced, Mary started to tell him what had happened, but he silenced her with a hand. "I know all 'bout it and thar ain't no need fer me to tend them brothers of mine 'cuz them is stone dead! Shot to pieces by them Galtreys. It whar a miracle they lived so long after."

Mary stared at him in shocked dismay. Though she thoroughly despised his family and thought them lazy and shiftless and violent, she certainly wouldn't have wished this upon any of them. She murmured, "Oh, Zachary Thomas, I'm real sorry. How'd you find out?"

"I was comin' back up th' mountain when Emma waylaid me an' told me both my brothers is gone. I called in at Paw's place. We're gonna git together come dark an' go git us some Galtreys. They's gonna pay real big fer what they done t'day."

Mary was mortified. "Lord, Zachary Thomas, you cain't mean that. You've got to go tell th' sheriff, so he kin arrest them Galtreys responsible."

Zachary Thomas looked at her as if she had taken leave of her senses. "It ain't the way thungs work 'round here, Mary. Mountain folk have settled their own scores for hunnerds a' years an' we sure as heck ain't gonna change now."

"It ain't *got* t'be that way, Zachary Thomas. Fact is, it don't make no sense at all to keep up a quarrel year after year like you and them Galtreys."

"Don't believe you, girl! Them filthy swines jest kilt two of my brothers an' now you sayin' they ain't got it comin' to 'em?"

"Lord, that ain't true! I said no sech thing. Jest said it would make a lot more sense if'n th' sheriff took care of it, is all!"

Zachary Thomas snorted in disgust. "Man's gotta settle his own scores if'n he's a man."

Mary heaved on her breath helplessly. "Seems to me it takes more of a man to *stop* all the senseless fightin' an' killin'. If'n you go takin' revenge on them Galtreys, they likely to come after you agin after, and it jest goes on and on and on, whereas if'n you go to th' sheriff now, he'll take care of it an' that kin be th' end of that!"

"Ye're talkin' fool's nonsense, girl!" he said angrily. "Them Galtreys gonna come after us, no matter what we do. Now dish me out some vittles so I kin git goin'. It's gonna be a long night!"

* * *

Mary found herself sitting in front of the fireplace at the table, drinking mug after mug of bitter coffee brew, in the dim light of a single kerosene lamp. It was a black moonless night, punctuated by the mournful hooting of the gray owl that lived in a hemlock grove close by that seemed to complement her dark mood. She was used to being on her own at night, because that was when Zachary Thomas did most of his hunting, but this particular night had a sinister feel to it, and she shivered with apprehension. She shuddered to think what was happening right now. After all, the clan would be armed to the teeth as usual and, to be sure, all that target practice wouldn't go to waste! While it was true that mountain folk had sorted out their own disputes for centuries – the Blue Ridge had been plagued with such senseless violence that went largely unpunished – she knew that what she had told her husband made sense. Somebody had to stand back and let the law take its course rather than have these senseless feuds go on for year after year, gathering in intensity and violence in the bloody name of revenge.

She could understand how angry and upset the whole Buchanan family must be right now as the result of the shocking ambush, but it made no sense at all to her to risk other lives to get revenge. The brothers would very likely get caught in another ambush, because the Galtreys must know that they would not take the slaying of their brothers lying down and would likely be waiting for them! She supposed if that happened, it would make her prospects of escaping from the mountain that much greater. That being so, she wondered why it bothered her so much that her husband and his brothers might be wiped out, or possibly even put in jail or hanged if they murdered any of the Galtreys and the law did somehow get wind of it. Was it that in the event of Zachary Thomas getting killed or jailed, she would face the unnerving prospect of being left all alone to face his brother, Eli? As disconcerting as that was, she knew the reason was even more complex and deep-seated than that. Ominously, her monthly sick had stopped and she had started throwing up every morning, just as Maw had done whenever she was with child. She feared that she too was going to have a baby – *the result of one terrible night!* It was the worst thing that could possibly have happened! Not only would it make escaping from Claw Mountain that much more difficult, in a cruel twist of fate, it tied her to this ghastly clan – and Zachary Thomas – forever!

* * *

It was just before dawn when Mary heard a small sound outside. Jolting her-self from a light illicit doze, she rushed out onto the porch, holding the kerosene lamp aloft. The face that came into her circle of light was dog-tired and caked with dirt – *and blood!*

"Zachary Thomas, ye're hurt!"

"I'm alright – jest got grazed by a bullet, is all," he muttered as he climbed wearily up the porch steps, toting his long-barreled old Kentucky rifle in one hand.

"What happened?"

"Reckon at least four of 'em Galtrey boys won't be causin' us no more trouble," he said shortly.

Mary heard the words and felt like a big boulder had lodged itself in the pit of her stomach. It was even more bloody than she had feared. *Six* men had been murdered in a matter of hours! *Maybe more!* It could be that the Buchanans had lost more of their number in the exchange. "Were any more of yer own kin hurt?" she asked fearfully.

"Nah, even tho' they was a'waitin' fer us and thar was a big shoot-out, we got th' better of 'em. Killed two straight off then much later, after they had let their guard down thinkin' we was gone, Eli managed to get in close an' slit two of their throats."

Mary shuddered with horror and revulsion. This was a terrible nightmare! Grown men killing each other tit-for-tat like this and all for meaningless, long-forgotten reasons! It was truly barbaric! Zachary Thomas must have sensed her extreme repugnance for when she prompted him for more information he wouldn't say anything further, suddenly seeming closed and suspicious. Perhaps he thought she was pumping him for information so she could go tell the sheriff. To offset this impression more than anything else, Mary made him sit on a chair while she cleaned his grazed forehead with a clean cloth dipped in a bowl of warm water then she carefully wrapped a makeshift bandage around his large head that she had made from cutting up a pair of lace-edged white pantaloons she found in the chest. Mary noticed that while she worked, his face, usually so stoic and devoid of animation, was wracked with exhaustion and a kind of deep-seated pain. Though he didn't talk, Mary had no doubt that he was mourning the loss of his two slain brothers. After she had finished, without saying another word, he stumbled into the bedroom and dropped down wearily onto the pallet, face down.

13

The funeral for the two slain Buckos, Alvin and Samuel, was held at Horseshoe Hollow the next day, in the late afternoon, to allow time for the coffins to be made. (Because of the heat in summer, the dead were buried quickly in the mountains so that the corpses wouldn't decompose.) Unable to lessen their vigilance even on such an occasion, at least two of the Buckos and a few of their elder sons were acting as lookouts up trees in a wide perimeter surrounding the old homestead, old shotguns and squirrel rifles at the ready, to keep uneasy watch for possible avenging Galtreys, while all the rest on the ground carried their usual array of weapons.

It struck Mary that this peacock parading of weaponry of every description, was not simply some exaggerated male need to show-off as she had been wont to believe, but because a virtual state of war truly did exist between the two feuding mountain families. After what had transpired yesterday, how could she fail to know that hatred and tensions ran hot and deep between them? It didn't seem possible that a few cut trees all those years ago could have caused such bad blood between them as to result in such carnage.

The entire clan had assembled for the double funeral, even the children, who for once were quiet and well-behaved, as if the seriousness of the situation had been instilled in them by their parents. Mary had told Zachary Thomas she wasn't going to attend the funeral, since she didn't know the two brothers at all, and he had gone down to the main homestead without her. The real reason, however, was that she felt no loyalty to this disreputable family that had been the scourge of the Blue Ridge for so long. Yet at the last minute, something impelled her to change her mind, and she'd climbed carefully down the steep mountain slope to Horseshoe Hollow. Naturally, her husband had not expected her appearance. His eyes widened in surprise when he saw her and he came to stand dutifully beside her.

Inside a split-pole-fenced enclosure covered in periwinkle creeper, a double grave was being dug on the mountain slopes behind and above Obediah's homestead, next to where his wife, Hedina, was buried. Her grave was marked by a pile of rocks and a weathered wooden cross on which was crudely carved the scant epitaph: 'Hedina Buchanan. Died 12.-10.1889'. The makeshift graveyard was beneath a cove of towering hard-wood trees, a natural, cool, stately cathedral, which the sunlight struggled to pierce, amid the long slanting shadows of approaching eventide. Alongside Hedina's grave, running along the imperceptible curve of the mountain was a series of small, rock-piled graves, with smaller unmarked crosses wedged in them, which indicated that a good number of the clan had died in infancy and early childhood, making Mary aware that this was not the first time that tears had been shed in this family. Staring at the cross, wedged crookedly in the rocks above Hedina's grave, Mary suddenly felt the dead matriarch's presence in their midst as surely as if she were standing beside her. She shivered slightly. How poor, refined Hedina must hate what had been happening to her family of late.

Late yesterday evening, a bell had been tolled from the main homestead here at Horseshoe Hollow to announce the deaths to all those who lived on or near the mountain. What a desolate sound the bell-tolling had made! The mournful clanging had risen up to the heights of Eagle Spur, as eerie and lonely sounding as the wailing of a lost soul. Since she doubted any of the Buckos could count that high, she guessed it must have been Obediah doing the mindless tolling, which had dented the still mountain air like detonations in a mid-summer thunderstorm. Church bells were often rung to announce deaths to mountain folk, each toll indicating a year of the person's age, but here in the desolate, isolated region of the mountains, with the nearest church many miles away, oft'times ordinary hand-balls were used for this purpose instead. There had been two sets of bell-tolling for however many years old the two deceased Buckos were. Mary had lost count both times and thus didn't know exactly how old they were – she just knew they were much too young to have befallen such an ugly fate.

Some of the surviving brothers, who all looked exhausted from lack of sleep, took turns at digging the double grave, while others gathered rocks to pile on top of them, to prevent animals from digging up their remains. The digging was not an easy task because of the rocks embedded in the earth, but at last there was a depression deep enough to cover the two roughly hewn wooden box coffins of the corpses, which, to Mary's surprise, were still fully open to reveal the two corpses all decked out in fancy black suits and string bow-ties – and shoes. Yesterday, according to Zachary Thomas and mountain tradition, the mutilated and blood-splattered bodies had been washed and laid out by the womenfolk, and embalmed in containing bandages, but even so, dark patches of blood stained their suits. The murdered pair, both dark-haired, sun-browned and good-looking, looked very young and defenseless in death, eyes closed, their faces drained of blood, pale, waxen and sorrowful somehow. In this final irony, they hardly seemed made of the stuff of strutting Bucko legend.

The mourners were gathered around the graves in cowering bunches, women and children in vocal tears, while the men, these veritable hellers, were grim-faced, ashen and silent. Usually raucous and aggressive under the influence of moonshine, death had struck them with an odd silencing sobriety that seemed as alien amongst them as church attendance. It cast a cloud of stunned sadness and inertia, which hung over the assembled group like an invisible pall. Having tasted the bitter medicine so cruelly dealt out to countless others, a contagion of nameless dread dwelt in their haunted eyes, leaving them looking strangely vulnerable and afraid.

Only Eli, sullen and broody, stood unmoved and unmoving, among them. His slight lean figure was about as guileless as a coiled snake's, his two pearl-handled Owl's Head pistols stuck arrogantly in front of his belt, the knife that had no doubt been used to slash the throats of two of the Galtrey victims, for they were covered in a dark stains, hanging from the side of his belt. His bare feet and his arms, which were sticking out from the rolled-up sleeves of his white shirt, were brown as coffee beans. His pale-yellow eyes beneath his thatch of bright tawny hair, seeking Mary's, were as cold as winter ice, and his jagged knife scar, whitish against the brown of the rest of his cheek. With the blood of at least two men fresh on his hands, his was the chilling, calculated indifference of the soulless and the damned. Mary shivered involuntarily.

Alvin's scrawny, dark-haired widow, Lila, dressed in a shapeless black alpaca shift didn't look any older than fifteen, yet two young toddlers clung to her skirt and she carried a baby on her angular hip. Samuel's widow, Edna, was a tall, thin mousy-blonde, who wore her black widow's reeds, along with bright red lipstick and a funny straw hat that looked comical and sad at the same time. She had five children ranged about her, three girls and two boys, who were aged from about three to ten. Emma stood holding the hand of Beaufort, her little erstwhile lackey, who wore a white shirt under his blue denim dungarees. For once she had brushed her straight fair hair and half-heartedly washed her face, revealing a spattering of large dark freckles on her nose and cheeks. She had lost her usual tough, slit-eyed, spitfire look, for her thin face was puckered with grief.

The bereaved family dissolved into bouts of tearful hysteria which carried through to the children, who were wailing and weeping copiously. Moved by the sight and sound, Mary couldn't help but feel desperately sorry for these innocent victims of the violence . . . what a terrible shock it must have been for them all! Like the rest of the mourners, with the exception of the children who wore a variety of colors, Mary was dressed in black. She wore one of Hedina's handsome satin dresses from the treasure chest, complemented by a black hat and veil, black hose and the black, soft-kid button-up boots. But standing there amongst the poorly dressed barefoot womenfolk with their simple black alpaca frocks, set off by the odd outlandish, feathered or fruit-decorated hat bought from the general store, she felt so much a grandstanding outsider that she was angry at herself for having felt the ignoble need to lord it over this rabble, to show them in the only way she knew how, how vastly superior she was to them in every way.

The women deeply resented her presence among them, she knew, not least of all, for her imposing appearance today. Her Obediah-bestowed bounty from Hedina's chest must seem like an insult to them, especially since she was a newcomer to the clan. They eyed her now with undisguised, narrow-eyed malice and not a little envy. The men, though still all barefoot, had at least swapped their usual denim dungarees for black pants and white shirts, as a sign of respect for their fallen kin. The patriarch of the clan stood stonily apart from them all on a massive flat rock overlooking the operation with a dazed expression on his florid face. Obediah was all dressed up in similar get-up as the corpses in the coffins, and also wore shoes, as he had when he had visited them at Eagle Spur.

He looked glassy-eyed and tormented with grief, not responding to Mary's stumbling words of sympathy for his loss. She noticed none of his sons or members of their families dared to approach him and he seemed wild-eyed, lonely and confused, somehow, as if completely thrown by the recent passage of events. Mary felt she understood his bewilderment. Actively encouraged by him, his sons had been the instigators of countless bloody battles and bore the scars of such encounters on their lean, sun-browned bodies with boastful pride, yet never before had one resulted in the death of any of them. Now the overbearing patriarch was finding out the hard way that the Buckos were not as invincible as he had once supposed.

The coffins were closed without any ceremony being performed. The lids were nailed down then carried over to the grave site by the majority of the Bucko brothers, before being placed side by side in the shallow depression. As the brothers, including Zachary Thomas, shoveled dirt onto the closed lids, it caused the crescendo of grief to rise. The sound worried Mary's ears. Like Obediah, Eli did not get involved in this, but the sickening thuds caused even his head to drop. Mary was surprised to see that he had placed one arm tightly around the thin shoulders of young Jamie, whose slack-jawed face was raised guilelessly towards the heavens, eyes squinting, in a world of his own.

Mary had gathered some wildflowers, some golden ragwort and wood lilies, on the way down from Eagle Spur, and she moved quickly forward and placed a mixed bunch on the double mound of dirt before the brothers could start piling rocks on top of them. But she could tell her gesture was not appreciated. Some of the men gave her distinctly hostile looks as they began placing rocks and the womenfolk muttered darkly amongst themselves. There was no lay preacher officiating at the service and no hymn-singing either. Not even Obediah said a few words over the double grave of his two murdered sons when the rock-piling was completed. With her hulking great husband now standing beside her, head-bowed and mute with grief, Mary guiltily thought how the Galtrey clan, with four of their numbers slain, must be facing a similar – even greater – ordeal.

It didn't seem right not to say a prayer for those slain – the Galtrey dead, too – and when Obediah Buchanan, tears streaming down his face, turned away without even saying a few supplicatory words to the Lord over his sons' earthly remains, Mary surprised herself utterly by bowing her head and saying out loud, "Our Father who art in heaven . . . Hallow'd be Thy name . . ."

She was stunned and a little alarmed when nobody joined her in saying "The Lord's Prayer". Her voice faltered and she raised her head and took a quick peek at the gathered mourners, all of whose heads were bowed and their eyes closed, with the exception of Eli, who was staring at her with an oddly riveted look on his face that bordered on panic. Then Mary understood. It was doubtful that any of them had ever been to church, with the possible exception of Obediah! They didn't *know* "The Lord's Prayer"! And it seemed that they were allowing her, a despised stranger in their midst, to lead them in prayer because they didn't know how to pray themselves. It was pathetic and very sad. She finished the prayer and said, "Amen." She felt a tingling down her spine as a host of voices repeated, "Amen", as if driven to do so by some strange age-old instinct.

It was a fitting end to the funeral and, somehow, in that moment, the Buchanan clan did not seem nearly as threatening to Mary as it had been up till then. She knew the Buckos were hurting bad right now and it didn't seem to matter that they had caused so much hurt to others in the past. It was as if grief had lent them a slightly more human facade – for the time being, at least. Without faith to sustain them at this time of tragedy and trial, they seemed as helpless as frightened little children. By the streaming tears, the looks and silent nods they gave each other, by the hugs and the mute shaking of hands, Mary could tell the surviving Buckos were drawn together by a deep, fraternal bond that extended even towards her loner husband and the loathsome Eli. Although family ties and loyalty was the first commandment of the mountains, she sensed it was something more that bound these Buckos together so strongly. Was it just the extreme isolation in which they had been forced to grow up, or was there something else about them about which she had yet to learn? Mary closed her eyes, praying that she wouldn't have to stay on Claw Mountain long enough to find out.

14

The day following the double funeral of Alvin and Samuel Buchanan, a pall of gloom seemed to hang over the entire mountain, wrapping itself around the grieving inhabitants like the cloud that often hugged Claw Mountain like a preacher's collar. Mary did her work steeped in it. She felt weary and depressed – so much an outsider! How she longed for her old peaceful, contented life back on Lewis Mountain, in the midst of a warm, loving family, where violent death was as rare as snow in July, and the constant chatter of her sisters mingled with that of the birds, the chores were shared, and Maw cooked nearly all the meals and Paw told his stories – instead of having to live amidst these hostile outlaws and endure all this unending work and the unbearable silence of an uncommunicative husband. Indeed, she had come to the conclusion that silence was every bit as hard to endure as a beating. Silence could be beautiful when it was the silence of Eagle Spur. *The silence of Nature.* But when it sprang from another human being in a way that was not comfortable or at ease, when it was filled with tension and avoidance and curtness, and created invisible barriers, it was excruciating.

She heard a noise and looked up to see young Emma standing in the doorway, dressed in threadbare dungarees with a dirty white vest underneath, carrying the shotgun her uncle had given her. Her narrow face was once again smudged with dirt and her fair hair was scraggly and knotted. Her eyes were narrowed into slits and the tough little spitfire wore a mean, sulky look on her face.

"'Fraid yer Uncle Zack ain't here, Emma," Mary informed the child.

"I know," she retorted. "I've come t'talk to you."

"To me?"

She nodded. "Kin I come in?"

"Sure. Here, take seat. Want some milk an' cookies? It ain't fresh milk, tho'. It's canned."

Emma nodded and sat reluctantly on the chair, planting the butt of her shotgun on the floor right beside her, so that it was leaning against the table. Mary fetched a tin mug of milk and some cookies on a tin plate for her then sat on the chair opposite her. Emma didn't move to touch either of them. It was then that Mary noticed that the child was trembling and her pale-blue eyes were filled with tears. She looked at her with sympathy. The girl was clearly mourning the loss of her two uncles. How could she ever have imagined that she was so tough?

"Are you okay, Emma?"

Emma sadly shook her head, tears spilling from her eyes and running down her dusty, hollowed cheeks.

"What's th' matter, girl?"

Emma squinted across the table at her. "Aunt Mary, is Unc' Alvin and Unc' Samuel gonna go t'hell fer sure?"

It was the first time that Emma had called her 'Aunt' and Mary felt oddly touched by it.

"Well, Emma, I guess that's up to God to decide. Why, did they do some-thung bad?"

"Well, Unc' Alvin ain't done nuthin', leastwise nuthin' I know of. But . . . Unc' Samuel . . . he an' Unc' Eli an' Unc' Jake . . ."

Mary felt herself go cold at the mention of Eli's name. She breathed, "What about them?"

Emma's chin started wobbling. She dropped her head and muttered, "You gotta promise not to tell."

"I promise."

"I see'd them."

"What did you see, Emma?" Mary coaxed gently, dreading what she might hear.

Emma looked at her with stricken pale-blue eyes. "I's real skeer'd to tell you."

Mary got up, went around the table and crouched down beside the thin young girl. "Emma, you don't got to be a'feared of me. You kin tell me anythung you want."

Emma sniffed,then she swallowed hard and, gathering up her courage, she blurted it out. "I see'd Unc' Jake and Unc' Eli kill th' Galtrey boy, while Unc' Samuel look'd on."

Mary stared at her in dawning horror. "*You what?* What Galtrey boy and when did you see this?"

"Jamie. He was th' same age as me. He was fishin' in th' creek 'bout a week ago. They pounced on him from b'hind. Unc' Eli made Unc' Jake hold him to stop him from strugglin' while he pushed Jamie's head under th' water till he was drownd'd. Then Unc' Eli pull'd him up by th' back of his shirt from behind, and slitted his throat an' threw him back in th' water. They left him a'floatin' face down in th' creek. Thar was all this blood in th' water around him. Oh, Mary, it were *awful.*"

Oh, my God, those monsters had murdered a child, an innocent young boy out fishing! Mary was bludgeoned with shock. She felt sick to her stomach. She couldn't believe what she'd just heard. Little did she know what she was letting herself in for when she'd eloped with Zachary Thomas. She had ignored all mountain gossip, and her own innermost fears, about just how depraved the

Buckos actually were, and now she had been plunged right into the middle of this insane web of violence – of mass murder. And now this! *A child!* Steeped in the sheer horror of it, she could not speak for several minutes. Then she raised her head. "You're tellin' me they murdered a defenseless young'un?"

Emma nodded, looking miserable and shamed.

"Whar?"

"Down by Devil's Creek not far from whar Unc' Alvin an' Unc' Samuel got themselves ambush'd."

"So what ye're actually sayin' is them two were ambushed by th' Galtreys as revenge fer a murderous attack on one of their own? A small boy?"

Emma nodded vigorously.

"What were you doin' down by th' creek, Emma?"

Emma looked at her in stricken silence.

"C'mon, Emma, you kin tell me."

"I was fishin' too," she admitted in a small voice.

"With th' Galtrey boy?"

Emma nodded fearfully. "Yes, ma'am. But he was real nice. Not like them other bad Galtreys. He showed me how to use dragonflies fer bait."

"What happened thar, Emma? How come they ain't see'd you?"

"Well, I heard them a'comin' and I shimmied up a tree. They ain't see'd me up thar. But I see'd them. I see'd it all happen, Aunt Mary."

She burst into broken sobs, and Mary put her arms around her to comfort her, while her own heart constricted at what this innocent child had been forced to witness.

"Why ain't you told nobody, Emma, instead of carryin' this inside you all on yer own?"

"Who could I tell?"

"How about yer paw? Clyde, ain't it?"

"My paw is drunk near all th' time. 'Sides, he wouldn't have cared none, anyway."

"What about yer grandpaw then?"

Emma shook her head adamantly. "He hates all them Galtreys somethung fierce. Says th' only good Galtrey is a dead 'un."

"Does your Uncle Zack know about this?"

Emma shook her head. "Naw."

"Why ain't you told him? You two are real close."

"Well, I was skeer'd of gittin' a beatin' if'n he told Grandpaw I was fishin' with a Galtrey."

"Now you just listen to me, girl. You ain't done nuthin' bad, Emma! Foolish, maybe, but not *bad!*"

"Well, I know'd Grandpaw would be real mad. Figger'd Unc' Zack might be too. Anyways, I was thunkin' about how them that is bad goes to hell like you said. Oh, Aunt Mary, I surely want Unc' Samuel t'go heaven. He was my favorite unc' next to Unc' Zachary. Now, if'n he was with Unc' Jake an' Unc' Eli when they murder'd Jamie then I figger'd he might not get thar. Thought you might know."

"No, I'm afraid don't, Emma. Only God kin decide if'n a man is fit fer heaven, or not. But it seems to me if'n he stood by and did nuthin' while his two brothers kilt a little boy . . . !"

"Oh, he weren't happy about it, Aunt Mary! He begged them not to, but they wouldn't listen to him!"

"Well, maybe God will take that into consideration. All you kin do now is pray fer him."

"I don't know'd no prayers."

"You don't need to know any. You kin make up yer own. Would you like me to teach you how to pray?"

"Yeah, reckon I do! And I want you to teach me that one you said at th' funeral too. I liked it right fine." Her brow furrowed as if she'd just thought of something. She looked at Mary fearfully, her dirty, narrow little face wrung with anguish, and said under her breath, "Aunt Mary, you cain't tell Unc' Zack or Unc' Eli 'bout this, see? Unc' Eli would kill me if'n he knew what I see'd. I'm real skeer'd a'him."

"Don't you worry none, child. Everythung will be alright. I promise I won't breathe nary a word," Mary reassured her, pressing her lips to her forehead. But as she stood up, her blood ran cold. Emma was right. Eli didn't have any feelings for others at all. Anybody who could kill a child in cold blood was capable of absolutely anything – *even murdering his own blood niece!*

15

Though Mary kept her promise to young Emma by not mentioning a word of what she'd been told by her about the cold-blooded murder of the Galtrey boy, the sordid knowledge of it and of the subsequent massacres that had resulted from such a despicable act, boiled inside her like a laundry cauldron and her resentment towards her husband and his clan grew. Indeed, she could barely bring herself to be civil to Zachary Thomas. She did her endless chores steeped in a deep brooding silence that grew daily more cold and profound and easily matched the stoic silences of her husband.

She was convinced by now that her fears that she was with child were well-founded, for she had continued to be beset by the same type of sickness that used to bedevil her mother every morning in the early stages of her pregnancies. It complicated everything, but her determination to escape the mountain rapidly became an obsession with her. The thought that her baby could be born into a clan of child-killers appalled her. Indeed, her baby might even have a father with blood on his hands! She knew it had to be soon or else she'd have to leave it until after the baby was born when it would be much more difficult, if not impossible. As much as she did not want this baby, she could not possibly allow it to grow up among a bunch of thieves, indolents and murderers! After all, it wasn't *its* fault that it had been the result of the worst night of her life!

She dreaded having to tell her husband that she was going have a baby for she was concerned that this might make him more watchful over her. She had been hoping to avoid having to do that, but as the weeks wore on and she was already starting to show, she knew she could not delay telling him any longer. Indeed, he had probably guessed it already, since she had to rush for the forest behind the cabin to be sick nearly every morning. Gathering up her courage she tackled him one day after he came into the cabin, smelling gamy and of sweat. He looked tired and his face was grim and grimy. Lately, he had grown a full beard and this made him seem more formidable than ever. He placed his long-barreled old Kentucky rifle on its nail-perch over the fireplace then wearily sat at the table on one of the split-oak chairs. Mary gave him a tin mug of coffee trying to gather up the courage to tell him he was soon to be a father. After several false starts, she finally blurted it out. "Zachary Thomas, I am with child."

There was a deathly silence. She raised her timid gaze to find that he had stopped short and was staring fixedly at her with those startling turquoise-green eyes that burned into hers. Then he nodded and turned abruptly away. Mary felt a surprising pang of hurt. Though she told herself she could hardly have expected otherwise, she had anticipated that the idea of having his first child might have raised a little more enthusiasm than that. For all he cared, she might have just told him that the Leghorns he had purchased when she first arrived had started laying eggs at last. Well, that settled it! Even though he now knew, she was still determined to escape from the mountain at the first opportunity.

But since the massacres, Zachary Thomas did not leave her for long periods during the day like he had in the past. Mary began to wonder if he could read her mind and knew of her intention to escape, for whenever she resolved to do it, he would suddenly appear out of nowhere. Even when he went out on his daily tracking jaunts and to clear his traps, he wasn't gone for long hours at a stretch like before. Mary suspected, to her dismay, that he must even be confining his tracking and hunting to the Claw Mountain area rather than going into the vastness of the Wilderness below.

This rather unnerved her for it meant that she risked bumping into him on her way down. She planned to say, in that eventuality, that she had been very lonely of late and was trying to find Emma's family's homesite to go visiting. In truth, the girl came to visit her nearly every day when Zachary Thomas wasn't around. After praying with Mary for the souls of all those slain in the massacres and, especially, for the soul of young Jamie Galtrey, the surly girl would question Mary, demanding to know about many different things, showing such appalling ignorance about the world at large that it made Mary realize just what was brought about by such absolute isolation. Though young Emma was well-skilled with her shotgun and apparently knew everything that her Uncle Zack had taught her about tracking, shooting, hunting and the mountains, she had never heard about cities or school or books, let alone that these mountains were just very small part of a whole country governed by a president, who lived in Washington DC – stuff Mary had learned about through Emily's books and her own trips to the store. She certainly knew nothing about God and religion beyond the little Mary had told her.

"I sure wish I was smart like you, Aunt Mary," she would say wistfully.

Mary well understood her thirst for knowledge for she had been that way herself. Whenever she went to the store she always gravitated towards the menfolk, a mingling of mountain men and lowlanders gathered around the pot-bellied stove, for their conversation was so much more interesting than that of the womenfolk, who would chatter on about boring things like babies and recipes and quilting, or the girls close to her own age, who would talk about *boys!* Unable to join the exclusively male clique, Mary had a way of making herself invisible and, because she was always so quiet, nobody seemed to notice when she positioned herself close to them so that she might overhear what was being said – all this to satisfy her insatiable curiosity about the world outside the mountains. The men talked about grand, interesting things like politics and religion, fights and killings, snakes and boogers, stills and Revenue Men, moonshine and crops and, of course, the Civil War, which even though it had been over for some thirty-odd years now, was talked about as if it had happened just yesterday.

It was a touchy subject, for while some of the men and their male kin had gone off to join the regiments of the Army of Northern Virginia in 1851, others had ridden north to join the Union Army. Troops from both sides had crossed the Blue Ridge through the gaps, and bloody battles had ensued. The Confederate hero, General Stonewall Jackson, had camped on the river bottoms. Opportunist carpetbaggers, Reconstruction and the Yankees, came in for much heated discussion in the store, for hard times had come to northern Virginia following the war: institutions collapsed, banks were closed, the currency devalued and slave labor brought to a close (although a bid to free the slaves in a motion in the Virginia general assembly had been lost by just a single vote back in 1832). For her own part, Mary knew little about the bloody war, but she did know this. She didn't believe in war and she sure as heck didn't believe in slavery! She didn't like to favor either side, though, since clearly both sets of soldiers had mothers and siblings and sweethearts who had wept buckets over them!

Mary was tempted to offer to teach Emma how to read and write, but in view of the fact that she planned to escape as soon as she possibly could, she didn't think it fair to the child to start something she might not be able to finish. Instead, Mary pumped the child for information on the different homesites on the mountain, to get a better idea of the layout of the mountain's habitats and thus avoid them, trying to appear casual so as not to arouse Emma's suspicions. But time and again Mary's attempts to descend further down the mountain than the glade where the spring bubbled were foiled by the sudden appearance of her husband or Emma, so that Mary felt she could scream. She felt so trapped that even her daily trip to the edge of the ridge to gaze down upon the magnificent view below did not have the same calming effect on her that it once had.

Weeks slipped past and Mary, still obsessed by the need to escape from this desolate mountain, knew that her chances of accomplishing this were getting slimmer by the day. Ominously, her belly had swelled alarmingly with the weeks, making her wonder if she was carrying twins, and it was already late fall. Should she try to leave much later, winter snows would make it impossible. Even though she was only nearly five months gone, climbing down from the ridge to fetch water from the spring was becoming increasingly awkward. It would be hard enough if she wasn't pregnant, but with her big round belly to contend with, it would be slow, awkward and, indeed, dangerous, to attempt it, especially since she had no idea how she was going to get back to Lewis Mountain once she had successfully managed to flee the mountain. Yet she sensed that if she didn't make a determined effort to do it soon, it might never happen.

No, she could not live like this any longer! She had to try now, *before* the baby was born. *Tomorrow!* She would leave tomorrow! The more she thought about it, the more determined she became to succeed.

Mary woke up early the next morning. As usual, Zachary Thomas had made her a mug of coffee. She sat with him at the table to drink it in an uncomfortable silence, plotting and planning in her head, bringing to mind what Emma had told her about the various homesites on the mountain, so that she could avoid them. The girl usually came visiting late morning or mid-afternoon, when she could be sure of getting a glass of milk and homemade cookies, so instead of first doing her chores as she usually did, Mary decided to leave straight after Zachary Thomas left to go tracking or clearing his traps.

In case he was watching, she would take the water pail to make it look if she was fetching water then she would ditch it and make her way down. She knew that she could not take anything else, not even food, for if she was caught, it would be sure to arouse his suspicions. She would not be able to fly down the mountain like she had on the first attempt either – because of her condition. This time, she would have to keep far away from any footpaths, keeping a keen eye out for the Bucko lookouts in the trees, and make her way down the mountain with infinite caution. She groaned. *Who would have thought it would be so difficult to get off this wretched mountain?*

She made her husband a breakfast of corn-fritter pancakes covered with sorghum and he tackled the pile with vigor, eating with gusto and relish. He grunted his thanks when he was finished, belched loudly, then stood up and crossed to the fireplace to fetch his Kentucky rifle. He left, whistling for his devoted coon dogs, which bounded up to him, barking joyfully. As soon as he had ducked under the door, Mary rushed to feed the chickens and rooster and the cantankerous billy goat they had lately acquired then she tore back into the cabin's bedroom to change, choosing a wine-colored dress she'd never worn before from the chest. It was so loose-fitting she suspected it was one of Hedina's "with-child" dresses. Even so, it strained a little across her tummy. Still, at least if she did get caught, she had an idea that her husband might swallow her concocted tale that she was visiting kin if she was suitably dressed up for it. She thought about putting on Hedina's button-up boots, but soon dispelled the idea. She had to move quickly and surely and wearing high-heeled foot apparel, going down a treacherously steep mountain while heavy with child, would be madness.

She was about to leave the cabin when she thought of something. *Her good-luck charm!* Rushing to the mantel, she grabbed her eagle's feather from its bottle. She went outside and hurried across the yard, with the pail in one hand and the eagle feather clutched in the other.

She stopped at the top of the ridge for one last look at the valley below, keenly aware that this was the only thing that she would miss about Claw Mountain – this magnificent, incomparable view that was so profoundly inspiring. (Well, this and her vegetable garden, which had given her so much satisfaction and pleasure.) And indeed, the view was quite spectacular with the advent of fall. The intense richness of the red, gold and orange leaves was so vivid and alive it was as if God had set fire to the forests – a truly awe-inspiring conflagration! Wilson Run was but a murmuring brook, which mirrored blue in the valley floor below, while the flame of the forests looked so spectacular she felt moved to her core. *Food for the soul!*

117

As she stood on the edge of the precipice, seven giant eagles soared in the crisp blue sky above her, with lonely, haunting cries. She remembered how they had greeted her when she had first arrived on Eagle Spur and thought how she would miss them too. She and young Emma had spent hours searching for signs of their nests before finally coming across a single one, perched amidst perilous boulders, down a cliff a little. It was difficult to see from above and only Emma's fearless climb down aways had confirmed their suspicions. Mary drew in a deep calming breath. What wonders God had created here! What a pity they had been besmirched by the blood and ignorance of the iniquitous clan that inhabited this massive mountain. She gazed up at the eagles and watched them for a few moments, thinking that despite the fact that she had been largely wary of them, today it seemed as she was leaving behind her only true allies besides young Emma.

Mary turned and took a last long look behind her. The chestnut log cabin on a cleared patch of land, with its porch supported by wooden poles and a stone chimney puffing with smoke presented a scene of well-being and comforting domesticity, framed on one side by the giant chestnut tree she loved so much. Its nut crop in October had been truly awesome! The burrs that replaced the summer flowers had split open at first frost, dropping three nuts each, and the loft was full of flour sacks filled with the glossy brown nuts she'd collected. She'd told Zachary Thomas that what they didn't use through the winter, they could sell at the store. At the back of the cabin stood the row of huge guarding hemlocks, red spruces and Fraser firs and, behind them, the thick molten forest of fire that she had not dared to explore. *Her one big regret!* The whole scene was such a charming sight that for a moment, she actually felt a strong pang of something. She wasn't sure what for though for she didn't regret leaving here at all, what with its snakes, its wicked weather, its wicked inhabitants and a husband who never talked!

Perhaps it was just that she had poured so much of her energy into making this place remotely habitable that was searing her senses right now. She wondered if the cabin would revert to its disgusting state now that she would no longer be around to clean it and how long it would take for her garden to become infested with weeds and for the vegetables to go to seed, neglected and uncared for.

Feeling strangely numb, she took up the pail at her feet and climbed carefully down the narrow treacherous path, picking her way between the huge granite boulders. Once it was safely negotiated, she went to the glade of moss-covered rocks where the spring was. Crouching down beside it, she listened to the enchanting bubbling of the water – the captivating chuckles of Claw Mountain – the only ones she had ever heard on it, that's for sure! As she dipped her pail in the rocky pool – such a familiar chore – a big bloated green bullfrog stared at her from a boulder and she suddenly felt the pang again. She shook her head crossly and stood up, looking around furtively.

She was in luck this time. *No Zachary Thomas and no Emma!* She was shaking slightly, remembering what had happened the last time she had tried to escape when she had bumped into Eli. He had returned a few times after that first unsettling visit to the cabin, but thankfully, always when Zachary Thomas was there. During these times, she would try to keep her eyes downcast for it seemed that whenever she chanced to look up at him, her broody brother-in-law would be watching her with those oh-so-scary pale-yellow eyes. She shivered. More than anything, she dreaded the thought of bumping into him again. Well, this could be her last chance to get off this mountain and she would let nothing stop her this time.

Hiding the pail behind a clump of ferns and clutching her white-tipped eagle feather for luck, she crept down the mountain staying well away from the path, moving beneath towering red spruce and balsam firs, dripping with their long strands of grandfather lichen, treading on piles of fragrant dried pine needles underfoot. It was a beautiful fall morning and everything seemed crisp and new. Shafts of early morning sunlight dappled the earth. Wild birds sang and a few flew up at her careful passing. How she had missed walking through forests. She might have thoroughly enjoyed the walk were it not for the serious purpose at hand. The last time Mary had descended from her secluded prison up on Eagle Spur had been for equally serious purpose – to attend the double funeral of Zachary Thomas's two massacred brothers held at Obediah's homestead, Horseshoe Hollow.

Keeping a sharp eye out for lookouts in the trees, she stopped often to listen intently for anyone crashing through the forest, which was as thick and unyielding as any she had come across. This, along with the steepness of the mountainside, made the descent treacherous and tiring. But she had to be careful not to fall and endanger the baby growing inside her.

About two exhausting hours later, to her alarm, she heard raised voices in the distance and guessed that she must be coming close to Obediah's homestead. Hastily moving away from it, she headed deeper and deeper into thick, tangled forest. Then, quite suddenly, she stumbled over something and only just managed to stop herself from falling. She indignantly searched for the offending object and, to her surprise, found a half-buried glass jar. The unexpected object, in such a remote, unlikely spot, puzzled and intrigued her.

Moving forward, she carefully parted a tangle of brambles and fern immediately in front of it and found herself peeping in on a large glade of bewitching seclusion. It was obviously a place that seldom saw the sun for it was dark with gloom. Other than the sound of gushing water, there was a hushed brooding quality about the enormous, damp, dripping glen that lured her in to take a closer look. She was overdue for a rest anyway. *And what safer place to hide it than in here?* She spent a good few minutes forcing her way through the thick surrounding foliage that contained it almost as effectively as a shell does an egg, scratching her arms on brambles in the process.

As she wriggled her way through, silently bemoaning her big belly, still clutching the eagle feather, she heard a strange thumping sound above the sound of the gushing water. At last she was through. She glanced around. In an instant, she realized she had unwittingly stumbled upon the site of Obediah Buchanan's mountain still – *or rather stills!* For nestled amid a riot of ferns, in the center of a large sandy clearing, was a row of six stills. What's more, they were all in the middle of runs, for huge hickory logs fueled fires burning in the furnaces. They were giving off heat waves rather than smoke, which meant they must have been burning since before dawn – a common ploy used by moonshiners so that the smoke would escape detection by the despised Revenue Men. One of her uncles had once shown her his still site and had explained the whole setup to her, but his had been very crude in comparison to this! She studied the neat thumping stills with frank curiosity. They had rock furnaces chinked with clay, above which were huge wooden boxes with large copper-jointed cookers and condensers on top, which were attached to long funnels connected to large chestnut barrels. Several other barrels stood in a row to one side. There were row upon row of shelves on which stood vats containing sour-smelling liquid, along with neat rows of glass jars. The whole place had a distinctive smell to it, sour and ripe, combined with that of wood smoke.

A small waterfall, fed by a spring from high above, gushed over a ten-foot precipice of rock, into a rocky pool below, which spilled over into a clear, cold, fast-running stream. The surrounding rocks were weathered greenstone covered in thick green moss, on which trees, scaled with lichens, clung with exposed, twisted roots. Mary looked around in awe. So, if mountain gossip around the potbellied stove at the general store was to be believed, this secret little hideaway was where Obediah Buchanan produced the best home-brewed whiskey of all the Blue Ridge moonshiners.

Mary had heard it said that those few Revenue Men who had braved undertaking a search for it, had not been able to find it. Well, Mary was not at all surprised. It was a fascinating enclave, full of dark foreboding, and as effectively hidden as an eagle's nest. Well, as unruly, unkempt and wild as the brothers of the Buchanan clan were, there was little doubt they were expert and accomplished at one thing – *making moonshine!* For this was no ordinary mountaineer's still site. This was clearly a highly organized and thriving business! But where did all the crops necessary to sustain such a business come from? Mary wondered. Surely the Buckos couldn't possibly grow enough themselves? Well, whatever, it was certainly impressive, even to Mary, who had a keen aversion to the stuff.

16

Just then, Mary heard the voices of several men above the bubbling and thumping noises coming from the stills, not loud voices, but murmurous, and coming this way! She'd heard that mountain men were always cautiously silent around their illegal stills, as the sound of voices was one of the many ways that the Revenue Men used to locate them. She dived behind the row of large chestnut barrels, ducking her head down, trying to still her ragged breath, her heart pounding with fright. *If only she hadn't let her curiosity get the better of her!* Now she might just have ruined her one chance of getting away!

"Paw, they're runnin' real sweet," she heard someone say softly. She instantly recognized Eli's voice and shivered with apprehension. God forbid that they should find her! She would have to hide in here till they went away. Crouching down, she hastily stuffed the eagle feather into her bodice, and protectively clasped her bulging stomach, listening intently and shaking with fear. The fires from the furnaces made the enclave hot and airless, already moistening her skin, while the thick smell of sour mash and wood smoke assailed her nostrils. She strained her ears in anxious listening above the noise of the stills.

"Reckon I'll be the judge of that, you thick-skulled morons!" she heard Obediah say curtly.

In a crack between the barrels, she saw a thick curtain of foliage being dragged aside like a door. Obediah Buchanan and his two child-murdering sons, Eli and Jake, entered the clearing – the three people she least wanted to come into contact with right now! They pulled the foliage door closed behind them, thankfully returning the grove to the deep gloom her eyes had already adjusted to. One of them lit up a kerosene lantern and placed it on top of the very barrel she was behind. Mary immediately ducked lower and closed her eyes tightly, sure she would be spotted. She felt hardly able to breathe. Then she heard the men move away and she let out her breath and opened her eyes again. Through the crack between the barrels, she could clearly see the two Buckos and their father.

"See, Paw, it's goin' real smooth," said Eli earnestly, while his father grimly inspected the procedures on each still. "This here white lightnin's gonna be real good, yessiree!"

"Can't see how you can tell that when it's still thumping, you imbecile," Obediah said sharply. "I'll only know if you've done it right once the thumping stops and the whiskey comes. But let me warn you, here and now, it had better be good, else you'll have to answer to me. See you temper it right, boy, to get it back to a hundred proof, no lower than that. And see you don't sample too much either, you dumb popskulls! Get those lazy sons-of-bitches, Cletus and Toad, to flail more rye. I want to deliver twenty gallons before the week is up!"

"Sure, Paw," said Eli in a placating manner. "Sure thung."

There was more intricate discussion regarding the runs, then Obediah snapped, "See you morons keep a good eye on things now. You scorch any of this whiskey and I'll be forced to hold another hearing. I'll not have another run of good whiskey ruined through you stupid, lazy numb-skulls, you hear me?"

"Yes, Paw," said Eli and Jake meekly, in unison.

"And I want everything kept spotless, you hear? Smoke out those boxes with corn-meal bran when you're done. I've got a fine reputation to protect!"

"Yes, sir, Paw."

"How come I've always got to nursemaid you like you've never done it before? You put that stupid, feeble-minded, half-wit brother of yours to shame the way I've got to mollycoddle you like you're a bunch of girls."

Mary listened numbly as the despot carried on and on, mercilessly needling, berating and belittling his two sons to such an extent that despite what heinous things she knew about them, Mary actually began to feel demeaned and shamed for them. By the way even the unfeeling Eli placated and kowtowed to his father, there was no doubt that Obediah Buchanan was a feared tyrant to his sons. It might even be that unable to retaliate against his own father, Eli took out his frustration and anger on others instead. What on earth had Obediah meant when he said he would hold a *hearing?* She could not imagine. She only knew she could not equate the charming, gregarious man who had visited her soon after her wedding and regaled her with such interesting tales, with this thoroughly mean and despicable man.

"Lawdie be, what do we got here?"

Mary heard the words with a sense of extreme shock. She held her breath. *Had she been spotted?* She didn't have to wait long to find out. Next minute, Eli had moved aside the kerosene lantern, leaned over the barrel, grabbed her roughly by the hair and dragged her out from behind the barrels into the clearing, sneering, "Look what I caught, Paw! What do y'know! It's Zack's uppity wimmin."

Mary cried out in fright then awkwardly stood up in front of them with legs weakened by fright. She hugged her bulging stomach and stared sickly at the glaring trio, unable to speak. Eli still had her hair in his cruel fist and her scalp was stinging at the roots. She looked up to find Obediah's face twisted with fury.

"WHAT IN HELL'S NAME YOU DOING IN HERE?" he shouted.

"I ... I ..."

Mary stared at him helplessly, still at a loss for words.

"You *what?* Speak, bitch!"

She swallowed hard. "I was goin' to visit Emma, Paw Buchanan. I got lost."

"I'm not interested in that! How'd you find the stills?"

"I didn't. I mean, it were an accident. I tripped over a bottle outside then I just sort of . . . found it ...," she finished lamely.

Obediah spun around accusingly on his sons. "You hear that? You hear that, you cretin heads? She tripped over a bottle and found the stills! If she did that, what's to stop the Revenue Men from doing the same? Who left a bottle lying around to be tripped over?"

Eli and Jake's stunned faces were ashen in the light of the kerosene lantern. Then Eli mumbled, "Don't rightly know, Paw."

"*You don't know!* I put you in charge of these stills so I expect you to know! Well, we're going to have a hearing, alright – right now! Tie her hands together."

The faces of Eli and Jake fell at his scathing words, growing increasingly tense. Mary bit on her lip as Eli got a length of rope and tied her hands in front of her, pulling them together so tightly that the rope cut cruelly into her skin. As he worked, his face was grim, the terrible scar running the length of one cheek, taut and white, the small muscle in his jaw flicking with contained anger. She could sense his humiliation at what she could not have failed to overhear and suspected that it made him even more dangerous than usual. What would they do with her? Would they try to hurt her, even though she was with child? She was assailed by all the awful rumors that she had heard about this dreadful clan.

"Listen, I'm real sorry, Paw Buchanan," she blabbered to her belligerent father-in-law. "I was in a'fore I knew what was in here, I swar. I jest wanted to rest, is all. Then I heard yer voices and took fright. I sure ain't meant nuthin' by it. I never would have come in here if'n I'd a'know'd what it was."

"Quiet, girl!" Obediah commanded, with such chilling severity and such a terrible wrathful scowl that Mary shut up instantly.

Eli dragged her behind him out of the still alcove, after his father and brother had exited it, and Jake had closed the foliage "door" so that the still site was perfectly camouflaged once more.

"Now where's that bottle you tripped over?" Obediah curtly demanded.

"Up yonder," said Mary softly, indicating where with her head.

"Fetch it!" he demanded scathingly of Jake.

Jake returned a few minutes later with the mud-covered jar, his eyes downcast. Obediah took it from him with a torrent of curses, curtly instructing Jake to obliterate any signs of their presence before turning and plunging into the forest. Following unsurely after the furious patriarch, Eli pulled Mary behind him, tethered to him by the rope as if she were a cow. She stumbled along behind him, suffering from a mixture of terror and humiliation.

At last, they reached the clearing of Obediah's homesite where the remainder of the clan appeared to be assembled, as usual playing cards, horse-shoes or marbles, or just languishing on the spring-protruding sofas like wastrels, drinking moonshine. Obediah climbed onto his broken porch and just the way he stood then, swaying ever so slightly, Mary realized that the patriarch, if not exactly drunk, had definitely indulged in moonshine and was mean with it!

He bellowed, "YOU BUNCH OF USELESS WARTS, IT'S A HEARING I'LL BE HOLDING NOW."

The cacophony of the clan was instantly silenced by his shouted words. Suddenly, it was so deadly quiet you could hear the faint sigh of a quivering leaf. Astonishment turned quickly to fright! Never had Mary seen such raw fear. It was rabid amongst them, spreading like contagion, registering in staring moon-shine-glazed eyes, swallowing throats, nervously licked lips and on sweat-beaded brows, as Mary passed by them, bound and led like an animal. Eli tied the end of the rope to the porch rail.

Obediah waved his family towards him with an impatient hand, pale-blue eyes icy with anger. They stood in front of the porch in a clearly practiced, sprawling formation, with the filthy, raggedly dressed children in front, the scrawny womenfolk in their thin cotton dresses and cardigans behind them, and the men in their denim dungarees and holey vests at the back. The women looked starkly terrified and some of them began crying quietly. Even the children had been muted as if by mouth-gags and stared up at their irate grandfather with big, scared eyes. The air was thick with cold stark terror, including her own, since the "hearing" was no doubt being held especially to punish her.

Obediah did not waste any time at all in getting down to what the matter was about. "It seems that one of you stinking, miserable, ignorant worms has been careless and left a jar outside the still site to alert the Revenue Men to its whereabouts!" he roared, holding up the dirt-coated glass jar in one hand so they could all get a good look at it. "Now, I've warned you time and time again about such carelessness. I would have thought it was enough that you allowed the Galtreys to sneak up and kill two of your brothers in broad daylight! Now, you risk my being sent to prison for want of a few basic precautions? *Your own father!* You all know that I will not risk being put behind bars ever again, so you must know how serious this matter is. Now what I want to know is this: whose responsibility is it to take the glass jars to the stills?"

There was a stunned, deathly silence, laced with dread. Mary wondered if the offender would dare to own up.

"Did you hear me?" said Obediah, in a wheedling voice. "I *said* whose responsibility is it to take the glass jars to the stills? Eli?"

Eli's face looked drained of blood. He said nothing.

"Mine, Paw." Mary jumped as Jamie, the youngest Buchanan brother owned up guilelessly, his face earnest, even while his eyes roved queerly, without focus. "Eli always let's me help, doncha, Eli?"

Obediah span furiously on Eli. You mean you actually let this . . . this *useless half-wit* endanger me and my stills?"

Jamie fell back at his father's harsh words, blinking furiously, his jaw going slack and drool dribbling from his open mouth.

"Yes, Paw, and he's real good too!" said Eli staunchly. "He's done it plenty of times!"

Obediah's face was a mask of fury. "Now I told you to practice every precautions at all times to make sure those Revenue Men don't get those stills and use it as another excuse to incarcerate me. Anybody with an ounce of sense wouldn't let a numbskull with half a brain go anywhere near them! Now, he is never to go near them again, you got that? I catch him anywhere near them, I'll shoot him, you understand? *I'll shoot him!"*

There was a shocked indrawing of breath from all those assembled. Jamie's face fell with disappointment and shock, his jaw slack and eyes roving sightlessly to the heavens.

Eli answered softly, "I got it, Paw."

Obediah stood on the porch, scowling and slowly letting his eyes rove over his clan, building up the suspense, before pronouncing in a tight, cold voice, "And Jamie gets what's coming to him for being so goddamned careless."

Hands flew to mouths and there were little involuntary cries and shouts of dismay. Eli looked stunned and horrified. He said in a low controlled voice, "No, Paw, not Jamie! After all, we don't know how long that jar has bin thar, do we? Could have bin one of th'others." Then his voice turned placating. "Paw, he's only a boy."

Obediah turned on him then in an explosion of anger. "It doesn't matter a damned whit who *actually* did it! If a boy takes a man's job, he takes the responsibility for it, too!" He wiped a hand across his mouth, and then pronounced terrible judgment. *"Twenty-five lashes!"*

There was a collective gasp of horror and dismay, and Eli, his face darkly contorted, cried, "Naw, Paw, not *Jamie!* He cain't stand up to that kind of punishment! He's too weak and, what's more, he don't deserve it!"

"He doesn't deserve it? Doesn't deserve it? For exposing the stills so that even a dumb *girl* could find them? I'd say he deserves it just fine! Besides, nobody, but nobody, tells me I can't discipline my own son if he disobeys my rules! Now, get him ready or it'll be *fifty* lashes for you!"

Eli pulled up short, staring at his father with a look of stunned anguish. "You'll kill him, Paw."

"I said," Obediah enunciated, eyes blazing maniacally, "get him ready!"

There was a moment of eye-to-eye contention between father and son, before Eli finally backed down, seeming quite shattered. Mary watched in horror and sick foreboding as young Jamie was seized by Jake and Eli. The poor boy was dragged to the T-post, struggling and screaming. So this was what the contraption was for – *it was a flogging post!* The cowering, terrified youth was stripped to the waist by his grim elder brothers, and tied by ropes, face-forward, to the T-bar of the post by his wrists, so that his painfully thin pale rib-sprung white back was exposed. Eli seemed to be talking quietly to his youngest brother, trying to reassure him. But already Jamie was blubbering as Obediah took off his white shirt to reveal a chest and back that was covered in a mat of black curly hair almost as thick as fur, hanging the shirt over the porch rail, so that he was wearing only trousers and suspenders. He went into the cabin and came out a short while later, descending from the porch into the clearing. He held in one hand a short strong flogging whip with three leather strips with metal tips, and without any further ceremony, he flayed it forcefully across the back of his youngest child, immediately splitting skin and drawing blood.

"ONE!" he yelled as the boy howled in agony. The next blow landed with equal force. "TWO! . . . THREE!"

Mary could not bear to hear the poor lad's screams as the madman brought down his merciless whip again and again, to his shouted count. She tugged desperately at the rope keeping her captive, wailing and whimpering in keen distress. The children turned and buried their faces into their mothers' skirts, unable to watch as the cruel leather tongues kept raining down forcefully on Jamie's back. On and on, the madman went, counting and flogging remorselessly. Time and again, the metal-tipped leather thongs did their worst, splitting the skin on young Jamie's tender back, and mashing the thin layer of flesh below till it was raw as chopped meat. Rib bone was exposed in places and blood was flowing freely from his wounds! On and on, it went. *The lashes and the screams!*

Father, please make them do something a'fore he dies! Mary appealed desperately to the heavens. But the Buckos were cowering from the sight like a bunch of whipped dogs, turning their heads away.

On and on and on it went, minutes seeming like hours. Then at last, the boy mercifully passed out and his body went limp. But, unbelievably, Obediah continued to carry out his barbaric punishment without restraint. One of the wives, Pearl, vomited, and another fainted, as the lashes continued to land on the mangled back of the boy, who was dangling from the T-bar from the rope restraint by his wrists, his legs collapsed beneath him in a pathetic huddle. Blood ran from his back and soaked blackly into his overalls. Mary could no longer bear to look, sickened to her core, tears flooding her cheeks.

" . . . TWENTY-FOUR! TWENTY-FIVE!"

At last – finally – it was all over.

Mary looked up to see that Obediah was heaving with exertion, his fur-covered chest and back running with dark rivulets of sweat. He abruptly dropped the flogging whip and turned away. Jamie's restraints were quickly untied by Eli and Jake, who carried his limp adolescent, half-naked body to the edge of the clearing, next to the porch. The unconscious youth was carefully laid out on his stomach. Eli fetched him some water in the dipper from the water barrel beside the porch and, dipping a cloth in it, bent down and carefully wiped the side of Jamie's face with it with a look of infinite tenderness, silent tears streaming down his face. The boy stirred slightly, moaning. *Thank God!* He wasn't dead as Mary had feared!

"Are you alright, Jamie boy? Are you alright?" Eli asked worriedly. He looked up as his father went past, giving him such a blast of pure hatred that Mary felt it right where she stood. "If he dies," he warned his father. *"I swar I'll kill you!"*

Obediah was stopped in his tracks by his son's scathing words. He glared balefully at him, but was too exhausted to even speak. Spittle had gathered at the sides of his mouth and the mat of hair on his chest was drenched through with salty sweat. His longish silver-streaked hair, which was mostly flattened against his head with damp, was raised like devil's horns in places. If ever anyone looked a madman in that instant, he did!

Mary shuddered with fresh revulsion. To her alarm, just then, Jake spotted her and muttered, "What must we do with Zack's wimmin, Paw?"

Mary tensed, terrified, as she wondered what heinous punishment Obediah had in store for her. Perhaps he would strip her naked and flog her too! And nobody would try to stop him then either! But seeming utterly spent by the force of his earlier exertions, his eyes glazed, Obediah merely mumbled, "Get Zack to come fetch her. Let him deal with her."

Then he dragged himself up the stairs of the porch and disappeared inside the cabin. It was a signal for the assembled families to let go of their emotions. There were keening wails of despair and harsh broken sobs. Mothers comforted children while the men folk milled about and stoically stared, seeming dazed by the obscene searing moment. Though relieved by her seeming reprieve, Mary felt totally numbed by the brutal spectacle they'd all been forced to watch. Still tethered like a goat, her belly bulging in front of her, Mary dissolved into fresh sorrowing tears, feeling a harsh queasiness inside her stomach. What a terrible man was this Obediah Buchanan! Far worse than she had ever imagined!

So this then was the reason these Buckos were so intensely loyal to each other. It was them against this unspeakable monster! Yet how could one man wield this much power amongst his grown sons, even the callous Eli? Why did they not unite and stand up to him than submit meekly to his excesses like lambs to the slaughter, like helpless children? Was it the reason why they were such bullies themselves? Helpless under their father's yoke, did they take out their bottled-up rage on the world at large? But why couldn't they have tried to protect poor Jamie at least? Well, to his credit, Eli had tried. It was obvious to Mary that Eli deeply loved his younger brother and was fiercely protective towards him. Well, one thing was for sure. This wasn't the first time something like this had happened. Thank goodness, her husband had broken away from his family and was no longer a part of this shocking barbarity!

It was at that precise moment that Mary saw her husband enter the large dirt yard being dragged along by the hand by Emma. Dear child, she must have fetched him as soon as she knew what was going to happen. Mary had never thought she'd ever be glad to see her husband, but she was infinitely glad to see him now! Zachary Thomas's eyes widened in shock as they took in the whole sordid scene – the raw bloody back of his prone, unconscious, youngest brother, the weeping hysterical women, the wailing children. He crossed to Jamie and knelt down beside him, talking quietly to Jake and Eli.

"Git some kerosene," he demanded of Jake. Jake ran to the barn and came back with a tin of kerosene. Zachary Thomas unscrewed the lid and poured kerosene liberally into the bloody wounds to sterilize them. Even from his depths of his oblivion, Jamie screamed with fresh pain. "Now, move him to Cletus' cabin, well away from Paw," Zachary Thomas instructed Eli. "Make sure you keep him face down on th' pallet. Soak some bandages in kerosene an' keep his back covered. Be sure to keep him warm else th' shock'll kill him. I'll come by later with some resin from a pine tree to put over th' wounds to make sure they don't turn septic, else it'll kill him fer sure."

There was something very reassuring about the way her husband had taken charge. Even the hysterical crowd of women and children had fallen silent and was watching the proceedings raptly, while Emma, the scrawny little fair-haired waif, stood right beside her favorite uncle, holding tightly onto the shortened double barrels of her big upended shotgun with a whitened fist, her face closed and stricken. Then Zachary Thomas seemed to notice Mary for the first time as she stood tied to the porch by a rope, bedraggled and shamed, quivering, bludgeoned by the terrible cruelty she had just been forced to witness. He immediately stood up and came across to her. He knelt down in front of her, untying the rope tightly binding her hands together, his face set in stone. Without a word, he stood up and silently swept her into his strong arms and carried her through the group of stricken, staring kinfolk up the steep slopes to Eagle Spur. Though he was stoic and unspeaking all the way up, Mary, slumped across his one broad shoulder, saw his turquoise-green eyes were dull with pain. Then a steady stream of tears began rolling silently down his cheeks into his black beard. It made her feel strangely torn inside. *Oh God, what terrible things had he and the others been forced to suffer?*

* * *

In the troubled days that followed Jamie's flogging, when everything seemed sad and stricken and hard to get to grips with, and the same sort of all-pervading gloom that had followed the massacres sulked in the air, Mary tried to talk to her husband about what had happened at his father's homestead, but beyond mumbling that he was sorry that she had to see what she did, he consistently refused to talk about it, saying it was Buchanan business and did not concern her. She felt terribly guilty about the fact that if she hadn't been trying to escape and tripped over the glass jar, thereby discovering the illicit still site, Obediah would never have wreaked his terrible unwarranted punishment on the innocent boy. Zachary Thomas had not even asked her why she happened to be there, tied to the porch rail by a rope, but no doubt he had already heard about what had transpired from Jake and Eli. She hated the way her husband closed up and refused to communicate with her. Though he had never raised his voice or hand to her after their wedding night (and indeed, had never touched her since), his silence was a cruel punishment in itself. Coming hot on the heels of Obediah's shameful display of crass brutality, it made her feel isolated in a way she never had before.

From the little that she'd seen of him, she'd found Jamie a sweet and loving boy, quite unlike the rest of his brothers, who admittedly, all seemed to care for him. She'd had a soft spot for him ever since that first night. Now the idea that his own paw would deliberately set out to hurt him in such a barbaric, brutal and unfair manner pained her deeply, especially considering he was clearly not right in the head. She had nightmares about him being flogged to death and would wake up sobbing.

Naturally, Zachary Thomas was deeply worried about his ailing young brother after his terrible ordeal and would visit him several times a day, carrying his satchel of herbs and oils. He had told her that although he had given him more treatment for his wounds, some of them had turned septic, as he had feared. She badly felt the need to visit the dear boy herself and begged her husband to take her with him, but he was adamant that she must not accompany him. Though he refused to say why, she knew that it had to be that the clan was blaming her for what had happened to the youth. This caused her to have fresh lashings of worry and guilt. She might even have been tempted to visit Jamie on her own were it not for the fact that she had no idea where he was being kept. Instead, she gave Zachary Thomas jars of minced stew or soup made from the vegetables grown in her garden for his convalescing baby brother.

Since he was so thin to begin with, she suspected he was already badly malnourished and was not getting what he needed to regain his strength. In a way, she was relieved she had been forbidden to visit him, because she could not bear the thought of coming into further contact with Jake or Eli – or God forbid – that evil bastard, *Obediah!* She was so angry and disgusted at him for what he'd done to Jamie that she might well be tempted to rock him if she did!

One afternoon, Zachary Thomas came back from visiting Jamie, looking particularly harrowed and she managed to wring out of him that the youth had become quite fever-bound and delirious. Sick with worry herself, she suggested that they take him to a valley doctor on the buckboard, but to her dismay, he reacted violently.

"And git some quack report it to th' law an' git him removed from his own blood kin?" he snarled.

Considering that the youth had not been given the protection he needed from his 'own blood kin', Mary did not think it would be such a bad idea, but she bit her tongue against expressing her feelings. She sensed it was a case of a beleaguered family closing ranks, but it made her feel more the outsider than ever. This family, peculiar and dysfunctional as it was, was clearly one that stuck together no matter what. Zachary Thomas gave her such a stare of contempt that she never dared mention it again, though she was dreadfully worried about the boy. What if he died on her account, or because his family were so scared of the possible repercussions of taking him to see a doctor, he didn't get the treatment he so badly needed?

But thankfully, as the days wore slowly on, Jamie seemed to improve until it was clear that he had gotten through the worst. However, though the poor lad seemed to be recovering physically well enough now, the mental wounds went much deeper. Zachary Thomas told her he was very concerned about Jamie's state of mind, because he didn't seem to be registering anything that was going on around him, like he had before. Considering what he had experienced, Mary was not at all surprised to hear that the youth had retreated into a world of his own where he could feel safe from the brutal tyranny of his madman father!

Mary realized that her chance of escaping anytime soon had evaporated like mountain mist in the morning sun. Not only would everybody be watching her every move, she no longer had the courage to try since her last encounter with the Buckos had resulted in such terrible consequences! She had been lucky it had turned out the way it had for her, but knowing what the Buckos and their demented paw was capable of, she wasn't about to risk endangering the baby again. Next time, it might well be her getting the flogging! Her husband was so short with her these days, Mary began to suspect that he was not only angry with her for trying to escape (she direly doubted that he had believed the story she had told Obediah and his two sons about visiting Emma), but that he also blamed her for what had happened to his brother. She knew that Emma did, for she seldom came visiting anymore and was sullen and silent and slit-eyed as a Chinaman when she did. In the past, she had grown quite cheerful and talkative when she was alone with Mary, chatting on about all sorts of things, and Mary sorely missed that. She knew that the girl felt badly betrayed by the fact that she had tried to escape without telling her, or saying goodbye, even though to do so would undoubtedly have meant her reporting it to her Uncle Zack. Mary couldn't blame her in the circumstances. One thing for sure, it would be a long while before the girl learned to trust her again.

Falling Leaves and Mountain Ashes

Book 11

"Mountain of the Damned"

*'Oh, Winter,
Accursed and unrelenting,
cruel beyond imagination,
Why dost thou linger so?
Art thou the vengeance
Of an angry God or only
Nature's fickleness,
After all?'*

Brenda George

PROLOGUE

So severe was the winter of 1899/1900 that the superstitious mountain people feared that the looming new century boded ill for them. This calamitous winter was destined to become known as "The Big Freeze" by the mountain people, the worst natural catastrophe to hit the northern Blue Ridge Mountains in living memory, startling the unsuspecting mountaineers who dwelt in the secluded hollows and upon lonely elevated ridges with its suddenness and frightening ferocity. Sunny fall days, rich with the inherent colors of the season, with just a hint of exhilarating sharpness in the air, had overnight turned into intensely cold, dull, overcast days, with gray snow-clouds hanging sullen and low over the mountains ridges, casting them in perpetual thick swirling mist.

Not long after the migratory birds hastily beat their way south, temperatures plummeted, trees lost their dazzling amber, scarlet and gold leaves, and the first howling blizzards swept in on freezing arctic currents, whipping around mountain homes like frenzied white whirlpools. After that, snowstorms occurred with alarming regularit and, over the weeks, the snow gradually banked higher and higher, to a depth of over ten feet, with snowdrifts piled up to the rafters of mountain cabins, snowing them in, as roofs sagged dangerously beneath layers of snow several feet thick. Streams quickly iced up and waterfalls froze into twisted icy sheets, which hung suspended in mid-air. Loud cracks echoed through the mountain forests, like staccato rifle shots, as trees, visibly straining under the great burdensome weight of the snow, split resoundingly with the cold. But still temperatures continued their downward plunge, frequently dipping to an alarming 30 degrees below zero.

Some mountain families were so poor the only income they derived was from the harvesting of chestnuts from the forest, which they exchanged for basic essential supplies at the general store. They owned no hogs and so had been unable to adequately provide for their winter provisions, without the need to supplement their meager put-up vegetables with hunting, unlike the more fortunate among them who had timeously butchered hogs and cured the flesh by smoking it. The heads of these unfortunate kinfolk were forced to take to the atrocious elements by the growl of their empty stomachs and the hollow-eyed, hungry looks on their children's faces. Wading agonizingly through snow so deep and soft they disappeared in it up to their waists, they took their hunting rifles, laid traps and attempted to fish by picking holes in the ice covering rivers and streams. But their efforts were seldom rewarded. The wary forest animals, alerted by their primeval instincts, had long ago disappeared into their winter quarter and were too wise to brave such cataclysmic conditions. Even small mammals had disappeared into subterranean tunnels far beneath the ground while the ice covering former favorite fishing spots, was solid clean through.

Several of the men got trapped in howling snowstorms and died of exposure, their families anxiously awaiting their return in vain. With their providers perished, their wives and children faced starvation and death themselves, for travel to their nearest neighbors' homes was extremely difficult and the long journeys to the nearest general store, impossible. Those hunters who made it safely home, generally suffered severe frost-bite on their fingers and toes and their bounty was either non-existent, or pathetically frugal; perhaps the odd, tough, wiry squirrel or rabbit that had perhaps felt the constraints of their seclusion too keenly. But they were lean pickings indeed for the large, ravenous families they were meant to feed. The rest of the mountaineers, cruelly confined to their homes, chewed languidly on thick greasy strips of bacon, suffered stoically, fighting intense bone-aching cold, their minds geared toward only one thing: daily survival!

Feared as Godly retribution for their real or imagined transgressions, it cowed the humble mountain folk. For although winters of their past experience had often been severe, such extreme conditions – more suited to the Alaskan tundra of the far north – terrified and unnerved them. They huddled in their make-shift shingle-covered shacks and in their log cabins, helpless in the face of such adversity. A few of the more educated among them sagely reasoned that the start of a new Great Ice Age had been suddenly thrust up at them, while others grimly predicted that the end of the world was nigh. They all prayed constantly for surcease. But it seemed that God had truly forsaken them. For an agonizing long while, as weeks and months crept slowly past, the mountains were still locked in snow and ice and bitter cold. This stark white world was settled with a great engulfing silence, for the thickness of the snow muffled every sound, even the wails and wracking coughs of bewildered children and the frightened sobs of the womenfolk . . .

17

Winter closed in on Claw Mountain with frightening suddenness, washing the world white as cotton-puff clouds, and turning the air so sharp, crystal-clear and pure, it was exhilarating to breathe. To Mary, the high vantage point of Eagle Spur presented a glorious sight, for the surrounding mountains and the Wilderness Valley below were covered by a thick blanket of heaped-up snow.

Reflections from the sky and clouds and the brilliant multi-colored splashes of sunrises and sunsets, would give it the sparkling allure of millions of precious gems, while on the few clear days, Wilson Run, a mere trickle and stuffed with ice, mirrored the scrubbed blue of the sky. Such was its pristine beauty, it made Mary's throat ache to look at it. At night the view was equally incredible to behold, an intricate mobility of light and shadow. The whole valley would be a phosphorous white crust, with diamonds sparkling on snow-laden trees, while on partially clear nights, shafts of moonlight would send luminous beams to the mountains across the great vale, lighting them up in isolated ghostly picture shows, while others were smudged with deep purple and violet shadow. An icy, ethereal world, it was quite magnificent in its majesty and mystery.

But despite this particular compensation of living on Eagle Spur on the top of Claw Mountain, never had Mary experienced such bitter gnawing cold, and before too long, she felt trapped in a way she never had before. At the beginning of winter, before the sheer depths of snow prevented it, the wind would whistle through cracks in the logs of the cabin where the chinking was, sending in snowflakes that would lay an inch deep on the floor in places. Since the windows did not have panes of glass in them, there were only the shutters to keep out the cold. But the shutters also kept out the light, which meant the kerosene lamps burned throughout the day. The spring in the rock glade below where she used to draw water, had iced up and the stream lower down had been filled with slush before freezing solid into twisted and fanciful ice sculptures. Back-to-back blizzards began howling around their cabin in frenzied whirlpools and the snow banked higher and higher, huddling around their cabin like a thick winter wrap. The snow soon became too deep to even venture to the edge of the ridge, let alone risk attempting to descend down the treacherous ice-slicked path off the ridge, though Zachary Thomas managed to do it with the help of homemade snowshoes. When he went out to hunt for food every day, he would sit on the top of the pathway and slide down it on his back like he would an ice-chute, holding his long-nosed Kentucky rifle on high. Getting up was much harder for he had to use ropes hitched over huge, ice-slicked, slippery granite boulders along the way to haul himself up – a dangerous and tiring exercise.

The daily hunting trips were necessary, though, since her husband's brothers had left going to the general store too late for them to buy them winter provisions and now were prevented from going there by the extreme conditions. Indeed, the general store had become totally inaccessible by distance, snow and ice, long before expected and, knowing how the Buchanans' relied on store-bought necessities, Mary wondered about how they would survive the winter. Though their own last store order had fortuitously been a large one, Mary suspected that their own basics, like kerosene, sugar, coffee beans and flour would not last the winter and she rued the fact that what canned goods they had purchased the last time had quickly been used to enrich stews in the absence of fresh vegetables. She fretted that the produce from her carefully tended vegetable garden which had flourished in the rocky, but rich, soil, was not going to last until the spring.

She was especially proud of her cabbages. Some weighed nearly fifty pounds and they were sweet as sugar, a result of the high altitude, warm days and cold nights. She had made sauerkraut the way she had watched her maw doing it, by cutting the cabbage up and putting it in the big washtub. *Ka-suck, ka-suck, ka-suck* had come the familiar sound when she had beaten it repeatedly with a maul. After the juice came out of it, she had added salt before placing it in a wooden barrel, scattering green leaves on top and pressing it down with a wooden board with a big rock on top of it. She left this for ten days before packing it into canning jars. She had then put the jars in a pot of water on an outside fire she'd built and boiled them to seal the jars and cook the cabbage. She still had fourteen jars of the fine-tasting relish to show for her efforts. She had also strung beans all on her own (usually a communal task!) till her fingers were aching and raw. Threading a needle with cotton string, she had strung it with long strips of beans and hitched the string up on nails all over the walls and perches, so that they looked like fluttery, long, green fingers. When these dried, they were called "leather breeches" by the mountain folk. Rings of orange pumpkin were also strung from the roof and the two together made a colorful sight!

With the advent of winter, she had buried the cabbages, potatoes and turnips in three sections, in a circular trench she dug on a slope, as she had watched her father and Joe do, with a drainage ditch leading downhill and away from it so that surface water would not accumulate and rot them, covering them with leaves and brush to prevent them from freezing, pulling them out as she needed them. However, when the snow threatened to get too deep to access it, she had dug them all up and placed them in the shed under piles of sacking. When the shed, too, became out of bounds, she had moved them in sacks into the cabin loft, to join the flour sacks full of chestnuts, collecting what she needed as she needed it.

Since the Buchanan clan mainly depended on store-bought groceries, they owned no hogs like most mountain folk, who generally butchered them between Thanksgiving and Christmas, when they were sure of cold nights. Thus they could not depend on the sustenance the smoked ham and bacon would have provided. Sensing it was going to be needed, Mary was thankful she had gathered chestnuts by the bushel in late fall, blessing the plentiful bounty from the huge chestnut tree in the yard. Though she had warned Emma and Zachary Thomas to tell the rest of the clan to do likewise, she never learned if they had taken her advice.

Mary's life consisted of work, soul-deep fear as a result of the extreme elements, the constant dread of running out of food – and of giving birth! She lived an intensely lonely life of morbid introspection. Emma's visits, which had slowly picked up again after Jamie's terrible flogging, had stopped. Unfortunately, her only true companion could no longer visit because access to the ridge was all but denied to human passage. Mary was surprised at how much she missed the child. Though generally slit-eyed and surly, Emma was filled with such a quickening curiosity that it had made conversations between them lively and interesting. Her absence caused a definite void in Mary's life.

* * *

Mary was sitting on a wooden chair in front of the fireplace hugging the hard hump of her stomach over her gray shift, which brushed the floor, covering three sets of thick woolen socks and flat, buttoned shoes. She pulled her black shawl tighter across her thin shoulders. The dress, clearly one of the garments Hedina had acquired after coming to live in the mountains, was of a soft woolen material, ill-fitting, completely lacking in style and several sizes too large for Mary, which was fortunate, for it allowed room for the baby's growth. In the beginning, Mary had felt slightly uneasy to be wearing things belonging to a dead woman, but now she felt she intimately knew Hedina Charlemaine Buchanan through the disclosures in her diary, and felt oddly comforted by doing so. It was as if the musty-smelling cloth – the odor of which no amount of lye soap would wash away – exuded some sort of invisible strength she was somehow able to harness and use as her own.

She sat in front of a huge stone fireplace, in which hung suspended a big black metal cauldron, bubbling with boiling water, the steam audibly and vociferously lifting the heavy lid. She watched it, knowing that she should remove it from the flames, but feeling too weary to do so just yet. A few minutes more rest would not hurt any. She had learned to her detriment in the past that if she went any closer to the hearth, the skin on her bare hands would blister. This morning it had been so bitter that when she touched a metal pail she was going to fetch snow in to melt down and boil for coffee, her fingers had frozen stuck to it. Though she should have learned from previous lessons excruciatingly taught, without thinking, she had wrenched her hand away. The skin on her fingers had ripped off, and even now, they were raw and bloody and painfully stung, like the heels of her hands had when she fell down the mountain on her wedding day, only worse.

Studying the back of her hands now clasped over her huge stomach she saw that they, too, were chapped red and were sore-looking. She sighed, thinking how she had once considered them her only physical asset because they were small and well-shaped. Maw always used to say that her hair was pretty too, because it was thick and black and almost touched her waist when she unpinned it from the tightly-coiled bun she wore at the nape of her neck. But even though Zachary Thomas had once remarked on it too, she did not think so. It was straight and refused to take a curl like the beautiful golden locks of all three of her sisters, who were fortunate enough to take after their beautiful mother. Oh, how she missed them all and the happy, carefree times they had shared when they were all together. She remembered wonderful days filled with warmth and laughter and love and she fed now on those precious memories.

Existing as she was in a loveless vacuum, she so missed the closeness and warmth of her loving family. She sorely missed Lewis Mountain near the big logging camp, close to Devil's Ditch. She thought about each member of her family now with impassioned longing. She missed Joe most of all. With his solemn dark-brown eyes and hard-working ways, he had always been the one to whom she had felt closest. As children, in the spring, they had roamed the mountain forests together searching for polk greens, water cress, plantain, dandelion and mushrooms, picking wild strawberries, chinquapins, raspberries, blackberries, walnuts, hazelnuts and hickory nuts by the basket-load, while October was the time to collect chestnuts. They would run and take flying leaps onto thick grapevines, swinging with abandon from one to another, twenty feet above the ground. *Golly, what fun that had been!* None of her sisters were brave enough to do that. She sighed. Perhaps she had compensated for her lack of looks by trying to outdo the boys of her acquaintance. With just two years separating their ages, she and Joe had giggled together and shared secrets, while they dipped bare toes into the clear, icy mountain stream at Devil's Ditch. If only Joe knew what she'd done and how unhappy she was, she was sure he would not rest till he found her and rescued her from this pitiless place.

She got a warm fuzzy feeling in her stomach when she thought of pug-nosed and freckled, Percy, her baby brother, who was forever hell-bent on mischief. Nobody could stay mad with him for very long despite the lizards and frogs he hid in their pallets and the chores he left undone. Everybody spoiled him outrageously for he knew how to beguile to get himself out of any sort of trouble and worm his way into a body's good books, for he had such a cheeky grin, such captivating sass.

Mary's three winsome sisters, Lona, Laura and Nellie came next into Mary's mind. With barely three years separating them, they looked like triplets and their natures were the same too. Barely past the giggling stage, they were infuriatingly shallow and vain and they flirted shamelessly with the mountain youths. But for all that they were warm and loving and kind and there was always the tinkling sound of their irrepressible laughter to be heard whenever they were around. How could she have found them so tiresome when she was with them?

She missed her extended family too, who all lived on Lewis Mountain – her aunts, uncles, cousins and, most especially, her grandparents on her mother's side. (Her father's mother had died before she was born, and his father, when she was just three years old, so she couldn't remember anything about him.) Her grandparents lived in Meadows Hollow on the western side of the mountain, set in amongst trees, with an awe-inspiring view of the surrounding purply-blue mountains, and she loved going to visit them. She was especially close to her grandmother. Poor old Grandmaw's work was never done, it seemed. Whenever they visited their homesite, she was always busy with bucket and pail, washtub and broom-stick, feeding fowls or boiling fruit, baking, cooking, cleaning or scrubbing behind some dirty cherub ears. She made the most delicious cherry cobbler pie and would always give Mary a generous piece when she visited, sometimes with the rest of her family, oft'times on her own.

Grandmaw chewed snuff and always had a wad of it tucked inside her cheek. When she sat outside on the porch of an evening, though, she would smoke her long clay pipe. Grandpaw, on the other hand, tended to laziness, but all the kids loved him. He was full of fun and jokes and was a fine fiddler to boot. At community gatherings he and his fellow musicians would bring out their fiddles and banjoes and play and sing all the old mountain songs, soon getting all the folk quick-shoeing and stomping. Grandpaw's fiddle was homemade from the skin of a possum, while their neighbor, Mr. Clancy, had killed his black cat to make the head of his. *Poor old cat!* Lots of mountain folk used their big domestic cats for that purpose and Mary could never come to terms with it. Grandpaw could play the harmonica too. Clearly, Maw had got her musical talent from him!

Mary sighed. How she fretted for them all in the harshness of this merciless winter, like she did all the mountain folk – yes, even the blood-thirsty Buchanans. Though she knew her own family would be well-provided for food-wise, with a butchering day behind them to ensure smoked bacon, ham and the like, and would have plenty of vegetables in their dugout to last the winter, she knew her father's bad leg must be giving him plenty of grief in such extreme cold and that the rest of the family must be experiencing hardships too.

While the days on Claw Mountain seemed endless, Mary had always enjoyed winters on Lewis Mountain. Winter was traditionally an idle time, with the meat in the smokehouse, the vegetables in the dugouts, the food all stored and the wood cut. Snow had been grand fun back then. She remembered sliding down the hillside on homemade sleds as a child. Sometimes five or six young'uns would climb on a wide board and go sailing down the mountainside, shrieking and laughing. And when they were tired and cold, they would go inside and sit in

141

front of the fire, eating roasted chestnuts, apples and "simmers", as they called persimmons.

Christmas and New Year had passed on Claw Mountain without a single firecracker being let off. In fact, there hadn't been anything to mark these occasions, beyond mumbled greetings of "Happy Christmas" early on Christmas morning between herself and Zachary Thomas – and even that had been initiated by her. At home, though, if the harsh weather this year had not ruled it out, there would have been grand celebration on Lewis Mountain for sure. In past years, there hadn't been much in the way of gifts, mainly oranges and candy and cheap play-pretties in their stockings, though when they were younger, Paw would whittle wooden toys and whistles and Maw would make the girls the most exquisite corn-shuck dolls. There would be lots to eat and drink and lots of visiting too, of course.

They would start celebrating two weeks before Christmas and it would be January before everybody started work again. Neighbors and friends would bring banjoes, violins and fiddles and everybody would dance and sing. The kids would pitch horseshoes or flat rocks, light Roman Candles and set off great big thunder-bump firecrackers, which made the mountains sound like a battlefield! Maw would make "Hot Pot" for the grown-ups by putting spices and ginger into apple brandy and for the two weeks leading up to Christmas up until New Year, they would be visited by "Chris Cringlers", who would come calling with paper bags over their heads with holes for their eyes, nose and mouth. Carrying banjoes, guitars and fiddles, they would walk for miles every night. Entering a mountain home, they would disguise their voices while their hosts tried to figure out who they were. Once they were successfully identified, they would be given food and drink and would play their instruments and dance before moving on to the next home, often waking up sleeping families. What fun they were! *No chance of Chris Cringlers ever coming to Claw Mountain, that's for sure!*

Yes, home to Mary meant the sounds of laughter and singing, Paw telling his stories. Ah, what a master story-teller he was. He told such funny tales he would have all of his children weeping with laughter. Or he would tell ghost stories in the flickering light of a candle, which would have them deliciously thrilled and huddled under their bedclothes at night. *Maw playing her dulcimer with lovely lilting strains.* Paw had come across the instrument in the general store at Fletcher and had promptly bought it for Maw for her birthday, having been told by Mr. Fox, the proprietor, that dulcimers were rare on the Blue Ridge, being more common and popular among the mountain folk of the Smokies in North Carolina. It had cost Paw the barter of many beans, chestnuts, eggs and chickens to acquire it. Maw had been delighted with her gift. She was naturally musical and had soon taught herself how to work the fretted fingerboard, plucking the three strings with a melodious goose quill. She always played it at Christmas time, enriching the period for Mary. The sweet sounds of it rose up in Mary's memory now, filling her with aching nostalgia.

With pale, smooth, opalescent skin and hair the color of ripe corn, her blessed mother was a picture of the pure unspoiled beauty that nurtured so well in the rarified air of the mountains. Her smile was so warm, so sincere, so utterly love-ly, lighting flecks in her bright-blue eyes that it made scowls immediately vanish and taut lips stretch gladly in eager response. In Mary's eyes, her mother was the most perfect human being to grace God's good earth. She was serene and grace-ful, patient, understanding and terribly accomplished in the home. Why, she quilted the most beautiful and intricate of quilts that were the envy of all her kin and neighbors and she made the best jams and jellies and the best apple pies.

When she spoke, the cadence of her voice was low, almost a whisper, but the very sound of it brought an immediate lull in conversation, though she could inject a measure of sternness into it when the occasion warranted. And to be softly chastised by Maw was to invoke eternal shame within a guilty breast. For she was the epitome of a loving mother, who cared so feelingly for Mary, her only plain daughter among four, that she was always kindly bestowing comely physical and mental attributes upon her, which Mary well knew she did not possess. *Oh, Maw!*

How Mary missed her. If only she could talk to her. Or put pen to paper and send a letter to the general store to let her know where she was and beg her for-giveness. Though no one else in her family could read, they could get *someone* to read it to them. Mr. Fox at the Fletcher store, for instance. She should have done it long ago, but somehow she had lacked the courage, which was so terribly wrong of her considering how much they must have suffered on her account. But, alas, even if she could manage to persuade Zachary Thomas to take a letter for her, he would not be able to go there until spring, by which time her lying-in time would be imminent.

Her plans to escape Claw Mountain loomed daily more difficult. How was she possibly going to manage it with a small baby? She even thought about leaving the baby behind and coming back for it later with the sheriff, but she very soon let go of that idea. She would never get her baby back in that event. The Buchanans were ruthless in their family loyalties and it would probably end up in another bloodbath. She felt so hog-tied by the restrictions presently placed on her movements by the weather, so guilt-ridden, unhappy and homesick that she wished that she could tell Zachary Thomas how desperately unhappy she was, and beg him to let her go back to her parents with the baby. But though she prayed for the courage, she knew instinctively that Zachary Thomas would never willingly let them go.

Well, those happy days had long gone, to be replaced by days of toil and mis-ery. Of long strained silences. No love. No laughter. Mary felt a wave of longing and loneliness wash over her. Locked in an icy world on the top of Claw Mountain, she hadn't seen a soul other than her husband for over three unending months. Beyond just going outside onto the porch to fetch buckets of snow lowered down the narrow snow entrance on a rope by Zachary Thomas (since she was unable to scale the steep bank in her bloated condition) to melt down and boil for various household uses, she had not even ventured out the cabin for many weeks. She did her business in a foul-smelling bucket, which was removed and buried outside by her husband.

Effectively trapped inside by her condition, the filthy weather and the thick claustrophobic fog which constantly hugged the cabin in a ghostly pall, she felt so confined she wanted to scream. But to do so would be like having her voice swallowed up in a vacuum, such was the suffocating silence that persisted. Sound was so diminished in the thickness of the surrounding snow that it was necessary to talk loud or even shout in order to be heard. It was like living with wads of absorbent cotton permanently stuffed in her ears. She hated it and the terrible gnawing feeling of inescapable constriction.

Zachary Thomas had even moved the few surviving emaciated poultry birds and the billy goat, up into the loft, when the constantly deepening snow had made it almost impossible to feed them in the crude outside shed. The billy goat had appeared on the scene because she had begged Zachary Thomas to get them a cow so that she could have fresh milk and cream, which she so missed. Her husband had dismissed the idea as being too impractical, as getting a cow up onto the ridge would be too difficult, and had brought home a kid instead, saying they would have goat's milk in due course. Well, the kid had turned out to be a *billy*, much to Zachary Thomas's deep embarrassment, so getting milk was impossible.

They had kept the darned thing anyway and it had become something of a pet, answering to the name of Cedric. Though she had grown inordinately fond of the ornery creature, her husband hated the billy goat because it was forever butting him from behind. He was always threatening to kill it for the pot. He never did, of course, though Mary fancied they might have to resort to it in the not-too-distant future, when all the Leghorns had been devoured. Those Zachary Thomas's brothers had brought from the store had swelled to a score but were sadly diminished in number due to the effects of the cold and their systematic slaughter for food. Though their numbers had swelled considerably from their initial stock, they were kept principally for their eggs, and had never lain well. Whenever hunger threatened to overtake them, Zachary Thomas would wring another neck so they could cook and eat the tough stringy flesh on the carcass. Even now, Mary could faintly hear the eagle-eyed belligerent rooster and the few remaining hens clucking, scratching and fluffing out their feathers, in their roost above her head, and the goat forlornly battering his horns in boredom against a rafter. Odd bedfellows! *Doomed!*

Despite the fact that she daily risked the rickety wooden stairs to sweep up their droppings and scrub down the wooden boards at least once a week, the unpleasant stench of their excrement permeated the whole place. As well as caring for the fowls and goat, she cooked, cleaned the cabin and chopped logs of wood, hewn from trees previously felled and chopped into biggish logs by Zachary Thomas, to a more suitable size for the fireplace. The constant swing of the chopper had blistered the palms of her hands at first, but after the blisters had popped, gradually the skin below had toughened to form protective calluses.

But if she worked hard and felt forever drained by it, she knew that Zachary Thomas had even more exhausting toil. After every storm, he was forced to doggedly shovel snow away from the front entrance, clear thunderous masses of it off the roof to prevent the rafters from collapsing and to tunnel down below the window ledges to allow what little natural light there was to get in. Woodcutting was, of course, a major priority, and rightly so, otherwise they would likely freeze to death. They had to keep a fire burning day and night and it took a never-ending supply of logs to fuel the flames. A few days ago, he had chopped down a large tree fairly near the cabin, unleashing an avalanche of snow from its branches at the first stroke of the blade, which threatened to bury him, thus forcing him to have to jump back every time he chopped at the trunk. But thankfully a huge pile of roughly chopped logs now stood on one side of the hearth. It had been a dead tree with wood that was well-seasoned, but the fire, though it leapt high with flames and healthily crackled and snapped, seemed to have little warming effect, this, despite the added fact that he had also recently untidily papered the mud-chinked log walls with tatty pages torn from an old Sears, Roebuck mail-order catalogue in an effort to give the place a little added insulation.

He had used thick molasses as glue, but a few pieces had already peeled off, and hung wispily, without any conviction, as if they too had surrendered to the cold. And despite the added insulation and the snow banks surrounding the cabin, snow would still get through the cracks and lay in drifts on the cabin floor. She and Zachary Thomas slept on their pallet under the huge bearskin rug. Taken from a huge male that must have weighed nearly half a ton, for it was easy eight-foot long from nose to tail, the fur was a rich blackish brown and about six inches thick. Though she was grateful for the warmth it provided, she hated the considerable weight of it in her pregnant state and it bothered her that it still had its huge heavy head attached to it.

She would wake up in the morning staring at its dull, staring eyes and fearsome bared fangs, steeped in the awful gamy smell of it. Though she was tempted to ask Zachary Thomas to throw the skin with the head at the foot of the pallet, in truth, the head nestled between them like a third sleeping partner and did stop the cold air from sneaking under the bedclothes. Oh, for the lightness and warmth of Maw's wonderful quilts filled with goose feathers!

Mary shivered violently as she become conscious, once again, of the layers of cold air pressing in around her back. Although the work was hard and endless, it was the only way to keep even remotely warm. Besides, it broke the monotony a little, however dully. She sighed. Her back ached and she was sure that the constant tenseness of her body could not be good for the baby growing inside her. The time for her lying-in was drawing impossibly near. As far as she could figure, she could have as little as seven weeks to go. She often feared that the baby would come early, before the spring thaw, and she'd be trapped inside the cabin on her own, with nobody to help her. She did not know what to expect, other than a great deal of pain, for had she not heard Maw giving anguished birth to the four siblings who had come after her?

She was terribly afraid to give birth. *Afraid of dying.* Zachary Thomas, in answer to her timid questioning, had once gruffly promised to fetch Jenny Addis (the daughter of Ada, who had delivered him), the granny-woman belonging to the Addis clan on Bear Rock Mountain when her pains started. Though Mary did not like to doubt his word, she did direly doubt his ability to carry it out if the weather remained so appallingly bad. And even should it subside and travel became easier, they lived on such a high godforsaken ridge, there was no guarantee *anybody* would be able to reach them in good time, let alone an old woman.

Besides, Zachary Thomas often left her alone for long stretches while he hunted in the forests. He would put on his fur-lined coat with a hood attached, don his primitive home-made snowshoes made from strips of pine and cord webbing to defy the sheer depths and deceptive softness of the snow in places, take up his long-nosed old Kentucky rifle, from its place over the mantel, and his gunpowder horn and lead balls and be gone for most of the day. But she knew it could not be helped. They had not had any meat for three weeks now, the chickens were reduced to just three and their supplies from the general store were running pitifully low. They were nearly out of coffee, sugar and flour and had already run out of salt. Though they kept going on boiled vegetables, her bottled sauerkraut, thin watery broth, roasted chestnuts, chestnut stew and the occasional loaf of corn-bread, she longed for something more substantial and was forever feeling miserable and weak. Hunger constantly clung; a familiar aching hollow inside her.

Night hunting was, of course, out of the question and, day after day, Zachary Thomas would come back, his heavy black eye-brows and beard covered in snowflakes, shoulders hunched, his face grimly set and his deep turquoise-green eyes narrowed into unreadable slits, but his familiar thunderously crestfallen attitude telling her more than words that he had nothing to show for his efforts.

He looked achingly tired and Mary knew that the constant work and worry must be getting him down. But words of comfort (though she sometimes felt the urge to voice them) did not come easily. Indeed, their only, all-too-brief period of true communication had been on the day they met, in the slight touch of a hand, and a fierce unswerving gaze that had locked their eyes together for but a moment, yet in such a powerful turbulent way, that it had changed both of their lives forever. But the attraction, if it had ever existed for him, had not lasted long. Now for the most part, he seemed to purposely ignore her. And when he did talk to her, he was invariably brief and abrupt. Upon occasion, he would get drunk on moonshine. Mary hated it when he drank because it was the time he was given to his blackest moods, and he would sometimes cuss and shout to himself.

At night, feeling desperately lonely and unhappy, with the baby moving inside her, painfully reminding her of its unwanted existence, she would lay awake for hours listening to terrific blasting cracks as the wall logs and shakes in the roof were ripped asunder with the cold. It sounded as if the roof was about to collapse in upon them and it was easy to imagine that God was very, very angry with her. For without her parent's knowledge or consent, she had run away with and wed this man who was all but a stranger to her. Alas, when Zachary Thomas had asked her to go with him – rather demanded it – she had meekly followed and obeyed, like a young girl entranced, but gladly so, with her heart leaping with the joy and daring of it. Now she wondered at the madness that had swept her along this disastrous road. She bit hard on her lip, cringing at the very thought of it.

Once, she had plotted her escape with such an obsessiveness she'd thought of little else. But the winter had put an effective stop to any plans she might have once have had. Now she was well and truly trapped – a prisoner of the accursed elements and the unfortunate fertility of her own female body . . .

W eeks went by and the winter continued unabated. The mountains were still firmly locked in a grip of snow and ice. Zachary Thomas had reported drifts of up to fifteen feet against the mountain. A week ago he had gone to check on a neighbor on Beacon Mountain, after a particularly wicked blizzard that lasted four days, and had returned home more morose than ever. It was only two days later, as they supped on their sparse evening meal of a potato and a spoonful of green beans each, that he tersely revealed to Mary that he had found the tenant family frozen to death in their inadequate, crudely made shack. The shack door had blown open and the stiffened ice-encrusted corpses of Lon Ficks, his wife, Olga, and five children, had been grotesquely huddled around a makeshift fire in the center of the room that had long ago ceased to give life-sustaining warmth. Snow had blown in and covered the entire shack in a blanket of white drifting up against the wooden walls.

Unable to bury them and not knowing what to do with them, Zachary Thomas, worried by their stark staring eyes, had thought to cover their heads with rags he found in a corner underneath some logs. Mary had listened with horrified disbelief as her husband gruffly relayed his macabre tale without showing any signs of emotion. What a terrible fate for a family that lived right on their doorstep almost! She quickly lowered her eyes, unable to speak, ashamed that her first inner reaction had been one of heightened fear for her own survival. The full horror of it only sank in later. That night and nearly every night since, Mary had suffered awful nightmares about grim grisly corpses with fixed stares, crossing the snowy wastes with stiff frozen limbs, climbing up to Eagle Spur and bursting into their cabin, and she would cry out and thrash around on their pallet, according to her husband.

Once, Zachary Thomas had pushed the grotesque bear-head aside and grabbed her, holding her tightly in his arms until she had calmed down. When she came fully awake and realized what was happening, she had grown stiff with dread in case he tried to make love to her. But she needn't have worried. He abruptly let her go, placed the gamy bear-head back between them and turned over. She had lain awake for a long time after that, listening to his snores. Oh, for a way out of this nightmare! Maybe when the baby was born – if they survived at all, she could manage to escape and go home. *Home.*

18

*S*pring, *when it finally came, was as tentative as a whisper, a wondrous, tender benediction from the Lord, a welcome long-awaited sign of forgiveness. At last, the feeble winter sun gained infinitesimal strength. The snow began to slowly melt. It dripped from the trees, lightly at first, then like great plopping droplets of rain. Tiny creatures like mice, squirrels and weasels emerged from their subterranean tunnels far below the surface, dappling the snow with their footprints. Ice cracked; the streams began to trickle. As more snow succumbed to the melting power of the heartened sun, they began to gurgle and merrily dance. Then the great thaw started, and the waters, finally liberated, flooded streams and rivers down stream.*

There was a great stirring and shuddering as Nature resurrected Herself. In the forests, mushrooms and fungi pushed their way through layers of spongy humus and dead leaves on the forest floor. Ferns unfolded their fronds and tiny new leaves unfurled on stark bare branches recently shed of awesome loads of snow. Purple hepatica amongst fern fiddleheads soon gave way to multi-colored glories as millions of other buds burst forth into rapturous bloom; white and red trillium, jack-in-the pulpit, columbine, may apple, trout lilies, wild and crested dwarf irises and the ghostly Indian pipe. Pools contained the eggs of frogs and salamanders and tiny black-nosed dace and brook trout darted about. Opossums stared down from branches with red-rimmed eyes, most having lost the tips of their noses and tails to frostbite. The sharp barks of the secretive nocturnal gray fox indicated that the spring mating period was nigh. Tufted titmice fluttered between the branches. The ludicrous figures of woodcocks trampled brushy shelters and the low thumping sound of ruffed grouse accelerated to a fast drumming. Wild turkeys scratched for acorns and insects. Snakes slithered beneath fallen logs. Life, once so cruelly suspended, had returned once more to the Blue Ridge Mountains. But to the haunted eyes of the mountain people who had managed to survive the cruel rigors of the past winter, there were telltale reminders of their ordeal – the many broken branches of recently overburdened trees, the accumulated debris piled high on the banks of mountain rivers and streams, and most of all, the matchstick limbs, gaunt, hollow cheeks and haunted eyes of their neighbors and kinfolk, which spoke of the same deprivation and suffering they, too, had so recently experienced. So despite the fact that their bellies were at last full and the weather growing increasingly fairer, "The Big Freeze" had left in its wicked wake a trail of bitter memories . . .

It was early morning of the 6th April, 1900. Mary was preparing breakfast when suddenly her waters broke, spreading a yellow puddle on the floorboards. Then a first painful contraction hit her. Bending over double and clutching at her stomach, she gasped, and told Zachary Thomas, already seated at the table drinking his coffee, to hurry and fetch the granny-woman. With a petrified look on his face, her husband leapt up, rushed across the room and ducked under the door to go and fetch the mountain midwife, without even taking the time to fetch his Kentucky rifle over the mantel to tote along with him.

Lying down on the double pallet to await the birth of her baby, Mary felt quite terrified of what lay ahead. The pains, excruciating to endure, occurred regularly after that, but thankfully, still far apart, and Mary prayed that her husband and the granny-woman would get there soon. *What if the baby came when nobody was there?* When Zachary Thomas got back to the cabin about an hour later, he told her the crushing news that Jenny Addis, the only granny-woman in these parts, had been called away to another birth on Fork Mountain and that he had sent young Emma to fetch the doctor down in the valley town of Carlisle, instead. Knowing that this would take many hours yet, Mary was filled with panic and irrational anger at her husband for not keeping his promise to her.

After that, he waited in the other room as if afraid to enter the bedroom in case she gave birth in his presence. He might at least have tried to comfort and reassure her. But no, he didn't have it in him to be that considerate! Anyway, that was the last thing she wanted right now. She was sodden with sweat – even her hair was stringy and damp by now – and she must look a sight as she rubbed anxious hands over her swollen belly in a feeble attempt to ease the terrible pains. When she wasn't doing that, she was running her fingers dementedly through her hair and thrashing from side to side. *Lord, this was far worse than she had ever imagined!* It was hard stifling her cries when the contractions hit her, but she couldn't possibly let him hear her and know how much pain she was in – or how terribly afraid she was.

She heard him pacing outside the closed bedroom door, but she felt so alone and so scared, having to face such an overwhelming and traumatic experience all on her own. She bit hard onto the blanket each time a contraction ripped through her body, screaming inside her head as the agony rocked her mercilessly, causing silent tears to stream down the sides of her face. It went on hour after hour after endless hour, all through the long day, with the contractions coming closer and closer together, so she knew that her time was growing near, and *still* the doctor didn't come. She began to fear that the doctor had refused to come to Claw Mountain just as the other doctor had refused to come to tend to Hedina Buchanan all those years ago, only to be forced to do so by shotgun, later. Mary wondered if Emma had taken her shotgun with her and would do the same. She wouldn't put it past the child. She was a Buchanan through and through!

Eventually, the contractions were only minutes apart and Mary knew that the birth was imminent. A contraction of such intensity hit her so that this time she was forced to cry out loud, and she thrashed around on the pallet in a welter of agony, anguish and pure terror . . .

It was late afternoon and to Doc Adams, the signs of the ghastly winter just past were all but unnoticeable beneath the luminous pale-green flush of spring and the vast glorious beds of violets and snow trillium that carpeted the forest floor. His breath was coming hard and fast and he was wheezing as he doggedly climbed up the treacherous steep upper slopes of Claw Mountain by foot, physically weighed down by his medical bag, and mentally, by his fear of the hillbillies who lived on this notorious mountain, as well as the nagging feeling that he was almost certainly too late. He was on his way to attend to the delivery of a mountain woman as yet unknown to him. But that was not what was worrying him. From young Emma's earlier agitation, he feared that something was terribly wrong and that he would find the mother or the baby, or both of them, had died in terrible childbirth even as he struggled to reach them. He was beginning to doubt that it would ever happen for he had managed to wring out of Emma that this particular mountain home was in an inaccessible spot right on top of the darned mountain! Why, up here, there was still snow scattered everywhere on the ground and the forest was liberally interspersed with towering firs, which had scattered the earth with pine needles and spiced the air with their fresh, tangy scent, giving a good indication of the considerable altitude. And the top of the mountain looked to be fortressed in by huge granite boulders, so he was wond-ering how on earth he was going to scale them once he got to their lofty heights.

Trailing him, was little barefoot Emma, a sullen, filthy child, who was acting as his guide. Occasionally, she would dart ahead, climbing the tricky footpaths with the sureness and agility of a mountain goat, whenever she became impatient with his painfully slow progress. The going was further hampered by the fact that he was hardly dressed to go mountain climbing. This morning he had donned his black Sunday suit and waistcoat, a white shirt with a stiff upraised collar, around which he wore a black string bowtie. His best fob watch, the case of which was handsomely decorated in solid gold floral work, was attached to its gold chain and in his upper suit pocket. And he had worn his best black leather shoes. After all, it was the Sabbath and he had been expecting to attend church. Instead, here he was in the rugged heights of the Blue Ridge, totally exhausted, the fine serge cloth of his suit damp with sweat, sodden with river water from the knees down and covered in dust and stains, the top button of his shirt long ago unbuttoned, the bowtie loosened and his shoes badly scuffed, the once-proud shine hidden beneath scrapings of mud. But in his rush to get here, he had not wanted to waste precious time to change into more suitable attire, though, frankly, right now, he wished he had. But then he had not expected that part of the way would not be negotiable by Bessie, his faithful saddle nag, nor had he guessed at the sort of breath-stopping, difficult terrain they would have to negotiate even while he had sat astride her.

It had been about five hours earlier that the mountain child had come down to his handsome, red-bricked, two-storied house which adjoined his surgery, in the small valley town of Carlisle, situated in the lower valley where the Wilson Run flowed into the Rapidan River. The valley had been settled well over a century before by a wave of British immigrants from the coastal lowlands of Virginia. Large tobacco farms had been started here and in the Graves Mill Valley. In the wake of these pioneers came the courtly gentlemen of the plantation set, slave-owning cavaliers and planters of moderate means and sway, who had turned the wilderness into producing farms. However, hard times had come to the area after the Civil War. Former Negro slaves and their descendents had gravitated to the cities of the north and few Negroes remained in the area.

Doc had been born in the Virginian coastal town of Westleigh and, at the age of twenty-four, fresh out of medical college, upon the death of his wealthy uncle, Dr. Gladwyn Adams, he moved to Carlisle to take over his brisk medical practice. His uncle had been a well-respected doctor in the area, and had left the thriving practice to him in his will, as well as a considerable portion of his fortune. At the age of fifty, Doc was still a bachelor. Somehow, he'd never found the time to take a wife. Instead, he had acquired the services of a tyrannical housekeeper, Hilda Gross, a dour, pernicious woman of German stock, with the jaw of a bulldog, and thin lips permanently set in a downward bow.

It was clear that his medical status and elevated standing in the community did not impress her, for she bullied him dreadfully. With harsh, guttural tones, she bossed him around, ordering him to wash behind his ears, take his afternoon nap and eat all his carrots like any good boy knows he should! Of course, it wasn't quite as bad as that, but not far off. However, Hilda possessed the Teutonic love of cleanliness and good order, and the house was kept scrupulously dusted and cleaned and polished, so that it gleamed from the floor to the rafters like the proverbial new penny. His clothes always looked immaculate, the covers of his bed were nicely turned down for him at night and she was an excellent cook. He supposed it was good enough reason not to fire her.

However, this morning, Doc had felt in an unusually light-hearted and relaxed mood, because he had given Hilda the day off and she had actually taken him up on it to run some long-neglected errands. He still had a half-hour before he was due to leave for church and he sat on his high-backed armchair in the drawing room calmly puffing at a cigar, enjoying a time of rare, unbothered solitude. He looked idly about the room. As a young man, he used to think it was exceedingly depressing yet, in truth, it was an interesting room and, over the years, he had gained a certain comfortableness in it. His uncle had furnished it in solid walnut furniture, including a rather handsome desk, which had an intricately carved cigar case on top of it, a fireplace that was narrow and stately looking, topped by a mantel choked with family photographs in ornate silver frames. Above the fireplace was the obscenity of a mounted head of a bear that his uncle had hunted and shot himself in the great Wilderness Valley to the west. Though Doc had long ago resolved to take it down, he never seemed to get around to it. However, his eyes roved somewhat fondly over it now for he had shared many a one-sided conversation with the dadblamed thing over Hilda, so that it had become a sort of mute ally to him.

Just then, he heard a harsh banging on his front door and he frowned mightily, wondering, somewhat irritably, who had come to destroy his short-lived peace. He went to open the door and found, to his surprise, that it was an unkempt child; a tall, thin little girl in a state of extreme agitation. She was rather an appalling specimen. Her long fair hair was filthy and knotted and her narrow face smudged with dirt. She wore a stained grey-looking vest under stained baggy denim dungarees, which were damp and rolled up to her knees, and her lower legs and bare calloused feet were thick with grime. What is more, she smelled unpleasantly high, rather like a smelly wet mongrel. She was panting like a dog too, with her tongue hanging out.

With an involuntary wrinkling of his nose, Doc said, "Whatever is the matter, child?"

But for a few minutes, breathless and gasping, she was quite unable to speak. She stabbed a finger towards the mountains of the upper valley and spoke in garbled hysterics. It was only by some miraculous medical acumen he had acquired over the years, and her finally placing miming hands over a massive imaginary stomach, that Doc finally understood that he was needed up the way for a birthing. He felt a spurt of surprise. Mountain women had their own midwives among them, who were generally most efficient, and he was rarely called upon to be present at one of their childbirths. However, even when the child had calmed down and caught her breath (had she run all the way?), he was unable to make much sense of her demented gibbering. She finally fell silent and began a self-conscious shuffling of her bare feet.

It was obvious from her appearance that the child came from an extremely remote mountain hollow. Indeed, the child talked so badly he had trouble deciphering anything she said. The mountain folk from these isolated hollows were the most pitiful. They eked a meager existence, bludgeoned by unbelievable hardships, bartering what they grew or harvested from the forest in exchange for the goods they needed. They did not smell a dollar bill from month to month and usually could not afford the ministrations of a doctor, relying instead on home remedies and patent medicines to treat their ailments. Unfortunately, whatever their lack, it did not extend to moonshine, which was partaken of freely, often even being given to small children. This led to quarrels and fights and, all too often, barbarous and senseless killings! Many times, he'd had to pack up his probes, forceps, dressings, sutures and needles to patch up some bullet-ridden mountain man, who often miraculously survived. Such was the toughness of these people.

Yet even these poverty-stricken mountain folk were full of pride and, on the rare occasions when he was called upon by them, to spare them the indignity of receiving charity, Doc usually charged a tiny token sum and nearly always accepted the hospitality that they pressed upon him. Though many of the mountain folk were desperately poor, they seldom starved when the season was favorable for the forests provided a bountiful source of food. But the terrible winter past, the worst in living memory, had seen starvation visited upon most of them. The child before him was evidence enough of that. Despite her baggy attire, she was gaunt as a skeleton! He decided therefore that it must not have been only imminent childbirth that had sent this unlikely messenger to summons him. There must be some sort of serious complication.

Doc heaved a big sigh. Of course, there was no way that he would not go. There were times that he silently rued the dedication to his profession which would not allow him to ignore such pleas as this even when he was sure there would be little or no remunerative reward. Well, there was no help for it. He would have to miss the Sabbath service at the little Carlisle Episcopalian Church yet again. He ordered the child to remain on the porch while he went to his surgery to gather his medical necessities.

Later, when he was busy saddling his ageing nag, the child came warily down the porch steps. Emma, for he had at least managed to elicit her name, was watching him with a finger hooked on her bottom teeth.

"D'y'wan' me t'show y'th' way?" she lisped, squinting at him narrowly with pale-blue eyes.

Doc frowned. Besides the fact that she was appallingly dirty, he could not help thinking she had a mean, spiteful look about her. Mindful that the child had doubtless come a long way and had to get back somehow, but not exactly overjoyed at having her accompany him, he cleared his throat and muttered, "We shall see."

Emma was busy eyeing his horse with a round-eyed look of awe. Taking her finger out of her mouth, she said, "I ain't never see'd no live horse a'fore. Only ever see'd one in a picture once. M'grandpaw's got hisself some mools. Yer horsey's kinda big 'n bony, but he sure got hisself a purty face."

"*She*," Doc corrected, relieved that her speech was a little easier to understand when she wasn't all worked up, even if it still took a deal of concentration to decipher. "She's a mare."

"*A mare!*" Emma exclaimed with a cluck. "I alles thunked them thungs was what was only ridden at night. H'com you's ridin' this here one in th' daytime?"

Doc stared at the child in confusion before he cottoned onto what she meant. *Oh, the curse of ignorance!* She thought a *nightmare* was a horse that could only be ridden at night! *Dear Lord!* He cleared his throat, and said sternly, "Just where is this place, Emma?"

She began gabbling away in unintelligible sounds that could scarcely pass for English. Doc heaved a big sigh. It was doubtful the child had ever been to school – or taken a bath for that matter! Unfortunately, there were precious few schools serving these mountain areas and there was no doubt that the lack of educational services had far-reaching effects on these people. She gibbered and pointed fingers in all sorts of directions leaving Doc feeling utterly bewildered, but he had managed to divine that he was headed for, of all places, *Claw Mountain!*

He heard the name with a jangling of nerves, for of all the bad, lawless hollows and mountains of the Blue Ridge, Claw Mountain's reputation was surely the worst! Feuds, fighting, rockings and senseless killings fueled by moonshine madness, were commonplace in all these places, whose inhabitants were a law unto themselves. If Doc's memory served him correctly, from what his friend, Sheriff Coley, had told him, Obediah Buchanan was a squatter, who had quickly gained a reputation as a fierce, despotic moonshiner and had raised a whole tribe of rowdy liquor-ridden, fight-hardened and lawless sons. There were all sorts of rumors about the man; some insisted Obediah was descended from Scottish kings and was well-educated, while others said he was dirt-poor and ignorant. His sons would occasionally pitch up at general stores or at community functions down in the valley, descending *en-masse*, all liquored-up, to snatch wary, but unprotesting, female partners at valley square dances, cause fights, and lob jagged, fist-sized rocks at everybody coming and going. It was a fact that mountain men believed guns and knives to be their birthright, and the Buckos, as they were known throughout the mountain communities, were no exception. Flying bullets from their weapons would have everybody ducking and they drew their knives at the least provocation.

Once, the sheriff and his deputies had been called to a shindig at the dance hall at Wolftown that had been disrupted by the lawless sons of the clan. He had arrested two of them, including Eli Buchanan, who had been using his bullwhip to terrorize folk, as usual. The rest of the cracker clan had lain in wait for them and ambushed the sheriff's vehicle, training an artillery of pistols and shotguns on it, causing it to come to a standstill. They had released their kin, stripped the sheriff and his deputies buck naked, before taking off to where they had come from. Sheriff Coley had counted himself lucky to get away with his life, if not his dignity, and that was the end of that particular matter!

Of all the Buckos, Eli was the best known and the most feared. Word had it that nobody had dared cross Eli and lived to tell the tale. It was rumored that a traveling salesman had once sold him an alarm clock that didn't work. The salesman's body was found floating in Wilson Run the next day, with his throat slit from ear to ear. The sheriff strongly suspected Eli for his proficiency with knives and whips was well-known and, furthermore, there were witnesses who had told the sheriff that the salesman had last been seen going up Claw Mountain. The sheriff had gone up the mountain to question Eli and the rest of the Buckos about what they knew about the murder. Every one of them had sworn blind that Eli had never left Claw Mountain and, without any evidence or an eye-witness to the crime itself to prove otherwise, the sheriff had nothing on which to build a case against him. Doc had it on good authority from the sheriff himself that he strongly suspected Eli had been the perpetrator of a whole *spate* of unsolved murders by this same gruesome method over the past five years, but there was never any proof connecting him to the crimes and he remained mockingly at large.

Why, not so long ago, the Buckos had terrorized folk at the general store at Fletcher, nearly causing the proprietor, Harold Fox to have apoplexy. He'd been ailing ever since. Doc had heard the story of that particular nasty episode from the poor man himself. Sheriff Coley had told him they had no compunction about sending unwary strangers who dared to tread up Claw Mountain on their way with a barrage of blazing shotguns and rifles! There was also the harrowing tale about Obediah Buchanan fetching Doc Saunders to tend his wife, Hedina, who had pneumonia. The doctor had refused to go when sent for as he was fully aware of the clan's evil reputation. The next day, Obediah had fetched him by mule with some of his sons who had accompanied him on foot, and they had duly escorted him up the mountain by shotgun. After he'd given them the bad news that it was too late, and she died a few hours after his arrival, they'd forced the poor doctor to strip naked and sent him down the mountain dodging bullets!

Doc shuddered. All things considered, it was probably very wise to have young Emma along. She was no doubt kin or neighbor to the mountain woman concerned. Besides, he would never be able to find the place on his own. After placing one foot on the stirrup and heaving himself up onto Bessie's back, he leaned down, and rather meanly, pulled Emma up behind him, instead of in front. Mentally chiding himself for his lack of charity, he nevertheless had no mind to have the unpleasant odor of her right under his nose all the way there. They set off at a brisk trot and he felt unwilling repulsion as she snaked two thin grimy arms trustingly around his middle.

After leaving Carlisle with its cluster of modest frame houses, they rode for a long time along the valley flats, with neither of them saying a word; there was just the sound of Emma's periodic grunts as she made thudding contact with the saddle. Mountains rose majestically on either side, a series of ragged cliffs and rocky ridges emerging from the dense trees. They passed a couple of large to-bacco farms. In the days of slavery before the Civil War, these had been rather handsome places of some elegance. Now most were run down and forgotten relics, with an air of wounded neglect about them. In the echoey silence broken only by the roaring of the river waters, they rode along the debris-lined banks, leaving the small patches of civilization behind, heading towards thickly forested woodland. The river, which cascaded down through forests thick with ancient hemlocks and giant white oaks, had recently flooded with the melting of the formidable winter snows, and they passed rocky rapids and gushing waterfalls, thick with whipped foam.

After a while, they entered the great Wilderness Valley, on the other side of which rose the mighty mountain itself. Emma pounded him on his back with her small fist and indicated that they had to cross the river at this juncture. Despite the fact that the flood waters caused by record tons of melting snow and ice had receded, leaving the telltale debris of leaves, sticks, branches and logs all along the banks, the river was still a raging torrent, and Doc quailed at the very thought of having to cross it. The winter had been a bitter one throughout the land. There had been many back-to-back blizzards, causing records for cold temperatures being set in Virginia. Ice had formed on the rivers and in Chesapeake Bay. What made it so historic was the extent and severity of the winter weather, which affected the entire country, especially the South. It was so bad that ice flows in the Mississippi had made it all the way down to the Gulf of Mexico! So how those poor folk living high up in the mountains must have suffered!

The strong icy current pulled mightily around Bessie's flanks, drenching first Doc's shoes and then, as her hoofs touched the river bottom, his trousers almost to the knees. Emma waded through the strong rushing current that came up to her chest, pulling the mare behind her by the reins. Bessie was nervous and skittish and as the water lapped and surged around them, she whinnied in fright. Doc sat welded to the saddle by heart-stopping fear. Any minute now, the current must surely sweep them all away. And if not him, then surely Emma, for how could this wisp of a child withstand Nature's fierce insistence? Yet, somehow, she did. They made it safely to the other side and he helped Emma back up behind him, drenched to the skin, poor little thing.

Bear Rock, a giant, rocky promontory of Claw Mountain, loomed over the valley on one side, while the slopes of Fork Mountain descended upon the opposite bank of Wilson Run they'd just come from. In the distance, Buck Knob rose up in a misty haze and, almost directly ahead, the jagged heights of the dreaded Claw Mountain itself, a huge ancient forest-covered lofty land mass, with its fortressed summit of great, gray, granite boulders, a good thousand feet higher than any surrounding peak. It seemed infinitely lonely, somehow, and distinctly ominous to Doc.

Thinking about its unsavory inhabitants, he wondered what evil deeds had been committed upon its soil. They pressed on and, about three miles further on, they reached the foot of the dreaded Claw Mountain. As they started up the mountain slopes, Doc felt a thrall of fear run through him. What if Emma was kin to the Buchanan's feuding foes, the Galtreys? Doc wasn't sure if the Galtreys were squatters on this particular mountain or some other. Word had it that before the onset of winter there had been a massacre involving the two clans, which had resulted in much loss of life and that only the onset of the particularly nasty winter had calmed things down some. Might they, in that instance, feel no compunction to kill them both? After all, he had heard that not even children were spared these murderous louts. Awful heightened fear settled like a stone in his stomach and he found it difficult to breathe. The scamp could be leading him into the very jaws of hell for all he knew. Why had he not thought of this before setting out? *And why hadn't he paid more attention to the mountain gossip?*

Occasionally, Emma would yell some direction and point from behind to show him the way, when there were converging paths that led in different directions. Here, the land was mainly forested with the mighty chestnut, but it also gave fervent growth to vine-entangled stands of giant white oak, ashes, locusts, red maples, shagbark hickories and tulip poplars, while at a lower level, redbud and dogwoods, delicately laced with pink and white bracts of flowers, everywhere met the eye. There were glens entirely of hay-scented fern and breathtaking glimpses of the blossoms of flame azaleas and the elegant white cups of mountain magnolia. The whole mountainside was alive with the ceaseless bubbling of streams, the cries and twitters of a host of feathered fowl. But to Doc, an uneasy silence reigned beneath the sounds of birdlife and gushing water, lending the place an eerie air of malevolence, so much so, that Doc was much too nervous to luxuriate in the aesthetic value of the marvels he was seeing. His eyes darted about anxiously to see if any of the mountain crackers were hidden behind the massive trunks, watching them.

The path was steep and rocky, often blocked with fallen logs, alarming suck-ing and slippery mud-holes and elderberry bushes so thick, it was a nightmare to squeeze through them. Emma soon slipped unceremoniously off the mare's back again and led her by the reins, but poor Bessie, unused to such dangerous and unfamiliar conditions, was skittish and trembling, and often stumbled, scattering stones below. Finally, she shied and refused to go any further. Doc decided it was high time for a rest anyway. He climbed off the mare, talking to her com-fortingly, but quietly, in case anybody might hear him, feeling decidedly weary and saddle-sore. He sat down heavily on a moss-covered log. The child sat on the ground beside him, knees up, dungarees still damp from the river. Though she looked even more bedraggled than before, she seemed not in the least bit tired and it occurred to him that she was just humoring him by resting. She still smelled sourly ripe despite her drenching, but thinking of the way she had taken charge crossing the river, Doc couldn't help feeling a small, grudging stab of admiration for her. He took off his coat, laying it across the log and unloosened his bowtie, mopping his brow with his handkerchief.

"Why you s'fat?" Emma asked suddenly, her narrow face mean and slit-eyed.

Doc turned to look at her in bald astonishment. He had never considered himself fat before. A little stout perhaps. Distinguished-looking. A handsome figure of a man, actually. *But never fat!* But glancing down at the buttons of his shirt straining across his stomach, he cursed Hilda's undoubted expertise in the kitchen and sucked it in self-consciously, for a moment thrown off-kilter by the child's directness. He did not quite know how to answer her. Looking at her pencil-thin arms and slight, hollow chest, he was about to meanly point out that she could do with a good deal more meat on *her* bones, when he remembered what a terrible winter it had been for these poor folk and, instead, snapped rather severely, "How often were the pains coming?"

"Pains?" Emma screwed up her face in puzzlement.

"Why, the baby, of course."

But by the blank look on Emma's face, he could tell she didn't have a clue about what he was talking about. She shrugged thin shoulders and picked listlessly at a scab on her foot. Doc sighed, wondering what terrible ignorance he was up against.

19

Just then Doc heard a crashing noise, the distinct sound of snapping sticks, raised voices and raucous laughter. *Holy, Moses, somebody was coming!* He froze, his mouth turning instantly dry.

"Quick, child, hide!" he yelped.

He leapt up and hid behind a wild hydrangea bush as he saw two young mountain men coming down the mountain through the trees. They wore slouch hats, dungarees and vests and were barefoot. Each of them carried a shotgun over one shoulder. Forsooth, thought Doc, what if they spotted Bessie? Only part of the mare was visible from behind the bush where she was grazing on grass, but he daren't try to draw her into full cover in case she neighed or whinnied and gave away their presence. Even had he dared, his limbs were locked rigid by fear, and he couldn't move an inch if he tried. He glanced around to find Emma hiding right behind him as his nose had already detected. Engaged in low conversation, the two hillbillies passed right by without noticing them and continued on down the slopes. Doc let out his breath and sighed hugely with relief. *What a close call!*

"Who are they?" he whispered to Emma.

"They be m'kin," she replied with eyes narrowed. "Unc' Jake an' Unc' Eli. I be real a'skeered a' them two, especially *Unc' Eli.*"

"Why's that?" he croaked.

"'Cuz Unc' Eli be th' devil hisself."

Doc felt a moment of dizzy raw fear. If even this child felt that way about those two, he had just had a closer call than he cared to think about.

Nothing would induce Bessie to move further up the mountain even though

Emma pulled on the reins from the front and Doc pushed her sweat-slicked rump from the rear. Finally, they gave up. Tying her once more to the wild hydrangea bush and praying he wouldn't find her gone when he got back, stolen for horsemeat or used for target practice, Doc reluctantly left his nag to her uncertain fate. It had taken them a good few hours already to negotiate the tricky footpaths that led to the steeper incline to the top. Just when Doc had decided that the child had led him on some bizarre phantom search for a place that did not exist, he climbed a steep, narrow pathway through a complicated maze of giant granite boulders, crested a rocky ridge with some difficulty, and there, right in front of him, was a mountaineer's homesite.

Doc scrambled up onto a rocky ledge and stood up shakily, exhausted and panting, his knees creaking like unoiled door-hinges. He stared at the scene in front of him in awe. Although the past winter had left its calling card in sagging timbers and the broken-off gutters of the simple log cabin, the whole place looked like a magnificent painting! It was an idyllic setting, softened here and there with stubborn patches of snow, which was now beginning to shadow with twilight. There were majestic firs, giant brooding hemlocks and a glorious towering chestnut with a trunk of enormous girth, covered in pale new growth.

He turned to look for Emma and found to his alarm that she had disappeared. She had slipped away into the forest below without him even realizing it, or getting a chance to thank her. Now he felt more vulnerable than ever. That child may have been just a slip of thing, but she had been his only guarantee of safety, however tenuous. Now he was desperate and dreadfully afraid, stranded all alone right in the heart of Obediah's infamous domain. *How had this happened to him?*

As he glanced around to find her, his eyes caught the scene below, and he drew in a quick breath. For if ever a place had been sculptured by God Himself, this was it! The homesite overlooked a scene of breathtaking grandeur – a magnificent tree-shrouded valley which dropped steeply away from buttresses of craggy granite, Wilson Run lying thousands of feet below. The mountain seemed blissfully unscarred by the ravages of timbering or crop-clearing and, in that instant, Doc's tiredness fell away from him like a cloak. *What splendor!*

Then he heard a small sound behind him and froze. He turned around slowly to find that a black-bearded, barefoot hillbilly, a giant colossus, whose huge frame must cause considerable trepidation in braver mortals than he – stood a few feet in front of him. To his mortification, Doc saw he was pointing a long-barreled old-fashioned Kentucky rifle right at him. Doc could smell moonshine on the hillbilly right from where he stood. He stared at the long muzzle in dismay, his guts all aquiver, speechless with fright and fear.

"You th' doctor?" the hillbilly asked gruffly, eyes narrowed.

Doc could only nod.

"Whar in hell's name have you bin?" the hillbilly demanded. "I swar you quacks ain't good fer nuthin' 'sides pullin' th' odd tooth an' picklin' some poor fool's innards! I ain't forgotten that it was one of you lot who kill'd my maw! Would have brung me th' granny-wimmin 'stead of relyin' on a quack like you, only she was at another birthin'!"

He carried on his tirade for a good few minutes, scarcely pausing to draw breath, such was his wild-eyed agitation. The rest of Doc's scant courage fled in the torrent of the hillbilly's contemptuous words. Doc was used to being given a dubious reception: the wrinkled brows and anxious eyes of loved ones, the testiness of relatives fraught with fear and knowing dread, but to get on the wrong side of a Claw Mountain Buchanan was quite another matter! It could reap exceedingly dire consequences. He finally found his voice. "Uh, I presume it's your good wife who's about to have a baby?"

"Yeah, but it's a wonder she ain't dead, th' time it took y'all to git here!" complained the hillbilly bitterly.

"It . . . it was a long way and quite a climb," Doc, still panting, muttered weakly, keenly feeling the unfairness of it. "Your wife . . . how is she?"

"Well, I was hopin' you could tell *me* that," the hillbilly snapped.

"How often are the pains coming?"

"Well, she had one this mornin'. Ain't had none since that I know of."

"You mean . . . uh . . . your wife is not yet in full labor?" Doc was clouted with the knowledge. After all young Emma's histrionics, the hurry and panic and sheer effort to get here, expecting to find both mother and baby dearly departed, he was now told that the mother was not yet in proper labor! Likely it would turn out to be a false alarm! Doc didn't know whether to be angry, to rejoice, or to cry. He just knew that he felt inordinately shivery at the knees. Especially since the long, slender rifle was still trained squarely on him. He knew all too well how quick these liquored-up hillbillies were to use their guns and knives – Lord knows he'd mopped up after them often enough!

"This your first by any chance?" he asked finally, eyeing the long muzzle of the old-fashioned rifle nervously.

"Yeah. What of it?" grunted the hillbilly, narrowed eyes glinting ominously.

Doc pulled his gold-chained fob out of his pocket and studied its face carefully in the gathering gloom. "Well, it's just that if that's the case, it'll probably be a good while yet. Never comes quick with the first."

The hillbilly nodded and his shoulders suddenly sagged as if for a tiny instant he had submitted to intense relief, revealing to Doc the considerable strain he had been under.

"Doc . . . don't let her die," the hillbilly croaked and, with that small pitiful entreaty, all the menace in him seemed to melt. But that silly contention instantly vanished with the man's next carefully enunciated words. "'Cuz if'n you let her or th' baby die, I swar on m' good maw's grave, *I'll kill ya.*"

Still standing on the edge of the precipice, Doc felt a wave of fear-induced dizziness overcome him. And the man could easily do it too! If Doc wasn't able to save the woman and her baby, this wild goliath of a man could easily toss him over the side of this mountain, like a sack of grain, and who would ever think to look for him there? Oh, maybe in years to come somebody might come across a few bleached bones lying on the forest floor and wonder at the circumstances, but chances were good that he'd simply be swallowed up by the dense forest without a trace.

"Well," said Doc, mopping his wet brow with his crumpled handkerchief, before picking up his medical bag at his feet. "Perhaps I ought to go in and see my patient."

As Doc moved towards the steps leading to the porch, the big mountain man lowered his long rifle and allowed him to go past. Just then, a scrawny, rust-colored, red-combed rooster strutting lordfully around the yard, noisily trampling wild purple hepatica and snow trillium underfoot, followed by a tiny entourage of two winter-wizened hens, suddenly stretched its neck and gave full vent to an ill-timed crowing – at the exact moment a loud screaming wail sounded from inside!
. . .

20

The heart-wrenching cry sent Doc catapulting up the porch steps, through the cabin door, into the dim recesses of the big bedroom beyond the large main room. He found a young mountain woman moaning and thrashing about on a big double pallet, the hard hump of her pale stomach exposed and knees up and spread wide. It was obvious to Doc that her waters had already long broken, for he reached her just in time to catch the impatient infant that suddenly popped out from between her pale wide-spread legs in a wash of murky liquid and blood. Caught by surprise, Doc found himself fumbling and inept, as he hastily dropped his medical bag and caught the slippery infant just in time. After staring at it for a moment in stunned disbelief, he quickly cleaned out the mouth of the snuffling infant with a hooked finger then held the wriggling little boy-child, red as a beet, by the feet, to give it the customary sound whack on its backside. But before he had the chance to do so, the infant took a deep quavering breath and gave a loud wail. Chuffed, Doc held the squirming little thing in the cradle of his shaking hands for a breath-catching moment before placing it in the crook of one arm and taking a pair of surgical scissors out of his medical bag to carefully cut the umbilical cord.

"My, my, it's a fine little boy, dear child," he assured the panting, sweat-sodden young mother, who was watching them anxiously. "Never had one so keen to take on the world as this little fella. Heavens, I never even had time to get the water boiled!"

He cleaned up the blood-and-slime-blotched baby with a wad of absorbent cotton dipped in some liquid paraffin before handing it to the outstretched arms of its young mother lying on the double pallet, who stared at it with open awe as she carefully wrapped it in a blue woolen shawl. Doc was immensely thankful that both mother and child had managed to come through the birth so well, not least of all when he recalled the hillbilly's chilling threat to kill him should he have failed to save them both! Clouted with bone-numbing relief, he felt quite weak in the dizzy aftermath of his narrow escape.

Doc watched the mother, her long, stringy, black hair hanging from a middle path, staring tenderly down at her newborn baby. In the glow radiating from the lamp, Doc saw she was just a lass.. Alas, she had the same telltale sign of recent near-starvation – gaunt, hollowed cheeks, stringy neck and thin scrawny shoulders – that categorized most mountain folks these days, yet there was something indefinably gritty and determined about her. The way she had kept her contractions from her husband, for instance! It must have taken a lot of courage and endurance to face all that on her own, especially since this was her first baby. Of course, she would have to be gritty and determined in order to have survived the rigors of this past winter in the first place! He thought how extremely harsh conditions must have been up here at such an elevation. There was no doubt that they must have been snowed in for much of the duration. If so, what terrible hardships she must have endured, being with child on top of it all. How trapped she must have felt at times, cut off from the rest of world for months on end.

Doc gave her a smile of encouragement and glanced around the musty-smelling room. It was bare except for the double pallet and a big wooden chest (a surprisingly splendid piece!) on top of which a kerosene lamp burned in the dimness. The chest also had on top of it a basin filled with water and a water jug. A chipped cream chamber pot painted with blue flowers sat next to the pallet like an apology.

He asked gently, "Well, dear lass, have you got a name for him yet?"

She nodded. "Yes. Jediah Horatio Buchanan," she said shyly. "But I'll call him Jed fer short."

"Why, that's a fine name," commended Doc, "for a fine little baby boy. And what might your name be?"

"Mary."

"Ah, Mary, we need to put your husband's mind at rest. I fear he's been real anxious about you."

Mary quickly raised her head and narrowed her eyes as if in puzzlement. "Has he now?"

"Aye, very anxious indeed. I'll go get him then."

"*No!*" she cried, her eyes flaring momentarily. Then she quickly added, "Not yet."

"Is there something wrong, child?"

The young woman looked if she wanted to say something, but she stopped herself and instead stared at him dully. This niggled at Doc. Perhaps the reason she hadn't told her husband that she'd been having pains all day was because she was afraid of him? Was she being ill-treated? Her hands holding her baby were certainly rough and calloused, which indicated that she'd done plenty of hard work around here.

"Child, is there something you'd like to tell me?" he asked gently.

The young woman quickly shook her head, but her hazel eyes were mute with pleading. Doc mopped his brow. He was afraid to question this young woman. What if she repeated what he said to her husband? It was said that nobody got away with any real or imagined slight against this unruly bunch. What chance would he have right smack in the middle of the viper's nest itself? But how could he leave without establishing that she wasn't being held here against her will? Then it hit Doc with the force of a wielded club. *Mary!* Could this possibly be Mary *Harley*, the girl who had mysteriously vanished just days after the Buckos had invaded the store at Fletcher? Good grief! Why had he not thought of it straight off?

It had been the talk of every general store in Virginia how she had stood up to the evil, whip-wielding Bucko. Her sudden disappearance just a few days later had caused great consternation and was the headlines in all the local newspapers. There was much talk about her brave stance that day and also speculation about whether she had been abducted by the Buckos, or even killed by them. Had she indeed been abducted by this iniquitous clan and then forced to become a slave and concubine of this evil hillbilly? Doc felt impelled to find out. But he had to be careful in case he was horribly wrong in his suppositions.

"What is your maiden name, child?" he asked carefully.

The girl tightened her hold on her baby. For a long time she said nothing, then she whispered, "Harley."

Doc felt his spine tingling. Unbelievably, he had found the missing Harley girl! *Glory be!* And what was he to do now that he had found her? Flee with her and the baby during the night? There was fat chance of that happening! He had to struggle enough to get here with Emma as a guide in broad daylight. Lord knew it'd be useless trying to escape in the dark with her and her newborn baby –

164

especially with a hostile hillbilly hovering around. Well, he would simply report the matter to the sheriff on his way home. Yes, that would be the best plan of action.

Her poor family must have been beside themselves with worry, not knowing if she was dead or alive. Doc didn't have any time to ruminate on the matter, however, because just then the door slammed open and, in the doorway, stood the girl's husband – if indeed he be that! To Doc's dismay, the hillbilly's face was contorted with fury. Mary's face was a picture of fright and guilt. Doc felt a familiar loosening of his entrails.

"Ah, fine sir," he said quickly, "I was just about to call you."

"What were you two jawin' about?" the mountain man demanded to know.

"I was just asking Mary here what name you two have chosen for your firstborn son. Did you hear that, sir? You have a *son!* Congratulations on a fine baby boy!"

"*I got me a son?*" the hillbilly repeated hollowly, his eyes expanding in astonishment. For the first time Mathew saw how striking his eyes were – an unusual mixture of azure and emerald-green that reminded one of watery depths, yet with a brilliance as stark as a diamond. "I got me a son?" the hillbilly repeated, as if unable to believe it. He suddenly seemed stunned and unsure of himself. There was a moment of strained silence then he looked down at the girl and muttered, "You alright, girl?"

Mary nodded and Doc, while he inwardly quailed, managed with forced heartiness, "She's fine! Healthy as a horse and the babe slid out so easy, it was like he was on a greased sled!"

"That so?"

"Indeed. Now I think she needs something to drink before she gets some rest. Shall I make some coffee while you acquaint yourself with your new son?"

"No, I'll make her some sassafras tea m'self, and fer you too. It's all we got left. Ain't had no time to go down to th' store since th' winter thaw. By th' way, you'd best sleep in th' barn t'night and leave first light. It'll be too tricky to git down yonder at night."

"Well, thank you," Doc said, though for the life of him couldn't think why. He didn't relish spending any time at all as the formidable man's guest, albeit in the freezing barn. He just hoped he'd think of *feeding* him! He realized he hadn't eaten a thing since breakfast and suddenly felt quite weak with hunger. Mountain families were known for their hospitality, but this particular family was well-known for its *inhospitality!* He wished he was at home instead, being waited on and amply fed by Hilda. No doubt his housekeeper would scold him severely for not telling her he'd be away for the night. Somehow, even his dour housekeeper seemed far more desirable company than this evil fellow.

"What about my mare, Bessie?"

The hillbilly frowned. "Whar did you leave her?"

"Down the way a bit. Tethered her to a wild hydrangea bush alongside the path."

"Well, I'll go down and take her to my paw's barn whar he keeps his mules. I'll see she's watered and fed. Then I'll go with you and fetch her agin at first light and see you off th' mountain."

Doc's shoulders sagged with relief. He'd been worrying about what would become of his faithful nag, to say nothing of himself departing the mountain alive and fully clad! "Thank you, kind sir! That's most considerate of you. By the way, may I ask your name?"

"It's Zachary Thomas. Zachary Thomas Buchanan. And your'n?"

"Doc Adams."

"Thanks, Doc," Zachary Thomas mumbled before turning to go get the sassafras tea.

21

Mary stared down at the newborn baby in her arms and thought she had never seen a baby as beautiful before, even if he was bald as a coot and had a ruddy complexion. *Jediah Horatio Buchanan!* Little Jed! She felt full of raw emotion, full of powerful love for this innocent child of a loveless union, and curiously light-hearted, despite her exhaustion. After months of worry and dread of the actual birth, both she and the baby were miraculously safe and well. And despite how big she had carried, it wasn't twins, after all, as she had feared. It would be so much harder to escape with *two* babies to worry about. Even impossible!

It had been a nerve-wracking and awful experience just the same. Her baby was actually in the throes of being born when the miracle happened and the good doctor come flying through the door to the rescue, all afluster. A kind and portly man, the doctor had fortuitously been there just in time to catch the baby, cut the cord, mop up and make her comfortable. Despite the extreme discomfort and pain leading up to the birth, her baby had been born without any difficulty at all.

At last the nightmare was over and it had all been worth it for the peacefully sleeping baby was now lying safely in her arms. But equally as important, she was sure that Doc Adams now knew who she was, since recognition had clearly dawned in his eyes the moment she had told him her name. Surely he would report it to the sheriff or her family and they would come and rescue her and the darling child? She was wallowing in the import of this definite possibility when the door opened and Zachary Thomas brought in the steaming mugs of sassafras tea. The doctor took his gratefully and discreetly left the room. Zachary Thomas put her mug on the floor next to the pallet and stared down at Mary. After what she had been through she deeply resented his presence and wished he'd go away. She wanted him to leave her alone to enjoy her baby – and sleep.

"Mary . . . you sure you're alright, girl?" he mumbled finally.

Mary nodded. "Jest real worn out, is all."

"Thank th' Lawd. I've bin so worried. Prayed so hard fer th' doctor to git here in time."

Mary felt a jolt of surprise. *Zachary Thomas had prayed!* All these months of her saying grace before they ate and kneeling beside their pallet at night to say her silent nightly prayers, must have rubbed off on him. But the very fact that he had prayed at all meant Doc Adams was right. Zachary Thomas had genuinely been concerned about her and the baby. And looking at him now, she realized that he had also been through a lot. It showed on his tired and haggard face. After all, however much she wished otherwise, it was *his* baby too, not hers alone. It must have also been frightening for him to be helpless and uninformed in such matters, as he must surely have been, anxious about not having been able to secure the services of the granny-woman he'd been counting on, and then having to entrust such an important task as fetching the doctor to young Emma. Why had he not gone himself? Could it be he was afraid to leave her alone for such an extended period? Whatever, he had done his best to get her adequate care, she knew that now. Her proof was in the fact that he had acquired the services of a valley doctor, despite his father's keen aversion to such medical men. Her anger towards her husband left her in that moment and she looked up at him earnestly.

"Come take a look at yer son, Zachary Thomas. Take a look at Jed."

Zachary Thomas sat down on the pallet beside her. Mary moved the baby in her arms so he could get a good look. He stared at his tiny baby with a look of awe on his face. She held the bundle out to him. "Hold him, Zachary Thomas."

Zachary Thomas looked aghast. "I cain't do that. I'll drop him fer sure."

Mary shook her head. "No, you won't. You'll be jest fine."

Zachary Thomas held his breath, and reaching for the baby, gingerly took it and held the shawl-covered infant in the crook of his left arm. A slow smile spread on his winter-gaunt face. *"Jed*, you say?"

"Yes. Jediah Horatio Buchanan, if'n you don't mind, that is. I know we never discussed names a'fore, but I've always loved th' name Jed an' my paw's middle name is Horatio."

"Jediah Horatio Buchanan?" he said testingly. "Why, I reckon that's a real fine name."

He placed the baby on one huge hand and, with the other, spread the shawl to look at the squirming naked baby underneath, smiling as he saw its tiny male genitalia. He passed a slow shaking hand over his son's minute body and Mary was touched to see a look of infinite tenderness descend on his face as he took in the miniature attributes of his first-born son. It was a curiously touching scene, full of pathos and poignancy, and Mary felt distinctly moved by it. She had not expected this reaction from a man usually so taciturn and stern. But here he was, for once not the enemy – a member of the notorious Buckos who murdered innocent children – just a proud father viewing his newly born babe for the very first time. He grinned as the baby opened its mouth and gave a lusty yawn, opening its dark-blue sightless eyes. "Why, he's a real handsome little fella."

"He's coot bald!" said Mary with a smile.

"Me and my brothers were all bald as coots when we was born. Got long legs fer a baby, too, see? Jest like I had, accordin' to Maw."

Mary nodded in agreement. "Yeah, I reckon he takes after his daddy, fer sure."

Zachary Thomas looked up with an expression of pure joy on his black-bearded face. "You thunk so? Knew it was a boy all along. Jest thunk, Mary, I'll be able to learn him to shoot and hunt an' trap, jest like I done young Emma. I kin learn him to fish too." He raised his eyes to the roof for a moment, before leveling his gaze at her. "Thunk I'll learn him to skin right too, so you don't got to do it no more. Reckon thar's a whole lot I kin learn him about th' animals and birds and trees and sech. A man don't git to live his whole life in a place like this an' not git to know th' mountains real good. Reckon I kin make a real mountain man out of him."

Mary averted her eyes, as a pang of guilt hit her. She was surprised at the way Zachary Thomas had opened up and told her of his dreams for his child. It had not occurred to her that he might have been looking forward to the birth – and equally afraid that things might go horribly wrong, especially when he had appeared so disinterested when she had told him he was going to be a father. There was no doubt that he was excited at the prospect of raising his son and teaching him all that he knew about things essential to the survival of a mountain family. He would be devastated to lose them both when the sheriff came by to fetch them. Still, she couldn't let it influence her. She had to leave Claw Mountain, no matter what. For her own sake and, more importantly, for the sake of her child. *Please, Lord, let it be soon!* For she knew that the longer she remained here now, the harder it would be for Zachary Thomas – and the harder he was likely to fight to keep them.

22

A couple of days after the birth of her baby, Mary was busy serving Zachary Thomas at the table with a lunch of chunks of fresh corn bread dipped into the leftovers from last night's 'possum stew, when they heard some sustained distant gunfire down the mountain. She looked up worriedly, cocking her head to one side as she strained to listen.

Obviously seeing her fixed, alarmed expression, Zachary Thomas consoled her. "Don't fret none, it's jest target practice."

"But it don't *sound* like target practice to me somehow. I thunk it could be them Galtreys."

"Doubt it. Ain't heard no signal. 'Sides, it's stopped already. Reckon if'n it were somethung serious, it wouldn't have bin over so smartly."

He continued to wolf down his meal, but Mary got the impression that he was also listening acutely for, despite his attempt at nonchalance, his body had tensed. There was another sharp round of shots and then silence once more. Since gunshots were not an unusual occurrence on Claw Mountain, Mary had no idea why she felt so uneasy.

There were no more shots after that,and, after about fifteen minutes, feeling the heaviness of her milk-swollen breasts, she murmured. "Well, if'n you're finished here I'd best go feed th' baby."

She was just about to leave the room when there was a raucous squawking and screeching of eagles and, a few minutes later, loud banging on the cabin door. For the last couple of days they had suffered a steady stream of visitors from amongst Zachary Thomas's kinfolk, who had come to see the new babe. The women had cooed over Jed and pinched his tiny cheeks, and their loud cackling had woken him up. Even Eli, disturbingly handsome, had come to silently gloat, his pale-yellow eyes meeting hers over the baby's crib, as if to say . . . *oh so many things!* Like how close it had been for the baby to be his instead of her husband's! She was relieved that Obediah Buchanan had not shown his face. After what he had done to young Jamie, she did not think she could be civil to him. But as lacking as her husband's kinfolk were as to the social niceties, none of them had banged on the door like this. Unsettled by such a brash announcement, she and Zachary Thomas looked at each other in stunned surprise. Before they could react, however, they heard shouting from behind the cabin door. "ZACK BUCHANAN! OPEN UP! THIS IS SHERIFF COLEY!"

Sheriff Coley! Mary froze at the mention of the name. It was about to happen, she was sure! It was just two days since Doc Adams had left Claw Mountain and he had obviously wasted no time reporting her whereabouts to the law. She glanced at her husband in alarm, wondering what his reaction would be when he learned that the sheriff had come to fetch her and the baby off the mountain. From the gunfire they had heard, it was clear that the sheriff had received quite a reception from the rest of the Buchanan clan. Frowning heavily, Zachary Thomas cautiously stood up and went to open the door. Mary crept up behind him, her heart pounding inside her chest. They both froze at the sight that met them. For standing out on the porch was the sheriff and at least ten deputies, who surrounded him in a loose covey, all of them with rifles raised and pointed at Zachary Thomas.

One of the deputies had been shot in the arm, for his sleeve was soaked with blood and he had a handkerchief tied around it. With a sense of shock, she recognized her brother, Joe, among them, his hat low over his dark-brown eyes. His serious face brightened with relief when he saw her, but he held his tongue. Mary had never been happier to see anyone in her whole life, but she dared not acknowledge him at this stage. The air was fraught with tension.

Zachary Thomas glared at the sheriff, who had a brown handlebar mustache, and barked at him, "Zachary Thomas, I am arresting you for the kidnapping of Mary Harley!" With that, the sheriff clamped handcuffs onto the wrists of the stupefied mountain man. The sheriff then turned his attention to Mary. "Are you Mary Louella Harley?"

Shocked at what was happening, Mary could only nod.

"Good. Are you alright, girl?"

Mary nodded woodenly. "I'm fine, thank you."

"Good! Then we'll escort you back to Lewis Mountain and take this dastardly felon down to the jail at Madison to await trial."

Mary stood rooted with shock. Never in all her wildest imaginings about escaping the mountain, had she considered that such a thing might happen. For a brief moment, she wondered if she should let the official misconception stand. After all, if Zachary Thomas was arrested, he could not try to prevent her and the baby from leaving as he might well do otherwise. But Mary took one look at her husband's flabbergasted face and she stepped forward. 'I'll go with you, but you must release Zachary Thomas at once fer he didn't commit no crime."

"What say you, girl? Of course, he did! He abducted you from your home on Lewis Mountain and forced you to come here and work for him as a slave and to submit to his lusts, giving you a briarpatch child to boot, I hear!"

"No! No! You've got it all wrong! He didn't abduct me!" protested Mary.

Joe pushed forward and looked at her, aghast. "Mary, what are you sayin'? I know that you would never go willin'ly with a perfect stranger you ain't never even met a'fore – *let alone a Bucko!"*

Mary raised a calm, defiant head and addressed the sheriff. "Sheriff Coley,

170

I'm sayin' that I willin'ly eloped with Zachary Thomas. I saw him at the general store at Fletcher when I went thar with my paw and two sisters and . . . and we were both smote with love in that instant. He fetched me from Lewis Mountain and we got married the very next day. I have jest borne him a child. However, thru' no fault of his, I am real unhappy here on Claw Mountain, and wish to go back to my parents, so I would, indeed, be truly gratified if you could escort me and my baby home."

Zachary Thomas gave her such a horrified look at her final words that she was forced to turn away. "But, Mary, you cain't do that, girl. My young'un . . ." He let the words hang with import.

Sheriff Coley turned to Zachary Thomas. "Is this all true, Zack? Or have you coerced her to say such things? Wouldn't put nothin' past you Buckos!"

"It's true, damnit! *All of it!*" Zachary Thomas snapped, his eyes narrowed fiercely into burning turquoise-green slits.

Sheriff Coley's face fell as he considered the implications of Mary's explanation about what had transpired. He grated his throat. "Pity. For if what she says is true and she is your legal wife, then we can take her if that's what she wants, but we can't take your child away without your permission."

Mary looked at the sheriff in deep dismay, as he reluctantly unlocked Zachary Thomas's handcuffs. She had not anticipated that she would not legally be able to take her baby away from Claw Mountain without her husband's permission.

Zachary Thomas turned to Mary. "Is this true? Do you wish go back home, even after all we've bin through together?"

Mary nodded. She had no intention of leaving her baby behind no matter what. "I'm sorry, Zachary Thomas, but this ain't no place to raise a child. Even you must see it. Please don't make me leave without baby Jed."

Zachary Thomas lowered his head, letting out a despairing grunt. He was silent for a long time, then he said softly, "You sure this is what y'want, girl? You *real* sure?"

"I'm sure. I've bin wantin' to leave since th' day after I got here, you know that's true," she said meaningfully, so he couldn't fail to catch her drift. "It were a mistake, Zachary Thomas, I should never have bin forc . . . married you. I don't belong here."

Zachary Thomas stared at her with a look of utter devastation on his bearded face. There was a moment's charged silence then he thundered, "Then I guess you'd best be gone, wimmin!"

"You'll let me take Jed then?" Mary held her breath. She knew that Hollow tradition dictated that when a wife died, the young'uns were given to the nearest relatives to be raised. Perhaps the same applied when a wife deserted her husband. She shuddered at the thought that if he were to insist that she leave Jed behind, her darling baby might be raised by the likes of Cora, Ellie Mae or Agnes, until he remarried. *What a terrible thought!* Well, she could never let that happen. If he insisted that the baby stayed then she would have to stay behind too! But she could not bear for that to happen when she so desperately wanted to leave this accursed mountain. She couldn't bear to have to endure any more of the long, terrible silences. She thought how her maw and paw had long intimate conversations, punctured with laughter and knew how much her own marriage had been lacking.

But she had learned over the months that despite Zachary Thomas failings as a husband, he was not a wicked man. He had worked so hard during the winter to keep them alive and had bought everything she had asked for from the store in the beginning. She realized that it had been his way of trying to please her. She guessed it wasn't his fault he was such an uncommunicative soul.

It was strange but the extreme hardships she and Zachary Thomas had survived together this past winter had somehow wiped away her anger at being forced to marry him against her will and having to submit to him on her wedding night. So much had happened since then – the massacres, the flogging of Jamie and the accursed winter itself that it had dulled those particular transgressions in her mind. But she quickly made up her mind. If she had to, she would tell the sheriff that she had changed her mind about marrying Zachary Thomas, but that he had forced her to go ahead with the marriage anyway, against her will. It may mean arrest and prison for him, but if he wouldn't let her leave with her baby voluntarily, she would have no choice.

Zachary Thomas silently pondered on the matter then at last he swallowed hard and said with a break in his voice, "Thar ain't no way I kin look after a two-day-old baby, is there now? He needs a maw more than a paw right now."

Mary felt weak with relief. *She was going home!* And with baby Jed!

"Thank you, Zachary Thomas. Thank you. I'm ... I'm ... real sorry."

Zachary Thomas shook his head, unable to speak. The big mountain man ducked under the doorway and pushed his way through the milling deputies, with his head bowed. As he slowly descended the porch steps, Joe came inside and hugged her tightly.

"Mary, Mary, I'm so happy and relieved ye're safe. W'all thunked you were dead – murdered by th' Buckos fer darin' to speak out at Eli. We've all bin grievin' fer you somethung fierce. I've sure missed you, Sis."

Mary sagged against her brother's chest and wept with relief.

"I know. What I did was awful, but I was too ashamed to write. Do y'thunk they'll ever forgive me for puttin' y'all through all this, Joe?"

Joe pulled away and massaged her arms, looking at her with his warm dark-brown eyes. "Don't worry, Sis! Reckon they'll be so overjoyed to see you, they'll forgive you anythung."

Joe helped her get her few things together and then Mary lifted Jed out of the wooden crib that Zachary Thomas had finished for him just days before his birth. It was a plain crib, but nicely made and finished, and seeing it filled her with terrible guilt. Zachary Thomas had told her that he had worked on it for a whole month. She stood back and stared dully at it for a moment, tears coming to her eyes. It wasn't just the crib. The image of Zachary Thomas holding his baby for the first time kept coming to her mind. And since that time, when he thought she wasn't watching, he would gaze down at his sleeping child as if he couldn't believe that the infant was real.

Did she have the right to separate a man from his firstborn son? She forced herself to remember young Jamie Galtrey's hideous fate and the merciless flogging of Jamie Buchanan, and thought, not for the first time, how ironic it was that the youngest boys of the two feuding families were both called Jamie.

God knew she did not like to do this to her husband. One thing for sure, the marriage could scarcely have been a joyful one for him either. *Except for the baby!* The baby had brought Zachary Thomas joy. She briefly considered whether she should stay, after all. But the thought of living for year upon year with a husband who never talked, was unbearable. And she remembered how helpless a strong woman like Hedina Buchanan had been against the might of Obediah's will when it came to the raising of her sons and she knew, with all her heart, that she could not possibly allow him to be raised as a Buchanan. Right now, though she bitterly regretted hurting Zachary Thomas, she had no alternative but to leave *– for the sake of her infant son!*

Mary left the cabin wearing the plain brown work dress she had left home in, despite the fact that it was still a little tight for her after the birth of her child. In the circumstances, she did not think it would be right to take any of Hedina's clothes or the fine oak chest she'd been given as a wedding present by Obediah Buchanan. Zachary Thomas had secured her two dresses for Jed from a couple of his brothers' wives the day after he was born. Her precious baby wore one now and was also tightly wrapped in Hedina's blue shawl. She did not think that Zachary Thomas would resent her for taking these two things for their son. As she left the cabin, she had the absurd thought that she had not washed the lunch dishes. What would happen after she was gone? Would chaos return to Eagle Spur? *Of course, it would!* The Buchanans had not been raised for it to be any different! Outside, the sheriff and his deputies were getting restless.

"Mary, you'd best hurry now," Sheriff Coley thundered, fingering one curled end of his handlebar mustache. "There is the very real danger that we will be fired upon by the rest of the clan. Let your brother hold the baby and we'll surround you both to protect you."

After Joe had taken the baby from her, the other deputies hustled around her and would have swept her away had she not glimpsed Zachary Thomas standing at the edge of the ridge with his back to them. He was such a picture of utter desolation, with sagging shoulders and bowed head, that she was suddenly assailed by the terrible thought that he would jump over the edge the moment they left.

"Hurry, child! The sooner we get off this goddamned mountain, the better!" Sheriff Coley thundered.

But Mary stood firm, so that a couple of the deputies almost collided with her. "Sheriff Coley, forgive me, but I need just a few minutes alone with my husband to say goodbye."

"D'you think that's wise? An angry man, especially a Bucko, is a dangerous animal. Call him over here and talk to him in front of me."

"*No!*" Mary was surprised at the vehemence in her voice. "Zachary Thomas would never hurt me, I know that." Even as she said the words, she wondered how she knew that so surely. Maybe it was because they had been through so much together.

The sheriff heaved an impatient sigh. "Don't give me that nonsense! You don't know nothing! You're just a lass! These Buchanans never forgive a slight, no matter how small! I've been after them for many years and suspect them of some mighty horrible deeds, but they stick together like molasses. They bushwhacked us on the way up and something tells me it ain't gonna be any easier on the way down – especially when they realize that we've got you and the baby in tow! Don't trust that Zack won't try to get his own back on you, girl! While I grant you that he's kept his nose a mite cleaner than the rest of 'em, bad blood shows up every time. He'll heave you over the edge in a trice! So if you're wise, girl, you'll quit tempting fate and wasting time, and come with us right this minute!"

"*No!* I've got to go talk to him!" Mary insisted. "I'll jest be a few minutes, is all."

The sheriff looked at her in bald agitation. "Well, I can't stop you, but if you find yourself sailing over the cliff, don't say that I didn't warn ya! Now, you've got yourself five minutes! If you don't come then, we're leaving without you!"

Mary raced across the ground on bare feet, approaching her husband cautiously from the rear. She stopped just behind him.

"Zachary Thomas," she said softly. He stiffened, but did not answer her, or turn around. "Zachary Thomas, I . . . I've come to say goodbye."

Still he said nothing. The huge man didn't move. Outlined against the backdrop of immense blue sky, he was as solid and unmoving as a rooted tree trunk. Oh, what terrible things must be going on inside of him! What terrible pain and

174

anguish must be besetting him? *He was losing his first-born son!*

"Zachary Thomas, look at me, please."

Slowly, he turned to look at her. His face was distraught and his usually piercing turquoise-green eyes were dull with soul-deep pain. It shook her rigid to see the depth of his suffering. "What d'you want me to say, Mary? After you've plotted aginst me to take away my son with th' doctor that I specially got brung up to tend to you!"

Mary swallowed hard. "I didn't plott. I jest told him my maiden name when he asked me, is all. I guess he realized who I was and went to tell th' sheriff. I'm so sorry. I know how bad it must hurt, Zackary Thomas, but I've got to leave. But I want your understandin' . . . and forgiveness."

"Then you ask too much!"

"Zachary Thomas, I cain't let my son . . . our son . . . be exposed to th' dangers of life on Claw Mountain."

"We kin protect him. A wimmin is supposed to stand by her man!"

"It seems to me I've stood by you right fine up till now. But I cain't let him grow up to become one of them . . ."

"What d'you mean?"

"I mean ignorant and moonshine-sodden and violent like yer kin, Zachary Thomas! I cain't stand moonshine and what it does to folk. What it does to *you*. When you drink so, you never talk! Even if you *don't* drink you don't talk much, either. I hate it and I cain't stand th' silences no more. I want to hear th' sound of folk chattin' and laughin' and singin' agin. There ain't no laughter on this here mountain, Zachary Thomas. Not real laughter, anyways. Not *happy* laughter! Only cruel laughter and cussin' and cryin'. And thar ain't no *religion* on this mountain neither, Zachary Thomas. I know thar ain't too many lay preachers up in th' mountains, but it's th' same for Lewis Mountain an' other mountains in th' Blue Ridge, yet other mountain folk got religion, Zachary Thomas. I never knew how important religion was to me till I came here and found none."

Zachary Thomas drew in a deep, shuddering breath. "I don't want you to go, Mary. Please stay."

"I cain't, Zachary Thomas. I'm sorry, but don't you see? I ain't got nuthin' to stay fer."

"I'll change. I'll do anythung you want."

"Mary!" yelled the sheriff behind them. "Mary! Come, girl! Come on, now!"

"I'm sorry, Zachary Thomas, I've got to go. Goodbye."

Tears began pouring freely down Zachary Thomas's face into his big, black beard, like after the time Jamie had been so cruelly flogged, as if the pain of it was unbearable. She felt a terrible wrench inside her, a desperate grieving. Ignoring the sheriff's terse command, she turned to look at the magnificent sweeping scene below, densely forested slopes, spring dressing them in the pale green cloak of new growth, laced with the pink and white blossoms of the dogwoods, the blue of the sky reflected in the river in the valley below. *Eagle Spur!* What a beautiful spot this was! She remembered the first time she had stood here like this with her husband on her wedding day – *a whole lifetime ago!* – and how entranced she had been by it then. *And was still!* Only she wasn't the girl that she had been back then. She'd been thrust unceremoniously into womanhood and would never again be the same person that she was once.

Despite the sheriff's continued exhortations for her to hurry, she so keenly felt Zachary Thomas's pain that she didn't want to leave him like this. She felt the overwhelming desire to put her arms around him to comfort him, but the chasm between them was much too great to bridge. Instead, she took his huge hand and gently squeezed it, fully knowing the cruelty of what she was about to do to this strange, unfathomable man.

"Zachary Thomas," she murmured. "I kin promise you one thung. Jed will know who his paw is – and that he is a *good* man."

$\mathbf{M}$ary, her baby, the sheriff and the party of deputies cautiously descended the steep, narrow path off the ridge between the giant granite boulders, scattering pebbles, and began to make their way down the mountain path beneath balsam firs hung with long strands of grandfather lichen draped over them, and red spruces, keeping a wary eye out for signs of the Buckos. Mary felt a moment of panic when she recognized two shots from her husband's old Kentucky rifle from high above them, as quickly as he could reload the muzzle-loader. It was clearly a signal of sorts. Would the clan attack them, force her to back to Eagle Spur with Jed? Would there be another massacre? Mary was trembling with fear. The thought that she had put everybody in danger like this, including her baby, was horrifying.

Then an entirely different sound came from up above. It was terrible – a long sustained roar – so full of anguish and pain, and of such power and magnitude, that it seemed to reverberate around the entire mountain. They stopped in their tracks and looked up see Zachary Thomas standing at the top of the ridge with his feet braced apart, his arms raised, his Kentucky rifle in one hand and his head thrown back in an attitude of supplication, while the roar that erupted from his throat seemed to come from the very depths of his soul. It was enough to spook the sternest spine. It was all that the sheriff needed to hurry everyone along.

As it turned out their catapulted passage down the steep mountain slopes went unimpeded, with nary a sign of any member of the incorrigible cracker clan that had effectively held her hostage for nine unbearably long months. In the foothills of the mountain, were horses belonging to the deputies and the sheriff's van.

When Mary at last climbed into the back of it to begin her long journey home to Lewis Mountain, she realized with a sense of gratitude that the shots her husband had fired, had, in fact, been a signal to his clan to leave them strictly alone ...

23

Sheriff Coley drove them to Lewis Mountain, taking logging trails up to the Elderberry Hope Logging Camp, where he would leave them to walk the rest of the way. He parked his black van outside the gates of the camp. Being a Sunday afternoon, nobody was working at the camp and it stood empty and silent, with denuded tree trunks stacked in mountainous piles, the smell of sawdust, oil and freshly cut timber in the air. The familiar sight of it gave her a spurt of joy. She was nearly home!

After alighting from the vehicle and thanking the sheriff, Mary and Joe, who was still holding the baby, watched him leave in his chugging van, which had battled valiantly up the steep potholed track that served for a road, before climbing the slopes to the 4-acre Harley tract through fields of bluegrass interspersed with beautiful hawthorn blossoms, trillium, mountain laurel and hepatica, which lazily rippled in a light playful breeze that was blowing. Turning to look down on the logging camp, she saw that none of the lumberjacks were around the long bunkhouse next to the mess hall, and there was only an occasional snort from a horse in the stables behind the camp. The lumberjacks were probably in town down the valley someplace, out for a good time, or sleeping off Saturday-night hangovers.

As they neared the family homestead, Mary felt a twinge of apprehension. Despite Joe's reassurances, what sort of reception could she expect from her parents when they had suffered such terrible torment over her?

There were fields of newly planted corn rows and cabbage patches. What a wonderful familiar sight the family cabin was, weathered and welcoming as a warm summer breeze. It brought instant tears to Mary's eyes. Her eyes roved fondly over the familiar tub of pink and white petunias on the porch, honeysuckle and pink wild roses climbing up the corner porch poles on either side, pink, violet, white and blue sweet peas trailing up some wire fencing nailed to one side of the cabin, while delicate pink and white blossoms starred the crab-apple tree that grew beside it, the spicy scent of which stung her nostrils with its sweetness.

As they approached the cabin, Joe, proudly holding his baby nephew, yelled a warning signal and the cabin door was flung open. Harleys spilled through it in a shrieking, joyful mass. Her mother and three sisters ran squealing down the hillside to meet them with their arms raised in jubilation, laughing and crying at the same time, while her father, with his bad leg, hobbled behind them as fast as he could manage. Her blonde-bunned, beautiful mother, with tears streaming down a face contorted with a mixture of agony and sheer joy, met Mary first. She swept her errant eldest daughter into her arms, swinging around and around with her.

"Oh Mary, Mary, child! Oh, Mary," she whispered over and over again. "Thank th' Lord, oh, thank th' Lord. I thought I'd never see you alive agin. We all thought you'd bin murdered by them awful Buckos!"

Then Mary's sisters with their bright-blue eyes and lovely smiles, golden hair flying, came and joined them, jumping up and down and shrieking and laughing. They gave her a big communal hug that was joined by her father. Then making everyone else give way, her father too, gathered Mary into his arms and hugged her tightly to him. His small stature meant that he wasn't much taller than her. When they parted, Mary saw that his warm brown eyes were full of tears and his dark curly hair was now streaked with gray. Since he had never had any gray in his hair when she last saw him, she guiltily surmised that it must have been from all the worry she had caused him.

Then they spotted Joe with the baby and they all crowded around him, cooing and laughing at the tiny little thing. Mary was sure that Doc Adams must have told Sheriff Colby that she'd had a baby and that he, in turn, must have advised her family accordingly, for none of them seemed in the least bit surprised that she'd brought one home.

"His name is Jed – Jediah Horatio . . . after you, Paw," Mary told them proudly. "His father's name is Zachary Thomas Buchanan. He ain't like th' other Buckos, at all. He . . . he is a *good* man."

Having been given such an unrestrained rapturous welcome, Mary's heart was full. She was so thankful and relieved to be home at long last.

* * *

Mary had been home for three months. Her initial joy at returning home had lately plunged into a lingering depression. Though her parents had taken the tale of her voluntary elopement and marriage to a Bucko with surprising equilibrium – no doubt softened by her safe return without any physical harm having been done to her and with a baby that they already all adored – nothing seemed the same for her anymore. It was a case of innocence lost and the rose-tinted glasses she had worn to view the world back in the good old carefree days, had been trampled underfoot. To her surprise, as she lay awake at night on her straw pallet, she would twirl the stem of her precious eagle feather slowly between her finger and thumb and think back on her life on Eagle Spur. She would find herself longing with all her heart for that wild, lonely place on the top of Claw Mountain with its soul-stirring, magnificent views.

The feather had gained an unprecedented importance for her now and she had taken to wearing it tied onto a leather thong around her neck, for not only did she credit it with bringing her back home to Lewis Mountain, it seemed like a strange, spiritual connection to that far-distant place. Sometimes, in deep into the night, when she woke from a sleep, she even fancied she could hear the giant eagles of Eagle Spur calling her back there. Their calling was heard deep inside her, a mystical thing of the heart and soul, rather than of the ears, but it seemed to fill all her senses and cause her to experience a desperate longing. And she had strange, vivid dreams of meeting a very tall powerfully built Indian. Around his neck he wore a large gold circle which rested on his sleekly muscled bare chest, but very little else. He was a handsome, regal fellow, with black eyes, reddish-bronze skin and feathers tied to a top-knot in his long black hair which he wore in a wide swath in the middle of the head, the sides of which had been shaved. He wore nothing but the skin of an otter at his girdle with the tail strung between his legs and a leather pouch on the right-hand side of his waist. Ornamented around the bottom with a leather fringe, with an eagle feather attached it, it was fastened to a belt made of well-dressed skin. Buckskin moccasins adorned his feet.

The two of them would stand together on the edge of the ridge looking down into the Wilderness Valley below. He never uttered a word, but it was as if they were able to communicate in a deep and profound way. Zachary Thomas had told her once that the tableland forest that she had never dared to enter, contained an Indian burial site, and she wondered if the eagles really did do the bidding of the restless spirits of those long-departed Indians as her husband had once caustically remarked. Mary was highly superstitious and the spirit world was very real to her as it was to most mountain folk.

When she awoke from these dreams, she would realize anew how those incomparable views from Eagle Spur had sustained her while she was there. Indeed, feeding on them had been her connection to God in that godless time, the wondrous spectacle of that untouched tree-shrouded valley below and the mountains beyond, her church. Though she would never have expected to, she also sorely missed having her own home, feeling as cramped and out-of-place in this bustling, noisy household as she had in the strained, silent one of her estranged husband. Listening to her sisters while they settled down to sleep up in the loft, she realized that despite the fact that she had missed them so dreadfully, they still managed to try her with their constant giggling and wild, inane chatter about boys. How ridiculously ironic that she should now long instead for the deep, awesome silences punctuated by eagle cries that surrounded Eagle Spur!

If she really wanted to be honest with herself, she missed Zachary Thomas too. Despite the agonizing nightmare of his heavy silences, he had a solid, comforting presence that she had got used to having around. Theirs could hardly have been called a marriage, for they had shared no marital intimacy, but it had been partnership of sorts. But she didn't like to think of her husband too often. It wrung something out of her that she didn't have to give right now. Mary was surprised at how much she missed that scrawny little spitfire, Emma, too, knowing how betrayed she must feel now that Mary had left the mountain for good without telling her or saying goodbye, as before, when she had tried to escape.

Mary tried to temper these longings with memories of Bucko atrocities and boorish behavior and banks of ten-foot high snow that had deafened the world and chilled to the bone for long, gloomy, terrifying months on end, but for some unknown reason it didn't stop the longing. Finally, though it pained her to admit it, she had to face the awful truth. She was dreadfully homesick for Eagle Spur! Claw Mountain, with its loneliness, its wild, pristine beauty and bewitching views, had succeeded in capturing her soul! How contrary life was. When she had lived on Claw Mountain, she had spent all her time longing for Lewis Mountain, which now seemed so tame and civilized in comparison.

Her only consolation in her present circumstances was her darling baby; she actually ached with the depths of her love for him. He was a happy, contented infant, placid and uncomplaining, who gurgled and cooed and played with anything anybody handed him, seeming totally unaffected by the many stresses and strains that had marked her pregnancy. Yet even her joy in her child was tempered with guilt at having denied Zachary Thomas his paternal right to share in it. She only hoped time would heal the devastation and tragic sense of loss she so unexpectedly felt inside.

24

Doc had no idea why Jediah Horatio Buchanan, that ugly little new-born babe he had so recently escorted into this world, had struck such a chord inside him at the end of that sparkling spring day in April, but right from the start he had fretted about his general well-being. In his time, Doc must have delivered close to a hundred babies, yet none had affected him quite like that of the Harley girl and her huge, hostile, hillbilly husband, Zack Buchanan. Maybe it had been the distressing circumstances surrounding his birth, what with the wild rumors of kidnapping or murder, and the thought of the innocent little child being forced to grow up in such a lawless environment. Not least of all, his own desperate bid to reach the inaccessible spot just in time to catch him and cut the umbilical cord, had no doubt sparked this unprecedented interest in the child he had delivered – if "delivered" it could be called, since he'd had such little work to do. But as time went by, Doc knew it was more than that. It had been through his own direct intervention in the matter that Mary Harley Buchanan and that same baby had been rescued from a life of hell on Claw Mountain and, as a result, the child now had a decent chance in life. Thus he felt *responsible* for him in a way! He resolved to make time to visit the Harley homestead sometime soon to check on him.

It was a full three months after Jed's birth before Doc finally got the chance to visit his small charge at the Harley cabin on Lewis Mountain in the next county. He drove there in his horse and buggy, taking the logging trails up to the Hope Logging Camp, before hoofing the rest of the way up by foot, carrying his trusty black medical bag to the Harley tract. Summer heat had turned the valley below blue with haze and Indian pipe, blue-weed, rhododendron, thimbleberry and wood lilies pleased the eye as he puffed and panted up to the cabin.

Mary herself opened the door to his sharp rap, her mouth dropping open with surprise before her face brightened when she saw who it was. With her blue skirt brushing her bare calves, the tall barefoot girl's face was olive-skinned, with calm brown eyes and black hair parted down the middle and scraped back in a bun, from which a few thick strands of hair had escaped. She had a dignity about her that he hadn't noticed in her after the childbirth, but right now, she looked a little weary and disheveled with the heat. She welcomed him inside her parent's home with a tired smile.

"Why, Doc Adams, what a wonderful surprise! I am right pleasured to see you. I sure never figger'd on it. C'mon in and take seat." She ushered Doc over to the table, where he sat down on a wooden chair. "I'm afraid Paw has taken two of th' girls to th' store and Maw's gone to th' Franklin cabin. Irma Franklin ain't feelin' too good and Maw's gone to help with her chores. Joe's busy in th' fields and Lona is collectin' eggs. So thar's only me to entertain you till they all come back. Gee, Doc Adams, you sure look plum tuckered out to me. Would you care for some lemonade so as to recover from th' climb? Perhaps some whiskey?"

As a sensible concession to his ulcer and the early time of afternoon, Doc reluctantly refused the whiskey. Instead, he accepted her subsequent offer of some cold milk and a slice of corn bread. He sat on one of the hard wooden chairs

in the main room of the four-room cabin, while Mary went to fetch some milk from the springhouse. He glanced idly around the room. The cabin was basic and simply-furnished with solid home-hewn wooden furniture, the yellow poplar floor spread with a worn, but colorful rug and the walls hung with a few pictures of flowers and mountain scenes.

As in most mountain homes, the walls were fashioned from chestnut logs and chinked with mud to guard against the winter cold. There were still bits of newspaper stuck to them as added insurance against the bitter weather. Besides the fact that they had just passed through the most severe winter ever experienced in the Blue Ridge, Doc was aware that it routinely snowed waist-deep up here during normal winter months and that papering the walls was a common method of achieving added insulation.

The smell of wood smoke was stringent in the air and his eyes stung a little. A wooden ladder led up to the straw-covered loft above his head and the chimney above the massive fireplace was made of flattish rocks piled dry one upon the other. A big black pot bubbled with some delicious-smelling fare on the wood-fire stove. He sniffed the air appreciatively. He had no doubt that before his departure he would be invited to sup with the Harleys. And he had no doubt that he would agree to do so, despite his good intentions not to overstay his welcome. He sniffed, peeved at the way that his mind inevitably returned to his stomach.

A short while later, after Mary came back inside and he had taken his mild refreshments, Doc made discreet enquiries into Mary's health and into that of her baby.

"Come," said Mary. "It's time for him to wake up from his nap."

Mary stood up and ushered Doc shyly into a small adjoining storage room, the gleam of pride in her eyes telling him how anxious she was to show him her precious babe. This tiny, narrow room contained only a plain wooden crib, a few odd boxes and an old tailor's dummy. Wearing a light, sleeveless, cotton dress, the baby, Jed, was lying quietly in the crib, sucking on one curled fist. And staring down at him, Doc was amazed at the transformation in the child. His unlovely newborn appearance had been magically transformed. The ruddy complexion was now a healthy pale brown. His initial baldness was replaced by a wild little mop of brown hair. Why, he was a *beautiful* child by any standards!

When he saw Doc, Jed's little legs moved rigorously with excitement, lifting his plain cotton dress to his waist, and he crooned softly. Doc saw that the cloth-diapered babe was completely devoid of fat. And as Doc moved towards him with his stethoscope, the babe even gave him a small winsome smile, dimpling a tiny cheek. And it was right then that the little thing irrevocably captured his heart!

Though it was probably caused by wind, Doc couldn't help but be delighted by this special tribute. All other babies seemed to do was scream when they saw him and his stethoscope. And then as Doc prodded and poked his little body, Jed gurgled and cooed all the while. But what struck Doc the most was that he seemed to have an unusual awareness of his surroundings. His eyes, lacking the placid vagueness of most infants, moved with uncommon alertness for one so young. They would follow every tiny sound, every slight movement, even catching on the motes of dust carried on a ray of sunlight that streamed into the room and, in the brilliance of their blue, Doc thought he discerned some innate intelligence . . .

25

"Mary, I've got a real dandy surprise fer you." Her mother stood at the opened doorway, smiling fit to bursting, her bright-blue eyes shining with anticipation.

"What is it, Maw?"

"We've planned a little shindig to celebrate yer safe homecomin' come Saturday night!"

Mary stared at her lovely blonde-haired mother in dismay. She knew all about Maw's "little shindigs". That was the very last thing she wanted – a whole load of prying friends and kin asking her about Claw Mountain and the Buckos! She groaned and shook her head fiercely, "Oh, please, no, Maw, I don't want no shindig!"

"Sure you do, darlin'. You've bin mighty full of th' miseries of late. It's all arranged. Everybody's a'comin'. Hit'll be jest like old times."

"But Maw . . ."

Mary might have known it was no good arguing with her mother. Whenever there was a slightest cause for celebration, she and her father would throw a shindig. That was the mountain way. Weddings, funerals, birthdays, infant-sprinkling ceremonies, corn huskings, apple-butter boilings, you name it, mountain folk from miles around would gather and dance and drink the night away. And this time, her parents had planned one to celebrate the safe return of their eldest daughter who had been rescued from the jaws of the hell that was Claw Mountain, so what hope did she have to avoid it?

All week was spent preparing. The barn was cleared out and laid with fresh

straw, bales of hay had been brought in, and Maw and Mary had been busy cooking and baking up a storm. There were mountains of corn loaves, persimmons,
pumpkin and Indian puddings, fried peach, goose-berry, elderberry and vinegar
pies, apple dumplings and buckwheat cakes, sourdough pancakes and currant
buns, fried chicken and sausage and hush puppies. There was also a huge cake
covered in honey-bee icing. The guests would all be contributing too, of course,
as was the custom. It would be a grand feast!

Whenever a shindig was planned, there was always an atmosphere of
excitement in the Harley household and, this time, was no exception. Mary's
sisters were beside themselves because there would be boys from other hollows to
ogle, and flirt and dance with – it was all they chatted about. It irritated Mary that
they didn't deign to help with the food preparation – even if they did help look
after Jed and half-heartedly tended to the other chores. However, caught up in the
familiar hustle and bustle, even Mary, who was dreading the occasion, felt the
odd flare of excitement when nostalgia came into play. There had been no good
clean fun at Claw Mountain, after all. Her wedding celebration had been more
like a barroom brawl than a party!

* * *

W hen Saturday finally dawned, Mary was feeling wary and tense, but she had
decided that she was going to pretend to enjoy herself so her mother would cease
to worry about her. Grandpaw and Grandmaw Meadows were the first to arrive
on Saturday afternoon, Grandpaw armed with his fiddle, banjo and har-monica,
Grandmaw with one of her delicious cherry cobbler pies, her long clay pipe and
the wad of chewing tobacco in the pouch of her wrinkled cheek. They made a big
fuss of Mary and said how happy they were to see her. Grandmaw kept looking at
her with those shrewd faded blue eyes of hers, as if she was dying to say
something more, but Maw's bright-blue ones warned her off each time. Her
grandparents would be sleeping in the cabin after the party, on her parent's
double pallet, while most other folk, would just doss down in the barn.

The other guests began arriving towards evening, carrying kerosene lanterns,
guitars, a Jew's harp and more banjos and fiddles, as well as some plates of
pastries, cakes or pots containing steaming vittles. The men and boys, at her
mother's insistence, dutifully shed their weapons in the storeroom in the cabin – a
wise decree when there was 100-proof hooch around! – before heading towards
the barn with their moonshine jugs. More and more guests arrived, till it seemed
that the whole of Lewis Mountain was here at Harley Hollow! As the guest of
honor, so to speak, Mary had been instructed to greet the guests as they arrived.
Though everybody gathered her in their arms and soundly kissed and hugged her,

nary a word was mentioned about her elopement or what she had experienced on Claw Mountain.

Considering their love of good gossip, Mary knew her mother had somehow spread the word that nobody was to broach the subject with her. Since this had been her main concern, she began to relax a little. Before too long she went into the barn lit up with many kerosene lanterns as the fiddles began sawing and the banjos playing and the square dancing commenced. Soon, everybody was grabbing partners and quick-shoeing, tapping and stomping to numbers like "Turkey in the Straw", "Flop-eared Mule", "Pull Your Shades Down, Mary-Ann", "Hush Me, Baby" and "Golden Slippers". Grandpaw Meadows and Earnest Clancy were the fiddlers, while banjoes were being energetically plucked by Hedley Scuttle and Sam Yates, these elderly fellas being a familiar foursome at communal gatherings. Those not dancing stood around the sides and clapped and joined in the singing. Some old folk sat on chairs or hay bales, smoking pipes and tapping their feet in time to the music, while the children played or joined in the dancing too.

Soon, different musicians joined the main foursome, some playing guitars, others, banjos or fiddles, and one, his Jew's harp, all with such naturalness and precision, it was as if each number had been practiced a hundred times before instead of them just joining in spontaneously. Grandpaw Meadows also played his harmonica intermittently and did most of the singing, but others sang randomly too, or sang duets with him. Mountain people, with their fun-loving natures, loved their music and never had it been clearer to Mary than on this sparkling summer night. As the strains of familiar songs like "Carry Me Back to Old Virginny" "Shortnin' Bread", "Down Yonder" and "Ragtime Annie" met her ears, the medley caused a curious ache inside her. She felt warmth and a love of her mountain people with their honest, generous and hard-working ways that filled her senses. How proud she was to be one of them.

Even Paw with his bad leg joined in the dancing. In the early stages, he and Joe made sure Mary was no wallflower, while her sisters danced every dance with a different boy, gold ringlets flying. Mary, wearing her blue best dress, danced dutifully, stomping away with her bare feet and a fixed smile on her face, as if the nine months she'd spent on Claw Mountain had never happened. Only they had and they kept intruding on her thoughts, as the shindig gathered in intensity. It got so boisterous sometimes, the young fellas, barefoot and already high on hooch, were jumping high as a tall man's waist, with rip-roaring yells. And after a while, every uncle and male cousin she owned came to claim a dance from her.

She knew it was their way of saying that they loved her, and that despite her bad behavior, they had forgiven her the terrible worry she had caused her family. These were her people and she had known them her whole life, yet as the night wore on, loving kin and close friends suddenly began to seem like strangers to her. It was as if she was mentally drawing away from them and, as she did so, they were becoming less and less familiar to her. It was a strange unnerving sensation. She wondered why that was and why she was feeling so oddly removed from them.

It was during the playing of the lustily sung "Little Brown Jug" that Wiley Holbrook suddenly appeared in front of Mary and asked her to dance. Mary felt a stab of annoyance. *How could Maw have invited him!* And where had he been hiding all this time? Surely he hadn't just arrived? She was about to refuse then hesitated. A refusal would seem so pointed and rude when she hadn't refused a single dance up till now. He stood there so forlornly, middle-aged and melancholy, his face hangdog, his big nose red as a ripe plum, brown eyes mournful as a bloodhound's beneath mousy thinning hair, as if half-expecting her to say no. She guessed it was hardly surprising considering how rude she'd been to him in the past, and suddenly, she felt terribly sorry for the man even as he snorted and wiped a hand across his runny nose. She dipped her head in consent, wanting to gag, but trying not to seem too repelled, and his face immediately brightened. He drew her into the center of the dance space and they square-danced without speaking or touching, while the dancers all around them made merry, the ladies, lifting their skirts, and the men, foot-stomping up a storm, both "yee-haaing" and flying their elbows, in time to the raucous tunes. Mary danced without much animation, staring off at the other dancers, not daring to look at Wiley in case he gained some slight encouragement.

However, she was soon to bitterly regret her small concession, because thereafter, Wiley planted himself squarely at her side. He fetched and carried homemade lemonade for her and kept coming back from the overloaded trestle table for the eats with odd tidbits on a plate for her to try. And suddenly, nobody asked her to dance anymore, as if this was an outcome they had all planned, for everybody kept sneaking sidelong glances at them. Mary was furious. *She was a married woman with a tiny baby!* Had they all forgotten that? And for anyone to think they could possibly ease her doldrums with *Wiley Holbrook,* for heaven's sake! He was half the reason she had left the mountain in the first place!

Though Wiley kept asking her to dance with him again, she refused, pleading weariness, but this didn't seem to dampen his spirits a wit. He stood at her side positively beaming as if he were the owner of the finest rooster on the mountain. To make matters worse, the music had calmed down considerably. Now there were ballads and love songs being plaintively played and sung, and couples cuddled up. Then Maw got in on the act plucking the fretted fingerboard of her flat-laid dulcimer with a goose quill and singing with her soft, pure voice, "Don't give your heart to a rambler, little girl".

Mary couldn't help thinking she was trying to tell her something by her choice of song. (Like give her heart instead to a dull, boring oaf like *Wiley Holbrook!*)

Nevertheless, her mother looked so beautiful in the lantern-light with her blonde hair swept up in a loose bun and a look of sweet ardor on her face it was as if she really felt the pain of the lost love of the lyrics as she sang "Bring Back My Blue-Eyed Boy to Me". Normally, Mary would have enjoyed listening to these melodious mountain ballads, but since she had the awful feeling that they were being aimed especially at her and Wiley, she felt humiliated tears smart her eyes. *She had to find some excuse to get out of here!*

Finally, in desperation, she stammered to the idiotically grinning, hog-reeking fellow at her side, "I've got to go feed my baby," before fleeing from the barn, though in truth Jed had already been nursed and put down and she had checked on him a couple of times since. Entering the cabin, Mary climbed swiftly up the ladder to the crowded loft and sat on the pallet next to Jed's crib, cross-legged and miserable, before laying down her head and crying herself to a light sleep that was interrupted by the sounds of the hellbent hilarity and merriment throughout the long night . . .

The next morning, feeling horribly guilty for opting out of a party thrown especially for her, Mary helped her mother and several of the lady guests with the late communal breakfast, hiding her desolation and heartache behind as bright a smile as she could manage. To cover her sudden disappearance from the party the night before, she had told her mother she had fallen asleep while checking on Jed, but Maw's all-knowing eyes were full of concern as she served bacon, eggs, buckwheat cakes and pancakes to countless mountain men nursing massive hangovers and their smilingly complaining wives, before serving the young'uns.

The breakfast was served in the barn, which was still littered with innumerable passed-out bodies. (Thankfully, Wiley was nowhere to be seen!) Many would only leave in the late afternoon to return to their own homesites. Grandpaw Meadows spoke for them all when he and Grandmaw left, Grandpaw, carrying his musical instruments, and Grandmaw, piles of tasty leftovers, when he told his devoted daughter, "Why, Ellie Harley, it were th' best darned shindig I've bin at fer a long, long time …"

Three days later, her mother cryptically informed Mary in the kitchen that she had a "caller". Mary gave a huge sigh. It was probably another lost-lost cousin, since several of them had called on her since her return to Lewis Mountain, no doubt hoping to get the lowdown on what had happened to her on Claw Mountain. She went reluctantly into the living room and immediately was plunged into panic, her relief at not seeing Wiley Holbrook the morning after the shindig, shattered. For standing in front of the fireplace was the dadblamed man himself. Even dressed in his best Sunday clothing, he presented a sorry sight, hat in hand and thinning mousy-brown hair standing on end.

"Hello, Mary," he said when he saw her, looking at her eagerly, like a devoted puppy. He was the *last* person she had expected to see and she was angry at her mother for not telling her who it was so she could have made some excuse to avoid seeing him. As it was, she was trapped by politeness.

"Hello, Wiley," she said without enthusiasm, as she sank in the furthest chair from him. "What brungs you here?"

Wiley cleared his throat. "Why, *you* do, my dear."

"I cain't thunk why!" she snapped, suddenly furious about being put on the spot like this. "Surely you know it ain't seemly to call on married ladies?"

"Oh, I thunk ye'll change yer mind soon enough, once you hear me out," he said staunchly.

"What do you mean?" she asked warily.

"I mean, I'm here to solve all yer problems!"

Mary stared at him in bald astonishment. "All *what* problems?"

He frowned. "I mean all the . . . er . . . talk you have bin subjected to since yer return from Claw Mountain, of course."

Mary felt her face blushing to the roots of her hair and she tightened her fists so hard that her fingernails dug into her palms. So there had been talk that Maw had somehow managed to keep from her. But she wasn't going to allow him to get away with such tactlessness.

"All *what* talk?" she asked pointedly.

Wiley looked perplexed and scratched at his head, off-loading a shower of dandruff onto his one shoulder. "Well . . . er . . . well, you know . . . that . . . uh . . . unfortunate business with . . . that . . . that . . . *lowdown Bucko critter.*"

He said the last words with such disgust in his voice that Mary was left in no doubt about how much he wanted to insult her husband. Mary felt herself go cold with mortification.

"*That lowdown Bucko critter* jest happens to be my wedded husband *and* th' father of my young'un!" she said scathingly. "And I'll thank you not to refer to him as sech!"

"Yeah, well, I apologize fer that, dear child, but thar ain't no need to defend him no more fer I'm here to tell you, you kin put all that behind you now. I am fully prepared, despite all th' scandal, to wed you once you and he are divorced. As you know, I've been mighty lonely since Blanche departed this world and I've got a mean passel of hogs to offer you. Largest herd on Lewis Mountain, in fact," he said importantly, hitching up his pants with his thumbs. "You'd be hard-pressed to find a better deal than that in yer unfortunate circumstances."

Mary stared at the man, utterly flabbergasted by his words. It took her a moment to recover her wits.

"And what makes you think I'd want to marry you even if I were divorced?" she asked in such an even voice, she felt outside of herself. She reminded herself of her mother, even though she wanted to explode with outrage.

Now it was Wiley's turn to look flabbergasted. "You mean? I don't thunk you fully understand th' situation, girl! Thar won't be many men willin' to take you on after what you done, or take on another man's young'un fer that matter, but hit jest so happens I've bin real sweet on you fer a long while now, so I'm even prepared to put up with th' young'un to make you my bride."

"*Put up with . . . ?*" Mary stood up, and with as much dignity as she could muster, said coldly, "Wiley Holbrook, even if thar be naught willin' to take me or my young'un on, as you say, I wouldn't marry you even if'n you were th' last man left in th' Blue Ridge. Now please leave me be and be on yer way. And be sure not to come back here neither, y'hear, else I'll send you packin' with Paw's rifle m'self!"

By the aghast look on his sagging face, it was clear that Wiley knew how massively he had blundered, for he spluttered, "But . . . but . . . I didn't mean it that way . . . I . . . Mary, my dear, I am yer devoted servant, yer . . . "

"Wiley Holbrook, if'n you don't leave right this minute, I'll go fetch Paw's rifle right now and *blow you clean in half!*" she said scathingly, narrowing her eyes into slits (blatantly borrowing some of Emma's tough tactics, even though she didn't even know how to shoot a darned rifle!). She pointed her finger at the door and the mean look on her face must have done it, for Wiley Holbrook suddenly skedaddled to the door like a raccoon with a hunting hound after it. He flung open the door, turned and yelled back, "Seems I totally misjudged you, girl! I thought you had class and manners! Now I see that that thar mountain has bewitched you and changed you into a vicious harlot!"

"Yeah, well, you might jest consider tryin' to improve yer *own* manners, Wiley Holbrook! Sech as usin' a handkerchief from time to time!" she yelled after him in a rare fit of temper.

Mary met her horrified mother at the kitchen door, and balked. Her mother did not take kindly to her offspring arguing or being rude to company. She looked stern and her deliberately even tone, which had always been as effective as any switch, told Mary how miffed she was. "Mary, what he said was unforgivable, but you ought to know better than to threaten to shoot a man, especially considering why he was here in th' first place! It sure ain't like you to be so rude! I surely did not raise you to . . ."

Mary was in no mood to have her behavior questioned, especially after the way *he* had behaved, but Maw had always had the power to make one feel they'd committed the worst crime on earth, no matter how minor the deed, or legitimate the motivation.

"Oh, Maw, I'm right sorry, but I couldn't *help* it! He was downright insultin' and what's more, *you* put him up to this!"

Her beautiful mother had the grace to look a trifle sheepish.

"*Why*, Maw?" Mary groaned. "He's th' last man on earth I'd turn to, don't you know that by now? *I cain't stand him!* Did you smell him? He smells of hogs, Maw! *Hogs that have bin wallowin' in a heap of shit!* I swar he must sleep with them precious hogs of his!"

"Well, I admit he may not be as swashbucklin' a fella as yer Bucko, that I don't know, but he's a good decent man, if you'd jest look past his . . . physical . . ."

"*Maw, you cain't be serious!*"

Her mother looked at her with pleading. "I realize now that it was much too soon to encourage him, but Mary, honey, you really do need to close that chapter of yer life and look to th' future. And you could do a lot worse than Wiley. He may not be young and handsome as ye'd like, but one thung fer sure, he's far better than any Bucko could ever be!"

Mary eyed her mother, aghast. "*No!* Ye're wrong about that, Maw. I couldn't *possibly* do any worse than Wiley Holbrook! And Maw, thar be one thung you kin be real sure on – whatever my future may hold, he ain't *never* gonna be a part of it. Now, please leave me be."

Mary pushed past her mother and out of the back door. She ran out into the yard, past the clothes fluttering on the wash line, fleeing her childhood home as fast as her legs could carry her. She went up towards the top of the mountain and, when she reached there, she turned and sank down onto the ground amongst the lush bluegrass and wept bitterly into her hands, feeling a tumult of emotion inside her. Was Wiley right? Had Claw Mountain had such a bad effect on her that she had actually threatened violence on another human being for the first time in her life?

Then she remembered what he had said and she rather wished she'd actually carried out the threat. Calling Zachary Thomas a *critter* as if he had no worth and her baby as if her precious darling had no worth either! She stayed on the top of the mountain a long time, absently fingering the eagle feather around her neck, as had become her habit of late, while she gazed out across the magnificent valley stretched out in front of her in a haze of purple and blue. Normally, taking in such a view would have filled her with joy and serenity and peace. Today, however, despite how long she let her eyes rove over the splendor, she still felt anger and turbulence inside her. It sickened her that her mother actually felt that a sniveling little worm like Wiley Holbrook was more worthy than Zachary Thomas. Well, her husband might well be a Bucko, but at least, for all his faults, he was strong and handsome and dependable – and he sure as heck didn't reek of hogs! But much as she hated to admit it, Maw was right about one thing. She had to stop thinking about Claw Mountain else she'd go clean mad!

26

Mary's melancholy continued unabated. As much as she tried to hide it from her family, she couldn't fool her maw, who called her aside one day.

"Mary, what's eatin' at you so, girl? I figger'd you'd tell me in yer own good time, but it sure don't look like that will be anytime soon. Now I know you've jest had a baby and that sometimes sets a wimmin to moonin', but I reckon it's much more than that that's got you so blue."

"I'm fine, Maw," Mary lied.

Her mother pulled her down onto a chair at the table and sat down on a chair beside her. Taking Mary's hand in hers, she said softly, "Mary, honey, this is yer maw ye're talkin' to. What happened back thar on Claw Mountain? It'll make you feel better to talk about it, you'll see."

Mary stared into the bright-blue eyes of her lovely blonde-haired mother that were clouded with concern and tried to deny that anything at all had happened on Claw Mountain, but found she could not. What had happened there had not only changed her whole life, after all, but had changed her, *as a person.* And suddenly, it all came tumbling out in a rush.

"Aw, Maw, it was awful . . ."

She started off by telling her mother all about the clan and how drunken and loud and mean they were. About how they indulged in moonshine all day long, and were slovenly and dirty, and how target practice took precedence over everything else for them. That the only one of the clan she had befriended was young Emma. She told her mother how tough the past winter had been. Then almost without conscious volition – for she didn't want her mother to fret over what she'd been through – she found herself telling her mother about the bloody massacre between the Buchanans and the Galtreys, and the double funeral she had attended as a result of it. She could see how much this revelation disturbed her mother, but she was unable to stop herself, as if she was being swept along by some flash flood she could not resist. She gushed on about how it had all started when Eli and Jake had drowned young Jamie Galtrey at Devil's Creek, and how Eli had split the boy's throat, even after he was already dead, the terrible words pouring out of her mouth like bitter bile. She simply had no control over them. It was if there was something separate inside her was seeking to purge her of the nightmare she had lived through on Claw Mountain. She could see the expressions of horror and disbelief descending on her mother's face, her hand flying to her slender throat in shock.

"Oh, Mary, I don't believe what I am hearin'! Poor, poor little thing," she groaned. "You've got to tell th' sheriff, Mary! They cain't be allowed to git away with sech a wicked crime!"

"That's jest it, Maw! *I cain't,*" said Mary miserably.

"Why not?"

"'Cuz it were *Emma* who saw it, Maw, and she won't rat on the clan, that's fer sure. She's sore a'feared of Eli! A'feared he'll harm her if'n he finds out she witnessed th' whole thung. One time, Obediah Buchanan – he's their paw – flogged his youngest son, Jamie, who's only fifteen, so bad, he almost died, fer hardly no reason at all. He gave him twenty-five brutal lashes with this here horrible short steel-tipped three-pronged floggin' whip! Jamie's so thin, he's all ribs and skin and, what's more, he ain't right in th' head, Maw. His back was . . . raw as a piece of meat. " Tears sprang to her eyes and her mouth quivered as the horrific memory of it flooded back. "It were sech a bloody mess, you could see rib-bone even! I was right thar, Maw! That fiend, Obediah, showed Jamie no mercy even after he'd long pass'd out!"

Mary was about to tell her mother how she had been forced to watch the whole ghastly spectacle while tied by a rope to the porch rail, when she was still with child, but thought she'd better spare her that much at least. She stopped herself with an effort, her face puckering up with crying.

"Oh, my poor darlin', what dreadful thungs you've bin thru'," said her mother soothingly, tenderly brushing a strand of hair off Mary's face, before taking her in her comforting arms, squeezing her hard as Mary shuddered with great uncontrollable sobs. "Why do you think them Buckos are so hated and a'feared amongst decent mountain folk? Do you even wonder that we thunk'd you'd bin murdered by them, too, after you stood up to Eli Buchanan at th' store that day? The sheriff told us he suspects they've bin involved in plenty sech killin's over th' years. Them's real bad folk, honey. *Evil!* But you knew that a'fore you left so no one believed you'd willin'ly go gittin' involved with th' likes of one of 'em. How did that happen, honey? Tell your maw all about it."

She released Mary and stared at her expectantly. Mary swallowed hard, tears streaming down her face, wondering how much she could admit to her mother without being an added burden to her. Certainly, she couldn't tell her how Eli had tried to rape her, or how Zachary Thomas had forced her to marry him and had raped her that first night. Or even about the dreadful state of his cabin when she got there. For some reason, she didn't want her mother to think badly of her husband, even though he *had* been guilty of forcing her to do something against her will, and tended to downright slovenliness.

"Maw," she began at last, "how did you feel about Paw when you first met him?"

Her mother drew back in surprise. "Well, I first saw him at an apple-butter boilin' at yer Aunt Trudy's place. We were hardly more than young'uns then and I didn't thunk too much about him one way or 'nother. But after that, he seemed to be plum everywhar I went. He was always tryin' to git me to notice him too – foolin' around and showin' off. He made me laugh at th' funny stories he told. I guess I grew into lovin' him as I got to know him."

"Oh dear, then you ain't gonna understand what I'm about tell you, Maw. When I first saw Zachary Thomas, it was as if I'd bin struck by a bullet in the heart! We looked at each other and neither of us could look away. It were powerful, Maw, *real powerful.* I ain't thunked about nobody but him for th' next two days and then, all of a sudden, he was standin' in th' doorway of th' barn, tellin' me that he felt exactly th' same way and that he wanted to marry me. Now I know how crazy that sounds, Maw, but I thunked about that *awful* Wiley Holbrook, and . . . well, I *wanted* to go with Zachary Thomas more than anythung in th' whole world. I was so smote by him that I allowed my heart to rule my head. Anyway, Maw, it was a frightful mistake. We . . . we ain't suited."

"Tell me about yer husband . . . this Zachary Thomas?"

"Aw, Maw," Mary said despairingly. "I don't know what to tell you about him. At first, I hated him somethung fierce."

Maw's brow furrowed in puzzlement. "But I thunked you jest said it were love at first sight, honey."

Mary started at her slip. "Well, it were, but then . . . well, th' very next day, th' day of the weddin', I woke up and decided I'd made a horrible mistake and wanted to go back home."

"Well, why didn't you?"

"Well, it ain't easy to leave Claw Mountain, Maw, if'n a Bucko wants you to stay."

"You mean he *did* force you to marry him and stay aginst yer will?"

"Yes . . . no . . . I mean, he said it were jest weddin' jitters, is all, and he got th' preacher to marry us anyways. I was real mad about it at first, but later . . . well, this past winter was so wicked and we were thrown together so much . . . I know this sounds real strange after what I done told you about th' clan, but Zachary Thomas ain't a bad man, Maw. He ain't like th' others. He's a real hard worker too. Trouble is, he's a real quiet sort. Don't say much at all. Fact is, his silences were a real strain on my nerves, Maw, and that's why I couldn't stay no longer. It were terrible livin' with them. It made me yearn fer home like nuthin' else."

193

"Do you love him, Mary?"

"No . . . no, of course not!" Mary said quickly, blinking her eyes rapidly in disconcertion. "That love-at-first-sight stuff wore off real quick once I realized what I had done. And he don't love me neither. I thunk he needed a housekeeper more than a wife. But I did grow to respect him, Maw. And even tho' he only knew his son fer a few days, I know he loves Jed somethung fierce." Even as she said the words, the truth in them caused a curious ache in her heart. "He didn't leave th' cabin fer two whole days after he was born. And he had all these big plans fer him too, like teachin' him to hunt and shoot and fish. All th' thungs most paws do with their sons."

"Poor man," sighed Maw sympathetically. "It must have been real hard on him . . . yer leavin', I mean."

"Reckon it clean tore his heart out."

Her mother studied her with shrewd, canny blue eyes before she spoke again. "That's what's a'gittin' to you, girl, ain't it? Ye're feelin' real guilty about takin' his young'un away from him? Well, honey, you stop thar right this minute. Zachary Thomas may be a mite better than th' rest of them, but he's still a Bucko! You did th' right thung by gittin' your baby away from that evil place. You'll git over it in time, honey. All you got to do is remember it were fer th' best."

Mary gave a weary acknowledging sigh. "I guess."

* * *

Ten days after Doc Adams' unexpected visit, Mary was breast-feeding her baby while sitting on a chair in the small storage room where the crib was, when she heard a faint knock on the front door of the cabin and soft voices. A few minutes later, there was a hesitant knock on the storage-room door, before her mother came in and closed the door behind her. There was a worried expression on her lovely face and her bright-blue eyes were stricken with alarm. "What is it, Maw? Not that Wiley agin. I swar . . ."

"Oh Mary, it ain't Wiley. It's *Zachary Thomas* . . ." She lapsed into silence, clearly unable to continue.

Mary felt a surge of shock. *Something terrible had happened to him, she just knew it!* He must have taken his own life like she had feared he would. She remembered his anguished roar as they left Claw Mountain and felt a moment of raw panic and guilt. He had killed himself because he could not bear to be parted from his infant son. She was responsible for a man's death! *Her son's paw's! Her husband's!* Obviously the sheriff had come by to let her know. She could hardly bear to have her thoughts confirmed.

194

"What is it, Maw?" she said finally, feeling scarcely able to breathe. *"Is he dead?"*

Maw shook her head vehemently. "No. He's *here* and he wants to talk to you!"

Relief and alarm rose up inside of Mary all at once. *Thank God!* She let out her breath, feeling herself begin to shake. She quickly withdrew her swollen nipple from her suckling infant's mouth and tucked her breast back inside her bibbed shift, pulling her under blouse down then she hastily stood up and put Jed back in his crib.

"What if he has come to fetch Jed?" she said worriedly. "Oh, Lord, Maw, did he say he's come to fetch th' young'un?"

"No. He jest said that he needs to talk to you."

Never in her wildest dreams had Mary anticipated this. And how foolish of her not to have! Did she really think she could walk away from the Buckos' domain with one of their kin so easily? After her revelations to her mother, the dangers of Claw Mountain seemed to cling to her like a burr on the hindquarters of a mule. She stood up and creased down her apron and skirts with her spread hands, before patting her hair and drawing in a deep breath.

She said in a low, urgent voice "Maw, please stay and watch Jed. Listen at th' door and if'n you hear me say *'Zack Buchanan'* real loud then take Jed and escape with him thru' th' winder. That's th' signal, see? Will you do that fer me, Maw? Please! I cain't risk losin' my young'un!"

"Of course I will, honey. Now you go, quickly. I'll listen at th' door."

Maw pushed her through the door and Mary went into the other room, filled with trepidation. Her gaze fell upon her husband who was standing in front of the fireplace, exactly where Wiley Holbrook had stood so recently. But Wiley Holbrook's sorry countenance was a far cry from the huge, well-built figure that stood before her now. Zachary Thomas had shaved off his beard and wore the same big black mustache that he had when they had first met. Both the mustache and his hair were freshly greased and he was dressed in gray trousers and a clean white shirt. On his head he wore a gray fedora, with a single brown-and-white hawk feather in the hat-band, which he removed as soon as he saw her. Except for their wedding day and the day of the funeral, she had never seen him look so handsome and spruce and it had a profound effect on her. Her heart began a fearsome pounding. Their eyes met and riveted. Her mouth fell open, as she felt renewal of the intense attraction for him that she had experienced that first day that had been the root cause of all her troubles. She wrenched her eyes from his with an effort and murmured, "Zachary Thomas."

"Hello, Mary," he replied softly.

The silence stretched between them like taut elastic.

"I . . . I believe you wish to talk to me," said Mary.

"Yeah, I sure do, but not in here. Let's go fer a walk outside whar nobody kin hear us."

Mary gave a quick, nervous glance at the closed door behind which was her precious baby. Why had her husband come? He sounded nice and sincere, but was it a ruse to get her away from the house, so his brothers could sneak up and snatch the infant away? But according to the sheriff, he could take Jed away anytime he wanted. Well, that may be true, but it wasn't the Bucko way of doing things, so they'd likely snatch him away, anyway, and would never let her see him ever again! Mary was in a quandary of indecision.

"Please, Mary, thar be some things I've gotta say to you."

Despite her strong reservations, her natural optimism and good manners finally won out. "Oh, alright then, I know jest th' place."

Mary walked to the door and exited it in front of her handsome husband. They descended the porch steps and he fell into step with her as they strolled away from the cabin across fields of gently waving bluegrass. Mary was intensely aware of him walking by her side, but she forced herself to look straight ahead.

"Whar's th' rest of yer kin?" asked Zachary Thomas.

"Joe and Paw are in th' apple orchard. My sisters and my baby brother, Percy, are a'hoein' out in th' fields."

"How come you didn't introduce me to yer maw?"

"Well, she . . . she had to tend to Jed," she began, then seeing his skeptical face, she added, "His diaper needed changin'."

She could tell he still didn't believe her. Well, she thought in annoyance, did he really expect that he could come to her home and be treated like any other visitor, with politeness and the usual hospitality, instead of someone who had whisked her off into the wild blue yonder (even if she had gone willingly)? He couldn't possibly imagine that he would be welcomed into the bosom of her family, surely?

They entered the forest and leading him down a number of paths, Mary took him to a secluded little glade, to which she used to escape as a child. It was where her cousin, Emily, had taught her to read and write and cipher. It was thickly surrounded by purple and blue hydrangeas, flame azalea bushes, splashed with bright clusters of orange flowers, and calawba rhododendrons with brilliant sprays of pinky-orange blooms. The overhead trees dripped with vines of hanging moss and tangled grape-vines. Right in the middle of it was a huge fallen tree trunk covered in moss. Sunlight dappled her precious little hideaway in pretty sketchy patches, giving it an atmosphere of light and peace. At least it was a place where they could talk without being disturbed by a single soul! With that thought, Mary suddenly remembered what Sheriff Coley had told her about how Buckos never forgave a slight. Zachary Thomas could easily murder her here and take off and it might take ages for somebody to discover her body! *If ever!* After all, she may have lived with him for nine months, but she had never really gotten to know him at all. She shivered slightly with apprehension.

"This is jest fine," murmured Zachary Thomas approvingly as he entered her childhood sanctuary through the dense surrounding bushes.

Throwing off her worst fears, she said, "Well, at least we kin talk private here, tho' thar ain't nuthin' more to be said that ain't already bin said."

"Please jest hear me out, girl." He took her hand and led her to the fallen tree trunk. They sat down and he turned towards her, squinting his striking turquoise-green eyes at her, his face deadly serious. "This is real hard fer me 'cuz, as you know, I ain't much of a talker, but I ain't leavin' till I tell you what's on my mind."

Mary nodded. Studying his smooth handsome face, she felt a terrible ache in her throat, for it was still so gaunt. It reminded her of those long, bitter winter months they spent together, fighting for survival. Their shared experiences held her in a kind of stricture now. She'd slept beside this man for nine whole months, with nothing between them except the bear's head in winter. She'd cooked and cleaned for him. It made her feel close to him in a way she never had when she was with him. He seemed so lonely and vulnerable somehow, full of nervousness, as if he was dreading this confrontation. She knew how much he hated talking. He could not seem to find ease in any company, let alone hers. What was it that he had come for? Perhaps something had happened to Emma. After all, he couldn't fail to know how close they had become while she was at Claw Mountain.

"How's Emma?" she asked as casually as she could.

"Fine. Misses you somethung fierce tho'."

"Yes, I miss her too."

Zachary Thomas straightened his frame, looked her straight in the eye and said in the firm voice he always used when he was taking charge of a situation. "Mary, I've bin doin' a whole heap of thunkin' since you've bin gone. Now, I know exactly why you left an' I ain't blamed you none! But I've come to ask you to come back to Claw Mountain with me."

Mary closed her eyes, her heart sinking at his words. How could he possibly ask such a thing of her? "You know I cain't do that, Zachary Thomas. You've wasted yer time comin' here if'n that's what you've come fer."

"Mary, kin you look me in th' eye an' tell me you ain't missed me even a little bit?"

Mary opened her eyes and gazed at him distressfully. "What are you tryin' to do, Zachary Thomas? I ain't a'goin' back with you and that's all thar is to it!"

"Have you miss'd me at all?" he insisted doggedly. "'Cuz I've sure miss'd you, girl!"

Despite his firm resolve, she could detect a tone of pleading in his voice. She knew how hard this was for him, but how could she possibly admit to something like missing him when it would only serve to encourage him? Yet, it would be real mean of her to send him away thinking that their time together, however strained, had meant absolutely *nothing* to her. Well, if nothing, what *had* it meant to her? Somehow that was impossible to answer. It had dragged her into a harsh reality like a babe plucked screaming from the womb. Yet it had also taught her many things like self-reliance and how to run a home. And most of all, it had given her Jed. *The one really good thing to come out of all this!* She could not pretend then that it had meant nothing to her when it had taught her practically every valuable lesson she had learned in her young life. She owed him a lot for that alone. Still she mustn't raise his hopes. That would be too cruel.

"Well, if'n you must know," she murmured non-commitally, "*I've* miss'd you some, tho' I cain't thunk why when you hardly said two words to me all th' time I was thar! I'm sure it must be right hard fer you bein' on your own agin. What with all th' work an' all."

"Yeah, it is, but it's much more than all th' work you did, Mary," he said earnestly. "It was *you!* It was yer . . . yer . . . yer, well, doggone my skin, wimmin, it were yer doggoned *spunkiness* that I miss so much. Th' place is real empty now with you and th' babe gone."

Mary's eyes grew wide with astonishment. "Oh, don't give me that nonsense, Zachary Thomas. You hardly even know'd I was around. You'd drink yer moonshine an' clean forgit I was even thar. Have you any idea how lonely I was? I swar I could never go back to that life ever agin."

"An' I sure wouldn't expect you to. I know I ain't bin th' best husband to you, Mary, and I apologize right good fer that. But I say thungs *won't* go back to what they were. You see, I've changed, Mary. I ain't th' same man I was back then."

Mary heaved a skeptical sigh. "Jest how have you changed, Zachary Thomas?"

"Well, fer one thing, I ain't touched a drop of moonshine since you done left."

Mary's eyes widened in astonishment. "You've stopped drinkin' moonshine?"

Zachary Thomas nodded, eyeing her solemnly. "Not a single goddamned drop has passed my lips since you've bin gone. I would have come to fetch you sooner, but I figger'd that I had to prove to you, and to m'self, that I'd lick'd th' drinkin' habit fer good. You've got to understand that I've bin drinkin' real hard since I was six years old, so it sure weren't easy to stop. But I did it!"

"*Six years old?*" Mary echoed incredulously. "You started drinkin' hard at six years old?"

Zachary Thomas nodded again. "Paw made every one of us git drunk on his moonshine on our sixth birthdays! Said it were our 'initiation into manhood'! He'd put a shotgun in one hand an' a jaw of raw moonshine in th' other even a'fore we was out of knee-britches. Made us drink till we puked! Hit's probably what saved our lives, mind! And he's bin feedin' us on th' stuff ever since."

"*Six years old!* Oh, Zachary Thomas! Didn't your maw ever tried to stop him?"

"She tried to, but thar ain't nobody stops my paw from doin' what he's got a mind to! Said it was to make us into genuine mountain men. You told me when you left that you hate th' way that my kin drinks moonshine th' way they do. Well, that thar's th' reason. We all grew up t'be hellers 'cuz of it. But we drank mainly to forget."

"What do you mean, Zachary Thomas? *To forget what?*"

"To forget all what Paw done to us . . ."

And then began a tale of horror, the likes of which Mary had never heard before in her life. If Zachary Thomas had been deeply uncommunicative in the past, he made up for it now, spewing up the horrors of growing up on Claw Mountain under the mean and vicious influence of his evil father. It seemed that for all what Obediah termed as "misdemeanors" or the more serious charge of "civil disobedience" committed by his sons, which meant that they had willfully, or unintentionally, disobeyed any of the many rules he held dear, Obediah would hold a "hearing", during which time he would hear whatever "evidence" was available, and for which he would be sole judge and jury. He called it "Buchanan justice". Mary shuddered. *Buchanan justice!* So that was how the term was coined that Eli had used several times. And how well she knew about those awful hearings!

"As you know I weren't thar at Jamie's floggin', but I reckon it must have bin one of th' worst. It were th' first time Paw had flogg'd him, 'cuz we all tried to keep him out of Paw's way. I reckon Paw considers Jamie a personal insult to hisself. He had his own special treatment fer him. He liked to tease and taunt him, tell him what a useless dimwit he was, how stupid. He would ask him questions he knew Jamie couldn't understand, let alone answer, an' then scoff at him, or he would make him do chores that would confuse him, jest so he could belittle him. Paw's real good at doin' that. Has a tongue on him that is almost worse than th' lick of his whip!"

Remembering how cruel Obediah's tongue had been while taunting Eli and Jake at the still site, Mary was forced to agree. Zachary Thomas paused a moment before continuing his harrowing tale. He told her how Obediah used various methods of punishment for those he deemed guilty. For lesser "offences" he loved deeming punishments that humiliated, like stripping the "culprit" or "culprits" naked and have them run a gauntlet of pails of ice-cold water thrown by the others, or have them wear a chamber pot on their head for a week, or nothing but an apron on for that same length of time and have everybody call them a girl. Zachary Thomas told her that the chamber-pot sentence was one of the worst punishments for it had to be one that hadn't yet been emptied and, after the stinking contents had been poured over their heads, they had to endure the reeking stench of themselves for a whole week before they were allowed to remove the chamber pot and wash. It got so they all hurried to empty their chamber pots at the crack of dawn. But it seemed there was always someone who had forgotten on the day of a dreaded hearing.

Other punishments handed out by Obediah ranged from forcing the child deemed guilty to miss meals for as long as a week, to running up and down the mountain non-stop for several hours. For what he deemed more serious offences, he would beat the younger boys with a strap until they were old enough for an even more vile form of punishment – *being flogged at the flogging post!* They all lived in terror of the flogging post! The word "hearing" evoked such terror in them, for they all knew it might easily lead to this ultimate punishment. And such was Obediah's cruelty, he would sometimes use it for a relatively minor offence just to keep them off-balance and unsure. Mary listened to Zachary Thomas's macabre tale, told in a deadpan voice, with growing horror.

"Did he flog you too," she managed to ask her husband.

In answer, Zachary Thomas stood up, removed his shirt and vest, and slowly turned his back on her. Mary gave a cry of horror and jumped up. In all the nine months she had lived with him, Zachary Thomas had never removed his vest. Now she knew why! His back was nothing but a mass of terrible twisted, tortured, and obscenely pink flesh. As she looked at the warped product of a madman, Mary's eyes became blinded with tears and she began to sob brokenly. She had known the patriarch was wicked and mean and brutish, and lacked even a spark of decency after the flogging he had lavished on his poor backward son, and his shocking treatment of Pearl after she had tried on one of his late wife's garments without permission, but she was bludgeoned by the full extent of his cruelty and depravity. *What a life of hell her husband and his brothers had endured!* She felt a powerful anger towards Obediah and a terrible all-consuming grief for the whole clan that had suffered so acutely under his warped tyranny.

She forced herself to control her sobbing, instinctively knowing how this would affect her husband, who stood stiffly with his back to her as if he were rooted there. With a compulsion born of the helpless need to comfort him, she moved forward and ran one trembling hand over the deep pitiful scarring that would forever mark her husband's huge muscular back.

She noticed that the winter trials he had suffered had wasted it in size, making him seem so wounded and vulnerable, so stripped of his usual stoic strength, which was the barrier he used to shut her and the world out. To feel the twisted gnarled flesh beneath her fingers made fresh hot tears sting her eyes. It was the first time she had touched her husband since the night Jed was conceived – and that had been to fight him off – and it stirred deep emotion within her. One she was unable to easily identify. There was searing pity, yes, but a strange indefinable longing too. But he flinched beneath her touch as if burned by a branding iron, and he turned around immediately, pulling on his vest and shrugging his shirt back on and bowing his head.

As he slowly buttoned up his shirt, his face set like granite, she could tell that he hated the pity and was embarrassed by it. She gazed at him in mute sympathy. What had it cost him to open up to her the way he had? *To reveal such terrible things to her?* To show her his disfigured back? Was this why he and the others had been too afraid to take Jamie to a valley doctor after his flogging, even though his life was at risk? Were they afraid that somehow the terrible secret of the wholesale abuse of the clan would somehow be let out? Did they fear exposure above all, because it would somehow weaken what little power they did have? *Their ability to cope with it?* It was hard to believe that this sort of thing could have gone on for so long, unchecked. But she knew why – it was the sheer isolation of the mountain. For despite the general lawlessness and their grim reputation, not even a hint of this dark family secret had ever come out – at least not in any mountain gossip she had heard. Even she, who had known about the flogging post, had not even begun to suspect the full extent of Obediah's evil abuse of his sons.

After her husband had exposed his back to her, she was sure that he would clam up again but, to her surprise, he sat down on the log and carried right on talking about his tortured childhood. He told her that while Obediah loved to use his fancy flowery language, which he called "King's English", to constantly belittle his sons, telling them how stupid and ignorant they were, he had refused to allow them to be educated, despite the fact that their mother had begged him to allow her to at least teach them to read and write.

He refused pointblank saying that mountain children were not educated, and besides, they had no need of such things. He even refused to allow her to name her own children such was his fear of being sent back to jail. He needed people to believe they were just common mountain folk so that they would thus not suspect that he was an "aristocratic" fugitive from the law. Such was his warped thinking that he did not consider *he* was the biggest danger to himself, in that respect. So while Hedina wanted names like Charles, Pierre and Ferdinand for her children, he gave them typical mountain monikers.

His word was law no matter how oppressive and draconian, and his dangerous and unpredictable moods, one minute smiling and jovial and charming (the Obediah Mary had once witnessed) and the next hair-trigger moment, mean and malicious, kept his boys in a state of constant fearfulness and dread.

Furthermore, he would use his sons against one another, in that they never knew who would be called upon to help him administer punishment, so that it caused ill-feeling and suspicion between them. Fortunately, as they grew older, and understood his tactics more, so a strong bond borne of common suffering and hatred of him was forged between them, uniting them in spirit. Even adulthood had not spared the clan. And he had a whole new generation under his control now too. Obediah still physically abused his own sons, with the exception of Eli and Zachary Thomas, that is, for they were the only ones who stood up to him. All the other brothers were weak and aimless, acting like cowed dogs in his presence, seeking oblivion from their fear by imbibing in moonshine. But Obediah used their children as a means of controlling them. For instance, he might beat a son if the father transgressed.

Mary stared at her husband in horror. *What an evil, evil man!*

"How come Eli ain't a'fear'd of your paw like th' others?" she murmured.

Zachary Thomas gave her a transfixed look, before he finally mumbled, "Thar is a good reason, but I ain't gonna tell you what it is. Thar be some thungs best left unsaid!"

Mary wanted to press him then she decided she really didn't want to know, after all.

"Eli always was an insolent kid. Like he didn't care what happen'd to him! I cain't remember how many beatings he took 'cuz he would imitate Paw's speech, that fancy lowlander talk of his. But," continued Zachary Thomas, "Eli may stand up to Paw some, but even he obeys his orders. I know you couldn't believe it when none of my brothers stood up to Paw when he flogged Jamie. Well, you don't know Paw and his maniacal will. How much mind-power he has over them – yes, even Eli. He does it by using the others when he punishes a 'culprit'. So even though they're all grow'd, they obey him, jest like they did when they were young'uns. They're all sore afraid of him, Mary."

Mary was bludgeoned to silence when her husband finally finished talking. Having purged himself of such truly monstrous revelations, he seemed utterly exhausted and emotionally spent. Mary groaned at the torment and brutality suffered by her poor husband and his brothers over the years, under the cruel yoke of their father. While Zachary Thomas had told her this dreadful tale of horror in a monotone, his face stoic, now tears were streaming unchecked down his cheeks. Mary stared at him in dismay, feeling terrible knowing that the fam-ily she had so hated and condemned without reservation, had hidden so much raw pain and anguish beneath their brash, obnoxious exteriors. She laid a hand on her husband's arm and he immediately covered it with his own huge hand. She lifted his hand and kissed it then held it against her cheek.

"I'm so sorry, Zachary Thomas," she whispered, unable to comprehend the depths of the clan's suffering. But as much as the story, with its pathos and gut-wrenching pain, had horrified and revolted her, it made her more determined than ever that her son should not have to grow up on Claw Mountain where he would be subject to the barbaric rules of his depraved grandfather. For Obediah *still* ruled his family with a rod of iron. She had witnessed it for herself!

"But don't you see, Zack," she said, using the diminutive of his name for the first time. It seemed to create a form of intimacy between them she had never experienced before, "it's th' very reason I cain't go back. Your paw ain't never gonna change. He's a real mean, *evil* man and I don't want my young'un to grow up anywhar near him."

Zachary Thomas narrowed his eyes and said, "I wouldn't let nuthin' bad happen to him, Mary, ye kin be sure of that! 'Sides, you don't got to worry about Paw no more. He ain't bin th' same man since th' Freeze. He caught th' pneumonie real bad an' is real sickly an' weak. His lungs clean got th' better of him. He coughs real nasty all th' time and he's real skinny 'cuz he don't hardly eat no more. All my kin suffered real bad this winter. They ran out of store-bought groceries real quick. Some of them had collected chestnuts, like you done told Emma to tell 'em to, and they managed to survive okay.

But nearly all my brothers lost young'uns to starvation and th' cold. Willie lost Pearl. She always was so skinny and weak-lookin', but she looked like she ain't had more than a single layer of skin on her bones a'fore she died. I lost another three of my brothers too. Jamie's gone. He never did git over th' floggin'. But Ebenezer and Emma's paw, Clyde, died from that thar cold, tryin' to hunt fer vittles fer their families. I came across them both froze to death in th' Wilderness. Couldn't git them out on m'own with th' snow so deep, so I had to bury 'em in th' snow then go back in th' spring to give 'em a proper burial. Even in th' best of times, they ain't never hunted. Never bothered. Were real useless at trackin'. Emma always kept her family in vittles. She always took on more responsibility on her young shoulders than was right. But even tho' he were a real bad 'un to his family at times, in th' end, Clyde proved he loved 'em. He wouldn't let Emma out in that filthy weather and snow! Their baby, Thompson, died too."

Mary stared at him in shocked dismay. "Oh, my Lord, Zachary Thomas, why didn't you told me any of this a'fore?" she asked incredulously. "You suffered all that on yer own right thru' th' winter?"

"Well, I didn't want to worry you none when you had your own fight on, what with th' baby comin' and all. 'Sides you done took on so badly when I told you about Lon Ficks and his family."

"Oh no, poor, poor Jamie . . . and poor Emma – and her family too!" Mary felt the tragedy and sorrow of Jamie's young life and a spurt of fierce longing for the tough little spitfire that she had left behind on Claw Mountain. If the fiery little girl had been upset at the loss of her two uncles after the ambush, how must she be feeling after the loss of her own paw and her baby brother and all her other lost kin? Mary longed to be able to comfort her young friend. How must the man sitting beside her be feeling, too, having lost so many of his kin like that and then,

shortly afterwards, his own wife and son when she left with Jed? She gazed at her estranged husband with deep sympathy, saying softly, 'And you, Zachary Thomas? Losin' all yer kin like that then losin' me and Jed both so soon after. I'm so, so sorry that you had to suffer so much all on yer own," she added chidingly. "You *should* have told me!"

Zachary Thomas shook his head, swallowing hard. "Anyway, it affected Paw so bad, bein' so ill an' losin' more boys like that . . . it's like he's had all th' stuffin' knocked outta him and, somehow, he ain't this terrible monster no more. At least, not to me. My brothers have taken to scoffin' at him whenever they kin, knowin' he cain't git back at them no more."

Mary drew back. "Well, don't you dare go feelin' sorry fer *him*! Fact is, he's still that monster he was when he beat Jamie an' did all them other awful things to y'all. An' if'n he was fit an' well, you kin be sure he'd still be at it!"

Zachary Thomas bowed his head, and shook it slightly. "I cain't forgive him fer all th' wicked thing he's done, but thar are days when I *do* kinda feel sorry for him the way th' boys take to mockin' him so, when they ain't dared even raise thar voices to him when he was able-bodied."

Remembering how she had felt when Obediah was chastising Eli and Jake at the still site, Mary guessed that as much as it miffed her, she could understand his feelings. Then Zachary Thomas continued, "Guess it's 'cuz I'm th' firstborn and I'm th' only one who's got some good memories of Paw, a'fore th' drink took him and th' devil got inside him. I remember him playin' with me, holdin' me on his lap and crawlin' around on th' floor with me. Thungs he ain't never done with any of th' others. When I thunk of them times, it's like I'm rememberin' a whole different person. I jest wish he could've bin that kind of Paw to them too. Fact is, I don't thunk he's gonna last much longer. And if he goes, thungs'll change on th' mountain fer th' good, you'll see! Fact is, they already have.

"Mary, I'm askin' you . . . no, I'm *a'beggin'* you to come back to Claw Mountain with me. Jed's my son too, y'know. He deserves to grow up with a maw and a paw. I know full well how much a boy needs a paw who loves him. So if'n you don't do it fer yerself, then do it *fer Jed,* Mary . . ." Zachary Thomas crushed her hand in his, forcing her to look up into his piercing turquoise-green eyes, as he turned towards her. "Mary, I ain't never told you this a'fore but . . . *I love you.* I love you, girl. I fell in love with you in that thar general store an' I ain't stopped lovin' you since. I've bin thunkin' real hard an' I reckon you an' me was meant to be. I never go anywhar with my brothers an' I'd never bin to th' Fletcher store a'fore that particular day, neither. I thunk th' reason I went thar that day was 'cuz I was *meant* to meet you and we were meant to be together. I felt it strong then and I feel it strong now. *Right here!"* He pounded over his heart with his fist. "Mary, I ain't never told you a'fore that I love you, 'cuz I ain't much on expressin' my feelin's and 'cuz I know full well how much you hate me. But

Mary Louella Harley Buchanan, I *love* you more than life itself an' I'm a'willin' to do *anythung* you want to become a better husband to you."

Mary stared at her husband in astonishment. His words had created a storm of feeling inside of her and she couldn't trust herself to speak. Then he took off his hat, laying it carefully on the ground beside the log, before turning towards her. Then he reached behind her head and unclipped her bun, slowly raking her loosened long black hair with his fingers so that it fell on either side of her face down almost down to her lap, before he kissed her gently on her lips. She felt his mustache brush her cheeks and smelt his distinctive smell of tobacco and faint sweat. At first she resisted, her body tensing, and then she gave a little sigh and surrendered to the moment. Closing her eyes, she put both her arms around his neck and drawing him to her, passionately returned his kiss. They finally drew apart, breathing hard.

Then gazing into his eyes, Mary heard herself whisper, *"I love you too, Zachary Thomas."*

The truth of those whispered words reverberated throughout her being, and thinking back, she realized for the first time that sometime during their long arduous months together when they were fighting for their very survival, it had happened – love for him had grown deep inside her, unacknowledged but there, nevertheless. No, it was before then even, when he had carried her up the mountain after she had witnessed Jamie being flogged almost to death, after failing to escape. Zachary Thomas had a stunned look on his face as she continued softly, "I ain't know'd it fer sure until right this minute, but hit's true. I ain't never wanted to admit it to myself, but I've had this great big empty hole inside of me th' whole time I've bin away, an' I would never admit to m'self th' real reason why."

"You love me too?" her husband asked incredulously, his eyes searching her face. "You love me too? I thought that mebbe you had miss'd me some an' we could use that as a start. I never dreamed . . . how come? I did you wrong. I forced you to marry me aginst yer will, and I . . . forced m'self on you, too, that first night. I hated myself fer it and swore to m'self that I would never touch you agin less'n you asked me to."

"Well, I did hate you some at first, 'cuz I was so mad you were forcin' me to marry you, but I guess that wore off in time and, even tho' you ain't talked much, you sure worked hard an' looked after me real good. Then you carried me back to Eagle Spur after Jamie's floggin' and somethung changed inside me back then. I suddenly knew you ain't no bad man. That underneath th' moonshine and th' heavy silences, you were a good, decent man. You proved that when Jed came along. I saw th' way you look'd at him."

"Kin you let me see him when we git back? I was so hopin' you would show him to me, but I was jest too plum nervous to ask back thar."

"Of course. He's so beautiful, Zack. Ye're goin' t'be so proud of him."

With that, they kissed again, without touching at first, just a melting meeting of lips, as they slowly twisted their heads this way and that. Then he took her head in his two big hands and gently kissed her mouth over and over again. Then he stood up and lifted her up by her hands, before laying her down on the leaf-strewn, grassy ground. Muttering words of tenderness and love, he kissed her again before he ran his hand over her full breasts and the dampness caused by her milk, causing a flare of fire in her loins. He pulled the bibbed top of her skirt down and lifted up her under-blouse, revealing her naked upper torso, and the feather on its leather thong.

Zachary Thomas frowned, staring at it in bewildered consternation. "Is that what I thunk it is?"

"Yes, it's the eagle feather that landed on my foot when we climbed up Eagle Spur on the day of our weddin' when them eagles acted so strange."

"I remember. *Why did you keep it?* I would thunk you wouldn't have wanted *anythung* that reminded you of Eagle Spur."

She eyed him seriously, staring into the brilliant turquoise-green of his eyes. "Maybe I kept it, 'cuz I *did* want to be reminded of it, after all."

Her husband smiled at that and resumed his gentle love-making, which was so different to his rough love-making on her wedding night. Her nipples were leaking milk and he smiled tenderly down at them, before covering one of them with his mouth and sucking softly on it, causing her to shudder with unfamiliar and thrilling sensations. She arched her back and closed her eyes, reveling in the feeling. He slid his hand up under her skirt and pulled her bloomers down and off. He fumbled with his flies then mounted her, thrusting himself gently inside her. She was ready to receive him this time; all the secret places of her sex were swollen with blood and slippery and oiled and moist, in the breathtaking heat of passion. Unable to contain the feeling that swept through her, she hung onto his back with both arms as he rode her with slow, aching tenderness.

Filled with joyous passion, Mary felt herself laughing and crying at the same time, and he nuzzled his face into the crook of her neck, kissing it. He raised his head and she grasped his long black hair in her hands, staring into his strong, handsome face with great wonder, taking in its every feature. The heavy black brows above the startling turquoise-green eyes, the straight nose, the commanding mouth beneath the black mustache, the wind-whipped brown skin and the deep lines around his eyes, and she wondered how she could have once found him so hard and forbidding, so unapproachable. Underneath all that, beneath the quiet strength, lay the sensitive soul his mother had written about in her diary. He had shown great courage in revealing himself to her so totally, after suffering such rejection from her.

She felt an incredible closeness to this man, as if she were able to see right inside his soul. She ached to get closer to him still, to get right inside his skin, for her body to somehow merge with his, till they were a single physical entity, so that she was him, and he, her. And suddenly, that's exactly how it felt. It was if their union was complete, in every sense of the word, as if it was filling all her senses, her entire being, and that they were one, that she, in turn, was filling all his senses, his entire being. There seemed no limit to the depths of their passion, to the height of their love! And just as suddenly, for the first time, she felt like a bride. It was a wonderful feeling that flooded her with joy. He was wonderful. *She loved him!* Oh God, how she loved this enigmatic mountain man, who had suffered so much pain and brutality in his life. *Dare she go back with him . . . ?*

27

When Zachary Thomas and Mary got back to the cabin and opened the front door about an hour later, they gasped in shock for it was to find that her whole family awaited them. Not only that her paw, Joe and Percy were all aiming their hunting rifles at her husband. It was the second time this had happened to him in just three months and Mary keenly felt the helpless indignity of it that lighted on his startled face. Percy had a fierce look on his freckled face, only one calculating, aiming eye opened, while her three sisters were huddled fearfully behind their lovely mother, who stood tall and chin-raised. Paw looked feisty as a bantam rooster, and Joe, with his narrowed eyes topped by his heavy black brows, downright ferocious!

"Leave her be!" snarled William Harley from his lowly stance of at least a foot-and-a-half beneath her towering husband, his beady brown eyes as hard as marbles. "Git away from this here place this instant! We don't want yer kind around here!"

"Yeah, leave my sister alone!" Joe said scathingly. "Ain't you done enough to mess up her life?"

Totally flabbergasted by this hostile reception, the pair of them stood there dumb-struck. Then all eyes turned on Mary and widened in surprise. Looking down at where their eyes were directed, Mary was horrified to realize that despite having brushed down her dress with her hands after her love tryst with her husband, there were still bits of grass and leaves clinging incriminatingly to it. She brushed at her hair with a flustered hand and, to her dismay, she discovered bits of debris clinging to that too. A crimson blush spread over her face, but she managed to recover enough to raise a defiant chin and say clearly, "Listen,

Zachary Thomas is my husband and I won't have you talkin' to him like that!"

Her mother took a step forward. "What are you sayin', Mary? I raised th' alarm as soon as you left th' cabin. I thought he'd forced you to leave with him agin."

"*Agin,* Maw? He ain't never forced me th' first time, remember? Now I know y'all are jest tryin' to protect me, but thar ain't no need. I told you all a'fore that Zachary Thomas here is a *good* man and I still firmly believe that." Now it was her family's turn to be dumbstruck. "Well," Mary continued. "I'm real glad ye're all here together, 'cuz I got me an announcement to make. I'm a'goin' back to Claw Mountain with Zachary Thomas and we're taking baby Jed with us."

There were huge gasps of shock and dismay. A great silence engulfed them all as her family digested this highly unpalatable piece of news. Then Maw found her voice. "Mary, have you taken leave of yer senses? What are you thinkin'? You cain't possibly go back and expose both of you to all that danger! Not after all that happen'd thar!"

"Maw, you don't understand! It's whar I belong now – with my husband an' my young'un. Th' reason I have bin so unhappy since I've bin home is 'cuz I missed Zack so much, Maw. What's more, I've discovered that I truly love him. I miss Eagle Spur somethung awful too. I miss havin' my own home. I ain't yer little girl no more, Maw. I'm a grown wimmin now and a wimmin belongs with her husband!"

Maw looked totally mortified. "Mary, honey, yer're lettin' yer heart rule yer head agin!" she warned severely. "Nuthin' has changed. When you git back thar, it'll be jest as awful as you told me it was th' first time. Please, girl, you must take time to consider yer position … and little Jed's safety!"

"Maw, you ain't got to worry about that!" Mary was about to tell her anxious mother about the way Obediah Buchanan had been struck down by illness, and how the winter had sadly decimated his family, making them far less of a threat than they were before, but after hearing her husband's harrowing tale about how his family had suffered all these years, she felt she couldn't do it to him. She just couldn't denigrate his wounded family in front of her own. Instead she said quietly, "I appreciate yer concern, Maw, I surely do, but Zack and I will be thar to protect little Jed. And Maw," Mary took one of Zachary Thomas's huge hand in her own. "It will please you to know that Zack don't drink no more neither. I'm so proud of him. Whatever else we've bin through together, he's always bin a good husband and a good provider. And we've decided to try and make our marriage work so Jed kin grow up with a proper family, not one without a paw. Maw, Zack tells me that y'all kin visit us thar on Claw Mountain then you kin see fer yerself how I'm a'doin'."

The whole family stared at them goggle-eyed, as if they had no idea how to respond to this audacious idea. No doubt, it was the last thing any of them wanted. Then Joe frowned mightily and found his tongue.

"Mary, the last time I went up Claw Mountain with Sheriff Coley and th' deputies, I damn near got myself kilt! Reckon I wouldn't want to put Maw and th' girls thru' that."

"Well, it won't happen that way ever agin! Zack'll make real sure of that, won't you, Zack?" Anxious to get off the subject, she didn't wait for him to answer and instead quickly turned to him and said, "Zachary Thomas, please forgive my appallin' manners. I must introduce you to my family. Everybody, this here is my husband, and Jed's paw, Zachary Thomas Buchanan. Zack, this here is my paw, William Harley. He used to work fer th' Hope Loggin' Camp a'fore he had his accident a few years back. Now Maw complains he gits under her feet mostly," she teased with a smile, hoping to alleviate some of the tense atmosphere that reigned in the cabin. When her father looked thunderously crestfallen at her words, she hastily added, "Of course, she's jest enjoys teasin' him. We couldn't do without Paw's hard work around here. He's bin teachin' Joe how to run th' place."

Zachary Thomas cautiously outstretched his hand and Paw lowered his rifle and took it with a look of consternation on his face.

"How do you do, sir?" Zachary Thomas said gruffly, but politely. "Sir, I know you are real concerned about Mary and th' baby, and I sure as heck don't blame you fer that. But I want you to know that I sure intend to look after them real good from now on in, so you ain't got to worry none."

Her father nodded stiffly, looking totally unconvinced.

"This here is my maw, Ellie Harley," said Mary hastily.

Her mother reluctantly stretched out a hand to take Zachary Thomas's proffered one, a look of concerned pique on her face. He bowed over her hand in a courtly manner and Mary saw that some of his father's old-world charm had rubbed off on him.

"It's a right pleasure, ma'am," he said.

"These here are my two brothers, Joseph and Percy, and those three little darlin's back thar are my sisters, Lona, Laura and Nellie."

Zachary Thomas solemnly shook the hands of each of them in turn. While Joe and Percy regarded him with distinctly hostile eyes, her sisters smiled at him winsomely, their male-greedy bright-blue eyes taking in his handsome looks and mighty build.

Then Laura gushed, "Why, blow me down, Mary, I remember him now! He was thar at the store that day. Lawdie be, Mary! *Good fer you!*"

"Quiet, Laura," rebuked Maw sternly.

"Now you wait here, while I go fetch yer son fer you," Mary told Zachary Thomas, her hazel eyes glowing warmly. She went into the storage room, and lifting her sleeping baby carefully out of the crib, wrapped a pale blue shawl around him, before taking him through into the next room. "And this, Zachary Thomas," she said quietly, "is yer son, Jediah Horatio Buchanan. Ye'll see he's grown some since you last saw him."

She smiled softly up at her husband as she placed the precious bundle in his arms. She watched as he carefully drew aside the shawl covering his son's face. A smile of rapturous joy spread slowly across his face. "Why, Mary, I swar he's th' finest-lookin' man-child I ever laid eyes on …"

When Zachary Thomas muttered that it was too late to get to Claw Mountain before dark, Maw reluctantly invited him to stay overnight so that they could set off early in the morning. Supper was a stiff and joyless affair. It was summarily decided that Mary should sleep in her old pallet in the loft while Zachary Thomas bedded down with her brothers in the adjoining shack. To Mary's dismay, her mother used her time away from her husband to try to talk her out of going.

"Mary, I cain't believe ye're so trustin'! I'll grant you he's a charmer alright, but you've got to remember he's a Bucko and is *not* to be trusted!"

"That ain't true, Maw!" replied Mary tartly. "I'd trust him with my life."

Her mother stared at her in consternation. "I kin see what he's done! He's had his way with you and filled yer head with all sorts of romantic notions! You cain't let yer heart rule yer head a second time, honey, and put little Jed in danger!"

"Maw, ye're forgettin' one thung, and that is, I've bin married to him fer a whole year now. He's my husband and th' father of my young'un!"

Her mother snorted with derision. "You said yerself that you wanted to leave a'fore you got married an' he wouldn't let you!"

"That may well be, but I stayed, and what's more I'm *glad* I stayed! *I love him, Maw!* I'm a'goin' back with him and that's final!"

It was the second argument Mary had had with her mother of late and she felt just awful. It was a most uncomfortable situation and, remembering all she'd put her family through the first time, she felt terribly guilty and upset. If only they could accept that this was something she *had* to do and give her their blessings, it would make all the difference. As it was, she spent a sleepless night thrashing around on her pallet, thinking about this terrible new burden she was placing on her family.

Yet even in the midst of all her anxieties, she couldn't help thinking about her husband and remember the way they had consummated their love in her secret childhood refuge earlier, feeling an odd excitement and a melting warmth for him deep in her loins. He had even broken the curse of his silence with her, telling her of so many things. *Terrible things!* Hopefully, it had been the moonshine that had made him so grimly uncommunicative before. She felt such an incredible closeness to him now and a terrible longing to just lie with him and hold him.

Beside her, in his night cradle, her baby, usually so good, grizzled as he teethed, and Mary was sure that he sensed something was going on. Was her mother right when she said that she was allowing her heart to rule her head a second time? Was everything as Zachary Thomas had made out, or was he using her vulnerability to get her back to Claw Mountain for less than noble reasons? Would she be putting her baby in danger? Then she remembered Zachary Thomas' face as he held his baby after an absence of three months, and shrugged off all the doubts that were plaguing her. Nevertheless, she was infinitely relieved when the sun rose, pushing dazzling rays of light through the tiny holes in the shingles.

Feeling weary with lack of sleep, Mary breastfed Jed then packed all her things, including all her personal belongings and clothes that her cousin, Peggy, who had several young children, had passed on to her for her baby, into her old suitcase, as well as all the writing materials and books her cousin, Emily, had left her, while her unusually subdued sisters climbed out of bed and got dressed in a sober silence.

When she had finished packing, Mary climbed down the loft ladder, before her sisters lowered the baby down in his cradle at the end of a rope as was the usual routine, before the suitcase was lowered by the same method. Zachary Thomas came in from the outside shack, huge and rumpled-looking, wearing the same clothes as yesterday, his jaw shadowed with dark stubble. He, too, looked tired and Mary was sure he'd also spent a sleepless night, but he gave her a slow smile when he caught her at the wood-fire stove after she had placed a kettle of water on it to make newly ground coffee. Putting an arm around her waist, he kissed her soundly on the mouth. She slumped against him gratefully, her fears that he would retreat into himself overnight, falling away. It wasn't until that moment that she was completely sure that she was doing the right thing by going back with him to Claw Mountain.

Her whole family had risen early to see her and the baby off and they breakfasted in a tense silence on corn-meal mush, covered with fresh milk and lashings of fresh cream (oh, how she had missed such luxuries on Claw Mountain!), before she and Zachary Thomas made preparations to leave. Her unsmiling mother handed Mary a basket of food to take for the long journey back to Claw Mountain, saying she had put in boiled eggs, cheese and corn bread, fruit, pickle and some thick slices of ham. Mary hugged her gratefully, knowing it was her way of saying she had forgiven her for their fight last night. Mary wanted to reassure her she had nothing to be concerned about, but considering what she'd put them through the last time, she knew there was nothing she could say to comfort her mother, or subdue her fears, right now. In her mother's eyes, Mary was off to the notorious Claw Mountain to live among the scourge of the Blue Ridge and, after the terrible disclosures she had made to her about them, she was understandably upset and terrified for her and her infant grandson.

Later, her family assembled out on the porch with dark-smudged and swollen eyes. One look at their gloomy faces told Mary they were totally unreconciled to her leaving and were desperately worried and heartbroken, not only at the thought of losing her for a second time, but losing baby Jed too. Everybody in the family was enchanted with him and he had been thoroughly spoilt. Maw and her sisters had picked him up at every opportunity, dressing him in his handed-down baby dresses, and gladly changing his cotton diapers whenever the occasion demanded it. But Mary knew that of them all, Joe would be the most sad to be losing his young nephew. Perhaps because he had been the family member to rescue the pair of them from Claw Mountain, he had taken on the role as sub-stitute father to the newborn baby, and was so taken with him that he would carry the cradle out into the orchids with him on fine days for hours at a stretch.

"You kin come see him real soon, Joe, then if'n ye're convinced thar ain't no danger fer th' others, they kin come too," Mary reassured him as he stuck a tan hooked finger for his baby nephew to grasp, sniffing loudly. He nodded quickly, his intense dark-brown eyes full of sorrow and worry. She would deeply miss Joe. They had always been so close, and they had often sat outside on the porch at night to talk while she was here. He knew more about her life on Claw Mountain than anyone and she knew he was deeply concerned for the two of them right now.

When she turned to say goodbye to the rest of her grieving family, their restraint fell away and they surrounded her in a weeping mass, hugging and kissing her and crooning soulfully at Jed, who was perched on her hip, all but ignoring her poor husband. Zachary Thomas packed the two mules with Mary's and Jed's belongings then he went inside to fetch the portable cradle. He took Jed from Mary, placed him in the cradle, and then tied the cradle with Jed still in it to the mule tethered behind the lead mule. After lifting Mary onto the front mule, he climbed up behind her. Mary couldn't help thinking of the day he had come to fetch her and had lifted her onto that fine horse! Still, she was going *home* and that was the only thing that mattered. As her husband clucked the mules forward, Mary turned to take one last fond look at her family to find they all had their hands raised in a solemn farewell.

It was a long tiring trip with the two mules, and Mary was infinitely relieved when they finally arrived at the foot of Claw Mountain, feeling exhausted and drained. Unfortunately, before making for Eagle Spur, they had to return the two mules to the barn at Obediah Buchanan's homestead at Horseshoe Hollow. Zachary Thomas had already told her that since Obediah's illness, it was no longer the daily meeting place for the clan and, sure enough, when they arrived there, the place was eerily deserted and a great unnatural silence reigned over all. And though Mary did not miss the cacophony the clan had made when they had gathered here in the past (when the sound of it would rise to the heights of Eagle Spur, a blot on her peace), their absence gave the place an added sense of desolation and gloom which hung over everything like persistent mist.

It unsettled her to remember all the unspeakable things that had occurred here over the years. The yard was as ugly and unkempt as ever, with its horseshoe posts, the ugly old sofas standing on bricks with their springs bursting through, huge piles of shattered glass from wild practice shoots, rusty tins, bottles, broken barrels, wagon wheels and other rubbish. *It was a desolate and depressing sight!* She shuddered when she saw the whipping post standing in the middle of the yard as stark and accusatory as a hangman's noose. She felt an aching sadness as she envisioned frightened young boys cowering beneath a madman's tyranny, too afraid to speak out against the brutalities he was committing against them. The pain and terror they must have felt under the strap or the flogging whip! Made to feel totally worthless and unloved under the lash of an equally cruel tongue and the indignities he made them suffer. She thought of her own baby and felt she would die rather than have him suffer in any way. *What made a monster like Obediah Buchanan?* What made him behave that way with his own flesh and blood? It seemed too awful to comprehend.

As they were leaving Horseshoe Hollow by foot to complete the last leg of their journey, Zachary Thomas, with his son's cradle strapped onto his broad back and carrying Mary's suitcase in one hand, Obediah himself came out onto the porch. Mary was shocked at the change in him. Gone was the robust, handsome, virile-looking man she had met less than a year ago. In his place was a hugely-shrunken, spindly, pathetic-looking creature in filthy long underwear, with disheveled hair that had turned completely white. Clearly the patriarch of the Buckos had been very ill as Zachary Thomas had reported. Well, he had got far less than he deserved! Yet he looked so pitiful, so devoid of any dignity, that even she might have felt a little sorry for him if she wasn't so terribly angry and disgusted at him for having caused so much pain and suffering to his own family. Well, to be sure, to be reduced to this and have his family desert him must be a tremendous blow to his pride, to say the very least. *Good!* Let him suffer, like he made those poor helpless young'uns suffer! Like he made poor Jamie suffer, the most helpless of them all! Beside her, Zachary Thomas tensed.

"I'm surprised at you, Zack," Obediah railed at his eldest son, in a wheedling voice. "Fancy trying to sneak off without coming to pay your due respects to your own father?"

Zachary Thomas took off his hat and said apologetically, "Sorry, Paw, hit's jest that we're dawg tired after th' long journey. Reckon I'd rather come by another time."

"Hhmmph, seems to me it's been a mighty long time since you were last here." His voice had taken on a curiously whining tone. Deserted by a family who had previously obeyed him at every click of his fingers, he was clearly feeling real sorry for himself, trying to evoke guilt in his eldest son. He turned to Mary with a scowl on his flesh-shrunken face. "Aah, you're back, I see!"

"Yes, Paw Buchanan, that I am," she replied as politely as she could manage, though it was hard with Zachary Thomas's recent heinous revelations about him buzzing around inside her head. "Fer good this time."

"With the babe, I see. Bring him here so I can see him!" demanded the patriarch.

Mary shuddered at the thought of him casting his evil gaze upon her innocent son. "Why, when you ain't never bother'd to come by to see him when he was born?" she asked accusingly.

Obediah snorted with derision. "Got so many grandchildren now, I lost interest in them years back. But I think I'd like to see Zack's offspring. Zack always was the one with the most sense. Takes after me in looks and talents, he does, but unfortunately, he's got some of his mother's weak nature in him too. But thank God he at least has a brain inside his skull, because all the rest are nothing but a bunch of bleeding idiots! A sniveling bunch of rat-assed cretins!"

Mary felt her ire rise at the man's ugly, scathing words which revealed such a naked contempt for his own sons. After all, if they were idiots at all it was because he had got them addled on moonshine from the time they were knee-high to a grasshopper, she thought furiously. Maw always used to say that a drunk man was naught but a fool, and she was right. Obediah had the cheek to pontificate when he was directly responsible for raising naught but a bunch of fools! Furthermore, he'd treated them with such ghastly cruelty that it had bred in them a positively virulent hatred for, and disrespect of, their fellow man. Thank goodness that Zachary Thomas had his maw's "weak" nature in him! Perhaps because he was the eldest and closest to his maw, she had been more of an influence on him than she had been on the others, and it showed. Despite his size, his mother had seen a measure of sensitivity in him that Mary had only caught glimpses of in the past.

Unable to let her father-in-law's shameful comments pass, she retorted coldly, "Well, frankly, Paw Buchanan, I reckon they'd all be fine young men if'n it weren't fer th' overindulgence in moonshine that you encouraged in them so!"

Zachary Thomas threw her a pleading, cautionary look. She was fully expecting to have to lock horns with Obediah on this but, to her surprise, he threw back his head and shook with thin, reedy laughter that was quite unlike his rich, hearty laughter of before, emphasizing his present weakened condition.

"You sound just like my Hedina!" he chuckled gleefully. "She reckoned that moonshine was no good for a body too. Well, I've been drinking my own moonshine for nigh on thirty years now, girl. Best in the whole goddamned Blue Ridge, it is, and it sure never did me any harm. Made a man of me and men of my boys. Got to get them young and raise 'em tough! But my Hedina would rather I had hired them a French governess to teach them to read William Shakespeare and drink tea with their pinkie fingers raised in the air. Imagine – out here in the wilds! I'd have ended up with naught but a bunch of nancy boys. Instead, everybody in these here hills knows who they are and not to mess with them!"

Mary had no idea who this Shakespeare fella was, but she thought he must be someone fine if Hedina thought him worthy of reading. "And you thunk that bein' a'feared of by yer own neighbors is a good thung?" she asked caustically.

"Of course! A man's got to show the government who's boss in his own back yard! You can never let the government get the best of you. Seen any Revenue Men today?"

"No," replied Mary, wondering what the government had to with anything. The man was clearly losing his mind!

"How about Galtreys? Seen any of them scum-of-the-earths in your travels?"

"No, no Galtreys neither."

Obediah snorted with smirking satisfaction. "We licked them real good the last time. Got their tails between their legs, whole bunch of those yellow-bellied sons-of-bitches! Still gonna get that filthy old man Galtrey right between the eyes before I die! Always vowed I would and I intend to keep that vow!"

Mary heaved an exasperated sigh, her eyes flashing. In the so-called 'licking' of them Galtreys he had lost two of his own sons and, even in his weakened state, when he might have used his time reflecting on a life ill-spent, all he could think about was creating more violence in the name of vengeance!

"Don't you thunk thar's bin enough killin' around here already?" she snapped. "Have you forgotten th' funeral of your two slain sons so soon, or are you plannin' on diggin' even more Buchanan graves?"

"Old man Galtrey cost me six months of my life!" roared Obediah peevishly. He bent over in a paroxysm of coughing and spat out a glob of thick dark-yellow phlegm, which landed in the yard right in front of them. Mary felt her stomach heave and she looked up at the culprit with narrow-eyed disgust.

Zachary Thomas was looking decidedly edgy by now. "Thunk we ought t'go on home now, girl. You upsettin' Paw."

"Well, he's upsettin' me so's I reckon we're about even!" she quipped, turning her attention back to the visibly agitated soul glaring at her from the porch. Clearly, Obediah was a man not used to a dissension of opinion. "And how exactly did he manage that, Paw Buchanan?" she challenged. "How did Dean Galtrey manage to cost you six months of yer life?"

"Caught me cutting down trees on the mountain and reported it to the landowner, he did! I ended up in the Madison County Jail for six months!"

"Well, if'n that indeed be th' case then it seems to me that hit were yer *own* doin's that got you in jail, and not his!'"

Obediah looked stunned by her temerity. *"What do you mean?"* he asked darkly, looking highly disgruntled.

"I mean you said that even if'n you *ain't* guilty of a deed, you're fit fer th' punishment! Jest like you said a'fore you flogged poor innocent young Jamie twenty-five times fer somethung he didn't do. You said even if he weren't guilty of leavin' th' glass jar whar th' Revenue Men could find it, he had to take th' responsibility fer it, anyway, as I recall! So it seems to me that since you *were* guilty as sin of cuttin' down them trees, knowin' full well it were aginst th' law, you *fully* deserv'd th' punishment to my way of reckonin'!" she announced, with flashing hazel eyes. Obediah blinked his eyes owlishly, caught out in the full thrust of his own arguments and misdeeds, and thus quite unable to answer her baiting logic.

"You talk utter nonsense, woman!" he finally muttered sourly, turning around and wandering back inside the cabin, without bothering to gaze upon his latest grandchild, after all.

"C'mon, Mary," urged Zachary Thomas. "He ain't worth it. 'Sides, it'll start gittin' dark in a while. Thar's lots I need to show you a'fore then."

"Oh." Mary smiled at him ruefully. "Guess I'm gonna be real busy fer th' next few weeks. I kin jest imagine all th' work that's piled up since I've bin gone."

"Yeah," grinned Zachary Thomas sheepishly. "Reckon so."

Mary felt a deep churning excitement in the pit of her stomach as they scaled the steep heights of Claw Mountain to reach the craggy granite-walled cliffs that supported and surrounded the outcrop of Eagle Spur and the rest of the tableland, breathing in the fresh tangy scent of pine, as they passed beneath an increasing number of balsam firs draped with grandfather lichen, and red spruces. Eagles were circling the skies in growing numbers and the sound of their wild cries sent goose bumps over her entire body. She had missed this place so much and couldn't wait to look down from the summit once more. At last they topped the ridge and stood up together, breathing hard. She immediately rushed to the edge to look down at the view below. Zachary Thomas came to stand beside her, setting down her suitcase at his feet. It was all as she remembered! The great magnificent tree-shrouded valley with Wilson Run running through it, the sound of its jubilant waters faintly heard. Utterly spellbound by the breathtaking scene below, she drew in a deep, satisfied breath as Zachary Thomas shyly took her hand in his.

"Oh, Zack, ain't hit glorious?"

Jed's cradle was still on his back, and half-moons of sweat showed on his white shirt beneath his armpits. "Sure is. It's what brung me here to live way back. I used to come up here reg'lar when I was a young'un, an' begged Paw to let me come live up here, when I was twenty-four years old. Since I topped him by at least half-a-foot back then, I guess he took that as a sign that he ought to give his permission! Yeah, reckon thar ain't 'nother view like it in th' whole wide world!"

"Ye're so right! You've got no idea how much I missed bein' here, Zachary Thomas, lookin' down on all this. I dreamed about this here view. Don't reckon heaven itself kin look much better. And th' *eagles!* I missed them too! And th' air up here. It's so pure an' sweet."

Finally, after standing there for a long time in silent homage to the spectacular scene below, they turned around, still holding hands. Looking upon the homesite she had so recently left behind, Mary froze. Her mouth dropped open and she stared ahead in awed surprise.

When she left here three months ago, it too had an unkempt air about it, especially after the ravages of winter, with broken gutters and sagging timbers on the roof of the chestnut-log cabin, as well as caved-in timbers on the porch. The barn roof had also caved in and the yard had been weed-strewn. Well, the makeshift old barn had been torn down and in its place stood a brand-new barn, hewn from chestnut logs, the roofs on the cabin and the porch had been replaced, the gutters fixed or replaced, and what's more, a hand-split chestnut fence now surrounded the homesite. The magnificent chestnut tree was full of green summer leaves and eight-inch spines of small creamy-white blossoms, like when she had first came here. It spread its branches over a spotless yard that was completely free of weeds.

As she walked over to it in a daze, still clasping Zachary Thomas's hand, she saw that a large hen-house had been erected, which was full of healthy-looking Leghorns, and four shoats trampled the yard near a water trough, while two more of the baby hogs snuffled around the cabin. What's more, there was a spring-house and a field beside the homesite was two-feet high with stalks! The Canadian mayflowers encrusting the guarding hemlocks behind the cabin were in full bloom. Mary was stunned. It did not look anything like the decrepit homesite she'd left behind. This was Eagle Spur in all its glory!

"I don't believe it!" Mary whispered. "Hit's simply incredible! Did you do all this work yourself? *Fer me?"*

Zachary Thomas nodded, grinning at her surprise. "Most of it, anyways. My brothers and Emma helped some. Fact is, we Buckos had ourselves a real genuine barn-raisin'."

Barn-raising was common practice in the Blue Ridge, being part and parcel of a well-refined community spirit in the mountains. *Fancy it happening on Claw Mountain!* Mary could scarcely believe it "Lawdee be, Zack, I swar you and yer brothers are genuine mountain men now, that's fer sure!"

"Raised merry hell too, they did!" Zachary Thomas continued proudly, chuckling to himself. "I know my brothers are usually bone-idle an' shiftless, but they came right smart when I asked 'em to. Th' men and their older boys came to do th' work and th' wimmin provided th' refreshments, while Emma minded th' young'uns. Well, they all got likkered up an' started fightin' amongst themselves as usual, but I managed to keep 'em workin'. I stayed stone cold sober and chivvied and shouted at 'em, and a'fore too long it was up. I did all th' finishin' touches mind. Reckon they were right proud of themselves, they were."

Mary felt a moment of keen regret at missing such a momentous occasion amongst the clan. "Oh, Zack," the diminutive came so easily to her tongue now, "I don't wonder. It sure looks magnificent as kin be. And my vegetable garden?"

"Go see. I'm jest gonna put Jed in his crib inside first. Wait thar fer me."

While Zachary Thomas disappeared into the cabin with the cradle, Mary rushed around the back of the cabin and went over to the edge of the forest to inspect the product of her labors that had sufficed them so well throughout the grim winter months. To her delight, she saw that her vegetable garden was weed-free, freshly hoed, and filled with rows of small cabbages. Mary waited till she heard Zachary Thomas coming up behind her before she turned to him, her face beaming with pleasure.

"Oh Zack, I reckon you did right fine here too!"

They went inside the cabin and to Mary's astonishment everything was as shiny and clean as the day she'd left it! She gasped in surprise. "Zack, how on earth did you manage all this?"

"Weren't easy but I worked like a dawg . . . had to do somethung t'git my mind off of moonshine – and you and th' young'un! That day you left I vowed I'd git you both back. I thought about what I needed to do to achieve that, and figger'd that b'sides givin' up moonshine, I'd best keep everythung clean an' neat th' way you like it. I swar I like it that way m'self these days.

Fact is, when you saw it that first day, I couldn't abide th' look of disgust on yer face when you saw th' state of th' cabin. I felt sech hot burnin' shame I ain't know'd whar to look, 'cuz I suddenly seen it all thru' yer eyes. I would have preferr'd that you spat out yer revulsion, reviled me fer my uncleanliness and sloth, but instead you jest hugged it all to yerself, not sayin' a single word. Jest cleaned it up real smart-like. Heck, these days it sickens me when I visit my kins' homes and see how they live in filth an' muck, jest like I used to. So I made real sure I cleaned it good as you.

"It ain't come easy at first then a funny thung happened! I started to enjoy it! If'n you keep it clean and don't let thungs pile up too much, it gits to be a whole heap easier. Had Emma come do my washin' tho'. That's jest *too* darned wimminish, I reckon."

"Why, Zack, fancy you turnin' into a genuine hen-husband on my account." She laughed, as his face turned dark red. "I cain't believe all what you've done in jest three months! I was expectin' to work my fingers clean to th' bone like last time! Now all this! Why, I feel like I've clean died and gone straight to paradise!"

"Got somethung real special fer you in th' barn too!" declared Zachary Thomas, beaming fit to bursting at her praise.

"You do? As if all this ain't enough already! What is it, Zack?"

"C'mon and see." He took her hand and led her outside to the barn. And there inside a stall piled with freshly turned hay was a great big beautiful black-and-white Holstein milk! Oh, wonder of wonders! *Fresh milk and cream!* More than anything, she had missed fresh milk and cream! She grinned at him in delight.

"Zack, what a *wonderful* surprise! How on earth did you git this beautiful creature up here?" She went up to the cow and patted its forehead.

"Believe me, it weren't easy!" said Zachary Thomas, with a foolish grin on his face. "Had to hitch her up here on a winch rigged up special-like!"

Mary turned to him with her heart full. She raised her eyes to his face, and reaching up a hand, laid it on the side of his cheek, saying solemnly, "You did all this fer *me?* It jest don't seem possible that you did all this fer me . . ."

"Well, I figger'd it were one thing to git you back up here an' quite another to *keep* you here! Reckon I wanted ev'rythung jest perfect so you wouldn't ever want to leave me agin."

"I won't leave you, I promise!" she whispered. "I won't ever leave you agin."

Falling Leaves and Mountain Ashes

Book III

'A New Role'

*'No one knows the
Dark illicit dance
Of the true Pretender
Or how the art of
Imitation truly
Becomes the
Man …'*

Brenda George

8

LATE SUMMER, 1900

It was the first time that Eli was to go to Stony Man Camp instead of his father to sell moonshine produced from their stills, which had been running extremely well since he had taken over the helm. Former production figures had more than tripled. In addition to using their own extensive moonshine crops, he was now procuring crops at outrageously low prices from the Ficks and Addis clans of Beacon Mountain. He often wondered why his father had insisted on selling his moonshine to Skyland, which was a day's ride away, when he had no shortage of customers at much closer general stores and private customers to whom he delivered rather than have them collect – since no person was ever permitted to set foot on Claw Mountain without Obediah's express permission!

But the summer resort had attracted the patriarch of Claw Mountain right from its inception about six years back. After hearing about it from a customer, he had gone to satisfy his curiosity about the place and was away for a whole week. He'd come back in a good mood and was full of praise for George Freeman Pollock, its founder, whom he described as 'one of Nature's gentleman' and 'a real man's man'. He praised the man's 'vision' and from all his tales about the place and the high caliber of the guests there, Eli fancied that his paw was so taken with it because it afforded him a taste of his former life amongst rich folk without the necessity for him to leave the mountains.

After packing four of the mules with twenty five-gallon kegs of moonshine, Eli went to see his father for last-minute instruction and advice, nervous in case he managed to do anything wrong and invite his wrath, which even in his father's present state of ill-health was highly unpleasant to face. While his brothers, except for Zack, seldom had anything to do with the decrepit old man anymore, Eli was forced to since he still relied on his experience and expertise when it came to producing first-class liquor. He was determined not to allow the quality of the liquor to deteriorate since this was something his father had repeatedly predicted would happen, having little faith in the ability of his sons to manage without him. It had become a matter of pride and determination to Eli to outshine the mean old bastard yet!

Dressed in his usual faded dungarees and threadbare shirt, Eli was barefoot as usual. On entering the cabin, he found his father lying on his big brass bed, white hair awry, evilly shrunken, stinking like the worst polecat. He was breathing stertorously and his thin white-furred chest seen through the unbuttoned top of his long johns rattled with phlegm. His father took one look at him and snorted in derision.

"Eli Buchanan, George Freeman Pollock will take one look at you and boot you right out of camp. I always go to Stony Man Camp looking like one of the guests, never like a mountaineer, and I expect you to do the same. Pollock always treated me like one of his guests, too. He not only invited me to be his guest at Freeman Lodge, he allowed me to sell my moonshine to his guests. He always buys himself a deal, too, at two dollars a barrel more than the five dollars a barrel he pays the other mountaineers for their crude moonshine, because he says my whiskey and apple brandy are the very best he's ever tasted. At the parties and balls he holds there, all the mountaineers only get to peek in the windows at the fun, but because of my undoubted caliber, I was able go in and dance with all the rich young ladies from the big cities like Washington D C, Baltimore, Philadelphia and New York. I won't have my son treated any different."

He rummaged under his mattress and brought out a crumpled bank note and handed it to Eli, who took it from his father warily. The old man was not given to dishing out money to his sons. Eli straightened it and stared at it suspiciously. It didn't look like any other he had ever seen. "How much it fer, Paw?"

"That there's a fifty-dollar note! Yankee dollars, too! Not useless Confederate bank notes!"

"Fifty dollars?" Eli stared at the bank note in a state of shock. He'd never seen such an enormous sum in a single note in his whole life. "Paw, whar'd you git this from?"

"Never you mind. Just take it down to the store at Graves Mill and buy yourself the finest suit in there and some shoes and hosiery and a tie and a hat, and then you ride into Skyland like you own the whole world! Mind, don't you dare choose anything yourself! Get the proprietor's daughter, Sally, to do it. She's got fine taste and she's a looker too. Been living in New York, but came to help her father out a while back. Brought the latest New York stock with her as well." Obediah chuckled gleefully, his pale-blue eyes gleaming. "But don't make any trouble for her, else she'll try to get her own back on you and will likely send you into Skyland looking like a carnival freak! Mind you be mannerly and don't get fresh with her. You can keep the change to keep yourself well-clothed. This is real important, boy! Don't forget - *clothes maketh a man!* But don't tell your brothers that I gave it to you else they'll get all jealous. Would be wasted on those morons anyhow. And don't change till you get near the camp so you look smart and clean, not with a day's dirt and dust on you. And remember to take off all your weapons before you get into the camp. Only Polly, himself, and the mountaineers, are allowed to carry weapons inside the camp. And take a bath before you leave here! Can't go to Skyland smelling like a long-dead animal. Remember that you're a gentleman come from genteel stock."

Eli stared at his father in stunned amazement, suspecting the fever had addled his brain. Though his father liked to brag about his "aristocratic" background, never had Eli considered himself a gentleman of any sort simply because he was his paw's son. (His father claimed his own mother was addressed as "My Lady" by the locals and their slaves, right up to her death, and he talked like a rich lowlander with a flourishing hoity-toity accent, which Eli had gloatingly mimicked behind his back all his young life.)

Indeed, gentlemanly habits and pursuits were quite beyond any of Obediah's sons simply because they had never been exposed to the like, except occasionally at the store. It had never mattered to Obediah in the past that they dressed roughly and never took a bath. Indeed, they had long been considered a cracker mountain clan under their paw's harsh rule and had been taught that toughness, wildness and being feared by all in the mountains, but especially by the law, was the thing to be desired above all else. This they had accomplished without a doubt and his father took grim pride in it. Yet here he was hinting that Eli should drastically amend his usual behavior. It puzzled and annoyed Eli.

"Shucks, Paw, since when do you care about sech things?"

"Since a Bucko's always got to have respect! You know that I taught you to let no man be your superior. And no man is. Your bloodline is flawless. Well, at Stony Man Camp things are a little different to how they are around here. To stay superior we've got to play them at their own game. When you get into the camp, you ask to see George Freeman Pollock right off. Tell him who you are and don't act all ignorant, or touchy, either, for that matter. Pollock is a very important man in those parts and all the mountaineers around Stony Man look up to him. He can introduce you to important people, who, if you play your cards right, can allow you to take your rightful place in society."

"What rightful place in society?" asked Eli indignantly, scowling fiercely at his father, not enjoying this talk at all. "I ain't one fer no airs an' graces. You know that, Paw."

"Not yet, you aren't. But there's no reason in the world why you shouldn't be. And I'll tell you why. Not only is it your birthright, like your dear saint of a mother believed, it's good for business too. Maybe you can expand the business – even move to Washington, if you play it right."

"Hell, I don't want to leave Claw Mountain, Paw! What I want to do that for?"

"You need to broaden your horizons, Son. See a bit of life. Experience good clothes, fine food and rich women! Somebody's got to get this clan known on the outside. I'm 'King of Claw Mountain', but you can become 'King of Washington'!"

"You mean, you want me to become *th' president?"* asked Eli incredulously.

"Hell no, you're no Abe Lincoln by any stretch, darned fool that he is, freeing all the slaves that way, but if you play your cards right, you could end up providing the president and all those in his administration with Buchanan-stilled liquor! You're the only one of my sons who's got the balls to pull it off. Zack would never move off the mountain. He doesn't care about money. *But you!* You're different from the others! You're smarter than the lot for a start! You could easily learn to appreciate what money can buy. It's *power*, boy. You already know all about that. Besides me and Mr. Pollock, you're the most powerful man in these mountains."

"Yeah, an' I done it without two cents t'rub together, so what I need it now fer?"

"Because you're wasted here on this godforsaken mountain, I can see that now. You've got the gumption to get ahead where it matters – in the nation's capitol! Those fancy folk at Stony Man Camp always treated me like I was a member of their own family. And you know why? Because they know breeding when they see it. Now that this dratted illness bears upon me, it's up to you to find your own way. Oh, and see you treat the rich girls with respect, not like common mountain wenches . . ."

Eli left his paw's pus-and-decay-smelling room several hours later, stunned by his delusions of grandeur about him, thinking that the fever must certainly have eaten right into his brain. Nevertheless, he decided it was too late to start for Stony Man Mountain. He unloaded the mules in the barn, deciding to go to the Graves Mill general store instead and leave for Stony Man at first light in the morrow. After unsaddling the mules, he spotted the old bathtub in the barn and reluctantly pulled it out into the yard. It was coated with thick dust. He couldn't even remember the last time anybody had used it.

The road up the mountain into Stony Man Camp was in appalling condition. Narrow and tortuous, it was full of ruts, gullies and potholes and strewn with rocks and boulders. On the way up, Eli, leading the four mules loaded with five-gallon barrels of whiskey and apple brandy, along the extreme left-hand side of the track, was passed by a splendid four-horse team pulling a Western-style covered wagon, full of crates which was obviously taking supplies up to the busy summer resort, as well as gaily laughing, well-groomed guests on buckboards, driven by hired drivers. Others had hired horses, while a few of the guests opted to walk the four strenuous miles up to the resort. By the time Eli strode into Stony Man Camp, or Skyland, as it was becoming increasingly known, it was late afternoon and the long shadows of tall trees lay across it. The air was crisp and cool. There was a bustle of business and activity in the place and Eli noticed mountaineers working as stonemasons, handymen, carpenters and builders all over the place.

A short while ago, in the cover of the forest coming up Stone Man Mountain, Eli had changed into his new quality clothing chosen for him by Sally French, the comely daughter of the proprietor of the Graves Mill general store. Sally, true to his father's advice, had given him sound guidance and had fitted him out in unquestionably good taste. Indeed, he looked quite the lowlander dandy! He wore a gray flannel suit, a pale-blue shirt, red braces and a blue-and-red plaid tie, a gray Derby hat with a gray feather in it and gray shoes.

Eli could not believe that he now owned such splendid apparel when he'd been forced to live like poor white trash his whole life (not that he had cared much before!). Though it sat on him oddly, like glorious finery on a scarecrow, he felt these fancy threads gave him a stature previously only won for him by the skill and indiscriminate use of his guns, knife and whips. However, he was feeling somewhat strange and foolish right now, leading the string of four packed mules, on foot, since his father had warned him that only fools rode mules. The new shoes were pinching his toes, despite the fact that he wore socks. Adhering to his father's strict instructions, he had taken off all his weapons and packed them carefully on one of the mules at the same time he had changed his clothes, but because he felt quite naked without them, he carried his long bullwhip in his hand.

As he entered the camp he saw a stand of glorious hemlocks, with logs arranged underneath them. He heard laughter and loud singing of sorts and turned to see a line of six donkeys on which rode a motley group of city folk dressed in formal clothing, who were entering the camp from a westerly direction. Seated on the lead donkey was a little ginger-haired man wearing a ten-gallon hat. He was carrying a bugle and was yodeling on the top of his voice, causing the camp dogs to start howling. On the two rear donkeys were two spiffy-looking young men – one wearing a wide-brimmed straw hat and the other, a straw boater – and sandwiched between them and the yodeler were an old man and two elegant young women who were riding side-saddle.

Tying his mules to a post, Eli walked purposefully towards the group, who were busy dismounting. One of the young ladies alighted with the help of a big, portly man with white hair, muttonchop sideburns and a florid complexion, who was wearing a monocle attached to a gold chain clipped to the lapel of his light summer suit.

Suddenly, there was a loud shriek of alarm and Eli spun around to see what had caused it. A large coiled yellow rattlesnake had reared up from under a rock, with its fangs bared and a fierce rattling of its tail. It was ready to strike one of the young ladies who had obviously alighted from her donkey, far too close for its liking. Acting instinctively, Eli unleashed his whip in a flash. It struck like a lick of lightning, the thin end wrapping itself around the neck of the rattler. That accomplished, he drew it sharply back before lunging forward so that it went soaring through the air in a high wide arc, landing deep in the forest surrounding the camp. There were great cries of relief and amazementand a flurry of spontaneous clapping from the riders and other onlookers.

The man in the ten-gallon hat and strange garb strutted over to Eli, a beaming smile on his youthful, open face. *"Why, thank you, kind sir!* You sure know how to handle that whip of yours! I have no doubt that this young lady is extremely grateful to you for your quick reaction, which undoubtedly saved her life. But, in so doing, I fear you just lost out on two dollars. That's how much I'd pay for a large live rattler like that."

"You collect rattlers?" asked Eli in bald astonishment.

"Indeed, I do. All snakes, actually. Those I don't keep for my snake shows, I personally deliver to Dr. William B. Mann, who is the Superintendent of the Washington Zoological Gardens."

"Had me a pet rattler myself once," muttered Eli.

The man looked surprised and impressed. "Well, I never! Then you'll have to come and see my snake show after supper this evening. Name's George Pollock, but my friends call me Polly. What's yours?" He stuck out a friendly hand for Eli to shake.

George Pollock! So this was the man that his father so admired and looked up to! Eli felt a keen sense of shock. He didn't look like anything he had imagined a man of such magnitude and growing fame would look. Weighing in at some 130 pounds and about thirty years old, he presented an almost comical figure with his wispy red mustache, bugle, ten-gallon hat, high boots, corduroy trousers, a corduroy fringed hunting shirt, which dropped almost to his knees, and hauled in at the waist by a United States army canvas belt, with a .45 caliber revolver stuck in it. Yet, Eli had to admit that despite his odd, eccentric appearance, the man carried himself with such authority, he somehow managed to carry it off.

"Eli Buchanan, son of Obediah," replied Eli, taking the man's firm hand.

Pollock's eyes widened in surprise. "Well, there's a thing! *Obediah's son!* How is the old son-of-a-gun?"

"Mighty poorly. That's how come I'm here in his stead."

Pollock shook his head in sympathy. "Why, I'm real sorry to hear that. He seemed brimming with health the last time I saw him. It just so happens my mother is in a very poor state of health as well."

Just then, the young woman entered the conversation, turning to Eli and saying breathlessly, "Why, sir, I think I owe you my very life."

Eli got to see her close-up for the first time and what he observed quite took his breath away. He was instantly grateful that he had taken his father's advice regarding taking a bath and buying a new set of clothing that behooved the wealthy gentry who frequented the place. He had never seen such an exquisitely beautiful and refined young woman in his whole life and he became instantly tongue-tied.

She wore a voluminous black satin skirt trimmed with small black pearl buttons that fitted snugly under her bodice, a white satin blouse with muttonchop sleeves, with a huge black satin bow at her throat. Her skin was pale and so flawless it looked like fine porcelain. Her lips were the color of dark rubies, while her jet-black hair was swept up under a small straw boater hat, wrapped in black voile, which floated in two long strands down her back. She viewed him with dancing green eyes beneath a short black veil that had been lifted. Then remembering what his father had told him, Eli whipped his hat off his head and smoothed back his bright-yellow hair "Heck, it was more a'skeer'd of you than you were of it, ma'am."

"Just the same, it was ready to strike me. You saved me from almost certain death. How can I ever repay you?"

"Thar ain't no need." Suddenly aware of the crudeness of his speech, he immediately amended it to resemble his father's. "I mean . . . there ain't . . . isn't . . . no . . . er, any need."

"My name is Annabel Cotterell. What did you say yours is?"

"Eli, ma'am," said Eli, blushing furiously. "Eli Buchanan."

"Father, do come and meet Mr. Buchanan here. He saved my life getting rid of that awful rattler with his whip." She went and slipped her hand through the arm of the portly, prosperous-looking gentleman with white hair and muttonchop sideburns, who was standing nearby, watching the proceedings with a cold critical eye, amidst a curious group of onlookers. "Mr. Buchanan, this is my father, Reverend Cotterell."

Reverend! Eli recoiled inwardly, but managed to keep his face impassive. He hated men of religion more than he hated most men, because he hated God, and he'd had a hand in chasing an enterprising preacher or two away from Claw Mountain in his time. He gave the man a flat, baleful stare. The reverend stopped as if struck by the force of it. He did not stretch out a hand. Instead, he nodded at him shortly, staring at the jagged scar on Eli's left cheek with a look of extreme distaste, before hurrying his daughter away from such obviously undesirable company. Furious at the pointed insult, Eli considered striding over to his tethered mules, drawing out his dual pearl-handled Iver Johnson pistols and shooting the departing man squarely between his meaty shoulder blades. Had his paw's long lecture not still been ringing in his ears, and the man his paw respected so much not been standing right beside him, he would have done it without a second's thought.

However, he felt slightly mollified when Annabel looked over her shoulder at him and said with a small winsome smile and a fluttering of long black lashes,

"Perhaps I'll see you later, Mr. Buchanan."

Annabel's comely curves and the female swaying of her hips made Eli smart in a strange, unfamiliar way. It somehow compounded his humiliation at the hands of her father and caused the small muscle in his jaw to flicker with anger.

Pollock clapped a placating hand on his shoulder. "I can understand how you may be smitten, son, but you would be well-advised to forget about that charming young lady. No man is good enough for the reverend's only daughter. He keeps an eagle eye over her virtue. Since he got here, he's sent any number of eager lovelorn suitors packing. Come, unload your mules then let me show you around the place, after which we'll retire to my quarters and enjoy some of your father's famous apple brandy – after I've purchased a keg or three of each of what you've got to offer, of course. It's been a while since I enjoyed the rare pleasure . . ."

After allowing him to offload, stable, water and feed his mules, for the next two hours, Pollock, accompanied by his white-and-brown pit bull, Nellie, showed Eli proudly around the place. He told Eli he had purchased the dog nearly a decade before from a Negro in Washington, as protection, and let the animal sleep beneath his bed. The affable fellow then regaled him with colorful tales of the early days at the camp. Eli had to admit that it was all very impressive. Built on a shoulder plateau, Stony Man Mountain, with Stony Man Peak looming up behind it, was carved out of the wilderness, with lovely views in close proximity – though nothing compared with those from Claw Mountain, of course! His father had described Stony Man Camp as a 'colony of tents', so it was clear to Eli that many improvements had been made since his father had last visited the camp a year ago, at the time his brother, Zack, had taken the Harley wench for a wife.

Although there were still a good number of tents, there were also a fair number of rustic log cottages and cabins, a large rustic log dining hall, commodious bath houses supplied with hot water from boilers and wood-stoves kept fed by employees and even the odd guest, a log stable covered with hand-made shingles, kennels and a kitchen, all lit up with a newly-acquired acetylene gas plant, which also lit up the grounds.

Close to the observation point on cliffs at the head of Kettle Canyon, Pollock introduced Eli to Augustus R. Heaton, a bearded gentleman whom Pollock described as an artist, poet and author, smilingly referring to him as the "Patriarch" of the camp. Heaton's plot, called "Indian Rock", consisted of a number of colorful striped tents and a picturesque rustic log cabin, which were surrounded by a decorative wooden fence, with an elaborate wooden feature over the entrance gate. Pollock told Eli that all the tents in the camp were provided with a wooden floor and a double roof and were comfortable even in the wettest weather. A large windmill at Kagey Spring drove water up to a tank in the camp and there were well-tended gardens in which grew a large variety of vegetables, as well as all manner of berries, fruits and flowers, for use at the resort. There was a small bluegrass pasture rent from the forest to graze half-a-dozen cows to provide fresh milk and cream to the guests.

"I go down to the wharves in Washington once a week myself to buy seafood direct from the boats – bring back lobster, oysters, shrimp and fish packed in ice-packed sugar barrels for shipment back to Skyland," the little man said pridefully.

Eli wondered what type of food the first three might be if they weren't fish.

Pollock went on to tell him that mountaineer women worked as cleaners, cooks and dish-washers and that a mountain woman named Mrs. Park did all the laundry, having set up large laundry cauldrons at a spring a mile away from Skyland. Eli spotted a mountaineer so entirely covered in baskets that he looked like a giant tortoise on the move.

"Whar's he from?" he asked Pollock curiously.

"Corbin Hollow. They make fine Century baskets from white oak, which they sell to my guests." He went on to say that Skyland was also a ready market for the mountaineers' eggs, vegetables, moonshine and cordwood. Indeed, Pollock provided jobs for at least fifty mountain men and women in the Stony Man region, paying them fifty cents a day to clear brush, act as porters for the camping gear and dig up tree-stumps, in addition to those he hired for their building capabilities. Eli could see why his father had been so impressed with the man. Mountaineers did not usually take kindly to strangers and he'd heard that they were a mighty rough bunch around here, though not in the same league as the Buckos, of course.

After the grand tour, the two young men sat in easy chairs sipping superb Buchanan apple brandy out of fine crystal goblets in Pollock's log cottage called Freeman's Lodge, which was situated just below the Dining Hall. A huge buffalo robe lay in front of the log-burning fireplace and several of the walls were filled with shelves bearing Pollock's collection of "beer stein glasses". They were of every size and description, some as small as thimbles. They chatted for a while about the failing health of their respective parents, Pollock, his devoted pit bull, Nellie, lying beside him aas well as his two lead brown beagles, Ringwood and Tripod (they slept in some outside kennels along with other dogs used for the resort's "coon chases"). Then he casually remarked, "Ever thought of making money from that remarkable whip of yours?"

Eli gawked at his host in astonishment. "What do you mean?"

"I mean, if you could work up some kind of show with it, I'll pay you five dollars a night for a week. I'm always after new types of entertainment in this place. You interested?"

Eli stared at him in a thrall of astonishment and disbelief. Through handling moonshine sales and getting supplies from the store, he had learned how to count money. He discreetly used his fingers to help him to mentally calculate how much that would come to. *Thirty-five dollars!* It was more cash than he saw in a whole year (until being handed that fifty dollar note by his father, that is)! And he could earn that in a single week!

"Hell, yeah, I'm interested. Only trouble is, I ain't brung no change of clothing. Figger'd I'd do my business and be gone by now."

"That won't be a problem. We're much the same build, although you're a bit taller. You're welcome to take whatever you need from my wardrobe and take full advantage of our laundering service."

"That's mighty generous of you, Mr . . . er . . . Polly."

"Nonsense! We'll dress you up like a cowboy for your whip show. Have plenty to offer in the way of costumes from our Wild West Shows. You can take your pick! 'Eli Buchanan's Amazing Whip Show' can start immediately following my snake show in the Dining Hall tonight. Tomorrow night you can do something around the campfire. We'll change the venue every night to make it more interesting and exciting. Of course, I insist that you be my guest at Skyland while you're here. You can stay with me right here in Freeman Lodge. Your father always did. Quite a fellow, your father. Many a time we've swopped stories till dawn."

"Yeah, sir, quite a fellow . . ."

While Pollock went to take a refreshing hot bath, followed by a short nap at Freeman Lodge, Eli nipped at the moonshine keg – Buchanan "white lightning" bought from him by his genial host, along with a keg of apple brandy. He was feeling totally out of his depth here at Skyland, despite his host's efforts to make him feel at ease.

His father had been right to wise him up about how things worked here else he'd be looking the complete fool by now. He thought of the young lady he'd saved from the rattler with an excited feeling in the pit of his stomach, knowing she was like no woman he had ever met before. But when he thought of the reverend it was with slow-burning anger at being so humiliated in front of her. Denied the instant retaliation he was so used to venting without thought, already he was keenly aware of how differently things worked in this place.

When he returned from his bath, Pollock donned a black "tuxedo", as he called it, and was ready for the evening's supper and entertainment. In ebullient mood, his host walked with Eli, who was dressed in his new clothes, across to the rustic Dining Hall. The front of the hall was set up on stilts with a decorative low wooden railing surrounding the balcony, set amongst big trees, with flowering bushes below.

Eli was placed next to Pollock, who sat at the head of the long table and there followed a sumptuous meal, the likes of which Eli has never seen or tasted before, all served by black-uniformed Negro waiters wearing white gloves, while music was being performed by an all-Negro orchestra, led by a man named Will Grigsby, a rather handsome young Negro with a long down-turned mustache, who played a golden horn that Pollock called a cornet. A couple of Will's brothers were amongst the other well-attired members of the orchestra. The musical instruments consisted of two guitars, two violins, a bass and Will's cornet.

Alarmed by the vast amount of cutlery he had no idea how to use and, sorely embarrassed by his own ineptitude, Eli tried hard not to be noticed. Since he was unable to read, the menu was a complete mystery to him, but Pollock, spying his discomfiture, came swiftly to his rescue by suggesting various dishes. Used to spooning meals out of opened cans, it was a terrible ordeal for Eli and he felt like the worst kind of ignorant hick, though nobody seemed to notice that he was the only mountaineer seated at the table – fooled by the quality of his clothing, no doubt. His paw had been right about that, after all. He studied the other diners, the women wearing fabulous jewels and dressed in shimmering evening gowns, the men in black tuxedos and bow ties, and tried to imitate their moves, but the Hawksbill clams completely dumbfounded him, his food kept falling off his fork, and some peas accompanying the succulent roast lamb shot across the table between two guests on the other side then went skidding along the floor before being swiftly retrieved by the discreet gloved hand of one of the waiters.

Afraid to make an even bigger ass of himself, Eli skipped dessert and instead settled for a glass of what the waiter called champagne, to steady his nerves. It completely lacked the punch of moonshine, but it tasted pleasant enough, he supposed. He was innately thankful that the ravishing Annabel Cotterell and her father were seated right at the other end of the long dining table . . .

Afer supper, while George Pollock was changing from his tuxedo into his clothes for the snake show, he gave Eli the key for the Annex Cottage, which was situated to the east of Massanutten Lodge, where he said Eli would be able to find a suitable "cowboy" costume to wear for his whip show, describing the one he always wore to his Wild West Shows, which he said was sure to fit Eli.

The darkened cottage was a hotchpotch of a building. El entered it and found it full of shadows and strange shapes. He turned on the gas light at the entrance. It was clearly used strictly for storage purposes for the sallow light was thrown onto a large horde of George Pollock's belongings. Among the paraphernalia, there was cloth-covered furniture, antiques of all descriptions from elaborate lamps and chandeliers to a stately grandfather clock. A large collection of wines was stored in a rack against one wall and at least six trolley racks of different kinds of fancy costumes, as well as shelves full of shoes, boots and an odd collection of hats. Aware there was not much time, Eli wended his way through the dusty assorted bric-a-brac to the racks and began wading through the hanging garments. There was a large variety of colorful apparel in velvets and satins and laces, with ostrich feathers and masks, mostly vastly unfamiliar to Eli. He moved to the next trolley, then the next. Finally, he drew out the "cowboy" outfit that Pollock had described to him and changed quickly into the strange garb. True to Pollock's prediction, the red shirt was a perfect fit, as were the black cowboy jeans, chaps and black cowboy boots. Finally, he tied a black kerchief around his throat, stuck two fake silver revolvers into holsters on either side of his hips and placed the black ten-gallon hat with a silver band on it, upon his head. He frowned, feeling mighty ridiculous in this loud get-up.

Just then, in the stillness of the night, Eli heard strange sounds coming from behind an interleading door. They were almost whispering sounds, with sighs and hisses and slippery slurps that were impossible to identify. His curiosity aroused, he slowly opened the door, turned on the gas light and entered the small room. The sounds were clearly coming from a white Victorian ball-and-claw bathtub with gold taps that was set against the far wall. Tiptoeing forward to see what was making the strange sounds, cursing the fact that his chaps were loudly squeaking, Eli ventured forth with caution. Then he gave a startled cry, his heart pounding with fright for, in the bathtub, was an inches-deep writhing mass of live snakes - *deadly yellow and black rattlesnakes, reddish-brown copperheads, black snakes, pilot and ringnecks!* Several of the snakes, clearly disturbed by the noise of his chaps and sensing his alien presence, rose up their heads and assaulted him with an array of cold staring eyes and black flickering forked tongues. Rattles began an ominous censure in his ears. Eli hastily backed out the room and slammed shut the door, thinking that George Freeman Pollock was sure one brave and unusual son-of-a-bitch!

29

Later that evening, Eli entered the large dining hall for a second time, after the long dining table had been cleared and moved away and chairs positioned to give a good view of Pollock's snake show at one end of the room, providing seating for about one hundred persons. Eli quailed at the size of the audience. He spotted

Annabel Cotterell and her father sitting in the front row. To his surprise, she turned in her seat and beckoned to him. Eli, dressed in the loud outlandish cowboy outfit which made him feel awkward and conspicuous in this grandly attired group, carrying his prized bullwhip, cautiously wound his way, chaps squeaking, through a maze of chairs to find there was an empty seat right beside her.

"I've saved you a seat," she said, by way of explanation. He sat on it with a feeling of impending doom, which had everything to do with his ludicrous appearance. The thought of his forthcoming act in front of this bunch of rich, snobbish strangers unnerved him. Reverend Cotterell, leaning forward in his chair, threw him a dark withering look. Eli didn't know how much more provocation he could stand from the pompous ass before he might be forced to retaliate. And when he did, neither the reverend nor his daughter would be likely to approve. The young man on the other side of him looked him up and down in pure cynical distaste, before craning his neck around him in annoyance. He was dressed in a tuxedo, had a white scarf draped around his neck and wore a top hat and gloves. He sat with his two hands casually covering an ivory cane and was smoking a smelly cigar in a long black holder. It was obvious to Eli that he had been conversing with Annabel Cotterell and was highly annoyed at his arrival. Eli felt good that he had effectively cut him off from her considerable charms. He was acutely aware of the young lady's presence himself and was surprised that she did not seem to find his appearance in any way odd.

She, on the other hand, looked incredibly beautiful in a long lilac dress and shiny purple slippers, her raven hair, stemmed on one side with a sparkling clear-stoned clip, flowing in waves past her shoulders, pale alabaster skin gleaming like pearl, green eyes shining with pleasure at seeing him – well, so it seemed to him. She smelled of flowers and sweetness and her voice was warm as she whispered, "How lovely to see you again, Mr. Buchanan. I wasn't sure if you had left the resort already."

"No, I'll be stayin' a week yet."

Just then her father grated his throat noisily and Annabel turned dutifully away from him to face the front. But it seemed to Eli, her smile was full of secrets and she was decidedly pleased . . .

At the sound of a bugle blast executed by Pollock, the snake show began in the Skyland Dining Hall, before an avid audience of richly attired city folk. From the start it was clear to all the audience that George Freeman Pollock was a born showman with a flair for the dramatic. Dressed once again in his Wild West garb, he opened a snake box, lifting out rattlesnakes, one by one, in the middle of their long sinuous bodies with his bare hands, before putting them back. As each of the highly poisonous reptiles hung, churning slowly in mid-air, submissive but menacing-looking, the audience watched breathlessly, fascinated and revolted at the same time, the silence broken only by an eerie hissing sound. Pollock swirled and handled each of them with complete ease and familiarity. Then the audience gasped as the sinister sound of rattles started up, man's ingrown fear of snakes rising richly to the fore and reflecting on their horrified faces.

At first, the small red-mustached young man played the reptiles individually, stopping and starting the rattles on them on command. Eventually, he allowed the large rattlers, three yellow with their intricate diamond markings, and two black, with markings that were not so easily visible, to slide sinuously up his arms, over his shoulders and around his torso, causing the ladies to shudder with horror and revulsion, hiding their carefully painted faces, while the men gave the odd involuntary whoop despite the fact that Pollock had called for complete quiet during the performance so as not to upset the delicate creatures. There was good reason for that. Rattlesnakes are exceedingly jittery creatures, after all. They have a great natural fear of man and the secret in handling them is to allay these fears and calm them down. This, Eli noticed, Pollock did with the sound of his voice, just like Eli had once done with his own pet snake.

As a fitting climax to the show, Pollock announced he would perform a feat equaled only by the Hopi Indians of Arizona, performing their famous snake dance. Because of the danger involved, he called again for absolute silence from the audience once more. Tension filled the air as the orchestra began a dramatic musical build up. The members of the large audience instinctively leaned forward then, as if suddenly fearful that the snakes might strike out at them despite the fact that they were seated well back from the "stage" area, they hastily drew back again. The orchestra began playing a dramatic tune announced as "Song of India". A tall dark-haired woman in a long narrow flounced gown, with red satin binding sewn onto the bottom of each flounce, and red satin shoes, commenced playing a wailing instrument that looked similar to a fiddle. Pollock then performed the Indian Snake Dance, picking up a large king rattler with his mouth, to the awed "oohs" and "aahs" of the audience. It was a feat Eli would not care to imitate and a thrilling display of daring. His respect for his host was growing by the minute.

Just then, the pompous-looking young man sitting beside him stirred. He sneered in a loud, bored voice, "The man is a fake I tell you! Not only is that outfit he's wearing a clear copy-cat of Theodore Roosevelt's Wild West duds, it's obvious to even a fool that the poisonous fangs of that reptile have been removed."

Eli felt a surge of anger inside him. There was a shocked gasp from the rest of the audience, which he could tell did not appreciate the man's raised caustic remarks. Eli was not surprised by this clear support for his host for in the short time that Eli had been around Pollock, it was clear that he was a highly popular man, to whom people flocked to hobnob or pass the time of day with, his capacity for extending friendship with everyone, from his staff, to his guests and to the mountaineers, quite remarkable.

Indeed, Pollock's welcoming overtures towards himself had both surprised and flattered Eli. Never having had a friend of any description before in his life, save perhaps his brother, Jake, Eli realized what a rare attribute this was. Now Pollock was being openly insulted by this fool, who was also clearly endangering Pollock's life by so breaking the silence at such a crucial point in the act. And what he said about the king snake was simply not true. Eli could tell from where he sat that its fangs were very much intact. In any event, from his own experience, he knew that rattlesnakes that had their fangs removed or had lost, grew others, a fact of which this fool was clearly ignorant!

It was clear that Pollock, too, had heard the loud cynical remarks above the sound of the orchestra and the wailing fiddle-like instrument, for his head jerked up momentarily before his concentration necessarily returned to the dangerous reptile he was busy holding in his mouth. Feeling compelled to stand up for his heroic host, Eli turned a deadly stare upon the arrogant young man, coldly informing him in a low compelling undertone that the fangs hadn't been remov-ed at all. He then inquired of him who Theodore Roosevelt was to try and dispel that notion too if he could. Evidently the crusty Reverend Cotterell had nothing wrong with his hearing, for, to Eli's everlasting humiliation, he leaned around his daughter and glared at him with bulging cold blue eyes, one clearly enlarged through the lens of his monocle. He dangerously broke the required silence once more.

"Good gracious, man!" he snapped loud enough for the whole audience to hear, "You jest, of course. The man he was referring to only happens to be the vice president of the United States . . . !"

After the stunning finale of the snake show, Pollock put the reptiles back into the snake box to hearty applause, carefully locked it and took up a bullhorn. "Ladies and gentlemen, we now have a slight change to our printed program. We have amongst us a skilled proponent of the whip, the likes of which I have never seen before. Why, just this evening he saved the life of a young woman by using his whip to remove a dangerous rattlesnake about to strike her. I witnessed this remarkable incident myself. We are fortunate that this young man has agreed to give you a short display of his whip skills. I am privileged to present to you young Eli Buchanan, a member of the famous Buckos, whip-handler supreme, who hails from the heart of Texas."

While the audience clapped politely, Eli frowned at his host, angry at the deliberate deception about from where he sprang. Then he realized that Pollock was only trying to create a "cowboy" image for him to go with the garb and this was very likely appreciated by the audience. And while his paw must have told him that his clan was known as the Buckos, he very much doubted that he would have told him anything bad about them, such was his determination to impress the owner of Skyland he held in such high esteem. And, quite suddenly, Eli was glad of the cover of "Texas", wherever that was, thankful that no one in this highfaluting audience was likely to know of the Buckos and their mean reputation in the Blue Ridge Mountains.

After all, he would hate for Annabel Cotterell to learn his real identity and discover that he was just an ignorant hillbilly. All he wanted to do right now was impress the young lady, dazzle her with his considerable skills. He had no doubt that he could achieve this. After all, he had practiced daily with a whip from the tender age of ten. He had become increasingly skilled with it, soon using it to intimidate, humiliate and hurt others.

Eli, in his loud cowboy duds, with two fake silver revolvers stuck into holsters on either side of his lean hips, reluctantly rose from his seat and walked to the center of the hall with loudly squeaking chaps, holding his bullwhip. He turned to face this well-attired audience, the men in their tuxedos and top hats, the women in their glittering gowns, ostrich feathers, ermine stoles and fox-furs, while Negro waiters moved among the audience dispensing glasses of champagne on round trays. Eli stood silently, his handsome scarred face coldly unsmiling, eerie pale-yellow eyes fixed on the audience. He could tell that his flat incurious stare spooked the hell out of them for the whole audience fell silent and watchful.

As the silence stretched, he knew he emanated such an aura of menace that it completely unnerved the onlookers. He had always had this power to disconcert and he enjoyed exercising it now on this snobbish, tenderfoot mob, with their toffee-nosed airs and graces. It felt good to be in command and superior again after the acute embarrassment he'd suffered a short while ago at the hands of Reverend Cotterell. The audience began to shift and squirm in their seats, clearly disturbed by his unmoving broody presence. He bowed to them slightly then, quite suddenly, flashed them a mischievous little boy's smile. With that, they let out their collective breaths.

He began slowly. Raising his twelve-foot long leather bullwhip high above his head, he swung it around and around, till it made a loud whirring sound and created a draught, gradually increasing in speed till it was just an invisible blur that caused a chilly air-current that ruffled hair and ostrich feathers. After a few minutes, he slowed the whip down until it was once again visible to human sight. Then with the audience mesmerized, he lashed it against the floorboards on either side of him making them jump in almost comical unison.

After going through a series of more mundane whip tricks, he turned his attention on a bowl piled with fruit on a table on one end of the "stage" area. One by one, he whipped the fruit out of the bowl; first an apple then an orange then a pear then a banana. Each rose in the air and sailed back towards him, till the air was full of flying fruit. He neatly caught each in his free hand before casually tossing them into the audience. The menfolk sportingly lunged to catch them to impress their womenfolk with their athleticism. There were loud cheers and warm clapping, and Eli knew that already he had their undivided attention and support.

He then called for a volunteer and, to his grim satisfaction, the officious young man, who had so recently insulted Pollock, raised a casual white-gloved hand, an amused smirk on his face. Eli smiled to himself. He had no doubt that the young dandy had volunteered in order to try to show him up or to gain favor with the ladies, especially Annabel.

"What is your name, sir?" Eli asked him, casually beckoning him onto the floor.

The intrepid volunteer got up and went to stand beside Eli. "Chester Blake," he informed the audience at large with an amused smirk, tipping his top hat. "Though most of you know that already, I would imagine."

"Ah, Mr. Blake, I trust you will not get sore at anything I do?"

Leaning on his cane, his black top hat set at a jaunty angle on his head, Chester Blake nodded urbanely. "Of course not." he said smoothly. "Do your worst!"

"You real sure now? You don't want to change your mind?"

Blake shook his head. He stood there with an air of complete bravado, leaning on his cane with one hand, while he used the other to puff at a smelly cigar, having left his long holder lying on his seat. Eli distanced himself from the man by some twelve feet.

"Well, Mr. Blake, anytime you wish me to stop, please let me know. I'm sure that nobody in this hall would blame you any if you wished to pull out at any time."

"I wouldn't dream of it, Mr. Buchanan!" replied Blake, though he suddenly looked a trifle unsure, as if wondering what he had let himself in for.

At that, the whip suddenly curled around the man's cane and jolted it from beneath his extended hand to make him falter and almost fall, causing a howl of laughter to come from the audience. It was done so suddenly and with such incredible speed that it had caught everybody by surprise. The cane itself, an elegant piece of sculptured ivory with a black onyx top, was sent hurtling up into the air. It pin-wheeled on the way down and Eli caught it deftly in one hand, to the gasps and cheers of the audience.

No sooner had Blake recovered from the sheer ignominy of that when Eli whisked the cigar out of Blake's mouth with a lick of the whip and sent it sailing up to the ceiling. It swirled in mid-air then plummeted straight down. Eli quickly positioned himself under it and it landed plum in his mouth. He clamped his teeth over it and started puffing away nonchalantly, causing the audience to break into loud, appreciative laughter and applause. Blake looked decidedly disconcerted by what had happened, but soon recovered his composure and sneered with disbelief. He gamely bowed his head towards to Eli in grudging acknowledgement of his skill. Though he was smiling urbanely, Eli could sense his intense chagrin simmering below the surface.

Then Eli began a dazzling display of whip-wielding that had the audience gasping. First, he let his whip loose so that it became an entity all on its own. It flickered to and fro, to and fro, making a loud cracking sound in the air. It licked at his astonished volunteer like a striking snake, but never once did it actually land on the person of Chester Blake, who, to his credit, did not shriek, bawl like a baby or squirm, like the cowardly Hannibal Hanford had done. Though he could not stop himself from rapidly blinking every now and then, he managed to remain upright and fairly unconcerned looking, which took some doing considering the steadfast attack of the rampaging whip. But every now and then Eli would lash the whip down on the floorboards beside him, making him jump.

From long experience, Eli knew that the removal of a man's hat left him feeling the most vulnerable and, next minute, the end of the whip snaked around Blake's top hat and sent it skidding across the floorboards. Then he began slowly undressing the man. He whipped the white scarf from around his neck. His bowtie became miraculously undone and was whipped out from around his neck. Each of his shirt buttons in turn were ripped off his shirt and sent spinning around the floor like a series of tiny tops. Blake's braces came in for it next, whipped out and tossed to the floorboards with skillful little lightning licks of the whip. It was nothing short of sheer, dazzling wizardry and the audience fully appreciated the unbelievable skill it took.

By now, Chester Blake was consumed with white-faced anger. It was obvious to Eli that he had never imagined that such things could be achieved with a whip. Perhaps he had expected that he would have to hold apples in his hand or on his head, to be whipped away by the whip while he remained stoically upright and unblinking, displaying his bravery to all. Instead he stood hatless, hair wildly awry, disheveled, his collar open, his dress shirt agape, his braces gone, so he had to clutch at his tuxedo pants to make sure they didn't fall down.

By the look in his eye, Eli knew that Blake knew he was being systematically humiliated by this upstart from nowhere. But his assurances to Eli that he would not take affront at anything he did, stopped him from calling an immediate halt to the proceedings. He struggled to hang onto his dignity, chin arrogantly raised. And seeing his defiant posture, Eli could not resist. His whip wound itself several times around the man's legs and unceremoniously upended him. The oaf landed smack on his ass and squealed as petulantly as a child. Aware of where he was,

Eli sportingly went to him to give him a hand up. Blake vehemently slapped his hand away. He stood up with considerable difficulty, after shedding himself of the binds of the whip with shaking hands, and flounced out of the room in a furious rage, hanging onto his tuxedo pants for dear life. There were a few sighs of regret but, by and large, everybody seemed to remember the pompous ass doing his best to humiliate *George Pollock*, their well-loved and popular host, and felt he deserved no less a dressing-down.

It was a fitting end to the show. With a flourish, Eli took up his whip again with one hand and, with the other, took off his ten-gallon hat, swooping it low as he bowed from the waist, to tumultuous applause. He was standing right in front of Annabel Cotterell, who had stood up and was clapping loudly, a broad, amused smile on her lovely face. With George Pollock barking his praise over the bullhorn, Eli was flushed with triumph.

Not only had he totally demolished his pompous, opinionated rival, he had clearly won the approval of the audience, not least of all this beautiful young woman with jet black hair and laughing green eyes, who was watching him now with a look of pure admiration and awe. Only the portly Reverend Cotterell with his white hair and flourishing side-burns, sat stonily unmoved and coldly unamused, his monocle clamped within the fleshy surrounds of one twitching blue eye. Used to fear and horror meeting his former displays of whip-wizardry, it was a novel experience for Eli to be so widely admired. He decided he liked it just dandy!

30

Eli was jolted awake at the crack of dawn the next morning by a god-awful loud blasting noise. He leapt up in his long johns and staggered to the window of the spare room in Freeman Lodge where he had spent the night, to see the red-haired and slight figure of George Pollock, hale and hearty as a bright-eyed child despite his late night, standing with his legs astride and his bugle to his lips, in front of the log Dining Hall where a large group of guests had gathered to commence on a hike. One of his beagle dogs stood beside him, head lifted, baying at the raucous sound.

Pollock saw him peeping out the window and shouted for him to join them, but Eli shook his bright tousled head furiously. His host had already tried hard to convince him to accompany them on their excursion last night, but Eli had lived his whole life in the mountains and had no particular wish to explore this one. Led by Pollock in his "Teddy Roosevelt" garb, the well-attired guest hikers set off, the women wearing sensible skirts several inches off the ground, most of the men, tight-fitting trousers fitted into knee-high boots. Eli frowned when he spotted Annabel Cotterell and her father amongst the hikers. He had been hoping to see her at breakfast. *Damn, now she'd be gone the whole day!* Had he known she was going he might well have joined them, but they were already on their way and would be gone by the time he got dressed.

Now that he was well and truly awake, Eli decided to get up. He was habitually a late riser, after invariably drinking himself into a stupor every night and passing out. He chose some clothes for himself from Pollock's expansive wardrobe. He was walking across to the Dining Hall for breakfast in an immaculately starched white linen shirt and the most subdued pair of trousers he could find amongst a bunch of loud plaid ones. Since he had need of it twice already, he decided on the spur of the moment to take his whip with him. But as he neared the Dining Hall, he felt a bit of a fool carrying the thing, surmising it was not the mark of a genteel man. He would leave it somewhere outside the Dining Hall, and hope nobody around here had long fingers. It was then that he noticed Chester Blake on a buckboard tethered to four mules on the dirt road near the entrance to the camp. He was in the driver's seat and held the reins. The buckboard was piled high with luggage – four trunks and a bulging carpet bag – which indicated that Blake had intended to stay a lot longer. (Pollock had told him that most guests spent at least a month at the resort, while some spent the entire summer.) So, thought Eli in disgust, unable to face his fellows after last night, he was slinking away like a mongrel dog with its tail between its legs. Eli strolled over to him, approaching from the rear of the buckboard.

"Goin' someplace?" he asked casually.

Blake jumped and his head spun around guiltily. Then he recovered himself and gave Eli a contemptuous glare. When Eli was level with one of the hind mules, he turned and looked up at him with icy pale-yellow eyes. Blake was dressed in an expensive-looking dark brown, vested serge suit, a stiff white collar, a dark-brown tie and had a brown derby hat on his head.

"As if that's any business of yours!" Blake snapped.

"Well, it might be if this is Mr. Pollock's buckboard you're takin' away."

"I have his permission," Blake said coldly. "I'll leave it at the Sours farmhouse at the bottom of the mountain then I'll take a carriage to Luray, and from there, take the train back to Baltimore. Pollock said he'd send somebody to fetch it."

"What a shame. I was kinda countin' on usin' you as my volunteer fer my whip show agin t'night."

Blake drew himself up haughtily. "I have no wish to remain here in such undesirable company. You, sir, are no gentleman! You don't fool me for a minute. You're nothing but a monkey in a fancy suit, pretending to be something you're not!"

The remarks hit home hard, delivering a blow to Eli's stomach like a brawler's punch. Since it was altogether too close to the truth, Eli felt an invasive chill steal over him. Despite its uncanny relevance, he could not believe the insult just leveled at him. He had just been compared to a *monkey!*

Eli had seen one once at the general store. A tiny, wide-eyed, little scrap of gray fur, dressed in miniature human clothing, trousers and a gold-trimmed bolero, with a boxed cap on its head. It was collared and attached to a thin metal chain. It had performed to the sound of a music-grinder being wound up by its gaudily attired tinker master, the tiny creature hopefully holding out a cup to him to add more cents and dimes. Eli pretended to delight in the pathetic creature which had looked him with such expressive, blinking eyes, while it gripped the cup with tiny furred fingers. The sight sickened Eli for some reason; chained and dancing to somebody else's tune?

Later, he had surreptitiously given the monkey some oleander leaves he nicked from a bush outside, to chew. The leaves were highly poisonous. The monkey died a painful death that nobody could explain. Thus being likened to a monkey playing at being a human had particular meaning for Eli. Indeed, the notion filled him with murderous rage. This pompous piece of shit in his expensive clothes, holding the reins with white-gloved hands, had likened him to a *monkey!* The insult rankled deep inside him, stirring up old ugly feelings like a dying fire being stoked, churning the glowing embers in him, till the flames licked.

Eli considered taking one of his mules, presently being well cared for in the Skyland stables and ambushing the buckboard further down the hill to get his due revenge, but he was in strange territory here, outside his usual range of influence. His father had warned him to stay out of trouble, since Pollock often got the sheriff from Luray up to sort out matters at Skyland. If they found Blake someplace with his throat slit the night after he'd thoroughly humiliated him, he might easily become the prime suspect.

Besides, Chester Blake was important, a wealthy businessman from Baltimore with political aspirations, Pollock had told him, not some traveling salesman or some bothersome mountaineer that nobody would care too much about. Eli reluctantly decided he could not afford to get into trouble here. It was a novel idea for him to let an insult pass – especially one that had angered him as much as this one had. And for a moment, he still burned inside with the pique of it. He ached to teach Blake some respect right here and now.

He forced himself to give the man a thin cold smile. His eyes were dead, showing no animation, and he could tell that Blake was unsettled by his stare for he shifted on the buckboard seat, though he tried to hide his unease beneath a superior, raised chin.

"That so?" Eli asked thoughtfully, "Well, I guess ye're right 'bout one thing, at least. I sure as hell ain't no gentleman."

With that, thankful for it thrice at the resort, Eli gave a loud, blood-curdling yell then he turned and unleashed his whip, hitting the nearest hind mule square on its rump, sending the panicked team galloping down the rocky trail of the mountainside at breakneck speed, to the alarmed shrieks of Chester Blake . . .

To Eli's considerable astonishment, starting at breakfast and continuing throughout the day, he found that his whip show had made him into an instant celebrity amongst the guests. Not all of them had gone on the hike and, of those left behind, the men heartily slapped his back, put their hands on his shoulder and shook his hand and the women gave him warm, secret smiles and followed him with their eyes, while even the children, obviously having been told of his exploits with the whip by their parents, looked at him with something akin to hero worship in their eyes and begged him to show them some whip tricks.

Eli didn't mind the kids too much, but hated to be touched by another man and whenever one of them got too chummy he would shrug his hand off and slay him with a withering glare. Though they hastily withdrew, they seemed not to want to distance themselves from him as other more discerning folk had in the past. It occurred to Eli that city folk lacked a presentiment of danger and were more open and trusting than mountaineers, at least those who had traveled the bumpy half-day ride on a buckboard up Stony Man Mountain. In fact, the more aloof and distant he became, the more they seemed to seek his company.

It was a novel experience for Eli to be so universally admired, instead of despised and feared by everybody, and it worried him that it felt so good. It was not something that he wanted to get used to. *The approval of his fellows!* To add to this sudden personal popularity, word had got around about how fine his liquor was and, by lunchtime, he had sold all of his moonshine to the guests. Pollock had warned him not to sell any to his staff, since liquor caused him far too many problems. He complained that most of his employees were fond of their liquor and if they managed to get hold of any, they would get drunk and start rows or neglect their chores. Even Sam Sours, the farmer who lived at the foot of Stony Man Mountain and was the resort's official Mail Carrier, bringing up mail every day by his donkey called Cupeper, or a mule, was extremely partial to apple brandy and would do his numerous other chores, including cobbling at Skyland at night, while steadily getting soused.

* * *

It was a strange, somewhat disturbing, week for Eli, although not without its excitement. He found himself changing in a way he never would have expected. Used to being aloof and feared and totally in command, he found himself getting involved with other people to an extent that bothered him. After all, even his own family, with the exception of Jake, mostly kept their distance from him. Yet these rich socialites actually sought out his company, asked his opinions, drank apple brandy out of huge brandy goblets with him in their cabins (alcohol was frowned on in the resort though). At first he had felt like an ignorant fool in the company of the rich and influential people who vacationed at the summer resort, but his instant acceptance by them, made him respond to them in a way he never would have imagined just a few days ago. For one, he found his speech increasingly changing to resemble that of his father's. He had not realized before what an impression his father's flowery "King's English" speech had made on him, but now he was easily able to recall and successfully parody it, dropping the rough mountaineer's speech he had used all his life.

Indeed, a natural mimic, he'd been scornfully parroting his father's speech for years (and been whipped for doing so, whenever his father overheard his insolence), so his ability to switch to something closely resembling the locutions of the rich at the summer resort came rapidly and with remarkable ease. And his clothing was no longer the coarse clothing of a mountaineer, albeit mostly drawn from the wardrobe of George Pollock.

Eli was aware that he was falling into a role here that his father had mostly already created for him. Many of them knew Obediah well and did not doubt his authenticity, because many of his claims were genuine. They extended this trusting acceptance to his son. Eli lied easily and marveled at how gullible city folk were. Now, despite a fine family lineage, his family was no longer squatting on Claw Mountain, neither were they crackers and moonshiners, feared by all in their range of exploits. Though admittedly his father was known universally as "The King of Claw Mountain" and that they lived on the mountain, Eli brashly claimed that his father owned vast tobacco plantations in the Graves Mill Valley and he freely bandied about the false (as far as he knew) claim that the former President James Buchanan, a Pennsylvanian, now long deceased, was a direct ancestor, after somebody had questioned whether he was descended from his bloodline. This had given Eli the lie that despite his misgivings, he was holding his own in this exulted company.

Eli was, in fact, acting out the role that the great Obediah had so recently predicted for him and was becoming increasingly skilled at it. It was easy when everybody was so courtly and charming, to become courtly and charming too, though admittedly, his manner was a good deal more aloof than those with whom he came into contact, and his eyes conveyed none of the warmth theirs did. But through it all, he had felt his own appalling ignorance at every level, though he used his eyes and ears, paid close attention to everything and everyone, was quick to learn, and seldom making the same mistake twice. He wondered if there were others, like Chester Blake, who were not fooled by his thin veneer of civility. But if there were, they didn't show it, except for Reverend Cotterell, whose contempt was clear to all. Still, Eli hoped that the others attributed this to his interest in his daughter rather than showing up his lack of manners and education.

After that first night, when the two shows were followed by an evening of musical entertainment by the six-member Negro orchestra, most of the nightly entertainment was around the campfires, which was fueled by tree stumps dug out by mountain men. But the guests would gather wood for the campfires, too, and there would be sing-songs, the telling of stories and the playing of guitars. Every night, Eli's whip show would commence the campfire entertainment and it always caused a mild sensation. Then the young folk would have a campfire Virginia Reel to music provided by talented Tuckahoe musicians. Eli had been informed by his host that "Tuckahoe" is an Algonquin Indian word and a name applied to Virginians who lived to the east of the Blue Ridge Mountains, while those living to the west side of the mountains were referred to as "Cohees". He had stored the information in his memory for future use.

After that first whip performance, however, Eli refused to appear in the cowboy costume again. He despised the squeaking chaps and the outsized ten-gallon hat which hid his most distinguishing feature besides his scar – *his bright golden hair!* He remembered his mother telling him once when he was small boy that she had drunk a daily cup of sunshine while she was bearing him to produce such a head of hair! It was one of the few memories he had of his gentle, refined mother and was the one that he treasured the most. He had mixed feelings about his mother though. *Why hadn't she stopped Paw?*

He had paid another visit to Annex Lodge, keeping well away from the bathroom with its eerie slippery and hissing sounds, and had emerged as a buck-skinned frontiersman. The hide breeches and mackinaw shirt had long fringes on them and the top boots were made of finest deer hide and were fringed around the tops and down the sides. He added a hide belt to which he attached his hunting knife, which he then included into the act. The outfit was not as colorful as the cowboy costume and Pollock appeared quite disappointed by his more subdued choice, but conceded, after the first show he wore the new outfit, that it did indeed suit his unique character far better, right down to the scar, which Eli had told Pollock was due to a "childhood accident".

Eli knew that while the brash cowboy costume had detracted from the man, this other costume, in its very simplicity, revealed the man. His skill and cunn-ing, accompanied his moody good looks, heightened by his scar and his bright head of gleaming yellow hair, were an instant hit with the guests, especially the young ladies, who sensed his badness and were clearly attracted to it, the way that women often were. Though several of them had shown keen interest in him, he kept himself coldly aloof from them. There was only one lady that he was interested in – *Annabel Cotterell!* –and he was determined to bed her before he left.

Following his first whip show, Pollock had warmly congratulated him on putting up a fine performance but had warned him against upsetting any more of his guests, while readily admitting that Chester Blake was a 'smug, condescending prig', who had badly needed a lesson in manners. Although Eli didn't understand Polly's words, he easily caught the man's drift. He also understood his own position and was careful not to humiliate any more of Polly's guests, treating further intrepid volunteers a lot more kindly than he had Chester Blake.

Indeed, Eli was careful not to antagonize Pollock, who, to his amazement, generally treated him like a long-lost pal. He knew that this easy acceptance of him had definitely entrenched his position with the other guests, making everything else possible for him. Pollock's friendship – and Eli was intensely wary of the word – he knew had sprung initially from his host's friendship with his father, but as the days went past, Eli became increasingly aware that his own relationship with the man had proceeded way beyond mere courtesy towards his father.

This unlikely relationship with the owner of Skyland had started when Eli had so gallantly saved the life of Annabel Cotterell and had gained momentum when Eli displayed his expertise with the whip. A great showman himself, Pollock loved another performer! From there, it had developed rapidly, through long nightly conversations that dug deep into the night, while sipping from barrels of Eli's apple brandy or moonshine whiskey. Used to keeping himself tightly in control, for the first time in his life, Eli actually found himself unwinding a little, relaxing in front of the flame-roaring fireplace with its the buffalo robe in front, at Freeman Lodge. They talked about their respective upbringings.

Pollock's father was in Washington real estate, while his mother was a schoolteacher and had a kindergarten school there. His father was one of the major stockholders who owned this 5,371-acre tract at Stony Man Mountain as well as another 5,000-acre tract on Hayward Mountain, in Madison County. They had been bought to mine copper during a brief copper boom in the Blue Ridge Mountains. The two mines on Stony Man and Dark Hollow proved worthless, however, and it was only when Pollock visited the area at the age of sixteen and saw what a paradise Stony Man was, reporting its potential back to his father that the land was developed. Eli listened, fascinated, as the small red-haired man told him that he'd always longed for the wilderness and for adventure. He had been keen to become a naturalist and had managed to get himself hired at the

Smithsonian Institution as an assistant to one of the finest taxidermists in the country. Eli was suitably impressed when he learned what a "taxidermist" was.

The tale of Eli's childhood, on the other hand, was a fantasy of his imagination. He told Polly how he and his father would go hunting and fishing together, and of a beautiful mother who had held the family together. In truth, although his father had taught him how to shoot, he had never taken him hunting or fishing, and his mother was a shadowy figure in his life, who barely spoke, she, like all her offspring, completely dominated by her husband, despite the fact that he had never laid a hand on her, except to bed her and use her to make more sons. Of the true sad tale, he told nothing. Especially, he neglected to tell of his father's brutality towards his children. He did not want to put Pollock against his father. It would not benefit him.

So instead, he told Pollock of an idyllic childhood spent in the grandeur of the mountains. He could tell that Pollock really liked him – at least this ingenuous, fake Eli that he had presented to him. Although he told himself that he was only courting the man's favor to gain benefit for himself, Eli had to admit that Pollock was totally likeable. He felt a respect for him he extended to few others. His knowledge of the mountains, his fearless handling of highly poisonous snakes, his dogs, his boundless energy and enthusiasm and his keen sense of humor, all served to evoke a grudging, but growing admiration for him. And like any respectable mountain man, Pollock carried a pistol around with him. (Apparently some mountaineer outlaw called Fletcher had once threatened to kill him and he wasn't taking any chances.) No wonder his father, who respected so few in authority, respected him so highly.

To his disappointment, Eli didn't see much of Annabel Cotterell at all over the first couple of days, since she and her father went hiking and, at night, they barely did more than exchange greetings with him at supper, for, worn out by their daily hikes, they retired early.

Eli was getting restless hanging around camp. At first he had watched guests playing tennis on the lawn tennis court, an alien game which had fascinated him to begin with, but quickly began to bore him, and he finally resolved to go along on the daily planned entertainment, hoping to bump into Annabel. What amazed Eli was the capacity of rich city folk for play. There appeared no end to the entertainment provided by Pollock at Skyland – torch-light processions, euchre parties (a card game of sorts), tennis, hikes, parties, picnics and balls, there was no limit to Pollock's imagination. Eli had no idea what most of them were, but Polly eagerly filled him in on details. His host had lately hired what he called "a social editor" who ensured that every big event was published in the Washington Star in a half-column devoted to Skyland on Saturdays and, sometimes a full column for special events like a Flower Ball, Fourth of July Party, a Wild West Show, etcetera. Clearly, the fame of George Pollock and Skyland was spreading.

Eli went on a "Gumbo Picnic" up to Stony Man Peak with the guests, but though it was a lot more fun than he had anticipated, to his annoyance, Reverend Cotterell kept his precious daughter well out of his way. Annabel looked miserable while her father slurped his way through bowl after bowl of the delicious Louisiana-style soup thickened with okra pods.

The morning following the picnic, Eli went on one of the exciting chases held twice-weekly through the mountain forest. Apparently, beforehand, for one of these chases, a live coon would be led for some miles and then put into a tree close to camp. The camp hounds would then be put on its trail with the guests following on foot. They would set off from the Dining Hall, the departure point for everything that happened in camp.

The morning Eli went to the Dining Hall for the start of the chase, he found, to his bitter disappointment, that there were only men gathered around and that only Pollock carried a shotgun. Evidently, this rugged type of entertainment was not the type enjoyed by Annabel and her father, or the other women, and they did not put in an appearance when Pollock blew his bugle and set the dogs loose. Soon the pack was in full joyous cry, with Polly and the other male guests catapulting through the trees in their wild wake, yelling and whooping like boys, the hounds eventually ending up barking frantically around the tree in which hid the hapless coon. To Eli's surprise Pollock did not shoot the coon; seemingly, it was nothing more than a Skyland prop. Eli doubted that any of these city tenderfoots would appreciate coon pie, however, especially in view of the glorious food provided by Pollock's table, to which even Eli was getting all-too-well accustomed.

Pollock left camp one day and came back in the afternoon, having been on his once-a-week excursions to market to buy luxury food: lobsters, shrimps, oysters and crabs, which were shipped back to Skyland in sugar barrels packed with ice, among other delicious delicacies.

Getting a little desperate about ever seeing Annabel alone, Eli told Pollock that night in front of the fire that he would like join him and the guests on a planned overnight trip down into White Oak Canyon, the next day. His host seemed enormously pleased by the concession by him to join him and the others on a hike, and told him he wouldn't regret it.

"You're in for a grand experience," he told Eli with hearty enthusiasm. "Weather permitting, of course …"

"Of course."

31

The overnight trip to White Oak Canyon cost Eli five dollars to be deducted from his whip-show wages. He was told by Pollock that this was to cover incidental expenses, such as payment to the mountaineers, some of whom would go ahead to prepare the campsite, while others would carry the hikers' baggage. The advance team would thrash the surrounding underbrush to scare away any lurking snakes, cut firewood and make improvised mattresses. Normally, Eli would have balked at paying such a hefty sum, but he figured that if he refused, it would make him seem cheap and ungrateful after the hospitality extended to him by Pollock thus far.

Since going on the trip would mean canceling his whip show for one night, Eli offered to stay on an extra night, a proposition to which Polly readily agreed since it had become so popular amongst the guests that they attended night after night, such was their amazement at his whip skills. (He made sure he always included something new in his act each time for this very reason.) He also introduced his knife skills to the act, turning his back on three different targets specified beforehand, spinning round and throwing his three knives one after the other at great speed, always hitting each target square in the middle, or he would throw vegetables and apples high in the air with one hand, and slice them in half with a knife expertly thrown with his other hand. All this would cause his awed audience to gasp and clap and cheer with amazement.

The morning of the hike Eli was relieved to see that the Cotterells were amongst those guests gathered around the Dining Hall. Annabel's smile of pleasure and little wave when she saw him made the five dollars seem infinitely well-spent. As a concession to the long hike ahead of them, she and most of the other women wore long-sleeved blouses, black skirts that reached their lower calves, rather than the ankle-length ones they normally favored and black stockings, with either sensible walking shoes or button-up boots and an assortment of hats. Reverend Cotterell, a portly figure, wore a wide-brimmed suede hat and he carried a staff. His trousers were tucked into knee-high hiking boots, in common with most of the men, including Eli. He was much less friendly towards Eli than was his lovely daughter. In fact, his face looked positively thunderous when he realized that Eli was to accompany them. His jowls were set in concrete, bulging blue eyes, cold. He failed to respond to Eli's stiff greeting. *The old goat!*

Eli watched as the staff spread large pieces of heavy striped canvas on the

Dining Hall porch, one for each guest, on which they placed several blankets, a change of clothing, and nightwear (for those who chose not to sleep in their clothes), bathing suits, and a small packet containing their toiletries and other personal requirements. Thankfully, Pollock had loaned Eli blankets to take with, and had already given him a new toothbrush and toothpaste to use the night he arrived. (He'd never used a toothbrush before that! He'd also begun taking daily baths in the bathhouse, since Pollock and, quite a few of the other guests seemed to, and he was determined to follow their lead. He found, to his surprise, that he greatly enjoyed the feeling of hot soapy water all over his body.) Pollock rolled up each canvas, tying it with clothes line, making a big weighty bundle. When the packing up was ready, Pollock blew his famous bugle and announced departure. (Eli had soon discovered that Pollock had made the bugle his Skyland trademark – it aroused the guests to the glory of each new day, announced the daily mail brought up by Sam Sour, summoned the guests to the Dining Hall, announced the departure of the daily hikes and signaled the start of the evening festivities.)

They started for the canyon in single file, Pollock taking the lead, followed by the twenty-odd guest hikers. Falling in behind them trekked a similar number of hardy mountain men with the large bundles hoisted onto their shoulders. The mountain men were easily distinguishable by their ill-fitting clothes, suspenders and battered old hats. The camp caretaker came up in the rear. Eli slotted himself behind the last guest and the first mountaineer. He was right behind Annabel Cotterell and her father and this gave him enticing glimpses of her from the back from time to time, but not as often as he had hoped because of her father's considerable bulk. He could tell that Reverend Cotterell did not enjoy having him right behind him. He seemed intimidated and kept throwing wrathful glances over his shoulder at him.

Even though there were blazed trees (chopped grooves in their trunks) to guide the hearty group who were laughing and joking, the going was rough since the mountain paths were crude and overgrown with brush and often barred with fallen logs. After a while, the hikers found the going extremely strenuous, their faces becoming red and sweaty. Reverend Cotterell was also huffing and puffing, but his pride somehow kept him going as he struggled to keep up with the group. Occasionally, a mountain man behind Eli would get weary and throw down his bundle to sit on till he had regained his strength.

But Eli, used to scaling the steep heights of Claw Mountain his whole life and unimpeded by such a load, found the going remarkably easy, except for the fact that he was wearing hiking boots borrowed from Pollock, which he found heavy on his feet. But the pace was far too slow for his liking and he had to fight his irritation. After a while, Eli could no longer contain his impatience and made his way past all the other guests to join Pollock in the lead. As he went past Reverend Cotterell, the man gave him a glare and a satisfied snort but, on passing Annabel, he could have sworn that she reached out a hand to briefly brush his. His hopes soared that she would be willing to escape the eagle eye of her father after they got to the campsite. He was eager to have her all to himself.

The headwaters of the several falls located in White Oak Canyon were only about a mile-and-a-half from Stony Man Camp, on the east side of Stony Man Peak, but the falls themselves were considerably further away, right at the bottom end of the canyon. At one point, the canyon, heavily forested, became steep and narrow, with high surrounding cliffs. The lusty, jolly group, comprising of city folk of all ages and sizes, became increasingly quiet and bedraggled as they negotiated the tricky paths. Most of them were inexperienced hikers and had come along for the pure adventure of it. After a long exhausting trip, towards evening, they finally arrived at the foot of an enchanting waterfall, called Nigger Run Falls, deep down in the White Oak wilderness. The surly mountain men quickly removed the huge bundles from their shoulders at the campsite, and departed, making their way back up the steep slopes, leaving the city folk behind to enjoy their bold adventure. The mountain men would return the next morning to carry the baggage back up again.

When the ladies, hot and exhausted, saw the crystal-clear rocky pool surrounded by ferns, below the falls, they squealed with delight. After hurriedly changing into their long striped bathing suits, retrieved from their bundles, behind some bushes, they waded in for a refreshing swim. Eli was disappointed to note that Annabel was not among them. He and Pollock watched with amusement as the other females splashed and squealed like girls, before he started helping Pollock with the unpacking. Then he spotted Annabel standing at the edge of the pool, looking wistfully at the other young women. For once she was all alone, without her father standing fierce guard over her. The reverend was sitting on a fallen log, red-faced, mopping his wet brow with a sodden handkerchief amidst a group of some other male hikers, who stood around also trying to catch their breath. Eli could not believe his luck!

He casually strolled over to Annabel. She sensed his presence and turned to face him. She looked flushed and tired, but very beautiful, with damp tendrils of black hair framing her face beneath her wide-brimmed straw hat, which was kept on by twin lengths of white voile threaded through two holes in the outer brim close the head, and tied becomingly in a bow beneath her pointed chin.

Used to the coarse women of Claw Mountain, with the exception of Mary perhaps – though she could hardly be considered beautiful – Annabel seemed a vision of loveliness to Eli, and he realized anew that he was totally smitten by her. So this is what his father had meant when he had talked about the rich city women. Annabel gave him a wan smile that made his heart lurch. Eli could not believe that she could have this effect on him. Normally, he lived in a dark, bleak place and had a heart of stone that nothing and no one had been able to pierce with the exception of young Jamie, who'd died during the winter. They'd lost him a long time before that, though. He was never the same after the flogging.

"WHY AIN'T . . . AREN'T YOU IN THERE WITH THEM?" Eli shouted in Annabel's ear to be heard above the roar of the waterfall, his voice taking on the haughty timbre of his father's.

"OH, FATHER THINKS BATHING SUITS ARE FAR TOO IMMODEST," she shouted back, her light breath against his ear raising goose bumps all over his body. "HE SAYS THEY ARE AN INVENTION OF THE DEVIL."

He led her some way away from the falls so that they could hear each other better. "Is that what you think too?"

She turned and looked towards the cavorting women with longing. "Well, right now, I think I'd very much like to be in there with them!"

"Doesn't he ever leave you alone?"

"Not for very long. But I don't mind," she hastened. "He's just looking after my interests and reputation, so important you know."

Eli frowned. "How so?"

"Well," she explained earnestly, "There are all sorts of wicked cads out there who would take advantage of a young lady if they could. That's why we need to be chaperoned."

"Sounds like your father talking to me. I get the feeling there are times when you're really chomping at the bit to be rid of him!"

She lowered her eyes modestly then mouthed, 'Maybe.'

"*Then do it!* I'll meet you here tonight after the others have gone to sleep. Shouldn't be too long with everybody so beat and all."

Annabel looked up at him, wide-eyed and shocked. "Why, Mr. Buchanan, what are you suggesting?"

"I'm suggesting you take that swim you've got your heart set on."

"But I don't have a bathing suit," she protested.

Eli looked at her with frank, lusting pale-yellow eyes, "Well, far as I can tell, it don't take no bathing suit to swim."

She gave a little gasp of shock. "Oh, Mr. Buchanan, sir, you surely jest."

"Hell, no! Just be here."

She didn't reply, but gazed at him with the side of her lower lip caught by her teeth, her green eyes glinting with a strange excitement. He knew she was caught by the daring of it, by his badness. *She would come!*

They ate heartily around the campfire. There was a log table in the middle covered with chestnut bark. Will Grigsby was the cook and there were piles of fried chicken, potato and French salad. It was rounded off by delicious sweet corn from the Skyland garden that Polly had cooked in the ashes of the campfire and served swarming with butter. Eli's eyes met Annabel's as she sat across the campfire from him, next to her father, daintily chewing on her corncob, the firelight glinting red in her eyes. She looked away, flustered. He could tell she was thinking of their tryst planned for later tonight.

He could not wait for the others to go to sleep on the makeshift beds prepared for them by the mountaineers, but Pollock, the perfect host, whose energy seemed inexhaustible, had other ideas. He started telling tales, which were soon taken up by others. There was much hilarity and amusement. Even Eli found himself grinning, as he viewed the jolly group in fascination. Then Polly ordered a sing-song, which he led himself. Soon everybody was yelling, "HOW MUCH IS THAT DOGGY IN THE WINDOW" at the top of their voices. Eli felt amazingly relaxed and happy. He was beginning to feel more and more comfortable around these rich city-folk. Nevertheless, he was immensely pleased when Reverend Cotterell excused himself and his daughter, saying they needed their rest. It wasn't long after they settled down on their assigned mattresses that Eli heard the reverend's loud snores. It was music to Eli's straining ears.

Fortunately, the retirement of the Cotterells was the signal for the others to likewise retire and people started drifting off to their forest beds. Eli's "mattress" was next to that of Polly's. The "mattresses" had been made by driving spikes into logs at six-inch intervals and weaving clothes line across them, placing on top of these makeshift frames, ten inches of soft, freshly cut, sweet-smelling boughs of hemlock. They proved enormously comfortable. Eli lay down on his, fully dressed right down to his boots, covering himself with the two loaned blankets.

He gave it a good half-an-hour before he sat up, checking to see if Polly was asleep, which he was judging by his light snores. All around him he heard heavy breathing and snores, which blended into the roar of the nearby waterfall. He stood up and crept to the spot where he had arranged to meet Annabel by the obliging light of an almost full moon. He sat on a rock to wait for her. There had been a slight drop in the temperature, but it was still a warm summer night, rich with heavy natural perfume. An hour passed, filled with the roar of the waterfall and the familiar night sounds of a mountain forest.

As the minutes passed, he began to fret. Had she been playing games with him? Leading him on with her eyes when she had no intention of meeting him? He felt a spurt of anger and disappointment at the thought that he might have been made a fool of. Then he heard a slight sound and saw her dark figure quickly approaching, her footsteps soundless against the might of the waterfall.

He stood up and held out a hand to her as she neared him. She took it. Her slender hand was trembling like a fall leaf about to break from the bough. She was dressed as before, but carried a wrap tightly around her shoulders and was holding herself stiffly upright, as if guarding herself against who knew what. She'd let her hair loose so that it hung long and heavy around her shoulders, black as night, the moonlight cutting a silvery sheen across it. The moonlight played on the pale pallor of her skin, making it appear so white, it looked like molded candle wax. She looked like a statue almost. She was so different from the mountain women he had known, with their bad teeth and bad breath.

Don't treat the rich girls like common mountain wenches! His father's words came back to him. Normally, he was rough with his women, taking liberties for himself, with or without their permission. He forced himself to restraint. He pulled her gently towards him and she melted into his arms. Her perfume filled his nostrils and he could feel the female softness of her body against the hard, mountain-bred leanness of his own. He found the rest of her body was trembling also. Either she was sorely afraid she would get caught out in her daring, or it was excitement.

He found he was only slightly taller than her as he pressed his lips to her fragrant hair. Then he bent and kissed Annabel's neck with a tenderness born of the new Eli, playing at being civilized. Not that she didn't evoke powerful emotions inside of him as their lips met, their mutual attraction exploding. They kissed long, deep and passionately. All Eli could think of was getting her out of her clothes.

"ANNABEL, ANNABEL, WHERE ARE YOU?"

They heard an angry roar above that of the falls and instantly sprang guiltily apart. There was a loud crashing through the trees. *Reverend Cotterell!* Annabel fled from Eli's embrace like air from a burst balloon. Eli ducked quickly behind the rock and peeped cautiously around it, knowing the bright moonlight would have easily exposed him had he stayed where he was. His heart was thudding painfully with fright. He had no more wish to be caught out than she did. *Polly had warned him not to upset any more of his guests.*

"HUSH, FATHER," he heard her shout, as she rushed up to the comical figure in long-john sleepwear and a sleeping cap that was clearly visible in the bright moonlight. "HUSH. YOU'LL WAKE EVERYBODY!"

"WHERE HAVE YOU BEEN?" he thundered suspiciously.

"I COULDN'T SLEEP AND THOUGHT I'D COME AND SIT BY THE FALLS A WHILE UNTIL I GOT SLEEPY."

"WHO WERE YOU WITH?"

"NOBODY! EVERYBODY IS FAST ASLEEP! COME, FATHER, I'M READY FOR BED NOW." She feigned a big yawn as she took her father's arm. She turned him around, leading him away.

Eli hit his fist against the rock in frustration. *Damn Reverend Cotterell!* Eli's whole body ached with disappointment. He'd almost had her. He had visions of her swimming in the pool, hair let loose, her naked skin like white marble with big droplets of water all over it. Nipples puckered from the cool water. He realized then that if he wanted Miss Annabel Cotterell he was going to have to get rid of her father.

He spent the next half-hour scheming how he would do it. A fall would be the easiest if he could somehow do it in a way that nobody would suspect him. He would position himself behind Cotterell like he had in the beginning. A little tap at his ankle could send him tumbling to his death. But if he succeeded and they recovered the body, how willingly would Annabel fall back into his arms if she was mourning the loss of her father? And she'd probably want the body shipped back to Washington for the funeral right away. Then he'd never see her again. *Damn!* Thwarted, he stewed in frustration. He'd go mad he didn't bed her before he left.

When he'd allowed enough time to pass, he decided to go back to his bed. He had to make absolutely sure that nobody saw him. If anybody was to mention that he came back to bed a lot later than when he had retired, he was sure that Reverend Cotterell would cotton on to his planned tryst with his daughter immediately. He would denounce him to his host, who would no doubt banish him from Skyland. And already Eli could not abide the thought of being denied access to the pleasure resort of the rich now that he'd had a little taste of it. He crept back to his bed like a thief in the night, using the forest trees as cover. He fell asleep listening to the roar of the falls, and dreamed of the delectable Miss Annabel Cotterell.

The next morning, Pollock aroused them early with a blasting of his infernal bugle. The hikers, still exhausted after their long arduous trip down the canyon, groaned when they heard it and begged to be allowed to sleep on. But Polly was adamant and they arose reluctantly, grinning sheepishly, and stretching stiff and aching limbs. Sunlight pierced the forest with swords of golden fire, raising mist on the ground. A light mist floated over the pool at the foot of the gushing falls at White Oak Run. Bits of mist broke off from the cloud and wandered wispily through the trees in smoke-like tendrils.

High cliffs surrounded the campsite like an embrace. It was a glorious summer morning. Polly, as chipper as ever, cooked them all a bacon-and-egg breakfast, the savory, delicious smell of it rising through the trees, sharpening their appetites, as they listened to the twittering sounds of early-morning birds and the pleasant roar of the falls. As they sat eating their delicious fare, Eli, still smarting from his brief aborted encounter with the reverend's daughter last night, surreptitiously watched her. But Annabel, much to his disappointment, did not once look in his direction.

After breakfast, they waited for the mountain men to come back to the campsite to take the baggage back up. Polly and Eli set to tie the bundles up again. The mountaineers arrived in due course, having traversed in a couple of hours, what it had taken the group a whole day to traverse the day before. The hikers looked up the steep slopes in dismay. The going would naturally be far more strenuous going up and they were still worn out from the descent.

Reverend Cotterell held them up by stopping to rest often, his face blood-red and covered in sweat. Climbing behind him, Eli found himself hoping that he would have a heart attack. Then, remembering his own reasoning last night, should he die, praying he would not! Nobody chatted as they had going down, saving all their breath for the rugged climb. After many long arduous hours, they at last emerged from the canyon and the hikers fell about on the ground in total exhaustion. The mountain men gratefully dropped their heavy bundles. Polly allowed them all a long rest and liquid refreshment, before making them rise to set off back to camp.

Since most of their limbs had stiffened up during the break, he kept them going by making them place one foot after the other and marching in single file. "DO YOU THINK IT'S RIGHT-RIGHT-RIGHT TO LEAVE THE CANYON YOU JUST LEFT-LEFT-LEFT?" he loudly sang.

Each hiker had to put their right foot forward when he sang "right" and their left foot forward when he sang "left". It kept them going alright, but even so, some of the hikers were so fatigued, they barely made it back to camp. But refreshed by a bath and a long nap, most of them were ready to take part in the evening's entertainment. Others, however, didn't appear for a couple of days, including Annabel Cotterell and her father – much to Eli's bitter disappointment.

32

Tonight there was to be what Pollock called a masked "Colonial Ball" with period costumes he had procured from Van Horn Costumers in Philadelphia, two weeks before. Pollock insisted that Eli come along and join in the fun, saying that it would be an elaborate affair that would be chronicled in all the Washington, Baltimore and New York newspapers.

Apparently there were different "themes" for every lavish affair put on at Skyland and Pollock did everything in his power to stay true to the stated theme, sparing no expense. Now Eli knew why Annabel had not been surprised at his cowboy costume that first night, because in this playland of the upper middle-class and the rich, costumes were commonplace among Pollock and his guests. Practically every night they wore costumes to complement whatever entertainment he had arranged.

However, Eli felt so embarrassed when he donned the elaborate Colonial costume (one especially procured for him by his host), he told Pollock to go ahead of him and that he would join the party later. Though in truth, he had decided not to go. The outfit consisted of a maroon velvet, gold-brocade jacket, black-satin knee breeches, black, gold-buckled shoes and a ridiculous white curled wig. He knew he would feel totally out of place at such a high-society affair dressed as he was. Besides, he didn't even understand what "Colonial" meant, and furthermore, he couldn't dance. When later challenged on his non-appearance, he would simply pretend that he had fallen asleep and unintentionally missed the whole thing.

But as he had sat in Freeman Lodge in front of the fire with the buffalo robe rug at his feet, Annabel consumed his thoughts, especially the memory of their trip down White Oak Canyon. Their burning kiss at the falls was still searing his senses. The thought of seeing her again, perhaps for the last time (he was leaving the day after next), made him decide to go to the ball, after all, though it was by now several hours after it had started.

He reluctantly left Freedom Lodge and went to the log Dining Hall. Pollock always allowed the mountain men to observe the festivities in the Dining Hall from the outside and Eli found them packed around the windows and the doorway, staring in at the lavish costumes and the elaborately decorated hall, taking swigs of "mountain dew" from flasks and jugs, big spare-looking folk in coarse clothing. Though he was actually one of them, it was funny how far removed he felt from them these days. Certainly, they did not suspect his true origins, regarding him as one of "them rich city guests". Indeed, he felt infinitely superior to them, far more worldly and knowledgeable, after his week's worth of hobnobbing with the rich and prominent folk who vacationed here. All the same, peeking in the windows with the other mountain men was like looking in at a whole different world yet again.

The women wore enormous white domed curled wigs with little ringlets hanging down from them, splendid crinoline gowns with plunging necklines, in a rainbow of colors and hues that shimmered and sparkled in the lights. The men wore fancy costumes with satin knee breeches, brocade velvet coats and lace frills around collars and cuffs and short white curled wigs. In addition, everybody wore eye-masks to hide their identity. Tonight, despite the fact that he no longer felt in the same lowly league as these mountaineers, Eli would have preferred to hang around outside with them rather than enter such an unfamiliar and grand domain, badly feeling his own humbleness and inadequacies. Then remembering Annabel

Cotterell, he determinedly pushed past a tall, bearded mountain man and entered a world of pure make-believe.

George Pollock was the Master of Ceremonies and he kept things moving with assurance and aplomb. Music was once again provided by the accomplished colored orchestra led by Will Grigsby. Eli stood just inside the doorway, watching the festivities, feeling silly and spare in his Colonial costume, thinking how his brothers would rib him if they could see him now. The revelers danced what Polly announced as "minuets", which were performed with much pomp and formality, but every now and then there would be more lively tunes.

Eli felt a stirring in his loins as he stared at the pale bursting breasts and half-masked faces of the rich city girls. Even plump and ageing matrons wore these highly revealing gowns. *Why, they were practically naked!* He found the anonymity of the women tantalizing. His eyes eagerly searched out Annabel with her fine porcelain skin, her dark ruby lips. But most of these women were pale as slugs and, without the clue of her raven hair to go on, he found he could not recognize the reverend's daughter anywhere. *What if she wasn't here?* Since her father did not approve of bathing suits, no douubt he would also be shocked at so much flesh being exposed, and had either whisked her away from the ball, or had forbidden her to come in the first place. Actually, he could not see a likely candidate for her father, with his distinctive portly figure, either.

Well, if he did not spot Annabel soon he would leave. All this mincing and curtsying was quite nauseating! What was he doing here amongst all these genteel folk pretending to be someone he wasn't, anyway? He felt like the worst kind of sissy! What had happened to Eli, the tough, notorious Bucko, who took shit from nobody and dished it out freely? *Damn!* He was still that man! He had to get out of there. But he badly needed a drink first. No alcohol was sold at the resort and supper usually kicked off with a single cocktail – thereafter, there was limited champagne for the guests, though he'd spotted any number of surreptitious swigs being taken from hip and pocket flasks by the men and by a few of the matrons. Mountaineers would discreetly knock on cabin doors selling tots of their moonshine, and Eli had to be equally circumspect when selling his own barrels of stuff, at Pollock's request.

He headed for the nearest punchbowl and was served by a Negro waiter, who was likewise suitably attired in Colonial costume – a white wig, a gold-brocade black velvet jacket, black-satin knee breeches with gold buttons and black shiny shoes with big gold buckles on them. Eli gulped the punch down and found it sickly sweet and mild as baby piss. It didn't have the throat-scorching kick of his moonshine, that's for sure! Nevertheless, he stuck out his glass for a refill and gulped that one down too. Another waiter, also in Colonial dress, sailed past carrying a round tray of filled champagne flutes. Eli grabbed at one, gulping down the contents. *Better.* He was developing a taste for this strange golden bubbly liquid. After swallowing it down, he headed for the door, sticking to the edges of the room to avoid colliding with the dancers when he felt a hand catch at his arm.

"And where do you think you're going?"

Eli instantly recognized the soft female voice and his heart lurched. He turned slowly towards her, hardly trusting himself to speak. "You're here ...," was all he managed to say, for Annabel Cotterell was truly a sight to behold. She looked exquisite, her green eyes behind the mask, dancing, the high domed white wig, with its few ringlets, giving her an undeniable elegance. Smelling as sweet as honeysuckle, she wore a pale-green shimmering gown that matched her eyes. Her breasts were white marble orbs bursting out of the tight bodice of her dress, her tiny waist emphasized by the long, crinoline skirt. She wore a diamond necklace and matching bracelet, and waved a white ostrich-feather fan. *She was easily the most eye-catching woman at the ball!*

"Where's your father?" he asked sourly.

"Oh, he's sleeping. He hasn't yet recovered from the climb out of White Oak Canyon and is totally worn out. That, and a sleeping draft, helped me slip away to come here. I'm forced to resort to that every now and then if I want to enjoy myself. He doesn't approve of dancing. I love it!"

He was pleased by Annabel's daring. *Sleeping drafts, no less!* She wasn't as innocent as he had first suspected. She had spirit and he found he enjoyed that in her. He hated timid, insipid women. Since the night they'd kissed he'd been obsessed with making love to her. Maybe tonight was to be the night!

"Come dance with me." She pulled pleadingly at his arm.

He resisted. "I . . . I can't dance," he admitted grudgingly.

"I'll teach you," she said, dragging him, protesting hotly, onto the dance floor. "Just follow me and do what the other men do. It's easy."

It wasn't long afterwards that Eli had got the hang of the minuet, the stately court dance of the 17th and 18th centuries, according to Miss Cotterell, his natural grace assisting him, his odd mistake seemingly going unnoticed. But it was the girl who held him there as he minced and curtsied and circled with the best of them, hand upheld with other hands. She had him bewitched and enchanted, a slave to her dark ruby smile, her perfect rich girl's teeth. Soon she had him tackling square numbers, old-fashioned schottisches, one-steps and waltzes with increasing confidence.

"You're a natural," she complimented him.

And indeed he was. Like almost everything else, it came easily to him, as if he had been doing it all his life. He'd always had the power to imitate almost everything he saw or heard spoken, with the greatest of ease. It was a talent he intended to use to its fullest degree to win the heart of this young woman. He told himself that it was only because he wanted her body, but he knew that wasn't strictly true. Several young men had tried to claim dances from her, but he darkly told them to get lost, and when they realized who it was by his snarl and his partly visible scar, they'd turned around and speed off to ask some wilting wallflower to dance. Though, in truth, Polly was such a good host, he made sure that everybody joined in the fun. And Eli found that he, too, was having a lot of fun pretending he was some aristocratic gentleman of yore, courting this beautiful young lady.

Drawn irresistibly to Annabel, in the midst of all the revelry, lulled by the sweeping music, he found himself bending and quickly kissing those sweet ruby lips in the middle of the dance floor. He thought the stolen kiss had gone unnoticed but, the next moment, to his horror, he saw Reverend Cotterell at the doorway, ravaged-looking, eyes half-closed, hair wildly awry. The reverend squeezed through the knot of mountain men, dressed in a long black cassock and a white clerical collar. In a furious rage, he ordered the music to be stopped with such an outraged howl and a waving of upraised waving hands that it achieved instant silence, and Will Grigsby and the other Negro orchestral members obediently lowered their instruments and stared. The fabulously costumed couples stopped dancing and stood around, also staring at the guilty pair and the enraged black-cassocked madman, as the festivities came to an abrupt halt.

"MR BUCHANAN!" the demented Reverend Cotterell roared. "You have insulted both me and my daughter with your vile conduct! How dare you kiss my innocent daughter in full view of all present, and besmirch her honor in front of her peers!" Ladies put shocked hands to their delicate mouths and men muttered beneath their breaths at the bold affront. "I demand a public apology!" The reverend turned on his shocked-looking daughter. "As for you, Missy, you will go back to the tent and remove that . . . that licentious garment immediately then you will burn it!"

Annabel's face, visible beneath the half-mask, reddened with embarrassment. She lowered her head submissively, pulling her hand away from Eli's. George Pollock rushed forward to defuse the situation, obviously mindful of Van Horn's Costumers in Philadelphia, as well as the need to placate his enraged guest presently being so disruptive.

"Reverend Cotterell," he said light-heartedly. "I am sure that it was just an innocent kiss in the spirit of the Ball and that Mr. Buchanan did not mean to insult either you or your daughter by it. However, I am sure that he would be perfectly willing to apologize publicly to you both and retire immediately."

Eli swallowed hard, feeling blood infuse his face, and ice, his veins, as the attention turned on him. While many of the guests remained incognito, not even a mask could hide the revealing scar that slewed down his left cheek that had caused the reverend to make him as the culprit right away. How dare this wild-eyed piece of lard spoil another night – perhaps his last – with Annabel! It would take so little to lay him out on the floor, his hands at his throat, but with Annabel's anxious eyes on him, he had to resist the temptation.

But the reverend wasn't finished. He turned on the Master of Ceremonies, who was busy removing his mask, with an outraged bellow. "And you, sir, are a disgrace for allowing such sinful cavorting to carry on. These . . . these costumes are positively *lewd."*

"Now, now, Reverend," placated Pollock. "These are historically faithful costumes of our fine Colonial ancestors. It's just meant as a bit of fun."

Dour and ascetic by temperament, with Calvinistic fervor in his well-known attitude against drinking, dancing, card-playing, Sunday amusements and other "frivolities", the reverend was livid.

"Fun? *Fun?* Dancing and cavorting like medieval worshippers of the devil and you call it *fun?* Sin, is what it is! *SIN!* And God will surely punish you for it by casting you all upon the Lake of Fire in the afterlife!"

Eli gave the man a cold smile, pale-yellow eyes bright with anger, but he managed to keep his tone level.

"Mr. Pollock is right, Reverend. I meant no harm. It was nothing more than an innocent peck," he said in his best "Obediah Buchanan" voice, trying to maintain his dignity under the weight of this outrage and the shocked gazes of all these rich and influential people wearing these elaborate costumes of a different era, who had come to respect and admire him over the past week. He cursed himself inwardly when he saw their raised eyebrows and disgusted sneers.

Clearly, he had taken a liberty that was not acceptable in such high society. His father had warned him about it. In his ignorance, he'd treated the young lady without the proper respect! After all, even mountain wenches were usually heavily chaperoned. Public kisses, though pernicious liberties he'd formerly taken without compunction, were even considered, by staid mountaineer parents, as an outrage. What's more he had insulted his host. He had a lot to learn yet. *Damn!* He had to save face. To convince everybody that he knew how to behave in such circumstances, else he'd have gained nothing from the past week. Following Polly's clever lead, he said in a voice ringing with sincerity, using flowery words he'd heard used before and that had stuck in his memory to be used now like poured honey, "Dear Reverend, I apologize most humbly if I have unintentionally offended you or Miss Cotterell, or indeed, any of the other guests, in any way, and for embarrassing my host. Naturally, I will leave the ball immediately. Goodnight."

He nodded shortly at the startled reverend, then Annabel and then Polly, before he ripped the mask from his face and threw it on the floor, stalking out of the Dining Hall with outward dignity and calm, but with blood-boiling rage simmering just below the surface. Though he felt he'd done a good job in the circumstances, his time here had been ruined by that so-called "Man of the

Cloth"! How he hated such men who used God and the devil as their weapons, lambasting all and sundry with their sweeping judgments and their pompous talk of sin!

*   *   *

Eli spent a rough night in Freedom Lodge, stewing in impotence and anger over the reverend's audacity to denounce him in public, right in front of his daughter. He had not known that he possessed so much restraint. His agitation was compounded by the sounds of revelry which recommenced a short while after his departure from the Dining Hall and, later, the grunting and squealing of a family of wild hogs belonging to the mountaineers, which had been set loose in the forests to feed on mast.

They had entered the camp and Eli could hear them rubbing their backs on the foundation posts of the cabin. Had this been Claw Mountain he would have put a bullet in each of them, but here, he could not afford to cause trouble for Pollock with the mountaineers. Night-time at Skyland wasn't always as peaceful as one might expect in a mountain resort. If it wasn't hogs keeping him awake at Skyland, it was stray dogs which invaded the camp and set to howling and barking. They were forever being chased away by the staff, but the next night, they'd be back again.

Or cows belonging to Valley farmers, with their damned annoying bells, would wander into the vicinity. One night, a herd of about fifty of them had broken down fences and swarmed into camp with jangling bells, awakening everybody in the camp. Polly and Eli had hurriedly got up and dressed and, along with Polly's white pit-bulldog, Nellie, and his two favorite beagle dogs, they and the workmen and waiters had driven the intruders away, yelling and whooping, since as well as the disturbance they caused his guests, they were eating grass Pollock needed for his own stock.

It was nearly dawn when Eli finally fell asleep. Thankfully, the next day was Sunday and Pollock did not sound his bugle at seven o'clock as he did the rest of the week. But habit over the week made Eli wake up at that time anyway. When he arose and got dressed in his own new clothes, he found Polly already dressed and sitting in the living room. After Eli's abject apologies to his host, they had a long chat about the previous night's debacle. He told Eli that despite his public apology regarding "the kiss", Reverend Cotterell had not been satisfied and had demanded that he kick Eli out of camp. Polly had told the reverend that he would consider it. He had, however, decided against it.

To Eli's surprise, he was most sympathetic over the matter. Apparently, something remarkably similar had happened to him fairly recently at Skyland. Amazingly, it had also occurred at a Colonial masquerade ball and involved the niece of a bishop, both of whom were guests of Augustus Heaton, Skyland's "Patriarch". To start off the ball, Pollock had asked the young lady to dance and, with her permission and those of the other guests, he gave her a kiss. All was fine until Heaton heard about it. He, too, had demanded that the music be stopped and, in a rage, told Pollock that he had insulted his guests and further demanded a public apology for his outrageous behavior. Pollock denied that he had insulted the young lady in question, but immediately retired, after which the ball came to an abrupt end. So, his host assured Eli, he knew exactly how Eli was feeling right now over an innocent kis and, as then, he wasn't going to bow down to such unreasonableness and narrow-mindedness.

Eli thought it prudent not to tell his host that his kiss had not been an innocent one at all. He had listened in astonishment as his host related the tale. The incidents had indeed been remarkably similar. So similar, in fact, that it bordered on the ludicrous! Both of the ladies in question had been a relative of men of the cloth, both had been kissed at a Colonial ball, both balls had been interrupted by enraged persons, one by a father, the other, by a host. The whole scenario struck a distinct chord of kinship between the offending pair, as if they had just been united in some sort of bizarre blood-brotherhood!

"I guess truth is stranger than fiction, after all," mused Polly with an impish grin and a twinkle in his brown eyes. "Quite remarkable coincidence, I would say. Ah, the outcry over a couple of innocent pecks," he sighed.

Eli thought about the situation and decided that the best thing to happen all round would be for him to leave the camp today instead of tomorrow, as planned. As he saw it, there was no way that he was going to get to be alone with Annabel after what had happened last night. That way, Polly would save face at least. The trip had soured for Eli anyway. And all this play-acting was beginning to wear on his nerves. It would be good to get back to a place where he could kick the dog and unnerve the population with a single glance. *Where he called the shots!* He saw that the longer he remained here, the more his power waned and the more he became subject to the whims of others. But he'd be back! One day they'd all bow down to him.

He greatly admired Pollock, though, with his dogs and his snakes, and would continue to use him to get into the lifestyle of the rich that his despot father had envisioned for him. For sure, he would leave Skyland a completely different person to the one who had come. He knew that he would never again wear old denim dungarees and filthy vests, or go barefoot. This trip had given him a taste of the good life and he found he definitely wanted more of it. He wanted Annabel Cotterell, too, and, some day he would have her.

"Look, if you don't mind me missing tonight's whip show," he told his host, who was busy fondling Nellie, with one hand. "I'm going to leave today. I've already caused you to lose one guest. I don't want to feel responsible for your losing more. You can tell the reverend you booted me out to smooth his ruffled feathers." (His father had used the expression upon occasion so he knew in what context to use it.)

"No, no, I won't hear of it!" wailed Pollock.

"I'm going whether you agree to it or not."

"Well, if that's the case, I insist on your coming back as my guest whenever you'd care to. I've thoroughly enjoyed your company, as indeed as I did your father's. I'd ask you to stay for the Sunday service, but Reverend Cotterell is giving the sermon and, somehow, I don't think you'd be in the mood to listen to him. Still, the Sunday services are good fun. We sing grand Moody and Sankey hymns."

"Who're Moody and Sankey?"

"Famous evangelists."

Eli nodded. He didn't want to show his ignorance by asking him what "evangelists" were, but he'd find out.

"You know you don't have to do this, Eli?"

Eli gave his ginger-haired host his most boyish, mischievous smile. "Oh yes, I do . . ."

After enjoying a sumptuous last breakfast with his host, Eli thanked Polly for everything as they left the Dining Hall, shaking his hand, and assuring him that he would be back next year at the same time, to bring more of his moonshine, having already been paid the money that Pollock owed him for his whip shows, less the five dollars for the hike. Eli headed to the stables, where he saddled and loaded up the four mules, while his host departed for the Sunday service. Eli led the mules out of the stables and walked them past the spot Pollock called "Cathedral Pines" where guests in their Sunday finery already sat on logs under giant hemlocks listening to the sermon by Reverend Cotterell, who was again wearing his black robes, his voice raised in fervor. Eli felt a blazing hatred towards the bloated toad for having denied him . . . so many things. Solemn mountain men, wearing hats, sat on the outer logs, or stood behind the group. Eli's eyes sought out Annabel, who was wearing a black dress, frilled with long layers of black lace and a black hat and veil. She was sitting on a log close to where her father was standing, facing Eli's direction. Though he willed her to look up, she kept her head submissively downcast. Certainly, he could not risk shouting goodbye to her while her black-attired father was speaking, rocking importantly on his heels. The reverend ended his sermon just then. After spotting him leading the packed mules past the worshippers, Pollock saluted him a quick farewell then started playing his banjo. The congregation began singing a staid hymn to his able accompaniment and the mournful sound followed Eli all the way down the hill, echoing a strange ache in his heart . . .

33

In the months that followed Mary's return to Claw Mountain, she was to discover that life was as rewarding as it was challenging and unpredictable. Who would have dreamt she would return to this mountain in a twinkling of an eye, the way she had, and that it would turn out so well? There were many reasons for this, the most compelling one being that her husband was most certainly a changed man since he'd given up drinking and, what's more, she was deeply and irrevocably in love with him. He had proved his worth, not only by putting so much hard work and effort into the homesite, but in his sheer determination not only to get them back, but to "win" them back.

Furthermore, he had not slid back into being the deeply uncommunicative soul that he had been in the past. She realized now she had been partly to blame for that. Because she did not understand the complicated and tragic background of this backward and deeply wounded clan, she had condemned them outright, and he, seeing and sensing this, yet welded in a close bond with his brothers through shared suffering, was unable to stand up for them, yet neither was he able to condemn them, with the result that he had escaped inside himself. By her rigid attitude towards him and them, she had made him feel inferior and unlovable, further exacerbating their differences – and so the invisible wall between them had grown higher and higher, till neither could see over it, into the other's soul.

Zachary Thomas was still given to long periods of silence because that was part of his shy basic nature, but now that they were so close and shared so much, they were comfortable silences, not the excruciating silences of before. It was as if her husband had finally learned how to communicate and, though they pretty much fell into the same routine as they had before she had left, they now shared closeness and intimacy that had been completely missing in their lives together before now. They made love often and she slept in his arms with her head on his broad shoulder. This physical intimacy deepened and strengthened their once-non-existent marital relationship.

And of course, there was baby Jed. Their shared adoration of their beautiful baby son did more than anything to cement their once-torturous relationship. On warm Indian summer evenings, Zachary Thomas would lay Jed against his chest as they sat on the swing he had made for the porch, and Jed would gurgle with contentment. It was surely a picture to warm the heart, this big, tough mountain man being so tender towards his baby son. At the risk of being called a hen-husband, he even changed Jed's diapers on occasions when she was busy doing something else, and he didn't seem to mind doing it one little bit.

Though Mary had much more to do than before with the added responsibility of caring for her baby, she was blissfully happy and content, especially now that Obediah Buchanan had ceased to be such a threat. Indeed, his illness and fall from autocratic power had the effect of changing the whole atmosphere on the mountain from one of terror and fear and the underlying undercurrent of unease and malevolence, to a much lighter and more relaxed one, even if strangers, and of course – the despised Galtreys – were still not welcome on it!

Remembering all the terrible deeds the Buckos had committed in the past, Mary still didn't know how she would feel about the other Buckos when she saw them again, but she did know that she would never, ever feel right about Eli. According to Zachary Thomas, Eli had taken over the whole of their father's lucrative moonshine business and had big plans to expand it even further. He'd even been to Stony Man Camp, instead of his father, and had come back looking, talking and acting like a rich lowlander. *And, for pity's sake, he now wore shoes even in warm weather!* At least now she knew the Buckos' behavior wasn't prompted by sheer meanness on their part. It was clear to her that every destructive act they had ever committed was a cry of pain and anguish from a tortured past. She knew this with a sureness that came from the very depths of her soul. She so wished there was something she could do to change things on the mountain. To channel all that deep anger and resentment and hatred into something that would raise them out of the depths of degradation into which they had slumped. But she was only one person and they were the mighty Buckos – used to having their own way, no matter how violent, imbecilic and trying that way might be. Well, at least she had somehow managed to make a good impression on one of them!

The first time young Emma had come visiting Eagle Spur the day after Mary arrived back on the mountain with Jed, Mary was delighted to see her, but she scarcely recognized her, for although she carried her trade-mark shotgun, her face was washed clean and shiny, albeit that her hair was still somewhat dirty and tangled. Used to seeing her pale-blue eyes through a raccoon-like mask of dirt, Mary was stunned. Even at her uncles' funeral, she'd still had a few smudges of dirt on her face. Now she looked so different, for the ravages of the winter had imprinted itself cruelly upon her and her already narrow face was now so gaunt that her eyes peered out of deep hollow holes in her skull. There was no doubt that the child had suffered enormously during the recent hellish winter, yet the fact that she had survived at all was a miracle, considering what a slight little thing she was to begin with. Mary fancied that she wouldn't have made it if she wasn't so naturally spunky. However, today, she seemed sad and dispirited, despite the winsome smile she offered Mary.

"Oh, Emma," said Mary as she gladly swept the girl into her arms, kissing her soundly on the top of her head. "I sure missed you, child. I swar I scarcely recognized you when you came thru' th' door! You sure are a purty un' underneath all them layers of dirt!"

Emma pulled away and eyed her warily. "Well, Unc' Zack said you thunk cleanliness be next t'godliness, so's I reckon'd I'd best clean up some from now on, 'cuz I aim t'git me to heaven no matter what. Don't want to burn in hell like you done tole me happens to them that's bad and don't listen t'God."

"Well, it's true real bad folk don't git to go to heaven, Emma, but God sure wouldn't chase you away from heaven jest 'cuz you got a dirty face. Jest th' same, I reckon He must be mighty pleased to be able to see your sweet face proper-like, same as me."

"Well, when Unc' Zack done tole me how important bein' clean was to you, I figger'd mebbe I'd chased you away to yer nice clean kinfolk 'cuz you couldn't stand lookin' at me no more."

"Oh, Emma, how could you thunk sech a thung? Why, not a day went by without me thunkin' on that cute dirty little face of your'n. I missed you real bad, honey."

Emma looked up at her pleadingly. "Aunt Mary, please don't go away 'gin! I miss'd you somethung fierce, and thar ain't nobody else I kin talk to like I kin talk to you."

"I won't, Emma, I promise."

Emma looked hugely relieved then she remembered something and her face brightened, "Guess what, Aunt Mary, I found 'nother eagle's nest right on th' other side of th' spur."

Mary and Emma had been eagle-nest hunting in the past and had only located a single nest in a rocky overhang. With the number of eagles that flew around Eagle Spur, they had figured there must be lots more, but all their attempts to find them had been unsuccessful.

"Oh, did you now?" Mary enthused. "You're goin' to have to show me real soon."

Emma lapsed into her sad demeanor. Then Mary remembered that Emma's father and baby brother had perished in the winter and how badly the deaths of her two uncles had affected her. She led the girl across the floor to sit her down on the puncheon bench.

"Heer'd about your paw an' young Thompson and all yer other lost kin, Emma. I'm real sorry."

Emma's eyes instantly dropped to the floor. "Oh, Mary, I thunk I kilt Thompson. I thunk I kilt m'paw, too!"

"No, no, honey, of course you ain't kilt him. Th' freeze got him, is all. It got a whole mess of mountain folk!"

"No, you don't unnerstan'. Paw was drunk all th' time, an' he ain't never should'a tried t'go out in sech a miserable state t'hunt. I should'a bin th' one t'go. I done all th' huntin' fer my family a'fore th' winter come bad. Well, I tried real hard to git him to let me go, but he wouldn't. He insisted on a'goin' with Unc' Eben that day an' I should'a *stopped* him. I should'a gone instead! Then my sisters an' brothers would still have a paw."

Mary looked down at the earnest little wisp of a girl sitting beside her. She'd had so much on her shoulders from such a young age that her sense of responsibility was so very keen. She was filled with terrible guilt about her father's death, and it was gnawing at her soul like a hungry dog on a bone.

"Oh, honey, you should have done no sech thung. It were yer *paw's* responsibility, not your'n! He was th' head of th' family, not you! All I kin say is he must have loved you somethung fierce, not t'let you go out in that fearsome cold. 'Sides, without snowshoes, you would've disappeared in that snow clean over your head. Don't y'thunk that your paw knew that *you* were th' one who needed to stay by th' family? He was countin' on you t'be thar fer them, honey, not jest thru' th' winter, but after, too. He knew you could help them survive whereas he couldn't."

"But I couldn't save *Thompson*, Aunt Mary. I felt so bad when he went. Maw cried so hard and I ain't know'd what t'do t'comfort her, especially after Paw had disappeared. Now Paw was given to beatin' her sometimes when he got too drunk, we young'uns too, but she loved him somethung awful, I swar."

"Now, honey, you gotta stop feelin' so responsible! God's th' *only* one who decides who should live and who should die! He must have decided that he wanted yer paw and yer baby brother by His side, is all."

"Well, He must'a bin mighty lonesome, 'cuz He sure done took a whole lot of m'kin. Only He never took th' one I done *told* Him to."

"Oh, who's that?"

"*Grandpaw!*" she said scathingly, her eyes narrowing into slits. "*I hate him!* He kilt Unc' Jamie! I was prayin' God would first freeze him good then send him straight t'hell to burn fore'er and e'er, so he look'd all black and twisted like a burned log, jest like Aunt Cecelia that time."

Expecting her to say it was her Uncle Eli, Mary stood staggered by the depths of the child's virulent feelings towards her grandfather. Then she remembered how Obediah would have all the children lined up in neat little rows to watch his cruel, fiendish punishments. How they had shook and cried when they had been forced to watch as he flogged the back of young Jamie bloody raw. How many other floggings had they been forced to watch? Mary bit on her lower lip distressfully. What terrible things Emma must have witnessed in her tender twelve years. And from her own horrific experience, Mary knew that to watch something like that was almost as unbearable as having to suffer through it personally. No wonder Emma felt this way about her grandfather. Obediah had robbed the children of Claw Mountain of their precious innocence. But hatred was so destructive to the person bearing it, and Mary could see that it was tearing this poor girl apart. As much as Mary despised the patriarch of the Buckos herself, it pained her to see how it was affecting this innocent victim of his evil doings.

"Oh, Emma, honey, I know it's real hard not to, but you mustn't hate yer grandpaw. It's true he's done lots of real bad thungs, but Jesus tells us we must forgive and show only love and compassion to those who sin aginst us. 'Sides, he's so weak now, he cain't hurt nobody no more."

Emma's pale-blue eyes grew big and round. "So it's true about Grandpaw bein' so poorly?"

Mary nodded.

The girl looked grimly satisfied. "Is he gonna die?"

"I don't know, Emma, but he sure looks real sick. Thunk how miserable he must be now that his whole family has deserted him. He's done sowed so much bitterness and hatred right thru' his life and now he's got t'live with all that. Sure cain't be an easy load. You shouldn't hate him. You should rather pity him." (Though Mary guiltily allowed that *she* wasn't able to forgive the monster for what he had done to his family, she had felt compelled to tell this impressionable child the way it *ought* to be, according to Jesus – for *her* sake, not Obediah's!) Emma's eyes narrowed into slits and for a moment she looked like the tough little spit-fire of old.

"Pity him!" she said vehemently. "Pity him! Thar ain't no way in hell I'm gonna pity him! An' I sure as heck won't forgive him neither! Not after what he done to Unc' Jamie. Why, I swar he's meaner than a mad dawg. *I hate him!* An' when he dies, I aim t'spit on his grave . . . !"

34

Mary's talk with Emma that first day back at Claw Mountain had a profound effect on her. For the first time she fully realized the damaging effect that being forced to witness Obediah's cruelty on so many occasions must have had on the children of this mountain clan. Previously, she had thought of them as a bunch of filthy uncontrollable, rowdy brats with no manners at all, and now she realized that beneath all that must lay a welter of deep, unresolved feelings and untold insecurities. She remembered how cowed and upset they'd been at Jamie's flogging. How frightening and confusing it must have been for them to have had to watch their fathers and uncles and brothers being flogged and demeaned and punished and persecuted by their own grandfather, over years. Surely, besides the pure anguish of that, they must have wondered if that would one day be their own fate and be filled with deep-seated fear and dread. The likelihood was that unless something was done to help them, the whole bunch of them would follow in the footsteps of their drunken parents and turn into lazy, shiftless, piddlediddlers with no sense of direction or pride. There *had* to be something she could do to prevent that!

The question lingered with Mary throughout each day, into long sleepless nights. And then, one night, lying on her husband's broad shoulder with her hand rested on the vest of his hairy muscular chest, listening to the comforting sound of his snoring, Mary got it. She knew what it was what she had to do to break the curse of ignorance that was so rife on this mountain. *She would teach the children to read and write and cipher!* She remembered how the whole world seemed to open up to her when her cousin, Emily, had taught her these basic skills all those years ago. She didn't know much, but at least she could teach them what she *did* know. Of course, she wasn't a trained teacher, but then Emily hadn't been one either. Mary thought how lucky that she had thought to put all her books that Emily's parents had given her after the death of their daughter, into her suitcase, as well as the paper, pencils and chalk Emily had used. Mary was filled with a quickening excitement. She would do for Hedina's grandchildren, what Hedina had not been allowed to accomplish with her own sons. And this time there would be no one around to oppose the idea now that Obediah had lost his position of absolute authority in the family. But that was where Mary was wrong . . .

Mary's first opposition to her idea of introducing basic learning skills to the children of Claw Mountain came from her own husband. She couldn't wait to tell him her idea the moment she woke up and she was devastated by his angry reaction.

"What th' devil fer?" thundered Zachary Thomas. "Paw was right in that at least. Best they learn th' thungs that will git 'em to survive in th' mountains, like huntin', fishin' an' trappin', so that what happened last winter cain't never happen agin. Fact is, I aim on teachin' them thungs to *all* my brothers' young'uns jest like I done learn'd Emma. Got me another shotgun I kin use to teach 'em to hunt."

Mary already knew that the Buckos' sons did not rely on their fathers to provide fresh meat, because she had heard from young Emma that even the younger children, both boys and girls, did have their own means of catching small prey, which they would roast over a fire and eat. According to her, they would make snares by bending a pole over and making a circle of twine with a piece of apple in the middle. Although most of them had no hunting rifles, they were good aims, throwing rocks at rabbits, coons and squirrels, invariably hitting them square on the forehead. Most were proficient with their slingshots too. Even so, they all seemed so emaciated, it was clear they weren't getting sufficient to eat. No doubt the young boys of the second generation of the Buckos would all leap at the chance of being taught to hunt with a shotgun by their Uncle Zack, who, according to Emma, they all looked up to for his many accomplishments.

She didn't like to point out to Zachary Thomas just then that none of the skills he aimed to teach his nephews would have helped this past winter anyway, because of the wicked weather. After all, her husband was an expert hunter, trapper and fisherman, and, Lord knew, even he had enjoyed scant success. She kept her mouth shut because she considered it a wise move anyhow. The Buckos young'uns *did* need to learn the skills necessary for survival in the mountains and to become self-sufficient. After all, as much as Obediah had wanted them to seem like other folk living in the mountains, so his fugitive status wouldn't be exposed, the Buckos lacked even their most rudimentary survival skills – if you didn't count making moonshine, that is!

"Well, I thunk that's a real fine idea, Zachary Thomas and, while you're at it, tell them to gather plenty of chestnuts and store them in sacks fer th' winter months and to keep hogs to slaughter, so they won't go hungry when the weather gits too fierce and not to rely jest on store-bought stuff like a'fore. I kin help you with that! You an' I kin teach 'em to be proper mountain folk, Zack." Mary felt herself filled with a soaring zeal to do just that. "But it don't got t'be *all* we kin teach 'em!" she added earnestly. "I kin teach th' young'uns to read and write and cipher like I said. You ask how learnin' to do them thungs kin help them in th' mountains. Well, it teaches a body how to *thunk*. How to be a better person."

Zachary Thomas stared at her, aghast. "We're jest ain't good enough fer you, are we, Mary?" he said scathingly.

Mary stared back at him in dismay. How could he choose to twist her words that way, when nothing could be further from the truth? "I never said I was better than you an' yer kin, Zachary Thomas!" she replied testily. "Don't you see I'm aimin' on *helpin'* 'em not hurtin' 'em?"

Zachary Thomas eyed his young wife skeptically. "Well, maybe we do got to change our lives some to survive better, but we sure don't need t'learn book stuff in these here mountains, whatever you say. That's pure hogwash!"

Mary stared at him in bald frustration. What was he afraid of exactly? *Change?* Or was his resistance to book-learning a peculiarly male thing? After all, even her own father scoffed at it, thinking it a complete waste of time, so why did it surprise her that this backward, backwoods clan should think any differently about the matter, especially in view of Obediah's total aversion to it? Indeed, to this day, her father did not know that she could read and write. Though her mother had expressed pride and satisfaction when she told her, she had warned her to keep it a secret from her father. When she asked her mother why, she had just smiled wryly and said, 'Oh, men have got sech big heads, they jest cain't bear th' thought of any female bein' smarter than them!'

But perhaps it was understandable that something not directly linked to survival must seem paltry and unnecessary to her husband after the tragic loss of so many members of his family, and that learning to survive future winters must seem far more imperative for the clan under the circumstances. *And of course it was!* But that did not mean that they couldn't learn to do *both*. They could learn some survival skills *and* the basic rudiments of literacy – even if it was just through her untrained endeavors. She wanted to hotly defend her stand, but these were the first cross words spoken between them in the two months she'd been back, so she forced herself to calm down.

"Your maw knew that it were important too," she said softly, but chidingly. "If'n you were able to, you could read it yerself in her diary. 'Sides you done told me so yerself! How she wanted you boys to learn all that y'could so thar'd be choices fer you in life."

"Y'mean leave th' mountain, don't ya?"

"Only if'n that's what you wanted."

"Well, I got news fer you. No Buchanans will leave this here mountain *ever!* Claw Mountain is th' home of our clan an' hit'll be our home forever. An' all a man needs in these mountains is a huntin' rifle an' a knife!"

Mary thought she heard a ring of patriarchal rhetoric in his words. For sure the whole of Claw Mountain was regarded by Obediah Buchanan as being his own personal kingdom and the rightful home of the Buchanan clan. Now her husband was perpetuating that line of thinking. *It was the Buchanans against the world!* How could she, as an outsider, hope to make a difference? Through being brainwashed by his father into thinking that book-learning was stupid and unnecessary in these mountains and, by some misguided sense of family loyalty, he didn't like the idea that even the most basic form of education might conceivably one day splinter the clan by driving some of its members off the mountain in search of a better life. Well, that sure wasn't her intention at all. She just wanted to cut through the appalling ignorance, so they could have a better chance at life while living *on* the mountain. But it was clear that she and her spouse had very different thoughts on the matter and they both lapsed into cautious silence, neither wanting it to spill over into something more serious between them. But the silence sulked like a nagging toothache between them and, that night, their love-making was deep and passionate and contained an element of desperation. They clung to each other as if terribly afraid that their differing ideas might drive them apart once more, knowing that their newfound happiness together was yet too tender and fragile, to be too toughly tested.

* * *

Despite her husband's heated opposition to the idea of teaching the Claw Mountain children the rudiments of education, Mary couldn't let her idea go. In fact, the more she thought about it, the more she realized that it was *exactly* what was needed on the mountain to change things for the children in a more positive direction. However, due to Zachary Thomas's stubbornness on the matter, she realized that change would have to come slowly if the Buckos weren't to feel threatened or exposed. She decided she would have to forget all her fancy ideas of transforming the whole mountain community overnight. She would have to secretly teach Emma first and then take it from there. Though she hated to do it behind her husband's back, he had left her no choice. She broached the subject with the sullen fair-haired tomboy the next time she faced her across the table. Emma had a tin mug of fresh milk topped with cream and a tin plate piled with honey-dew biscuits, made with honey and sour cream, in front of her. Her first sip of the creamy milk had left a white mustache on her top lip, while she chewed languidly on one of the tasty biscuits, spilling crumbs.

"Emma, how would you like it if'n I were to teach you how to read and write and cipher?" Mary asked testingly, not knowing what her reaction might be. These Buchanans were a strange bunch, after all. She had certainly not expected the reaction she had gotten from Zachary Thomas!

Emma looked at her with big, rounded, pale-blue eyes. *"D'you mean it, Aunt Mary?* D'you mean you'd truly learn me?"

"Of course!"

Her narrow little face brightened. "Oh, Aunt Mary, I'd be right beholden t'you t'learn me. I want t'be real smart like you!"

"Forsooth, ye're sech a bright little thung already, you'll ketch on in no time at all. Jest one thing tho'. It's got to be a secret from yer Uncle Zack. He don't thunk it's sech a good idea and I don't want to tell him till I thunk he's about ready to hear about it."

* * *

274

And so it came to pass that every morning, except for the Sabbath, after Zachary Thomas had cleaned his long-barreled old Kentucky rifle, clipped his gunpowder horn to his belt, scooped up a pile of lead balls and went off to go tracking with his coon dogs, Emma would arrive at Eagle Spur like clockwork. Mary would sit with her at the table, books and paper and pencils would come out, and she would begin Emma's lessons. Zachary Thomas was habitually gone the whole morning, at least, but just in case he should come back while they were still at work and, because she had so many of her chores to attend to, Mary limited the lessons to just two hours a day. And she was right about Emma's ability to learn quickly. She might be as ignorant and unworldly and unlettered a young'un as ever there was one, but she was far from stupid.

Indeed, like most mountain folk, she was bright and canny, with a whole heap-load of horse sense. Before too many months had passed, not only could she read and spell and write painstakingly with a pencil, she had read Mary's entire small collection of Emily's books, which they spent many delightful hours discussing. While Mary was doing her daily chores, the girl would follow her around, asking dozens of questions about great American classics like *Tom Sawyer, Huckleberry Finn* and *Uncle Tom's Cabin.* Mary was so proud of the girl for her achievements, she felt fit to bursting.

One day, Emma brought with her to Eagle Spur, her spike-haired, small cousin, Beaufort, who was dressed in ragged denim dungarees rolled up to his knees. He was filthy and his beady, bright, brown eyes peered out at her beseechingly from an appealing mask of dirt.

"Mary," said Emma. "Beaufort also wants you t'learn him t'read an' write an' cipher, jes' like you done learn'd me."

And so it began. The lessons were to open up a whole new world to the cracker children of Claw Mountain, as one after another of them, on hearing about Mary's "secret" lessons, joined her, Emma and Beaufort in her little impromptu classroom, till there were finally a whole whopping giggling seventeen of them and they were forced to sit in two crammed rows on the floor, while she sat on the table facing them and baby Jed lay gurgling contentedly in the cradle beside her.

They were a pitiful lot, filthy and so malnourished they were thin as string beans, with bad teeth and lice in their hair. They were beset with headaches, sniffles, wracking coughs, running noses, septic sores and festering scabs. Mountain folk invariably treated their ailments with home remedies rather than rely on doctors whose ministrations they could rarely afford, but it was clear to Mary that these children had not been given the benefit of either. Their parents had not even sought the help of Zachary Thomas's apothecary for ailments they considered minor! In any event, she had no doubt that these children were so badly neglected because their parents were drunk on moonshine most of the time. Mary worried herself sick about their health and whether they were getting enough food to eat. She always made sure she fed them plenty of cookies and milk and thick slices of cornbread spread with molasses. Just the way they bolted the fare down seemed to confirm her suspicions.

What delighted her, however, was their sheer eagerness to learn, even though some of them spoke so badly that even Mary, who was mountain born-and-bred herself, had great difficulty understanding them. Disciplining them had been a big problem at first for they were used to being allowed to run hog-wild, but she soon realized that idleness had been the main cause of most of their unruliness and that if she managed to capture their attention by making the lessons interesting and fun, they would be reasonably well-behaved. She also insisted that they should be clean and their hair brushed when they entered her cabin. Those who didn't have the washrag habit, which was all of them, she would wash, herself, on the porch, using a pail, suds, a washcloth and a scrubbing brush. Though they elaborately groaned and rolled their eyes as she scrubbed and wiped the dirt off them, it was all part of the fun and she suspected that they enjoyed this break with routine and it was part of the reason they came. She soon ran out of paper and got each of them to find a flat piece of mountain slate to bring with them, so they could write upon these with chalk she provided.

There was another serious problem, however. Right from the start, she noticed that some of the children seemed unduly sleepy and dazed when they came for lessons. Some threw up or would find a corner to curl up and sleep. It didn't take Mary long to figure out they were sleeping off the effects of moonshine overindulgence. Since some of the children were still small, she was horrified to realize that Obediah's tradition of force-feeding excessive amounts of moonshine to his own children once they had reached the tender age of six, had been passed down to his grandchildren via their parents.

One skinny little ten-year-old boy, Tommy, a tough, foul-mouthed child, habitually came to lessons in a drunken stupor and would get loud and abusive. And it wasn't only the boys either. One little girl, Allie, who couldn't be more than eight, came to lessons with her eyes red and sore-looking and decidedly glazed, and she kept throwing up. So, both the sons and daughters of these mountain crackers were being induced into this sinful pastime from an early age. Mary knew that in some mountain families, the brandy bottle was passed around the breakfast table every morning in the belief that it was good for children and helped to keep away diseases, but she was convinced that the moonshine given to these young'uns did not stop at medicinal doses!

Indeed, they were obviously allowed and encouraged by the parents and grandfather to freely indulge in 100-proof alcohol, not only risking their lives by doing so, but running the real risk that they would all grow up to be drunks and wastrels like their parents – unless she could persuade them to give up their destructive habits. So Mary embarked on a program whereby she would tell them of the terrible effects moonshine had on their ability to think and act rationally, and she strongly advised them to give it up. She did this on a daily basis before she started her classes, since she considered the subject so important. Fortunately, it gradually began to pay dividends, as she noticed a big drop in the number of incidents involving drink and outright drunkenness.

* * *

If Mary considered that their parents must wonder what happened to their children during the time they spent with her being scrubbed shiny-new and saying their 'ABC's', she didn't have to wait long to find out. One fine fall morning, a deputation of moonshine-bolstered mothers came up to Eagle Spur to confront her. With the aggression that was typical of them, they flung open the door without knocking and stalked in. Cora, mousy-haired and toothless, was the vocal ring-leader, who blasted Mary clear across the room with her moonshine-laden breath, shaking her bony fist at her as she nervously rose from the table to confront them, while her classroom of children sitting crammed in rows on the pine floorboards with their slates on their laps, in front of them, all fell to a stricken silence and watched the drama with big, frightened eyes.

"How dare you fill my boy's head with devil's nonsense!" Cora shrilled. "Tellin' him he cain't even take his own grandpaw's fine hooch no more! Why, wait till I tell Obediah what ye're preachin' now."

The other mothers, following after her, started yelling and haranguing Mary, who stared at them nonplused.

"The devil's nonsense?" Mary said indignantly. "Why, Cora, hit ain't th' devil's handiwork at all! You're welcome to tell Obediah that I thunk it's a wicked sin t'force hooch on young'uns, so they cain't even thunk straight no more. And less'n you want your son dyin' of too much likker, you'd best be with me on this and all you others too."

"Oh *you!*" said Cora disgustedly. "You're jest a troublemaker, you are. Knew it from that first day you got here and paraded 'round in Hedina's finery jest liked you owned hit! What's more you ain't a'begged our permission t'take our young'uns."

"Are y'sayin' you would have given yer permission, Cora?"

"I ain't sayin' no sech thung!"

"Did you know that Tommy kin read 'n write now, Cora?"

Cora looked taken aback, but wasn't to be outdone. "No, an' don't care a whit neither! He ought t'be home doin' chores, not comin' up here ev'ry day havin' his head filled with sech hogwash!"

The other mothers murmured approvingly amongst themselves.

"Readin' an' writin' ain't hogwash, Cora. Why, the young'uns kin now read classic stories wrote by great American authors. They're a real bright bunch and I'm so proud of 'em."

Cora looked confused, her eyes blinking owlishly. "What's *orthers?*"

"An author is somebody who writes books an' sech. Well, Tom kin now read 'em all an' he kin write his ABC's too, real fine."

"What he need ABC's fer on this mountain?"

"Well, he may not *always* be on this here mountain, Cora. 'Sides, what else is thar fer him t'do, 'sides git silly on corn-mash whiskey?"

Cora shifted under her direct, challenging gaze. "Well, like I said a'fore, he's got t'help his paw with chores and in th' fields."

"It's only fer two hours a day, Cora, so thar's still plenty of time fer doin' that."

"Well, he cain't come no more an' that's that!"

Mary felt her heart sink. She had been so afraid of this. "But he loves class so, Cora. *They all do!* Haven't you noticed a big difference in him an' th' others lately?"

"And neither kin Katie and Orville come no more!" interjected the flame-haired Ellie Mae, who had once loaned her ring to Zachary Thomas to complete his and Mary's wedding ceremony, in support of the ring-leader, Cora. "We've come t'take our young'uns home right now and, what's more, if'n they come up agin, they'll git a fierce beatin'!'

"What . . . what are y'all so afraid of?" Mary exploded in frustration. Did they, like the Hardshells of the southern Blue Ridge, also think that ignorance was something to be admired, or was it something else? Then she thought of something. "Are y'all 'fraid that they'll end up smarter than you? Well, let me tell you somethung. They're *already* heaps smarter than you! At least they're keen to learn as much as they kin in life even tho' you forced their innocent heads into moonshine jugs practically a'fore they could even walk a step!"

There was a quick indrawing of breath, and the women looked at her as if they'd been scalded. Mary knew why. Deep in their heart of hearts, they knew how terribly wrong it was. They knew that it was shameful to allow young'uns to indulge freely in moonshine, to get drunk and disorderly, yet they rationalized everything in their twisted liquor-sodden minds just to prevent themselves from feeling guilty. Just then, there was a disturbance and, to Mary's horror, Zachary Thomas ducked under the opened door.

"What in hell's name is a'goin' on in here?" he asked angrily.

Mary stared at her huge husband, aghast, knowing how furious he would be when he discovered what she had been doing behind his back. She thought about the excuses she could make to hide what was happening here, for the children's sake. But it was no use. She been caught red-handed in the act of going directly against his wishes and there was no use trying to cover it up or deny it. She raised a defiant chin. "I was learnin' these young'uns to read and write like I told you I aim'd on doin', and your brothers' wives don't like th' idea any more than you do. They're here t'take them back."

Zachary Thomas's piercing turquoise-green eyes beneath black bushy eyebrows, narrowed instantly. "You tellin' me that you went ahead even tho' I warned you not to?"

Mary shrugged. "*Somebody's* got t'help these young'uns, Zachary Thomas!"

"I thunk you oughta give her th' strap, Zack!" yelled one the women, "Messin' with our young'uns' heads, she is. She ain't got no right."

"Yeah, you ought to tie her to th' floggin' post an' git her sorted out real smart!" leered Cora spitefully, her dark-brown eyes, marble-hard.

"I'll do no sech thing!" Zachary Thomas thundered. "Now you take your goddamned young'uns and be gone, the whole darned lot of you!"

Just then Emma stood up. She wore old dungarees with a faded threadbare white vest underneath and her feet were bare, but her face was clean and the dark freckles sprinkled over her sun-browned nose and cheeks could clearly be seen. Her pale-blue eyes could not be seen, however, for she was slit-eyed and fiercely indignant, a tough little spitfire filled with zeal.

"I ain't a'goin', Maw," she coolly informed her mother, Eliza, a tall thin woman with brown hair that was already graying despite the fact that she wasn't yet thirty. "Aunt Mary here is a real good teacher. She done learn'd me how t'read in no time at all. I'll show you right now."

With that, Emma took up her copy of *Tom Sawyer* and started reading it with a loud, clear voice, while the invading adults stared at her in transfixed astonishment.

"My word," Cora whispered in awe, after the thin, fair-haired girl had read a whole page without stumbling once. "I do b'lieve th' girl *kin* read."

Samuel's tall, thin, mousy-blonde widow, Edna, was staring at Emma with a peculiar expression on her countenance. Mary was teaching two of her children, Lisa and Sam. Emma finished reading and stood looking clean and proud.

For a moment, there was stunned silence then Cora stormed over to Tommy sitting on the floor and yanked him up roughly by his one arm. "So she kin read! *So what?* It sure don't change th' fact that hit won't do 'em th' slightest bit of good on this here mountain!" she shrieked, parodying the familiar old refrain.

With that, all the other hags came forward to drag the children away, to their loud squeals of anger and dismay. Eliza tried to take her daughter by the arm, but Emma wrenched herself free and stood her ground, eyeing her mother with her mean, slit-eyed, spitfire look that was no match for lesser wills than her own. Her mother left without her.

Mary was finally left staring sickly at her huge black-haired husband, who eyed her with a strange look on his face, while Emma stood aside from them, a worried look on her face.

"Unc' Zack, please don't be mad with Aunt Mary. I ask'd her to learn me!"

"Now you know that ain't true, Emma. I won't have you lyin' fer me," Mary scolded gently.

"You ain't gonna go away agin now, are ye?" pleaded Emma.

Looking directly at her husband, Mary, filled with anger and disappointment, stood unbowed by what had happened. She knew without question that what she had done was the right thing to do! No matter that it angered her husband, she would not submit to his archaic thinking.

"No, I ain't *never* gonna go away agin, Emma," she said softly. "Claw Mountain is my home now and this is whar I intend livin' out my days – with th' man and th' son that I love with all my heart."

Zachary Thomas's shoulders sagged a little then and his face softened imperceptibly. Letting out a long, tortured sigh, he turned to Emma and said gruffly, "You sure kin read right fine, girl. If'n I was you, I'd best keep this learnin' thung up . . ."

35

To Zachary Thomas, as with all mountain men, except his brothers, that is, hunting and trapping wild game was a way of life in order to provide food for his family and to enable them to buy provisions. He generally went tracking during the day and if he found fresh tracks, he would take his coon dogs back that night. Occasionally, he would stay out the whole night, though since the Galtrey massacre, he didn't like leaving Mary and the baby alone too often, or for too long. He would also go out during the day to bring back creatures he had trapped for their furs. Raccoons were admired for their fine tails and because coonskin hats had become a firm favorite amongst city children, ("Davy Crockett" hats, they were called), while foxes graced the necks of rich city women throughout the land.

His favorite hunting ground was in the upper Wilderness Valley that lay in the vast basin below Claw Mountain, because it had remained a primeval wilderness where he seldom saw another human being. The unspoiled beauty of the untouched timberland got him thinking how much he'd love to show it to Mary and that he ought to take her along with him sometime. It would only be for a few hours and they could leave Jed behind with Emma, whom Mary trusted with looking after him. And so it was arranged . . .

Since Zachary Thomas did not intend to do any hunting, he put the two coon dogs in the barn for Emma to let out later. They whined and scratched and howled indignantly at being left behind, as he and Mary climbed carefully down off the ridge. She carried a basket full of goodies while Zachary Thomas carried his bedroll, his trusty old Kentucky rifle, with his gunpowder horn attached to his belt and a knapsack containing lead-ball ammunition on his back. He had brought along his trusty muzzleloader for protection purposes only. There were always Galtreys and wild bears to consider.

As they made their way down Claw Mountain, the sun was rising and throwing yellow shafts of light across the earth. Once they were off the mountain, they headed west, barefoot, along Hollow Trail, before entering the vast untouched Wilderness. Zachary Thomas walked in front of his wife, who seemed full of awe and wonder at the sights he had to show her, helping her over the difficult parts. The forest of giant ancient hemlocks, great white oaks and chestnuts was awesome in the early morning light, hallowed and silent. It smelt of fresh conifer and was still damp from a short storm last evening. Beads of moisture were still dripping from the leaves and pine needles. Such was the reverential silence and the haunting beauty of the place that Mary said the forest felt sacred to her. *A holy sanctuary!*

Though Zachary Thomas treated the vast, undeveloped timberland as his own domain, he admitted to her it was actually owned by two brothers, John and Hamp Fray. Except for a horse trail to The Sag, a partly constructed trail along the slope of Little Buck Knob and a stock path, the land was undeveloped.

"Confederate soldiers used to hide out in this here place durin' th' Civil War away from them damn Yankees. Otherwise thar ain't many folk entered it except for a few hardy hunters and trappers, like m'self. It's a favorite haunt of bear-hunters. It sure gauls me a lot, but it is th' best bear-huntin' place of all, even better than Bluff Mountain, Jones Mountain Point or Bear Huntin' Rock.'

He told Mary that over-hunting had already almost wiped out a sizable elk and deer population in the mountains and the settlers had rid the mountains of the wolves and mountain lions also, mainly because they were afraid of them. Now, it was the turn of the bears to be under threat of attack and extinction. Although most mountaineers did at least eat the meat of the bears they had shot, the lowlanders were just thrill hunters and, after skinning a felled bear for a trophy, they left the meat to rot. He sounded regretful about this state of affairs and Mary quickly espoused, "Reckon folks oughta leave them poor critters well enough alone if'n they don't need to kill 'em fer eatin'. Seems to me thar's room fer *everythung* in th' wilds. Truth be known, I simply *loathe* huntin'."

Her husband grunted, non-committal, not wanting to be drawn onto such delicate ground by his rash crusader of a wife. A born hunter and trapper, he had far too many pot-quarries and pelts to his credit to start getting all holier-than-thou about it. But he did admit to her that because the bears were now so scarce, he never hunted them anymore. Nevertheless, an expert tracker, he was able to show her several sure signs of the presence of bears; clawed trees, raked out patches under chestnut trees where they had gone in search of mast, old rotten logs which they had broken into to search for grubs and larvae. Mary said she was glad to have him with her because the idea of confronting a bear made her somewhat jittery. Zachary Thomas told her not to worry since bears usually fed at night and slept during the day.

They trekked for hours through the fragrant forest and he showed her many delightful glades filled with wildflowers, ferns and colorful groups of mushrooms – yellow coral red-cups and tiny puffballs nestled at the foot of trees – fungi with bright-orange, curly layers resembling cabbage leaves growing on bark, and trickling streams. They didn't talk much, yet there was such a bond between them, there seemed no need for words. He sensed her deep unbridled pleasure at what she was seeing and experiencing and would throw her occasional satisfied glances, his eyes meeting her warm hazel gaze, as he checked her step and gallantly helped her over rocky patches.

They decided to eat their lunch under the shade of a giant oak tree. It had been a long walk and Mary seemed grateful for the break, though Zachary Thomas, used to traipsing through the Wilderness on an almost daily basis, didn't have need of it. He unrolled his bedroll for them to sit on and Mary spread out a folded cloth napkin between them. They had skipped breakfast because they wanted an early start so by now they were both ravenous, feasting on pieces of pot-roasted chicken, egg sandwiches, corn fritters and honey-dew biscuits, parching their thirst on homemade lemonade. In the midday heat of the perfect summer's day, the sky was a brilliant scintillating blue above them. Mary admitted to him that she was thoroughly enjoying it all, even as she rubbed her bare, dusty chestnut-stained feet, to ease the ache in them.

After they'd finished eating and had rested a while, they set off again. Zachary Thomas took her to the headwaters of Wilson Run. A mere ripple at its head-springs, it sprang amidst a lofty forest of ancient hemlocks. They followed the river's banks until the river turned into a roaring torrent, reaching a full-tilt climax at waterfalls in the lower hemlocks, spray rising at least thirty feet in the air. It was a beautiful scenic setting and Mary was clearly enchanted with it. With the good summer rains, the roar was so fierce that they could not hear themselves speak and they were soon covered in fine spray. Zachary Thomas shouted into her ear that the river flowed more sedately further on, dropping to the middle valley, where there were deep pools and shallow riffles. He assured her that the next time they would explore the full length of the river, right to where it plunged over more rocks and boulders before joining the Rapidan River in the lower valley.

The mist was deliciously cooling and they got their hair wet, but Mary didn't seem to mind. She looked so beguiling that he couldn't resist bending down to kiss her. It was a long lingering kiss, before they broke away, breathless. They stared into each other's eyes, both seeming filled with intense longing and a sense of wonder. It seemed the most natural thing in the world when he laid her down on an enormous, flat, slippery rock lifted her shirt and made long and urgent love to her, their cries when they came, lost in the wild noisome voice of the river.

Later, they swam in the shallow river, Zachary Thomas shedding all his clothes, but Mary, too shy to look at him or to be so completely exposed, kept her eyes averted and her long bloomers on, wrapping and tying her shawl around her bosom, to further protect her modesty. They frolicked like carefree children, splashing and dunking each other.

After following her husband on a barely discernable trail for some time, Mary was surprised when he suddenly hushed her to silence and put out a cautioning hand for her to stay behind him. Peering through the trees, she saw that a wooden stand had been built in the hemlocks about four feet high, with ramps leading off it to the ground. To her shock, she saw that two old brown horses had been led up the stand and slaughtered. One horse had collapsed with its large head coming to rest on the bloodied corpse of the other horse, which lay eyes open and staring. Both their throats had been slit and blood dripped over the edge and onto the forest floor and there was an awful putrid smell in the air, which poisoned the fragrance of pine. Mary raised both hands to her face and stared at the terrible scene in horror, utterly appalled. She had always loved horses, not least for the fact that she had eloped on one with Zachary Thomas (albeit, a borrowed one) and even the old runty horses at the logging camp she found endearing. She couldn't imagine why this ghastly thing had been done to these two poor animals.

"What's happenin' here?" she exploded angrily, feeling her face grow hot.

"Hush, girl, they're jest usin' them old horses as bait."

"Fer *what?*" she whispered distressfully.

283

"Fer bears. They'll come feed off them horses and git themselves shot."

Mary stared at him in acute horror. "It's bad enough killin' them poor bears off, most of th' time without even usin' them fer food, but to use poor old horses, *two* of them, mind, to do it is jest plain despicable," she rejoined in a fierce undertone. "Why have they gotta kill the bears" After all, even *you* know they've bin killin' them out. Why cain't they?"

"Oh, reckon it's 'cuz huntin' bears gits a man's blood pumpin' like nuthin' else kin."

"You mean that's th' *only* reason they kill 'em? *To fire th' blood?* Don't they know that once they're all gone, they'll be gone *forever?* And to use them poor innocent horses!" she wailed.

"Yeah. Don't like it too much myself, no more, though I was guilty of doin' it in th' past. Always used up all th' meat of the bears I shot tho', and dished it out to th' clan, but I still feel kinda ashamed when I thunk back on it. Them hunters like to chop the heads off the beast and stick it up on a wall someplace as a trophy so's they kin sit and look at it all day and thunk what big men they are. Still, guess one of *my* trophies ain't nuthin' more a floor rug now, to be tramped on underfoot, or to warm my bed come winter, so's I guess I ain't no better than they are. I've jest learned to see thungs a little different now."

"Well, I'm sure proud to hear you say that, Zachary Thomas," said Mary evenly, though she was still seething with anger. Then she noticed that her husband's attention was elsewhere. He was staring straight ahead into the thick surrounding forest.

"Listen, I'm going to load my Kentucky jest in case we need to use it as protection," he breathed. "Thar's bears around here fer sure."

Lowering his knapsack carefully, kneeling down on one leg, he took a patched piece of greased cloth out of the weapon's patch box and some lead balls out of his pocket, and loaded them into the muzzle with the patch before pouring a measure of gunpowder from his gunpowder horn into the flash pan. Then he slowly stood up again.

"Hush now and stand real still," he whispered, his voice taking on a cautionary tone as he stared into the clearing.

Then she suddenly saw why Zachary Thomas had hushed her. She actually smelt the beast before she saw it. With a strong, wild smell, a huge black bear down on all fours, with shaggy black fur, a humped curved back and a large head on a long thick neck, which must weigh close on five hundred pounds, had entered the small clearing and was sniffing around the ramp with its pointed, inquisitive nose, clearly attracted by the blood of the slaughtered horses. Mary pressed behind her husband and peeped at the impressive wild beast from behind his large frame. Zachary Thomas slowly raised his long-barreled muzzle-loader, cocked the hammer back and aimed it at the beast. Although the barrel was so long, it didn't dip down as she had previously been wont to believe. Her strong husband was able to hold it remarkably straight and true. Remembering how straight Emma could hold the heavy double-barreled shotgun given to her by her uncle, she reckoned the Buchanan clan was blessed with extremely strong arms and hands.

She watched in breathless fascination, strangely unafraid, as the bear cautiously began to climb up the ramp to reach the stand where the bait provocatively waited. When it reached the stand, it stood up on its hind legs, an awesome creature, easy seven feet tall with strong claws on its feet. Mary felt privileged to see such an impressive sight. It made a strange noise, baring its fangs, and starting swaying slowly from side to side as if suddenly wary. Mary wondered if it had caught their scent. Apparently satisfied, it dropped down on all fours again and began to feed on the corpses of the aged horses with little grunts and snarls as its fangs tore into the horse-flesh.

Suddenly, the surrounding silence was rudely dented by the unholy sound of repeated shotgun blasts. Mary's screams were swallowed up in the brutal cacophony of noise. The bear, riddled with enormous bullet holes which immediately oozed blood, grunted, screeched and thrashed about in fright and pain, before falling off the ramp onto the ground below. It landed with a great big thud and air was expelled from its mouth in a loud, terrible sigh. It twitched several times before laying still, stone dead. There was a moment of horrified silence, during which time Mary could not believe what had just happened before her very eyes, the stink of sulfur and fresh blood thick in the air.

At first Mary thought that Zachary Thomas must have fired his weapon, but this notion was soon dispelled when four chortling, elaborately mustached lowlanders, dressed in knee britches tucked into shiny knee-high boots, handsome tweed jackets and wearing burlap caps, emerged from the brush, carrying shotguns and looking mighty pleased with themselves. They bellowed and roared with laughter as they went and stood beside their fallen quarry, slapping each other's backs, while Mary shuddered with soul-deep horror. Though she'd known what the ramp and the slain horses were for, she had failed to grasp that the hunters had been hidden close by waiting for just such an eventuality.

Then three of the hunters gathered, chests puffed, chins raised, grinning, behind the bullet-riddled, blood-oozing carcass, each carelessly placing one dusty booted foot on it, and proudly placing their shotguns upright beside them, butt on the ground and muzzle in one hand, while the fourth went to stand in front of them with a large camera he had set up on a tripod, both of which had been hastily retrieved from the forest to record forever the disgraceful scene.

Covering his head and part of the camera with a large black cloth, his left hand sneaked out and removed a cap from the front of the camera. Holding up a broad, narrow-headed flashpan on a long handle in his right hand, there was a loud unseemly click and an explosion of light accompanied by a "phoofing" sound. Smoke rose from the flashpan and the smell of magnesium chloride mingled with that of the sulphuric smell of detonated gunpowder from the recently fired weapons. The photographer then quickly replaced the cap on the front of the camera and emerged from beneath the black cloth with a triumphant smirk.

Mary stood stunned. *What a wicked, wicked desecration!* How could they destroy the sacredness of the forest this way? Turn it into a slaughterhouse! A place of unholy carnage! Filled with indignation and rage against the unfeeling monsters, Mary found herself ducking around her huge husband and flying into the clearing. Placing her hands on her hips, she screeched, "You thunk ye're so doggoned smart, don't you? *Well, you ain't!* What chance did it got aginst them big guns of your'n? Not a one! And them poor horses! It's downright disgustin' to say nuthin' of cowardly! You ain't nuthin' but a bunch of cruel lowdown cowards! It's different if it was fer vittles, but this here killin' fer fun and a trophy head, is an abomination aginst God!"

The four prosperous-looking lowlanders, all strangers to her and no doubt from one of the surrounding valley towns, gawked at her in stunned shock, their mustachioed faces aghast. Next minute, she became aware of Zachary Thomas standing at her side and realized what she had done. She looked up to find he was staring down at her in a quandary of embarrassment, confusion and shame . . .

36

Doc Adams moved himself around on Bessie's saddle to get the circulation going in his large behind, which was feeling quite numb and saddle-sore. He'd left Carlisle at first light, with his trusty black medical bag and a black tin trunk containing medical supplies and was presently heading towards Claw Mountain along the banks of the quietly flowing Wilson Run, steeped in the remembered foreboding of the mountain he was riding towards, inexplicably missing the strong reassuring presence of the hillbilly child, Emma, despite her filth and bad smell that day, and feeling some strong residual fear despite the assurances of Mary Harley Buchanan that she would guarantee his safe passage once he reached there. Her heart-rending letter, written in a large childish scrawl, had touched a cord in him and he had found himself unable to resist its call, especially knowing how much the mountain people of the Blue Ridge had suffered during this frightful past winter.

It promised to be a long tiring day with little remunerative reward attached, but the thought of it excited him somehow, as if the good Lord had set him on a path of glorious salvation through enormous good works. After all, it was well-known that doctors in the valley towns refused to go anywhere near the vicinity of Claw Mountain, which rose above the Wilderness like a grim reproach, lonely and wild and forbidding. He wouldn't have dared himself a little while ago. Yet here he was doing just that for a second time in less than nine months, despite Zachary Thomas's dubious welcome of the 45-inch barrel of an old-fashioned Kentucky rifle aimed at his gut!

Young Mary had taught him something by her letter. She had taught him the true meaning of the Hippocratic oath and, although venturing up a mountain full of fearsome and bloodthirsty hillbillies who'd likely slit his throat on the slimmest pretext, to practice non-remunerative medicine, wasn't exactly a role he had earlier envisaged for himself, it had been thrust upon him by strange circumstance, and he felt himself rising to the occasion with a fire in his belly that had nothing to do with his dyspeptic ulcer.

It seemed that destiny had more in store for him than he had earlier bargained for, and the comfortable, but mundane, existence he had carved for himself in a picturesque valley town, was to be livened up somewhat. So despite the knot of fear deep inside his gut, filled with a fine missionary spirit, he wondered if he couldn't extend his work even further afield while in the vicinity, to the other squatter and tenant families who lived on the neighboring mountains. But perhaps he should wait and see how the day turned out. Could be he would not enjoy working surrounded by a host of hostile hillbillies!

It was late November and the first snows of winter had already swept across the mountains, dusting them with powdery snow that had soon melted, leaving a bone-chilling residue of cold. Snow capped the higher peaks, however, including the granite-bolstered plateau of Claw Mountain, which loomed ominously in the distance. It was so high, it was surrounded by a collar of thick cloud. Several recent sub-zero nights had brought heavy hoary frost, which blackened the tips of bushes and turned blades of grass to spears of tinkling crystalline glass. Rime ice had started to encase the limbs of tree and the branches of bushes. Mist rose from the river in chilling spirals. Thin ice had crept over the banks of the river and clung to the water's edge, ready to spread across it, causing a crunching sound as Bessie's hoofs made contact with it. It was bitterly cold, and Doc's warm breath caused trumpets of steam as the air condensed. The air was so crisp, it caused his eyes to water and his nose to burn when he inhaled through it, causing it to run, so he had to keep sniffing, or wiping it with his handkerchief. His greatcoat and gloves were lined with sheep-skin, but he still felt miserably cold. Bessie, too, did not seem to be enjoying the trip, humphing and snorting crossly with regularity. No doubt she would much rather be in her nice warm stable of straw, lazily chewing from her trough of oats than once again stamping through the wildness of the Blue Ridge on a mad escapade.

Larks, sounding their sweet song, flocks of white-tailed ptarmigan and the occasional eider or harlequin duck were some of the few birds to be seen so late in the season, while he spotted a weasel, several shrews and a fiery red fox with a splendid white bushy tail along the way. They crossed the two-foot deep stretch of river at the point where he'd crossed it before on Emma's instruction and valiant effort. It was hardly the brutal deluge of water that had been caused by the mammoth spring thaw as it had been back then, so he was not at all afraid of having to cross it on his own.

He headed towards the base of Claw Mountain at a gentle canter wondering what he would do if young Mary was not waiting for him as he had instructed. Would he dare go up to Eagle Spur on his own without even the hillbilly child as an escort? No, he'd be insane to do that! A large hawk with immature plumage flew overhead and then, inexplicably, soared slowly in front of him as if to show him the way.

When he at last reached the foot of Claw Mountain, he was relieved to see Mary sitting with a child on a fallen log. He shouted and raised a hand in greeting and, when he reached them, climbed wearily off his snorting horse, Mary and the child quickly rose to meet him. Mary wore a woolen shift that was mostly covered by a thick long gray coat. She wore thick black cotton stockings and flat black lace-up shoes. Her dead-straight, long black hair was loose, hanging on each side of her face almost to her waist and she wore an oversized woolen, turned-up gray cap on her head. Despite her somewhat frumpy attire, with her clear, high forehead, hazel eyes and pale olive skin she looked quite becoming, Doc thought. She possessed a straight-backed dignity that far outweighed her tender age. The child, on the other hand, seemed immune to the cold for she wore only denim dungarees with patches at the knees and a white vest underneath and, unbelievably, she was *barefoot*. Mary's eyes held genuine warmth at seeing him and he moved forward to hug her, asking her about the health of her and her baby. After Mary confirmed that they were both fine, the child at her side mumbled, "'Lo, Doc Adams."

Doc turned to her with a smile on his face. "Why, hello, young lady, and who might you be?"

"Shucks, Doc, don't you remember me? I'm *Emma!*" she scolded with one hand on her skinny hip and her eyes fiercely screwed up. "I done show'd you th' way th' las' time you came."

"*Emma!*" Ye Gods! Doc Adams stared at the child in bald astonishment."Well, blow me down. I don't believe it!"

He stared at a child who, although she was still washboard-thin, not only didn't smell, but had a perfectly clean face and brushed fair hair instead of the tangled mess of before. Furthermore, her lower legs and broad callused feet were reasonably clean too. *What a transformation!* The only familiar thing about her was her slit-eyed, surly expression. He'd also noticed to his alarm that she was carrying a shotgun. Seeing the thing served to remind him about where he was. He gave her a sickly smile and patted her awkwardly on her shoulder. "My, Emma, I never would have guessed. You look fine as can be."

While Emma glared at his praise, Mary smiled broadly. "I thunk so too. Emma kin read an' write and cipher now too, Doc. Learn'd her m'self."

"Well, I never! That's quite remarkable! You must be real proud of her."

"Oh, I am, indeed."

Emma turned her attention to his horse, and immediately brightened.

"See, Mary, this here horsey is th' nightmare I done tole you about. Ain't he purty?"

Doc was about to correct her for the second time, but figured: *What's the use?*

"Sure is. Oh, Doc Adams, thank you so much fer comin'. It means so much to me."

Doc nodded diffidently, and asked, "Well, where have you arranged for the examinations to take place?"

"Well, Zachary Thomas figger'd th' main homestead at Horseshoe Hollow is th' best place since it's closest for everybody. It's got a real big yard an' you'll also be able to ride your horse thar without too much difficulty . . ."

"How thoughtful," mumbled Doc, while his mind zeroed in on the fact that he would be going to the homestead of *Obediah Buchanan* whose hatred for doctors was legendary! "Eh . . . did you gain permission from Mr. Buchanan – Obediah, that is – for me to go there?"

"Well, not exactly, but Zachary Thomas said it ought to be okay."

"*Ought to be?* You mean you're not sure?"

"Zachary Thomas says it don't matter none what he thunks."

Doc felt his insides grow even colder. "*Indeed.* And will your husband *be* there by any chance," he asked hopefully, feeling that if at least that giant hillbilly was around, there might be a slim chance of him surviving the day.

Mary shrugged. "Don't know fer sure. Zack war'n too keen hisself, in th' first place. Listen, Doc, I don't know fer sure how many patients you gonna git this time round. Zack said none of 'em seemed too keen."

Doc felt like he had on that other occasion when he had near broken his neck to get to the top of Claw Mountain to tend to Mary's childbirth, only to find it wasn't at all appreciated by her giant hillbilly husband. He frowned mightily. "I rather expected more from you, Mary. I'm a doctor with a busy practice. You can't expect me to keep coming here on wild goose-chases!"

Mary blushed and averted her eyes. "I know that, Doc, and I'm truly grateful to you fer comin', like I said. Jest thought I'd warn you that we might got to overcome some thungs a'fore these folk allow thar young-'uns to be examined by you, is all. They're mighty suspicious and I fear they don't got too much respect fer doctors."

"So I've heard. Well," he said resigningly, "perhaps you'd best show me the way."

The trio entered the large clearing of Obediah Buchanan's homestead, Doc Adams, sat atop Bessie, his heart thumping so hard it felt as if it were jumping right out of his chest. His dear nag was being led by the reins by Emma, who had marched all the way up like a fearless Joan of Arc, while Mary followed behind them. The yard was partially covered by a thin layer of ice and disgustingly untidy, littered with rubbish and broken bottles, with any number of spring-sprung sofas standing on bricks all over the place. A buckboard stood next to a derelict barn and a T-post stood in the middle of the yard – probably for pitching horseshoes, Doc decided, since it was a favorite pastime of mountain men.

He felt enormously vulnerable. Here he was in the middle of Obediah's den of iniquity with naught to protect him but a young woman who was an outsider herself and a surly mountain child he very much doubted would hold much sway either. He kept his eyes fixed on the rundown cabin, expecting to be gunned down through one of the closed, shuttered windows at any second. The Buchanan clan was notorious for chasing unwanted strangers off Claw Mountain in the most undignified of ways! Emma finally brought Bessie to a halt in the middle of the yard and Doc climbed off his rump-shuddering, tired old nag with his own limbs locked in stiffness.

Well, Mary was right to be concerned. It did not look as if a single person had braved to come. Only a few painfully thin mongrels roamed the yard in search of scraps.

"Well, where can I set up?" he muttered, to offset the annoyance he felt at being so shunned after it had taken so much effort to get here.

"In th' barn," replied Mary.

"Can you make sure Bessie's watered and fed?" he called pleadingly after Emma as she walked the old mare towards the barn. "And be sure to unsaddle her. Know how to do that?"

The hillbilly child turned around and nodded sullenly, and Doc stumbled miserably after her, Mary at his side. The barn was large and ramshackle and stabled four mules in separate stalls. Emma led Nellie to an empty stall and started removing her saddlery, while the mules snorted and squealed as if in objection to sharing their living quarters with a horse, albeit for a short time. The barn was littered with straw and mounds of dung, around which lazily buzzed a few cold-resistant horseflies. A few smelly animal pelts were nailed to the wall and there were any number of drums and pieces of broken machinery piled everywhere. Gray spider webs spread across every conceivable corner, and several broken wagon wheels lay in a haphazard pile, while he could see a fair-sized rat right from where he stood.

Doc snorted in disgust, looking around the place grimly. Not a patch on his antiseptic surgery, he thought wryly. What might Hilda think of it? Still, he noticed a workbench had been cleared and dusted off in one corner and there was an empty stable right next it with a blanket strewn across it which might be useful if it were necessary for any of the patients to disrobe. If he got any patients at all, that is! It would have to do. He asked Mary to get a pail of water and some lye soap in it to scrub down the workbench while he busied himself getting out phials, salves, ointment linctuses and his stethoscope from his bag medical bag. He then extracted probes, forceps, dressings, bandages, sutures and needles from his medical trunk. Mary was quick to do as he asked and, after lighting two kerosene lamps, she went outside. She came back a few minutes later holding a tin mug of steaming coffee, which he took from her gratefully.

"Thank you kindly," he said, sitting on a rusty and dust-covered trunk over which he'd spread a clean handkerchief, before gulping the evil-tasting, but warming, brew down. Although it was much warmer in the barn, he still felt chilled to the bone. He handed the empty mug back to Mary and wiped his mouth with the back of one hand. "Where'd you get it?"

"Had it brewin' on a fire outside fer a long while now. Reckon'd you'd be needin' it."

Mary smiled bravely at him, but he could see she was worried.

Doc remained seated on the trunk. An hour had passed, Emma had long disappeared and nobody had come yet to take advantage of his medical services, during which time he tormented himself by thinking of what he might be doing with his precious time instead. Why, he could be snoozing in his armchair in his study. Reading a good book. Attending the service at the Episcopalian Church. Leisurely smoking his pipe in his favorite armchair. Dealing with long-neglected correspondence. Minutes ticked slowly by and he kept taking out his fob watch to check the time. A slice of Hilda's delicious Apple Strudel made with sweet apples, currants, and raisins, spiced with cinnamon, wrapped in pastry with fresh breadcrumbs and baked until golden and hot, and a nice hot cup of tea would go down well right about now. His stomach rumbled and he discovered he was starving. He wondered what the chances were of getting any lunch. Perhaps Mary would think of it. She seemed a considerate child, born of a mountain family to whom such hospitality was habitual.

"Doc, don't lose heart yet, please," Mary murmured earnestly as she sat beside the trunk on an upturned pail. "You'll git at least one patient. Zachary Thomas is due to bring baby Jed down right about now."

As she spoke, the barn door creaked open, a large shadow darkened the doorway and in strode the huge mountain man himself, carrying the baby in the crook of one arm. The door swung closed behind him. In the light of the kerosene lamps, Zachary Thomas looked mighty unfriendly to Doc. Could be he still blamed him for his young wife leaving him and taking his newly born baby with her, to go back to Lewis Mountain a while back. Doc leapt up and found himself fawning and being overly familiar with the huge black-haired hillbilly.

"Why, Zachary, my good fellow, how good to see you again!" he blustered. "I see you're in fine fettle! How's hunting going? And how's the little tyke?" He lifted the baby swaddled in blankets off his father and laid him down on the hard metal bench. The baby seemed to recognize him for he immediately started a frenzied kicking and glad little gurgles, bestowing on him a dazzling little smile, showing two rows of minute sporadic teeth. Doc felt a melting rush of warmth, suddenly feeling that the trip had been worth it for this alone.

"Why, Jediah Horatio Buchanan, what a bonny little fella you are," he said softly to him, as he fitted his stethoscope to his ear, lifted the child's long woolen smock and listened to his tiny chest. It was clear as a whistle and, after peering into his eyes, both ears and down his throat, he was happy to announce a clean bill of health for the baby and good, sturdy development. He handed the baby to Mary, who welcomed the mite with outstretched arms, gentle coos and a loving smile.

"You next?" Doc inquired of Zachary Thomas.

The huge hillbilly shook his head firmly. "Don't believe in quacks!"

Doc felt a flash of indignant fury not only at the blatant insult, but at the lack of gratitude, which he tried to conceal beneath an airy disregard. "What, you got no complaints? No ague? No sore throat? No cold? No *hemorrhoids?*"

Mary turned to her husband in angry dismay. "Why, Zachary Thomas Buchanan, you apologize to Doc Adams this instant! He's come miles to tend to us and you've got th' awful cheek to say sech a terrible thung to him. You don't got a stitch of manners, let alone a scrap of appreciation."

Zachary Thomas looked sheepishly shamed at his wife's strident outburst. He drew in a deep calming breath then pursing out his mouth, he stuck out a placating hand to Doc. When Doc uneasily shook it, squinting under its crippling squeeze, the hillbilly mumbled, "I'm sorry if'n I offended you, Doc. I guess I was kinda rude at that. Still, I don't aim to be no guinea pig!"

Guinea pig, indeed! "Well, *that,* sir, is your prerogative!" Doc said huffily. "It might help you to know I practice medicine, not hoodoo! I may have stuck a few needles into people from time to time, but never pins!" He could see the pointed analogy went straight over the hillbilly's head. "Will there be any more patients, or shall I be on my way?"

"If'n you want my honest opinion, Doc," replied Zachary Thomas, "I thunk you've wasted yer time comin' here. Buchanans don't hold with doctors an' you ain't likely to git any more patients if'n you hang around here fer a week!"

"In that case, let me be on my way and I won't chance to waste your time or mine ever again!" snapped Doc.

Doc hastily gathered up his medical paraphernalia and began packing them back into his medical bag and medical trunk, shaking with anger and humiliation.

Just then the barn door opened with a creak and a small voice piped up. "I'd be mighty beholden to you if'n y would take a look at my young'uns, Doc."

Doc stopped what he was doing and turned to find a tall, thin, young hillbilly woman with mousy-blonde hair, who was holding the hands of two small children, while another three peered from behind her skirt.

"I'm Edna," she said. "Widder of Samuel. Reckon Phoebe's got th' flu an' Lisa cough's awful bad, too. Sam cain't keep his food down and Lila cries all night without stoppin'. Tim got a real nasty cut on his foot on th' way over. Thunk you kin help 'em?"

Doc smiled broadly at her and said heartily, "Well, Edna, I can certainly try." He looked up haughtily at Zachary Thomas. "I trust you don't mind if I tend to these children before I go?"

"*'Fore you go?'*" said Edna. "But I thought you was here fer th' whole day?"

"Well, I was supposed to be, but it seems I'm not wanted around here and as soon as I'm finished with you and your dear family, I'll take my leave."

"Well, a'fore you do that, Doc," said Edna seriously, "I thunk you ought to take a peek outside an' check exactly what's a'goin' out thar. Don't thunk you *kin* leave!"

Doc was immediately struck with the certainty that Obediah Buchanan had a shotgun trained on the barn and would strike him down in a hail of bullets the moment he tried to depart it.

"*Why not?*" he croaked, feeling as vulnerable and afraid as he had ever been. He'd been a fool to come! This devilish clan would doubtless consider him a fitting candidate to avenge their matriarch's death for which they had blamed an innocent doctor, who'd probably done naught but try to save her!

"Jest take a peek thru' th' hole in th' door if'n you like," suggested Edna, obviously seeing his terror.

Doc walked over to the barn door with his knees knocking together and his stomach a watery pit, and peered through a peephole in it. He sucked in his breath and barked out a sound of pure shock! For, to his astonishment, he saw that the whole yard was *full* of hill folk – scores of hillbillies and their passels of children – and they were all lined up outside the barn door, in their rags and winter coats, silent and scared-looking, as if afraid what this outside contact might bring down on this old doomed mountain, rather than the reverse. Doc could scarcely believe the evidence of his own eyes. Whatever Mary's reservations and Zachary Thomas's misgivings, they had badly misjudged the mood of their kinfolk, for the members of this clan had somehow managed to overcome their prejudice and their deepest fears and had come to seek medical treatment for their family's ailments. Mary, handing over her baby to her husband, rushed over to the door and summarily pushing Doc aside, peeped through the same hole, letting out a squeal of sheer delight.

"Knew they'd come," she exclaimed. "I prayed so hard fer it! Ask'd God to lift their fear an' ignorance and fer them to come forward in their droves. Reckon my prayer got answered right smart, don't you, Doc?"

"Indeed," smiled Doc, feeling the full flush of triumph himself.

37

The afternoon progressed well. Doc applied ointments and salves on suppurating sores, treated ague, sore throats, worms and lice, and pulled out any number of rotten teeth. Some patients, in their teens and twenties, had glaucoma, for which he poured eye-drops that would have little effect. He gave countless spoons of cough syrup, palpated emaciated chests and listened to heartbeats, dished out hundreds of pills, amidst the overwhelming stench of filth and long-unwashed bodies. Indeed, Doc felt that Hilda would swoon if she could see his latest clinic and patients. He doubted that even her stout Teutonic heart could take it. Some cases among the children were so severe that he urged their parents to take them to the nearest hospital. By the anguished looks on their faces, he knew that they were unable to afford such medical care and that before too long more graves would be dug on Claw Mountain.

But he did what he could for them, rummaging around in his apothecary chest for anything that might help them survive their ailments. Still, despite his concerns, the whole exercise was energizing for him. He felt his missionary zeal expand like pure oxygen pumped into his lungs. Mary was a wonderful help. With not a day's training to her credit, she proved a natural nurse's aide, her caring and anticipation, combined with her eagerness to help, was a joy to his weary body. She kept him going with mugs of coffee and sandwiches and cookies, which he nibbled at between patients.

At last, as the shadows were growing lengthy, the long line of mountain crackers waiting to enter the barn had evaporated, although most of those already tended were still loitering in the yard outside for Doc could clearly hear their murmuring. When the last patient was dismissed, Mary helped him to pack up his things. She had invited him to stay the night up on Eagle Spur (this time not in the barn like before, but in the cabin on a made-up pallet). He had accepted, out of necessity rather than choice. Besides the fact that he was so weary, it was far too late to start for home now. It would mean traveling far into a freezing winter's night. Nevertheless, Mary's hillbilly husband badly inhibited him. He was so taciturn and fierce-looking, with those black eyebrows coming down like thunder-clouds over those lighting-bolt turquoise-green eyes.

Still, he noticed that for all his threatening appearance, Zack Buchanan was sure gentle with baby Jed and his eyes followed Mary around with surprising softness. Doc remembered when he was last here to deliver Mary's baby, how frightened and troubled Mary had been and how he had thought she had been kidnapped and abused. But it was very clear that a deep bond had since been forged between these two. Quite a remarkable turn of events, by any standards.

After making sure that his beloved nag, Bessie, had been watered and fed by Emma in one of the stalls, Doc and Mary left the stinking barn together. As he exited, he heard a loud retort and something whizzed past his ear and imbedded itself in the barn door, barely an inch to the right. Doc gave a cry when he realized that it was a bullet. Before he had time to see where the danger came from, he heard somebody yell, "YOU QUACK! WHO GAVE YOU PERMISSION TO COME ONTO MY MOUNTAIN?"

Doc ducked as a second bullet missed him by a hair's breath. He stared in horror at the shotgun being leveled at him by a skinny, white-haired creature standing on the porch of the cabin that was barefoot and wore filthy long johns. Obediah Buchanan? *Surely not!* Doc could not believe it was him. He had heard what a fabulous-looking fellow Obediah was, how elegant and virile-looking. But the man's next words betrayed that he was indeed the infamous father of the infamous Buckos of Claw Mountain.

"I AM OBEDIAH BUCHANAN!" the man screeched haughtily. "I AM THE KING OF CLAW MOUNTAIN! I REPEAT – WHO GAVE YOU THE RIGHT TO ENTER MY KINGDOM WITHOUT PERMISSION?"

Doc felt the urgent need to run fleeing down the mountain before there was time for these ferocious hillbillies to strip him naked and send him on his way – a ludicrous figure of plump white flesh and goose pimples – as he had heard had happened to a colleague in the medical profession and others who dared to displease this heinous clan. He knew he would never be able to stand the humiliation of such an eventuality happening in front of this fearsome lot he had just so nobly treated. But he couldn't run if he tried for his legs had totally seized up and his breath was coming hard and fast.

"Why," he croaked, "a request was made by young Mary, who wrote me and asked me to come and tend to your family's ailments. I was most happy to oblige."

Obediah snorted with derision. "You *dare* to insult King Obediah in his own kingdom by coming to treat his subjects without his permission?"

Doc balked. The man clearly was having delusions of grandeur in referring to himself as a king and to members of his own blood family as subjects! There was a wild and frightening look in the man's eyes as he discharged another bullet in Doc's direction. As it too missed him by a whisker, Doc gave a wailing scream and feared that he would have to change his trousers. Mary rushed between him and Obediah, who was standing barefoot and wavering on the porch – the very caricature of a heinous hillbilly that legend had lent this place! There were loud wails of anger and railings against the patriarch from the assembled clan.

Mary spoke up first. "Paw Buchanan, I cain't believe you would rather see more of yer family die than allow this wonderful doctor here to treat them. *Especially th' young'uns.*"

Obediah drew himself up, scratching at the great mat of white curls at the open neck of his filthy long johns. "Damn right I would! A quack killed my wife and I swore that day that no quack would ever set foot on my mountain ever again. Now move out the way, girl. This one is headed for Devil's Creek!"

Doc felt himself shudder with fright. It was rumored that Devil's Creek was the place where a massacre had taken place between the Buchanan and Galtrey clans and it clearly signified the fate the man had in mind for him.

"But Paw Buchanan, the young'uns . . ." But Mary's cry died on an icy breeze that had whipped up and the shotgun was pointed right at Doc again. Zachary Thomas rushed forward and pushed his wife out of harm's way, leaving the path unobstructed to Doc's trembling body. His knees were knocking as he awaited death in this undignified and humiliating manner. Oh, well, at least he had tried to bring medical succor to a back-ward and primitive people – primitive in their lifestyle and their urges – and whatever else happened, he had honored the Hippocratic Oath, rather grandiosely, in the circumstances. Perhaps history would dictate that he would go down as a genuine hero of this new century in these parts. But these were irrational flashes as he tried to stand his ground nobly and hold onto his guts.

The shotgun was wavering in a circle in Obediah's weakened hands, as he lifted it up to aim the thing at Doc's thumping chest. A shot through the heart would be nice – quick! Better than a messy stomach wound. The hillbilly clan had gathered around the doctor in a loose circle, but a wide one that did not threaten intervention in any way. Mary turned anguished hazel eyes on him as she struggled to get out of her husband's firm grasp. In a few seconds, it would all be over – he'd be another victim of the wicked Buckos and their evil patriarch! Oh, well, how foolish he had been to think it might turn out well. Doc raised his head to face his enemy and they stood for a moment eyeing each other in a moment of mutual contempt. Then an astonishing thing happened. There was a shrill whizzing sound and a sharp crack and, the next moment, the end of a whip had wrapped itself several times around the barrel of the shotgun and ripped it right out of Obediah's hands. It flew through the air and was deftly caught by Zachary Thomas.

Doc shuddered with shock and relief. The whip-wielder could be none other than the most feared Bucko of them all – Eli! Without a doubt, he had just saved Doc's life, though for what possible purpose Doc was at a loss to comprehend. He turned gingerly to look at his unlikely savior. With his thatch of bright-yellow hair spilling over his eyes, Eli gave a first impression of being rather boyish and innocent – an impression that was quickly quashed when one saw his evil pale-yellow eyes, hellish scar and the two Owl's Head pistols stuck in the front of his pants, the knife at his side – and the famed, devilish whip!

However, despite the jagged identifying disfigurement that rent his one cheek, Eli was much more handsome and well-dressed than Doc could possibly have imagined. He wore a jacket over a clean white shirt and gray pants rather than the dungarees worn by most of his brothers. His coat looked new while theirs were of threadbare cloth raised by hunched, bony shoulders, with holes at insistent elbows. His shoes looked far newer than the pitiful gaping specimens of winter footwear that clad the feet of his kin. If he wasn't so dreadfully unnerving to look at, he would be a fine specimen of young manhood, though slightly built and not at all tall. Yet, despite his lack of height, he had a power of command that was most disconcerting. Obediah gave a little shocked screech as Eli strutted forward, with the confident swagger of a famed gunfighter, a menacing figure of immense and chilling presence compounded by that awful scar that slewed down his left cheek. His words to his father were just as chilling.

"You old fart," he said scathingly. "Thar ain't gonna be no more murdered young'uns on Claw Mountain, you got that? Now git back inside a'fore I turn this thung on you."

Obediah's face was a study of shock. His eyes were wild, his lower jaw hung slackly open, and he had started to drool. His whole body was shuddering. His eyes beseeched his other "subjects" to no avail. Nobody came forward to defend him. Indeed, the mob raised fists and jeered at the emaciated old man on the porch. They spat at him and filled the air with loud curses. Obediah's eyes, filled with fear and anguish, rolled around as if they were on stalks. It was with cold shock and some relief that Doc realized Obediah Buchanan was no longer a force to be reckoned with on Claw Mountain – except to himself, of course! Indeed, it seemed his own family had turned against him. It was quite painful to watch, even though Doc could only imagine what might have caused such a reaction in them. Perhaps after the bitter winter, the pitiful state of their health and the medical treatment they had received, and which was now threatened, was enough to do it, but Doc was not convinced somehow. Clearly there was a usurper of Obediah's tawdry throne and it was none other than the Bucko of the most ill-repute – *Eli Buchanan, himself!*

"You gutless piece o' shit! Git back in yer kennel whar you b'long," Eli sneered at his father.

With a peculiar little whimper, Obediah turned and staggered back into the cabin, a thoroughly humiliated man. Doc stared dumbly at Eli. Despite the fact that he had saved his life just minutes ago, he could not help but believe that this young man would easily eclipse the evil reputation of his father. Doc slumped with relief and he looked at Eli gratefully, wanting to thank him for saving his life. But the look Eli turned on him was so strafing and hostile that Doc swallowed over a coal-sized lump of fear in his throat. Would his antagonist merely switch? If so, he felt he would rather have died at the hands of the first than the second, known universally in the mountains as "The Whip-Wielder" and "The Throat-slitter"! But as he went past Doc, Eli said to him under his breath, "Jest see you come back here agin, y'hear? And don't you let no young'uns die."

Once again, Doc slumped inwardly with relief. "I'll do my level best, son. You can be sure of that."

And suddenly the whole ugly incident was over. The hillbillies broke ranks and started moving off to their individual homesites. It had been such an ugly display that Doc felt totally bludgeoned by it, to say nothing of the fact that he had almost lost his life just prior to it. He was glad to escape to Eagle Spur with Zachary Thomas, Mary and Jed shortly thereafter.

Even after the effort to get there, Eagle Spur was wickedly cold and snow lay around the place, while ice crunched underfoot. Inside the log cabin, young Emma, whose virtues Mary could not extol enough, had put on a coon stew and lit a warming fire before escaping to her own hollow. Before too long, Doc's belly was full and he and Mary were quietly talking about the long eventful day.

"I'm right sorry I got you into sech a bother," Mary apologized profusely. "But you kin tell jest how badly yer help was needed here."

Feeling calmed down by his generous, delicious meal and quite relaxed for the first time that day in the dim light of the two kerosene lamps, Doc felt he could downplay the alarming events because the concern in Mary's eyes was so evident.

"Indeed, I have to agree. Their health appears quite pitiful and, despite everything, I was glad to help."

"Then ye'll come agin?"

After his ordeal, Doc felt clouted by the thought of having to go through anything quite as harrowing again any time soon. But his words belied his feelings. "Indeed. Perhaps in two or three months' time – depending on the weather, of course. If the winter promises to be anything like the last one, it could be a while longer, of course."

"I understand. Jest come. I know they'll leave you alone after what you've done fer them today. Perhaps we kin arrange a signal fer yer arrival."

Zachary Thomas offered Doc a nip of moonshine and, when he agreed, poured a generous tin mug of the stuff from a jug that had been sitting on the mantelpiece above the fireplace. Despite his ulcer, Doc felt he needed the stuff like never before after his life-threatening ordeal earlier. Besides he could not resist partaking of what was reputedly the best whiskey to come out of the Blue Ridge. He was not disappointed.

38

One afternoon, about a week after Doc Adams' highly successful visit to Claw Mountain, Mary heard the eagles making a huge racket again and opened the door to find out what was going on. To her great surprise, her brother, Joe, and – of all people – *Reverend Hubbly,* wearing a black suit and white clerical collar, were standing out on the porch, in front of her towering husband. Although Mary was delighted and excited to see her brother, Reverend Hubbly, despite his religious calling, was not her favorite person since he was so highly judgmental and critical of everybody. Therefore, she was immensely relieved to hear that his visit was to be a brief one.

Tall, thin and balding, the stern-looking fellow, who seldom smiled, declared he was staying just long enough to take some refreshment and enquire of her life and circumstances before going on his way again. As it was, he eyed the moonshine jug on the mantel with extreme distaste before sitting down at the table, making the blush rise in Mary's cheeks. She wanted to blurt out that Zachary Thomas no longer drank moonshine and that she had never indulged in it, that the jug was just on the mantel because it had always been there and to supply the odd visitor. But she knew that only a total ban on the stuff would satisfy him and, since it stood there in all its incriminating unglory, she didn't want to risk being shot down in hell-licking flames by him, so she kept her mouth firmly shut about it.

Soon they sat at the table chatting and nibbling still-warm Johnny ash-cakes, which she had made by wrapping cornmeal with cabbage leaves and leaving them in the ashes until they were golden brown. They were all drinking coffee, except for the reverend, who had opted instead for a glass of milk laced with a thick layer of cream. Still hunched in stern disapproval, he had a white mustache after taking a big gulp of his milk that somewhat ruined the dignified demeanor he clearly liked to convey. Mary, sitting across the table from him, gave him an unsure smile.

"What a nice surprise, Reverend," she politely fibbed. "Whatever prompted you to visit me here?"

He sniffed haughtily. "Oh, it didn't start out that way."

His eyes shone with glee as he told her the story. It seemed the good reverend had been visiting the Harley family at the same time that Joe was getting ready to leave to visit his favorite sister on Claw Mountain. Concerned about Mary's spiritual welfare on the heathen mountain, the reverend had insisted on accompanying him. Mary glanced up nervously at her husband seated at the head of the table, at the reverend's condemnatory words about the mountain, to find he was eyeing the reverend stonily.

Thankfully, Joe took up the story. Since none of the Harley family could write, he explained, he could not let her know of his plans to visit and it had been extremely fortunate that Zachary Thomas had come across the pair in Reverend Hubbly's horse-and-buggy in the foothills of Claw Mountain when returning from tracking in the Wilderness with his two coon dogs, and had escorted them safely up the mountain.

The reverend rejoined the conversation, wanting to know everything about Mary's spiritual life since she had left his congregation. Had she backslid, or did she still say her daily prayers? After assuring him that she did, he wanted to know if she went to church and, if so, what *denomination.* Learning of the lack of churches of any description within twenty miles of Claw Mountain, he blustered sternly, "For goodness sake, girl, that is simply not acceptable! You cannot allow this to sway you from proper worship."

He glowered at her as if the lack of churches hereabouts was all *her* fault. "*Do something!* Get them to build a brush arbor and I'll come by once a month to hold services!"

Mary stared at him in bald astonishment, hardly able believe her ears. She couldn't help thinking that such an offer was extremely brave of him, since everybody knew that the Buchanans despised preachers almost as much as they did doctors, and the odd preacher who had ventured up here in the past had been sent packing in a less-than-dignified manner. And look how Obediah had nearly killed Doc Adams so recently. Though, admittedly, the preacher probably hadn't heard about that one yet. *Build a brush arbor on Claw Mountain?* What a *wonderful* idea! Why hadn't *she* thought of it? She so missed going to Reverend Hubbly's monthly services in the brush arbor on Lewis Mountain, even if it was for the singing and fellowship rather than his boring, droning services of Old

Testament vengefulness, which were invariably interspersed with scathing attacks on other religions and denominations.

Nevertheless, whatever she thought of his merits as a preacher, his services always attracted hundreds of mountaineer worshippers, who loved anything that broke the monotony of life in the mountains. Zachary Thomas started grumbling under his breath at such a preposterous notion, but he didn't say anything, perhaps because he did not want to deny her religion in front of her brother, who would no doubt report such a thing to her parents.

Ignoring her husband's meaningful glare, she said, "Oh, Reverend, how awfully kind of you! God must surely have moved you to make sech a fine and noble offer. I'll surely see what I kin arrange."

The reverend stared at her with rapidly blinking eyes as if was the last thing he expected to hear. She wondered if it was a genuine offer, after all. Perhaps he already regretted his words and had been counting on her admitting that such an idea couldn't possibly work on this mountain. Still, he had been brave enough to visit her here, so perhaps she was being uncharitable in thinking he might not have meant it. But Mary was soon to discover that the reverend was in fact all fired up by the possibility of bringing his particular brand of Christianity to Claw Mountain.

"In that case," he declared pontifically. "I'll be back here first Sunday of next month, at eleven-thirty, for noon! See that the necessary structure for the Lord is in place, because I've got no time to waste. I have many more souls to save besides those of this bunch of sin-ridden and godless heathens! I've heard it on good authority that the Episcopal Mission Board is considering building a mission someplace in this vicinity." He snorted in a contemptuous manner. "However, if there is a good response by the inhabitants of this mountain to services, I will strongly recommend to my own Presbyterian Church Board that *they* build a church right here on Claw Mountain. Needless to say, my word carries considerable weight in the right circles. That will pip those pushy Episcopalians! They and the Baptists are taking over the mountains with their missions, and mollycoddle their congregations as if they are a bunch of helpless infants!"

He rubbed his hands gleefully and Mary could see him mentally notching up converts for himself to brag about to his Church Board. No doubt the Buchanan clan would be one worth aiming at in that respect. Mary could not believe such an extraordinary turn of events. *A brush arbor right here on Claw Mountain and the first service a mere two weeks from now!* Though she had no idea how she would succeed in getting the arbor built, or how she would drum up a congreg-ation, she was determined not to give the pontifical circuit-preacher an opportunity to backtrack on his offer.

"You kin count on it, Reverend," she said with firm conviction. "Ain't that right, Zachary Thomas? My husband is a fine carpenter and will have th' arbor up

301

in no time at all." Zachary Thomas frowned mightily at being summarily roped into her plans, while the reverend nodded in grim satisfaction. Mary stared gratefully at the reverend, quite overcome at the thought of a proper church being built right here on Claw Mountain. Not even Lewis Mountain had one anywhere near where the Harleys resided. Oh, how she had prayed that her husband's kin would be guided to cease all their violent and sinful practices, and now she had just been told that God had been listening all along! After the abrupt cessation of her book-learning classes, it was exactly what was needed to channel their energies into more positive things! Well, she didn't know how, but she'd get them there. *They'd get that promised church here on Claw Mountain, if she had anything to do with it!* She beamed at Reverend Hubbly. "Thank you, Reverend. Thar ain't no place that needs it more."

Reverend Hubbly puffed up his narrow chest airily. "Always knew the good Lord had a special mission in mind for me. Didn't expect it to be this, mind, but I can see now that the conversion of this mountain would show those nincompoops at the Seminary . . ." He paused when he saw the eyes of the siblings directly in front of him widen in shock. He clawed at his white clerical collar with long bony fingers, making a grating sound in his throat. "Can't let those show-off Baptists get a hold here first either, now, can we? Fact is, what we need to do is have a good old-fashioned *revival!* Nothing whips up a religious fervor like one of them. No reason to think that the folk on Claw Mountain and hereabouts should be any different." Caught up in ecclesiastical rapture, his light-brown eyes were blazing with zeal. While Mary thought a revival was mighty ambitious at this early stage, she, too, began to plan in her mind how that could possibly happen.

After Reverend Hubbly left with Zachary Thomas to be escorted to his horse-and-buggy waiting in the foothills, Mary turned to her dark-haired brother, who was studying her with intense dark-brown eyes. She was so happy to be alone with him. She showed him Jed who had just woken up from a nap. He lifted the baby out of the crib and threw him into the air, clearly overjoyed to see his infant nephew again. Jed kicked and gurgled in excitement, goo dribbling from his tiny chin.

"Oh, how he's grown, Sis. What a bonny little fella he is."

"He's crawlin' around jest everywhar! Lord, I've got to have eyes in th' back of my head. Oh Joe, I'm so happy to see you!"

Her brother smiled gleefully at her. "I would have come sooner, but you know how it gits. Paw's leg's bin playin' up pretty bad and I didin't want to leave him on his own. But it's bin much better of late and I knew I had to come a'fore th' winter sets in or else I'd have to wait till next spring. And Maw and Paw are so worried about you . . . I thought I'd have to walk, so it was sure nice hitchin' a ride on Reverend Hubbly's horse-and-buggy, even if he did jaw me silly all th' way here. And you, Mary? You sure look so happy and content. I reckon we've bin frettin' ourselves senseless over nuthin', all this time."

"Oh, I *am* happy, Joe. Zachary Thomas is a real good husband and I love him so much."

"Well, I must say I'm mighty impressed with yer place. It some beautiful up here with that view an' all. Looks real well-tended to, too. Must say, seems yer Zack has proved us all wrong."

Mary smiled at her brother, thrilled by his words. "That surely means a lot to me, Joe. Now that that's settled, while you're here, we'll make definite arrangements for th' rest of th' family to come visit in th' spring. I'll git Zachary Thomas to take Obediah's buckboard-and-mules to fetch whoever wants to come."

"Well, I thunk you kin count on Maw. She wanted to come with me on this trip, but I managed to persuade her it would be wiser to wait and see what I found here first."

"Oh, Joe, please kin you stay fer hog-butcherin' day? It's th' day after tomorrer and th' Buckos and thar kin will all be here to help, 'cuz Zachary Thomas has promised them good pickin's. Reckon we'll have to slaughter all six of th' hogs. They've fattened up fine on all th' acorns and chestnuts they've bin gorgin' on in th' forest. Came across a good three-hundred-pounder at the edge of th' forest th' other day. Reckon we'll git a fine lot of vittles from them all. Only trouble is, th' Buckos ain't never slaughtered no hogs a'fore."

Never one to shirk work, Joe's response was immediate and sure, his dark-brown eyes glowing with eagerness. "Sure, Paw said he kin spare me for a few days and we kin have our own hog-butcherin' day when I git back. I'll be glad to oversee it, if'n Zack agrees, that is."

Mary smiled with relief. "Reckon he'll be real glad of yer help. He's real good hand at butcherin' an' skinnin' an' sech, but he ain't never kilt no bunch of hogs a'fore neither. The clan ain't like proper mountain folk Joe. Thar daddy has them so befuddled on hooch, they ain't no good at nuthin' much!"

Joe grinned. "Wondered if'n I'd git to meet all th' Buckos. You got all th' equipment you need?"

"Sure hope so. I told Zack what to git. He fetched it from th' store by mule and it's all packed in th' barn. Two big scaldin' vats, two 35-gallon cast-iron kettles, a lard press, puddin' kettles, picklin' and cannin' jars, pans, buckets, sacks of salt for curin', butcherin' an' parin' knives and sech. Near took all of his credit at th' store. Oh, and a grinder fer makin' sausage too." She paused. "Jest hope I didn't forgottin nuthin'."

Remembering what a huge operation butchering day always was, Mary was so relieved her brother was going to stay to oversee it all. In truth, the day had been looming over her with ever more apprehension. She had always hated the annual day of slaughter with its ugly sights and smells. Especially, she didn't relish the idea of killing the poor hogs, but had been forced to harden herself to the necessity. She was concerned, too, over the fact that her sisters-in-law had been at loggerheads with her over her decision to teach the children book-learning without their permission. Even though the day-long medical session with Doc Adams had relieved the tension some, she knew that unless all the women worked as a team under her direction, the day could still prove to be a disaster. Butchering six hogs and preparing the meat would be a long and arduous task, after all, which would require great combined effort.

Fortunately, to Mary's relief, Zachary Thomas and Joe seemed to have hit it off and, after her husband had come back from escorting the preacher off the mountain, he readily agreed to Joe helping out on butchering day. They had sat for hours discussing strategy for the big day. The first job was to build a meat house, or smokehouse, next to the springhouse her husband had built while she was away, in which the meat could cure. The pair of them worked on the meat house the whole of the next day, finishing it in the early afternoon, when Zachary Thomas's ten surviving brothers (including, most disconcertingly, Eli), and their older sons, started arriving at Eagle Spur. For once Eli was dressed in his old clothes and winter boots, rather than the fancy duds he had worn since his visit to Stony Man Mountain. They gathered in a loose crowd in the clearing in front of the cabin, where Zachary Thomas introduced them all to Joe and made it quite clear that the two of them would be running the show together. He stressed that everybody had to do what was asked of them by either one of them.

Clearly this did not set well with the other Buckos who were not used to listening to anybody, least of all a youthful stranger. They muttered and threw Joe a lot of dark, menacing looks, which he met with calm, unafraid eyes and a raised chin, making Mary proud to be a Harley. Zachary Thomas made another stern stipulation. *"Thar's to be no drinking moonshine from now until th' work is over in th' morrer else you forfeit what's comin' to you!"*

Ignoring their grumbling, he set seven of them to chopping wood for the fires the next day. While they were busy doing that, Joe, Zachary Thomas, and his remaining brothers, Toad, Eli and Johnny, strung several strong poles together between two wide trees for a double gallows under Joe's capable direction and, when this was done, they arranged the two scalding kettles for the next day's work. The hardest thing to arrange was enough water. The annual hog slaughter required a great deal of it and Buckos and their offspring formed a long line down to the spring below Eagle Spur with pails. Two old bathtubs had been brought up from Horseshoe Hollow and these and every available tub and container at Eagle Spur were filled as well as the scalding vats and kettles. Then the hogs had to be rounded up from the forest and penned for the night in a structure Zachary Thomas had knocked up for the purpose, which took hours. There was much too much to do the next day to still go looking for hogs before they even got started.

Surprisingly, the Buckos all worked hard and with purpose. It seemed that the thought of the fresh hog-meat coming their way was enough to keep them off the hooch, for a short while, at least. Zachary Thomas stressed to his brothers that they had to be back at daybreak the next day. Since the Buckos oft'times rose late after bingeing on moonshine all night, Mary couldn't see them obeying her husband's strict instructions to not drink at all, in which case, she doubted they'd see them before noon when it would be far too late to start the operation, since it would need a full day to get everything done.

That night, Zachary Thomas and Joe sharpened knives long after Mary had gone to bed, fretting that things could still go horribly wrong. She would hate for Joe to have to report to her parents that her first "butchering day" was a complete disaster . . .

39

Against all the odds, the surviving Buckos and their older sons, all dressed in dungarees and thick coats, were all back at Eagle Spur by daybreak the next day, ready to get to work. The air was freezing cold this time of the morning and their breath formed trumpets of steam. Frost lay on the ground in patches. They shivered and blew in their bare hands to warm them.

In true Bucko style, they came armed to the teeth with their pistols, squirrel rifles and double-barreled shotguns, causing Joes wary, dark-brown eyes to meet Mary's. Many of their younger sons had been left to act as lookouts for any Galtreys. They assembled once again in the big clearing in front of the cabin, with their rotten teeth and threadbare clothing. Zachary Thomas reminded them again that nobody was allowed to drink moonshine until all the hogs had been slaughtered and prepared. Though they again grumbled loudly, soon they were too busy to think about it.

Joe sent some of the Buckos and their sons to drive the hogs from the temporary pen to the barn for the slaughter. The women and children arrived not much later, carrying all manner of utensils in which they clearly hoped to carry away as much of the day's hog bounty as possible. The younger children, including the babies and toddlers, were sent to the cabin where Emma was to supervise them with a couple of the older girls. She was very good with children. She brooked no nonsense. They respected her for it and listened to what she said. Mary was pleased to see all her former pupils among the young'uns, and that they had made an effort to wash up before coming to her cabin, in marked contrast to the others, who were filthy, bedraggled and lice-ridden. She made Emma promise to scrub them up before allowing them to enter.

Mary enlisted the help of the women to arrange the pans and start the fires. As she had feared, they didn't take kindly to her entreaties and worked slowly and reluctantly, scowling and grimacing and muttering under their breaths all the while, except for Samuel's widow, Edna, with her gaunt features and mousy-blonde hair, who leapt to start one of the fires. Mary sensed she had a staunch allay in the slightly older woman. Ignoring the other women's belligerent behaveior, Mary got them to raise the water temperature in the scalding kettles by heating rocks in the fires and dropping them in the water, sending clouds of steam into the still fall air to combine with the smoke from the fires.

After a short while, there was a great deal of noise as the hogs were driven from the temporary hog-pen near the entrance to the forest, to the barn, by yelling and cussing Buckos and their youngsters, wielding hickory switches. The hogs, all mammoth, dark-brown, hair-bristled creatures, burst into the homesite clearing squealing and grunting loud enough to wake the dead. Five of them must weigh between 200 and 250 pounds, while the last was easy the gargantuan 300-pounder.

After a concerted effort all but one of them were driven into the barn. The remaining hog, the heftiest one of all, was a stubborn, ornery critter and, clearly outraged at this rough treatment, it turned on Clem and chased him up a tree. Then it turned on its hoofs and charged down Johnny, who had to run and leap onto a huge boulder near the edge of the ridge and hang onto the top of it for dear life, while the rest of them fled out of harm's way.

This broke the tension amongst those watching, especially the women, who shrieked with laughter, yelling loud and derisive remarks at the two embarrassed Buckos currently being menaced by the grunting, enraged hog. Every now and then, the beast would turn from its trapped foe and charge around the clearing causing them all to scatter and take refuge behind whatever they could find. It was hilarious and Mary found herself joining in the howling laughter. At last, a chortling Zachary Thomas, Joe and Eli managed to draw the rampaging hog off with whistles and switches and some hasty side-stepping. They finally got the beast, snorting and grunting, into the barn as well, enabling Clem and Johnny to get down off their perches, red-faced and scowling.

A short while later, a shotgun blast went off in the barn. There was a terrible squealing noise and Mary heard Joe yell, "NO! MAKE IT A CLEAN KILL OR I'LL DO ALL TH' REST M'SELF!"

There came a second blast almost immediately. A short while later, there was a third blast, and a single grunt. *A clean kill!* After being bled in the barn, the two slaughtered hogs were dragged from the barn on sleds made of wooden boards, to the scalding barrels. The hogs' throats had been slit and their huge ungainly carcasses, immense dead weights, were then hauled up sloping boards set against the scalding kettles and tipped into the bubbling cauldrons, after Joe had done a finger-test in each vat used by old-timers to make sure it was hot enough, since this was very important. This he did by quickly dragging his finger twice through the water; if he was unable to do so a third time – it was hot enough! It was hot enough, in both cases and, as the huge carcasses were tipped into the vats, it caused much of the water in the cauldrons to splash out, causing everyone to jump away from them to avoid getting burnt. After that, the two hog carcasses were turned by two men with ropes to scald their other sides. The raw stink of scalded hog-hide and bristles filled the air, which had thankfully warmed a little with the risen sun.

After about five minutes of rolling and turning, the carcasses were then removed from the scalding kettles using the ropes again, till they were back on the sleds. Under the quiet direction of Zachary Thomas and Joe, several Buckos took up paring knives to scrape the hides from top to toe to remove all the hairs and bristles. After that, the two carcasses were hoisted up on the gallows by stout gamboling sticks, which had to be inserted into the hind-leg tendons to suspend them from the securely strapped horizontal poles. Even so, the poles dipped dangerously in the middle with the combined weight. Joe decided it might be wiser to let one of the carcasses down and do them one at time rather than risk breaking the gallows, or having to strengthen it at this late stage. It had been Zachary Thomas's idea to build the double gallows to save time, but he could see the sense in Joe's caution. Mary then marshaled three of the women to scrub the suspended carcass down with scrubbing brushes. When they were finished, Joe made to slit the belly of the carcass, having placed a large tub beneath it to catch the viscera.

"Lemme, lemme, I wanna do that," insisted Cletus. "I'm right handy at it!"

With that, Cletus wrenched the sharpened butcher's knife from Joe's hand and set to work. Remembering the pitiful job he'd made skinning the hare the first night she arrived on Claw Mountain, Mary rolled her eyes. He soon showed his lack of experience. He slew clumsily down the hog's belly through a thick layer of skin and shiny white fat so that viscera spilled out in a hot gluttonous blood-speckled mass. Unfortunately, in doing so, he had clipped the large intestine without tying it off first and got himself unceremoniously covered with putrid-smelling hog shit!

The others shrieked with unkind laughter, but Mary tensed. It would be just like a Bucko to blame Joe for his own stupidity and take out a pistol and shoot her brother dead – and no doubt the rest of them would consider it fully justified. Clearly hugely embarrassed at having made such an ass of himself in front of this stranger, Cletus sneeringly scrapped the goo off himself, to the continued gales of laughter from his own kin. He glared at Joe, with a finger itching at the trigger of one of the Owl's Head pistols in his pants. Joe defused the tense situation by gallantly springing to his defense.

"Don't worry, Cletus, did th' self-same thung m'self first time I tried it. Shucks, it's so darned common, folks call it a 'hog christenin'! Reckon we oughtta call you 'Cletus Hogshit' from now on," he added, with a huge grin. Mary was worried that this might make the Buckos feel so humiliated and angry that the danger had not yet past. Or he might pointblank refuse to do any more work, but once again, Joe deftly saved the day. "You've got to tie it off with strong twine a'fore you cut it to prevent what jest happened from happenin'," he told Cletus solemnly, instructing the Bucko to watch carefully.

Her brother raked out hot, steaming piles of entrails, thick blister-like intestines containing hard lumps of manure, followed by the liver, kidneys, heart and lungs, and the rest of the innards with his fingers, before carving the head down to the spine with a butcher's knife, then chopping at the back bones with an axe, while Cletus looked on in awed fascination. Then quite suddenly, Cletus grabbed the detached head and, setting it on top of his own, so that blood ran down his face in an estuary of red rivulets, began to chase the women.

It was such an unexpected development, and the hog's head looked so ludicrous on top of his head – like some grotesque Halloween mask – that it had everybody howling with laughter, including Mary, who laughed so hard she got a stitch in her side. After a while, Cletus pompously delivered the hog's head to Mary on a blood-swimming platter, presenting it to her as if it were the head of John the Baptist. She giggled and bowed ceremoniously to him as she accepted it from him. He reeked so badly of hog shit that she had to resist the impulse to hold her nose.

"Go wash up in th' rainwater barrel, Cletus," she called after him. "Emma'll give you some soap."

The head was set up on three-foot-long sharpened stake with its long snout pointing upwards. Mary got some of the women to rescald, rescrape and shave it until it was completely clean of hairs. She noticed they did it much more willingly after that bout of fun and nonsense. After they were done, the head was delivered to a trestle table. Joe obligingly stopped what he was doing to come over and cut it in half, starting at the mouth and moving steadily towards the neck. The jaw bone he clipped with a wood axe. He split the head-bone down the center with an axe. Mary then showed them how to carefully clip out the tongue and remove the brains, putting them into different pans and to remove the remaining skin and meat. The eyes, ears and snout were then removed from the ravaged head. By this time, the women's arms were greasy and bloodied up to their elbows. The top part of the head would be put into the large kettle for pudding meat. It would be cooked at a rapid heat until the meat came loose from the bones. Later, the hearts, kidneys and livers would be added because they required less cooking time. The tongue would be kept for canning. But that would only be done when three of the hogs had been made ready for it. The other half would be done in due course.

In the meantime, Mary had set two of the women to scrub the inside of the first carcass. She sent Cora running to the cabin with the quivering liver in both hands to put in the pot to be cooked for the midday meal. Two of the huge livers ought to do nicely for the whole bunch of them along with the mountains of cornbread, Johnny ashcake biscuits and baked potatoes, she had already prepared for the mob. Zachary Thomas, Joe and Cletus went to work on quartering the carcass. While the toothless Cora was gone, Mary and Edna started separating fat meat from the ribs to start the pudding and lard kettles, which had already been fired.

By now, the third hog had been shot in the barn – cleanly again – for beyond an initial grunt, there was an abrupt silence. After being bled by cutting its throat with a knife in the barn, it was duly delivered to the scalding kettle's sled. Some of the boys had built up the fires again and more water had been added to the kettles to replace what had splashed out. It was heated by adding more hot stones. The second hog was presently being hoisted onto the gallows and, without Mary having to ask, several of the women moved forward to scrub it with scrubbing brushes. Sportingly, Joe allowed the ever-eager Cletus, who had washed up in the rain barrel and was bare-chested and rib-sprung as a starving stray hound, to slit the carcass' belly. The smell of warm blood and sour, rancid-smelling viscera soon assailed Mary's nostrils again.

This time, Cletus carefully tied off the big intestine to avoid getting covered in hog-shit a second time, after Joe had showed him how to make a small incision beneath the hog's tail and to draw out a loop of the large intestine, tying it securely before severing it with a knife. After it was beheaded, the head was placed on a sharpened stake and dealt with as had the one before.

The third hog was tipped into a scalding barrel by Alvin, Ezekiel and Toad. This time it was Otis who insisted on slitting the hog's belly. Mary noticed a sense of satisfying order was coming into all their labors. Her handsome, husky husband, dripping sweat, was busy dragging a fourth slaughtered hog on a wooden board from the barn with the help of Elmer and Eli, gave her a tired happy grin and a wink, which showed her that he, too, believed the whole operation was going well. This hog too – a good 250-pounder – had been shot between the eyes and had had its throat slit, before being blooded. Heat from the fires made it hot work and sweat freely flowed. Hours passed as they all worked hard at their allotted tasks.

Without the aid of moonshine to get them all riled up over nothing, Mary saw a side to the Buckos that she hadn't suspected existed in them before. She fancied it even surprised the Buckos themselves.

Like a bunch of playful puppies, they cavorted and romped, chased one another, danced jigs and pulled faces. They told silly jokes, cackling like laying fowls at them, themselves. After slicing off the hog's head, Otis cut out one eyeball from its socket and pelted Cletus in the back with it. Cletus turned around and chased Otis around the cabin. Johnny trotted crazily around the pudding kettle before cheekily hooking a half-raw kidney out of it. He bit into it, causing blood to run down his chin, before tossing it back in. Even Eli – usually so sinister and silent – was smiling and laughing, joining in the merriment. There was singing, too, from several quarters, but none like that emanating from Toad's wife, Ellie Mae. She had a bird's nest of shrieking red hair and a homely face full of freckles, but she had a beautiful voice, as sweet as a mix of hominy and honey, which soared into the air and sprinkled on the heads of the slaving mountain folk like pearly dew-drops.

The third and fourth hogs were out of the scalding kettles and being scraped of all their hair, while the second hog was being quartered. The third hog was dragged to the gallows and was hoisted up onto it. This time, Willie insisted he wanted a turn at butchering a carcass. After giving him careful instruction, Joe handed him the knife. Despite some fierce and leering glares aimed in his direction, Mary could tell that her elder brother had managed to command the respect of her husband's brothers. Whereas, at first, any direction from him was met with scowling faces and hostile eyes, now they went to their work without such deliberate obstinacy. Mary imagined that it must be hard for them to kowtow to somebody else when they were so used to doing things their own way. The dogged, hard work continued, interspersed with ribald and funny quips from all those participating.

There were another two shots from the barn as the last two hogs were killed. The third and fourth heads were delivered to a trestle after being removed from the stakes. Joe dismembered them as before, and the women started working on the heads as Mary had instructed them. Despite the fall air and the heady heights of Eagle Spur, sweat broiled from the heat of the fires and the stench of warm blood and viscera polluted the air. By now everybody was exhausted with the non-stop, tiring work.

There was a welcome break at lunchtime, when Emma and some of the older girls brought out the meal. There were steaming piles of liver, which had been sliced and a little of the tenderloin, fried golden brown, served with brown gravy and hot cornbread, baked potatoes and Johnny ashcakes, which they set down on a trestle table set up for that purpose. It was eaten in two shifts, because one group had to be watching the kettles as the others took a break from their labors and ate. Those from the first group took a tin plate from a pile of them and helped themselves to the abundant fare. They sat around on the grassy ground, tossing leftovers at Rufus and Red, Zachary Thomas's two coon dogs that had sniffed around hopefully the whole morning.

Mary made more coffee, pouring it into a whole array of extended tin mugs, while the older children had milk. The atmosphere was happy and relaxed and everybody was chatting amicably, the women with their knobbly knees beneath plain cotton shifts covered with blood-splattered aprons, the men in their denim dungarees, wolfing down their tasty fresh-meat delicacies with their fingers. Mary noticed that the early-morning scowls on the women's faces, which were flushed with hard toil, had turned to weary grins, many of them toothless.

Mary smiled to herself, thinking how shared tasks had always kept the mountain folk close and neighborly, something the Buchanan clan was learning for the first time – no, the barn-raising at Eagle Spur had been the first time, and now she felt genuinely sorry that she had missed that special event. Mary realized that it was the first communal meal that she had ever known the Buchanan clan to have. There was no doubt it had united them, not only physically, but soul-wise too. The absence of moonshine had definitely made such a difference, with nobody cussing, yelling or fighting. On Lewis Mountain, such gatherings were held every Sunday, when friends and family would get together, either at the Harley home, Grandpaw Meadows' place, or at one of their neighbors'. And after shunning her for weeks, at last the members of the clan had let down their guard and were talking to her again.

As was the custom on the mountains, after the second group of adults had been fed and given coffee, the smaller children were led outside the cabin by one of the older girls to get their lunch. Mary asked where Emma was and was told she was seeing to Jed. After each group finished their coffee, they got up, dusted off their clothes and returned uncomplainingly to their labors. Mary, her hair disheveled and hanging in strands down her face, helped some of the men divide the meat and fat for the kettles, while the women finished working with the hogs' heads.

And so it went on, the fifth hog being dealt with in the same fashion as the first four had been. It was dragged on the sled up the sloping boards and tipped into the scalding barrel before being scraped of hair. Then the slaughtered hog was hoisted onto the gallows, where it was first scrubbed by the women and then butchered by one of the men, before the women tackled its head, first at a stake and then on the trestle table after Joe had done his bit. The huge 300-pounder had been left until last. It was simply too big for the scalding vat. Even if it hadn't been, it was so heavy all the water would have splashed out and there would have been no way to turn it. So it was left on the board and buckets of boiling water were thrown over it instead. Soon the terrible smell of scalded hair and parboiled flesh filled the air.

Mary gazed at the poor thing in sympathy. The massive dead razorback hog had lost its mean look as it lay trembling and vulnerable-looking on the makeshift scalding board, its light-blue eyes opened and sightlessly staring, its pale underbelly quivering. It was shaved of bristles and hide, reducing it to a smoothly shorn embryonic-looking thing, devoid of any dignity whatsoever. It was much too spirited a beast to have come to such a dreadful and ignoble end. When it was at last hoisted up onto the gallows, it was such a dead weight, it caused the poles of the gallows to dip alarmingly in the middle.

Two more heads, after having been scrubbed and cleaned and shaved on the sharpened stakes, were duly delivered to the women waiting at the trestle table, who were chatting loudly. The piles of ears, tongues and jaws on the pans were steadily growing higher. The hoofs were to be used for pickling. Ezekiel's wife, Mabel, was about to toss the hog tongues into the pudding kettle, but Mary snatched them away from her just in time, explaining that such good meat ought to be kept for canning. Despite a flash of annoyance, Mabel surrendered the delicacies without her usual carping. The tenderloins, of course, were much savored and those not served at lunch were also to be kept for canning.

Mary then got the women to start grinding a large pile of meat scraps into sausage after having checked it to remove any skin or too much fat, and to reduce large pieces so they would get through the sausage grinder. One of the older boys, boasting of his strength with typical Bucko swagger, volunteered to take over hand-cranking the sausage grinder as the women fed the meat into it. Mary got Ettie, Alvin's sour-looking wife, who had a bulbous nose and close-set eyes, to grind sage in the coffee-mill to season the sausage after it had been ground, along with salt and pepper.

Mary stuffed some of her share into pre-sewn sacks for summer sausage, handing out a few to the womenfolk who said they wanted some as well. The rest of the ground meat was shoved into casings that the men had prepared by flushing out and cleaning the hogs' large intestines. Mary gathered up some of the hogs' ears, feet and jaws and boiled them in a big cauldron suspended over one of the fires. When the meat was falling off the bone, she had one of the men remove the cauldron from the fire. She drained off all the liquid and removed all traces of bone. Mashing the meat with her fingers as she had seen her mother do so many times, she added vinegar, and salt and pepper, and set it aside to jell to make souse. She did this several times over.

Meanwhile Joe had got the men to strain off the pudding meat and divide it amongst the various pans, while the women prepared the mason jars and cut backbone, ribs and tenderloin, as well as a few livers and feet for canning. Soon all that was left in the pudding kettles was a greasy sludge on the bottom. Mary got Zachary Thomas to fetch some sacks of flour and cornmeal and she added these to the kettles with a little salt and pepper for seasoning to make scrapple or *ponhoss*, the mixture thickening as she stirred inside each kettle in turn.

Mary, who could feel the strain in her lower back, asked Johnny to fetch the lard cans from the barn and, after the mixture had cooled, she got a clean cloth and strained the liquid through it, from the kettle into the large cans. All that remained on the cloth were the cracklings, which, when cooked crispy, were a favorite treat of the mountain folk. Squeezing the liquid from the dried skins, she then divided them among the various pans, so that each family would get some.

She then set some of the women to rendering the lard. She showed them how to slew the fat in thick slices with a sharp knife and then to slice first one way and then another, causing it to become little cubes, which could easily be melted down. The women, taking up knives started dicing the layers of pork fat heaped in pans. Soon their hands were shiny with grease, while sweat slicked their foreheads. When they were finished, one of the cast-iron kettles was used to render the fat into lard. It had to be cooked slowly in order to render the most lard. The hot grease was then poured into the press until it was full and the press handle was turned down to a snug pressure. They ended up with twelve 50-pound cans of lard in all, enough to share amongst the whole clan. When the *ponhoss* from the two pudding kettles had cooled, Mary sliced it and divided it among the various pans as well.

She ordered the men to build up the fires, and instructed the women to wrap the meat-filled jars with cloth to provide protective padding while they boiled in the kettle during the canning process. While the kettles boiled, the families congregated at the trestle tables where bacon was being carved from layers of meat and fat with paring knives, and hams, shoulders and side meats were being divided. Even the viscera were equally divided to be fed to the chickens and coon dogs. The last thing to be done was the salting of the meat. Carrying the sacks of salt from the barn on Mary's instruction, the women then set to sprinkling the hams, shoulders and slabs of bacon with it, ensuring each side was covered, before they were sacked for curing in the smokehouse. Zachary Thomas had promised his brothers he would help them build smokehouses in which to keep their bounty, over the next few days. Mary had already set aside some bacon for Joe to take home to her own family, as well as a few jars of her sauerkraut and green beans for them to sample. Though they were unlikely to need the extra bounty, it would further convince her family of how well things were going for her now on Claw Mountain.

Finally, as the shadows were growing long, after many long strenuous hours of bone-breaking hard work, it was all done. Eli and John helped Joe and Zachary Thomas take down the gallows and the knives and pans were washed up by the women and older girls, before being packed up. Unbelievably, the day had gone off without a major hitch. Indeed, the Buchanan clan had surprised Mary with their capacity for hard work when the occasion demanded it. Everybody looked weary, but happy and satisfied with a hard day's work well done. They had worked as a team and done one heck of a good job too!

40

The weary mountain clan sank to the ground and were sitting in bunches chatting and laughing amongst themselves. Released from Emma's eagle eye, the bedraggled children surged from the cabin, laughing excitedly, joining their parents on the ground. Zachary Thomas brought out some moonshine jars from the barn to be passed around. But the Buckos and their wives, weary and content for once, hardly took more than a few sips each before they stood up and said it was time to go home.

Remembering that Reverend Hubbly was coming in less than two weeks' time to hold his first church service, Mary decided that this was the perfect time to tell her husband's kin about it. She was real nervous, especially as she had not yet fully discussed the matter with Zachary Thomas, with Joe still around, but she knew she'd never get a better opportunity than this. She leapt up and stood in front of the milling group.

"Well, folks, I want to hank y'all so much fer comin'. You sure did a real fine job. Never could have done it without y'all." She cleared her throat, her heart hammering inside her chest. "I've got a real important announcement to make. We're aimin' to build a brush arbor on Claw Mountain and Reverend Hubbly has promised to come preach in it on th' first Sunday of each month."

The whole gathering instantly froze and Eli turned furiously on her, his pale-yellow eyes blazing. "*What did you jest say?*"

Alarmed by the swift change of mood and by the astonished glare her husband threw her, Mary stood firm. "Y'all heard me. We are buildin' a brush arbor for a monthly church service to be held. I sure hope ye'll all attend."

"And *who* gave you th' right to make sech decisions about our mountain?" Eli demanded to know.

There was such menace in his voice, such anger glinting in those disturbing eyes that Mary felt a chill run down her spine. She could see Joe eyeing her worriedly. Just when she'd been thinking how hard Eli had worked today and with such good humor that he'd almost seemed likeable and that perhaps there was hope for him, after all, here he was acting like the ugly Eli of old again.

"Nobody," she said, feeling flustered. "But I live on this mountain too now, and surely I've got me a right to git a preacher up here if'n I want to."

The small muscle in Eli's jaw began to ominously flicker. "Jest git this straight! You ain't got *no* rights whatsoever on this here mountain, you got that? This is *Buchanan* territory! And you sure as heck ain't no Buchanan."

Mary swallowed hard, brushing her blood-and-grease-stained apron with her hands. She strove for a measure of reason and dignity after the thorough slap-down from the most feared Bucko of them all, knowing how his antagonism towards the idea could sway his kin against it.

"Well, even if that be th' case, my husband *is* of Buchanan blood and he sure does got rights. He's with me on this, ain't you, Zachary Thomas?"

All eyes, including Mary's pleading ones, turned to her husband, who was standing there, staring at her, in mortified horror. After a moment of tense, expectant silence, he finally nodded grimly. "Yeah, reckon, a little religion might be a good thung, at that."

Mary's shoulders slumped with relief. Perhaps he had remembered what she'd told him when she'd left with baby Jed about how important religion was to her, and how there was no religion on this mountain, for him to have supported her in this. Perhaps he was also mindful of the fact that Joe was looking on, and would report what he said to her parents.

"It don't got to concern you, Eli," she said in a placating voice. "Those of you who are not interested, don't got to attend, of course, but you'd all do well to come, Eli. The good Lord's word is fer us all to hear. Ye'll all enjoy th' sangin' too, I'm sure. And Ellie Mae, a voice like yours belongs to God, that's fer sure. I thunk we'll need to start a choir a'fore too long. So please come."

"What's a choir?" the flame-haired freckled creature asked petulantly.

"A group of sangers."

"Thar ain't no chance *I'll* go to no church!" Eli said scathingly. "Not till hell freezes over!"

"Well, I guess that's yer decision, Eli. But if'n anybody else would like to come help us build th' arbor, please be here early next Sunday mornin'. We'll choose a good site with yer help, build it, an' then ye're all invited fer vittles. Th' first service is th' Sunday after that. I thunk you should be real honored that Reverend Hubbly has decided to include Claw Mountain in his monthly roster and will also recommend that a permanent church be built on th' mountain if'n th' response is good. So I beg you to make an effort to come."

No one else said a single word, not a person stirred. Mary did not know what she had expected, but certainly not this total unresponsiveness. Eli did not say another word either, but was staring at her as if she'd gone mad. She looked away from his intense gaze to see how the others were taking it, but they moved their eyes away evasively and were muttering under their breaths. They turned and started silently filing down the mountain, carrying the pans and utensils and buckets filled with hog bounty – hams, bacon, sausage, *ponposs*, lard, plus jars and cans of pickled meat. Mary stared after the departing bodies in dismay.

Upset that such a successful day should end on such a flat note, when the last person had disappeared over the ridge, Mary turned and trudged wearily towards the cabin. As she looked around the yard, she suddenly felt a great pressure bearing down on her chest. There was a putrid stink in the air. The fires were still smoldering and there were piles of singed hog hair entangled in the grass. There was blood in the grass too – some blackish and some red with recent spilling, and smelling ripe and foul. Fat and gristle and bits of skin were everywhere. All the buckets and utensils were covered in blood, some dried, some fresh. Suddenly, the successful day turned dark and ugly in her mind.

She had been out to feed the hogs some slop in the pen last night and they had come sniffing up to her with their long snouts, squealing and grunting, hungry and inquisitive. *And so trusting.* She had thought then how the poor creatures were doomed and that all that awaited them in the morrow after long months of roaming wild and free in the vast tableland forest and feeding on mast, was this . . . this *carnage.* Her hands were greasy and streaked with blood. *The blood of those poor critters.* She was filled now with a terrible aching sadness.

She kept telling herself it was a necessary evil – and it was! *Survival!* – but the thought of the spirited hog and its eventual ignoble fate sprang to mind and, somehow, it seemed so unnatural and cruel. And now she had failed in her bid to persuade the Buckos to support Reverend Hubbly's offer. She heard the sound of Dapple's cowbell as she came in from the forest to be milked. Later, she would have to go out and milk the poor thing, of course, but right now, she was just too bone-weary. She felt exhausted, defeated and deeply depressed as she went into the cabin, wiping tears from her eyes. Joe and Zachary Thomas were busy returning equipment to the barn.

Dear Joe! What a blessing he had been. They never would have coped without his able assistance and direction. Well, not nearly as well, she was sure. He seemed to be everywhere at once, guiding and instructing and helping in his quiet, able way, gathering Bucko respect as he went along. She was going to miss him something fierce when he left in another day or so. (He was staying on to help Zachary Thomas with building the other smoke-houses.)

Emma was still inside the cabin. She was holding Jed, who was crying inconsolably. His face was bright red and tears were streaming down his small cheeks. Mary felt her heart sink. She'd been so busy all day she hadn't even had any time to think of her poor baby.

"Don't know what's wrong with him, Aunt Mary," Emma said worriedly. "He's bin like this th' whole day. It sure ain't like him. He hardly ever cries."

"Emma, why didn't you come tell me?" Mary asked, as she took her baby into her arms and tried to comfort him.

"Y'all were so busy, I didn't want to bother you none. I done gave him a honey sugartit, but he wouldn't take it. Jest spat it right out."

"Guess he must be teethin' bad, poor baby. Don't you worry none, Emma, honey. I'll rub some oil of cloves on his gums. That'll fix it. Best you git on home to yer family now, a'fore all them crisp cracklin's are gone. Thanks fer all yer help."

"Alright, Aunt Mary. Sure hope he'll be okay . . ."

But even though Mary rubbed oil of cloves onto Jed's gums with a little finger, he kept on crying for hour after wretched hour. There was such a heartbroken sound to his crying that it was very upsetting to listen to. When she gave him to Joe to hold while she went out to milk Dapple in the barn, she could still hear the sound of his anguished crying. And here at the scene of so much carnage, the smell of hog blood was powerfully heavy in the air, making Mary feel slightly nauseous. Pools of dark blood lay in the straw where the hogs' throats had been slit and on the wooden boards. Then a crazy thought entered her mind. Was it the extensive blood-letting that had upset her baby so? She knew she felt profoundly affected by it, herself, right now, but how could it possibly affect an eight-month-old baby inside the cabin? She shrugged off such a ridiculous assumption.

Though she was totally exhausted from the day's labors, Jed kept her up all night. Indeed, his heartbroken crying continued uninterrupted the whole of the next day and night, until Mary began to fear that there might be something more seriously wrong with him than just teething. She decided to get Zachary Thomas to take him to Carlisle to see Doc Adams by buckboard that morning, before taking Joe back to Lewis Mountain. The whole of the previous day, the pair been busy building smokehouses at other homesites on the mountain, and they looked dog tired, especially after the exhausting butchering day! But they too looked very worried when she told them about Jed's distress throughout the long day.

Then, on an intuitive hunch, before she sent Zachary Thomas and Joe away with little Jed, she set about erasing all marks of the butchering day from the barn and out in the yard. She ordered Zachary Thomas and Joe to return the old bathtubs to Horseshoe Hollow since she had discovered the water in them was red with blood, since some of the clan had tried to wash up in them. She scrubbed the wooden boards, buckets and sleds clean with clean water and lye soap, covered the pools of dark blood in the barn, and outside, with fresh soil and buried the bloodstained straw that was in the barn, replacing it with fresh straw. She swept the yard with the yard broom, burying the thick matted piles of hog hair, gristle, bone and bits of fat that was lying about in the grass and threw pail after pail of water onto the grass to get rid of the dried blood clinging to it. The moment all the evidence of the day of carnage was removed, little Jed suddenly stopped crying and became her calm, serene, smiling little baby again . . .

Falling Leaves and Mountain Ashes

Book IV

'Spreading the Light'

*'When Light approaches the darkness
It is not the Light that vanishes,
But the darkness ...'*

Brenda George

41

The following Sunday, Mary rose long before dawn to cook lunch for those she desperately hoped would join them to help build the brush arbor for Reverend Hubbly to come preach in, the next Sunday. The idea of having regular worship on the mountain was thrilling to her and she prayed that Eli's antagonism towards the idea would not stop the others from coming. Mary felt that she had made some strides in her relationship with the other women, after the hugely successful hog-butchering day the week before. But because of their non-responsiveness to the idea of building the brush arbor when she had raised it, she had no idea what to expect. Would any of them be brave enough to defy Eli and come? Well, she had to believe that they would. She had prayed hard enough about it. And she was preparing for it, in any event.

She had baked six loaves of cornbread the night before, along with honey-dew biscuits and buckwheat cakes – she just wasn't sure if anybody would be around to eat them! She went to sit outside on a blanket beneath the leafless giant chestnut tree, to wait for those brave enough to come help build the brush arbor. The grass was covered with chestnut leaves and empty chestnut burrs covered in bristles that had fallen to the ground after the nut harvest. She played with Jed, while Zachary Thomas wandered about doing odd chores to keep himself occupied. His face told Mary that he doubted that any of his kin would put in an appearance.

By eleven o'clock, reckoned by the height of the sun at this time of year, not a single soul had ventured up to Eagle Spur, with the exception of her little stalwarts, Emma and Beaufort. Another estimated half-hour passed, and still nobody came.

Then, just when Mary was despairing of anyone else coming, Ellie Mae's flaming head peeped up over the ridge. She came with her five children and her husband, Toad, who, no doubt badgered by his waspish wife, whose visions of starting a choir had been fulsomely aroused, looked as if he had been dragged there very much against his will.

"Mary," said Ellie Mae, "reckon we've come t'help build that thar brush doo-dah of your'n."

Mary leapt up and rushed forward with grateful, outstretched arms.

"Welcome, y'all. So glad you could make hit. Do you know if'n anybody else is a'comin'?"

"Mebbe," was all Ellie Mae would commit to.

A few minutes later, the mousy-blonde head of Edna popped over the ridge. She was trailed by her young brood of five. No one else came. That meant there were five adults and twelve children to do the work. Worried about the lack of support, Mary bit back her disappointment. Well, at least it was a start and the others might come around to the idea later. Feeling that where the arbor should be built should not be her decision alone, and that she probably *had* made too many decisions of her own of late, Mary prompted Zachary Thomas to ask for some suggestions. While they were busy discussing the matter, Cletus came up over the ridge, grinning and showing his rotten teeth. Mary smiled him a warm welcome and Zachary Thomas shook his hand. At least there were now six families represented here in all.

"No place near Obediah's homesite," railed Ellie Mae, scratching her bird's nest with a filthy long nail. "Lookit how he was with th' doctor. Reckon he'd kill a preacher fer sure."

After Obediah's showdown with Doc Adams some two weeks ago, nobody was keen to have Reverend Hubbly run into the patriarch anytime soon. It was decided among them that the arbor should be easily accessible to all those who lived on the mountain and that they should look for a suitable spot at about the same elevation as Horseshoe Hollow, midway up the mountain and well to the east of Eagle Spur. Mary thought she knew just the spot. The assembled members of the clan descended to take a look at it. It was perfect – a large clearing with little undergrowth. It was intensely cold in the deep shade provided by a tall canopy of trees above it, with a few purple leaves still clinging to the branches of oaks, but it could easily provide space for at least a hundred worshippers, besides a pulpit. The families set to work, the men felling young trees and saplings with axes to provide the poles for the structure. Deep holes were dug for the poles then a rectangular overhead structure of poles, with interlinking poles for the sides of the arbor, all bound together securely with ropes. Great progress had been made.

Usually grasses were used to provide the roofing of brush arbors, but Claw Mountain was a heavily forested mountain with no store of blue-grass except at the bottom in the foothills. However, with the onset of early winter, this was short and dry and could not provide such lush means necessary to provide a suitable roof for the arbor. Personally, Mary felt the forest itself was a good enough cathedral, in which to hold services, but it did not provide any protection against rain – and winter downpours were particularly freezing and uncomfortable. She did not think that Reverend Hubbly would take too kindly to getting wet. Instead, the children were sent to collect any branches they could find with foliage on them. They were soon joined by the womenfolk.

They all worked hard at gathering, while Ellie Mae's sweet voice rang through the trees with spring-water clarity. She was as coarse and repulsive-looking a creature as Mary had ever encountered, yet God had seen fit to bestow upon her the voice of an angel. Unfortunately, they found that many of the bushes were almost leafless and Zachary Thomas had the idea to use sacking to cover the roof area of the arbor, before using whatever other kind of foliage they could collect. He fetched the sacking from his barn and then Toad and Cletus shimmied up the poles to nail it to the poles of the roof structure before they collected branches and foliage, which were laid intricately and thickly upon it.

When this was done, Zachary Thomas chopped a pulpit from the trunk of a felled tree. Several hours later, the brush arbor was all done. They all sat on the ground outside the newly erected structure to admire their handiwork. Through the open back of the structure they were able to see the tree-stump pulpit and the canopied foliage roof. *Their very own brush tabernacle!* Mary felt a deep sense of satisfaction she knew was shared by the others. Soon after that it began to rain and the weather turned cold. Mary thought how fortunate they were that Reverend Hubbly was prepared to come so late in the year. Most preachers only serviced their circuits in the warmer months. The rain was an icy-cold, drenching downpour that soon turned to sleet. It sent them all scurrying up to a foggy Eagle Spur to eat the goodies and warming coffee that Mary had promised them.

They gathered in the cabin, the young'uns sitting on the floor. Mary stacked some kindling on the hearth and the fire soon caught, crackling heartily, warming them. Mary placed the chairs around the cabin for the adults to sit on, and told them to help themselves to the food laid out on the table. There were many gratifying "oohs" and "aahs" as they all tucked in. When the visitors finally made to leave, looking happy and content, despite the fact that she had served them coffee rather than moonshine,

Mary stood on the porch with Zachary Thomas to see them off as thick white mist enveloped the cabin.

"See y'all encourage th' others to come worship next Sunday," she called after the departing souls. "And be real careful goin' down. It gits real treacherous when wet."

42

The following Sunday, Zachary Thomas, Mary and young Emma, carrying Jed on her strong skinny hip, met Reverend Hubbly, who arrived at the foothills of Claw Mountain in his horse-and-buggy wearing a black suit and his white clerical collar and a stern look on his face. The party climbed the mountain, with ice crunching beneath their feet and the air sharp with cold, to where the brush arbor had been built the previous Sunday. Mary was awfully worried in case there was not a large enough congregation to satisfy the busy circuit-preacher. If too few people pitched up, he might think Claw Mountain was not worthy of a regular monthly visit. After all, his Lewis Mountain brush arbor congregation numbered hundreds and mountain folk swarmed to his revivals in their thousands, to be saved. A tiny congregation might not satisfy his grandiose spiritual plans for the mountain.

She had pondered on this problem long and hard during the week. She figured there could be a fair number of people living in the remote regions of the mountain, including Beacon and Bear Rock Mountains and, even if she could get half of them to come it would be a start. Though she was unable to consult with Reverend Hubbly first, she had gone to Toad and Ellie May's homesite to ask Ellie Mae if she would sing an opening hymn to start their first service.

She arrived at the crude tin-roofed shack on foot. When she knocked on the door, it was opened by a scrawny child, who immediately ducked around her and dived out of the shack, showing none of the aggression Mary had found in the other children of Claw Mountain thus far. The little girl stood peeping at Mary from behind a bush. Like most mountain children, this little fair-haired scrap was shy of strangers. Mary gave her a warm, reassuring smile before she stepped inside the dim shack. To her dismay, she found Ellie Mae and Toad sitting at a table with a jug of moonshine between them.

There was a dirt floor inside and it was windowless and gloomy, lit by a single kerosene lamp. Sparsely furnished, the only adornment in the place was a sepia photograph of Toad and Eli taken by some brave, or foolish, traveling photographer, which was mounted on one wall. The two sneering Buckos were both dressed in black suits, white collar shirts, black bowties and black hats. They were turned toward each other and each had their dual Owl's Head pistols drawn and pointed upwards in a cocky attitude. To Mary, it was a pose that shrieked of their lifestyle of violence and intimidation. She removed her gaze from it with a sense of apprehension. These Buchanans had known no other life and she knew how difficult it would be to change such an entrenched outlook.

The shack was filthy and smelled abominably. She wondered how they all managed to sleep in such cramped quarters. The cold was awful inside the shack. Mary marveled that they had managed to survive the past winter with such inadequate shelter. Then she remembered that two of their children had *not* survived. After having made a comprehensive list of all the children of Claw Mountain for Doc Adams, Mary had memorized their names, taking special note of those who had not survived "The Big Freeze", as the last winter had already become known by the mountain folk. She knew that this unfortunate couple had lost a girl called Mae in infancy, and another two, Josephine and Hasten, to the wicked winter. The pair seemed horrified to see her, their eyes aching with shame at being caught out in the misery and squalor of their existence.

"What d'you want?" Ellie Mae demanded aggressively, her eyes bright and beady, her bird's nest of shrieking red hair a sight as ever and her face pale and liberally freckled with large orange dots. Then she added in a voice dripping with sarcasm, "Y'come to join us in a jug?"

Mary's smile was uncertain. "Why, Ellie Mae, you know full well that I don't drink. Fact is, I've stopped by to ask you somethung much more important."

Curiosity rose in Ellie Mae's brown eyes. "What might that be?"

"Well, I haven't had a chance to consult with Reverend Hubbly about it yet, but I'm sure he'd be well-disposed to let you sing th' openin' hymn at our first service on Sunday."

Ellie Mae scowled, but Mary saw that her brown eyes were bright with interest.

"Hmmph," she snorted "*Him?* Don't know no hims, 'cept th' two-legged kind. Fact is, I don't know nuthin' at all about that thar church stuff."

Mary took the opportunity to sit down at the table with them. "Well, that is th' reason fer the brush arbor, Ellie Mae. So you kin find out about these things. And don't worry, I know lots of hymns. I teach you some then you kin decide fer yerself which one you'd like to sing on Sunday. I'd like to dedicate the hymn you choose to all th' folks on th' mountains hereabouts that were lost in 'Th' Big Freeze', yer own Josephine and Hasten included."

Ellie Mae looked astounded. She clasped Mary's hand gratefully across the table, her eyes filling with tears. Even the usually mean and ornery Toad began blinking away tears and Mary felt a deep welling of pity for them both. To have so recently lost two of their children about the same time like that must be real hard for them to bear. She couldn't even begin to imagine how she would feel if she lost Jed.

Mary and Ellie Mae practiced singing hymns together for the next couple of hours, Ellie Mae's rich, sweet voice filling the tiny dirt-floored shack like wafts of perfume, with Mary's melodious tone blending in. Mary then took off for Beacon and Bear Rock Mountains to invite the Ficks' and Addis' clans to join them in worship and acquire faith, going from shack to humble shack, each more pitiful than the last. These two outcast clans were a wretched lot, appallingly thin with hollow eyes and rotten teeth and they spoke so badly, they were difficult to understand. Some of them were squatters, but others were tenants who had been given a patch of land on which to grow their crops in return for their looking after the grazing of cattle belonging to the owners of the mountain tracts. They would graze them on the bluegrass slopes and the summit of the mountain and would salt them too. Mary had come across one of their salt licks – a block of salt mounted on a waist-high stick for the cows to lick – a common enough sight on Lewis Mountain. Wild animals, like deer and hares, craving salt, would lick at the salt-block too.

The mountain people of Beacon Mountain regarded Mary with narrow-eyed distrust and suspicion, but considering they had been subjected to all sorts of nasty things in the past by the bullying Buckos, Mary could scarcely blame them. Unfortunately, they lacked the gumption and fighting spirit of the Galtreys to stand up to their hostile neighbors.

Mary strongly doubted they had even heard of religion or had any conception of the Almighty God of heaven and earth. Certainly, they listened to her stumbling words about the revival without a trace of comprehension, or interest, in their eyes, but they did open up little when she told them it would likely be dedicated to those lost in the past cruel winter. At first they had been reticent, but Mary had broken the ice by telling them of her own travails during the bitter winter months spent on top of Eagle Spur, saying she knew that they must have suffered considerably as well. Gradually, but with increasing confidence, they told her of their own difficulties during that terrible time, making Mary's heart ache for them. They gave her the names of those lost, too, which she recorded in an exercise book she had brought along for the purpose.

Only one gray-haired old woman, wearing a faded pink frilly bonnet, in a crowded one-room shack, showed any interest in what Mary told her about the revival. She had stood up painfully and limped across to a small wooden box. She took out an old Bible with a black leather cover and took it to Mary for her to examine. Mary opened it to find that births and deaths had been faithfully recorded in the front of it since 1702. There were no recent entries, however, which seemed to suggest that the remoteness of the clan's abode had robbed them of literacy.

"Do you ever read this, Gerta?" Mary asked hopefully, indicating the Bible resting on her knees.

The old woman, her skin as wrinkled as a dried prune, sadly shook her head. "Did when I was young, mind. Don't no more. Eyes too bad. We used to go to church when we lived in th' valley too. Ain't never bin since we come to this here mountain. Too far. Always did enjoy hit tho'."

"Then you simply must come to th' revival Sunday, Gerta."

"Aye, I'd love to, only cain't walk that fer, no more. These old bones don't git me around like they used to when I was a girl."

"Well, why don't you git some strong lads to bring you across to Claw Mountain on a litter then?" Mary suggested.

Gerta looked doubtful. "Reckon it would take more than th' askin' of an ugly old woman like me to git them thar."

"Well, please try, Gerta. I'd sure love to see you thar. I thunk I'll give you directions jest in case ..."

* * *

Mary returned to Eagle Spur that day feeling, she'd had an enriching experience by reaching out to the poor folk who lived on the neighboring mountains. She now knew their names, which of their loved ones had died in "The Big Freeze", and something about their lives. She wasn't sure if any of them would come to the revival, but she was very glad she had gone to them anyway, feeling that the missionary jaunt had bestowed its own rewards.

The Sunday of the planned revival, Mary would have loved to have been able to decorate the arbor with fresh flowers but, being winter, that was out of the question. Instead, she and Emma had collected armfuls of ferns from some of the more protected glens. Some of the tips of the ferns had already been blackened with frost, but when they entwined them with the assorted foliage on the sacking on the roof of the arbor and down the sides, it gave the place a lovely look of naturalness that was so appropriate for their forest sanctuary. Mary had even stuck several ferns into cracks on the stump-pulpit, but felt it needed some color. Then a thought struck her. She went to where she knew a sumac bush grew. She collected some of its green flowers and bright red fruits, which she added to the pulpit and around the front of the structure. Mary thought it looked very beautiful.

Even Reverend Hubbly, who'd been fetched from his horse and buggy from the bottom of the mountain by Zachary Thomas, snorted with satisfaction when he saw it, but his next words quickly dispelled her sense of achievement. "It's all very fine, Mary, but *where are the worshippers?*"

There wasn't another soul about and Mary's own heart sank. "What time is it, Reverend?"

Reverend Hubbly removed his fob-watch from his top jacket pocket and looked at it peevishly. "*Half-eleven!* As I recall, I specifically instructed you to tell them *half-eleven,* for twelve. I know how tardy these mountain folk are. They have no sense of urgency whatsoever!"

"Well, at least thar's a half-hour to go yet. They'll come ... I'm sure."

"Well, I should hope so after all the effort I've made to get here," he grumbled. Clearly all his former enthusiasm for the project had vanished.

"You've got to understand it ain't easy to make changes on this mountain, Reverend. Progress will likely be slow. Have you asked your Church Board if'n you kin build a church here yet?"

Reverend Hubbly sniffed contemptuously. "Of course not, child! The Board would have to be convinced that the mountain is *worthy* of such a privilege before I could sound them out. Quite frankly, it doesn't look too hopeful to me."

They waited another ten minutes and still nobody came except for Emma and Beaufort. Of course, Mary reckoned young Emma would follow her through fire, if she asked her to, and that little Beaufort would do the same for Emma. Mary was so disappointed she could feel it seeping into her bones. She'd had such high hopes. Still, all was not lost. It was still twenty minutes to service time on Reverend Hubbly's watch. Mary tried to distract the reverend by telling him of her plans for the first service and her idea to dedicate it to those lost in "The Big Freeze". The preacher agreed somewhat reluctantly, writing down notes and names on a small notepad, saying crossly that he couldn't read Mary's 'illegible scrawl', which took a good while. Then, the job at last done, he raised his balding head and peered around the surrounding forest expectantly. *Still nobody else had come!*

Then just when Mary was about to give up hope, as Reverend Hubbly's watch hit the midday hour, Ellie Mae, Toad and their five surviving children, Kate, Orville, Pete, Fanny and Clancy hurried up through the forest. Almost at once, Cletus arrived at a trot, and Edna and her five children appeared through the trees. Instead of welcoming them to their new place of worship, Reverend Hubbly sneered and looked pointedly at his watch as they rushed up out of breath.

"It is a great shame that some people find it fitting to keep the good Lord waiting!" he said severely, making Ellie Mae's freckled face go blood-red.

Mary felt similarly bludgeoned by his pointed disdain. Most mountain people did not have watches to go by and reckoned the time by the sun, so they were rarely exactly on time, often having miles to walk, even if they did live on the same mountain. They all looked at him with such mortified faces that Mary quickly went behind a big rock and took out a basket of put-up vegetables, eggs and a ham to give to Reverend Hubbly for coming out to tend to their spiritual needs, which she'd only intended to present to him after the service. She gave it to him now with a look of pleading in her eyes. The reverend took the basket with an ungracious grunt, hardly bothering to give it a glance.

He was much more concerned by the small turnout, which he seemed to think was a direct reflection on him personally, despite the fact that he was hitherto unknown to any of them, but Mary. Actually, Mary was feeling a deep disappointment herself. Besides the poor turnout from Claw Mountain, none of the folk she'd spoken to during the week at Beacon Mountain had showed up, not even Gerta.

"Hmmmph! *Some revival this is!"* Reverend Hubbly said with a sour scowl. "I've given service to more folk than this in Seminary class!"

"Oh, please bear with us, Reverend," Mary said beseechingly. "It ain't too bad fer a start. It's only th' first service, after all. I know more will come in time."

Looking entirely unconvinced on that score, the reverend snorted, "Well, let's begin so I can be smartly on my way."

With that, Reverend Hubbly marched to the front of the arbor and moved behind the tree-stump pulpit, standing there with bumptious dignity in his black clerical garb and white collar, while the tiny congregation entered the arbor cautiously and stood inside, in two raggedy rows, facing him. The ground was etched with ice and the breeze filtering into the arbor carried a ruthless chill, making the worshippers wrap their threadbare coats closer to them, reddening their noses and causing them to run. The reverend laid down his Bible before him on the pulpit with an irked expression on his face then looked up and regarded them with open antagonism, as if highly peeved that his imminent presence had not provoked a greater response than this.

"I want all those carrying weapons of any kind to take them outside and leave them there till after the service," he said pointedly. "I will not have tools of destruction in the house of the Lord!"

Cletus and Toad looked stunned at first then reluctantly obeyed, shedding their guns and knives between the gnarled roots of an oak tree close to the arbor. To Mary's surprise, two of the older boys also went out, depositing their knives in the same place, while Beaufort gave up his slingshot. When they returned to their places, the reverend closed his eyes to say the opening prayer. It was obvious that Emma saw that her cousins did not know how to pray for she hurriedly went along the ragged row, whispering to them to close their eyes and place their hands together in front of them, as Mary had taught her to do.

"Oh Lord," Reverend Hubbly began pontifically, "bless this modest brush arbor built in Thy name and to Thy glory. Sorry about the pitiful attendance, Lord. *Thee,*" he intoned meaningfully, "surely should be treated with more respect than this! All I can say, Lord, is that I hope that many more worshippers come this way else I fear I will not be a party to such a willful slighting of Thee."

Considering that those who had braved to come here had helped build the arbor and, furthermore, had risked the wrath and displeasure of Eli Buchanan, Mary felt a cutting hurt inside her both for them and herself. But then Reverend Hubbly opened his eyes and redeemed himself somewhat. Referring to the lengthy notes he had scribbled on the notepad, he said, "It has been requested that this service be dedicated to all those who lost their lives during what has become known amongst mountain people as 'The Big Freeze'. I find this entirely fitting. So saying, here are their names . . ."

There was a breathless silence as the names rolled slickly off his tongue as if he had been rehearsing the list for weeks. "Clyde and Ebenezer Buchanan froze to death while out hunting to provide food for their families. Jamie Buchanan died due to complications of an illness. Pearl Buchanan was lost to pneumonia. Johnny and Cora Buchanan lost two children, Aaron and Alice, due to starvation and the cold. Ellie Mae and Toad Buchanan lost Josephine and Hasten to similar ravages."

The reverend continued with the list of names and the causes of their deaths, moving on to members of the Ficks and Addis clans who had lost their lives during this terrible and trying time, his voice droning on and on, during the long liturgy. Unbelievably in all, thirty-six people on the three mountains alone, had lost their lives to hyperthermia, starvation and illness caused by the extreme conditions, including Lon and Olga Fick and their five children, who had frozen to death in their wooden shack. Never had Mary been more conscious of the extent of the winter's devastation and what it had done to the folk living on the mountains, than now.

Reverend Hubbly continued, "It is clear that you all suffered terribly during that harrowing time. We pray for those who lost their lives and pray too that Jesus Christ has seen fit to save their souls, especially those of the innocent children. We therefore commit their names to Jesus . . ." He began another somber countdown. When the names of Josephine and Hasten were mentioned a second time Ellie Mae's pale orange--freckled face puckered with crying. The preacher ended the dedication by saying, "May heaven be the reward for all those who practice sobriety and clean-living and, if perchance, the burning fires of hell be the fate of those who sought only liquor and violence before death, well, it can't be helped – it's too late now! But it's not too late for the sinners left behind. May they see the Light, oh Lord, before it is too late for them too, and you are forced to strike them down and cast them into the burning lake for all eternity!"

It wasn't *at all* what Mary had hoped for with its emphasis on damnation for sinners rather than comfort for those left behind and she was worried in case the Buckos in attendance would take umbrage at the not-so-subtle sideswipes at their lifestyle, but surprisingly, they seemed neither angry nor offended. Instead, they listened attentively, sober-faced.

Next, it was time for Ellie Mae to sing the opening hymn, which Reverend Hubbly announced was in dedication of those he'd just named. Wiping the tears from her face, she went and stood next the pulpit nervously facing the congregation as Mary had instructed her. She wore a shabby brown coat over her gray dress and flat black shoes, her flaming red hair, its usual tangled bird's nest, her nose bright red with her misery and the cold. Reverend Hubbly's nose flared at her sour smell, but her voice soared with such aching sweetness and richness that even the grumpy preacher looked wide-eyed with amazement, and suitably impressed. And as "Amazing Grace" rose to the makeshift rafters of their crudely made shelter, Mary suddenly noticed, to her considerable surprise, that some of the other Buckos and their families had crept out of the trees to listen from afar, no doubt attracted by curiosity, and were presently mesmerized by Ellie Mae's full rich tones.

Mary devoutly hoped that they had heard Reverend Hubbly's dedication too, because it had seemed such a crying shame that it could not have reached more of their ears, especially those who had lost loved ones during "The Big Freeze".

"Praise the Lord," said Reverend Hubbly when Ellie Mae had finished. He did not commend her on her exquisite rendition even though she had clearly practiced so hard and sung it so flawlessly and beautifully. She looked disappointed as she returned to the congregation. The preacher then opened his Bible and read from Samuel, Chapter 12. "'And they cried unto the Lord and said, We have sinned, because we have forsaken the Lord, and have served Baalim and Ashtaroth: but deliver us now out of the hands of our enemies, and we shall serve Thee . . . If ye will fear the Lord and serve Him and obey His voice and not rebel against the commandment of the Lord, then shall both ye and also the king that reigneth over you continue following the Lord, your God.'" The reverend paused to see if he still had their attention, then continued, "'But if you do not obey the voice of the Lord, but rebel against the commandment of the Lord, then the hand of the Lord shall be against you, as it was against your fathers . . . and you may see and perceive that your wickedness is great.'"

After that weighty pronouncement, he closed his Bible with a snap then proceeded to commence his sermon. It was about a subject Mary knew was very dear to his heart. *Moonshine!* He mildly railed and grumbled about its evils, and though Mary agreed with his sentiments, she felt it was an extremely unfortunate choice of theme for the first service and likely to alienate those who listened. She had hoped for something far more soul-stirring from the preacher to get these crackers all fired up about religion, but he was frankly boring, his voice a monotone and sternly rebuking, as he droned on and on. Had she known he was going to take this attitude towards his new parishioners, she might not have been so keen to get the services started.

But despite Mary's doubts about the preacher gaining converts among the Buckos and their kin and neighbors, listening to Ellie Mae's beautiful voice singing the beloved hymn, closing her eyes in prayer and worshipping her God communally, had been succor for her starved soul. If only Reverend Hubbly would not alienate them. Next, the reverend sang the invitational hymn and gave the altar call, inviting the congregation to come forward to be saved from sin by Jesus Christ. He looked around expectantly, but nobody moved. They stood their ground, shifting uncomfortably, gawking at the preacher as if he were mad. Then Emma saved the day. She stirred, surrendering Jed to Mary from her slim hip. Then she and Beaufort moved forward together hand-in-hand to the rail that Zachary Thomas had knocked up on Mary's instruction just before the service, and knelt before it. Mary's heart melted to see them kneeling there together like that.

The others looked at each other warily, clearly made undecided by Emma's brave move. Mary looked up at her tall husband expectantly, willing him to go forward, but he stood rooted to the bare ground, his mouth pursed obstinately. *Poor Reverend Hubbly!* His altar calls usually attracted hundreds of sinners who wanted to accept Jesus Christ as their savior. Now, a measly two – young'uns at that – had answered his call. Reverend Hubbly's grim face said it all as he blessed the pair and made them repeat their commitment to Christ after him.

After the unsuccessful and disappointing altar call (Mary had been hoping that at least Ellie Mae or Edna might have been brave enough to go up), Ellie Mae, Mary, Emma and Beaufort lustily sang the rehearsed hymn "Bringing in the Sheaves". Mary's heart lifted a little with the singing and, looking around, she saw that the various clan members were looking quite enraptured. Maybe they could be brought around after all. Boredom played a big part in their mischief-making, to be sure. Church services were beloved among most mountain folk because they not only provided worship, they were a major distraction from the monotony of their lives, a welcome bye from boring routine.

Even though there had been no sign of Eli as yet, Mary had grown increasingly worried in case he should come and try to disrupt the service. As the Buckos outside drew closer, her eyes anxiously searched for sight of him. She knew that if Eli did cause trouble of any sort, there was every chance that the lay preacher would simply abandon Claw Mountain from his circuit. But as the service progressed, Mary began to be hopeful that he had simply decided to stay away. Despite the poor turnout and Reverend Hubbly condemnatory and lackluster service, it had all gone relatively well so far, so perhaps the whole thing would pass without incident. Then suddenly, to her deep dismay, she saw Eli and some of his brothers come strutting through the towering trees like an unsightly bunch of fallen angels ...

They came carrying shotguns and with pistols sticking out of their belts. There was no mistaking Eli's bright-yellow hair. Mary's heart began to pound when she spotted it. He wore clothes fit for attending service, but there was no doubt in anybody's mind that he wouldn't be joining the worshippers. Except for butchering day, he'd worn the fancy clothes – and shoes – since returning from Stony Man Mountain. Eli was with that awful Jake! *That evil pair had murdered a helpless young'un!* Ezekiel came leading a saddled mule by the reins and Alvin, Otis and Clem came through the trees, flanking them. They all halted when they came to the arbor and stood around, grinning fiendishly, at the small knot of worshippers in the arbor through the "side wall", which comprised of six vertical poles and four vertical ones. The atmosphere was suddenly thick as hog-fat and there was a fearful whispering amongst the small congregation as they viewed the lean, arrogant, yellow-haired youth, who stood with a mocking smile on his handsome disfigured face, outside the arbor.

"HEY. YOU, PREACHER-MAN! WHAT DO YER THUNK YE'RE DOIN'?" Eli demanded of the preacher, his tone so menacing, so undeniably scathing, that there could be no doubt in anybody's mind that he meant trouble.

"I'M HOLDING SERVICE FOR THE LORD!" Reverend Hubbly called back loftily, standing straight-backed and grim-looking, as he peered through the poles of the arbor at his would-be tormentor.

"WELL, I GOT NEWS FER YOU! YOU DON'T GIT TO DO IT ON CLAW MOUNTAIN!"

With that, Eli picked up a rock and threw it forcefully at the arbor. It hit one of the arbor poles before entering the arbor, narrowly missing one of the children. Reverend Hubbly started to reply, but his voice faltered when the outside bunch started cussing and yelling and firing their shotguns into the air, causing the entire congregation to jump with fright and Reverend Hubbly to cover his ears with his hands. It was the signal for all the troublemakers to pick up rocks and lob them at the fearful worshippers. Soon a barrage of missiles rained in on the arbor. There was panic among the worshippers as they tried to take cover behind each other and the poles.

It was Mary's worst fears come true. Zachary Thomas went to the back of the arbor and yelled furiously at his siblings to stop, but they had clearly been imbibing in moonshine and were mean with it. Rocks whizzed past Zachary Thomas's head and others glanced off some of the children so that they yelped in fright and pain.

Although Zachary Thomas kept yelling for his brothers to stop their bombardment of rocks, there was nothing to do, but duck. One of Edna's sons, Sam, got hit on the chest with a rock, winding him. The seven-year-old screeched with shock and pain, and then howled, rubbing his fists in his eyes. Edna quickly knelt solicitously beside her son, an anxious look on her face. This infuriated Mary and she rushed and stood in front of her husband to confront the sneering Eli, having surrendered Jed to his usual minder. Eli stood challengingly in front of the other mischief-makers, his straight yellow hair flopping over his pale-yellow eyes, which met her with studied insolence.

"Cease this abomination this instant, Eli!" Mary's voice shook with emotion. "This here brush tabernacle is a house of th' Lord! To rock it or them who worship here is a terrible sin aginst Him!"

"As if I care a jiff whose house it be!" replied Eli coldly. "I told you that I didn't want no church on Claw Mountain and thar ain't gonna be no church on Claw Mountain while thar be breath in my body!"

"Well, you cain't speak for everybody, Eli! Thar be folk here who want to be able to praise th' Lord and you don't got no right stoppin' them from doin' that! Fact is, Eli, we'd be right happy if'n you would join us."

Eli stared at her as if he couldn't believe what she had just said. *"Me,* join *you?"*

"Yes, you, Eli, and Jake and Otis and Ezekiel and Clem and Alvin, too. Don't let th' devil be your master! Come join in th' altar call and be saved. Jesus loves you all."

Eli stared at her with loathing tawny eyes. In answer, he picked up a hand-sized rock and aimed it straight at her head. She ducked sideways to avoid it and it glanced off the side of her temple, causing a long gash that quickly drew blood. Zachary Thomas bellowed with outrage. There was an uproar as the children behind her screamed and scattered. Zachary Thomas gave an almighty roar and tried to charge down his brothers, but Mary held grimly onto his one arm with both hands, as blood trickled down the side of her face from her wounded temple.

"Don't," she whispered fiercely. "Listen to me, Zack. This kin turn even uglier, real quick. If'n you fight them now, who knows what kin happen. *Leave them be."*

Though she was quaking with fear, she could not let Eli and his evilly grinning cronies know that. She stood firm with her head held high, her shiny black hair coming down from beneath one of Hedina Buchanan's bonnets on either side of her face, even as more rocks were hurled. The Buckos' evil reputation for brutality and bloodshed had never been more prominent in Mary's mind. She'd never forgive herself if they killed Reverend Hubbly. She knew they would use any – or no – pretext to resort to it, using pistols or knives. If they could slit the throat of an innocent without a qualm, slitting the throat of a despised man of the church, would be as easy as pie for them. She tried another tack. "Now you don't only go aginst th' good Lord Himself, Eli Buchanan, you go aginst yer own kin. You ought t'be real ashamed of yerself! Never know'd sech a thing to happen in this here family a'fore. Now you've set brother aginst brother! I hope ye're right proud of yerself." Eli glared at her so fiercely that she forced herself to temper her tone. "Eli, *you* don't got to worship if'n you don't got a mind to, but it ain't fair to stop th' others."

"Fair? *Fair?* Who said anythung about bein' fair? This here mountain b'longs to th' Buchanan clan an' nobody does nuthin' on it without *my* permission!"

It was Obediah Buchanan's archaic rhetoric all over again.

"Well, I'm askin' fer it now, please," pleaded Mary hoarsely.

"Permission denied!"

With that, Eli and his siblings threw ropes around the roof poles of the arbor and tied them to the saddle of the mule. Then they beat the mule mercilessly with switches. It neighed stridently with indignation and fright. It immediately became obvious what their aim was, and Mary cried, "NO, NO, ELI! This here's a house of th' Lord! Don't do this terrible thung, please! I beg you."

As the arbor began to tilt dangerously to one side, the women and children inside it began to scream and clutch hysterically at one another. Mary thought quickly. Eli was clearly in a very dangerous mood. Not only was he agitating against his own kin, there was no telling what he would do to Reverend Hubbly next. The poor man was looking positively terrified and distraught, and Mary could scarcely blame him. First the rocking and now this! *The destruction of the arbor!* She had been a fool to think she could get Eli to accept this.

The assaulting force engendered more fear by firing their pistols in the air and over the roof of the arbor, whooping and hollering. Mary turned to Zachary Thomas and said urgently, "Git Reverend Hubbly away from here, Zack!"

Her husband groaned. "I ain't leavin' you an' Jed, Mary!"

"You've got to! They wouldn't dare hurt me!"

"Eli's done it already! Look at yer head. It's bleedin' bad."

"Zack, we cain't let them kill th' reverend. We've got to protect him! If'n they kill him, thar will be big trouble fer th' whole clan, that's fer sure! You want t'see yer kin behind bars over this?"

"SATAN IS AMONGST US! DELIVER US FROM EVIL!" wailed the beleaguered preacher, who was cowering behind the tree-stump pulpit.

"Don't worry, I'll look after her, Unc' Zack!" Emma, pale and grim-faced, came to stand beside Mary, the freckles on her nose and cheeks looking like a scattering of tiny currants, Jed perched on her lean angular hip. It was only then that Zachary Thomas moved.

"Go!" Mary urged. "A'fore hit's too late!"

"Alright, I'll go," he said reluctantly, "but only if you and Emma and Jed go straight back up to Eagle Spur. *Now!* Don't wait around and try to reason with any of them when they're in this sort of mood! I'll take care of that wound of your'n when I git back! Take care, girl!"

Mary nodded in agreement.

"Hey, Toad," yelled Eli just then, "sure never figger'd *you* fer a hen-husband! Never thought I'd see *you* in no church even if it's jest a pile of old logs!"

Toad stirred uneasily. Mary knew that he hadn't wanted to come in the first place and that his younger brother's scorn must surely rankle. It was clear that it would take very little to make him walk out.

"You used to be a man! Now you ain't nuthin' but a girl!" Eli crowed scornfully.

Then Eli made a big mistake. He threw a rock which bounded off one of the supporting poles and hit Toad's nine-year-old son, Abner, on his head, laying him out cold on his back. Ellie Mae screamed and rushed over to her prostrate son.

"You've kilt him! You've kilt him!" she shrieked in anguish.

Mary rushed over to the boy but, after a few heart-stopping moments, he thankfully began to stir.

The effect on Toad was dramatic. Filled with terrible fury, he spat at his brother. *"Damn you, Eli!"* he roared. "I swar if'n you touch another single one of m'family, I'll kill ya!"

"Take more than a hen-husband like you to do that!" jeered Eli.

It was clear that the other Buckos with Eli were growing uncomfortable about badly injuring one of their sibling's children. They stopped lobbing rocks and stood around, looking somewhat shamed and sheepish. Cletus went and stood beside Toad, his eyes blazing.

"You've gone too far this time, Eli! Go away an' leave us be!"

Zachary Thomas looked astounded. Mary knew it was because it was very likely the first time any of his brothers had stood up to Eli. Her husband then took the opportunity to rush over to the lay preacher. Grabbing him by the arm, he pulled him out from behind the tree-stump pulpit, hurrying him out of the arbor even as it began to groan ominously, the mule straining to move forward under the furious flaying of switches.

The last Mary saw of the pair was them scurrying down the mountain with Eli lobbing rock after rock at them, and screeching obscenities. The rest of the congregation had no sooner rushed out of the arbor when the whole thing crashed sideways to the ground, amidst the drunken laughter of the miscreant Buckos and the screams and wails of terrified children. Mary was appalled. Never had the Buckos fought against each other in this manner, she was sure. And for the very first service to end in such a terrible way! There was real fear in Emma's eyes when she came up to Mary, carrying Jed on her hip. Mary knew that she too could sense just how dangerous Eli's mood was as she grabbed Mary's hand. After all, she had watched her uncle murder the Galtrey boy not so long ago, and as tough a youngster as she was, it was obvious she deeply feared for Mary's safety, and that of little Jed, right now. Mary decided that her own presence was inciting the situation and it was, indeed, time to go. She rushed over to the huddle of worshippers staring dazedly down at the flattened structure that it had taken them so much hard work to build.

"Ellie Mae, Toad, Edna, all you young'uns!" she said quickly. "Thank y'all fer bein' so brave and comin'. But it's time to leave now. Go home a'fore this gits any worse!"

Leaving her precious baby ensconced on Emma's hip rather than risking taking him herself, as she knew she was the desired target, Mary scrambled up to Eagle Spur, with Emma and Beaufort, to jeers and lobbed rocks that crashed around them dangerously. Thankfully, they escaped unscathed and their attackers did not come after them as she had feared they might. As they climbed, Mary felt shock, bruising disappointment and hurt, overwhelm her. She had harbored such high hopes that the members of this wild and inhospitable clan would be healed by being given some religious succor, but she'd been wrong. The service had not healed, but *hurt* them. Indeed, it had driven a deep wedge between them so that brother had fought against brother, and even young children had suffered.

Safely back at the log cabin on Eagle Spur, Mary reassured the two stunned children with milk and cornbread. She wanted to tell them how happy and proud she'd been that they'd accepted Jesus as their savior, but she did not know what to say after what had just happened. Zachary Thomas came in some time later looking tired and haggard. Mary thought he might berate her, blame all the trouble on her, but instead he took a good look at her wound, expressing murmured concern. It had stopped bleeding already, but he cleaned it carefully, applied kerosene to it with a clean cloth, which he pressed against the gash before winding a bandage around her head. He worked in silence,and, bludgeoned by the day's disastrous events, Mary, too, was silent and subdued.

"Thank you," she murmured when he had finished. Zachary Thomas took her by the shoulders and stared into her eyes with his intense turquoise-green ones. "Listen, Mary, I know you're right upset, but don't worry. I got Reverend Hubbly to agree to come back next month if'n th' weather ain't too bad by then. Then he's promised to come back th' month after that and so on, but come what may, he *will* be back!"

337

Mary stared at her husband, speechless with shock. Then she finally managed, "What are you sayin', Zack? He cain't possibly come back here after what happened today! *It ain't safe!* Not fer hisself, nor fer any of us!"

"We cain't let Eli win, Mary!" Zachary Thomas said quietly. "We'll rebuild th' arbor and if'n they pull it down agin then we'll build another one. And we'll keep right on buildin' 'em till they git sick an' tired of pullin' 'em down an' leave us be."

"But what if they kill somebody with their rockin', or if they kill Reverend Hubbly? After today, you surely cain't expect him to . . ."

"The reverend was all fired up by th' time he left. Said we've got to fight Satan's fire with fire! It's true, Mary. We've all bin lettin' Eli git his own evil way around here fer far too long. Now, he's gone too far. He's turned on his own kin."

"But he almost kilt little Abner. How will Ellie Mae and Toad feel about puttin' their young'uns at risk like that agin, Zack?"

"I already spoke with them. They're as mad as I am. They reckon they're with us on this one. Said they really appreciated th' service and was mad as kin be when Eli an' th' others broke it up like that and then turned on 'em."

"But . . ."

"But nuthin', Mary! It ain't jest yer fight no more. I expect this sort of behavior aginst us from them Galtreys mebbe, but not my own kin! We're gonna rebuild that arbor and we'll all be thar – *all of us!* And what's more, we'll make th' next one much stronger. We'll put double poles in and fill in th' sides with poles too so th' rocks cain't git in like they done today."

Mary listened to her husband speak with stunned silence, marveling at his quiet strength. She had been feeling so terribly upset and defeated and now this . . . this amazing turn of events! Some of the Buchanans were actually prepared to stand up against Eli. They were prepared to fight him and all those who had opposed them today to hold service for the Lord. Mary was astounded to hear what had transpired, and also of Reverend Hubbly's immense courage in saying he would return to the mountain despite what had happened here today. The man wasn't much of a preacher, but he was truly a brave man when faced with the specter of Satan. Still, Mary was filled with knowing dread. Where would this family insurrect-ion lead to? Death? Destruction? Or something great and beautiful? Mary wasn't feeling too hopeful. Her husband saw her anxious face and took her in his arms, hugging her reassuringly.

43

"Mary..."

The grim tone of Zachary Thomas's voice made Mary look up from the cabin floor she was scrubbing to see her huge husband standing in the doorway. He looked strangely devastated, his eyes screwed-up with wariness. *Something terrible had happened!* Mary hastily stood up, smoothing her white apron down.

"Lord, what is it, Zack?"

"Hit's Paw."

Mary quickly crossed to him and put her hand consolingly on his arm. "Has he finally taken his leave of this world?"

Zachary Thomas shook his head. "That's jest it. I don't know, Mary. He's gone a'missin'. You know how his mind's bin wanderin' of late? Ev'ry time I pop in at Horseshoe Hollow, I figger on findin' him dead. Sometimes, he'd be passed out with booze and I'd have to go right up to th' bed to see if'n he was still breathin'. When I saw him yesterday, he looked so doggoned weak and skeleton-like, I figger'd he couldn't possibly last much longer so's I went back thar t'day to check on him, and he weren't thar! Now you know he never leaves the cabin these days."

Obediah missing! The notion was preposterous.

"What could have happened to him, d'you thunk?" Mary asked her husband.

"I don't know, Mary. I've looked fer him ev'rywhar. In th' cabin, up in th' loft, in th' barn, in th' yard, in th' surroundin' forest. I haven't bin able to find him noplace. I even checked fer spoor in case some rogue bear came up from th' Wilderness and snatched him. I'm goin' to organize search parties to go look fer him."

"Of course," she murmured sympathetically, "he might be injured someplace."

"Thought I'd come tell you first what's bin happenin' and see if'n you wanted to help."

Despite her fierce repugnance of the man, Mary knew that she had to support her husband in this. It was his father, after all. She remembered how Zachary Thomas had told her how his paw had been good to him when he was a toddler, before the booze got him and turned him mean as a maddened hog. She knew that Zachary Thomas clung to those few good memories of his father, like a drowning man gasps for air. Knowing this, she readily went down the mountain with him to the dreadful old homestead at Horseshoe Hollow to help look for her father-in-law, leaving Jed in the able care of Emma, who pointblank refused to join them.

It was a remarkably somber group that had assembled at Horseshoe Hollow.

There was a dreadful air of desolation there. The Buckos, their wives and elder children turned haggard faces and haunted eyes on her, as if expecting her to tell them what to do, but it was Zachary Thomas who took charge immediately, giving orders, splitting them into groups and saying who must search where on the mountain. Mary was glad of his direction and strength right now.

A huge search of the entire north side of the mountain was undertaken. It took three weary days and yielded no sign of the patriarch of the clan, nor gave any clue as to what could have happened to him. Mary had thought that the clan would be relieved and express grim satisfaction that he had so unceremoniously disappeared out their lives after the abominable way he had treated them, but that wasn't the case. Instead, it was clear that the sudden disappearance of the tyrannical patriarch had a very unsettling effect on them. Perhaps it was because they had not been able to establish their father was dead that made the members of the clan so gloomy and distracted for weeks on end. Only one person was clearly overjoyed by Obediah's mysterious disappearance – *Emma!* Not only had she refused to join the search party, when the search had been abandoned after failing to discover any trace of her grandfather, she came up to see Mary at Eagle Spur with her narrow face flushed with triumph.

"I'm so darned happy!" she whooped. "Now, I don't got t'see that miserable piece of shit ever agin!"

"Emma!" Mary scolded. "Don't talk about yer grandpaw that way. It ain't respectful, no matter what he's done."

"Well, he weren't no grandpaw to me! Don't thunk he even knew my name. I'm real *glad* he's dead!" she said gleefully, before adding defiantly, *"Praise th' Lord!"*

"Well, we don't know that he's dead fer sure, Emma. Could be he's alive someplace and will still be found. I suspect his mind was wanderin' and he walked right off th' mountain; likely he cain't remember who he is to tell folks he meets up with. That sort of thung happens, y'know."

But Emma looked at her with a face that reveled in confidence. "Oh no, he won't! *He's dead!"* she announced with boundless certainty.

Mary frowned. "I told you you cain't know that fer sure, Emma."

"Oh yes, I kin," snarled Emma.

Those surely spoken words and the look on her face made inexplicable cold shivers run down Mary's spine. How come the girl was so sure? Surely, no matter how much she hated her grandfather, she wouldn't have had anything to do with his disappearance? *His death even?*

"Emma," Mary said cautiously. "You didn't . . .?"

"Didn't what, Aunt Mary?"

"Oh, nuthin'." Mary shook her head to rid herself of the disturbing thought. She couldn't make herself question the girl any further because she did not want to know if Emma Buchanan had anything to do with the disappearance or death of her own grandfather. Because if she *was* somehow involved – and he might still pitch up unharmed – she couldn't *bear* to have the burden of something like that weighing on her mind. Besides, the dear girl, her staunch little ally, couldn't possibly be responsible for such a wicked thing, could she? As tough and sullen as she was, she wasn't capable of such a dreadful thing. After all, she had been saved during that first tumultuous service in the brush arbor and already knew that such a terrible sin as murder would be severely punished by the Almighty, for all eternity.

How many times had Emma told her that she wanted to go to paradise when she died? That made Mary feel a little better. But then she suddenly remembered Emma's vehemence when she told her how much she had wanted her grandfather to die in the winter and how she'd said that she would spit on his grave if he did. And suddenly, Mary felt unsure again. There was no doubt that Emma hated her brutish grandfather. It worried Mary that she had seen so much violence in her short life. After all, she'd lived amongst this wild and hoary horde long enough to witness how they solved all their problems by simply eliminating whoever and whatever stood in their way. Would it be any wonder then if she had chosen a similar way out of hers? But she could never have done something as terrible as murder her own grandfather, surely? *No!* Mary refused to believe it. Nevertheless, the whole thing badly unsettled her. She didn't want her dark suspicions to poison her relationship with this precious child whom she loved like she was her own. With that, she went to Emma and put her arms around her, planting a kiss on the top of her head, determinedly pushing ugly, searing thoughts from her mind . . .

By the time the next monthly Sunday service was due, another stouter brush arbor had been erected. But it snowed heavily a couple of days before, and word had to be sent to the reverend not to come. It was three months before the weather was fair enough for Reverend Hubbly to visit Claw Mountain again to give another service and, even then, snow was still patchy on the ground. Mary thought that the time-lapse was probably a blessing since it had given tempers and nerves time to settle. As the Sunday loomed to accommodate the second service, Mary and Zachary Thomas went to inspect the arbor only to find, to their dismay, that it had been pulled down again by Eli and his cronies in the interim.

However, the same group of volunteers mucked in and soon another one was built. This time they even made rough log pews for them to sit on, amidst many voices raised in hymn. Taking courage from each other, they had first debated about finding a new site for the arbor rather than have Eli know exactly where it was, but Mary and Zachary Thomas both dug in their heels on the matter. Eli had to learn that no matter how hard he tried to destroy their services, he would not succeed. They would stick to the old site, which was easily accessible to most of them, and thus the perfect spot.

Once again, they built a much sturdier structure than before, even though there was far less brush for the canopy than the first time. They covered the top with sacking as before and placed branches and heaps of pine needles on top of it. It turned out well enough, considering. Amazingly, the mountain folk turned out in far greater numbers than for the first service, including members of the Addis and Ficks clans. Even the old lady Mary had visited, Gerta Addis, had taken Mary's advice and managed to persuade her scrawny-looking kin to carry her to the brush arbor on a litter. Mary was amazed to see that Otis and Ezekiel, who had helped Eli pull down the first structure, stood in front of the rough log pews with their families en-tow. What had persuaded them to join their ranks in defiance of Eli? Had they little heart to go against their own kin once again? Mary felt it was a real good sign. And viewing them as they quietly filled the pews after obediently leaving their weapons outside to Reverend Hubbly's grim, finger-pointing instruction, it seemed to Mary they were all drawn inexplicably to a God previously unknown to them, either by curiosity, or some indefinable longing deep in their souls.

This time at least fifty brave mountain people faced Reverend Hubbly, who stood behind the tree-stump pulpit, stern and grim, as he began another dull service that remonstrated and condemned. He referred at length to the horrible fiery fate of those who would dare to defy God, obviously referring to Eli and his cohorts. But, although his service once again left Mary feeling vaguely uncomfortable, the hymn-singing was a delight, Ellie Mae's sweet voice leading the throng of voices that joined in even though they scarcely knew the words, until the repeat choruses.

All the while, Mary nervously kept a sharp eye out for Eli. There was a sharp indrawing of breath when he and his remaining cronies suddenly came into view through the forest, armed, as usual, and looking dangerous. The entire congregation tensed, the atmosphere instantly becoming thick with dread. On the last occasion, Eli had crossed a boundary they had never suspected he might, and now, they were all on tenterhooks about what new outrages he might dream up. Even Reverend Hubbly wavered in his sermon before defiantly carrying on with a suddenly fervently raised voice that was so unlike him.

Eli, Jake and Clem and some of the elder Bucko sons who liked to emulate Eli, proceeded to jeer, cuss, shout, whistle and threw rocks that fortunately failed to penetrate the more tightly built side walls. While the congregation shivered with apprehension, clearly feeling helpless and naked without their weapons, and Reverend Hubbly struggled to keep the service going above the general din coming from outside, Eli committed the ultimate outrage. He leisurely urinated against a tree in full view of all, showing such mocking insolence and irreverence that it filled Mary with shame and made her blood boil.

But the increased numbers seemed to deter the blasphemers from trying to pull the arbor down like before and, though they made general nuisances of themselves, miraculously, the second service passed without major incident or injury. Mary knew the mountain people would be back, bolstered by this success, and ever more of them, as word spread. Mountain folk had so few distractions in their lives they would not be able to resist the lure of religion for long. *She would get a proper church built on Claw Mountain yet!*

Even when they found that the arbor had been pulled down again afterwards, Mary did not lose heart. Like Zachary Thomas had said, they would keep building them as long as it was necessary! From that time onwards, however, although the services were held regularly, there was always trouble of some sort with which to contend from Eli and his lackeys, who admittedly, had dwindled in number. It was highly disconcerting to have rocks or bullets whizz over their heads while they were bent in prayer, or to have to listen to the sermon above an unholy racket coming from outside.

Once, during a service, the attackers set fire to the brush with burning torches so that the worshippers had to flee to avoid getting burned, as flaming sticks fell and embers floated down. Since the arbors were pulled down almost as soon as they were put up, erecting them was left till the day before and some of the Buckos volunteered to stand guard over them until the commencement of service the next day. This stopped them from being torn down before service, but did not stop them from being torn down immediately afterwards. This was done unfailingly.

It was a major battle of wits and wills between the two opposing forces, but though the worshippers refused to bow down, they always felt under siege. The children, particularly, seemed to feel vulnerable and afraid, their little faces screwed up with worry as they glanced fearfully about the place. It was all very disheartening. It was a miracle to Mary that despite this constant drama, the congregation was steadily growing.

Then a strange thing happened. Suddenly, there were no more attacks. The monthly services came and went blissfully free of interference and intimidation by Eli and his cronies. Mary was reminded of the time old Duke Colby down at the Fletcher general store had told her a story about how, in 1754, all the Indians, under the influence of the French, had suddenly and unexpectedly left the Shenandoah Valley, leaving the settlers with a sense of ominous disquiet that was soon to bear fruit. For the Indians, with their French allies, launched the bloodthirsty attacks that would become known as the "French and Indian Wars", which took the lives of many of the early settlers.

Old Duke had been an Indian fighter out West before the start of the Civil War. He'd hastily returned to Virginia to join the Confederate army. He would trap people in the general store to whom he'd spin his yarns. While her sisters would quickly duck out of the way whenever they saw him coming, politeness constrained Mary to stay and listen, at least for a while. As a result, the old buzzard always made a beeline for her, doffing his gray Confederate hat at her before launching onto another long tirade about his adventures. Though she sometimes felt trapped and dismayed, he did tell her a lot of interesting stuff. And Mary fancied she felt the same sense of disquiet and unease now as the settlers must have had when the Indians suddenly disappeared from the valley back in those long ago days. *The calm before the storm!*

But perhaps Zachary Thomas was right. Perhaps Eli had come to his senses at last and had recognized the fierce resolve of the worshippers, as her husband had predicted, and had given up tormenting them. But Mary was not so sure. She had a sickening feeling that Eli never gave up on what he'd set his mind on and she was unable to attend monthly service again without the fear of some sort of Eli-inspired violence erupting out of nowhere. The feeling of dread was almost worse than the deeds themselves, because it wore on the nerves so.

44

The past winter had thankfully been much milder than the crippling "Big Freeze" of the year before. Even so, on Eagle Spur it had been harshly cold and unrelenting, with several bad snowstorms that had snowed them in, though for just days at a time rather than weeks and months. Mary was glad that warmer weather was well on its way, though the elevated tableland of Claw Mountain was, of course, still had patches of snow here and there. Indeed, life on the Blue Ridge was universally invigorated – the winter thaw was busy flooding streams and rivers, the air was sharp and sweet and the forests were awash with pale-green new growth with dogwoods sending exquisite snowy-white and pale-pink blessings throughout, making the view from Eagle Spur a sight to behold. The creatures of the forest, released from winter's cruel bind, rejoiced and mated, frolicked and gamboled, with renewed vigor.

One morning, Mary went to fetch water at the spring. While she was kneeling beside the bubbling spring, scooping up water in a pail she heard a loud thrashing sound behind her and looked over her shoulder. To her considerable alarm, a huge black bear was lumbering out of the forest, the first she had ever seen on Claw

Mountain. She immediately dropped the pail and stood up slowly, frozen with fear, for Jed was in a hide "papoose" on her back that Zachary Thomas had made for her, and the bear was tossing its great head around and growling as if it were in a bad mood. It was no doubt very hungry after its winter hibernation and its foraging had brought it a long way up the mountain. She considered making a run for it but the bear was so close, she knew she could never make it to safety. And if she fled and it attacked her from behind, Jed would be in terrible danger. No, she had to stand very still and hope that he would get bored and move away.

When Jed saw the huge beast he shrieked with delight and gurgled merrily away, causing Mary to quake with fear. To her horror, the wild-smelling bear came right up to her, sniffing at her trembling hand. It circled around to her side and stood up on its hind legs swaying from side to side and sniffing at Jed, who continued to coo fearlessly at it. The bear with its thick coat of black fur towered above her and Mary screwed up her eyes in abject terror, barely able to breathe. One swipe of the bear's huge paw with its long curved claws could mean the end of her baby, before it finished her off too.

Never had Mary felt such raw terror, so vulnerable and exposed to danger. She could feel the bear's hot, putrid breath on her neck and hear a deep growl that seemed to emanate from the depths of its stomach. Any minute now, it would attack them, swat at them with those fearsome claws and sink its fangs into them, tearing them apart, the way the bear in the Wilderness Valley had done to one of the slaughtered horses up on the ramp. But minutes passed and nothing happened. When she finally dared to open her eyes again, it was to find the bear had dropped down onto all fours again and was wandering lazily back into the forest. She only realized then the narrowness of their escape. She almost wept with relief . . .

Later, Mary learned that Toad and Eli had shot the beast and divided the meat up between the clan. Remembering how the bear had left her and Jed alone, she felt deeply saddened that such a great rare beast had ended up as a temporary balm to a bunch of stomachs, and she firmly refused the meat offered, much to Zachary Thomas's indignant protests. Though she had told him about the incident of the bear and how it had refrained from attacking her and Jed, he failed to understand her reasoning in refusing its meat. But Mary stuck to her guns. She felt that the spirit of the slaughtered bear would somehow understand and appreciate her return gesture. Of course, according to Reverend Hubbly, Christianity taught that animals did not have souls but, for some reason, Mary had always found that mighty hard to believe.

One mid-morning, not long after the incident with the bear, Mary, wearing an apron over a brown working dress, was busy cleaning the cabin floor with a scrubbing brush and soapy water, which smelt of strong lye. Little Jed had turned a year old the day before, on the 6th April, and was crawling around everywhere like greased lightning. He had tried taking his first few steps a month ago – early for a boy, she was assured by some of her sisters-in-law, but he still wasn't up on his feet permanently yet. He would totter a few steps before landing on his bottom then would revert to crawling again. What a sunny baby he was though, serene and sweet-natured, with a smile to break a body's heart. He was crazy about Zachary Thomas's two faithful coon dogs, Rufus and Red. Indeed, animals seemed naturally drawn to him. Even Cedric, the goat, seemed to become less ornery when baby Jed was around and would gently buff its horns up against his tiny chest, while Jed patted him with sticky little hands and gurgled and cooed incoherently at him. The shoats, too, would shuffle up to him, while the fowls would cluck and strut around him, fluffing out their feathers. Indeed, baby Jed always seemed to have a little coterie of furred and feathered friends fussing around him, like he was the one who fed them instead of her. And how strange it was that the bear had not harmed either one of them . . .

There was a knock on the cabin door just then. When Mary got up from her calloused knees to open it, she was surprised to find Edna and her three elder children standing on the porch, two of whom, Lisa and Sam, having once been her pupils. She noticed with a touch of pride that their faces were washed and their hair neatly brushed. She invited them inside with a warm, welcoming smile. While they sat a the table, she busied herself around, pouring glasses of milk from a tin jug on the table for the children, who reached eagerly for the oatmeal cookies she placed on a tin plate, reachable by all. Then she placed a tin mug of coffee poured from a pot in the hearth, before her thin, mousy-haired sister-in-law, saying brightly to her, "Well, what a lovely surprise, Edna. To what do I owe this here pleasure?"

Edna turned earnest brown eyes on her. "Got me a real big favor t'ask a' you, Mary."

"Oh, and what's that?" asked Mary.

Edna suddenly seemed nervous and shy and Mary encouraged her with a smile. Finally, Edna burst out, "I want you t'teach me an' all my young'uns how to cipher and spell and read and write. Of course my two eldest already know some 'cuz they came t'yer classes a'fore, but I'm sure thar's plenty more you kin learn 'em . . ."

Mary's mouth dropped open, unable to believe ears that rang with possibilities. She felt a swift surge of excitement. "You want me to teach you an' yer young'uns?"

Edna nodded eagerly. "Yeah, I sure do. I want my young'uns to be smart like you, and I want t'be smart too. I don't drink moonshine no more, ever since you told Lisa and Sam how bad it is. And now I kin see fer m'self how bad thungs

346

were on this here mountain. Thanks to you, thungs have improved of late, what with Doc Adams a'comin', and them church services at th' brush arbor and hog-butchering day, and all."

"Oh Edna, of course I will! Do you thunk any of th' others would come if'n I started up classes agin?"

Edna shrugged. "Hard to tell. But I'll be sure to try to brung them around much as I kin. Thar's more . . ." She paused as if to gather courage. "I want you to learn me how t'cook proper-like and do thungs round th' homeplace. But th' young'uns' schoolin' is th' most important, of course."

"Oh, Edna, I'm so happy you feel this way. I'd be delighted to teach you anythung you'd care to learn. I've bin thunkin' real hard about thungs ever since th' wimmin folk come took their young'uns away that day. Clean broke my heart, it did, and I swore that if'n I ever started th' classes up agin, and things went well, then mebbe we could git ourselves a *real* teacher to come teach all th' kids around here and Beacon, Bear Rock Mountain and Buck Knob Mountain too. Y'know - in a proper schoolhouse."

Edna face fell into an alarmed frown. "*Buck Knob Mountain?* Ain't nary a'one of us here would agree to any of them Galtreys steppin' foot on this here mountain, Mary. Surely you know that by now? Thar's bin too much bad blood between us."

Mary sighed. "Well, I was thunkin' how nice it would be if we didn't have to worry none about th' Galtreys raidin' us all th' time. How wonderful if'n they didn't have to have lookouts posted in trees an' sech, and th' young'uns could play together without bein' in danger."

Edna nodded. "Yeah, it sure would be nice. But I thunk you should jest forgit it, 'cuz it ain't never gonna happen, Mary."

"I guess not."

"And a paid teacher? How kin we afford that?"

"Oh, I don't know," mused Mary. "But I'll thunk of somethung."

It was the beginning. Gradually, after Mary began teaching classes again, more and more children were permitted to join and re-join Mary's classes by mountain mothers previously resistant to the need. Most of the mothers were those attending the religious services and Mary was convinced that it was a burgeoning faith in the Lord that had touched their hardened hearts and enabled their previously moonshine-addled eyes to see what they had failed to see before.

The numbers soon swelled to a point that made it necessary for Mary to move them outside under the giant chestnut tree in fine weather. She followed the same teaching protocol as before, but soon began to realize her limitations. Her own education was so rudimentary, and her teaching aids and books so limited (even though she had managed to persuade Zachary Thomas to use some of his trapping credit at the store to purchase more pencils, paper, rulers, chalk and erasers), that she realized she had reached the zenith of her own tutorial scope.

She began to concentrate on pushing for a school on the mountain with a proper paid teacher, who could teach the children much more than she could ever hope to. But the folk on this mountain were still desperately cash poor, even though life had improved much for them since Eli had taken over his father's moonshining business. While his efforts to keep religion away from Claw Mountain may have thus far failed, he had turned his attention to business, quickly expanding it by increasing crop production and adding more stills, enabling the Buchanan families to buy shoats and chickens and a few luxuries unheard of during their paw's mean reign. Though Mary was still as wary as ever of the whip-wielding Bucko, she had to grant him that much at least. But she knew Eli was just biding his time, all the more dangerous for having been thwarted as far as the church services went. She well knew that he wasn't going to let her get away with much more. She vowed to discuss the matter of getting a paid teacher with Doc Adams on his third visit, scheduled for anytime now.

He had been back up the mountain on horseback, toting his black medical bag and his pharmaceutical trunk as soon as the snowy conditions allowed, and he'd had another highly successful day treating the mountain's inhabitants, thankfully, this time, without having to contend with that mean dangerous old despot, Obediah.

No trace had ever been found of the missing patriarch of the clan, no clue as to what had happened to him. His sudden disappearance remained a lurking mystery, which teased the imagination at odd unexpected times, but it was as if a collective sigh of relief had escaped from the mouths of the entire mountain community. Mary, too, felt that something awful and evil had gone from the mountain but, fearing the retribution of his youthful successor, she still felt decidedly vulnerable and afraid.

45

After Edna asked Mary to teach her how to cook, Mary gave the matter a great deal of thought. It came to her that *all* of the Bucko women could benefit from such instruction. Though their drinking had been curbed somewhat through her preaching and that of the highly disapproving Reverend Hubbly, they still indulged in the moonshine jug. She decided that they drank mainly because they were bored! They didn't grow vegetables or cook for their families, relying heavily on store-bought stuff for their meals, which Obediah had given them money for, though he had been mean with it, according to Zachary Thomas, controlling their lives even to that extent. He also paid their humble clothing, most of it, second-hand. Mary wondered how he managed to support the whole clan on moonshine profits. Had he had another source of income, stolen it, or extorted it out of Devon Ansley before he was sent packing to California?

Mary had sent a message to her mother through Reverend Hubbly, confirming that Zachary Thomas would be fetching her from Lewis Mountain soon for a two-week visit and she had a brainwave. She would get her mother to teach the women of the Buchanan clan how to do needlework, so that they could make quilts and clothes for themselves and their children, while Mary would teach them how to make vegetable gardens, cook, can and preserve, since she had never been too good with a needle.

Knowing her mother, Mary was sure that she wouldn't mind. The same day the idea came to her, Mary approached Zachary Thomas to go and fetch her mother so that she could implement her plan soon as possible. Zachary Thomas acquiesced to her request with a wry smile and suggested she and Jed come along with him, leaving dependable Emma in charge of the feeding of the livestock and the milking of the cow.

They arrived at the Harley family's Lewis Mountain tract in the buckboard drawn by two mules in the afternoon, to a clamorous welcome, which was even extended this time to her husband, so Mary knew that Joe must have given a good report of him to her family. The log cabin and outbuildings were surrounded by a glorious show of spring blossoms, including sweet-smelling flowering cherries and apple blossom. Mary couldn't believe how grown up Nellie and Percy were and was told that while Laura and Nellie had several admirers, but no steady one as yet, Lona had a young man named Benny Chase from the Swift Run Gap area calling on her now. It seemed Lona only saw him on weekends, though, because he had to travel the considerable distance on foot. Apparently, every Saturday evening he would pitch up, hat in hand, and the pair would sit in the parlor under the eagle eyes of her parents. (Mountain courtships were always heavily chaperoned.) Benny would sleep with Joe and Percy in the shack built onto the cabin and would go with them to the brush arbor the next day (if it fell on the day of the monthly service) then have Sunday lunch with them, before walking all the way back home. Such long-distance courtships were common in the mountains.

While Paw and Joe, holding Jed up on his shoulders, showed Zachary Thomas around the four-acre tract, Mary helped her mother pack up a big trunk to take to Claw Mountain with her.

The next day they left Lewis Mountain early in the morning and traveled to Claw Mountain in the buckboard, with her mother riding up front next to Zachary Thomas and Mary riding in the back with her small son. It was a bumpy, uncomfortable journey, but with Mary and Maw chatting all the way, it seemed to go a lot faster than it had the day before. After they reached Claw Mountain, Zachary Thomas gave the special "all-clear" two-shot signal with his long-barreled Kentucky rifle, which allowed them unimpeded passage up the mountain.

With the sulphuric smell of detonated gunpowder rich in the air, Maw gained Zachary Thomas undying devotion when she admired his proficiency at loading the muzzle and said what a magnificent weapon he had. She admiringly touched the beautifully engraved polished brass inlay on the stock and the hinged brass patch box, and murmured, "Jest look at this here fine workmanship. And this here stock is maple, ain't it?"

"Sure is. Done by a master craftsman, ma'am. Barrel is all of forty-five inches long." He sounded enormously pleased by her interest.

Sitting in the back of the buckboard, Mary smiled to herself. Maw always knew exactly the right thing to say to get everybody eating out of her hand. She had discovered right off what made her husband proud.

They left the buckboard at Horseshoe Hollow and pushed up on foot to Eagle Spur, Zachary Thomas holding her mother's heavy trunk on his head, while Mary carried Jed in his papoose, and she and her mother, a few sundry items between them. Her mother seemed a trifle apprehensive when she saw the ugly homestead at Horseshoe Hollow and spotted surly lookouts with shotguns in the trees, but once she crested the steep ridge of Eagle Spur and was hurried over by Mary to see the stunning view spread below them like a magic carpet, her nervousness seemed to instantly vanish, and she was smiling and relaxed. Mary knew that she felt the same sense of safeness on Eagle Spur that Mary did herself.

"Oh, Mary, it's truly magnificent!" Maw whispered in awe as she stared all around the place.

While Zachary Thomas chopped wood, Mary gave her a tour of Eagle Spur. Her mother said admiringly, "Mary, what a fine home you have made here. I'm so proud of what you two have done. I'm happy to say you were right about Zachary Thomas and I was wrong. And I couldn't be more pleased about it. One look at you tells me how happy he's made you."

Those words and receiving such high praise from her beautiful mother were like receiving showers of blessings from heaven!

* * *

It did not take long for the home-craft "classes" to get started, her mother proving a patient and talented teacher. At Mary's request, she had brought with her all her sewing baskets containing needles, threads (sewing and embroidery), and thimbles. She also brought bales of cloth and bits of left-over fabric she had gathered over the years, great big piles of it and it was soon put to good use.

Edna had told the other Bucko wives about the sewing lessons, and they came, hesitantly at first, but more eagerly, as the word spread. Her blessed mother soon became a popular and admired figure amongst the women of Claw Mountain, her smile as lovely and captivating as ever, as she bent over her charges in expert instruction. She showed them how to make rag dolls and quilts and drapes and clothing, moving from one group to the next like a kindly school teacher.

She had a positive effect on them too, for they seemed to take greater pride in their appearance when she was around. Those who didn't have the washrag habit quickly adopted it and knotted, unkempt hair suddenly became brushed and tidy-looking. They cried when she left, as did Mary, when Zachary Thomas took her back to Lewis Mountain. Maw promised to return before too long, leaving a legacy of fine home craft and pride in her lovely wake.

And before too long, industrious quilting parties and sewing bees became a favorite pastime for the women of Claw, Beacon and Bear Rock Mountains, who badgered their menfolk to get them bales of cloth from the store. Many of them proved to be talented seamstresses, although some of the more elderly women of the Addis and Ficks clans merely watched in curiosity and sucked at clay pipes at these industrious bees.

Sometimes they gathered at different homes around a quilting board suspended from the ceiling, which Zachary Thomas had rigged up for them upon her maw's instruction, to hand-sew fabrics onto colorful patch-works. Cabins that once had bare windows now had pretty colorful curtains fluttering in the breeze and the women and children came to monthly service wearing newly sewn clothing made of brightly colored calico and cotton.

Mary's gardening, cooking and canning lessons also proved popular. Since the time of "The Big Freeze", Zachary Thomas had been teaching his brothers and nephews to hunt rather than waste their time doing target-practicing, so now, instead of relying on store-bought canned goods, the women fed their husbands and large broods on delicious stews from the hunt, and supplied them with cakes and cookies that they had baked themselves. They started vegetable gardens and flower borders, which they filled with hollyhocks, zinnias, marigolds and sweet Williams.

Through it all, as the womenfolk turned increasingly from hooch to home craft, tension on the mountain lessened. Mary was immensely proud of them all.

The members of the Buchanan clan had become proper mountain folk at last . . .

* * *

The third time Doc Adams went to Claw Mountain to tend to the myriad medical complaints and illnesses of the clan, he taught basic hygiene while he applied salves and dished out pills, telling them to wash their hands after doing their "business" and before eating, a revolutionary new theory he'd read about and had cottoned onto. Though his treatment cost a tiny nominal fee as before, this time he was surprised to be given baskets of wild strawberries, blackberries and youngberries, mushrooms, eggs, ears of corn and bottles of honey to take away with him. Used to having these sort of things pressed him by other mountain folk whose pride and abhorrence of charity was well-known, it warmed his heart no end, coming as it did, from this once fierce and disreputable clan. Relieved at not having to contend anymore with mean old Obediah and, armed with Eli's blessing, the sporadic visits up Claw Mountain were proving a small balm to his conscience, a pious penance for living down in the prosperous lowlands with a brisk medical practice, a handsome red-bricked, two-story house and the finest horse-and-buggy for miles around, while the mountaineers, for the most part, lived in totally inadequate housing with no schools and no proper medical care.

After the long line of patients had been tended to, he was approached by Mary, his able and willing nurse's aide, who said there was something important she wished to discuss with him.

"Doc," she said, as she faced him in the yellow glow of the kerosene lanterns in Obediah's barn, seated on his packed-up black medical trunk, "As you know, I've bin teachin' th' young'uns to read an' write, but I haven't bin taught all that much m'self and they need a proper teacher. I want to git a schoolhouse built on th' mountain and to hire one. Kin you please tell me how to go about it? And find out if'n thar be a teacher someplace who'd be willin' to come here?"

"You want to start a school on Claw Mountain?" Doc was clouted with the knowledge of how far Mary had brought this backward mountain community already. She'd told him how she and her mother had taught the women home craft and gardening, brought a circuit-preacher to the mountain, proudly showing him the brush arbor where he preached, how she'd taught the children to read and write. And of course, Doc, himself, now visited the mountain every three months or so to give practically free medical treatment, a most unusual circumstance of which very few folk on these mountains could avail themselves. (Of course, seeing young Jed proved a strong motivation for that too. He frankly adored the

little fellow.) Now a schoolhouse and paid teacher, no less!

It would take a brave soul to agree to teach on Claw Mountain, that's for sure, especially with Eli Buchanan reportedly running things around here now. Remembering his encounter with the yellow-haired youth that first day and his evil reputation, Doc was worried about Mary coming up against him on this like she had about the circuit-preacher coming to Claw Mountain. He had to sound a word of caution.

"Well, always supposing that you can get one to teach here . . . I mean the place doesn't exactly inspire confidence in valley folk . . ." Then seeing her face, he changed his tack, "Er . . . first thing is, do you have enough money to *pay* a teacher?"

"I don't rightly know, Doc," she said warily. "How much you reckon one would cost?"

"Well, I could enquire for you, but I think you could count on at least fifteen dollars a month. Then you'd need extra for buying books and equipment. Of course, you'd have to build the school and someplace for the teacher to stay. After all, he or she would have to live on the mountain. It'd be much too far for anybody to travel here everyday."

"Well, I kin git Zachary Thomas and his brothers to build th' schoolhouse and th' desks – Zack is real good at carpentry – and someplace for th' teacher to stay too, using timber from th' forests on th' mountain. And since I intend fer th' school to service Bear Rock Mountain an' Beacon Mountain too, and one day, even Buck Knob Mountain, I'm sure thar'll be more than thirty young'uns to learn all told, 'cuz I'm learnin' more than that right now. And if'n we charge each child fifty cents a month that'd be th' fifteen dollars we need fer th' teacher."

"Now that th' clan is raising chickens and shoats an' I've got them gatherin' eggs and berries an' chestnuts for barter at th' store, I thunk they're much better off than they've ever bin.

"Still, you might find it difficult to find the cash, since you can't hire a teacher on barter. It's hard cash you'll be needing, Mary."

"I know," Mary said worriedly. "I did think of that. I guess I'll got to approach Eli to let me have some cash from th' moonshine sales every month."

"And you think he'll let you have it?"

"Well. I ain't his favorite person right now, but somehow, I'll git him to be with me on this."

"I believe he'll been fighting against having a preacher here every month. Heard at the store how he keeps pulling down your arbors."

"Not anymore!"

"Well, how do you think he'll feel about a school?"

"I'm hopin' he'll feel different about schoolin'. Thar ain't many folk Eli is close to, but I know that his family is real important to him. And he seems to have some feelin' for th' young'uns ... fer th' Buchanan children at least," she hastily qualified. "And he used to be very gentle with his younger brother, Jamie."

"I think you may be right, Mary. I've never told you this before, but on the first day I came to Claw Mountain, after I faced old Obediah's wrath, Eli told me to make sure none of the children died and stressed that I must come back again. Guess the young man has a soul after all."

"Well, let's hope so, Doc," she said skeptically, "but I have my doubts. I've jest got to convince him that the school would be fer thar benefit."

Doc Adams regarded the determined young mountain woman thoughtfully, the smell of straw and fresh mule dung assailing his nostrils in the decrepit old barn.

"Mary Buchanan, what inspiration you are to me, girl! I'll certainly do what I can for you . . ."

46

After much thought about the matter, Mary decided to send Zachary Thomas to see Eli about the fifteen dollars a month needed to hire a schoolteacher, knowing full well that he would never listen to anything she had to say on the matter. Indeed, he would almost certainly have opposed it simply because it was *she* who had raised it.

Amazingly, as it turned out, Eli actually *agreed* to give the cash needed for the teacher's salary every month out of the monthly moonshine sales. It seemed too good to be true. Mary couldn't help wondering if her husband did, indeed, have some kind of hold over his younger brother, or if the unexpected concession had genuinely sprung from his concern for the children, as Doc and Zachary Thomas had felt. But considering how her husband was unable to influence him to stop pulling down the brush arbors, perhaps not.

Certainly, in some ways, Eli was very different since coming back from Stony Man Mountain. Edna had told Mary that he called himself a gentleman now and said that he expected to be treated as one. Thankfully, though, he had largely dropped the lowlander speech he'd adopted since then, except for those occasions when he wanted to lord it over them. She reported, with a measure of awe, that he bathed at least once a week now, and wore fancy city clothing most of the time, and how he was now much more reasonable and mannerly when dealing with other members of the clan. Why, she exclaimed, he never went barefoot anymore! What was even more remarkable was that these days he no longer led his brothers on their wild valley forays, in fact, frowning so sternly upon them, that they were no longer wild at all, but rather dull, boring affairs, if clan gossip was to be believed. It was clear that a remarkable change had come over him, though Edna said he still drank heavily.

His mean streak was still there, too, as he had shown in his violent opposition to having the monthly church services on the mountain. Mary shuddered. One thing for sure, whatever had been the cause of these radical changes in him, he was still as dangerous as a rattlesnake! But she couldn't help wondering who or what at Stony Man Mountain could have had the power to cause such a remarkable change in one man's thinking and personal habits.

Once Mary had gained through her husband an undertaking from Eli that he would pay for the schoolteacher, she got Zachary Thomas and those of his brothers who attended monthly service, to agree to build the schoolhouse with an attached room beyond the schoolroom, where the new schoolteacher could live. So the church-going male members of the clan felled the trees, cut them into logs and chinked them with mud after building the structure with them, purchasing ready-made pine floorboards from the sawmill at Graves Mill and installing them with neat precision under Zackary Thomas's expert direction.

There were thirty desks for the pupils, a table and stool for the teacher, a blackboard, a potbellied stove in the middle of the room and a bucket and dipper in one corner to provide fresh water from the creek. Zachary Thomas had ably built every one of the desks that stood as proudly as thrones in the schoolroom. Doc had brought up a loaned desk from the elementary school in Carlisle on old Bessie, for him to copy and her husband had made an even better job on them than had been done on the original, Mary felt.

The schoolyard was surrounded by a split-pole chestnut fence. A school bell had been rigged up an old oak tree and could be rung by pulling on the end of a rope. Mary could hardly believe that she had overcome all the obstacles and now formal schooling for the deprived children of Claw, Beacon and Bear Rock Mountains was fast becoming a reality. It was to be called "The Emily Tuttle School" in honor of her late cousin, whose early tuition of Mary had been indirectly responsible for all this.

The schoolteacher's new living quarters at the school, which led off from the back of the classroom, was of a decent size, if modestly furnished. Besides also boasting a pot-bellied stove, most necessary in these parts, it had a small wood-fire stove to cook meals on. (The latter was much envied by Mary, who was still cooking all her meals in her fireplace in primitive fashion.)

Mary agreed with Doc Adam's contention that there had been no question that the new teacher could live off the mountain and travel there every day. The mountain was just too remote and inaccessible for that. Though Doc Adams had warned Mary to hang fire on building the school until they could find somebody willing to come and teach in it (which might not be such an easy task with the

355

lawless reputation of these parts), she had waved his concerns away, saying she knew that they would find somebody suitable, and had gone ahead anyway.

But none of this would have been achieved without dear old Doc. He had proved a staunch ally. He had recently brought a young doctor, Jason Darwin, into his practice and was now semi-retired, so he had spent much time helping Mary to organize the new school. He'd even been to visit other mountain schools to check them out, so they could hopefully gain from their experience. Furthermore, dear Doc – bless his sweet soul! – had donated a handsome sum of five hundred dollars towards the building costs, educational supplies and furnishings for the teacher's living quarters.

It had taken four whole months to get this far . . .

But they were still without a teacher, and Mary had other concerns. "I need to know more about schools, Doc." Mary confided in the good doctor. "I'm frightful ignorant about how they work and th' different grades and so on. Do we need permission from th' authorities to go ahead with classes?"

"I doubt it, Mary. I happen to know the Department is desperately short of funds. "Besides, you won't be asking them to build a public school, and will be paying for the teacher yourselves. I'm sure they'd be only too happy with any private attempts to educate the mountain children. But I tell you what. I'll take you down to see the folk at the Virginia Department of Education and the County School Board in Madison, to find out about grades and curriculum and what educational supplies you'll need and so on. I'm sure they'd be most willing to answer any questions you may have and will help you in any which way they can."

So it was arranged. Mary and Doc Adams had gone to see the educational authorities in Madison, traveling there in Doc's fine horse-and-buggy. Mary was dressed in one of Hedina Buchanan's fine dresses, a blue watered-silk shirt-waister, with tiny silvery blue buttons, and wore a matching blue hat with a black ostrich feather in it and her button-up soft-kid black boots. Even so, she had an idea that the outfit was outdated and unfashionable compared to those of the rich lowlanders, judging by the fashions she had seen in the streets of Madison.

Of course, her idea of fashion had been geared to the Sears, Roebuck catalogues in the past, so she didn't know (or care, for that matter) much about such things. But Doc Adams had waved away her expressed concerns and had said he'd never seen such a true and fine lady in all his born days. 'Besides,' he had assured her. 'Madison's naught but a village. What do they know about fashions around here?' And since his look of admiration was so genuine and open on his face, she figured he couldn't just be trying to humor her. She did so want to give a good impression at the meeting, even if she would have to admit to terrible ignorance on her part.

At Madison, they went first to the Virginia Department Education where they asked to see the head to gain official blessing and advice for their new school. The department was headed by a black-suited, scholarly looking man with a full gray beard and little round spectacles, whose name was Arthur Soames. He ushered them into his tiny office and regarded them over his wide cluttered desk with a somewhat puzzled, polite smile on his face. He seemed to have mis-understood their mission completely for he immediately launched into a long spiel about how Virginia's large debt from building canals and railroads throughout the state before the Civil War and the Civil War, itself, had deprived the children of the Commonwealth of Virginia of education, and how it was not until the 1880s that Virginia had started up a proper system of education, with each county being responsible for educating its own children.

"Naturally, the more populated towns are serviced first," continued Soames. "So while I think it's admirable that you wish to get a mountain school built, I'm afraid, at this stage, the less populated mountain areas are of secondary import-ance. Besides, schooling is not mandatory and we have found that since moun-tain parents need their children to help out on the farms, they rarely insist that they go school, so it's all a bit of a waste of time really. And, frankly, a waste of money better spent elsewhere. So," he sighed regretfully, "as much as I would like to oblige, I'm afraid we are not inclined to fund, or even partly subsidize, the building of your proposed new school."

"But it's already built!" spluttered Doc Adams indignantly. "And what's more, the mountain people will be paying for the school teacher themselves. We just need your advice on how to start classes and to give advice on matters such as curriculum, grades and so on."

Arthur Soames looked astonished and immensely relieved. He raked his long gray beard with his fingers reflectively, before saying, "Well, that's a different matter entirely. Most commendable. On Claw Mountain, you say?" He frowned as he seemed to recollect the sordid reputation of the mountain, which Mary knew was very widespread.

"That is correct," Doc Adams confirmed. "Thanks to this young lady here. She's been the driving force behind the whole project."

"Is that so?" Arthur Soames turned to Mary in puzzled surprise. "Are you a teacher then?"

It was clear from the way Mr Soames stared at her that he couldn't quite equate the finery she wore with her mountain speech and she felt the need to tell him that she might be largely unlettered, but she was nobody's fool. Instead, she said, with a proudly raised chin, "No, I ain't no teacher, Mr Soames. I live on th' mountain with my husband and th' rest of th' Buchanan clan and have long felt the need to start a school thar fer th' young'uns. Idle hands and all that."

Her reply seemed to delight the old academic, for he chuckled softly. "Ah, very commendable indeed," he said with a wry, pleased smile "My sentiments exactly. How many pupils are you expecting to attend?"

"About thirty or so to begin with," answered Mary. "But I hope to expand it later."

Mr Soames raised a surprised black eyebrow. "*Thirty?* That's a fair number. Well, first thing you've got to determine is how many and how long your terms will be."

Mary bit her lower lip. "What are terms?"

"Well," he replied kindly, "terms are periods when you teach, and then there are breaks in between to rest both teacher and pupils. In my experience, I have found most of the schools erected by the mountain folk themselves, are only open a couple of months in the summer."

"No," said Mary firmly. "I thought that at first too. But I've changed my mind. I want th' young'uns of Claw Mountain to be taught right thru' th' year, straight off."

Mr Soames seem astounded to hear the extent of her ambition, but before he had time to comment, Mary went on, "I thunk thar ought to be three or four terms then. Of course, th' longest break would be durin' th' summer so that th' young'uns kin help in the fields with th' crops."

Mr Soames cautioned that she might find that this plan was a little too ambitious to begin with, but Mary replied archly that she was determined to try, anyway. She saw Doc's amused smile with a sense of triumph.

*   *   *

In all, it was a very fruitful day, Mary felt, as she and Doc Adams rode back to Claw Mountain over rough, rocky trails, in the horse-and-buggy. The benign Mr Soames had been most apologetic about being only able to give her advice and a few teaching aids, such as a couple of text books and several boxes of chalk, in the way of assistance, but he had sent them away with the names of several qualified teachers who might be interested in teaching school on the mountain. What's more he had promised that he would be willing to come to Claw Mountain during the next week to inspect the schoolroom and make any suggestions he saw fit, and would come again when they had appointed a teacher with whom he would consult.

Their visit to the Madison County Board had been equally positive, especially as it came with Mr Soames' relayed instruction to 'treat them right'. So, all in all, she was well-pleased with what had transpired.

Used to having to walk most places, Mary allowed herself to appreciate the sheer luxury of the nifty, fringed horse-drawn transport that she had not been able to appreciate on the way there because she'd been so nervous. She had been afraid that their humble efforts would be scoffed at, rather than encouraged, and now that Arthur Somas was firmly on their side, she felt an extraordinary lightness inside her. That was because God was on her side, too, she felt sure! He knew how much she wanted the best for the young'uns.

The early autumn air was invigorating and God was busy setting the forests afire, the spectacular scarlet, gold and amber colors of the leaves, already rich against the brilliant blue of the sky. *Oh, it was so good to be alive!*

* * *

A week later, after the clan had been duly warned of his impending visit, Arthur Soames had come to Claw Mountain to carry out his promised inspection. He was a tall, spare-looking man, filled with the love of knowledge of the true academic, whose stately old-fashioned appearance brought to Mary's mind a picture of the Founding Fathers she had seen in one of Emily's old books. His patrician sageness and solemnity was somewhat nerve-wracking for the anxious threesome of herself, Doc Adams and Zachary Thomas, who followed him around meekly as he first checked to see if the building itself was structurally sound, before seeing if the teacher's living quarters were adequate, and then inspecting all the educational equipment. Though not a public school, Mr Soames had suggested that regular state textbooks should be used, in case any of the pupils should want to move on to public schools later on.

Mary had seen the sense of this immediately and she and Doc Adams had bought a load of these text books, as well as other worthy supplies from an educational supply store, for which Doc had so kindly paid. Mary was pleased to note that when Mr Soames saw the neat piles of the recommended stacked books, he gave a grunt of satisfaction. To Mary and Doc's considerable relief and satisfaction, Arthur Soames declared he was greatly impressed with their efforts and, after giving them his blessing and good wishes for the school and promising to come back again after a teacher had been appointed, he went on his way back to Madison, on horseback.

Doc had already written to each of the five prospective teachers on the list Mr Soames had given them, asking if they would be willing to teach on Claw

Mountain for the not-too-princely sum of fifteen dollars a month. He and Mary
were deeply disappointed when all five of them summarily declined the position.
But Mary refused to give up, saying that God would provide the perfect teacher
for Claw Mountain. Then Doc placed an advertisement with the *Warren Sentinel*
newspaper, in Front Royal, which attracted a single reply from a Miss Violet
Prescott.

Miss Prescott was duly appointed as the teacher for the new school, by mail. A
couple of weeks later, she arrived on the mountain on mule-drawn buckboard
driven by Zachary Thomas, who had been sent to Winchester to collect her. With
her long black broadcloth nobby skirts, crisp white cotton blouses and big black
bows, the new schoolteacher was a demure-looking twenty-two-year-old with
long brown curly hair which she kept tied in a black bow behind her head. Her
gray eyes were accentuated by thick, dark lashes and these and her pale skin and
rosy cheeks all conspired to make her a very attractive young woman. But despite
her ladylike demeanor, she had a pert little figure that made her seem as feisty as
a bantam rooster and, indeed, she might well need such fighting qualities to
survive here, Mary surmised.

Despite the appalling reputation of the Claw Mountain community as demonic
and lawless, which she calmly professed to know about, the beguiling Miss
Prescott had taken up the challenge with the fire of ambition lighting up her
lovely eyes, clearly earnest and eager to start her first teaching assignment. And
this pleased Mary immensely. She was concerned that her comely looks would
invite unwanted attention, however. She had not forgotten Eli's attempt to force
himself on her when she first came to the mountain and she was not pretty at all.
She felt constrained to warn the newly appointed teacher about him. She told her
to report any problems she might encounter, especially with Eli Buchanan,
directly to her, and she had promised that she would attend to them. With not
much separating their ages and a common goal to do the best for the children on
this mountain, she and Mary had struck up an immediate rapport, and Mary felt
that God had ably answered her prayers concerning the matter.

Arthur Soames had been back to consult closely with the teacher, as he had
promised, before the school was due to be opened and it was decided between the
long-bearded academic, Miss Prescott and Mary that the new school should go up
to the fourth grade to begin with and be upgraded to the sixth or seventh grade
once enough pupils had achieved that initial upper grade.

* * *

The miracle had happened! Today was the day that the new school was to be opened and, in a few days time, classes would commence. Mary stared wondrously around the large, one-roomed classroom with joyous pride bursting from her breast, the smell of freshly cut pine strong in her nostrils. Through the opened windows, she could see the early morning sun shining through the trees and hear wild birds chattering, as if they too were excited about this grand day.

Mary was filled with heady expectation. Both Doc Adams and Arthur Soames had agreed to be there for the Grand Opening to give speeches, and Mary had galvanized the Bucko wives into assisting her in baking cakes and cookies, making sandwiches and bringing homemade lemonade. She could hear Miss Prescott bustling around in her room at the back now, but she called out that she would be out shortly to help Mary.

Since the school had been named for her father's niece, Mary had invited Emily's parents, the Tuttles, in Richmond, to attend the opening, sending a letter to them through the Fletcher general store for onward posting, even though she did not expect any of them to put in an appearance. Thus she was overjoyed when Emma, with Jed bouncing on her angular hip, ran to the school, where Mary was busy making preparations for the day's events, to tell her excitedly that her brother, Joe, had rolled into Horseshoe Hollow with her parents, in a horseless carriage, with her Richmond aunt and uncle, and Frankie Tuttle, one of her male cousins.

Mary raced back to the main homesite with Emma to greet them and bring them across to the school, especially pleased to discover that her father had made the long journey, since he had not been to Claw Mountain before. There were squeals and whoops of joy and many hugs when the long-lost relations greeted each other. Her aunt and uncle were in their city finery, their black Cadillac, handsome and gleaming. Her beautiful aunt wore a gracious long purple dress, splendid wide-brimmed hat and a fox fur around her neck, while her mother looked as young and lovely as always in her simple mountain dress. Shamed by her cousin's city threads into wearing shoes for once, with her silvery-blonde hair drawn behind her head in a bun, she looked radiant.

Mary noticed anew at how much her father had aged. His limp seemed more pronounced, his curly hair had gone much grayer, his brown eyes seemed to have lost a little of their luster and he had a persistent cough that worried Mary's ears. But he was smiling fit to bursting and she had fondly linked her arm in his as they all walked over to the school through the forest, as there was no remotely navigable track leading there.

Back at the school, while her father and her aunt and uncle sat at desks in the schoolroom talking to Joe and Zachary Thomas, her mother helped her and Miss

Prescott organize things. Because the schoolroom would be too small to accommodate everyone, the teacher's table was dragged outside into the schoolyard and four chairs placed behind it for their two honored guests, herself and Miss Prescott. She had wanted Zachary Thomas to sit up front beside her, but he had declined. Knowing how he, with his reserved nature, hated the limelight, she didn't press the matter. Everybody else would have to sit on the grass beneath the towering trees or at some of the school desks that had been pulled out for that express purpose. The proceedings were to start at eleven to give folk plenty of time to get there.

Doc Adams and Arthur Soames arrived early. The tall, bearded academic had even brought along a newspaper reporter and photographer to record the event for prosperity. Shortly before eleven, the children came trickling in accompanied by their parents, the boys in overalls and sweaters and wearing over-sized caps, the girls in dresses and sweaters, many sporting the same pudding-basin hair-styles as the boys. Members of the Ficks and Addis clans from Beacon and Bear Rock Mountains were there too. Mary had told all the congregants about the school during the monthly Sunday service and the turnout had been quite remarkable, because, with even Eli's blessings on the project, the parents of the mountain clans had gone along with the idea just fine. All but a few of the children were barefoot, but to Mary's satisfaction, their faces glowed so redly from being scrubbed with homemade soap that it looked as if even the boys were wearing rouge.

It all went magnificently. After calling for quiet, Mary shakily stood up to introduce the two honored guests, Mr Soames and Doc Adams, who were dressed in their best Sunday suits, and the new school teacher, Miss Prescott, who looked charmingly captivating in a long black taffeta skirt that buttoned up to beneath her bosom, white satin blouse with billowy sleeves, tied with an enormous black bow at the neck and a pert black hat atop her head, attracting many admiring glances.

With heartfelt pride, Mary started by telling them how she had been taught to read and write many years ago by her young cousin, Emily Tuttle, for whom the new school was being named and how the magic of the printed word had taken her into many different worlds and filled her with wonder and the deep desire to learn all she could about the world they all lived in. She said that the joy of learning was a precious gift to give a child and how much it pleasured her to have played a small role in giving this gift to the children of these mountain parts in memory of her beloved cousin, who had died at an early age of consumption.

At that point, Mary noticed her glamorous aunt sitting at one of the school desks was sniffling, raising a handkerchief to her nose, and that her eyes were moist. Then Mary used the opportunity to thank everybody individually, who had contributed by giving of their time, labor and money to make her dream for Claw Mountain come true, especially her faithful friend, Doc Adams. She thanked the mountain folk for helping to build the school and for having the courage to send their children to school. She thanked the schoolteacher for being brave enough to come to such a remote area to teach. She thanked the Tuttles for coming and bringing her parents. Lastly, she thanked her husband, Zachary Thomas, who had given so much material support, hard work and meaning to her dream.

She sat down to warm appreciative applause. Both the honored male guests, when called upon to talk, gave long and entertaining speeches, filled with good humor that seemed to set the tone for the whole day.

Miss Prescott was the last speaker and after she had stood and said a few words, telling the assembled pupils and mountain people of her plans to educate the children of the mountain, Emma gave a reading from *Little Women*. Mary felt such stirring pride as she saw the tall, thin, barefoot mountain girl, with her long fair hair primly scraped into a neat little bun, with her soap-scrubbed shiny face, and wearing a clean shapeless blue shift for a change instead of her habitual dungarees, standing in front with opened book in hand, and heard the clear, perfectly pronounced words ringing through the forest. To be sure, Emma represented all her heartfelt dreams for the mountain children. Bright as a button, the girl had been the pick of her own pupils in their informal classroom.

After Emma had finished her faultless rendition and closed the book matter-of-factly, the audience clapped rapturously. Though Mary doubted the words had much meaning for them, it had given the coarsely, if neatly, dressed mountain people, seated on quilts and old threadbare blankets, a sense of pride and achievement unthought-of before now and a little taste of what awaited their own children in the classroom.

Their faces were flushed with hope, their gap-toothed grins a sure measure of their growing determination to do the best by their offspring. With a wildly leaping heart, Mary suddenly noticed for the first time that even Eli had put in a late appearance and was nonchalantly leaning against a rail of the chestnut fence in his city suit, talking quietly with his closest cohort, Jake. She just hoped he wasn't there to start trouble! She wouldn't put it past him to destroy everything they had built here out of sheer spite!

47

Soon after the opening of the school, Eli found the comely Miss Prescott busy grading papers at her desk one evening before retiring into her back room for the night. She wore a black, fringed shawl across her shoulders and tendrils of her curly brown hair fell about her face so that she looked very appealing in the sallow light of the kerosene lamp on her table. She looked up with beautiful, startled gray eyes when he entered the room silently, only a slight creaking of the floorboards, beneath his leather soles, alerting her to his presence. When she saw him, she gasped with fright. She stood up and backed nervously away. So the bitch knew who he was – *his distinctive scar was always a dead giveaway!* Often, he resented the reaction of strangers to his scar, when he would mentally curse Sloane Galtrey for inflicting it on him but, tonight, the notion that the awesome power of his appearance always managed to give sway, gave Eli a heady rush.

"Good evening, Miss Prescott," he said in his father's 'King's English' and his best cultured voice, which he could tell surprised her. "I don't believe I've had the pleasure."

Her eyes looked around wildly.

"I know who you are. *What do you want?"* she asked crisply.

"Whatever you've got to offer."

She sucked in her breath in alarm. "If you think you can take advantage of me, I swear I'll scream so loud they'll hear me in the next county."

"Don't reckon anybody would hear you," Eli said softly. "There's nobody anywhere near this place."

In actual fact, the closest homesite was at Horseshoe Hollow, which was not all that far away and somebody might well hear her screams in the still night air. He viewed her perky bosom inside her white cotton blouse with interest, almost tempted to do something about it. But no, there were much more important things at stake here. He advanced slowly on her and she took up the wooden pointer on the ledge beneath the blackboard, brandishing it like a baseball bat.

"Hey, calm down, sweetheart. All I came for is for you to learn me whatever you got to learn."

Her eyes widened with sick apprehension. "What do you mean?"

"Lessons, of course," replied Eli. Slowly, Miss Prescott let out her breath and lowered the pointer stick. "I want you to give me private lessons for two hours a day every weekday evening after regular school is out."

"And what if I refuse?"

"Oh, I wouldn't advise that, Miss Prescott. Shucks, lady, don't you know it's me who's paying your salary?"

Miss Prescott bit her lower lip and said haughtily, "I heard what you did to the brush arbors . . . how you pulled them down, that is. You planning to do the same with the schoolhouse?"

"Heck no, if you turn out to be a lousy teacher, I'll just set fire to it," he said in a voice dripping with sarcasm, his sallow yellow eyes as cold as winter ice.

Miss Prescott swallowed hard, the color high in her cheeks. Then she got a haughty, determined look on her pretty face. "It'll cost you an extra five dollars a month."

Eli regarded her soberly, chagrined by her demand. He had not expected her to dare try something like this. *Five dollars a month!* But if he refused, she might just decide to leave and he had no time to waste. For the same reason, he knew that he mustn't give in to the fleeting attraction he felt for her. She really was very pretty, and spunky, too. He always liked that in a woman.

"Alright, five dollars extra a month," he agreed grudgingly.

"What subjects would you like me to teach you? Reading? Writing? Spelling? Arithmetic? History? Geography?"

"All of them – but first of all I want you to learn me to read and write. Oh, and one more thing. This here is to be a secret between you and me. I hear it from anybody else and you'll be on your way sooner than a greased hog slips through a man's hands."

"You mean *teach* you to read and write, don't you, Eli . . . ?"

W ith his ability to do everything easily and well, Eli was reading fluently and writing with a large childish hand inside of two months, Miss Prescott proved to be an exceptional teacher, who demanded much of him, correcting his every tiny little grammatical mistake. She also loaned him books on which to practice and to broaden his knowledge. Despite the fact that he knew that the idea of starting the school had originated from Mary, whom he despised, he had gone along with it because it had suited him to get himself an education. Now he would be ready to return to Skyland next summer on a more equal footing than he had the last time, when only his wits had kept him ahead of the game. Indeed, he knew he would feel a lot more confident than he had acted the last time, when he was nothing more than an ignorant mountain cracker beneath his calculated veneer of civility mimicked from a madman.

Now he was ready to make a concerted play for Miss Annabel Cotterell when he returned there at the same time next year, having learned from George Pollock that she and her father had vacationed there at exactly the same time every year for the past three years. He hoped that the incident of the public kiss at the Colonial Ball had not turned the dour reverend against Skyland as a summer resort and that Eli's voluntary leaving after that had lulled him into thinking that the coast would be clear for him and his daughter to return there. But it hadn't only been for selfish reasons that Eli had agreed to pay for a teacher to come to Claw Mountain.

He realized now that if the Buchanan clan was to stay strong, they would have to learn to compete in the world outside these mountains, just like his father had said. The isolation had kept them in ignorance for too long. After his week at Skyland, he could understand that for himself. He now had his sights firmly set on Washington D.C, where Annabel Culverwell and her father resided ...

Falling Leaves and Mountain Ashes

Book V

'Mystic Child'

*'How can a mere babe be blessed
With wisdom such as this?'*

Brenda George

48

Mary was frantic. *Little Jed had disappeared again!* These days, though still unsteady on his feet, he would carefully climb backwards down the porch steps then hurriedly toddle off before Mary even knew he was out of the cabin. Jed's calm, but intense, inquisitiveness had got him crawling at five months, and walking at eleven months and, though he had not yet uttered a single word, his early sense of awareness had very soon given way to an urgent urge for discovery that had Mary always on the hunt for him.

He was not always easy to find either – in the barn, right under Dapple's big warm belly, under a haystack, under bushes, between boulders, up small trees, in the fowl hock; there seemed to be no limit to his infantile wanderlust. Yet she had never had to search for him this long before – one moment he had been playing happily beside her in the cabin and, the next, he had vanished. Though she had been looking for him for well over an hour now, she still couldn't find him anywhere.

Unfortunately, Zachary Thomas had taken his two coon dogs with him and gone off tracking in the Wilderness, as usual, and Emma had already left to hunt for vittles for her family so Mary had nobody to help her search for him. She had considered going to seek help from the Buckos and their families, but decided she couldn't risk taking the time to do that when Jed might be in need of her urgent help. Terrified that he had gone too far to the edge of the ridge and was lying injured or dead on some rocky precipice far below, she had been searching all the way around the edge of the ridge, dreading what she might find, shouting till she was hoarse.

But though she craned her head over the edge to find her eighteen-month-old toddler, coming across a huge eagle's nest some ten-feet across by twenty-feet deep, made out of sticks, a huge bulky structure lined with grass and moss which had been built into the cliff below, there was no sign of him.

In utter despair, she slowly turned around from the ridge and saw the dark, foreboding forest of the tableland behind the row of hemlocks at the back of the homesite. It seemed to beckon her towards it. Though she had repeatedly forbidden little Jed to go anywhere near it, she wasn't sure how much he understood. She supposed it was entirely possible, even likely, that he would eventually seek it out. If so, she might never find him in the vast forest that lay so close to their doorstep.

Feeling frightened and threatened by the forest, she had not yet had the courage to enter into it since returning to Eagle Spur. Afraid of snakes and the giant golden eagles that were gathering overhead, soaring in silent watchfulness on the air currents above, she knew she had to find Jed before he came to any harm. Taking a deep breath to bolster herself with courage, she forced herself to stumble towards the virgin forest, passing under the giant chestnut tree that had dropped its magnificent bounty of nuts on the ground below that had seen her gathering basketful after basketful over many weeks. She walked between two of the hemlocks, feeling a thrall of fear enter her being. *This was forbidden territory.*

The forest was hushed and still and dark and oppressive. Not even the slightest breeze quivered a leaf. Even in the full glorious flush of fall, the forest seemed hugely subdued and sinister. The only sign of life in the forest were hundreds of monarch butterflies fluttering in the undergrowth, on their way south to Mexico for the winter. *Where were all the birds, the animals?* The silence got to her, making her jumpy. There was the fragrance of rich loamy earth, of fallen leaves and damp humus, acorns, stagnant water and the fresh pungent smell of hemlock needles.

"JED! JED! WHAR ARE YOU, MY SWEET BABY? TELL ME WHAR YOU ARE."

But she knew that Jed could not answer, because Jed did not speak. Venturing further into the forest, pushing through bramble bushes that scratched at her arms, passing huge groves of fern and masses of red and orange wildflowers, she searched on and on, calling his name, growing more frightened with every passing step. Oh, where could her precious baby be? Then, quite suddenly, as she plunged through thick verdant growth, she at last came upon her wayward child. And what a nasty shock she got. She cried out in intense alarm.

Wearing just his cloth diaper, his dress cast carelessly to one side, the toddler was sitting on top of an ant nest and had so many large black ants running all over him that she could scarcely see an inch of bare flesh. The insects caked his little sun-browned chest like dollops of thick black molasses. They coated his bare arms and legs and crawled like feasting flies all over his face, doming his head like a thick black cap. She remembered having attended a mountain picnic as a child that had been ruined when it was invaded by the tiny black insects, and all the children, including her, had wept with their painful nips.

Though Jed should be screaming with pain right now, instead he was pointing at the insects and gurgling delightedly. She hastily pulled him off the ant nest and dementedly dusted the clinging, scrambling, panicked ants off him, causing him to back away from her, squinting with alarm. She stripped him of his diaper, letting loose the insects that were thickly bunched inside. As she shook his diaper, they fell to the ground and scattered in a black mindless mass.

When at last he was completely shed of the marauding ants and standing as vulnerably naked as a newborn, she fully expected to see scores of nasty red bites all over his body, yet, unbelievably, his skin was completely smooth and clear and untouched. She turned him around checking his diminutive genitalia and the crease in his bottom, to find that they too had not a mark on them. Weak with relief, she scooped him up into her arms and pressed him against her chest, wondering how it was possible that not a single ant, out of the hundreds that had covered his entire body, had nipped him!

With Jed safely snuggled in her arms, she suddenly felt a safeness that she could not comprehend. Seconds before, she had been shaking with fear and now all she felt was calm and an inner peace. What's more, the forest had lost its sense of menace. Instead of turning and heading back in the direction of the homesite she had vaguely worked out from the position of the sun, she felt an urgent need to explore further into the dense woods. Slowly, she wandered around with Jed, a naked little cherub, on her hip. He was gurgling in contentment, gazing peacefully up at her with sage brilliant blue eyes and bestowing on her, his heart-wrenchingly sweet smile.

She saw the beauty that lay everywhere around her in the forest, and it filled her heart and sang in her senses. Virginia creeper had started the mighty conflagration just before the first frosts had singed the leaves of the hardwoods. Now the bright fruits of the dogwood splashed the understory, white baneberry and the fire of sumac, red oaks and maples, the rich red of the cherry tree, were mixed with the brilliance of beeches, golden asters, shiny yellow birch, redroot and goldenrod.

Then a sound carried on a sudden breeze that blew up from nowhere, rustling the fallen leaves at her feet. It was the light, eerie sound of rattles and drums and flutes, soft as a whisper, but so rhythmic and compelling, it stirred the blood. It lured her forward like the song of the Pied Piper, through coves of fern, bramble bushes and trees whose barks were thickly scaled with lichens. Then abruptly, she came across a large clearing. In the center of it was a huge mound some thirty feet by fifteen feet in length and width, and some fifteen feet high. It was covered in wild grasses, moss and flowering wildflowers, which grew out of its sides in sweet surrender.

Mary stared at it in astonishment. What on earth could this be? Too orderly and precise to be of a natural order, it spoke of rendering by human hands. But what was its purpose? It was then that she saw him. *The Indian of her dreams!* Some splendid seven feet tall and with a great nobleness of stance, his chest, hung with the large gold circle, was muscular and well-developed, not in the thick-set way of a white man's, but sleekly so with the sinewy grace of a deer, his shoulders broad and his skin a warm reddish bronze. The sides of his head were shaved and his long sleek shiny black hair was tied at the top of his head with a leather string, into which were stuck hawk and eagle feathers. His eyes were black as glowing coals. He had a broad flat nose, full lips and no facial hair. One eye was circled with red ocherous earth, while black soot encircled the other. He wore nothing but the skin of an otter at his girdle with the tail strung between his legs. As before in her dreams, at his right side, hung his bag that was ornamented around the bottom with a leather fringe, with an eagle feather attached it, fastened to a belt made of well-dressed skin. She instinctively knew it was to carry medicinal roots and herbs, which seemed to indicate he was a medicine man of sorts. *He was quite magnificent!*

Although Mary started when she saw him, she felt strangely unafraid. Once again, he said not a word. She noticed his piercing black eyes were fixed on Jed. Jed seemed to see him, too, for he responded with a happy gurgling laugh, before the Indian vanished in a flash. One minute he was standing there in all his magnificence and, the next, there was nothing but the odd huge mound. *What was it?* What secret was the silent Indian guarding? Mary turned with reluctance to head for home. Her fear of getting lost went unfounded. She found her way back to Eagle Spur with amazing ease, merely by heading towards the place where there was a prolific number of eagles in the sky.

*   *   *

That night, in bed, Mary asked Zachary Thomas if he had ever come across the strange mound in the tableland forest. He turned to her with narrowed turquoise-green eyes.

"What were y'doin' back thar?"

"Lookin' fer Jed. He'd gone aways into th' forest and I almost went mad tryin' to find him. What's th' mound fer, Zack? It sure don't seem like somethung natural to me."

"It ain't. That thar is an old Indian burial mound."

"Good heavens!" Mary's eyes widened in shock. "You mean that's th' Indian burial ground you told me about b'fore?"

"Sure is."

"They buried their dead *above* the ground?"

"Yep."

"How d'you know fer sure that's what it is?"

"Well, when I first discovered it, I was still a boy. I took a shovel and dug down into the top of it. I came across a skeleton covered in wood ash about two feet below. It were all of seven-foot long. That thar mound is full of human skeletons and remains; men, women and young'uns, all covered in wood ash and buried in blankets along with thar personal possessions. "Of course, all them blankets have disintegrated by now."

372

Mary gave a little involuntary shudder. *An Indian burial mound!* "Well, that thar mound must have bin made a real long time ago then, 'cuz Duke Colby at th' store told me all th' Indians left th' Shenandoah Valley hundreds of years ago. You thunk they died natural-like, or were kilt by some enemy?"

"Oh, I thunk it were of natural causes alright. Who would bother to bury an enemy way up here if'n them was murdered? Reckon they must have had a village on th' banks of Wilson Run and buried their dead up here whar their enemies couldn't disturb 'em. Seen signs of long-gone Indian habitation down thar by th' river, m'self."

"Still, seems a mighty big haul to do that every time somebody died tho', don't you thunk?"

"Yeah, but thar may have bin other reasons fer it?"

"Sech as?"

"Thar beliefs an' sech."

"Guess so." Then Mary thought of something. "How come you don't hunt th' tableland, Zack? Must be plenty of game to be had in thar, though I must admit I didn't see none."

"Well, after I come across that thar mound, I found I couldn't hunt thar no more. Seemed too disrespectful somehow. 'Sides th' eagles wouldn't let me."

"What do you mean?"

"I mean every time I went in thar, they'd attack me and chase me away! I finally figger'd out they didn't want me thar. That's when I started to hunt th' Wilderness below. Swar th' forest up here gives me th' wobbles."

Mary knew exactly what he meant. She considered telling him about the giant Indian she had seen in her dreams and in the vision in the forest today, but she decided against it. Perhaps she had been so worried about Jed she'd been hallucinating like some dippy old hag drunk on moonshine. She sure wouldn't want Zack to go thinking she was losing her mind. He was awful fond of saying it actually. Every time she thought of something new to try, he would say. 'Mary, have you lost yer mind?' She'd sure hate to give his words any credence.

49

Jed was now two years old and a healthy child, but one thing about him worried Mary. Though he seemed to understand everything said to him, he still didn't talk – not a single word – no matter how patiently she and Zachary Thomas and Emma tried to teach him. She had helped her mother look after all her younger siblings and knew they had all started talking at a much younger age. Doc Adams always examined Jed on his by-now regular visits to the mountain to treat the various ailments of its inhabitants (which he had expanded to include Beacon and Bear Rock Mountains), but when Mary told him her fears that Jed might be backward or dimwitted, he objected strongly, saying that, if anything, the child had always appeared more than usually alert and aware to him. However, to put her mind at rest, he would thoroughly examine him with that specifically in mind.

Fortunately, Jed adored the good doctor, who was so taken with him that he invariably brought him some candy in wrappers, which he'd put in a different pocket each time. They always played a little game. He'd ask Jed in which pocket he'd put the candy and Jed would always, without exception, point to the right one. Doc Adams would shake his head in perplexed amazement and fondly tickle him under his chin.

After giving him his usual medical examination, Doc proceeded to test Jed's reflexes at the knees with a small wooden mallet, stared into his eyes with his old orthoscope, clicked his fingers on either side of the head of the child, while the mite sat on a bench in the barn at Obediah's homesite, totally calm, not in the least nonplussed by all the untoward activity. Doc then pronounced the small boy healthy in every respect. He told Mary that she had no cause for worry about his tardiness in speech since some children were just slower than others, but quickly caught up once they got started. Indeed, he insisted that he did not doubt the little boy's intelligence.

This mollified Mary some and she began to appreciate that for all his muteness, Jed did indeed seem to radiate with discernment and a lucid comprehension that went far beyond his tender age.

* * *

It was early afternoon and Mary had completed most of her daily chores. She decided to take Jed out for his daily walk in the tableland forest. These had become entirely necessary of late for, if she didn't do this, the toddler would go there all on his lonesome. There was just no stopping him! He'd be down the porch steps and away before she had time to blink! With the face of an angel and a lean, hard, nut-brown little body that was completely devoid of infantile chubbiness, he'd simply disappear and Mary would have to search frantically for him, always worried in case he'd gone to the edge of the ridge and fallen over it.

Invariably though, she would find him somewhere in the great forest of the tableland behind the homesite as she had before. Indeed, the tableland forest seemed to have the attraction of a magnet for him. Many times he would be at the burial mound, chortling and talking his nonsensical baby-speak, though she hadn't seen the giant Indian again.

Once, soon after Doc's visit, Jed disappeared again and she found him sitting on the forest floor, gazing up at the canopy of trees overhead with a rapt look on his angelic little face, ears sticking out beneath a wild mop of brown hair. He gurgled delightedly when he saw Mary and pointed upward, as if to show her something. She looked up and, for the fleetest of moments, she saw a bright all-embracing intense light that was hazed at the edges with golden brilliance. It flooded down on them and her entire being was suddenly filled with an incredible feeling of intense joy and ecstasy. She felt a love so intense, so powerful, it was almost as if it could squash the earth flat. Simultaneously, she felt such a heightened awareness, such *knowingness,* it was as if she understood the workings and mysteries of the entire universe. The beauty and glory of the entire firmament and all of creation were revealed to her. Then she blinked and it was gone. *A blissful moment that had lasted an eternity!*

She stared up in open-mouthed amazement at the rustling Indian summer leaves of green and gold and could see nothing out of the ordinary. She must surely have imagined it! But her skin was tingling, there was a weak, fluttery feeling in her stomach and she was trembling all over. She looked down at her child who lifted his head to gaze up at her. She felt herself drawn into the depths of his brilliant blue eyes. She felt as if she was drowning in them, as if she could see right down to the very depths of his soul. She had the overwhelming feeling that despite the fact that he was just a toddler and had not yet uttered a single word, he was so much older than her, and infinitely wiser. She was thoroughly disconcerted by this certainty, this powerful revelation.

"Forsooth, Jed, you are naughty to go off like this all on yer own!" she scolded with a severity she seldom used on him, for he was an extremely sensitive child who hated raised voices. She was instantly ashamed of these harsh words coming so soon after experiencing something so extraordinarily beautiful and profound. Suddenly, decidedly spooked, she swooped him up onto her hip and ran through the forest on fearful, fleet, bare feet. *What did it all mean?*

For a long time after that Mary couldn't sleep at night for thinking about what had happened that day. It had been such a strange and thrilling and uplifting experience; it was as if time had stood still for a moment and she and Jed had received some sort of divine benediction. It was as if God had revealed Himself to her and her son. If so, He was not a robed king in the heavens as she had been taught, but everywhere, in everything! It seemed the only explanation! But why did He choose to show Himself to her and her blessed son?

After that brief moment of pure rapture and powerful revelation, she and little Jed communed silently together at a level she did not understand. Indeed, Jed, calm and beatific as a monk, pure and innocent as new-fallen snow, seemed to exist on a much deeper level than all those around him. Whenever she took him into the forest, leading him, toddling, by the hand, he would point things out to her. He would croon and smile a smile of the angels and his little face would light up, so that she would feel herself go weak-kneed and melting with love for him – a love so deep and profound that it scared her. Somehow, she seemed to understand more about these things of Nature that he brought to her attention than she did before, something deep and intuitive and subliminal – *he* was the teacher, the wise one always, the wisdom he exuded, needless of words, all-encompassing, ageless.

The first day she had entered the forest, she had not seen any animals, now she knew they were everywhere. A red-tailed fox, usually so coy, would stand still and unafraid at their approach. A bobcat, with its reddish-brown fur, dark spots, tufted ears and short tail, would watch from a rocky ledge, without stirring. Shy deer would not dart away at their presence, birds did not fly up at their passing. It seemed that wherever he walked, there was peace and calmness and quiet inner joy.

She had spent a lifetime exploring mountain forests, yet seeing them through her small son's infinitely knowing eyes somehow enriched everything, as if she were seeing them for the very first time. As if she had been blind before! Colors on birds and wildflowers would take on a new dimension: a red-back salamander would seem almost luminous, wood lilies were like brilliant glowing splashes of red paint, fern and forest would pulsate with green lights of different hues. Her awareness would expand so that she seemed to perceive that there was a connectedness between everything.

She would experience her most intensely religious moments at these times, for she knew without question now that God was everywhere, in everything, and this sure intuitive knowledge brought with it a joy that was boundless. It would expand in her chest to such an extent that she felt it would burst. She would be so thankful that she would kneel beside little Jed and press her lips to his forehead, silently thanking God that she had been blessed with this special child that she felt such a strong spiritual connection to, in addition to the natural bond of a mother to her only child.

And so the daily jaunts into the forest had become as important and necessary to her as they were for Jed. They became a deep-seated need in her, a restorative for her craving soul, so compelling and intense that she lived for them and she knew that without them, she would feel like a drowning person gasping for air.

* * *

This particular day was no different. She and Jed were silently marveling at a glade of glowing lavender geraniums beneath a clump of ancient oaks, when they appeared out of nowhere – two strange, bony, mountain crackers, with long, matted, black hair and beards and piercing coal-black eyes, who looked far wilder than even the most ferocious-looking Bucko. They were carrying double-barreled shotguns. They brought with them such a feeling of foreboding and darkness, it was as if the sun had been suddenly obliterated by a black cloud.

Mary felt an immediate presentiment of extreme danger. It washed over her in sickly waves, leaving a knot of raw fear in the pit of her stomach. In addition to the shotguns, they each had an Owl's Head pistol and a large hunting knife hooked onto their belts. One wore a slouch hat, while the other wore the hat of a Confederate soldier pulled low over his eyes. Mary knew it was a Confederate hat because it was the same type that Duke Colby always wore at the store. They were dressed in blue denim dungarees and were barefoot, their feet big and splayed and stained with the tannin of chestnuts. She had smelled the unsavory-looking pair before she saw them. They exuded a powerful stench of stale sweat and, to her dismay, Mary could also detect the unmistakable smell of moonshine on them. *Men who were drunk could seldom be reasoned with!*

To her knowledge, besides those long-dead Indians buried in the mound, no human, other than Zachary Thomas, had ever traversed this tableland forest, and no sane person dared to set foot on Claw Mountain. *Except the Galtreys!* Only the Galtreys had dared invade Bucko territory in the past! She gave a little involuntary cry when she realized who they must surely be. Now they had gone even further and scaled the great granite heights of Eagle Spur! Her heart lurched and her hand tightened on little Jed's.

The little boy immediately started crying – unusual for him, for he seldom cried – as if he too acutely sensed the danger they were in. How on earth did this hoary pair escape detection all the way up here? The last raid between the two feuding clans had been the massacres, before Jed was born.

Had Buchanan vigilance lapsed into complacency after such a long time? Did they imagine their age-old enemies had at last been vanquished once and for all? Mary's eyes feverishly searched the skies. Why had the eagles not warned her of their presence? Though great numbers of them wheeled the sky on air currents, with huge widespread wings, they were watchful, but silent. If only they would attack these two like they had Zachary Thomas and Obediah and countless others in the past, chasing them away from these sacred burial grounds they appeared to guard.

Mary was terrified, more for her child than for herself, though she'd heard terrible stories about what had been done to Buchanan women by the Galtreys in the past, probably in retaliation for similar atrocities committed on Galtrey women by the Buckos.

She had never felt more vulnerable and afraid, except when she had been at the mercy of Eli while trying to escape from the mountain. Had her family been right, after all, when they had said she should not expose little Jed to the dangers of raising him on Claw Mountain? She had felt so safe here on Eagle Spur, she had never dreamt her son could be endangered while they lived here. But right before her was the proof that he was. That she, herself, was.

One of the men gave her a leering grin, exposing rotten and missing teeth, his black eyes glittering with manic lust. "At last, a Bucko bitch all on her own. And a boy too. Not as old as our Jamie, but he'll do."

Mary heard the words with palpating terror and instant realization. They wanted to avenge their murdered brother, Jamie, by murdering little innocent Jed. *Oh God, no!* She found her whole body shuddering with the force of her feelings. "No, you cain't mean that. Don't you dare touch him!"

"Who's gonna stop us, huh? That spouse of your'n be down th' Wilderness, a long, long ways from here. Reckon he's surely gonna be mighty surpris'd to git home an' find th' two of you with your throats a'slitted, jest th' way Eli slitted th' throat of our baby brother, and two of our other brothers," snarled the second cracker, his voice harsh, his black eyes fierce, the hate emanating from him so powerful and raw that it burst upon Mary like a summer thunderstorm, leaving her weak and trembling.

She couldn't talk, couldn't breathe, terrified out of her mind. *They mustn't touch Jed!* Desecrate this holy forest with the blood of her and her child! She had to stall for time, to gather her wits and think of some way to escape their sordid vengeance. She had to get them to take them back to the cabin. Back there, she might find something with which to defend herself and Jed, since a desperate glance around her had soon told her that there was nothing here in the glade within close range. No handy branch or stick. Not that they would of any use against those weapons. Also, if she got them to take her and Jed back there, Zachary Thomas might return early and stop this madness. Otherwise, he would never be able to save them for he no longer ventured into the forest of the tableland, having been scared off by the guardian eagles of Eagle Spur years ago.

"Zack won't thunk of lookin' here," Mary cried. "He never comes here. If'n ye're goin' to do it so's he'll know about it, you best do it back at th' cabin."

"Oh, he will come here soon enough when he finds you gone. Heer'd Zack boy got hisself a real mean search goin' fer that precious paw o' his." the first cracker sniggered.

Mary lifted her head and stared at the two crackers, who were grinning and watching carefully for her reaction. "What do you know about that?" she asked warily.

"Oh, more then you know, wimmin. More than you know," replied the one with the slouch hat, cryptically.

So that was it! The *Galtreys* had been responsible for the mysterious disappearance of Obediah. It hadn't been Emma, after all. Oh, how could she have believed Emma capable of murdering her own grandpaw? The Galtreys must have kidnapped him from the cabin and taken him back to Buck Knob Mountain with them. It wouldn't have been that hard now that she came to think of it. Obediah had often been left alone at the homestead. They'd probably crept up in the dead of night.

Why hadn't she or the Buchanans thought of the Galtreys? Or had the clan, after all? Perhaps they'd been so glad to get rid of the dastardly old despot that they just didn't *care* enough to seek revenge. God knows what the other clan must have thought up to punish Obediah. *What tortures!* All she knew was he would never have come out of it alive. After all, he was the one who had started this long-running and vicious feud in the first place. But the Galtrey's bloodlust had not been sated with the life of Obediah, now they wanted even more folk to die. And what a coup this would be. *The wife and child of the eldest Bucko!*

"Please!" she begged. "We ain't do you no harm! Please leave us be!"

"Jamie ain't done them Bucko animals no harm neither, but that sure ain't stopped 'em none!" snarled the one with the Confederate hat.

"Don't sink to thar level then! Don't let them make you into animals, too."

They looked appalled by her logic and stared at her with wild uncomprehending eyes. The one with the Confederate hat on shook his head. "Ye're crazy, wimmin! Reckon they'll be well rid of you."

"What . . . what are yer names?"

"What you wanna know fer?" the same one asked suspiciously. Then his face cleared. "Aw, I git it. Want to know th' names of yer killers a'fore you and yer boy die, huh?"

Mary felt an icy ripple scale her spine. She had been right about their intentions! They couldn't make it any plainer than that.

"No," she said quietly, with more control than she felt. "I want t'know th' names of young Jamie's brothers."

They stared at her accusingly before the one in the Confederate hat muttered, "Reckon ye're entitled to know th' name of them you've wronged. I'm Sloane Galtrey an' he's m'brother, Quaid."

Mary took a deep nervous breath. At least she'd got them talking. She had to make them see reason. "Listen, I kin understand how you must have felt when Jamie was murdered like that. It were a wicked thung. I prayed fer him, I truly did. I know you must have loved him to want to do this, but it's wrong. Killin' an innocent child were wrong then and it's wrong now!"

"So what? We ain't gonna let th' Buckos git away with what they done to Jamie!" snarled Sloane.

"They *won't* git away with it," she blurted.

"What you mean?" Quaid said darkly.

"I mean th' wicked *will* be punished. They will have to answer fer their evil deeds."

"To who?"

"To God!"

"Who tole you that?"

"Th' Bible!"

"Well, I heer'd of this here person called God a'fore, but I ain't never met him m'self!"

"That's 'cuz you don't go to church," she said imploringly.

"*Church!*" said Quaid mockingly. "Don't need no church!"

"Well, less'n you go, you ain't never gonna git to know God." Even as she said it, she realized how ridiculous that must sound to the two Galtreys when the nearest church was twenty miles away and they would definitely not think kindly of attending the brush arbor services on Claw Mountain.

"Reckon I kin live without him," Quaid decided. "How's 'bout you, Sloane?"

"Sure kin."

They were both grinning idiotically and, suddenly, Mary knew they had been stringing her along, lulling her into a sense of false security. Leaning their shotguns against a tree trunk and removing the knives from their belts, they leered at her. Mary glanced anxiously down at Jed beside her, holding trustingly onto her hand. The little boy had stopped crying and was staring up at the two mangy men with brilliant blue eyes in a mud-colored face that was frowning earnestly. It seemed to her that with that uncanny intuition he seemed to possess, he knew something bad was about to happen, yet he faced them with a placid bravery, though his eyes seemed suddenly, incalculably sad. She couldn't bear to have this tender, sensitive soul – *her sweet baby!* – murdered brutally before her very eyes. She stepped in front of him even knowing that her body would not protect him from what was coming.

"You cain't do this," she said, with quiet dignity.

"Oh yes, we kin, an' we will! Now, step out of th' way," sneered Sloane.

"I won't. Listen, thar *is* another way."

The two men advancing menacingly on her, slowed. "What y'mean?"

380

"I mean, you got plenty power right now without havin' to do this terrible thung that will taint yer souls ferever."

"How come?" asked Quaid testily.

"You got th' power to forgive and brung an end to it all."

"*Forgive!*" Sloane spat on the ground. "I'd rather die m'self than forgive them Buckos fer all they done to young Jamie."

"Well, vengeance has got th' power over you. An' vengeance don't feel too good now, does it?"

"Oh, it feels jest fine to me," snorted Quaid. "Now out th' way, bitch!"

"Hey, what's *yer* name? Reckon I'd like to say it as I'm slittin' y'throat!" said Sloane, his mouth twisted with loathing.

Mary swallowed hard, trying not to appear as terrified and intimidated as she felt. "I'm Mary Louella Harley Buchanan, wife of Zachary Thomas, and this young'un here is our son, Jed."

"Well, I got to admit, ye're a strange 'un," said Sloane.

"You ever kill a young'un a'fore, Sloane?"

Sloane raised guarded eyes of black glowing coals and stared at her without answering. Something told her that for all his bravado, he didn't relish what lay ahead. She had to play on that. "You think slayin' this precious innocent is gonna bring yer Jamie back, or give you peaceful sleep at night?" Sloane's thin mouth twisted further, but still he didn't talk. Mary couldn't believe it. They had stopped their advance and were actually listening to her. "You kill my son and you'll never sleep thru' another night agin yer whole lives. He's jest a baby! You will see his lamb's blood and his innocent blue eyes in yer mind fer th' rest of yer born days. *Don't do it!* Walk away and end it all, here and now. *Today!* I'll tell my husband what you done and I swar no Buchanan will ever touch a hair on a Galtrey head ever agin."

"Yeah, like you got th' power to stop *Eli!*" sneered Quaid, shaking his head in disgust.

"Maybe I don't, but Zack sure does. Eli respects Zack fer sure."

"Yeah, he respects Zack so much, Zack's done got him to stop pullin' yer brush arbors down," Quaid said sarcastically, spitting on the ground.

Was nothing a secret in these infernal mountains? Just when she had felt she was starting to reach them! She raised a determined chin, her eyes blazing her passion. "Don't you two become part of th' eternally damned," she said urgently, even as she realized with a deep, newfound certainty that there were none who were *eternally* damned, no matter how craven or depraved. "I don't thunk either one of you wants to do it, deep-down."

Then was a moment of silence that seemed to stretch forever and she felt a glimmer of hope. Then Sloane loudly cursed her, lunged towards her, throwing her roughly aside onto the ground, leaving Jed standing small and lonely and exposed. He lifted the child easily by the front of his dungarees and held him dangling with one hand, while with the other, he held his big knife across Jed's tender throat. "This here one is fer Jamie!" he snarled.

From the ground and the very depths of her soul, Mary screamed hysterically, "GIT AWAY FROM HIM! DON'T DO IT! Oh, please! Git away from him, you hear me? I beg you, *please!"*

She raised herself off the ground with what seemed like nightmare slowness, intent only on getting to her precious baby in time. *Oh, God! Oh, please, don't let my baby die!* But it was like running in a dream. She knew she wouldn't get near him in time to stop Sloane from slitting Jed's throat.

"LEAVE HIM ALONE!" she screeched with all the anguish in her soul, even as Sloane made to slash the throat of her innocent child, her blessed Child of Light.

Suddenly a loud, snarling voice rang out across the glade. "UNHAND TH' YOUNG'UN A'FORE I BLOW YOU CLEAN IN HALF . . . !"

50

*E*mma! Mary had never been more relieved to see the tough young tomboy in her life! She felt a flaring of hope. The surly slit-eyed thirteen-year-old slip of a girl had grown several inches taller since Mary first met her, but was hardly any pounds heavier. Now she stood barefoot, skinny and insubstantial and deceptively frail-looking, in her loose dungarees and white vest, her long droopy fair hair covering one pale-blue eye, her face brown and freckled, while aiming her sawn-off double-barreled shotgun at Sloane. There was a look of fierceness about the girl that even the two Galtrey crackers could not mistake when they wheeled in surprise at her scathing command.

Sloane slowly removed the knife from Jed's throat. When he'd recovered his wits, he made to put it back, but Emma fired a slug-shot at him with her double-barreled shotgun. There was a deafening roar that split through the glade like a cannon shot. The bullet hit his shoulder, shattering the bone and spraying blood everywhere. The impact spun him around, making him drop Jed, who fell to the ground in a surprised heap. Sloane screamed in agony, clutching at his shattered shoulder with one hand that quickly became blood-drenched. The knife fell on the ground with a gentle thud. Mary ran and grabbed Jed, dragging him away then holding him protectively behind her. During the whole horrifying ordeal, the solemn little boy had made not a sound. Quaid made for the Owl's Head pistol in his belt, but Emma fired into the ground just in front of him. There was an explosion of dirt, grass and leaves. He stopped dead.

"Now shet all yer weapons on th' ground whar I kin see 'em!" Emma demanded. Within seconds she had reloaded the weapon with two more slug bullets.

When the two were too slow to respond to her bidding, she fired another shot at their feet, making the earth explode in a shower of debris once more. Sloane was still howling with excruciating pain and was covered in blood by now. The hoary pair of crackers stared at Emma with wild, terrified eyes, before Quaid quickly dropped his knife and they both reluctantly started unbuckling their belts, Sloane sobbing with pain, awkwardly using the hand of his good arm, both letting their pistols drop to the ground.

"Now I'm gonna kill you both," Emma announced coldly. "You kilt my Unc' Samuel and my Unc' Alvin. And now you jest tried to kill *little Jed!* Reckon it'll delight me to git you both fer that."

Mary heard the words in alarm. She did not doubt that Emma meant it even though she now had the situation well in hand, and her life and that of Jed, were no longer in jeopardy. She suddenly realized that the girl had a presence that was almost as chilling as Eli's when aroused. Even a fool could tell she was more than capable of cold-blooded murder in the name of revenge. But was there any wonder when she had grown up in such a cauldron of violence?

Emma was about to fire her shotgun when Mary cried, "NO, EMMA, NO! No more killin', you hear me? *You want to spend an eternity in hell?"*

Emma turned slolwly on her, with a scowling face. She gave Mary a funny little smirk, her pale-blue eyes blazing a white-hot hatred for her captives that was long entrenched in this clan. Mary felt fear clutch at her throat. The girl was going to do it without a single qualm, despite her words.

"Maybe it'd jest be worth it," Emma spat the words out, "to put these two pieces of shit whar they b'long!"

Mary felt a spurt of desperation, almost as strong as earlier when facing the same ignorance from the Galtrey brothers. But she couldn't allow Emma, her young friend and confidante, to become a *murderer!*

She said urgently, "No! No, Emma! I won't let you do it! Now, please, remember th' Ten Commandments I learn'd you? The very first one is: *Thou shalt not kill!"*

Emma shot her an indignant look. "But they were tryin' to murder you an' little Jed! H'com you want me to let 'em off?"

"Because Jesus said, 'Turn th' other cheek', remember? Now, you've bin saved an' promised to serve him. You sure cain't do it this way. Don't you go puttin' yer own soul in eternal jeopardy fer th' sake of revenge!"

But Mary's plea to her conscience fell on deaf ears for Emma rose up in disgust. "Oh yes, I kin. They kilt my two uncles and nearly kilt Jed jest now. Th' Bible says 'an eye fer an eye an' a tooth fer a tooth' jest like Reverend Hubbly preached it."

Oh, drat the Bible with its contradictory messages! All Mary knew was what *Jesus* preached held the true merit. She wondered how she could reach the girl, penetrate all that searing hatred. "Emma, these two here are young Jamie's older brothers, Sloane and Quaid. Them were out to avenge his murder by th' Buchanans, today. Now, you were friends with that young boy. You know full well how he died. You thunk he'd like you to do this to his *brothers?* Whar's th' justice in that? And if'n it's an eye fer an eye you be wantin' then I reckon them Galtreys got a ways to go a'fore they git even with you Buchanan lot."

Mary could see that Emma was beginning to waver as her words sank in. She removed her one eye from the shotgun sight and looked at her with slit eyes, her face crumpled in thoughtful frowning.

"Well," she said grumpily, after giving the matter due consideration, during which time Mary's heart was in her mouth, "what would you have me do with this here scum then?"

"Escort them off th' mountain," said Mary hastily, bludgeoned with relief. "And for mercy's sake, girl, make sure that nobody sees you do it."

Just then, to Mary's considerable alarm, she heard Zachary Thomas's loud bellow and a distant crashing through the undergrowth. He must have heard the three shots and was coming to investigate. Since nobody hunted up here, he must have realized something was wrong. A short while ago, she would have done anything to have him here but, right now, if she didn't get these Galtreys off the tableland, Zachary Thomas would probably kill them, especially if he knew they had planned on killing his wife and son! Mary didn't want any killing whatsoever, especially here in this beautiful sacred forest.

"Quick, Emma, do as I say! You know your uncle will kill 'em both sure as eggs are eggs. Or worse, he'll hand them over to Eli to deal with and we both know what that will mean! He's th' last person you would want to git hold of them!" The two Galtreys clearly knew what that would mean too. They well knew by now of Eli's penchant for evil for their eyes flared with fright at the mention of his name! Mary reiterated, "Now, thar's to be no more killin' on this here mountain! Quick, girl, *go!* A'fore yer Uncle Zack gits here."

Emma began herding the two panicked men in front of her, Sloane weeping and whimpering with pain. Unarmed and in the heart of Buchanan territory, with the specter of Zachary Thomas and Eli looming over them, they had good reason to be. As they went past, Mary addressed the injured man in a low urgent voice. "Sloane, be sure to stop th' bleedin' by tyin' a handkerchief of a piece of yer shirt around th' top of yer arm, soon as yer're off th' mountain, else ye'll bleed to death. Then when you git back to yer mountain, pour kerosene on th' wound an' bandage it up to stop infection. If'n that don't work git some resin from a pine tree and spread it over th' wound, and bandage it up. That also helps stop infection," she said, remember Zachary Thomas's treatment of young Jamie. Then she turned and grabbed Emma's arm. "Emma, you cain't tell yer uncle what happened here today. *Promise* me that you won't ever tell him. It'll start thungs up all over agin, mebbe even worse than a'fore!"

Emma gave her a dark angry look. "How kin you worry about *him*," she snarled, "when he near slitted Jed's throat? I don't git it."

"But he didn't, Emma, he *didn't!* Turn th' other cheek, remember? Return hate with love. Jesus said, 'Love thine enemies'. *Now promise me, Emma!*"

Emma reluctantly rolled her eyes and muttered sourly, "I promise."

"Go now! I'll stay and hide th' weapons. I'll tell your Uncle Zack you were doin' target practice. He cain't ever know th' truth. He an' th' rest of th' bunch hate th' Galtreys so much, he'll want revenge fer sure, then more lives will be lost. I cain't let that happen . . .!"

* * *

After that terrifying incident, Mary could not take Jed into the forest without feeling vulnerable and terribly afraid. She had come so close to losing her precious son, to say nothing of her own life, that visits to the forest that were once memorable occasions of pure joy, had a nightmarish quality about them. Besides the fact that the forest had returned to its former comparative dullness, with the violent invasion and her fear, she was on her guard the entire time, and every sound in the forest, no matter how slight, made her jumpy and anxious. Unable to relax her vigilance even for a moment, the visits had ceased to be the rewarding spiritual pleasure they had once been. The two Galtrey brothers had violated her sanctuary and effectively destroyed her spiritual insight and her peace.

Even in the thick of the Galtrey reign of terror, she had never felt afraid of them or in imminent danger from them. After all, Eagle Spur was a virtual stronghold. It took a lot of effort to get up here and was largely inaccessible, especially to newcomers who would find it difficult to find their way through the maze of rocks. Furthermore, it meant passing several Bucko lookouts. It came to her that immediately after the massacre Zachary Thomas had not ventured far from home. She had thought at the time that it was because he had suspected her plans to escape, but now she realized that it had been to protect her and his unborn child from the enormous threat posed by a wounded Galtrey clan! They had promised a massive revenge attack that had never materialized. Instead, thwarted by "The Big Freeze", they had bided their time to avenge the murders of young Jamie Galtrey and those killed in the resultant massacre. Using stealth and guile, as well as patience, they had very nearly succeeded in wreaking terrible revenge on the eldest Bucko of the clan.

Thankfully, tragedy had been narrowly averted this time, but Galtrey memories were as long as those in the Buchanan clan! Just because they had been thwarted this time, did not mean that they would not try again now that they knew the way up. Just the thought of their vulnerability on Eagle Spur made life almost unbearable for Mary. She relived every minute of the terrifying ordeal over and over again in her mind, and she had nightmares about it at night. She felt insecure and vulnerable every time Zachary Thomas left to go tracking or hunting, especially at night. She knew her husband was very worried about her, but she couldn't confide in him. Little Jed felt the tension in her too. Holding her hand in the forest, he would gaze at her with brilliant blue eyes that were puzzled and perturbed. Though she was convinced that God sent special protection for her and her little boy in the form of Emma and Zachary Thomas that awful day – and she had spent many hours on her knees giving thanks for that ever since – she was desperately afraid that the time would come that evil would triumph once more.

She cursed this terrible feud. It had effectively destroyed her happiness and that of her family, to say nothing of the very real physical dangers it presented. Oh, the senseless loss of life and limb, the human suffering caused by a few felled trees three decades ago and a vain man's wounded pride. Though embittered by his stay in jail, in truth Obediah *had* done wrong and had rightly paid the price of that wrong-doing, as had so many other mountain folk who had resorted to stealing timber that did not belong to them. Why, when he'd been guilty of the crime, had he not accepted his punishment like a man, like he had always expected his sons to do, even when that punishment was totally *undeserved* in many cases? What right had he to cause such wicked strife in its wake? There had to be *something* she could do . . .

51

Mary felt an ache in her buttocks from it constantly thudding against the saddle beneath her. She felt as if she had been on the pesky mule for hours, but in fact, it wasn't that long. Leaving Jed in the care of Emma, she had saddled up one of Obediah's old mules and snuck it out of the barn at his old homestead at Horseshoe Hollow. She needed to take one of the mules since it would take too long on foot and she didn't want to be missed. She had even been forced to tell

Emma a white lie else the child would never have allowed her to go. She led the mule carefully down the mountain by the reins and was relieved not to bump into any of the Buckos, glad right now that their vigilance towards the Galtreys had waned somewhat of late.

She mounted easily in the foothills for she was wearing proper riding apparel. She had on Hedina's calf-length, black, pleated riding skirt, with its deceptive sewn-up slit between the legs. Mary had also chosen Hedina's white satin blouse with a lace collar, long muttonchop sleeves and pearl buttons down the front and at the cuffs to go with it. She had let her long hair down so that it swept almost to her waist in a thick shiny black curtain and made sure she was clean and well-groomed. Though she felt ridiculously overdressed for the all-important mission that lay ahead and the outfit was not at all suitable for a hot and muggy day like today, it was important to her that she looked her best. Somehow, she felt God would approve. However, Hedina must have worn this handsome-looking outfit to ride fine thoroughbred horses, not a miserable critter like this, Mary thought peevishly, as she jogged up and down on the mule's back!

She rode along the old stock trail that went towards Buck Knob Mountain. Due to her experience with old Sarah back at her parent's homesite on Lewis Mountain, she knew mules to be ornery – and this one definitely succumbed to the mold! After setting out well enough, he had suddenly stopped dead for no reason at all and refused to budge another step. She slipped off his back and tried to pull him forward by the reins, to no avail. Then, more as an experiment than anything else, she climbed back on his stubborn back and made as if to turn him around to go back home, pulling the reins in a wide circle and kicking his haunches. Fooled and contrary, the evil-tempered creature then moved forward, at such great pace, that she had been bouncing up and down on the saddle like a mad jack-in-the-box ever since!

Feeling thoroughly winded and trying hard to concentrate on just staying on the saddle, she nevertheless crossed the shallow waters of Devil's Creek with great trepidation, staring up at the huge overhang of granite and earth that joined the two mountains over a tunnel and deep gorge, feeling wholly intimidated. *No man's land!* She remembered Emma telling her how Johnny's first wife had been beaten, ravished and left for dead at this very place where young Jamie Galtrey had been so callously murdered. And it was here that Alvin and Samuel Buchanan had been ambushed and murdered in retaliation. It was here too, that the four Galtreys had been murdered in retaliation for that insane act! – *Devil's Creek!* - so aptly named! For it was a place where evil reigned. Malevolence hung in the air, thick as molasses. Even the mule seemed to sense the encroaching danger for he timidly slowed to a walk at last. In lonely, inadequate protection against a clan who knew no honor, Mary now held up in her left hand a stick with one of Hedina's dainty white handkerchiefs attached to the top of it, which she'd kept flat against the saddle up till now.

For once Mary was not concerned with the breathtaking view of the valley, the river and the great wilderness unfolding below and ahead of her. All her attention was drawn towards Buck Knob which rose up on her left. Despite the fact that it wasn't as high as Claw Mountain, it was still a daunting sight, steep and formidable. Her courage almost failed her. She closed her eyes briefly. *I lift up mine eyes unto th' hills from whence cometh my help. Protect me, oh, Father! Help me in this important mission, which I undertake in Thy holy name!*

Feeling an ominous mood in the air, she traveled warily along the stock trail until she at last came to a narrow footpath that ascended the mountain at a sloping angle. She urged the mule up the pathway with her hard, bare feet, and he thankfully obliged, seeming almost as chastened by the atmosphere as was she. It was only mid-morning, but already the summer heat was searing, the air heavy and laden with myriad sweet perfumes. Trickles of sweat slid down her face. She had no idea where to find Dean Galtrey's homestead and, as she followed the narrow path upwards, between towering trees and huge rocks, she felt hot, fetid fear invade her being. She was now well into enemy territory and was feeling acutely vulnerable and exposed. She wondered why she had not yet encountered a single human being. *No sign of life anywhere!* Just the same, she felt as if umpteen pairs of eyes were watching her every move. It was unnerving!

The first homesite she came to was little more than a shanty with a bark-shingled roof on it. She had no sooner veered off the path to start approaching it, when, to her alarm, she suddenly found herself surrounded by a dozen scrawny hags with thick matted hair and bare feet, dressed in thin cotton ankle-length dresses, with aprons over them. Some wore little cotton frilly caps on their heads and others, kerchiefs. Several of the older ones were smoking long clay pipes. Mary felt a surge of panic for they were as wild a looking bunch as she had ever seen in her whole life. Where they had appeared from she couldn't be sure. It was as if they had been lying in wait for her. Yet how had they been alerted of her presence so soon? She had heard no tell-tale signal shots though she had carefully listened for them. One of the hags hung onto the reins to stop her pressing forward.

"Who are ye?" one black-haired creature demanded to know.

Mary swallowed hard, praying silently for courage and strength before lifting her chin and saying clearly, "Mary Louella Harley Buchanan."

The words rang to a stunned, accusatory silence. Then a thin crone with dark hair snarled, "*A Bucko wench!*"

"Ye're a stupid bitch if'n ye thunk that thar weeny white flag's gonna save ye!" yelled another of them angrily. She was a spiteful-looking wench, mature and rather buxon in appearance compared to the others, who were all mountain-thin. A Galtrey by birth, if ever there was one, she had the same coal-black eyes and thick matted black hair as Sloane and Quaid!

Before Mary could form a suitable response, a dozen hands roughly grabbed her and dragged her off the mule. She fell heavily onto the ground on her back with a wounded cry. They proceeded to spit on her, before a barrage of flying heels plowed into her prostrate body from all angles. Mary didn't know what was worse! The pain or the humiliation! The vicious kicking of well-worn mountain-hardened feet seemed never to stop! One well-aimed heel booted her right ear causing a loud ringing noise and a great explosion of pain inside her head.

"I COME IN PEACE!" she cried. *"Please leave me alone."*

It earned her a fierce, bruising, rebuking kick in the ribs, and the response, "A Buchanan cain't come in peace! Them don't know th' meaning of th' word!"

"Please . . . take me to Dean Galtrey!" she begged urgently.

"What fer, you fancy prissy miss!"

Another swift blow to her ribs thoroughly winded Mary. One hag grabbed at her blouse now smudged all over with dirt and ripped one sleeve clean off from the bodice. The kicks continued, fiendish, hard and punishing. Somehow, Mary had never expected such foul treatment from the women. The men, maybe, but not the women! Duke Colby at the store had once told her that as blood-thirsty as the Indians had been, it had been their women who were the cruelest, and white women captured by the braves had always been given a torrid time by them. Mary fancied the squaws he had been referring to couldn't have been far different from these vicious Galtrey women. As more heels hit her, pain reverberated through her from a dozen different angles. Were they intent on kicking her to death? The very idea sent a fresh thrall of fear running through her. *She must not fail in her mission!*

"I need . . . I need to talk to Dean Galtrey," she gasped. "I've got to make a . . .a . . . deal with him!"

To Mary's amazement, the kicks slowed then stopped as curiosity got the better of them. A circle of hate-twisted female faces stared down at her.

"A *deal*?" repeated the one standing at her feet, a fiercely wrinkled crone with graying red hair. "What sort o' deal?"

"That is for him to hear. But I assure you it will benefit th' whole mountain."

"Oh yeah, sez who?"

"Sez me! Now will you please take me to see him?"

After considering her words for a few moments, the woman reached down a hand and helped Mary to shakily stand up. Mary glanced around at the crones surrounding her. The Bucko women had seemed drunken and loud-mouthed hags when she had first met them, but not nearly as threatening as this fiercely scowling bunch. The one with the graying red hair nodded shortly. "I'll take you. But ye'll got to leave th' mule here. It's too steep."

"Thank you. What's yer name?"

"Gussie Galtrey, wife of Jeremiah that got hisself killed by th' Buckos in th' massacre more'n two years ago!" she said meaningfully.

Her words chilled Mary to the bone. "I'm so sorry. It's one of th' thungs I came to tell yer father-in-law! It should never have happened."

"What are you sorry fer?"

"I'm married to Zachary Thomas, so I'm a Buchanan, too. Guess that makes me guilty same as them."

There was an angry murmuring among the women. It sounded like a swarm of disturbed bees and about as ominous.

"Did you take part in them killin's?" Gussie demanded to know.

"Of course not!"

'C'mon then, let's git this over with." Gussie grabbed Mary by the upper arm and dragged her up the mountain path limping and stumbling, after her. Mary's whole body was throbbing violently with pain. Gussie's fingers dug into her arm like a vice. The rest of the women trailed after them in a single line along the path.

"Ye're a real foolish 'un!" Gussie informed her. "Ain't too many would a'dared come up here, let alone all alone an' unarmed."

"Guess it was worth th' risk to me."

"Yeah?"

Mary nodded. That silenced the older mountain woman. Despite her heavily wrinkled face, she, nevertheless, seemed younger than Mary had suspected at first. Mary sensed it was a result of a hard life! She had experienced how difficult being married to a Buchanan man was like before Zachary Thomas changed. What must it have been like for her being married to a Galtrey? Not much different, she surmised. It surprised Mary to realize that despite their appalling behavior towards her, she did not smell moonshine on any of the women. Perhaps the Galtrey women did not indulge in the stuff to the same extent that the women of the Buchanan clan once did, because the patriarch of their clan was not as vicious as Obediah Buchanan? But who knows, maybe he was!

Gussie had a loose cough and kept hawking up great gobs of yellow phlegm and spitting them on the ground.

"You git lots of sickness on th' mountain?" Mary asked Gussie, who was heaving with the effort of climbing.

"Always. Especially th' young'uns."

"'Th' Big Freeze' hit us hard," said Mary, trying to get through to her. "Did y'all git hit hard too?"

Gussie nodded grimly. "Sure did. Reckon it claim'd twenty lives on Buck Knob all told."

Mary tutted her concern at the horrendous number of Galtrey casualties, feeling a small bond was somehow developing between her and the other woman. The Galtreys had had their troubles same as the Buchanans! "How awful for you," she sympathized. "Bad cough you got thar. Have you tried usin' kerosene with a spoonful of sugar?"

"No, I ain't."

"Well, if that don't work, boil some horsehound with wild cherry bark to make a syrup," suggested Mary, remembering the remedies that her husband generally recommended to his ailing kinfolk. "Failin' that, boil up a polecat and use th' grease to git all that nasty phlegm up! My husband, Zack, reckons that kin cure a horse!"

"I'll try it!" Gussie said shortly.

Finally, they arrived at a neatly built cabin in the middle of a tall, cool forest. Expecting Dean Galtrey's homestead to be as rundown as was Obediah's, Mary was pleasantly surprised. The cabin was neatly chinked with mud. The stone chimney was handsomely masoned. There was nothing derelict or broken on the cabin, or on any of a variety of barns in the yard: no broken shingles on any of the roofs, no broken gutters and the porch was well-made and intact, the doors of the barns, hanging right. The yard was clean and orderly. The livestock in the yard, comprising of chickens, ducks and several cats, looked well-fed and content. Two coon dogs lying near the porch, bounded over to greet them and their coats were clean and shiny. Mary couldn't see their ribs when she held out her hand for them to lick. However fierce Dean Galtrey was reported to be, the man had a deal of pride that was for sure! Perhaps Obediah's place had looked like this, once, before moonshine and malice had overtaken him!

Gussie led Mary up the solid porch steps and knocked on the cabin door. The door was opened by a fierce-looking man with a narrow, gaunt, parchment-white face, topped by a thatch of graying black hair, thin, dry lips and a long narrow patrician nose. Piercing black eyes stared at her in bald astonishment as the women crowded around her. He wore a pair of black trousers, a short-sleeved white shirt, braces and a pair of shoes, despite the fact that it was summer and the rest of the clan were barefoot. His arms were thin, flaccid and infirm but, despite his frail appearance, which was so different from the virile, robust appearance of Obediah when Mary had first met him, there was something formidable about him. It shone from his eyes like beams of pure steel and Mary's fear escalated. *This was not a man to trifle with either!*

"Paw, this here is Mary Buchanan, Zack's spouse, an' she's come to make a deal with you," said Gussie, her small black eyes glittering oddly. "He was part of th' group that kilt my Jeremiah!" she reminded him.

Suddenly, the human face Mary had seen briefly on Gussie on the way up, abruptly disappeared. She was just a bitter woman with a mighty big axe to grind!

The man screwed up his eyes angrily. "*A Buchanan has dared to set foot on this here mountain agin?"* he thundered with such vehemence that spittle flew. "Well, fer yer trouble, Missie, you're gonna end up in a ditch someplace whar th' Buckos kin find you."

Gussie looked hard at her father-in-law then surprised Mary by saying, "Why don't you hear her out, Paw! I, fer one, would sure like to hear what she's got to say."

"Please, Mr Galtrey," pleaded Mary. She was aching all over and could hardly stand, but she forced herself to hold herself erect and face him unafraid, even though her heart was pounding wildly inside her chest. "I came here at great risk to m'self to talk to you. Leastways, you owe me that much."

Dean Galtrey, Obediah's old arch-enemy, glared at her with coal-glowing eyes before grunting, "You've got yerself two minutes, an' if'n I don't like what I hear – and I'm bettin' on hit! – I'm gonna hand you over to these here womenfolk to dispose of. Well? Spit it out!"

As the hags crowded closer in on her, badgering her with barging elbows and foul breath, Mary gasped, "I'd like to talk t'you in private, sir."

"Well, you cain't'. I won't have you puttin' no curse on me," snapped Dean, indignantly hitching up his trousers by the braces.

"A curse! I ain't no witch! And what I offer you is th' very opposite!"

Dean glared at her suspiciously. "Beware of strangers bearing gifts," he muttered. "Ye're here to create a di-version, ain't ya?"

Mary shook her head adamantly, "Nobody knows I'm here. I snuck off without nobody seein' me."

"Well," snorted Dean, "Ye're not likely to tell me if'n you were."

"I am not. I come bearing an olive branch."

"What?" exclaimed Dean with a puzzled face, his eyes searching her person, as if he expected she had one hidden someplace.

"It's jest an expression. It means I come in peace."

"Peace! No Buchanan knows th' meanin' of th' word!"

"I beg to differ, sir. *I do!* I've come to seek an end to th' years of bitterness an' hatred an' killin'."

"Naw," Dean shook his head in disgust. "It's gone on fer too long to ever stop."

"No, that ain't true. If'n you want to, you kin stop it today. *Right now!"*

Dean snorted with derision. "Takes two sides to make peace. I'd never trust a Buchanan to make peace, let alone keep peace."

"Well, if'n you agree to it, I'll git th' Buchanans to agree. I know I kin do it. With Obediah gone, my husband is the head of th' clan now. They've changed a lot, Mr Galtrey. Most of 'em have stopped drinkin' and go to church services every month in th' brush arbor. God's what changed them, Mr Galtrey. He kin change you too, if'n you will let Him."

To Mary's shock, she saw Dean Galtrey's face grow red with rage. "Git out of here! *Nuthin'* will change a Buchanan, an' I won't have one preachin' at me. Take her away," he ordered the crowd of women. "Do with her what you will!"

Mary stared at the man in dismay. His face was set in rigid closure, his mouth a thin line downturned at the corners. His mind was so closed not even God could open it. *She had failed in her mission!* It was a signal for the women. Mary was dragged, struggling, from the porch out into the yard.

"What you goin' to do with me?" she asked nervously, quaking with fear as she faced a circle of evil-grinning women with spite and hatred in their eyes. Standing in the centre of this hostile group, she turned around and looked at them pleadingly.

"Oh, we're gonna git you good fer all th' sorrow you Buchanans done brought upon this here clan!" sneered one old crone.

"But I ain't done nuthin' to one of you! What d'you gain by makin' me suffer?"

Gussie Galtrey broke from the circle and came and stood right in front of her. She hawked up a gob of spittle and spat in Mary's face. Mary felt it running down her face and hastily wiped it away with the back of one disgusted hand. How could she think that she had begun to reach this woman whose face was so twisted with hate? "You told me yerself that you are guilty jes' by bein' a Buchanan by marriage so how come ye're squawkin' like a scalded cat now?"

"I meant, the *shame* of it is upon me, too. 'cuz of th' fact that am married to a Buchanan. I am aware that they wronged you and I came to beg yer forgiveness. This feud has carried on far too long. You must know that too. How many more husbands and sons will have to die a'fore it's over?"

"It won't never be over! Yer trouble is you talk too much an' pay too much mind to yer own self!" Gussie said in a vehement undertone. "I'm goin' to enjoy teachin' a Bucko spouse not to try a Galtrey too far."

Do with her what you will! What had Dean Galtrey meant by that? Mary had imagined that she ran the very real risk of being ravished by the *menfolk* by coming up here, but she had never expected something like this. Mary had vivid memories of Duke Colby's salacious tales of angry squaws cutting strips of skin off their victims, of tying their victims to stakes in the desert sun and pouring honey over them so that the ants would eat them alive, of disemboweling them. 'Never git on th' wrong side of an angry wimmin,' he had told her. 'They kin dream up all sorts a nasty things a man would never dream of.' These were white women, yes, but having lived in isolation for so long, they were wild and barbaric and given to cruelty as she had already found to her cost. What new tortures would they dream up for her now? *A Buchanan!*

Mary didn't have to wait long to find out. One of them picked up a jagged, fist-sized rock and forcefully lobbed it at her, a sneer on her thin face. It struck

Mary on the chest, badly hurting her, raising blood, for an angry red blotch appeared on her ruined, dirt-smudged and torn white satin blouse. The next minute all the others started picking up rocks and she realized in a flash what her fate was to be. *They were going to rock her to death!* All these bitter, angry, vengeful women, who had surrounded her in a loose, threatening circle, just like she was some woman of ill-virtue in biblical times!

As soon as she saw what they were about, Mary broke loose, pushing aside one of the women and bolting down the narrow path. There was a howl of outrage and rocks whizzed past, ominously close to her head and all around her, bouncing off other boulders and shattering, or thudding to the ground, reminding her of when she, Emma and Jed had escaped to Eagle Spur after the aborted church service. She felt the same kind of helpless panic now as she had then. One of the rocks found its mark, landing squarely on her back. She winced and threw her shoulders back with the agony of it, even as other rocks began to land on her. How had she imagined that she could somehow reach these people when the hatred ran so deep that they would kill an innocent woman – someone attempting to be a *peacemaker?*

"Ketch her quick, Gussie! She's gittin' away!"

Mary flew down the path again, dodging from side to side, to try to avoid the painful missiles. But next minute, she was pounced on from behind by two of the women, who landed on her back, winding her and grabbing her by the upper arms. She tried desperately to slip out of their iron grasps but they hung onto her with cruel hands, and between them, they dragged her back up to Dean Galtrey's neat yard. Well, he may not have a flogging post, but this sort of punishment was just as barbaric!

"Thought you could escape yer fate, did ya?" sneered Gussie, spitting in her face for the second time. "Well, I got news fer you, bitch!"

Ignoring the drool running down her cheek, Mary raised her chin and faced her attackers as calmly as she could. But she was trembling all over, her heart was pounding and she was badly frightened. These dreadful women were fully intent on killing her! Poor Jed would be without a mother! Zachary Thomas, without a wife! She raised her eyes to the heavens and prayed aloud in a ringing voice that sprang from she knew not where. *"Forgive them, Father, fer they know not what they do! Lord, give me th' courage to die with dignity. Be with Zachary Thomas and Jed and Emma and all the Buchanans. Be with Maw and Paw and Joe and Percy and all my sisters. Be with this here Galtrey family, too. Comfort and protect them all. If I am meant to be Thy sacrifice fer peace then I humbly accept it, oh Lord! I pray that th' Buchanans will not try to avenge my death. Please stop th' killin'. Help them all! Touch th' hearts of th' Buchanans and th' Galtreys and help them to see that thar ain't no future in it. Give me th' courage to face my death with dignity. Amen."*

She lowered her heavenward gaze to find the women staring at her with wide, startled eyes. There was a stunned silence and all Mary could hear in the hot, humid atmosphere was the rasping of a nearby bullfrog.

"What's a'goin' on here?" A male voice broke the spell.

Mary looked up to see the long black beards and matted hair of Sloane and Quaid Galtrey coming up the path and terror flared up inside her anew. Sloane, viewing her from beneath his Confederate's hat, was the one who had spoken and he wasn't likely to feel sympathetic towards her. His shattered arm and shoulder was heavily bandaged and in a makeshift sling.

Gussie found her voice. "It's a Bucko bitch! We're about t'learn her what we do with them lot."

Sloane came up to them and said urgently, *"Let her go."*

Mary felt a flaring of hope.

Gussie turned to her brother and said disgustedly, eyes glinting, "Ain't doin' no sech thung! I got me Jeremiah to account fer."

"I said let her go!" Sloane repeated.

"Sloane, I don't believe you would say sech a crazy thung. You ain't talked 'bout nuthin' but how we got to git back at them Buckos fer slayin' Jamie fer as long as I kin remember. Now them Buckos not only kilt my young nephew, they kilt my husband an' three of my brothers-in-law, so why am I goin' to let this one go?"

"You goin' to do it 'cuz she saved my life. An' Quaid's too."

"She what?" barked Gussie disbelievingly.

"You heer'd me. Even after I held my knife to her young'un's throat an' was about to kill him in revenge fer Jamie, she stopped a Bucko brat from shootin' us both. Th' brat had already shot my shoulder an' disarmed us both an' was aimin' on finishin' us off. Then Zachary Thomas was a'comin' an' she done tole th' brat to git us off th' mountain real quick-like so's he couldn't git his hands on us. Saved us from th' likes of him an' Eli by doin' it! One way or 'nother, we'd a bin dead 'uns fer sure if'n it weren't fer her. Now leave her be!"

"I don't believe it! Is this true, Quaid?"

Quaid, who'd been quiet up till then, nodded. "Sure 'nough is."

Gussie eyes narrowed. "How come a Bucko brat got th' better of you? How old is she?"

Sloane looked somewhat sheepish, and mumbled, "'Bout twelve, thirteen, I reckon."

Mary piped up in his defense. "Young Emma may only be thirteen but she's is a better shot than her Uncle Zack. Nobody with an ounce of sense would argue with that shotgun o'hers! Reckon they done th' only thung they could do in th' circumstances."

"Quiet, bitch! Weren't talkin' to you!" Gussie gave Mary a stinging slap across the face and addressed Sloane again, "Well, you an' Quaid may have bin saved by her, but all them others weren't. Paw said we kin git us our revenge on her an' I'm aimin' to do jest that!"

"OH NO, YOU WON'T!" a voice rang out across the yard. Everyone turned to stare at Dean Galtrey, who was still standing out on the porch. There was a stunned silence before he called, "Come here, girl!"

Mary pointed to herself. *"Me?"* she croaked weakly.

"Yeah, you, Mary Buchanan! Come here!"

Women broke away from the circle to let her through. She went up to the porch and stood in front of where he was standing, looking up at him, her face glowing hotly with the sting of Gussie's blow. She was shivering with fear. Was he going to let her go or add to her miseries?

"What you want with me, Mr Galtrey?" she asked meekly.

"I want to know if what Sloane said jest now is true. Did you save th' lives of my two sons?"

"Yes, sir, I surely did, Mr Galtrey."

"What fer?"

"I don't want no more killin' on th' mountain and I want th' feud to come to an end to make it safe fer my son an' all th' other young'uns of both clans."

"Why would you want to do that, girl?"

"Because it is destroyin' all of our lives, all our *peace!* It will destroy even *more* lives less'n somebody shouts ENOUGH! And now I've said it, I'll say it agin! ENOUGH! I have a young'un jest two years old, Mr Galtrey, and th' saintliest young'un you could ever meet. I don't want his life destroyed by hatred and bitterness. *He's an innocent!* He and all th' Buchanan an' Galtrey young'uns don't deserve to be th' victims of th' enmity that was festered between you and Obediah Buchanan so long ago!"

Dean Galtrey stared at her for a moment then muttered, "Come inside, girl!"

Mary limped up the porch stairs and stepped into a clean and neat mountain home. It had colorful rugs on the floor and pretty pictures mounted on the walls.

"Take seat," Dean muttered, waving her to a sofa. He sat on an upright wooden chair opposite her, his fierce black eyes in his white face giving him a ghoulish look.

"You want to now *why* I've carried on this infernal feud fer so long, girl?" barked the old man angrily. "'Cuz that arrogant, depraved son-of-a-bitch, Obediah, was wrong! I never told Devon Ansley that he cut down his timber, but Obediah was so full of bitterness from spendin' time in jail that he refused to listen to me. He wronged me an' he wronged my family all these years, punishin' us fer somethun' we ain't done an' now you expect us to jest *forgit* it!"

"No, I don't expect that," wailed Mary. "How could y'all when you have suffered so much out of that evil man's ignorance? But th' man who caused yer sufferin' is no more! It don't make no sense to carry on feudin'."

"But them sons of his, them foul Buckos, are of his seed! Pure dung, th' lot of them."

"That ain't true, Mr Galtrey. They suffer'd real bad under Obediah too. Much worse than you kin imagine. Now it's high time to cease this madness. I know it's not possible fer you to become friends, leastways, not right off, but at least you kin cease to be enemies. My husband, Zachary Thomas, is a real good man, Mr Galtrey. If you agree to end th' feud, I know I kin persuade him to agree to it, too. Th' rest of them will follow. Please say you will! *Please,* Mr Galtrey. I kin tell you are a decent man. What's more, I've got th' feelin' ye're a man of yer word. I will tell them that."

Dean Galtrey sat back on his chair, a thin, long-fingered hand held speculatively under his chin. He regarded her silently with hot black eyes under which it was grueling to suffer. After what seemed like a lifetime, he finally stirred. "Ye're a real brave young woman, Mary Buchanan, comin' here like this. Unarmed and preachin' nuthin' but peace. I've given th' matter some thought. As you kin see, I'm an old man now an' I'm tired. I ain't got nuthin' more to look forward to, but my grave. I ain't got no more stomach fer all this here nonsense m'self. I want to die in peace an' I don't know that I ever will when I'm so afraid fer my kinfolk. *Five dead in the massacre!* It's true that Obediah ain't around no more. *Him,* I could never forgive! Maybe now . . . I'll tell you what. If'n you kin git th' *whole* Buchanan clan to agree on it, including *Eli,* an' then git Zachary Thomas to meet me here tomorrow to shake hands on it then I'll do it. I'll agree to stop this infernal feud."

His words were pure velvet to Mary's ears. She leaned forward and covered both his hands with her own, her hazel eyes glowing with gratitude. "Oh, Mr Galtrey, God bless you, sir. Thank you! You won't regret this! I'll talk to them and git Zachary Thomas here jest a'fore noon tomorrow, I promise."

* * *

But later, when Mary, covered in dirt, blood and bruises, with dirt in her hair and under her fingernails, was riding back home on the evil-tempered mule, after having spent several more hours talking to Dean Galtrey about the hate-ridden years behind them, she wondered how on earth she was going to persuade her Galtrey-loathing husband and the rest of the clan to agree to make peace with them. But even more than Zachary Thomas, she wondered how *Eli* could possibly be persuaded to cease hostilities against their long-term enemies.

52

Mary returned the mule to Obediah's old barn, thankful that no one was around to witness her doing so. *Now if she could just get back to Eagle Spur and get cleaned up before anybody could see her.* Obediah's cabin was presently occupied by just two of the Buckos – Otis and Cletus – now that Obediah and Jamie were both gone and, not long ago, Eli had chosen to build himself a large cabin further up the mountain, near Beacon Mountain, with the help of his brothers.

Without the presence and evil influence of the patriarch of the clan to goad and bully her here at the homestead, Horseshoe Hollow had lost much of its sinister atmosphere. She could not look at the whipping post, however, without anger and despair rising up inside her for it never failed to evoke the memory of the wretched flogging of young Jamie, as well as the knowledge of countless other floggings she had not personally witnessed, going back over decades. Surrounded by long weeds and covered in creepers, the whipping post was barely visible these days, but she wondered why the Buckos did not destroy it now that their father was gone. But she thought she knew why they did not. Despite the fact that he had vanished such a long time ago and was almost certainly dead, they were still afraid that he might one day return and censure them for it – even as old and weak as he had become in his last days.

Indeed, Mary had seen clear evidence of their secret fear just recently. Zachary Thomas had fetched Obediah's big brass bed and taken it up to Eagle Spur for them to sleep on, since Otis and Cletus, distrusting their father's disappearance, refused to sleep on it in his bedroom, and still slept in the loft like children! Mary wondered at Obediah's awesome power to cower his sons without even being present, or even from beyond the grave. Probably they believed he'd haunt them if they did.

Her husband also brought up the rest of the furniture, the carpet, the talking machine, the record discs, the coal burner and the beautiful gas parlor lamp with clusters of grapes and leaves all over it.

"Paw ain't a'comin' back," he said by way of explanation. "He's dead, an' that's a fact. Pity to waste all them purty thungs he got. They would come to me in any event, seein'as I am th' eldest. 'Sides, they remind me of my blessed maw."

Knowing for sure that Obediah was indeed dead, Mary felt happy about receiving the stuff, as it was indeed her husband's rightful due. After beating the carpet on the washline for days and scrubbing it with soap and water, before leaving it to dry on the grass, she placed it in the front room, along with the talking machine with its big flower horn, on its fancy walnut table. She loved having music in the cabin and would play the cylindrical record discs over and over again on the talking machine. Music was something she sorely missed from home, though this kind was nothing like lively mountain music, even mountain ballads, being somewhat slow, somber and highbrow. It did grow on her though.

The rest of the stuff went into their bedroom, including the elaborate coal burner, which would make their future winters much more bearable. She was delighted with the parlor lamp, which cast such a pretty orange glow in their room at night. The brass bedstead stood handsome and grand, but the mattress was old and badly stained, and smelled evilly of vomit, urine, moonshine and sickness, and before Mary would consent to sleep on it, she had scrubbed it vigorously with soap and ammonia and left it out in the sun for days to dry when it wasn't raining. Fortunately, Obediah had never turned the mattress over and when Mary put it back on the bed, she made sure the stained side faced down and they didn't have to lie in Obediah's filth. The smell was much better, but she could catch a faint sickening whiff of it every now and then. To combat this, she had taken the mattress off again, put a blanket over the springs and sprinkled it with crushed dried lavender, and piled some freshly cut boughs of hemlock on it, before putting the mattress on again. This improved matters that would only be completely resolved with the passing of time. But the bed *was* gloriously com-ortable after the hard wooden pallet that had been their nuptial bed before. All things considered, Mary was thrilled with their new acquisitions and silently thanked Hedina Charlemaine Buchanan for them.

After unsaddling the cantankerous mule in its stall, Mary limped out of the barn and was shocked to come face-to-face with her husband. He was trailed by a worried-looking Emma, who held Jed on her skinny hip.

Zachary Thomas was livid. "Mary, whar in hell's name have you bin? Emma's jest told me what happened th' other day up on Eagle Spur with them murdering Galtreys. How could you keep a thung like that from me, girl?" he demanded heatedly. Then he registered Mary's condition – her torn, bloody, dirt-smudged blouse, her befouled black skirt and her tangled dirt-engrained hair – and he stopped dead and stared sickly, his hard turquoise-green gaze instantly softening with concern. "Mary, what on earth happened to you, girl? Are you alright? It were them Galtreys, weren't it? They done harmed you. Well, that's it! It's high time me and my brothers paid them another visit. And this time, it'll make the massacre seem like a Sunday picnic! We'll learn them not to mess with th' Buckos, once and fer all!"

"No, Zack, ye'll do no sech thung!" said Mary quietly, but firmly.

Mary gazed stressfully at Emma, shaking her head slightly. She felt a terrible despair descend upon her. Emma had broken her solemn promise by telling her uncle what had happened that awful day, which would make it so much harder, if not impossible, for peace to come about. Her husband now knew that Emma had stopped Sloane Galtrey from slaughtering his little innocent son by slitting his throat. It would only further fuel his hatred of the Galtreys and make him want revenge once more, in an unending cycle that went from atrocity to atrocity, on either side. How had she have ever imagined she could somehow break the cycle and bring to an end to all the strife? It was too deeply entrenched! The hatred, too scathing. She could see it in her husband's flaming turquoise-green eyes even now. *Oh Lord, will the violence never stop?*

Emma shrugged her thin shoulders, and muttered, "I'm real sorry, Aunt Mary. I ain't know'd what else to do when you went a'missin'. I was real skeer'd fer you. Figger'd them scum had kidnapped you and were goin' to finish off what they tried to do th' other day."

Mary sighed, knowing she had placed the child in an impossible dilemma. After all, she had witnessed a terrible thing that day and had acted bravely. Because of her, a terrible tragedy had been narrowly averted. She could not blame the child. She owed her, her very life and that of her precious son. Her eyes rested on her toddler, perched peacefully upon Emma's narrow hip. He was the very picture of purity and innocence, and such a beautiful child. His brilliant blue eyes, wise and watchful, were viewing her with placid calmness. His sun-browned face, topped by his wild mop of brown hair, was serious, as if he somehow knew what she had just suffered through. And seeing him, she felt a love so fierce and strong, she knew she could not give up now. She had to try her hardest to achieve peace for him, for all the other young'uns.

"That's alright, Emma," she said softly with an understanding smile. "Don't you fret none. I know you only done what you thunk was best." She turned to her husband, her eyes meeting his fierce gaze. "We need to talk, Zachary Thomas. Thar'll be no more killin' between this clan an' th' Galtreys. An' yes, I have bin with th' Galtreys on Buck Knob Mountain."

Zachary Thomas sucked in a harsh disbelieving breath. "You mean they forced you to go . . . ?"

"No, I went to Buck Knob on my own. They didn't force me t'go. I met with Dean Galtrey hisself. We need to call a meeting of th' whole clan, including th' young'uns. We'll meet outside under th' giant chestnut tree on Eagle Spur in a short while. I jest need a little time to go clean up."

Zachary Thomas made to protest vehemently. "You surely cain't expect me to. I won't . . ."

"Yes, I *do* expect you to, Zack. If'n you value th' life of yer son, that is, you'll do as I say. *Please.* Here, Emma, let me take Jed. You go help yer uncle round up everybody."

Fear leapt in Emma's pale-blue eyes. She swallowed hard. "Unc' Eli too?'

Mary stared at the child, startled for a moment, feeling the child's fears invading her own being. If anyone was a threat to her plans for peace with the Galtreys, it was Eli Buchanan. His influence over the others was profound and well-entrenched, although dented of late with the refusal of some of them to condone his behavior in rocking his own kin and pulling down the brush arbors where they worshipped. Emma, especially, had good reason to fear him. In addition to seeing him use violence against his own kin to stop the religious services, she had actually witnessed him slitting the throat of her ten-year-old friend, Jamie Galtrey. Mary nodded shortly.

"Eli, too."

*   *   *

A half-hour later, Mary stepped outside the cabin onto the porch. She had removed her ruined and bloodied clothing, cleaned up, washed up and brushed her hair, then changed into her best dress that she had brought from home, her dark-blue one, not one of Hedina's fine, city-bought creations. She no longer had the desire to lord it over the Buchanans, or to antagonize any of them by appearing to want to do so. She saw that the vast majority of the clan was already assembled in the welcome shade of the immense chestnut tree, men, women and children, in their thin cotton clothing, most of the men in their bibbed dungarees with short-sleeved shirts underneath and wearing straw hats.

As yet, they were not seated on the grass, but stood in anxious little groups, with sweat darkening the cloth beneath their underarms and glistening on their faces. The humidity was bad even though it was much cooler up here than in the valley. There was a dark murmuring among them, their curiosity clearly peaked. Mary wondered how they would react when they learned of her dangerous sojourn into enemy territory. She feared they would either be incensed by it, or strongly disapproving, even those who had stood by her side once a month on a Sunday and sang hymns.

After all, the Galtreys' past atrocities had been recited to her again and again since she had arrived at Claw Mountain. Mary felt a wave of despair as she mentally reviewed the crimes of the Galtreys in the eyes of the Buchanans. It didn't matter that the Buchanan clan had done equally bad – if not worse – things to their long-time enemies. *They would not remember those!* She knew she had a lot to do to overcome their prejudices if she was to succeed in her mission. *And succeed she must!* She said a quick mental prayer, asking God for His help in the coming ordeal.

She saw Eli and Jake join the sprawling group, and froze. Eli alone among the men, was bareheaded, his bright tawny hair the color of summer straw. His handsome sun-browned face was sullen, the jagged knife-scar on his cheek, pale and clearly visible. The clan's moonshine business had done well under his wily stewardship. She had heard, of course, that after his trip to Stony Man Camp, he had become journey-proud. Indeed, he was quite citified and looked quite the dandy these days. Now she saw the talk was true. Gone were the dungarees and bare feet. He wore trousers of fine gray flannel, held up by fancy red braces, a crisp, white long-sleeved shirt, with a gold watch chain attached to it that disappeared into his shirt pocket, and a red plaid tie. As a concession to the heat, however, he'd rolled up his shirt-sleeves, loosened his tie and carried a gray flannel jacket over his arm. And he alone amongst them wore shoes! Fine black leather shoes, so shiny, they must reflect the entire world around him. She doubted that even Hannibal Hanford would recognize him as his coarse, poorly dressed, barefoot tormentor that day in the store.

Ominously, she noticed that he carried a moonshine jug in one hand. After taking a swig from it, he handed it to Jake, who likewise gulped down some of its contents. Eli's pale-yellow eyes met Mary's, challenging and full of pure venom. His enmity towards her was open and virulent since Reverend Hubbly began holding services on the mountain and she knew he would welcome any opportunity to make her lose favor with the rest of the Buchanans, and bring her down.

She shifted her eyes from his unsettling gaze and stepped determinedly off the porch into a blast of sulking summer heat that presently made a mockery of the high elevation of Eagle Spur.

"Is everybody here?" she ventured to ask the large gathering as she approached. The glances she received were decidedly hostile, even the one thrown at her by Zachary Thomas, who was conversing quietly with Toad and Johnny. Without her husband's strength and support she had come to rely on, she felt particularly vulnerable and alone. Even Emma, standing near Zachary Thomas and her two uncles chatting with him, with Jed once again perched on her hip, seemed close-mouthed and sulky. Mary suddenly realized that in all the group there wasn't a single ally she could count on when it came to the matter of the Galtreys. Indeed, she could feel their collective animosity radiating towards her. It was clear that Zachary Thomas had told them she had been to Buck Knob Mountain and they were already resenting her for it.

"Jest Ebenezer and his family to come, is all." It was brave, fair-haired Edna, Samuel's tall widow, who smiled encouragingly at her. Mary felt a spurt of warmth towards her. Despite the fact that the Galtreys had killed her husband, she *did* have one ally, after all.

It wasn't long before the final Bucko family crested the ridge. It hurried up, panting and red-faced from the strenuous climb, seeming glad of the shade of the sprawling chestnut, which was full of luxuriant summer growth. The new spring growth known as "honeydew", which was cut by many mountain people and stored for winter feed for cattle, had not been harvested from this mighty chestnut. Indeed, its eight-inch spines of white blossoms had been so prolific they had attracted swarms of bees that buzzed around the tree even now, causing an underlying droning sound in the drowsy heat.

Mary gave the newcomers a quick nervous smile and asked everybody to sit down on the grass. They all sat down save Eli, Jake and Zachary Thomas. Eli and Jake stood leaning languidly against a huge boulder, eyeing her belligerently, making her lose even more confidence, while Zachary Thomas folded his arms and stared at her stonily, his face set like granite, his eyes screwed up against the glare.

What could she possibly say to change all their made-up minds about the Galtreys? Even in the remote possibility that she might get them to agree to make peace with them, could she trust Dean Galtrey to control his clan. Or Zachary Thomas, his? She didn't even know how or where to start. *Help me, Father! Give me the right words.*

She remembered the last time she had addressed the clan. It had been about building a brush arbor for monthly church services. Only then, they had been pleasantly exhausted from working so hard after butchering day and had faced her with mild curiosity and receptiveness, even though their reaction to what she had to say had been far from positive, whereas today, she was faced by a barrage of closed and hostile faces right from the onset.

She drew in a deep breath to infuse her with much-needed courage, still feeling traumatized by her violent encounter with the Galtreys. Her body ached all over, she felt weak and shivery and so, so exhausted. She began hesitantly, "I . . . I know you must be wonderin' why I asked you all to come here, even th' young'uns. Well, I needed them to be present 'cuz what I have to say concerns them. In fact, it affects everybody." She stopped, keenly aware that every pair of eyes was pinned menacingly on her. "This mornin' I went to Buck Knob Mountain and had a meetin' with Dean Galtrey."

Even as she said it, she knew that this, to them, was betrayal at its very worst. *She had met and consorted with their gravest enemies behind their backs!* There was a shocked intake of breath, before howls of outrage rose from those assembled. Several adults, their faces glowering with anger, shook angry fists at her. Even the children, taking cue from their parents, jeered and raised puny fists at her. Faces looked furious, unheeding.

"Why did you go thar, Mary?" questioned Edna quietly, a pacifier in the eye of the storm. "I'm sure you must have had a real good reason."

Mary's grateful eyes met the steadfast brown ones of Edna, whose five clean and neatly dressed children were seated around her.

"Oh, Edna, indeed I did! Th' best reason in th' world. I went thar to try to make peace with th' Galtreys."

"*WHAT?*" the Bucko clan howled in unified disgust, truly outraged by her words.

"Who gave you that right, wimmin?" demanded Toad.

"Yeah, seems to me you make a habit of takin' thungs upon yerself that affect this here mountain," said Eli cuttingly, straightening his sinuous frame, strafing her with icy pale-yellow eyes. "Don't you know you don't belong here an' never did? Thar will never be peace with them Galtreys as long as I draw breath!"

The others were all nodding, agreeing with Eli wholeheartedly.

Clem's wife, Rosie, said angrily, "Trouble with you, Mary, is you ain't suffered under them th' way we have!"

"Yeah, all you ever done was come to th' funeral of Al and Sam, and them weren't even yer kin!" snapped Mabel, Ezekial's wife, furiously. "It don't give you th' right to take it upon yerself to try to make peace with 'em."

Cora, mousy-haired and toothless, was equally vociferous. "It's treason, it is! Them Galtreys are butchers and murderers! How dare you go to them an' interfere in what ain't none of yer business!"

It was the start of a blistering personal attack on Mary. She understood their fear and their feelings and let them have their say without reply. Besides, she was too busy thinking of what to say next. Well, whatever they may think of her, they couldn't say she had never suffered under the Galtreys. She and her precious son had been attacked and nearly murdered by two of them and, she had, just hours ago, been mercilessly beaten and rocked by their vicious women.

She inwardly debated whether she should tell them of the Galtreys' latest atrocities, or whether it would be counter-productive to her argument that they should make peace with them. It could go either way. On the one hand, it might make them *more* angry and determined to never make peace with them. On the other hand, if they felt she had never suffered through them the way they had, they might think that she could never understand how they felt and had no right to ask what she was asking.

She had to make them realize that she *could* understand exactly how they felt, but that what they were feeling needed to be overcome, because there were much greater considerations at stake. *The futures of their children!* Their safety. There was no choice!

"Believe it or not, I know *exactly* how you feel. Whatever you may believe, I *have* suffered under the Galtreys! Jest two weeks ago, I was in th' tableland forest with little Jed, when two of them came up . . ." She was interrupted by another howl of outrage as they digested her words, but she ignored it and went on with her story. "They took out their knives and one of them picked up little Jed and held a knife at his throat. He would have slit it and killed me right after, if'n it weren't for young Emma here. She and her shotgun saved us both."

The crowd wheeled on Emma, who was sitting at Zachary Thomas's feet with Jed on her lap, seeking confirmation from her. She stared sullenly back at them.

"What you do with them, Emma?" Elmer demanded to know. "You bury them up on Eagle Spur?"

"No, she escorted them off th' mountain," supplied Mary glibly.

They turned back to Mary in disgust.

"What she do that fer?" Johnny wanted to know.

"'Cuz I told her to."

"You crazy bitch!" Eli snarled. "You turned them loose when they tried to murder yer own son. What kind of a maw are you?"

"A maw who is so afraid fer her son that she will do *anythung* to protect him, anythung at all, including approaching Dean Galtrey hisself to make sure that what happened that day never happens agin. Less'n it happens that way, we kin never be sure when they will strike agin or whose grave we will be diggin' next. Fact is, I used to feel real safe up on Eagle Spur. 'Sides th' fact that it ain't at all easy to git up here, I never figger'd they'd git past all th' lookouts. But it took a terrible experience to make me realize that no place is safe from them.

"Well, I discovered that I don't like to live with th' kind of fear that has filled me these past two weeks. I want my young'un and all th' young'uns of both mountains to be *safe!* They sure don't deserve to suffer fer what their parents or grandfathers have done!" There was a sober silence as the crowd absorbed what she had said. "Well, I got to thunkin' that th' only way they'll ever be safe is if somebody turns th' other cheek like Jesus said, instead of seekin' revenge th' whole time. *'An eye fer an eye'* jest keeps things goin' on and on and on. It don't solve nuthin'! I let them Galtreys go and it was what saved my life today. When I got to Buck Knob Mountain, I was surrounded by Galtrey wimmin – easy a dozen of 'em. They dragged me off th' mule and beat me bad an' kicked me something fierce. They beat me 'cuz I told them I'm a Buchanan."

"You told them that?" Ellie Mae stared at her in amazement, her eyes rounded, her cheeks, beneath her flaming bird's nest, bright red from the heat. She fanned her face with a limp rag.

"I didn't got no choice! I ask'd to see Dean Galtrey and they finally stopped kickin' me and took me to him, 'cuz they were so curious to hear what I had to say to him. Well, fact is, he didn't want'd to hear *anythung* I had to say about making peace, and he turned me back over to th' wimmin and told them to do with me whatever they put their minds to." Mary's voice quavered then as she relived the whole frightening experience. "Well, thar ain't no doubt that them wimmin want'd to kill me. They took me out into th' yard, surround'd me an' started poundin' me with big rocks. They were intent on rockin' me to death! Then SI . . .," Mary had been about to tell them the identities of the two Galtreys, who had attacked her in the forest, but she stopped herself just in time. "Then th' two Galtreys who tried to kill me an' Jed, came up th' path and told them to stop, 'cuz I had saved both thar lives.

"Well, Dean Galtrey standin' up on th' porch overheard what they said and demanded that I come to him. He asked me if it were true what his son had said, and when I said yes, he asked me *why* I had saved th' lives of his two sons. I told him it was 'cuz I cared about both clans and wanted to make peace with th' Galtreys so that my son and th' other young'uns on Claw Mountain and Buck Knob Mountain could be safe at last."

The assembled Buckos and their families were now so quiet Mary could hear nothing but the droning of the bees. No one made a sound. They were hanging onto her every word, all eyes riveted upon her. Angry faces had softened imperceptibly, although their owners were clearly still puzzled and perplexed by the questions she had raised in their minds with her tale. Only Eli, Jake and Zachary Thomas remained stonily unmoved. They groused and grumbled under their breaths.

"How many of you remember how this feud got itself started in th' first place?" Mary challenged.

Many of them shook their heads. She suspected that many had never known the reason, while others had simply forgotten, even Zachary Thomas, the oldest Bucko. It was Eli who raised his voice. "Sure do! Dean Galtrey reported Paw to th' sheriff when he cut down some trees that belonged to Devon Ansley. He got sent to jail fer six months while Maw was with child with Zack here. Paw sure didn't take too kindly to that."

"So you reckon if somebody cuts down trees that don't belong to him, he shouldn't git punished fer it?"

"Hell, no! This was Paw's mountain!"

"But them trees and th' land did belong to Mr Ansley, surely?"

"So what? It weren't no business of *Dean Galtrey's* whose trees Paw cut down!"

"And what if I were to tell you that it weren't *Dean Galtrey* who reported th' crime to th' sheriff? And that all these years Obediah blamed and punished him and his clan fer somethung they weren't guilty of?"

There was an alarmed murmuring amongst the clan, but Eli sneered in disbelief. "And I suppose Dean Galtrey told you that?"

"Yes, he did. What would he gain by lyin' to me about it?"

Eli blustered with outrage. He strutted forward angrily. "*He lied.* Paw couldn't have bin mistaken about that! All them Galtreys are liars an' thieves an' murderers!"

"I don't thunk so, Eli. You know fer yerself yer Paw weren't exactly th' listenin' kind! I believ'd Dean Galtrey when he told me that he didn't do it. He told me Devon Ansley hisself came an' *told* him that he'd witnessed yer paw cuttin' down th' trees, but when yer paw saw th' two of them together, he put two an' two together and came up with altogether th' wrong conclusion! He set y'all on a path of killin', violence an' destruction – *all over an imagined slight!* Them *Galtreys* were th' ones that were wronged, not th' Buchanans!"

Eli's mouth went oddly askew and his eyes went dull and distant for a moment, while Mary's roved warily over the rest of the clan noticing a sobering as the realization of what that meant descended on them. She saw dull recognition in their eyes that told her that they knew that what she had said was true. And they believed it because they knew what *Obediah* was capable of, not because it came from her! She pressed her advantage. "And now, ev'ry time thar's a new attack, it gits to be revenged upon, till hardly nobody knows what it's about no more. *Violence jest begets violence!* But they've had many more kilt on their side than ye've on your'n, and jest as much sorrow an' heartache.

"Now less'n we make peace with them, thar will always be heartache and sorrow in yer lives. In all th' lives on both mountains. *And what fer?* Thar ain't no profit in it fer either side! Long as I've bin on this mountain I've heard talk of mindin' th' Galtreys. Nobody knows when they will strike, or how bad it will be. We expected they'd git even fer th' massacre long a'fore now. Them two Galtreys who attack'd me and my son, said it was in revenge fer young Jamie Galtrey's murder two years ago. They've got long memories jest like y'all have got. It were little Jed who was targeted this time. Whose young'un will be next? Now, th' awful drowning and throat-slittin' of Jamie Galtrey is what got Alvin and Samuel kilt and started th' massacre in th' first place! So it were a *Bucko* deed that led to thar deaths."

"No! No Buchanan would kill a young'un," said Rosie sharply, her eyes sparking indignantly. "That had nawt to do with us! They blamed it on us so's they could kill our menfolk!"

Mary studied the woman silently. How would the rest of the clan react if they knew that Jake and Eli had been directly responsible for all the grief that followed that tragic event? Mary glanced at Emma, who gazed pleadingly back at her. She had promised the child not to tell anybody about who had been responsible for Jamie's murder and, even though she longed to denounce the heartless pair for what they had done, she knew that she could not. Besides the fact that Emma would never forgive her, it might put her young life in danger if Eli knew that she had witnessed him and Jake perpetrating the ghastly act.

Mary decided she couldn't accuse them outright, but she could get the clan thinking about who was responsible. She was fairly certain that deep-down every one of them knew who at least *one* of the culprits was, but either refused to believe it, or somehow justified the dastardly act in their own minds after the subsequent ambush and murder of Alvin and Samuel.

"If'n you thunk about it, it don't take too much figgerin' t'know that th' ugly deed was done by somebody in this here clan. Why would th' Galtreys kill one of thar own young'uns? That don't make no sense at all."

"Who would do sech a terrible thung?" challenged Rosie.

Then realization seemed to dawn on her face and she hastily lowered her eyes. Mary gazed solemnly at Jake and Eli, who stared back insolently, with the kind of careless ease that told her they thought she could not possibly know for sure that *they* had murdered the child. Mary shook her head determinedly, ridding herself of the temptation to just blurt it out. "I ain't sayin' who, 'cuz th' fact is, it don't matter no more. Real bad things have bin done on both sides. Each side has got a lot to answer fer and a lot to forgive. But always remember who started it in th' first place. It weren't no Galtrey. It were *Obediah Buchanan* – your paw! Now Dean Galtrey has said that if'n I kin git Zachary Thomas to come and shake hands on it tomorrer, he's a'willin' to make peace."

Mary gazed at her husband pleadingly, meeting his fierce turquoise-green gaze, as he looked at her, face scowling and quizzical. Through all of it, he had stood firmly against her arguments, she knew. "I stood and watched helplessly as a Galtrey held a knife to my Jed's tender throat and I'm askin' you to do that, Zachary Thomas, so it don't never happen agin. Nay, I'm *beggin'* you! I want my young'un to be safe. I want *all* th' young'uns to be safe! Are you willin' to risk th' lives of yer young'uns jest to keep this here senseless thung a'goin'?"

"I told you we ain't makin' peace with no Galtrey – not as long as I draw breath!" yelled Eli in disgust. "It don't matter a damn who started th' danged thung! See this here face of mine," he said, pointing to his scarred cheek. "Sloane Galtrey disfigger'd me fer life! *He's a marked man!* You've heer'd of mountain justice? Well, I won't rest till I git it, girl. Won't stop till every last Galtrey's in thar grave, too. So, so much fer yer crazy talk of peace."

Mary swallowed hard, thankful that she had not revealed the identities of the two Galtrey men who had attacked her and Jed. So it had been Sloane Galtrey who had caused the terrible scar on Eli's cheek – *Eli's badge of menace and bravado!* Perhaps Sloane was the Galtreys' *'Eli'*. The real bad one amongst them! Yet it was *he* who had saved her life today, even though his shoulder had been shattered by Emma's bullet and he must be living in agony right now. Miraculously, he had been touched by her expressing concern for him and for letting them go, even though he had tried to kill her child minutes earlier. It proved to her that love was stronger than hate. That just as hate and violence begets more hate and violence, love and compassion creates more of the same.

"Well, Eli, mountain justice won't make yer cheek whole agin or brung back all them that were kilt," Mary pointed out quietly, "I'm askin' you to do what Jesus said we must. *Turn th' other cheek.* Turn yer good cheek to them, Eli. Let bygones be bygones. And that goes fer th' rest of you, too."

"Hell, damn, I'll never do that, let alone on some dumb bucko called Jesus' say-so! Ye're crazy, wimmin! Comin' here an' settin' my family aginst itself with yer crazy notions. Turnin' them all into church-goin' freaks. Ain't nuthin' bin th' same 'round here since you come interferin' whar you ain't wanted. Now, nobody kin trust th' Galtreys to stand by no peace agreement. We all know that. They'd string us along an' then jest when we least expected it, they'd attack. *Wham!* Jest like they always do! Lyin' an' cheatin' and thievin' are all them murderin' swines is good fer. Every single one of you here knows that! So don't let this do-gooder outsider come in an' lead you like sheep to th' slaughter."

The crowd's mood changed with his words like a north-easter changes the weather. They were nodding forcefully in agreement and mumbling dis-contentedly. Mary knew at a glance that all the progress she had made with them thus far, had vanished. Mary stared at her young antagonist in keen distress. Standing here in front of this disreputable clan, she wondered how she had managed to reach this point in time. She had been on Claw Mountain for three years now, and, at twenty-one years old, was still one of the youngest adults here. Yet here she was trying to reason with the mighty Buckos. How had she assumed this huge mantel of responsibility for them all, anyhow? How come she felt an almost maternal caring about their welfare? It weighed heavily on her young shoulders now.

Suddenly, it was all too much for her and she felt hot tears scalding her eyes. She felt tired and defeated and direly wounded as a wave of dizziness overcame her. She didn't feel strong enough to battle such overwhelming odds all the time. Zachary Thomas sometimes called her *"The Crusader"*, with a touch of irony and affection, and she supposed that was part of it. She wanted to improve their lives. She desperately wanted peace and harmony to come to the mountain. But she was losing confidence of ever achieving that with every moment that passed.

"It's true that I was an outsider when I first got here," she began. "But I ain't no outsider no more. Fer sure, I no longer despise and fear y'all, like I did back then. 'Cuz I discover'd that underneath you're jest th' same as other mountain folk. Fact is, all I see when I look at you now, is *family.* You see, I've grown to love y'all like you are my own kin. If'n I felt thar was any chance at all that I was wrong about Dean Galtrey, I wouldn't ask you to do this here thung. But I talked with him a long time – several hours, in fact, and he done told me many things about how he feels and what has gone on between th' two clans over th' years – from thar point of view. Now, he done told me that he's old and tired and he ain't got th' stomach fer it no more. I believed him when he told me that! Now, I thunk I'm a real good judge of character. I wouldn't try to sway you to my way of thinkin', less'n I was real sure it wouldn't harm a single one of you. Don't you understand? *I care about y'all! Ye're my kin now."*

"Well, I got news fer you," said Eli ,with searing contempt. *"You ain't no kin of mine!* Now, this here mountain b'longs to me and I say *NO* to peace with th' Galtreys!"

"Hell, no, it don't b'long to you, Eli." A quiet, strong voice rang out across the clearing. It belonged to Zachary Thomas. To Mary's astonishment, he began picking his way through the large sprawling seated group, casually patting children's heads as he went past, until he got to where Mary was standing in lonely isolation. Then he slowly turned to face his furious younger brother, taking Mary's hand in his. Mary looked up at her huge, handsome husband in disbelief, immensely thankful for his solid presence at her side, for his undeniable strength. She felt as she had the day he had rescued her from the scene of Jamie's flogging by sweeping her up in his strong arms and carrying her all the way up to Eagle Spur from Horseshoe Hollow. She felt no harm could come to her now and she need not be afraid.

Zachary Thomas, fierce mountain man, her husband and protector, continued in a tone of reasonableness, "This here mountain done b'longs to all of us now! But with Paw gone, *I'm* th' head of th' clan, me bein' th' eldest and all. And this is th' way I feel 'bout thungs as they stand. Now y'all know Mary by now. You know that she's always wanted th' best fer yer young'uns, and fer you too. She was worried 'bout yer health, so she brung in Doc Adams to tend to all yer ills an' those of yer young'uns! She's learn'd yer young'uns to read an' write an' cipher, and brung a school to this here mountain so that they kin git a proper education and not be ignorant fools like th' rest of us. She's learn'd you wimminfolk to do some mighty useful things, too, so that th' lives of you an' yer families are much better than what they used to be. Why, Edna makes the best rag dolls I've ever seen and Lila makes a mean quilt and Ettie's jams are sure good. Why, thar be so many sewin' bees and cookin' lessons and vegetable garden lessons a'goin' on, that I wonder whar Mary gits all her energy from.

"But mebbe th' best darned thung Mary brung to Claw Mountain is religion. I never knew God a'fore I met Mary. And I got to be thunkin' that He must be somethung worth prayin' to 'cuz of her, 'cuz she be somebody who lives her religion ev'ry day. She does it by helpin' others whenever she kin! Now considerin' all that, d'you really thunk she would steer you wrong this time about makin' peace with our longtime enemies? Hell, I don't thunk so!

"I hate to say it, but Mary's right. It's high time to make peace with them Galtreys. Shit, I hate them Galtreys same as you. Why, right now, I could easily go an' finish off th' lot of 'em fer what they tried do to my wife and son and fer what they done to Mary today, but what good would that do? 'Cuz less'n I did git every last one of 'em, I'd be skeer'd to go huntin' in th' valley agin – like I was fer a long, long time after th' massacre. And what if I did go thar after, and th' Galtreys came up to Eagle Spur and kilt little Jed 'cuz me an' Emma weren't thar to protect him? 'Cuz, fact is, we cain't *always* be thar to protect him, not year in an' year out, we cain't. Lawd knows Jed is my only young'un, so he's real precious to me. Now, I don't want to do it, but good sense tells me that I must if'n I care enough 'bout my family, that is.

"Like Mary says, we owe it to all th' young'uns to be rid of this here threat hangin' over our heads, once and fer all! Now, who is with me and Mary on this?"

There was a moment's stunned silence before Edna's freckled hand shot up. Her children's hands followed in quick succession. This was followed by young Emma's hand. Then she took Jed's small hand in hers and raised it too. Hands all over the large sprawling group rose, hesitantly, at first, then with growing confidence, one after the other, after the other, until only Jake's and Eli's remained down. Mary could not believe the dramatic turn of events. She couldn't believe that she had managed, somehow, to sway her husband from his mulish obstinacy when it came to the Galtrey clan. But she knew that without his support, she would never have been able to pull it off. She gratefully squeezed his hand.

But as Eli watched his authority crumbling before his very eyes, he became more and more incensed. Mary could see he was seething with outrage, his eyes wild and scary – *a vision of hell!* Jake's face was likewise full of loathing and contempt. Could she ever reach a pair as twisted with hate as this?

"Well, I reckon that settles it then," said Zachary Thomas with a snort of satisfaction. "It ain't a job I look forward to, but tomorrer I'll go with Mary to Buck Knob Mountain and we'll make a peace pact with them Galtreys."

"Hey, wait a minute, Zack!" snarled Eli. "Me and Jake here don't go along with it so you'll do no sech thung!"

"Seems to me you're badly outnumbered here, Eli! Now I strongly advise you to go along with it. I advise it *good*," Zachary Thomas intoned meaningfully. There followed a moment of fierce eye-to-eye contact between the two brothers when something Mary could not fathom passed between them. Not for the first time, Mary had the feeling that her husband had some sort of hold over his younger brother. He seemed to be able to keep him in check, just as he had when Eli had almost raped her. And Zachary Thomas's hypnotic turquoise-green gaze did indeed win out over the yellow madness of Eli's.

Eli wrenched his eyes away first. But he turned his attention back to Mary, pointing a damning finger at her. "Ye're goin' to regret th' day you ever came to this here mountain, missy," he hissed scathingly at her. "You may thunk you've won today, but I'll never make peace with them Galtreys and a'fore too long all yer efforts will come to nowt! And mark my words, *I'll git you fer this!* Don't thunk I won't. This clan used to be strong! Everybody used to fear us! Now, since you came, it ain't nuthin' but a bunch of pussycats! Paw must be turnin' in his grave . . . if he's in one, that is! And, as fer you, Zack, you used be one of us, but she's turned you into a snivelin', yellow-bellied hen-husband, who kow-tows to everythung she says. It's like she's got you bewitch'd or somethung."

Standing at her husband's side, Mary heard Eli's scathing words and felt a nasty chill run up her spine, because they were delivered with such white-hot spitting fury. While she felt as if she'd just had a terrible curse placed on her and the worst insult heaped on her poor husband. Zachary Thomas's answering smile was surprisingly mild and ironic.

"Kin I help it if'n I got me th' smartest, bravest, most damndest wimmin in all th' mountains fer a wife . . .?"

53

Early the next morning, Zachary Thomas and Mary fetched a mule at Obediah's old homesite and started out for Buck Knob Mountain to make a peace pact with the Buchanan clan's most hated and ardent enemies. Members of the Buchanan clan had gathered at Horseshoe Hollow to see them off, silent, somber and scared. Forced to wear her dark-blue dress again, Mary sat on the mule with it draped about her knees. The mule was being led by Zachary Thomas, on foot. He refused to mount the beast and ride it to Buck Knob, saying he wouldn't be seen dead on a mule by a Galtrey.

Mary had protested, saying that if that was the case, she would walk with him, but her husband insisted that the trip would be too strenuous for her in her weakened state. Indeed, she did feel awful! Badly bruised and stiff and aching all over, she felt limp as a rag doll and quite exhausted, the beatings and the emotional trauma on Buck Knob Mountain and the harrowing meeting with the Buchanan clan afterwards, having taken their toll. Now that peace was about to come about, Mary also felt inordinately scared and unsure, as if she was about to walk on eggs that would shatter beneath her bare feet.

Though she was immensely grateful for Zachary Thomas's support and for the willingness of his family to make peace with the Galtreys, Mary felt weighed down by Eli's outright condemnation of any such notion and felt as if it was doomed to failure before it had even started. What if Eli carried out his threat and deliberately wrecked the peace pact? And what if a breaking of the peace pact fueled the feud to new and even more terrible heights? She could not bear it if she were to feel responsible for the loss of any more lives like she had been for young Jamie Buchanan's death, which still clung to her conscience like a burr sticks to a cow's hide. After all, his death had come about as a direct result of his terrible beating at the hands of his madman father, which would not have happened if she had not tried to escape from the mountain that day and tripped over the glass jar.

The early morning sun flooded the tree-shrouded valley below with bright dazzling light as they descended Claw Mountain. She could hear the faint roar of the river-rapids of Wilson Run far below and see the bright sparkle of the sun on the water. The Wilderness Valley was in the full flush of the season and the soft-white blossoms of mountain laurel and the delicate white blossoms of the red chokesberry, having shed its red fall foliage and scarlet berry clusters, graced the mountainside like dappled snow. There were clusters of the pink blossoms of the estern redbud. The sky was scrubbed shiny blue, but already steam was rising from the earth that was damp from yesterday's late-afternoon thunderstorm. It would be another hot, sultry day. One which was, for Mary, already fraught with tension and an aura of impending doom. She could not rid herself of the feeling that something terrible was going to happen. Maybe Eli was right and the Galtreys could not be trusted to keep up their end of the bargain. Maybe she was leading her husband into a trap! Perhaps Dean Galtrey had found a clever way to rid themselves of the new head of the clan, having rid himself of the old one. Zachary Thomas carried no weapon as Dean Galtrey had instructed and would not be able to protect the two of them should they choose to attack them. Remembering how the women had assailed her, Mary shivered in apprehension.

Thankfully, the mule behaved better under Zackary Thomas's firm lead and determined strides, and plodded happily along, perhaps sensing an even more stubborn will was involved than its own. As they crossed Devil's Creek, Zachary Thomas splashing through the shallow stream with his tough bare feet and the mule with sturdy hoofs, Mary was suddenly sharply reminded of a biblical tale featuring her namesake – Joseph leading the blessed Mary into the town of Bethlehem on a donkey, before the birth of Jesus. Zachary Thomas with his long hair made a credible Joseph-figure, while not only did she have her name in common with the biblical Mary, she also suspected she might be with child again, because her monthly sick was late. Of course, this dreadful mule was no match for a donkey! For some reason she also felt she was on some kind of a divine mission, even though it did not exactly embrace the whole of mankind. *Oh, heavenly Father, help us to please bring about a lasting peace!*

* * *

Whenen they at last reached the foothills of Buck Knob Mountain they took the same path that ascended up this mighty bastion of the Galtreys, as Mary had yesterday. When they reached the shanty, the womenfolk melted in around them, appearing out of nowhere like they had yesterday. Gussie Galtrey stood with her hands on her hips, glaring at them, her matted, gray-streaked, red hair streaming from her floppy felt man's hat. Mary stiffened on the mule, remembering the women's crudeness and cruelty. Their faces were as openly hostile as they were yesterday.

They viewed Zachary Thomas with eye-gleaming contempt and some curiosity. No doubt, Dean Galtrey had been forced to talk them into this, just as she had done to the Buckos. She nodded to them and they gave acknowledging nods, but no one spoke. The women urged them to carry on then fell in behind them on the narrow winding upward pathway. When it got too steep for the mule, Zachary Thomas stopped the snorting beast and lifted Mary off, tying the reins to a rhododendron bush, before they ascended the rest of the way to Dean Galtrey's homestead on foot. Mary felt a thrall of fear when she noticed a man with a shotgun high up on some rocks. Thankfully, he was not pointing it at them and soon disappeared from view.

When they got to the homesite, Dean Galtrey, his sons, Sloane and Quaid Galtrey, at his side, was out on his porch, apparently waiting for them, his eyes watching them shrewdly, while in the yard was ranged a vast silent crowd of fierce-looking men, women and young'uns. Mary clung to Zachary Thomas's hand and they climbed the porch steps, with her heart pounding with trepidation. *They were badly outnumbered here.* They wouldn't stand a chance if things went wrong!

Zachary Thomas's face was thunderous. He looked fierce and menacing to Mary, not at all like a man about to make an overture of peace with his neighbors after decades of violence. She wished she could tell him to relax and smile a little, but she knew how hard this must be for him. To make up for his lack of diplomacy, Mary gave the three waiting Galtreys a faltering smile, disconcerted by their steely expressions and the pointed lack of any sort of a welcome.

Sloane viewed them from beneath the brim of his pulled-down Confederate hat, with hostile black eyes. When he had made a plea to save her life yesterday, he obviously had not counted on such an outcome as *peace* with the entire Buchanan clan. She and Zachary Thomas were not invited into the cabin as she had been yesterday and she was disappointed, feeling a pressure in the presence of all these intimidating folk, none of whom looked as if they wanted peace at all.

"Mr Galtrey, Sloane, Quaid," she said unsurely, "this here is my husband, Zachary Thomas."

Dean Galtrey nodded shortly, his thin white face stern, his black eyes glowing like coals. Despite his steely countenance, he looked ridiculously refined in his neat attire, next to the picture presented by the matted black hair, long beards and coarse clothing of his two sons. Zachary Thomas did not extend his hand and Dean Galtrey and his two sons, fierce mountain men, did not move forward with theirs, each wary and keeping his own proud council. The three viewed her tall, husky, black-haired husband, equally fierce mountain man, with caution, but also with visible loathing, no doubt mentally heaping all his family's many misdeeds upon him.

Disconcerted and dismayed, she hastily continued, "Yesterday, we talked with th' entire Buchanan clan and all but two agreed that it's time to make peace with yer clan."

Sloane snorted with contempt. "Does them two include Eli?'"

Mary felt a surge of panic at his blunt enquiry, knowing there was no way that she could pretend that was not so.

"No, it don't," she admitted reluctantly, "but my husband is th' head of th' clan now, and he wants peace same as me."

Dean Galtrey looked highly skeptical. "I told you yesterday that peace depended on whether you could git th' *whole* clan to agree to it', including Eli. Nay, *especially* Eli."

"I know that, but it's got to start *someplace,"* said Mary pleadingly. "It's goin' to be jest fine, you'll see!"

"Indeed!" snapped Dean Galtrey. "An' jest what guarantee kin you give me that he won't bother my family agin?"

"NONE!" roared Zachary Thomas, joining in the conversation for the first time with a vengeance, seeming annoyed that Dean Galtrey was addressing his wife rather than him. "All I kin say is that if it does happen, *I* will deal with him."

"An' what power do you got to control that animal? Doggone it, everybody knows how crazy-sick he is! Don't reckon nobody kin keep him from doin' what he's got a mind to."

"I got my ways an' means," Zachary Thomas replied shortly, blasting Dean Galtrey with his sulpherous turquoise-green gaze, dislike, as bitter as bile between them. "Well, do you want to do this thung or not?"

The three Galtreys looked at each other. Then Dean Galtrey silently stared out at his assembled clan as he considered his answer. Mary awaited his decision anxiously, knowing their vulnerability in this viper's nest if he decided against it. The wait went on and on and on, the silence stretching to such an extent that just when Mary felt she could not bear the suspense a moment longer, Dean Galtrey suddenly delivered a surprising verdict to Zachary Thomas.

"Alright, we'll go along with it if'n you undertake to be *personally* responsible fer Eli."

"And what guarantees do we got that members of yer family won't break th' peace?" snapped Zachary Thomas, not to be outmaneuvered by the head of the enemy clan.

Dean Galtrey pointed a steely thumb back to himself. *"I* will personally deal with them."

"Kin we trust you?"

Dean Galtrey gave him an affronted gasp and his two sons glared balefully at Zachary Thomas.

"I am a man of my word," said Dean Galtrey staunchly, raising a proud, arrogant chin.

Mary believed him. Apparently, Zachary Thomas did too, for, after a moment's silent consideration, he nodded and said, "Then let's shake on hit. No more violence aginst each other. No more raids. We ain't allowed on yer mountain, you ain't allowed on ours. If anybody breaks th' peace on our side, you come straight to me, and if'n it's on yer side, I'll come straight to you, so we kin sort it out smartly a'fore it gits out of hand."

"Deal!"

Reaching forward, Dean Galtrey took Zachary Thomas's huge outstretched paw in his puny long-fingered white hand, adding, "But I've got to tell you, it never would have happened if it weren't fer yer wife here. It took a mighty brave wimmin to do what she did! Fact is, I trust her a deal more than I do you."

"Fair enough." Zachary Thomas nodded as he crushed Dean Galtrey's hand in his. To his credit, the man refused to wince though he trembled with the effort of withstanding the brief agony. It was the first physical contact between the two clans in over three decades that was not made in the cause of vengeance, yet even so, it contained more than a drop of the old poison. A mountain man's pride was difficult to overcome, especially when he felt it indicated some inherent weakness. They still had to learn what Mary already knew – that it was not a sign of weakness at all, but a sign of true strength. It took a big man to risk all when the odds were so high. Only time would show them that.

At that point the crowd erupted, not in triumph, but in an acknowledgement of the deed, the sealing of a peace pact on the strength of a single handshake – a deed craved on a certain level, yet on another, inwardly spurned by every last Galtrey here, Mary was convinced. Indeed, it was a strange strangled roar, in which relief, gladness and grief, was oddly mingled with fierce disapproval, outrage and the humiliation of capitulation to such a cause.

Mary couldn't help but think what a strong man her husband was in a way that had nothing whatsoever to do with his immense size. She felt that, ultimately, the Galtreys had recognized this quality in him and that it was at least partly responsible for their acquiescence in the end. They had to believe that he was, indeed, a man capable of controlling Eli, like he said. Mary wished she could be as confident, but fear sulked inside her, pungent as a raw onion, when she remembered Eli's threat. *I'll git you fer this! Don't think that I won't!*

Some of the womenfolk started crying, tough wild women, but mothers and wives and sisters who had suffered under Bucko tyranny. It was an understandable reaction, for Mary felt very close to tears herself. Her throat ached in sympathy for their sorrows and for her own. She closed her eyes in gratitude. *Peace!* Precarious, though it may be!

54

It was the first Sunday of the new month and Reverend Hubbly had come to the mountain to hold service once again. After another lackluster service, the congregants chatted gleefully with one another and the reverend, before dispersing into the forests on their way home, spilling down the mountain like driftwood down a river, such was their newfound contentment. Mary had no doubt that these services had added a positive new dimension to their lives despite Reverend Hubbly's limitations as a preacher.

Mary hoped the reverend was in a better mood than usual, for while his sermon had once again been most uninspiring, indeed glaringly condemnatory at times, the numbers in his congregation had grown appreciably, with mountain folk coming from Beacon and Bear Rock Mountains in increasing numbers, and so had the converts (even though he wasn't yet attracting anywhere near the vast numbers his services had on other mountains). Indeed, the brush arbor could no longer contain the numbers. They had gathered in their scores outside, once the rough log pews were filled, causing the reverend to raise his voice considerably so that they might hear him. What's more, Eli had left for Skyland and it had been a while, anyway, since any service had been disrupted by him and his contemptible cohorts.

Mary should have been happy and immensely relieved that Eli was gone, but instead, since he'd left, she had plunged into a deep depression and was weepy and full of both specified and unspecified fears which she had failed to hide from her concerned husband, hobbling around the cabin like a cripple. Her husband put her present blues down to the violence she had experienced at the hands of the Galtrey women –and it was true that the violence recently perpetrated against her person at the hands of so many had taken its toll on both her body and her spirit, and Mary felt strangely shattered inside. It seemed to her that all she had to hang onto these days was the spiritual experience she'd shared with Jed in the forest. As if seeking solace, her mind would return to it time and time again, making her wonder about its significance. Now she hoped to get some answers to her questions about it.

Mary had, as always, invited the reverend to share their Sunday fare with them, but Sundays were busy days for circuit-preachers in the mountains and Reverend Hubbly had many more stops to make and services to hold, and always declined. But Mary was extremely anxious to talk to him. Sending Zachary Thomas and Jed on ahead to Eagle Spur, she drew the reverend aside before he could escape.

"Reverend Hubbly, thar's somethung real important I wish to discuss with you."

"And pray tell, child, what might that be?"

The reverend, grandly pontifical in his black suit and white clerical collar, had a slightly miffed look on his thin, haughty face, as if he suspected that something unpleasant was going to be asked of him. Mary put a supplicating hand on his arm.

"It's . . . well, kind of hard to explain. A few weeks ago, I went fer a walk in th' forest back of Eagle Spur with little Jed. We had a kind of . . . well, *experience?"*

Reverend Hubbly clucked his tongue impatiently. "What sort of experience?"

"Well, thar was this brilliant light, see. It flooded down on us and it were brighter than any light I've ever seen a'fore. And in that moment, it was like I knew everythung there was to know about God and th' whole universe – though to be honest, I cain't seem to remember too much of it. Only some of hit."

Reverend Hubbly snorted with derision, ogling her as if she were demented. It was obvious to Mary that he did not believe her. He glanced furtively around, clearly afraid that she might have been overheard by the few remaining congregants still hovering around the arbor, who were clearly reluctant to have this welcome monthly distraction in their monotonous lives come to an end. He moved forward through the towering trees away from this danger, hands clasped behind his back, his face sullen and censorious. Mary grabbed at his arm, forcing him to stop and face her.

"I know it sounds . . . well, *crazy*," she said anxiously, "but it happen'd. That's why I'm talkin' to you now, Reverend. It was not of this world. It were so beautiful. I will remember hit all my born days."

"You mean it was something *supernatural?*" he asked skeptically.

"Yes, indeed it were, Reverend. I've searched for some other explanation, but thar jest ain't none."

"Well, I wouldn't be so hasty if I were you. Perhaps it was a moment of light-headedness. You probably felt faint. The mind can play strange tricks on one at times."

"No, I was as clear-headed then as I am now. I thought you might have some explanation. Was it *God,* Reverend? Did He show himself to me and Jed that day?"

Reverend Hubbly cleared his throat and stared at the ground, deep in thought, the top of his balding scalp gleaming through a sparse covering of black hairs. At last he looked up with a grim expression on his narrow face. "Have you told this to anybody else?"

"Nary a soul, Reverend. Not even Zachary Thomas. And as you know, Jed cain't talk yet."

"Well then, I strongly suggest you keep your mouth shut and just forget about it!" he said severely.

Mary felt a deep pang of dismay. *"Why?* What makes you say sech a thung?"

"Well," he said in a voice loaded with doom, drawing himself up righteously, "you must understand that such *mystical* things are to be treated with utmost caution. How could you possibly know all of God and the entire universe? Such presumption is heretical in itself when theologians have been studying such matters for thousands of years and none could presume to know it all. It was, without question, the devil up to his nasty old tricks again. Remember he is there to prey on your gullibility if you let him. *To snare you with false visions!"*

"Oh no, it couldn't possibly be that," Mary cried emphatically, shaking her head. "It were too beautiful! I was filled with sech joy and bliss, sech incredible *love,* as I've never known a'fore."

"You forget what a canny customer is the Prince of Darkness. He has ways to lure innocents to his side. I repeat, you must resist this and never think or speak of it again!"

Mary looked at the bumptious reverend in consternation. Unable to suitably explain the phenomenon, he was suggesting that the most beautiful, enriching and spiritual experience of her whole life was nothing more than a devil's prank, a ploy for the devil to win her favor? How could it be when it so strongly reaffirmed and strengthened a deep and passionate faith in God and the power of good? It made not a scrap of sense. Some stubborn part of her nature would not allow her to accept his explanation of the incident despite the fact that his white collar suggested she should.

"No, Reverend," she said firmly, shaking her head. "I'm afraid that explanation is out of th' question. And if you had gone thru' what I went thru' that day, you would surely know why I can say that with sech conviction."

"Child," he said, eyeing her with the severity of a teacher censuring a naughty scholar, "you cannot *possibly* speak with conviction! You completely lack experience in these matters."

"Have you ever heard of similar instances a'fore, Reverend?" she pleaded. "Please, I've got to know . . ."

There was another long moment of deep, sour introspection by the reverend, after which he muttered reluctantly, "Well, there have been reports of *somewhat* similar religious experiences that I've read about . . . but in this case . . ."

"Please tell me what you've read, Reverend. I must know!"

"Well, there have been a few reported cases of such . . . er . . . *fairly* similar happenings experienced by elevated men of the church, saints. These are known as 'The Rapture' or 'Beatific Vision'."

"And is it believed that those who have experienced them happenings are mere victims of a devil's hoax too?" she asked dryly.

"No, of course not!" he snapped. "They are imminently divine in nature! But such things are rare and precious and not given freely by God to just *anyone* . . . like I said before, such phenomena are the sphere of holy saints, not ordinary mortals. Besides, I very much doubt that's what you and Jed experienced."

"Why?" Mary insisted.

"Well, there are a number of *discrepancies* . . ."

"Sech as?"

"Well, for instance, you say this . . . er . . . *experience* occured while you and Jed were together?"

Mary nodded earnestly.

"Well, there's your answer alone!" he snorted triumphantly. "I've never read or heard of a *shared* experience of this nature before."

"That don't mean it ain't possible tho', does it?"

"How presumptuous of you to think yours might be the *sole* exception!" the reverend blustered sternly.

"Well, what if it were?" she insisted.

"Oh, I very much doubt that. Indeed, I can say with absolute certainty that it was not. Like I said, "The Rapture" is the prerogative of the saints. Monks and devoted men of God, who have spent years of study, silent meditation and seclusion. You, dear child, though you may have been minutely instrumental in bringing religion and possible salvation to the sin-filled creatures of this wicked mountain, are hardly such a saint."

"Of course not!" said Mary, feeling the heat glowing hotly in her cheeks. "Well, what about these 'Beatific Visions' then? What do they mean exactly?"

"Well, it is seeing the immediate vision of God Himself in His own proper glorious essence that only the angel spirits and the souls of the pure and the just usually enjoy in heaven itself. Matthew 11.27 tells us clearly that only Jesus Christ, 'the Son', chooses to whom God should reveal Himself in this manner. It is said that only a few blessed chosen ones are brought to a union with God in knowledge and love and that they share forever in God's own happiness," he intoned solemnly. "It is in this exquisite beholding of God face-to-face that the created souls find perfect happiness."

"But . . . but that's right, Reverend!" said Mary excitedly. "That is *exactly* what happened. It's what I have jest bin tellin' you . . ."

"Hmmmph," he snorted. "There you go again! Don't you see? If that had been the true case, you would not be the miserable wretch you've been today. Indeed, you make a mockery of *'sharing forever in God's own happiness'* with that long face when I arrived and the whole service through. Thought you were going to burst into tears at one stage. That signifies to me that the *devil,* and not God, precipitated the vision, if indeed, it was such a thing at all."

A jolt of shock hit her stomach, and Mary caught at her breath. *Was her unhappiness that obvious?* For a dizzying moment, she felt miserable and horribly exposed. What answer could she give him? There was no way that she could tell the reverend the reason for her present miseries. He would only use that to bolster his argument even more.

"No, I had it, Reverend! I experienced th' 'Beatific Vision', I know I did!" she said, with quiet certainty.

The reverend sneered skeptically, "No offence meant, but have you even bothered to ask yourself why God would choose to show Himself to a backward mountain woman and her mute child?"

Mary felt herself grow cold with mortification at his condescending words, feeling blood rush to her cheeks. After a moment of stunned disbelief, during which she struggled with a sense of outrage, she recovered herself somewhat. Regarding him with steadfast hazel eyes, she said quietly, and with great dignity, "Jesus' father was a humble carpenter. Are you sayin' that he was not worthy to be similarly blessed by God?"

Unable to answer her logic, Reverend Hubbly chose to ignore it.

"I say He would not choose to show Himself to someone who keeps a jug of moonshine on her mantel!" he said sharply.

Mary blinked her eyes in consternation then guiltily dropped her gaze to the forest floor.

"Then who *would* He choose?" she whispered contritely.

"He would choose those who have spent years working for Him and spreading

His holy word. *Deserving people!"*

Such as yerself, you silly old goat, Mary thought crossly. The real reason why he would not entertain the idea that she'd experienced something wonderful and divine was because he was *envious* of her. He felt she was far less deserving than was he, and rather than have her claim such a privilege, he would denounce it as something not to be desired. Something imminently *evil!*

"And you are quite sure that you've never heard of ordinary folk, seemingly no consequence like me, who have had them thar "Beatific Vision" experiences a'fore?"

"No," he said sharply, with wild-eyed emphasis, a little too quickly to be entirely convincing, suggesting to her that he *did* know instances involving folk other than extravagant do-gooders and saints, "and," he continued with haughty bumptiousness, "I have read extensive religious works of all denominations and faiths, even those of the infidels. I pride myself on the depths of my knowledge regarding religious matters. Now, I *reiterate.* Put this wickedness aside and never speak of it again!"

Wickedness? Mary looked at him in deep, disbelieving dismay. How could anyone be this willfully ignorant? She could tell there was not a jot of grace or understanding in him, nor a willingness to believe that she and Jed might well have been chosen by God to undergo a genuine religious experience. But then it was useless arguing with the likes of a stubborn, prejudiced man like the reverend. He was judgmental and harsh and dictatorial, without the simple grandeur of the truly wise. He preached religion, but did not practice its supposed aim for he was quite without a genuine love for his fellow man. He was highly suspicious of other religions and spent his life decrying them. It was no surprise therefore that, to him, such a miracle was not a magnificent manifestation of God, but instead, the blatant delusional trickery of Beelzebub! He *chose* to believe it, because the alternative was so distasteful to him.

Alas, Reverend Hubbly taught not the love of God, but the fear of God, and used this like a flail on the back of a slave to force his congregants into the acceptance of a narrow, fixed Old-Testament ideology. Mary couldn't help wondering if such a misguided ideology was, in fact, more damaging than no religion at all. Indeed, ignorance of God's true nature seemed infinitely preferable to being given a deliberate subversion of it. How much stronger would their faith be if they knew that God loved them with such deep, ineffable, unconditional love, He would never want fear or the brimstone threat of punishment to force them into acceptance of His word, just as He would never condemn sinners to an eternity of torture on a burning lake if they were unable, or refused, to accept it. Sinners worked out their own punishment under God's great natural laws.

She felt a deep, abiding pity for such willful blindness, such narrowness of insight, such woeful lack of wisdom. She wondered what had led this supposed man of the cloth to such a calling when he was so clearly unsuited to it. Nevertheless, she had the answer she had been seeking. Such experiences *were* of a divine nature! God *had* chosen to show Himself to her and Jed that day. And the experience revealed to her subliminally that God wasn't a man sitting on a throne up in heaven. *He was everywhere.* He was an omnipresent Being of infinite Love, of vastness and infinitude, of such wondrous magnificence that it must confound the most elevated mind of man. The Church, so puny in comparison, was important, but not necessary, for there were much greater things to be gained in the silence on the top of a mountain, in quiet meditation and contemplation. *God was all!* Within and without. All in all. Indwelling. For His sacred spark was within each, igniting her and all others. She – and all humanity – was thus part of Him, His individual expression upon the earth. But she knew He further resided in trees, in rocks, in the bubbling brooks, in the earth. Thus all such natural things were precious and sacred and must be treated with honor and respect.

It had showed her a vast and intertwined network of interdependence among all manner of bird and beast and man and Nature, both animate and inanimate, that existed upon this fragile earth, which were presently being plundered by man. She thought of the way the bears and the wolves and all the other animals had been hunted almost to extinction, and not just for survival either. How whole kettles of rattlesnakes were destroyed by the mountain people just for sport! How so many of the trees on the mountains had been felled, something she had never registered when she lived on Lewis Mountain.

Surely religion was only desirable if it brought man to true spirituality and the realization that they must live *as Jesus* lived in love, compassion and humility, helping his fellow man along the way. To recognize that since we are all part of God, all humanity shares a common brotherhood and a common destiny – eventual reunification with the One Most High. She knew all this with a burning awareness and intensity that had come to her as a result of that momentous day. She knew from the depths of her very soul, with such unsullied certainty, that she and her blessed child had indeed experienced that day, the so-called "Rapture of the Saints", or "Beatific Vision" and, what's more, had seemed to bask in its wondrous aftermath for at least two weeks afterwards. She and Jed – and she somehow knew that dear mute little boy had grasped the spiritual significance as much as she – had been the recipients of divine revelation, which had left them with a legacy of faith far greater than before, which she needed so desperately now that her faith in man had been so recently shattered, leaving her full of raw despair.

Mary wondered for the umpteenth time why God had chosen *them* –not because Reverend Hubbly had been so dismissive of her claim, but because it seemed such a miracle to be sought out by Him like this. Well, whatever the reason, she felt deeply honored and privileged and humbled and she hugged this to herself like a comforting wrap. She just hoped that she could live up to God's expectancy of her, whatever that may be. In the midst of the monumental ignorance and darkness that abided everywhere, how could she, frail and human and alone in the knowledge, in view of Jed's tender-aged complicity, shed and spread the Light . . .?

Falling Leaves and Mountain Ashes

Book VI

'The Improbable Path'

'The journey of one's life
Often has scant predictability
When reviewed by one
Whose path was once thought
To be set in stone.'

Brenda George

55

Eli found Skyland even more bustling and busy than before. A lot more work had been done at the resort – there were a lot less tents and lot more rustic log cottages and cabins. A good number of poorly dressed, scrawny Corbin Hollow mountain women, wearing frilly cotton bonnets, along with their thin, raggedly dressed children, had come to collect parcels of food and clothing that had been donated by Skyland guests. George Pollock, who was busy overseeing the distribution with some of his Negro staff, greeted him like a long-lost pal and promptly invited him to stay in his own abode once more.

Soon, the pair was drinking Buchanan apple brandy in huge goblets at Freeman Lodge and Pollock was getting him up to date about the various happenings and events that had taken place at the mountain resort since he'd left. Listening to the effusive conversation of the small red-headed man, Eli was astounded anew by his enthusiasm and sheer love of life. Apparently, the fame of Skyland summer resort was spreading like wildfire, with more and more of the rich folk of major cities being drawn here by the lure of its costume parties and balls, the pristine surroundings and the famed affability of the host himself.

By discreetly asking Pollock what had happened with Reverend Cotterell after he had left the last time he'd been here, Eli was immeasurably pleased and relieved to learn that the old coot had been satisfied by his swift departure and that he and his beautiful daughter were presently installed in one of the log cottages for the summer.

"I trust the good reverend will not take umbrage at my presence here in camp?" Eli enquired politely, not in the least bit bothered whether the reverend objected or not. This time he was staying put until he'd won his daughter!

Pollock got a slightly bemused expression on his face. "I think it's fair to say that the reverend will not be unduly concerned by your presence."

Pollock then told Eli that the next day they were holding their annual Skyland Tournament. He explained that the Skyland Tournament was held between six "knights" who had to name their choice of "Queen" in advance. The knight collecting the most rings on horse-back would be declared the winner of the Tournament, and his nominated young lady would become Queen of the Tournament, and duly crowned at a ball to be held in the evening.

Fine well-trained horses that had been used in various such tournaments at venues down in the Valley had been engaged a week in advance in order that the various knights would have the opportunity to get some practice taking rings. The horses were kept in a large tent which served as a temporary stable. Pollock had prepared a good course running the full length of Furnace Field to Field Cabin.

"Pity you didn't arrive sooner," he said to Eli. "You would have been able to enter. I assume you've had lots of experience riding horses?"

"Of course," lied Eli smoothly – he'd only ever ridden his father's mules. "I'm an expert horseman . . ."

*   *   *

As luck would have it, Eli and George Pollock arrived at the Dining Hall the same time as Annabel and her father that evening. Eli's heart leapt at the sight of her. She looked exquisitely radiant, her lustrous black hair piled high in a pompadour, held with a diamond tiara, her skin, milky and smooth. She wore a long shimmering pale-green gown, edged with white French lace, which matched her lovely green eyes that seemed not to dance the way he remembered, and was set off by a sparkling diamond necklace. She took Eli's breath away and set his heart pounding. He had forgotten just how beautiful she was.

"Miss Cotterell, how good to see you and your father again," murmured Eli with his most respectful voice, as if the fiasco ending his stay here the last time had not occurred. Annabel looked stunned to see him and seemed at a loss for words. Surprisingly, it was Reverend Cotterell who stuck out a hand and shook Eli's extended one. He grunted a stiff, "Good evening", in reply to Eli's own greeting. Had the man forgotten who he was or was he sporting enough to let bygones be bygones? But the man's eyes held a gloating smirk and Eli was soon to discover why as he lifted Annabel's left hand to his lips. *She was wearing a ring on her ring finger!* Eli felt his stomach drop to his feet as his disbelieving gaze lit on the huge single diamond. But as he stood up and their eyes met, attraction raced between them, searing and as hard to handle as a hot potato. The memory of their scorching kiss next to the falls at the bottom of White Oak Canyon passed between them, unspoken, but uppermost in both their minds, he knew.

He had dreamed of having this young woman from the time he left the resort. He was determined to make her his own and become worthy of her, even setting his eventual sights on Washington D.C. like his father had suggested he should. Indeed, he had come back to Skyland as a much improved person. He had felt mighty pleased with himself as, gradually, the strips of his ignorance were peeled away from him during his time away. He was now extremely particular about his personal hygiene, and had proved a quick and able student, who had finally impressed the feisty Miss Prescott. He now knew how to read and write and had done a smattering of arithmetic, history and geography. He also kept up on

428

current affairs by buying the *Washington Post* and other newspapers whenever he went to the store, which happened a lot more these days, as his curiosity of the world outside the mountain quickened.

At first, he didn't have a clue what most of the articles meant and he would discuss them with Miss Prescott to get a better handle on them. He was also careful not to become embroiled in any skirmishes off the mountain, afraid that any unruly behavior on his part might, somehow, come to the attention of nobler ears, and eventually reach those of Annabel or her father. For instance, it was said that Hannibal Hanford had Washington connections and he knew the man must loathe him for so humiliating him that day in the general store at Fletcher. Had it all been in vain now that Annabel was engaged? *No!* She wasn't married yet. And what's more, she felt as he did. Her reaction on seeing him had told him that plainer than words. He wasn't about to give up just yet.

* * *

The day of the Tournament dawned fair and lovely. Eli strolled to Furnace Field from Freedom Lodge to watch the competition, dressed in a brown serge suit, a stiff white collar and a white straw boater and, instead of a whip, he carried a white ivory cane with an ornate gold top on it. He now had a small but quality wardrobe chosen for him by Sally Fox at the Fletcher general store, bought from the change left over the last time and increasing moonshine profits and thus he did not have to rely on borrowing Pollock's somewhat gaudy attire like he had the last time. Pollock had asked him perform his whip shows for him again, but Eli declined, saying he left his bullwhip at home this time. Of course, he had anticipated Pollock's request and had done so deliberately. He didn't want Annabel to think of him as a hired entertainer this time, but a suitor.

Pollock had been up since the crack of dawn, making final arrangements for the Tournament. It had attracted a lot of interest, for when Eli arrived, there was already about two hundred people in attendance around the course, including some valley folk and a good number of mountain folk, who were identifiable by their drab, coarse clothing. In contrast to the mountain men, the lady guests were dressed in the elegant long dresses of the period, and the men, in top hat and tails. Annabel Cotterell was there too, walking around on the arm of her stiff, portly, black-suited father, who was wearing his white clerical collar. Annabel was wearing a long, plum-colored, satin dress, edged with white lace around the collar and the cuffs of the long sleeves, and dainty plum-colored slippers. She was carrying a lacy, white parasol.

The knights were resplendently costumed in outfits of gold-embroidered, long-sleeved tunics of different colors, elaborate caps, long sashes tied around the waist, and black leggings tucked into knee-high boots, which Pollock had acquired from his costumers in Philadelphia. They were strolling around, except for one who sat on a bale of straw, his head in his hands.

Just then, a harassed-sounding Pollock caught at Eli's elbow from behind. "One of the knights has taken ill and cannot complete the course. I need a replacement in a hurry. *You're it!*"

Eli span on him in alarm. "No! I can't possibly do that!"

"Why not?" Pollock looked at him in some dismay.

To Eli's surprise, he found his host dressed in a knight's costume and realized that he entered into the competition himself. He looked dashing in a black, gold-embroidered, long-sleeved tunic, with white ruffles at the wrists and a puffy, long white scarf tied in a bow around his neck, black leggings and knee-high boots.

"Well, for one thing, I've had no practice. I don't wish make a fool of myself in front of this mob."

"*Nonsense!* You can do it. You said yourself you're an expert horseman!" Pollock's look turned pleading. "We need the right number of competitors else it'll ruin the whole thing."

Eli stared at him in consternation. He knew what a stickler for detail Pollock was when it came to his special events, but Eli had never ridden a horse in his whole life and, somehow, he didn't think the experience he'd gained riding mountain mules would count a whit in a tournament like this, which he was fairly sure would require considerable riding skills.

"Isn't there anyone else you can ask?" he finally mumbled.

"I've already asked around and nobody else is interested at such short notice. Come on, Eli, I'm in a tight spot here. If you're anything as good at riding horses as you are at using that whip of yours, it'll be a cinch. Tell you what. I'll even give you a couple of practice runs."

"No! No! That won't be necessary," said Eli hastily.

"Does that mean you'll do it?"

Eli swallowed hard. It was the last thing he wanted – to make a complete fool of himself in front of Annabel Cotterell and her father – but George Pollock had been a good friend to him, extending him unequaled hospitality and an invaluable introduction to a whole different lifestyle. What's more his wholesale embracing of Eli had gained him instant acceptance amongst Pollock's peers. Eli realized with a sinking heart that if he were to turn down such a request, more especially since he had made the mistake of telling him he was an expert horseman, it would seem churlish and downright ungrateful.

He forced himself to grin at his host. "Well, I guess I can't possibly let you down now, can I? But you have to understand, it's been quite a while since I last mounted a horse. Been far too busy running the moonshine business to take time out for such pleasurable pastimes as horse riding."

Pollock grabbed his hand and shook it heartily. "Thanks, Eli, I knew I could count on you, boy!" he said with a broad grin on his boyish, freckled face, while Eli felt a lump of dread invade his stomach.

Then Pollock asked him for his choice of queen.

Eli stared at him blankly, before mumbling, "Annabel Cotterell."

Pollock shook his head as if he didn't think it was a wise choice, but he said nothing about it. Instead he said, "What knight are you?"

After a moment's consideration, Eli said, "The Knight of Claw Mountain," hoping nobody here was familiar with the reputation of the place. "What knight are you?"

"Why, The Knight of Skyland, of course!" replied Pollock, with an impish grin.

"Of course!"

Later, the stricken knight slowly undressed from his costume and handed it over to Eli to change into in the large makeshift stable tent. He was a pompous fellow, who did look somewhat green around the gills, though whether from genuine illness, a raging hangover, or the prospect of the upcoming Tournament, Eli couldn't be sure.

When Eli finally entered the arena dressed in the great finery of yore, a yellow, gold-embroidered tunic, a strange cap with gold braiding on it, black leggings and black knee-high boots that were a size or two too large, he heard Pollock's loud voice come over the bullhorn, "Ladies and gentlemen, there's been a slight change to our program. Unfortunately, Knight Ernest Riker, the Knight of Philadelphia, has had to pull out of the Skyland Tournament at the last minute due to illness. However, I'm happy to announce that Eli Buchanan, the Knight of Claw Mountain, has gallantly accepted the challenge to take his place, despite the fact that he has not had a single moment's practice."

There was a polite spattering of applause amongst the spectators, and Eli felt his face color. He promptly disappeared into the tent to fetch his horse, a huge feisty-looking black stallion, with silver livery and yellow ostrich plumes attached to the headgear on either side of its head. He was relieved when a groom helped him to mount and then led the horse out of the dung-littered "stable" to the start of the course.

Pollock quickly explained the rules to him. The idea was for each knight to complete the course on horseback at speed, within a designated number of seconds. Then with a long tournament spear, tied with a fluttering scarf, he had to scoop up rings, which were suspended on small wooden racks at elbow height along the way. The one to collect the most rings would be declared the winner.

A short while later, a blast from Pollock's bugle signaled that the Skyland Tournament was on. Eli was relieved that he was to be the third knight to go, since it would enable him to see how the feat was performed. Two grooms held the horse of the first rider.

Pollock announced over the bullhorn, "The Knight of Baltimore!"

The signal to go was given, the grooms released their grip on the horse's bridle and the first knight was off. The Knight of Baltimore, attired in a dark green tunic, thundered down the course, his long spear tied with a fluttering lime-green scarf, held aloft. He scooped up two rings with it to much applause from the crowd.

Now, it was the second rider's turn. Eli felt his stomach squirm with nerves as he now moved into the second position, holding his spear vertically to the ground, as he awaited his turn. His horse was a disturbingly frisky beast. It kept ducking its head, stamping its front hoofs on the ground and snorting.

Pollock announced, "The Knight of New York!"

The signal to go was given and the horse in front of him broke away from the grooms' grasps and tore down the course. But something must have alarmed it, for instead of continuing on the course, it took off down the path past the Dining Hall until it was out of sight and earshot. *One knight eliminated!* Eli was both relieved and terrified by the rider's seeming inability to control the horse. After all, these horses were supposed to be properly trained. Or was it because the hapless Knight of New York was a complete novice like himself?

It was Eli's turn next. He felt anything but a gallant knight of old. As the two grooms led his horse forward, he felt his mouth go dry with unaccustomed fear. After Pollock announced, "The Knight of Claw Mountain", upon the signal to go, the grooms holding the horse either side of his bridle, loosened their grips. Eli kicked the stallion lightly with his heels and, to his considerable alarm, the stallion reared and plunged, almost unseating him, before taking off at speed.

Eli couldn't believe what happened next. Like the horse before it, it did not head for the course. With Eli hanging on for dear life, quite unable to do anything to control the beast, the horse tore at a ridiculous speed towards a crowd of spectators gathered at the edge of the cliff, causing Eli's heart to pound with panic. Besides injuring folk, it was likely to plunge them both over the edge into oblivion!

Fortunately, the panicked cries of the spectators made the crazed animal turn abruptly and it cut diagonally towards the course once again, barging through another crowd of spectators. Sam Sours, the Skyland Mail Carrier, was hit. He rolled onto the ground, screaming, with a severe cut to the head. The demented stallion then plunged through another crowd of onlookers, knocking them sprawling onto the ground. Everywhere there was pandemonium! The cries of the injured followed after Eli as the horse took off again.

Then finally in the middle of the course, with a violent bucking motion, the spooked stallion bucked and reared up on its hind legs, unseating Eli and sending him flying through the air. Eli's long tournament spear struck the ground, twisting him and breaking his fall. Even so, he landed heavily on the ground on his back, thoroughly winded. His head bumped hard on the ground and he closed his eyes, seeming to lose consciousness for a moment. When he opened them, it was to find Annabel Cotterell bending solicitously over him, her delectable, marble-white lace-lined deep cleavage just inches away, as she clasped fervently at his hand.

"Oh, Eli, Eli, are you alright?" she crooned.

Eli shook his head to clear it, wounded more by the sheer indignity of it than by the actual fall. After finally recovering his breath, he mumbled thickly, "Yeah, I'm fine."

"Oh, thank goodness you're alright! For a moment there, I thought you were dead!"

He was stunned by the concern on her face. He lifted his head and looked anxiously around at the milling crowds at the edge of the field, seeing a whole lot of bodies lying on the ground, and hearing a lot of groaning. "Where's your father?"

"He's gone to help Dr. Johnson with the injured. But no doubt as soon as he notices I'm gone, he'll be along."

Eli lifted his head and clutched at her hand holding his. "I have got to see you alone, Annabel."

"I know," she whispered.

He stared her straight in the eye and said fiercely, "Tell me, what is that ring you are wearing?"

Crouched beside him, she had the grace to look slightly embarrassed. "I am engaged. My fiancé gave it to me."

"You're *engaged?*"

"Yes," she admitted shamefacedly.

"Annabel, how could you?" Even as he said the words, Eli realized how ridiculous they sounded in the circumstances. It had been over a year since he'd last seen her and they'd had no contact since. But she'd never mentioned being involved with anybody back then. Foolishly, he'd never expected anything like this!

"I . . . I thought I'd never see you again. Father was very angry after you kissed me at the ball. He forbade me to ever see you again. And you slipped away the next day without even saying goodbye . . ."

"It was the hardest thing I've ever had to do, I swear. I've never stopped thinking about you. But I was determined to see you back here again. Now, it means nothing ... you're promised to somebody else!" he cried despairingly,

433

feeling deep, numbing disappointment invade his being at hearing his worst suspicions confirmed. It was a feeling foreign to him, since in the past, he always got what he wanted, one way or another. *Still, she wasn't married yet!*

She lightly touched his arm, as he struggled to sit up. "I know, and I'm sorry."

"Do you love him?" He squinted at her warily.

She colored faintly. "I don't know. I think so. But I don't feel about him the way I feel about *you.*"

Eli felt hope rising, as he sat with one arm around his knee, his other hand still clasping Annabel's. "How *do* you feel about me?"

She blinked, flustered, at his bold unflinching question. "I . . . I think I love you."

Eli could not believe her words. "What did you just say?"

"I said, I think I love you . . . that kiss at the falls . . ."

Eli stared at her in bald astonishment. She had just admitted to him that she loved him, even though she was betrothed to another. He stared at her fixedly.

"You can't marry him!" he said shortly. "Not after that kiss."

"Oh, I must! Father has given us his blessing and you know how hard that is to come by."

Eli felt a spurt of loathing for the doughty old goat.

"What's your fiancé's name?" Eli grunted through clenched teeth, feeling the full thrust of jealousy hitting him like a prizefighter's slug.

"Alexander Montgomery. He's very well-known in Washington – he's a personal aide to Vice President Roosevelt and a member of one of Washington's oldest and most respected families."

A personal aide to the vice president of the United States! He felt all his carefully laid plans go instantly awry. How could he possibly compete with that when he was just an ignorant hillbilly? *Eli Buchanan from Claw Mountain, a member of the most respected family in all the Blue Ridge – but for all the wrong reasons!* Yet he knew he couldn't give up. Not after an admission like that from Annabel. And he vowed he wouldn't always be an ignorant hillbilly. He would become somebody who could compete with such a fellow! "Why isn't he here with you?"

Annabel looked slightly fed up and pouting, said, "I don't see him all that often. The vice president keeps him very busy."

Eli found some small comfort in that. He grunted and struggled up from the dust with Annabel's help. He took both her hands in his, and looking deeply into her lovely green eyes, he said fervently, "Forget him and marry me! I'll go back to Washington with you."

She took a small step back. "Eli, you can't mean that? We hardly know each other."

"Then let's *get* to know each other. Meet me after the ball to crown the Queen of the Tournament tonight."

"It's been canceled and so has the rest of the Tournament. Dr. Johnson insisted on it. He's only helping the injured on condition that Mr Pollock never holds another Tournament here again."

Eli groaned. *Damn!* In trying to help his friend out, he had actually failed him and caused all this chaos. He turned his attention back to lovely Annabel.

"Then pretend you're tired and retire early. Meet me at the back of the Dining Hall at nine o'clock. I know a place where we won't be disturbed. You'll need to dress as for hiking though."

She looked at him in wide-eyed astonishment. "What about Father?"

"Make sure you give him an extra-strong sleeping draft. One that will knock him out the whole damned night!" he replied, turning and limping awkwardly away before she could object . . .

56

*A*nnabel *was late!* At least twenty minutes late! And to Eli, impatiently watching for her arrival behind the Dining Hall, each agonizing minute seemed interminable. Then just as he was entertaining the idea that she might not come, after all, she came hurrying toward him, a black shawl wrapped tightly across her head and shoulders. Fortunately, she had chosen her clothing sensibly. She wore a black riding habit that covered her knee-high boots by some six inches and a black satin muttonchop blouse with a big black bow at the collar.

Eli was well aware by now that it was quite unseemly for a young man and woman to go anywhere without a chaperone, so he was immensely thankful that the grounds were deserted after the Tournament had laid low so many of Skyland's guests. Without saying a word, he grabbed her hand and, carrying a kerosene lantern aloft and two blankets beneath his opposite armpit, hurried her out of the camp. He knew exactly where he was taking her.

The last time he was here, Pollock had told Eli about a place he had christened "Pollock's Cave", where he would secretly rendezvous with a certain young lady. Afterwards, Eli had set out to look for it and had found it quite easily. It was tucked away in the cliffs above Skyland and was a quiet, charming place reached by a steep climb, up, over and around boulders. The beauty of it was that it was not too far from camp. Being mountain-raised gave El an excellent sense of direction and he was sure that he would be able to find it again, even in the dark.

The night air was bracing and the black velvet sky splashed with an array of glittering diamonds. Fortunately, the moon was a great pearl orb in the heavens, which gave them added light to climb by. After about a half-hour of painstaking climbing up the steep, precipitous slope, they came to the small cave, or depression, really, with overhanging rocks. It was so high that they were among the tall treetops. Eli went in first with the lantern, to make sure no snakes or wild animals had sought to shelter in the cave.

Fortunately, only Pollock's small cache of books and magazines was in there, neatly stacked on a rock ledge. Eli put the lantern on the same ledge and spread one of the blankets on the ground. After leading Annabel inside, he sat down on it, drawing her down onto it in front of him. She removed her shawl and he saw that her hair was not in its usual high pompadour but loose and long and lovely, a heavy curtain that glistened blue-black in the lantern-light. She gave him a smile, so lovely, that he felt he wanted to weep. He could hardly believe he was all alone with her at last, in a place where they could talk and make love without being disturbed by anybody, let alone her pesky father.

Sitting on the blanket, face to face with her, with the shadows touching her beautiful face with mystery and allure, he bent forward and kissed her on her dark ruby lips. She raised her hands to his face and responded passionately. He could not believe that here he was, a raw ol' hillbilly, making love to the most sought-after young woman in Skyland, the play-ground of the rich and powerful. It was in that moment that he realized that there was *nothing* he could not do. *Nothing* he could not achieve if he really wanted it. And what he wanted more than anything in the world, was this woman as a wife. It would mean totally reinventing himself, to an even greater extent than he had achieved so far. But it was not beyond his grasp. He was his father's seed, after all, and his father had told him that he had come from aristocratic stock. Perhaps that was why he had fallen so easily into this lifestyle of the rich – because it was his true destiny!

"Oh Annabel, how I've longed for this," Eli whispered against her ear. *"I love you.* I have never loved any woman before. It's all new to me and you are driving me crazy. I can't stop thinking about you."

"Oh Eli, Eli, I love you too. I do! I do!"

Eli drew her down onto to the blanket so they were both lying on their sides, facing each other. His body still ached from his fall from the stallion earlier and he smothered a groan. He tugged at the bow at her neck, loosening it, and unbuttoning the top of her blouse, planted a kiss in the porcelain valley between her breasts. To his surprise, he found that she wore only a camisole and not a corset as he had expected. He was relieved. He was not experienced at removing corsets, since the mountain wenches did not wear them. He stuck his hand beneath the camisole and ran it over her one firm breast. Her nipple instantly puckered and she shivered, arching her body back.

"So rough," she whispered.

He hastily withdrew his hand, feeling slightly panicked. His mountaineer hands had given him away. They were not the soft, smooth hands of the rich, idle and pampered young men who peopled her world. But she grabbed his hand and returned it to her breast.

"Don't," she murmured huskily. "I like it."

"Annabel, I beg you not to marry him."

Annabel sat up straight. "Oh, Eli, I did not come here to talk about Alexander!" she chided gently. "I came here to be with you. Please don't spoil it for me by reminding me of my fiancé. It makes me feel horribly guilty."

He eyed her evenly. "Well, perhaps you *should* feel guilty."

"Oh, but I won't let you make love to me, of course. That would be *too* wrong! But you must hold me tightly, my darling. I have longed for this moment for so long."

Eli felt certain that, despite her disappointing words, he could take her anytime if he really wanted to. After all, despite his presumptuousness, she had not objected to his feeling her breast. But then he remembered his father's words: *'See you treat the rich girls with respect, not like common mountain wenches . . .'* and he wondered how wise it would be to try for her complete surrender. Perhaps it would be better to leave her wanting till he thought of a way to damage her relationship with the toffee-nosed Alexander Montgomery.

He knew how their brief encounters in the past, so fleeting and full of spine-tingling lust, had stirred his own blood, always making him long for more. He knew it was the same for her. Besides, his whole body was sore from his fall earlier and he didn't exactly relish placing further strain on it. The climb up hadn't done him much good either.

He said gallantly, "Of course I respect your feelings, my dear Annabel. But the reason that we will not make love tonight is because my fall from that maddened beast today has left me full of pain and somewhat incapacitated."

"Oh, my poor darling, of course. You were almost killed!"

He gazed hotly into her eyes. "Just so long as you understand one thing – that the very next time we meet, you shall become mine . . ."

They spent the whole night together, lying in each other's arms, kissing and holding one another beneath the second blanket. He had turned the lantern right down and her skin was milky and smooth in the reflected light of the full moon that entered the mouth of the cave. And though his hands were everywhere, feeling her breasts, even creeping beneath her skirt and caressing the warm, damp crotch of her drawers, which had her groaning with desire, he did not attempt to further undress her, or himself.

In a way, he almost enjoyed the near-chasteness of it. Despite the wet, devouring kisses, the hot, heavy breathing, the feeling of blissful oneness with her, the woman of his dreams, he yet welcomed the feeling of holding himself back. He knew she was desperate with desire, her body crying out for him with its heavy musky scent, which he could smell above the heady sweet smell of her perfume, letting him know how much she ached to have him claim her.

Instead, he teased and cajoled, pressing himself urgently against her, so that she could feel the unmistakable iron rod of his manhood. Then worn out by his escapade at the Tournament, his fall and the climb, he fell asleep. About an hour before dawn, she roughly woke him up, insisting that he take her back to camp immediately so that she could slip back into her father's cabin before he woke up. To his dismay, she seemed anxious and upset, afraid now that she had been missed or seen by someone, who might report it to her father. He did his best to reassure her, but she stood up and hastily straightened her clothing and her hair and wrapped the shawl around her head and shoulders again, arranging it so that it half-covered her face.

He could tell that anxious fear and guilt had gripped her. He reluctantly stood up and straightened his own clothing, feeling as if he'd been hit by a steam train, before taking her by the hand and leading her outside the cave. The moon was low and cast an eerie light onto the tree-tops. A faint cool breeze soughed through the trees and strands of mist sailed through the trees like eerie wraiths. This early in the morning there was sharpness in the air and she shivered with cold.

He led her down the mountainside, holding the two blankets beneath one arm, and the lamp in that hand, using the other to hold her hand to guide her downward path, feeling stiff and sore in every muscle and joint of his body. He limped awkwardly, inwardly cursing horses that were clearly insults to the noble mules, cautioning her to be careful of her footing amongst the boulders. Fortunately, the way down was easier than going up had been. When they at last neared the camp, she left him without a word, scampering on fleet feet in the direction of her father's cabin.

Eli watched her go with his mind in a whirl of emotion, the memory of their passionate night-long tryst filling him with an odd mixture of bereftness, long-ing, dissatisfaction and pure joy. Her panic this morning, so obviously prompted by terror and guilt, bothered him, but he comforted himself by telling himself that she was most certainly in love with him and just needed a little time to decide what she should do about that snot, Alexander Montgomery.

438

57

During his last visit to Skyland, Eli had made a point of making friends with the many politicians from Washington who frequented the resort, so he wasn't all that surprised when Senator Huntington from Pennsylvania, who had bought some of his moonshine, approached him on his second day in camp, asking him to join him in a drink. They were presently seated on single stuffed sofas in the Dining Hall, nursing Buchanan apple brandy in big glass goblets, which had been brought to them by a uniformed Negro waiter. Although alcohol was not sold at the resort, the senator had given a barrel of the brandy to George Pollock requesting that he keep it on his behalf and have it served to him and his guests. Pollock had allowed this small concession, providing it was done discreetly. Since it was during the day, most of the other guests had joined in the daily activities and there was nobody around to disturb them to notice this lapse in the strict rules regarding alcohol.

The senator's large, flabby body was dressed in a white pongee suit to combat the late-summer heat. He had a craggy face that was pale and shiny, pale-green eyes that belied his shrewd nature, and he was freshly barbered and powdered. He had a large, bulbous nose, a full healthy head of white well-groomed hair, and thick, white eyebrows with long hairs sticking out of them and out of his large fleshy pink ears. He smelled strongly of men's cologne. A larger-than-life character, he seemed robust and was a little condescending in manner.

"I want to talk to you about this marvelously mellow alcohol you've been peddling around the place," the senator began, holding out his goblet to Eli. Eli sucked in a breath, eyeing him warily, as the senator continued, "Where is your distillery situated exactly?"

Eli frowned at the unexpected question. "Well, I don't have a distillery, Senator. Just produce from our own stills on the mountain."

"I could have sworn I overheard you telling somebody that your family owns distilleries in the Graves Mill area or thereabouts?"

"Sure. Cousins of mine," said Eli weakly. He remonstrated soundly with himself. He had to keep his tall tales straight in his mind or else he was heading for trouble.

The senator fell back in his chair in disbelief. "Are you telling me that such fine-tasting liquor is nothing more than illegally stilled moonshine? Most of that stuff is so raw it does nothing but fire the gullet. This is quite superb."

Eli felt a jangling of alarm. Perhaps the senator had something to do with the Revenue section of the government and was out to trap him. Nervous to incriminate himself, Eli merely grunted.

"Why, that's simply amazing!" the senator enthused. "In other words you run a little nickel-and-dime business and have never gone into mass production?"

"Guess so," said Eli nervously, wondering what was coming next, and not wanting to admit that his was far more than the average mountaineer's still site – ten stills now, producing a good deal more than the other Blue Ridge moonshiners.

"I've just taken over a distillery in Washington. A fella there couldn't come up with the mortgage payments. Drank too much of his own evil brew!" the senator snorted contemptuously. "I've been wondering what to do with the blessed thing. All the equipment is still there. I was able to get it attached to cover the back payments he owed me. Would you be interested in running it for a small wage to begin with – say twenty-five dollars a week – at least until it's up and running, plus a half-share of the profits? We could hire a chemist to do the actual mixing, but it must be under your strict supervision. With stuff like you've got to offer, we could make a killing. We could go into full mass production and ship it all over the country. Quite frankly, it's the best whiskey I've tasted, and I've tasted my share of them."

Eli sat stunned. *What a tempting offer!* Annabel and her father lived in Washington! If he took it up he would become respectable businessman in partnership with one of the country's leaders – and he'd heard from Polly that there were boundless rumors about what a sharp and ruthless businessman the senator was. He could win Annabel over if he were stationed there in the capitol, he knew it! Though the crabby and objectionable reverend might not be too happy with the type of business this was (though Eli had seen the old hypocrite was not beneath purchasing a ten-gallon barrel of his whiskey through Pollock), at least he'd have more to offer Annabel than as a fake gentleman and an ignorant hillbilly moonshiner. And with Annabel Cotterell on his arm, he would be the envy of every male in the nation's capitol.

Coming to Skyland the first time had broadened his horizons to such an extent that he had felt as restless as a trapped bear back on Claw Mountain. Besides, he badly wanted to get away from there. Away from *that* woman! *His brother's wife, Mary* – that constant thorn in his side. But he didn't want to seem too eager.

"Tell you what, Senator. I'll think about it and let you know tomorrow."

* * *

Eli spoke to George Pollock about the senator's offer that night, asking for his advice. After all, by the sounds of it, his friend had experienced more than his fair share of dealings and troubles with lawyers and accountants, fighting to keep Skyland more than once, and was likely to understand any pitfalls that might be encountered. And sure enough, Pollock had a fountain of good advice to offer. The proprietor of the Skyland resort told him to insist that he get a signed contract stipulating the conditions they agreed upon. Pollock had heard that the senator was a sly one and warned that he might try to take advantage of Eli if he went on only the man's word or handshake.

He also suggested that the half-share that the senator had offered seemed too generous for a man of the senator's ilk and reputation and suggested that if the senator used his own accountants, Eli might well find he ended up with a half-share of little or nothing. Armed with this insight, the next day Eli sought out Senator Huntington in the Dining Hall once again. He sat down opposite him.

"Senator, I've thought about it and I've decided I'd like to take you up on your offer."

"I'm delighted to hear that, my boy."

"There are a few conditions though."

The senator looked surprised at this, blinking owlishly. "Well, let's hear them then."

"First of all, any liquor produced at the distillery must bear the Buchanan name – it's my late father's liquor, after all, which he took great pains to develop, and had enormous pride in, and he sure deserves the credit for it." (Of course, Eli was determined to have the liquor called by the Buchanan name on his *own* account, not that bastard's, but the idea of honoring his father in this way, though deeply repugnant to him, sounded noble and was therefore much more likely to be respected.) "Furthermore many folk at Skyland have tried my liquor and I've no doubt that the word has already gone out among their friends and acquaintances back home – I bought three times the amount here that I brought the last time and it was all gone in a matter of hours. I am convinced that I could have brought any amount I wished and still sold it. What I'm saying is the Buchanans have gained a reputation for supplying good liquor. I think we can build on that."

To his relief, the senator nodded sagely in agreement. "Granted. What're the rest?"

"That there is to be a signed contract guaranteeing the use of the Buchanan name and which also stipulates that I and my brothers be allowed to continue to produce our same moonshine on the side. My brothers need the income still and they also need me to oversee it. I will have to go back there a few times a month to make sure production doesn't lapse, or deteriorate, but I wouldn't neglect the distillery, you can be sure of that."

The senator considered this for a moment, twisting the top of one fleshy pink ear speculatively. "I don't expect that it will eat into our profits too greatly," he finally said amicably, laughing with largess and waving an airy hand. "I never intended our sales should be directed at the mountain regions anyway. Nosiree, I want our products sold in all the finest restaurants and hotels from New York to San Francisco, Chicago to New Orleans. Done deal, young man," He clasped Eli's hand in his huge paw. "Now, let's drink to it."

"I'm not done yet, Senator. Just one last thing. I get to choose the accountants we use. You'd have the right to turn down my choice, of course, but only for good reason. No offense intended, sir, but a hick ol' mountain boy like me has got to safeguard his interests."

Senator Huntington audibly sucked in his breath, looking thoroughly shocked and offended. He took a good long while to think about this one, seeming tight-lipped and intensely annoyed, as he eyed Eli closely. Eli managed to stay calm and poker-faced under his intense scrutiny, as the silence stretched, taut as a bow. It was clear to Eli that he'd gone too far this time, but he didn't know how to put things right with the senator, so he remained silent and waited for him to speak.

"It seems I have greatly underestimated you, Eli Buchanan," the senator said finally, the light of admiration beginning to gleam in his pale-green eyes. "I guess I should be insulted, but I'm not. You're a shrewd young man. *A kindred spirit.* It'll be a rare pleasure doing business with you.

58

The rest of Eli's week at Skyland flew by, filled with endless parties, rich food and too much champagne. Unfortunately, although he saw a lot of Annabel and her father, he didn't get the opportunity to be alone with her again. Oh, she would give him long, meaningful glances when she thought nobody was looking but, to Eli's frustration, she refused to leave her father's side. Was it because her father had caught her out, or because she had decided she wanted nothing more to do with him after their all-night tryst? He could not bear the uncertainty. Had he not had Senator Huntington's offer under his belt, he would have been frantic, but now he could afford to let things lie until he got to Washington. Indeed, he couldn't wait to get there so that he could wrest Annabel from Alexander Montgomery's grasp. He was consumed with jealousy every time he thought of the man. Once again, he left Skyland without managing to say goodbye to Annabel.

* * *

Eli's return to Claw Mountain was met with great excitement by the other clan members for this time he had gone to Skyland with lots more to sell than just moonshine. Over the months, Edna had made a score of rag dolls that were beautifully sewn, with their cotton-cloth bodies filled with absorbent cotton, their hair made with different colored wools, their faces painted, wearing pastel gingham dresses, lace-edged long drawers, white lace-edged petticoats, white lace-frilled over-aprons, fancy white lace-edged caps and felt shoes, much of the materials to make them having been given to her by Mary's mother. She had told Mary that before Eli left for Skyland, she had begged him to let her accompany him to sell her rag dolls. He had refused pointblank, saying that she would feel out of place there. She had then asked if he would take the rag dolls along with him and try to sell them on her behalf. Though he had grumbled about it darkly, saying he would feel a fool peddling such "girlie" products, he had finally agreed to take them along and, what's more, had sold every one of them to the rich city guests at a whopping one dollar each, rather than the fifty cents she had asked for them, since the first lady he approached, with shame-faced reluctance, refused to give him a mere fifty cents for 'all that beautiful work.'

Word went out, and he had sold the twenty dolls almost a fast as his moonshine. He had brought back $20 in cash to his late brother's astounded and grateful widow. Mary knew her stalwart friend had never seen so much cash at one time in her entire life and was thrilled for her. What's more, the rag dolls could be sold at the general store on a regular basis, though admittedly, she'd probably only receive twenty-five cents apiece for them there.

But to Mary, it was the other Bucko widow, Lila, who was the most gifted sewer. Except for her mother, Mary had never seen the like. Such small, neat stitches! She had begun to make a quilt on her own as well as contributing to the communal ones at quilting bees. It had taken several months to complete and was quite exquisite. She made it with all sorts of beautiful and intricate designs, as if she'd been sewing her entire life. It had also been packed on the mule and sent it off with Eli to Skyland. He had sold it for a handsome six dollars. Lila had accepted the money from him with astonishment, and a sense of great accomplishment, Mary had no doubt.

Not to be outdone by the young women of the clan, the Buckos had got in on the act too. Much to Mary's sorrow, they had sent scores of rattlesnake hides with

Eli, which George Pollock had purchased for a dollar apiece to have made into belts. They'd obviously found another den, and, while Mary understood that cash was needed for their survival, she found such wanton wholesale destruction of the reptiles heartbreaking. Though she was still afraid of them she strongly felt that even these highly venomous creatures should be treated with respect.

Nevertheless, all the cash floating around the mountain was quite intoxicating and was met with great celebration and excitement by the once impoverished clan. Indeed, only Mary had deeply dreaded Eli's return.

59

Eli traveled to Shenandoah Junction by hired buckboard and mules then boarded the Baltimore and Ohio railroad coach to Washington D.C. He felt a burning need to get away from Claw Mountain, away from that bitch, Mary, away from all the dark, dreadful memories and secrets that sat inside him like a giant stone, forever weighing him down. After returning from Skyland, he could not bear to be on the same soil as Mary. Besides everything else, he could not forgive her for making a peace pact with the Galtreys. She had made his life on the mountain unbearable. Somehow she had managed to reduce his power amongst the clan and it infuriated him the way most of his kin fawned over her, and went to the services at the brush arbors, no matter how many times he had torn them down in the past. So the fact that he was now traveling towards a new life, hopefully with Annabel Cotterell, gave him a sense of great satisfaction as well as relief.

He was met at the capitol's station by Senator Huntington in a horseless carriage that easily equaled that fine specimen that had belonged to Hannibal Hanford. Taking his lone piece of luggage off the still-hissing steam train, Eli carried it to the parked vehicle filled with excitement. The senator helped him load the bulging carpetbag in his trunk then drove him into the city centre to show him around Washington. He carried his bullwhip in the cab of the vehicle with him. It was the first time Eli had ever been in a city and he was slightly alarmed at the size of the place and at how busy and noisy the streets were.

It was his first ride in a horseless carriage, too, and it did feel grand compared to being on the old buckboard pulled by his paw's old and ornery mules. It told him how much he had come up in the world already. The horseless carriages far outnumbered the horse-and-buggies in the streets and seemed to roar along at the pace of hares, sometimes causing the nostrils of horses to flare and their eyes to roll, as they passed. They drove past the White House and Eli was awestruck by the grand home of the president of the United States. How rich and powerful a man must be to reside in such a place? To enter its portals even?

He spent the next few days with his new partner (whose family lived back in Harrisburg in Pennsylvania), in his expensively furnished handsome brownstone in Georgetown, with its Rosenthal china, Persian rugs and vermeil cutlery. He openly asked about these valuable articles and the senator had expounded on them and other artifacts he owned at great length. It made Eli determined that, one day, he, too, would own such fine things.

The first thing Eli felt he needed to do, however, was to find himself a modest place to stay. He went the rounds of filthy, disgusting, noisy boarding houses, smiling grimly to himself when he realized that a short time ago he would have found nothing offensive about these dumps.

Using a horse-and-buggy borrowed from the senator, he finally found himself a room at a reputable, quiet establishment, in a neat flower-filled garden, which had been recommended by the senator. For seven dollars a week, the red-haired, buxom landlady offered him a large, airy, cozily furnished room with an ornate fireplace, and three meals a day, with Sunday dinners an extra fifty cents. It was a good deal more than he had anticipated paying, but it was worth it to him. It was important to him that Annabel Cotterell should approve if she ever chanced to visit him there. He thought she might find Betsy Dover's large, comfy home rather charming.

* * *

The distillery was in a rundown part of Washington, next to a tobacco warehouse. After assessing the place, which was in a deplorable condition, the next step for Eli was to get the new company formed and the partnership contract drawn up at a lawyer recommended by George Pollock. Armed with advice from his friend, Eli had another condition of his own built in: he had to be the one to do all the hiring and firing. He didn't want to be under the yoke of one of the senator's hand-picked men. He got Jake to join him from Claw Mountain at $15 a week, because his brother knew the production routine almost as well as he did, and then he hired, straight from the streets, a thin fifteen-year-old youth, called Tosser Daniels, at two dollars a week. Tosser wore a tattered brown cap and a ragged coat that was much too big for him. Eli had picked him out of a group of street youths, mainly because the boy reminded him of his dead brother, Jamie.

Jake wanted to stay with Eli in his room, but Eli hastily told him he was not permitted to share and that there were no more vacancies at the boarding house, quickly finding him a room in one of the cheap boarding houses he had over-looked for himself instead. Eli felt his brother would be more at home there anyway.

Eli's first goal was to get the distillery into decent shape. This was where all his father's manic insistence on perfection and cleanliness stood him in good stead. The giant copper kettles were tarnished green and covered with a fine layer of dust, putrid smells emanated from the grime-covered mixing vats, while old moldy sawdust covered the floor. Working like a regular demon alongside Jake and Tosser, Eli got the copper kettles cleaned, polished and shining, the mixing vats emptied, cleaned and polished, the old smelly sawdust removed and the floors spread with fresh sawdust.

Tosser proved a good choice for he was hardworking and uncomplaining and always arrived at the distillery every morning on time. Soon they had the whole place gleaming. Next, Eli bought bottles from a nearby bottling company and got labels made bearing the Buchanan trade name – "Buchanan's Famous Blue Ridge Mountain Whiskey" and "Buchanan's Famous Blue Ridge Mountain Apple Brandy". When they were ready to start production, Eli approached an account-tant who had been recommended by George Pollock. He readily agreed to look after the books of the new company, which was to be called "Buchanan's Finest Liquors". Senator Huntington duly gave Cecil Halsted, head of a small but reputable accounting firm, the nod.

Soon after hiring several more men to work the assembly line, production began. It went exceedingly well. Within six months, every restaurant and water-ing hole in the city was being serviced by "Buchanan's Finest Liquors", de-liveries being made in a large truck that had come with the distillery that could carry fifty crates at a time. They met some resistance from local gangsters on whose territory they were encroaching, but Eli was able to deal with this threat, quickly and effectively. He had brought his favorite whip, his bullwhip, his knife and his Owl's Head pistols to Washington with him, having reluctantly left behind his shotgun.

His other weapons he kept in his room, but he carried his bullwhip every-where with him and when some hefty fellows in cheap suits that were too small for them came into the distillery, demanding protection money, he used the whip to terrorize the pair, instantly ridding them of their guns with it. It happened a couple more times. Despite the fact that they carried guns, he always managed to outwit and outsmart them with his rampant whip. Finally, they left him alone.

Eli very soon discovered that Senator Huntington was not just a wily business man; he was a crook with a streetfighter's instinct. He had half the cops and judges in Washington on his payroll and was involved with just about every underhanded deal that went down in the city. Proud of the way Eli had handled the distillery and the handsome profits already being made from it, the senator soon begun to let Eli in on most of them. He seemed to find Eli's cool clinical approach to matters worthy of cultivating. Whenever he needed to lean on somebody, he sent Eli. Eli always came away with his job satisfactorily carried out, his menacing looks and disturbing air usually enough to get the job done without him having to resort to his whip, which had, by now, earned him the local street nickname of "The Whistle-Whip Kid". Soon, the business bought another four trucks and began making deliveries to New York and Baltimore. In another six months, the distillery had to be extended to cope with a growing demand throughout the country, and they bought another ten trucks.

* * *

Eli made the transition from mountain moonshiner to city distillery master with remarkable ease and, as the business prospered, so did Eli. His salary at the distillery doubled then quadrupled. Besides this, the split profits were pleasingly healthy. His clothes were now personally tailored and, like Senator Huntington, he visited a barber for shaves and to tame his bright-yellow hair. He bought the senator's horseless carriage from him, at a fraction of its worth, when the senator bought himself a newer model. Eli used it to travel to Claw Mountain and back. It was a 1902 Rambler Runabout which the senator had bought for $750, and had let him have for a mere $200. Eli was delighted with his new purchase. The handsome one-cylinder C Model with its spoke wheels, elevated steering wheel and carriage-like brown leather seat was a joy to a man whose previous transport had been a mule-driven buckboard belonging to his father or, more often, his own two feet.

His family had turned out in numbers to see it the first time he drove it back to the mountainand surrounded it in a big admiring covey, whistling and cheering. He had felt a measure of pride and satisfaction at having achieved so much in such a short space of time. What he didn't spend on cultivating his new image, he saved, including all the money he made from doing various deals with the senator. Though he ached to see Annabel Cotterell again, he had decided he would only attempt to contact her when he had something to offer her. Enough for him to knock out the opposition once and for all. A fine house, for instance.

President McKinley had been assassinated on 14th September, in Buffalo, New York, the previous year, when a crazed anarchist shot him twice in a receiving line at the Pan-American Exposition there, during the president's second term, and he died eight days later. Eli's only interest in the matter when he belatedly heard the news was what had happened to Alexander Montgomery now that his boss had become the president. Fortunately, Senator Huntington was a close friend of the new president, Theodore Roosevelt. From him, Eli learned, with considerable chagrin, that Alexander Montgomery remained the aide to the newly installed president. Eli had made the senator promise that he would always enquire of the president when his aide intended to marry Annabel Cotterell, whom the senator had met at Skyland with her father, of course, and so could legitimately express a personal interest in the match. This way Eli was able to keep track of her wedding plans, which appeared to be non-existent at this time, though she was definitely still engaged. According to the senator, '"Teddy" kept Alexander so busy 'the poor boy hardly had a life of his own'. This suited Eli admirably, of course. Obviously, if he heard that the wedding was on any time soon, he would be forced to make a move before then, but otherwise he felt safe to plan his new life and image.

* * *

Two years passed and the business was still booming. Knowing of his desire to purchase a house, but not his reason for it (which was to provide a home for himself and Annabel once they were married), Senator Huntington alerted Eli to the intended sale of a house that had belonged to a deceased wealthy old professor before it was put on the general market. The senator's bank manager had offered it to the senator initially and told him it was 'going for a song'. The senator told Eli that despite the apparent decrepit condition of the house, it made more sense for him to buy a rundown house in an upmarket area than seek a better house in a lesser area and, if he did it up, it could become a healthy investment for him.

Eli did not even go and view it, convinced that a house in the highly favored north Washington suburb would be sure to impress Annabel. He went straight to see the bank manager and told him flatly that he wanted to buy it and made him what the senator considered was a reasonable offer. Eli had saved enough for a sizable deposit, but would need a mortgage loan from the bank to purchase the place.

After much discussion, the bank manager, a snooty, condescending official, informed him that to purchase the place, Eli would need a high mortgage, far more than the bank felt he could afford. Eli was dashed but not defeated. Such was his grim determination to own the property named "Rose Haven", that he offered to put up his share of "Buchanan Finest Liquors" as security. Still the bank manager was not impressed, saying the business was too new as yet. It was only after Eli managed to persuade Senator Huntington to sign a personal guarantee in addition to his own security that he successfully secured the mortgage loan. (Of course, it helped that the senator had got word that morning that various products of "Buchanan's Finest Liquor" had won several gold medals at an exposition in San Francisco, which had resulted in a number of large export orders from England, Italy and Germany.) Eli found it hugely ironic that his father had given him something worthwhile after all.

Only once he and the senator had signed the necessary documents and the place was actually registered in his name, did Eli finally venture forth to look at "Rose Haven" for the first time. With a true mountaineer's superstition, he had been afraid that if he went beforehand, something might happen to spoil his plans. That morning he had got another piece of splendid news from Senator Huntington, who had summoned him to his house. There, the senator had informed him that he had taken over the sumptuous house of a wealthy banker he had financially ruined. In it, he said, were many pieces of antique furniture and *objects d'art* that he would allow Eli to purchase from him at a fraction of their value for his new home.

Eli was overwhelmed by the senator's generosity coming hot on the heels of his signing a personal guarantee for him to purchase the house. When he voiced this, the senator smilingly informed Eli that he fondly regarded him as the son he'd never had. Though Senator Huntington was a true scoundrel who preyed on the weaknesses of others, Eli considered how he'd been far more of a father to him than his own father had ever been. True, in the end, Obediah had recognized his potential and set him on the path to improving himself but, before that fateful day that he'd set forth for Skyland, his father had been nothing but a terrible burden to him and he had always hated him without reservation.

Elated by the way things were continuing to go his way, Eli drove to "Rose Haven" in his Rambler full of eager anticipation. It was all so hard to believe. He, Eli Buchanan, once a penniless hillbilly, was now the proud owner of a home in a fine Washington suburb at the tender age of twenty-three. He stopped in front of the house and stared at it in breathless wonder. Though the tall, stately brownstone did indeed look very dilapidated, the garden instantly captured Eli's imagination. The property was aptly named "Rose Haven" for the front garden beyond a low white picket fence, with a matching small gate, was a mass of magnificent roses of every description. Even the enchanting scrollwork front porch was covered in a mass of white miniature climbing roses. A sojourn through a wooden gate into the large back garden revealed that it was surrounded by high walls and a horticultural delight.

It was full of curving beds lush with a profusion of multi-colored flowers, exotic flowering shrubs, winding paths, secret grottos and fishponds of goldfish, over which were built charming little stone bridges. Beneath a tall oak with widely spreading branches, was a delightful white scrollwork gazebo. Eli was beside himself with joy. Buying the place was well worth it for the garden alone. How fortunate for him that the property had not gone onto the open market since he was sure it would have been snapped up in no time at all. But it had been destined for him! For such rare and exquisite beauty thoroughly complemented that of Annabel Cotterell, for whom he had bought it. He was more determined than ever to bring her home here as his bride.

He suddenly remembered how much his mother had loved flowers, though his father had forbidden her to keep them on the front porch out of sheer meanness, and part of him wished she was here to see all this. The memory of his mother gave him a slight jolt; he hadn't thought of her in a very long while. It always pained him to think of her, since he had such ambivalent feelings about her. Right now, it hurt him to do so and he brushed the memories impatiently aside, not wanting anything to spoil the magic of the moment.

However, if the outside of "Rose Haven" was quite heavenly, he was soon to discover that the inside was not. Indeed, it was dark, dingy and depressing. It was quite clear that Professor MacDougal, apparently a lonely old bachelor in life, had reserved all his love and efforts for his garden alone. The furniture which came with the house was heavy, old and musty-smelling, the wallpaper was faded and tatty and the carpets and rugs, ugly, moldy, frayed and stained. The plumbing was antiquated and all the lighting, gas. The windows were small and hardly let in any light. Its only saving grace was in its beautiful high, white, domed ceilings with their gold curlicues and painted Botticelli angels. Though disappointed by the dismal state of the house, Eli was determined to transform his new acquisition into a place worthy of Annabel Cotterell.

Within days, Eli, after seeking advice from Senator Huntington and reading numerous books on the subject of renovation and interior decoration and design – heady subjects for a mountaineer who a few years earlier had not known how to sign his own name – brought in an architect to make drawings of alterations to the place, and soon a team of workmen from a reputable firm of builders, decorators and general contractors, used by the upper-crust classes was employed to carry them out. His instructions to them were very clear.

For months the place was a terrible mess and the sounds of hammers and saws, scraping and sanding and the moving of ladders, resounded. Whenever he could escape from the distillery, Eli was there, inspecting and overseeing, breathing in clouds of dust and the smell of cement and sawdust, having inherited his father's obsessive need for perfection in what he valued.

The workmen removed old wallpaper from the walls with strippers, they water-washed the ceilings which necessitated using tall scaffolding to reach them, removed cracked and blistered paintwork with a paraffin torch lamp, knocked down walls to increase the size of both the drawing room and the dining room, knocked out two small windows and replaced them with big bay windows to let in more light, then used cement to stop up holes and accomplish the major structural alterations. Floorboards were replaced, the woodwork of the front and back staircases sanded and revarnished.

Besides this, the roof gutters were replaced, the roof cleaned and all the missing tiles replaced. The outside was a mess too with planks and wheelbarrows and piles of sand and cement everywhere and Eli, afraid that the garden might get damaged or neglected during this period, hired Professor McDougall's old Negro gardener, Timothy Gouch, who'd been kept on by the bank until the place was sold, to make sure that the plants were not damaged and the gardens were kept watered and well-maintained.

Finally, the house was nothing but a bare shell with bare walls, bare ceilings, and bare floors. And then the renovations and a magical transformation began. And nine months after the work started on it, it was finally ready to be filled with the antique furniture and arts and treasures he'd purchased from Senator Huntington, a collection that completely belied his mountain heritage and completed his personal transformation. Finishing touches were made by experts on interior decorating. *At last it was all done.*

Eli moved from his room in Betsy Dover's boardinghouse to his renovated brownstone as soon as the last workman moved out. He was delighted with his new home. Here he began to entertain Washington's finest, mainly the senator's friends and associates at first, but steadily branching out to encompass his own, though he escaped being part of the better list of the high-society Washington socialites, which was very exclusive and belonged only to "old money" and flawless blood lines, where even an old warhorse like Senator Huntington, serving his third term in Washington, was not welcome.

It was a state of affairs that did not satisfy Eli. Alexander Montgomery belonged to this exclusive set, and he was determined to be part of it himself one day. Eli was, however, invited to dinners and parties of the *nouveau riche*. However, despite his eloquence, his grasp on current affairs and his friendship with some of the highest-ranking politicians in Washington, he was considered a bit too risqué for many hostesses, too dangerous to trust with their daughters, with hints of his links to the underworld, his scarred face, bright-yellow hair and disturbing pale-yellow eyes, all of which were considered too much of a blemish on their finely coiffured and elegant worlds. But Eli did not care for it was time to call on Annabel Cotterell! It had taken him three whole years to get where he wanted, but now he was finally ready to claim her for his own . . .

* * *

Before Eli had time to go to the Cotterell home, however, an extraordinary bit of fate came into play. He was invited to accompany Senator Huntington to a meeting with the president at the White House. Besides wanting to meet the highest elected official in the land, Eli could not give up the chance of possibly meeting his rival for Annabel's affections, and agreed with alacrity.

They went to the White House the following brisk autumn afternoon in the senator's Rambler and entered its grounds through the new East entrance. The bright white mansion, off Pennsylvania Avenue, with its tall imposing front columns of the bowed South Portico, fronted by the South Lawn, and its huge grounds filled with gardens, trees and fountains, was definitely impressive. The "President's Park" surrounding the White House was filled with dogwoods, magnolias, pines, maples, beeches and oaks, among other trees.

The senator parked amongst horse-drawn coaches and carriages in front of the recently built one-storied west wing. Eli, who had been interested in building and renovation ever since he had done so many alterations to his own home, asked Senator Huntington about the extensive renovations he'd heard the president had done to the White House in 1902.

"Yes, the president had them done when he took office," replied the senator. "He moved into the White House with his wife and six kids and found the accommodations on the second floor were far too cramped, because they contained the staff offices as well. He ordered a temporary executive suite built, hence this new west wing."

In the latter part of the 19th century, it was possible for anybody to go up to the front door of the White House and wait in crowded corridors, anterooms, or even the state rooms, for an audience with the president, but since the assassination of President McKinley in Buffalo, New York, security had been heightened and this was no longer possible. Instead, there were lots of uniformed policemen and plain-clothed Secret Service agents guarding the famous mansion and the president.

Senator Huntington greeted them familiarly, telling them he had an appointment with the president. They returned his greeting, addressing him by name. He introduced Eli to them by name and said he was his associate. Though they threw Eli some dark enquiring looks, they allowed them unhindered access into the portals of the executive wing. They went to the president's office, situated next to the Cabinet Room, and knocked at a high white door.

"Come in," called a high-pitched voice.

They entered into a large rectangular room with a small alcove leading off it to the left through white sliding doors, where there was fireplace and a window with dark-brown velvet draperies. In the main room, at an antique desk, which stood opposite a neat fireplace with a white-marble mantel, sat the president himself. The senator had told Eli on the way over that Roosevelt was the youngest man ever to take office and, indeed, he was still a robust-looking man in his mid-forties. He had a long drooping mustache and thinning dark-brown hair. A tall earnest-looking young man stood in front of his desk holding some papers in his hand. He had taken his coat off and stood in his shirt sleeves, his stiff shirt collar unbuttoned and his tie undone.

As they entered, he looked up with an irked expression on his face, as if he resented the intrusion. He quickly did the shirt button up and adjusted the tie, taking his long frock coat, whose tails were dangling on the carpeted floor from the back of a wooden rocking chair in front of the fireplace and shrugged it on. He was clean-shaven, with a pale waxy complexion, dark darting brown eyes and dark hair cut in a short style with a middle path. He smelled faintly of tobacco and men's cologne. Without being told, Eli knew it was Alexander Montgomery and he felt his hackles rise. He loathed the fellow on sight. He had the look of a weakling about him, but Eli sensed an underlying intelligence.

The president rose and came round the desk, and stood with his jaw jutted out, a pleasant smile on his face. He wore a black frock suit and waistcoat in an expensive fabric, a white shirt with a stiff collar, and a black tie. The gold chain of a fob watch came from his waistcoat pocket. Eli smiled to himself, thinking that at least he didn't attend to Matters of State in his "Wild West" garb.

The president stuck out his hand to the senator. "Humphrey, always good to see you."

"Mr President," said the senator amiably as he shook the president's hand, handing him a complimentary bottle of Buchanan's whiskey. "I trust Edith and your family are all in good health."

"Thank you, Humphrey, indeed they are. And thank you for the whiskey. It's excellent stuff." He indicated the young man. "You've met my aide, Alexander Montgomery?"

"Indeed, we are well-acquainted by now." The senator turned to Eli who had removed his gray derby and was holding it in one hand along with his gilt-topped ivory cane. "This is my associate, Eli Buchanan."

"Ah, so this is Eli Buchanan," said the president, regarding him with interest. "Humphrey has spoken of you on several occasions and always in the most glowing of terms."

Eli dipped his head deferentially, and gave a modest smile. "Thank you, Mr President. I am truly honored to make your acquaintance."

Then the next minute, Eli was shaking the hand of the president of the United States. He felt a surge of emotion pulse through him at the unlikehood of it all. Here he was, the bad boy of the Bucko bunch, actually meeting the most powerful man in the whole world. Then Eli turned and shook hands with Alexander Montgomery and exchanged a few pleasantries with him, keeping his face impassive when he really felt like crushing the man's hand and loudly cursing at him, knowing what a hold he had on Annabel. The blue blood gave him a derisive stare, eyeing Eli's scar as if it was offensive to him. His handshake was soft as a woman's. Though he could not possibly know of Eli's intentions towards his fiancé, he must have sensed something instinctually, for dislike and challenge simmered between them as surely as if they were a pair of rutting bull mooses.

It was to be a brief meeting of only a half-hour, but not bad considering the president's busy schedule. After handing over the bottle of whiskey to his aide, with instructions to bring them each a glass of the stuff, the president moved them along to a corner where there were comfortable sofas. The senator set himself down in the middle of a three-seater brown leather sofa with a grunt, his large overweight frame practically taking up all the space, while the president sat in a brown leather armchair facing him. Eli sat in another similar armchair opposite him. Alexander brought the three drinks in cut-glass whiskey glasses on a small silver tray. When he offered Eli a glass, Eli had the feeling that it galled him to have to serve him this way, and he reveled in the feeling of power it gave him. He gave the young man a cynical smile, eyeing him with such icy pale-yellow eyes that he could tell he was disconcerted for he hurried away to the other side of the room.

While Senator Huntington chatted to the president on boring political matters, Eli, pretending interest, surreptitiously watched his rival doing his administrative duties while ignoring the presidential guests entirely. Eli might have wondered at such an "old-money" fellow like him doing such ostensibly menial work, but Senator Huntington had told him that the young man was ambitious and was only working with the president in order to gain invaluable political experience, before running for public office himself.

Political matters set aside, as the minutes loomed on the half-hour allocated to them, which had Alexander checking his fob watch every few seconds, the president asked Eli about himself and enquired as to his likes and dislikes. He was interested to hear that Eli liked hunting and looked at him with approval. He said that he was an avid hunter himself and that one day he planned to go to Africa on a safari to hunt for the greatest hunting trophy of them all – the African elephant. Eli tried to look suitably impressed thinking that once he and the senator were out of here, he would ask the senator what type of beast that might be.

The three men talked easily and jovially after that and, when a harassed-looking Alexander finally managed to bundle the visitors out of the office, Eli was to find that they had overrun their appointment by a full twenty-four minutes.

60

Eli used the ornate gold knocker on the handsome wooden door. Set in the top half of the door was an inset of pieces of leaded stained glass, depicting a fractured scene of Jesus on the cross. Though it disturbed Eli, he supposed it was appropriate since the home belonged to Reverend Cotterell. It was a tall, red-brick Georgian house, in a respectable neighborhood, but it showed marked signs of deterioration and had an asceticism that did the reverend proud. Even the garden reflected this, as if the reverend had taken a monk-like vow of austerity. Besides the odd sculptured bush, there was no garden, beyond a neatly trimmed lawn. Not a single flower bloomed to offset its plain appearance. Eli thought of his masses of roses and the other thousands of blossoms that covered his garden and how much joy they had brought him, touching him in a way he would never have thought possible. He often strolled in his garden towards sunset, when their multi-hued colors seemed to become enriched and the exquisite smell of them permeated the air. He felt almost bereft standing in such cold and dismal surroundings. *Living in Washington was turning him soft!*

For someone who had never feared anything in his life, except his father, granted, Eli felt surprisingly intimidated. He let out his breath and took a step back on the small porch that lacked an overhead canopy to protect visitors from the rain. It had been three years since he'd last seen Annabel, but he had known he could not see her until he had succeeded in business and had something to offer her – something that could entice her away from a presidential aide whose political ambitions were keen. Thankfully, "Buchanan's Finest Liquors" had swiftly flourished. He was suddenly assailed by the unthinkable notion she was already married, despite Senator Huntington's continued discreet enquiries on his behalf, which didn't seem to support that.

Eli wore his best tailored suit, dove gray, a stiff-neck white shirt, with gold cufflinks at the cuffs, a crimson tie, white gloves and gray hand-stitched imported leather shoes. His vest was made of dark-gray satin, and had a gold watch chain attached to its left pocket, and he carried an ivory gilt-tipped cane. He'd been shaved and barbered and wore a gray Fedora hat with a feather on it, which all but hid his bright-yellow hair, but for his flourishing sideburns.

The door was opened by an elderly Negro butler in a worn black suit and dull black shoes. He immediately raised a disapproving gray eyebrow when his dark eyes lit on Eli's disfigured face. Eli was used to people's reaction when they first saw him, but it never failed to irk him. Back in the mountains, he had reveled in the power it lent him to chill and make folk instantly wary of him. But here in civilized society it was a distinct disadvantage. He cursed Sloane Galtrey inwardly for the scar that marked him as a violent man and unnerved most people, making them instantly suspicious of him. Eli received evidence of this right away. When Eli asked to see Annabel, the butler became morose and grudging. He very reluctantly let him into the sitting room, taking his hat and cane from him.

Eli refused his instruction to take seat and stood looking curiously around the room instead. The butler seemed loath to leave the room and Eli fancied that he must think he was some sort of sophisticated burglar busy casing the place. But after a tense while the servant forced himself to leave Eli alone to go and summon his mistress.

The room was musty and old-smelling with an entire wall devoted to large leather-bound books that needed dusting. A large gas chandelier, the globes of which were grease-marked, hung from the ceiling in the center of the room. The Brussels rug was a deep maroon color and faded. A Victorian grandfather clock standing in one corner was not working. The furniture, arranged around a tall, prim fireplace, was heavy and upholstered in a worn drab cream-and-maroon floral cloth, while dreary heavy maroon velvet drapes completed the picture of doom and gloom. It was a sad and neglected room that smelt of dust and decay. Thinking of the somewhat dilapidated state of the house and taking in the humble furnishings, Eli wondered what it signified. At the same time he realized, with a good deal of irony, how far he had come in such a short time that he should even notice such things when it wasn't that long ago that he had lived in abject squalor on Claw Mountain.

He had learned a lot from George Pollock, the rich city folk at Skyland and Senator Huntington. And his own father, of course. That and his own innate ability to learn quickly and easily had stood him in excellent stead. Certainly, his talent as an accomplished mimic had served him extremely well thus far. Added to this was the fact that he now read voraciously to increase his knowledge on the subjects necessary for his successful transformation from mountain cracker to sophisticated city dweller and businessman.

Of course, he learned new things every day and made occasional blunders, which he felt were put down to his country roots since they did not seem to diminish his standing in any way, especially with Senator Huntington as his champion. In the three years he'd been in Washington, Eli had not had the chance to go to Skyland again as he was too busy running the distillery and overseeing the Claw Mountain stills.

Thinking back on the poor state of the house and garden, was it that, despite his good standing in the community, the reverend had either fallen on hard times or had not been a man of any great means to begin with? Or was it simply that his religion gave him a tendency to stinginess as if he believed the Lord favored those who had taken an added vow of poverty? If so, he was a complete hypocrite, for while he lived in such frugal austerity, he was a regular visitor to the heady, insular, high-society world of Skyland. That alone seemed to indicate that the man was mean rather than short of money. Or perhaps those Skyland larks had merely been a ruse to find a suitable husband for his daughter?

Eli shook his head. How his Annabel must hate living in this mausoleum. There was nothing here to suggest her sparkling presence. He heard a noise and turned around expecting to see her but found, to his annoyance, it was the reverend, himself, who frowned thunderously when he saw him. The stout fellow was hatless and his white hair completely awry. He was dressed in a cream seersucker suit and wore a starched white shirt opened at the neck and short of a tie, revealing white springy curls on his chest.

Seeming furious at being caught in this deplorable state of undress, his blue eyes maniacally bulged, the one behind his monocle, queerly enlarged and looming at Eli in rabid accusation. His bloated face within the sweep of his muttonchop sideburns was bright red and his chest was heaving as if he had been hurrying. The butler had clearly reported Eli's presence to him.

"*How dare you . . . ,*" the reverend began.

Eli hastily stuck out a placating hand. "Why, Reverend, how very good to see you again," he glibly lied. "I was thinking the other day about how remiss it has been of me not to have called on you when I've been here in Washington for nearly three years now. I do hope you will forgive my bad manners."

He had carefully avoided reference to his daughter, but the reverend was not easily fooled. "Haven't called on my *daughter,* you mean! Well, you could have saved yourself the trouble. It's not proper for you to call on a young lady who is betrothed to another."

"So she is not yet married? Even after all this time? My word."

"It is to happen shortly, so don't get any untoward notions."

"Sir, you misunderstand me. Alexander Montgomery and I have a most cordial relationship."

"You've *met* Alexander?" the reverend scoffed skeptically. "I hardly think you mix in the same social circles. And just *where* did you meet him?"

"At the White House," replied Eli casually.

"*The White House!*" the reverend exploded. "*A likely story!* What were you doing there?

"Meeting President Roosevelt. Nice fellow, Teddy. Talked about wanting to hunt elephants in Africa."

Reverend Cotterell narrowed his eyes suspiciously. "I don't believe you. You're a born liar! Maybe you fooled all the others at Skyland, but you didn't fool me!"

Eli smiled at him wryly. "Well, if you don't believe me, would you believe Senator Huntington?"

"Of course, he's a fine fellow. I know him well. But just because you drop somebody's name, doesn't give you an ounce of credence in my book. You probably met the senator at Skyland just like I did."

Eli eyed him with bored pale-yellow eyes. "Shucks, Reverend, if that's what you think, why don't you just phone the fellow and be done with it?"

Reverend Cotterell stared at Eli with narrowed, gauging eyes. "People like you trade on the assumption that the person you wish to dupe won't go that far. But I think I will call your bluff."

The reverend stomped across to a tall, elegant telephone sitting on an occasional table, grabbing the long stem in one hand and snatching up the corded receiver with pudgy fingers, demanding that the operator put him through to Senator Huntington's office. After a few moments, Eli heard him announce who he was and ask someone (presumably the senator) whether, to his knowledge, Eli Buchanan had been to the White House to meet the president.

Apparently, it was confirmed by the senator for the reverend snorted with disgust and replaced the receiver on its hook with a thump, looking barely able to contain his chagrin. "Hmmmph, said he took you there himself. I don't know how you managed to pull the wool over his eyes, but you haven't succeeded in pulling the wool over mine! And while the White House may have received you, you're definitely *not* welcome here. I'd like you to leave right now."

Eli felt a surge of anger, but he fought to keep his composure. He eyed the reverend narrowly. "I'll do that, Reverend, but not before I have paid my respects to your daughter. How would it look if I left without doing so? Why, it would be the very height of rudeness."

"Now look here, young fellow, your pretence of manners does not impress or fool me. I won't have my daughter associating with riff-raff like you. Leave, or I'll be forced to summon the law to have you forcibly evicted."

Just then Annabel burst impatiently into the room. "Father, who are you threatening now . . . ?" She pulled up short, gasping with shock when she saw Eli. She battered her thick black eyelashes, clearly enormously flustered.

"Eli," she whispered in astonishment.

She was wearing a black satin shirtwaister, with pearl buttons running down the front and a big tie under her white collar. Black button-shoes peeped out from beneath her voluminous skirt. It was a schoolmarm's outfit but, on her, it looked anything but. Her black hair was raised in a fashionable pompadour, filled, no doubt, with "rats" (a term Eli learned when he visited a high-class brothel recommended to him by Senator Huntington), and held up by two tortoise-shell combs. Her marble-white skin was perfectly textured and her exquisitely sculptured high cheek-bones marked her with incomparable beauty. Seeing her again almost took Eli's breath away. *How she had the power to consume him!* Her large green eyes reflected the shock she felt at seeing him, but such a reaction was heartening to Eli. She was not immune to his presence. She definitely felt something still.

He strode over to her and taking her one hand, raised it to his lips. "At your service, ma'am. I'm afraid your father doesn't feel I'm suitable company for you."

Annabel turned on her father with flashing green eyes. "Father, how could you threaten Eli that way? *Shame on you!* Have you forgotten how he saved me from almost certain death? *That monster rattlesnake! Uggh!*"

The reverend tutted his annoyance at being caught out at his game. "Might I remind you, young lady, that you are betrothed to a fine upstanding young man and are to be married next month? This is entirely inappropriate."

"Father, I won't have you treat Eli this way. Like some leper! Now, please leave us alone!"

Reverend Cotterell's chest puffed up with apoplectic effrontery, looking like some bloated bullfrog about to croak. "I will do no such thing. It's preposterous! I'd sooner leave you with a rattlesnake!"

"Father, considering the circumstances, that is in extreme poor choice of words. If you don't leave us alone then I guess I'll just be forced to leave with him."

It seemed to Eli that Annabel had gained a little gumption since he had last seen her, openly standing up to her despotic father this way. Oh, she had quietly slipped him a sleeping draft or two in the past but, in his limited experience, she had never openly defied him in this manner. He got a kick out of her spunkiness. He loved a woman with spirit when so many had cringed before him in the past. *Except his brother's wife, Mary, of course!* Reverend Cotterell scowled at Eli then he looked at his daughter. Her mouth was set in a firm line, which said that she had meant what she had said. Forced to capitulate and grumbling under his breath, Reverend Cotterell gave Eli one last parting shot before exiting the room. "You, sir, are the devil's tool!"

After her father left the room, Annabel's reaction was not what Eli expected. Despite her heated defense of him, her manner instantly changed towards him, becoming decidedly cool.

"He's right, of course," she declared regally. "I am engaged, as you are well aware, and will be married by this time next month. You cannot possibly call on me, especially after all this time."

Her meaning was clear. She was angry about the fact that he had taken so long to contact her.

He said softly, apologetically, "I would have come sooner only I wanted to have something to offer you."

"I thought you were already a successful businessman?" she said archly. "At least that's what you told everybody back at Skyland."

Eli had little trouble remembering what he had told Skyland guests about his background, since he had repeated it so often since then, he almost believed it himself.

"It is true we have many business interests, but in the mountains, and er . . . of course, there are the distilleries and tobacco plantations in the Graves Mills area, but nothing here in Washington. And besides, those were my father's interests. Now, since his death, I have made it all on my own. Besides that, I now own a distillery myself, here in Washington, in partnership with Senator Huntington. It has been such an amazing success and we are already exporting our liquors to Europe."

She gave him a critical once-over. "I can see that. You look . . . well, the very picture of elegance. Not that you weren't elegant before. You were. I can't quite put my finger on it. But there's something . . . *different* about you. You're far more well-groomed and confident than before."

"Ah, but confidence is something that I have never lacked. I came today to ask you to marry me."

"Marry you?" Her eyes widened in shock. "Have you gone quite mad?"

"I have my own house in a very prestigious neighborhood. Servants. I assure you, you will want for nothing."

She put her hands on her curved hips. "So you expect me fall into your arms and marry you just because you've made a success of your own business? Nay, my fine friend. For months I expected you contact me after, well, you know . . . and not so much as a phone call. I felt . . . quite humiliated. Now, three years later, you dare to believe . . ."

"I already told you why. I did not consider myself worthy of you until now."

"Well, that's very flattering I suppose, but it's much too late. I'm betrothed to Alexander and I *will* marry him."

"I've met him and he's not for you," Eli, fighting down jealous rage, said quietly, "He's much too staid and boring for the likes of you."

"What's that supposed to mean?"

"It means you like a bit of excitement, don't you? Even danger."

"What a preposterous thing to suggest!"

"But true, nevertheless."

Annabel took a hasty step away from him as if she suddenly could no longer trust herself in his proximity. She shook her head and said firmly, "Like I said, it's much too late. The wedding invitations have already gone out."

"It's not too late until the deed is done. A lady is entitled to change her mind."

Annabel considered this briefly. "Who says I *want* to change my mind? Besides, my father loathes you."

"Well, I wouldn't be marrying your father, would I?"

"I couldn't possibly go against his wishes."

"Seems to me you didn't mind doing that a few minutes ago!"

She glared at him, having no answer to his logic.

"Indeed," he continued, "seems to me you were quite happy to go against his wishes when you met me that night at that splendid falls down in the canyon too. And have you forgotten the night we spent together in that cave?"

He could tell that incredible night was, indeed, uppermost in her mind by the look on her face, but she managed to give him a dismissive toss of her head. She wanted him to think she was no longer interested, but he knew better. Her breathing had quickened with excitement and her beautiful face was slightly flushed, as she regarded him with emerald-eyed consternation. Eli pressed home his advantage. He moved over to her, took her in his arms and gave her a long, smoldering kiss that clearly took her by surprise. She tried to pull herself away, but only momentarily, before she slipped both her arms around his neck, buckling at the knees in surrender, responding just as passionately.

Both of them were breathing hoarsely as they broke apart at last. He cruelly pulled her head back by the hair at the back of her head, holding it firmly bunched in one hand so that her face was a couple of inches from his own, and hissed, "Does your precious Alexander ever kiss you this way?"

Her eyes were wide and dazed-looking, her ruby lipstick smudged, her mouth opened in bewilderment, her fevered look almost pleading. She swallowed hard. "That, sir, is not the way for a gentleman to behave," she managed finally.

"Nor a lady!" he responded coldly. "Listen, it's clear that your father will not permit me to call on you here again, so you're going to have to come to my home in future."

"In future!" she wailed. "On the contrary, I must never see you again! I have a reputation to uphold! You hear me?"

"I hear you, but that is not you speaking, Annabel. That's your father and the conventions of a prudish society speaking. One that has never known a love like ours. *Admit it!* You don't love Alexander. *You love me!* That kiss just told me so. I adore you. You cannot possibly marry that pompous dullard!"

"I do love Alexander," she insisted lamely, meekly lowering her eyes. "Of course I do."

"Well, if that is true then you've sure got a peculiar way of showing it."

She had the grace to look slightly embarrassed. "It's your fault. You tempt me so!" she said crossly. "Pray tell, why else would I be marrying Alexander?"

He reached out and took her angrily by the upper arms, forcing her to listen. "Only you can answer that. But I dare say it is because he is one of the few suitors, if not the only one, of whom your father approves. I cannot think of a more foolish reason to marry. Playing the dutiful daughter does not become you, Annabel. You'd be sentencing yourself to a lifetime of boredom. I doubt that Alexander would have much time for you even, with his job! You were meant for greater things! Here's my calling card. Come and visit me soon. I want you to see your future home. I promise you won't be disappointed. Make sure it's on a weekend. The rest of the time I'm busy at the distillery."

"You're mad"" she said staunchly. "Visit a man in his home without a chaperone? It's unthinkable."

"Oh, I'm quite sure you can manage it and think of a way to protect your precious reputation at the same time."

Though she glared at him, pretending mild outrage, he was gratified to see her slipping his calling card between the pearl buttons of her bodice.

With that, he kissed her on her delectable ruby-smudged lips again, lightly catching them between his teeth. Then he drew away from her, pushed her roughly aside and strode for the door. He felt her naked longing following after him with a sense of triumph. There was no doubt in his mind that she wanted him every bit as much as wanted her.

61

The next Saturday morning, Eli, wearing white gabardine trousers and a pin-striped navy jacket, a stiff-collared blue silk shirt, a navy-blue tie, and navy-and-white rubber-soled shoes, was sitting in a comfortable single sofa in his living room, contemplating the beauty of his surroundings. His skin had been freshly barbered and powdered and his bright-blond hair slicked down, but for an obstinate cowlick. How right his father had been when he had said that he was born to this life rather than the mountain life. He had slid into it as easily as a hen would lay a greased egg! In fact, going back to Claw Mountain was a real trial to him these days. His brothers sorely tried him with their coarse clothing and lack of manners and hygiene.

Just then, he heard a frantic knocking on the front door and he smiled to himself, already knowing who it was. He had given his servants the weekend off in anticipation of Annabel's visit, knowing she could wait no longer than he could for them to be together. He went to the heavy, paneled, wooden door and opened it to find a thickly-veiled woman dressed entirely in telltale black standing outside on the scrollwork porch, with its miniature white roses climbing over it. A hansom cab was moving away from the curb.

"You came!" he said triumphantly. "I did not doubt that you would!"

"Tut!" she said, as she hastily moved indoors and closed the door behind her, leaning back against it as if in relief. "I think I must be mad!"

She wore a black silk shirtwaister, soft-kid button-up shoes and black gloves. She moved forward and lifted her veils over her flattish, wide-brimmed black hat, revealing her pale, porcelain face and incomparable features. Her green eyes sparkled and her dark ruby lips were arranged in a winsome smile. She wore her raven hair in a luxuriant pompadour, with a long single ringlet lying across one shoulder. Eli thought she looked as exquisite as his favorite rose, with its narrow dark-red buds on long stems, of great beauty and elegance. He felt a deep thrill of admiration and joy, and was left smarting with it. He saw in this young woman the remedy of his life. *Redemption! Respectability!* She was the one shining light in the darkness of his inner world.

She seemed to sense the powerful effect that she had on him for her smile turned distinctly coquettish, her lovely green eyes dancing. She wrinkled a dainty nose at him and gave a girlish giggle. "I got to thinking about what you said about convention and decided it would quite become me to flout it on occasion."

Eli smiled back, feeling a rush of foolish gladness. "Then you will marry me?"

She gave a saucy little laugh, full of high spirits, fueled by her own intoxicating daring, it seemed. "Now you mock me, sir!"

"Where did you tell your father you were going?"

"To visit an old school friend. He might not have believed me had she not obliged me by putting in a surprise appearance at the house the other day."

"Quite the little schemer, aren't you?" he murmured appreciatively. He moved forward and encircled her in his arms. "You are so very beautiful, Annabel. But why do you so often wear black as if your whole life is a funeral you're attending?"

She let out a weary sigh. "Because that is exactly what it is. It is Father who insists on such sobriety. That's why I love going to Skyland so. All those colorful costumes! It's the only time he lets me wear color and the jewelry my mother left me, otherwise he strongly disapproves of ostentation. All my own clothes are black."

Eli smiled, viewing her with amusement. "Well, I am going to buy you a whole wardrobe of beautiful dresses made of all the colors of the rainbow and you can wear them whenever you come here."

She smiled enigmatically. "And who says I shall be returning?"

Now it was Eli's turn to smile enigmatically. "Oh, we both know that you will. Like I said, I never doubted that you would come at the first opportunity. Such eagerness is not considered ladylike, however," he teased lightly, "so I guess I should be exceedingly flattered."

She gave an impish curtsy and removed her hat and veils, by taking out the hat pins, giving her extravagant headwear to Eli to hang on a hook in the entrance hall. He took her by her gloved hand. "Come, let me show you around."

He led her into the living room and was gratified when she gave little gasps of awe and appreciation as she gazed around the large, beautifully appointed room, up at the high, white, domed ceiling, carved with Borticelli angels and hung with a huge French, crystal chandelier, with myriad sparkling prisms, at the pale-green and fuchsia floral watered-silk covering the walls, the dark cherry wood and glass display cabinet showing fine Meissen porcelain figurines and birds, the Louis XV chairs and English antiques, the comfortable sofa covered in pastel floral chintz, the long fuchsia chintz drapes tied back with cascading fuchsia ribbons, the white marble fireplace with its candelabra on the mantel-piece and brass andirons and the matching brass poker-set standing beside it, the Aubusson carpets and several ancient Chinese rugs with their silken piles, a richly carved, console table, on which sat a brandy decanter, crystal goblets, tumblers and champagne flutes.

"Eli, I don't believe this room!" Annabel waved an admiring hand around the room, her green eyes sparkling. "It's *dazzling!* Quite breathtaking! Did you decorate it yourself?"

Eli felt a spurt of pride at her words, at the tone of awed disbelief. While it was true that the house could hardly be considered a mansion, none who had entered its portals had failed to compliment his impeccable taste. However, although he looked the part of the wealthy aristocrat, with all the expensive trappings of wealth, in truth, he was still a long way off. The house still had a high mortgage, which he was busy paying off. Eli considered taking the credit for the room himself, but he had hired specialists in home decoration to assist him. He had been enormously pleased with the results and had paid them a handsome bonus.

"Hardly," he admitted. "I hired specialists, but I was careful to instruct them of my needs. I told them that it was for a woman of incomparable beauty who had captured my heart. I instructed them to spare no expense to furnish it with great delicacy and beauty to match hers – and to make green the predominant color to match her remarkable eyes.'

If he had expected surprise and pleasure at this great tribute paid to her, he was sorely disappointed. Instead, Annabel looked deeply alarmed. "I trust you did not mention my name?" she said sharply.

Eli felt a wave of crushing hurt. All she cared about was her precious reputation when he had done all this to please her. If only he could tell Annabel that he was so obsessed with her, he had left the mountains and changed everything about himself, improving himself, and establishing himself in business and Washington society, *all for her!* Though he was not yet on the visiting list of the better families, she would appreciate it surely? But there were things that she must never learn. Like about his fake past, for instance. But perhaps her own need to protect her reputation came with growing up in the reverend's strict household and he should not take it to heart so. He resolved not to let it spoil things between them. He had waited too long for this to ruin it now.

"Don't worry," he said stiffly. "Your secret is safe. But soon the need for such secrecy will be over when you agree to become my wife."

She gave him a quick, uncertain smile and he took her hand again and showed her the other rooms, her long black skirt and petticoats rustling beside him, as she walked in a waft of intoxicating perfume, her nearness as tantalizing to him as candy to a child. He wanted to grab her into his arms, but he'd waited a long time to show her all this and he wanted to savor it. The dining room had a mahogany table that was large enough to seat eighteen diners, with an oval cloth of fuchsia-colored lace in the middle, on which sat a twisted crystal centre-piece of exquisite design, affixed with a glass dish containing glass fruit that were delicately hand-painted, with an elegant silver candelabra standing on either side of it. Carrying through the color theme of the living room, the walls were covered with pale-green watered silk, encrusted with designs of ferns, edged with fuchsia-colored beading, and hung with delicate, whimsical paintings of flowers of fuchsia hues. While Annabel murmured appreciation and compliments, the mood had been somewhat ruined for Eli.

He resumed his tour by taking her into the large, well-equipped kitchen, with its set of copper pans hanging from hooks. Its Economy double-door refrigerator on heavy brass casters, with a matching double-door ice-chest above, was beautiful; the outer case was made of northern elm with a high-gloss golden finish and decorated with fancy heavy cast brass hinges, locks and strikes. The thick raised door panels were of an elaborate design. A large splendid Wilson kitchen cabinet in satin walnut of elegant design stood against one wall. There was a handsome gas stove too. Pale green-checker curtains fluttered at the large window. Then he took her back to the entrance hall and up the winding staircase to where there were bedrooms and bathrooms with modern plumbing. He showed her the charming guest rooms; each decorated in a different color, but declined to show her the main bedroom. *That would come later!*

They went back into the living room, and he poured her a flute of champagne from a bottle on ice, preferring to have Buchanan whiskey himself, which he poured into a cut-glass goblet. He sat in a chair opposite her, sipping at his drink, thinking how far he had come from Claw Mountain and slugging it down from moonshine jugs, as they engaged in polite and guarded conversation, two virtual strangers sizing each other up. Then they fell silent as if on cue and searched each other's eyes, the chemistry between them so strong that the air was suddenly fraught with tension. At last, he stood up and held out a hand to her. "Come into the garden now."

"No," she said quickly, "I'd rather not."

"I meant the back garden. Don't worry, it's fully walled and completely private."

She visibly relaxed then. "In that case I'd love to."

He took her through the back scullery door into the sizable garden, which was enclosed with high brick walls. It was graced by the huge old oak tree, from which hung a swing. Not far from the tree was the charming gazebo, the white metal scroll work of elaborate design. The garden was patched here and there with lawn and there were flower beds filled with a profusion of blooms of every color and hue, which sent up an incredible sweetness of mixed perfumes. There were winding red-brick pathways edged with flowering shrubs and bushes, and little bridges across ponds full of water-lilies and goldfish. White metal arches were covered with a profusion of wild white roses. Several pathways led into little secret grottos, containing fountains and cherub statues. A white birdbath, filled with water, stood in the middle of a bed of pink petunias in the middle of a stretch of lawn, and several birds were splashing around in the water.

As he showed Annabel around, she kept touching her hands to her cheeks in wonderment and delight. "Oh Eli, it's all so *beautiful!* It's like an enchanted garden. You must be so proud to own such a magnificent home."

"It's all yours," he said, touched by her enthusiasm, then laying his heart at his feet, he added, "It's nothing without you in it."

He led her into the gazebo and took her into his arms, his penetrative pale-yellow eyes searching her face.

She gazed back at him with sad green eyes. "Eli, it cannot be. You must know that."

He felt pain plunge into his heart like a dagger.

"Why not?" he said urgently. "I've done everything in my power to gain for you everything you could possibly desire."

"Oh," she cried. "Do not think that I am not grateful and enormously *flattered* by all this . . . your great devotion. And do not think that I have given the matter no thought! Indeed, it is all that has consumed me ever since you came to call on me the other day. But don't you see? Father would never permit it. This is all so exquisite, but such luxuries and possessions mean little to Father. It's status – reputation – that counts with him. I'm afraid he regards you as an evil, dangerous man. He told me so right after the episode with the rattlesnake, and warned me not to associate with you. I told him how unfair he was being since he did not even know you, but he insisted. And now you say that you earn your living through a distillery he would never accept you as a son-in-law. He does not approve of the imbibing of alcohol and heads the local chapter of the Temperance Society pressing to have it prohibited."

Eli snorted in derision. "Then he is a hypocrite! He bought a whole barrel of my whiskey from George Pollock at Skyland. The very *same* whiskey I now bottle and supply to the finest establishments in the land."

Annabel shrugged her slim shoulders. "Father contends he partakes of whiskey strictly for medicinal purposes."

Eli gave her a droll, disbelieving look, but he had no wish to pursue the matter further with her. "Anyway," he said shortly, "why should you care so much what your father thinks of me? You would be the one marrying me, not him! Furthermore, I have provided everything he could possibly want for you, including a deep and ardent love."

"None of that would have any import for Father. He detests you. And you have only yourself to blame. That first night at the whip show, you embarrassed poor Mr Blake so, after Father had even allowed him to sit close to me and engage in conversation. Father was most infuriated by that. And have you forgotten that impudent kiss at the ball? He considered that a personal insult and that you had irrevocably sullied my reputation. Quite frankly, I doubt there is anything you could do to get into his good graces now."

"I make no apologies for the kiss and Mr Blake was a pompous ass, who insulted a good friend, Mr Pollock, and endangered his life with the snake. He deserved no less."

"Perhaps," she admitted. Then she gave him a reproving look. "But you *were* rather mean to humiliate him the way you did."

"I admit it! I'd be mean to anyone who thinks he has a chance with you. You belong to me."

"I belong to Alexander, you mean," she said lightly.

He crushed her to him and snarled, "Then pray tell, what are you doing here?"

She was silent for a long while as she considered the question. In the quiet, Eli could hear the light breeze rustling the leaves of the oak and birds twittering.

"I couldn't stay away," she admitted in a whisper, her green eyes searching his. "You have this magnetic pull on me that draws me to you even though I suspect my father's assessment of you may well be correct."

"You mean you, too, think that I am evil and dangerous?"

She nodded, the pulse in the base of her lovely white throat flickering. "Oh yes."

He smiled at her sardonically. "Well, it's true, and that's exactly why you are here, Miss Cotterell. Admit it, you are attracted to the bad in me and you know full well that you will never be bored by me the way you are by Alexander."

"How can you suggest such a thing? I am *not* bored by Alexander!"

"Oh yes you are, and you know it. I've met him and he is a pompous bore. I, on the other hand, would never bore you, being both evil and dangerous." He bent and kissed her neck. She shivered deliciously.

"Eli, of course I don't think that you are *evil*, but I do know you are dangerous. You are always tempting me so, willing me to do things against my better judgment. You cause me to act with such reckless abandon with nary a thought of the consequences."

"I could never tempt you if some part of you did not want it too."

"I guess that's true. The trouble is . . ."

"The trouble is what?"

"The trouble is I'm madly in love with you still. These past three years, you have consumed my thoughts and my dreams. And when I saw you the other day, I thought my heart would surely explode with joy!"

Annabel's words had a powerful effect on them both, holding them in a thrall of tempestuous longing. Indeed, she looked at him with such a look of ardor that he could not mistake her desire, *her consent.* He took her hand and led her back inside then swooped her up in his strong arms and carried her up the staircase. They passed through a pillared marble doorway with cornices of pale green, into his large, thickly carpeted bedroom of pale-green shimmering silks and velvets, with charming glass lamps, a green marble fireplace, a giant gilt-framed painting of a mountain landscape draped in ethereal mist, which hung on the wall opposite a large four-poster bed draped with green silks. He heard her gasp with delight.

She stood while he undressed her, having learnt the intricacies of highborn dress in the high-class bordello the senator had introduced him to, kissing her all the while. Thankfully, her austere outer appearance in dress did not extend to what lay beneath the black dress. Frilly and feminine and fashionable, her underwear resembled the young woman herself. Sedate on the outside, wildly feminine and alluring on the inside.

He made her remove her dress and step out of her voluminous white satin petticoats, which were flounced and edged in lace through which pink ribbons had been had been threaded about six inches from the hem, along which it was decorated with intermittent pink bows. She was now down to her corset, her lacy, pink-ribboned camisole, her white satin drawers with billowing festoons of pink ribbon and the contrasting seductiveness of her black silk stockings. She had a dreamy expression on her beautiful face as he carefully untied the ties of her corset and removed it, throwing it on a dark pink sofa.

Now, Annabel wore only her white lace and ribbon-tasseled camisole that flared with the enticing fullness of her breasts, her drawers and her black stockings. She stood before him, a virginal vision of gentility and grace. He disrobed down to his trousers, then laid her down on the white silk coverlet, stretching out his lean, mountain-hewn body beside her, bending his bright-blond head and devouring her with his lips. Heat flooded his loins, but he forced himself to go slowly, not wanting to scare her. He rolled down her camisole and her skin beneath it was warm, flushed rosy and beguilingly damp. *So smooth and lovely.*

He felt a lump invade his throat as her perfect, pink-nippled breasts, so firm, tautly welcomed his mouth.

"Oh Eli, Eli," she whispered, writhing beneath him. She slipped her arms around his neck and clung to him, shivering with anticipation, ready to be plucked like a ripe peach from the bough. He untied the ribbons of her drawers and slipped them off, to reveal a small mound with a patch of dark hair, the sight of which increased his excitement. He then carefully unclipped her black silk stockings attached to her black lacy garter, and carefully rolled them down, admiring her shapely calves and the daintiness of her feet, which were so small and well-shaped compared to those of mountain wenches, who for the most part, went about without shoes. Then unbuttoning his trousers and removing them, he plucked the sweet forbidden fruit and began devouring it while she whispered wondrous words of love into his ear. He knew then that she was his for all time . .

.

* * *

Though their love-making was urgent and passionate, Eli took Annabel with a tenderness he had never used with any other woman before. The mountain wenches with their lack of underwear, he despised and had used with cruel contempt. Indeed, he had shown more respect to the whores of the bordello, since he wanted no complaints to reach the senator's ears. The young "ladies" of Mrs. Higby's establishment, with their beautiful teeth, mint breath and perfumed hair, were fascinating, if repulsive, creatures to him, and were all over him whenever he visited there, his broody good looks and aloofness, seemingly a magnet to them. They dressed like high-society ladies with their high pompadours and fashionable garments and even spoke like them. Eli had learnt a lot from them, not least of all, an intimate knowledge of the mysteries of high-born female underwear.

Annabel cried at the instant of her deflowering and struggled and thrashed about beneath him. Then when he was through her hymen, a powerful passion overcame the pain. Ecstasy followed, visible on her beautiful face, as she lay moaning under him. Their mutual passion grew till it became almost unbearable, then she shuddered violently beneath him and her ecstasy became his. In the pale natural light of the boudoir, her face took on a look of adoration and joy and Eli felt strangely moved. There was no doubt in his mind that she would consent to become his wife now . . .

They slept naked in each other's arms beneath pale-green satin sheets and, when they woke up, she looked flushed and her green eyes were lit with a gleaming light of satisfaction and triumph. She had pulled the "rats" and pins from her hair and it lay across the pillow, luxuriant, thick, and black as midnight.

"Oh, it was so wonderful, my darling and, what's more, I have the perfect solution to this mess," she whispered. "I will marry Alexander, but I will be your lover. And there will be no need for you to get jealous since you know that my heart belongs *only* to you! I will *always* belong to you, Eli. I just won't be married to you."

Eli stared at her in stunned dismay, too terrified to believe that she might actually mean what she said. "You mean you are prepared to be my mistress, but not my wife? You jest, surely?" he asked hoarsely.

"No. Don't you see? It's the perfect solution? This way, everybody's needs will be met, not least of all my own. Father will be happy because I will be marrying the man of his choice, Alexander will be happy because he really does want me to become his wife, and you . . . well . . . you'll be happy because you won't be losing me. And *I'll* be happy because everybody else will be happy, and I won't have to face a scandal, of course. *It's perfect!*"

Eli stared at her sickly, unable to believe her warped logic, the sheer selfishness of her thinking. He grabbed her one arm and hissed, "No, Annabel, you are wrong! Only *your* selfish needs will be met by such a bizarre arrangement. Oh, for sure, you would appear to be a dutiful daughter to your father. To Alexander, you would appear the dutiful wife. You would have respectability on one hand, and me, as a lover, on the other. Yet, in reality, all three of us would be cuckold to your vanity and deception!"

"Cuckold!" she repeated hollowly, staring at him with a look of honest puzzlement. "Surely you can't mean that, my love? *I love you!* Surely you know that by now? I think I just proved it to you."

"Love? You don't know the meaning of the word," he muttered dully. He thought of a love that existed between a man and a woman, and he could think of only one good example – the great love that existed between his brother, Zack, and his wife, Mary. Though she was his old adversary and their relationship had been fraught with animosity, Eli was not blind to her good qualities. *Mary had followed her heart!* She had fallen in love with Zack at first sight and had eloped with him, accompanying him to Claw Mountain. She had stuck to him through many trials, being helpmate, companion and lover to him, bearing him children. Annabel, on the other hand, wasn't even prepared to bear his *name*. And if she were to bear a child once married to Alexander, he would never know if it was his child or Alexander's. He didn't know which was worse. That, if it was his child, he would not be able to acknowledge it or raise it as his own or, if it wasn't, that the woman he loved would have given birth to another man's child. He wondered

why the need to have children was so strong inside him. Maybe he needed to compensate in some way for the one he had murdered.

"All I've done is tried to make the best of a bad situation," Annabel said plaintively. "Surely you can see that?"

"*The best!* You call this the best? The best and, without doubt, the most honorable, thing you could do is to call off your engagement right now and marry me instead."

"That's impossible! It would cause a terrible scandal. My father would be furious and would never speak to me again. Eli, you are so handsome, so strong, but I cannot possibly go against my father's wishes. He has his heart set on this."

"I don't understand why are you prepared to sacrifice your happiness for his?"

"Oh Eli, please try to understand. My mother left us when I was very young. It's always been just the two of us."

"Still, why the high road of filial loyalty when loyalty is hardly your strong point? I mean you've already been unfaithful to poor Alexander, even though you two are engaged to be married. *And you, a precious reverend's daughter, too!*" he added cruelly, suddenly wanting to hurt her as much as she had hurt him.

She wrenched her arm away angrily, her green eyes flashing. "How dare you! You mean cad! You tempt me so then blame me when I can't resist. It's all *your* fault! You spent one whole night with me and I didn't see you again for *three whole years!* Then you come back and expect me to dance to your little ditty without a thought for my present position." Her eyes filled with tears and she sobbed, "It's so easy for you, having grown up in the mountains with a kind and loving father. My mother's desertion left my father mean and forbidding and he has put the fear of God in me about reputation and such. Social mores have ruled my life!"

Eli snorted with disgust. "Hardly! Think of White Oak Canyon. Polly's Cave. Today. You have flown in the face of them before. Indeed, today, you threw all convention right out the window!"

"Well, at Skyland, you shamelessly pursued me, and I may have come here today, but my heart was thumping with trepidation so much, I feared I might explode, even though nobody could possibly have known it was me. I changed hansom cabs twice to get here and was heavily veiled. If I was really brave enough to fly in the face of convention, I would have visited you openly and not cared who knew. Have you forgotten that I am a betrothed woman? Visiting a single man at his home is unthinkable, even with a suitable chaperone. I love you madly, Eli, but I don't think I am strong enough to defy convention by *marrying* you. You're too bold and outrageous for me! There, I've said it!"

"And you don't think having *an affair* is defying convention? Would that be any less terrifying?"

"Oh, nobody need find out about it. We would be most discreet." She must

471

have seen the look on his face for she ran her fingertips lightly over his lips and said softly, apologetically, "Oh, you poor darling! You need to marry someone who is much stronger than me. Someone who cares nothing for society's dictates. Alas, I am without a doubt a slave to this awful thing called convention!"

To Eli her feminine logic was quite terrifying. She was quite prepared to go against convention, including entering a dangerous liaison, providing nobody found out about it – and so long as she could appear to be what she wasn't – *an honorable woman!* She was as much of a fake as he was. Maybe they deserved each other after all!

"So you are going to marry him, despite what has just happened between us? How could you, Annabel? *How could you?"*

She raised tear-swimming eyes to him. "Don't you think I would much rather marry you and live in this magnificent house than marry that stuffy fool? You're quite right, he *does* bore me. Everything is politics, politics, politics, with him and politics bores me silly. Frankly, I don't care a wit what President Roosevelt has in mind for the nation, or what bill is going through right now. I just want to dance and go to dinners and to parties. But Alexander is, after all, dependable, which is more than I can say for you – and he comes from a very old and respectable Washington family, whose ancestors came across to this country in *The Mayflower*, I'll have you know."

Eli refrained from asking what *The Mayflower* was, knowing it was something he should already know since she didn't explain further. He stored it away in the back of his mind to ask Senator Huntington about later.

Annabel began sobbing uncontrollably and Eli could not help but take her in his arms. She was weak and shallow and vain, but he loved her with every fiber of his being and he could not bear to see her so upset.

"And do you go to dinners and parties with him now?"

"No," she admitted, catching on her breath. "He's always too busy, but he has assured me that we will be admitted into polite Washington society once we are married."

"And what makes you think he'll have any more time for you then than he does now? After all, it has taken him more than three years just to get around to marrying you."

"I will insist! I will become a hostess and invite people around for suppers and conversation. And so what if he doesn't pay much attention to me? It'll be all the better for us. Don't you see? It'll give us more time together. Oh, Eli, I know how disappointed you must be, but it won't be so bad." She raised a hand and tenderly touched his scarred cheek. "Please, let's give it a try. I promise that if either of us feels unable to bear it, I *will* divorce Alexander and marry you."

Eli felt a dredge of deep disappointment inside him, knowing that if she went ahead and married Alexander, she would never become his wife, for divorce, with all its inherent scandal, would never be an option for one of such little courage.

"Eli," she said in a little girl's voice, tracing a cajoling finger on his bare chest. "Please, my darling, I don't want to lose you. I can't! *Not now!*"

And Eli, as angry and resentful as he was, realized, with a great sense of helplessness, that such was her womanly power over him that, God help him, he would do anything to keep her, including share her with another man if he had to. But the knowledge of his own weakness filled him with such scalding shame and torment that he could scarcely respond to her clinging and voluptuous kisses. *Where, oh where, had all his fine Bucko pride gone to now?*

62

Eli waited anxiously for Annabel to contact him again, sure that she would not be able to go through with the wedding to Alexander Montgomery after their passionate tryst the other day. Since that time, she had consumed his thoughts and fired his passions. His whole body felt on fire and tingled with longing for her, and he was filled with a tempestuous restlessness, hardly able to concentrate on his work in the distillery during the day and unable to sleep at night. Dressed in his green silk pyjamas, patterned with a large black dragon with red eyes, and matching dressing gown, he would pace the floor of his bedroom, with red-rimmed, hot, haunted eyes and guts that were aflame. He never went out, staying at home in case Annabel wished to telephone or visit him.

After more than a week of waiting in vain, though she had warned him never to do so, several times, he tried telephoning her father's house, but the Negro butler always answered and would coldly inform him she had gone away. Whether this was the truth or an instruction given to him by Reverend Cotterell as a ploy to prevent him for talking to her, Eli couldn't say. This uncertainty forced him to drive past their gloomy austere house a dozen times hoping to catch a glimpse of her, but there was never any sign of life. Once, he got up the courage to go up the pathway and heatedly use the knocker on the door, determined to force his way inside and go up to her bedroom if necessary, even knowing that she would be furious if he did. It was opened by the same morose, elderly, shabbily attired Negro butler, who gave him the same curt message. And something in the man's dark gloating eyes told Eli that what he said was the truth. It was obvious Reverend Cotterell had sent his daughter away to prevent him from having any contact with her before the wedding. He demanded to see the reverend, but the butler said that he, too, had gone away. He refused to divulge where the pair had gone to and Eli returned home in despairing defeat.

Then Eli got a terrible shock. The next evening as he sat in his living room in front of the fire languidly reading the Washington Post, his eyes lit upon a brief report, entitled: *"Reverend's Daughter to Marry Presidential Aide"*. It said that the beautiful Miss Annabel Cotterell was to marry Washington's most eligible young bachelor, Alexander Montgomery, in a small but high-society wedding to be presided over by her father, Reverend Augustus Cotterell, in ten days' time. After quickly perusing the short article, Eli slowly lowered the newspaper.

All his hopes, so high after their glorious love-making the other day (despite her subsequent words), were dashed. She was going ahead with it! She was going to marry that boring political lackey, even though Eli was the one that she truly loved. He felt physically ill at the thought of it. Frustrated and helpless. He threw the newspaper into the fire, watching it go up in smoke along with his dreams. Would those few exquisite hours of love-making be all he would have to remember her by? Surely there was something he could do to stop the wedding from going ahead? In his desperation, he even thought of bumping off his rival but, after giving it some serious thought, he knew he could not risk that. This was not the mountains with its simple code of frontier justice, after all.

Here, the murder of a presidential aide would be thoroughly investigated and he would be the very first suspect if Reverend Cotterell had anything to do with it. Besides, it would hardly endear him to Annabel, if she had even an inkling that he had anything to do with it. But even more than that, the new Eli railed against murdering his opponent; that old Eli, the violent, evil one, he'd determinedly left behind on Claw Mountain. Washington had spawned a new Eli. Here, he had found that he wanted to change who and what he was and to redeem himself – *so that he could learn to live with himself . . .*

* * *

Early on the Saturday morning a week before the scheduled wedding, Eli was out in his rose-filled front garden, feeling heavy-hearted since he had still not heard a word from Annabel and had lost all confidence that he ever would. His eyes roved over the profusion of glorious blooms, still dappled with dewdrops, in the garden of the home he had selected especially for her. He thought of his machinations to buy this place and of all the work that had gone into transforming it into a place of unsurpassed beauty. All for her – his beloved Annabel! But it had all been in vain. She was cleaving herself to another, in spite of her feelings for him.

He filled his mind with memories of her, roving over the time he'd first met her at Skyland, when he'd saved her from the rattlesnake, the first momentous kiss at the waterfall in White Oak Canyon, the Colonial Ball, the fiasco of the Skyland Tournament, when he'd nominated her as his queen and the night they'd spent together in Polly's Cave. Right here in his bedroom . . .

He realized then that all of their times together, with the exception of the other day, had been at Skyland. Indeed, their whole relationship, such as it was, had been developed in the play-play world of the famous mountain resort, not here in the real world. *Of course!* He'd been nothing but a hired hand when he met her. *A carnival act!* She probably thought of him as that handsome cowboy in squeaking chaps, who'd brandished his whip and rescued her from certain death, not somebody to marry in the soberness of Washington, where money and politics and etiquette were all that mattered.

How could he have expected anything other than what had happened? Despite all this sumptuous splendor, she had not witnessed for herself how far he'd come socially. She knew nothing about the high-society dinners and parties he was invited to, even though the better list was still not available to him. If he was only able to see her again, he could tell her all this, convince her that the social life she aspired to would be available to her should she marry him. Surely if she knew this, it would be enough to change her mind? But how was he to get hold of her before she married Alexander? It seemed hopeless. Just then, as if the heavens had heard his plea, he heard the sound of hoof beats and looked up to see a hansom cab stopping outside his house. His spirits soared when a heavily veiled woman dressed in black stepped out of the cab and entered by the front gate. *Annabel!*

She had come just as he willed that she would. But such was her hurry, she did not even notice him in the garden and rushed straight for the front door, banging the knocker then waiting impatiently in the scrollwork porch while the hansom cab moved off. He silently moved onto the porch behind her and gathered her to him from behind. She jumped and gave a little screech of fright. He hustled her inside and took her into his arms and they kissed madly, ravenously, as if they wanted to devour one another. Then they raced up to his bedroom, hand in hand, and she helped him undress her, her hands trembling with eagerness and anticipation. When they were both disrobed, they made passionate love on the four-poster bed, on the thick pale green rug on the floor, in the private adjoining bathroom of pale-green marble. Neither of them spoke.

But two hours later, she was gone and he was left with nothing but the lingering sweet smell of her perfume and the exquisite pain of heartache, his belated efforts to try to stop her from marrying Alexander Montgomery doomed to failure. She was quite adamant. As much as she loved him, she was marrying Alexander in one week's time.

It was the dreaded day of Annabel's wedding. On a crisp but sunny autumn morning, driven by a morbid compulsion, Eli drove his chugging Rambler Runabout to where the nuptials were being held at a stately Methodist Church, arriving just after the appointed hour. As he parked at the curb outside the church, he could clearly hear the organ playing the bridal march, so he had clearly just missed her entering the church. He didn't know whether to be relieved or not. She was obviously so anxious to wed Alexander Montgomery, she had not even kept him waiting as tradition dictated.

Anticipating that he would brazenly enter the church, Eli had dressed in a white morning suit with a carnation in his buttonhole, a white straw boater on his tawny head and had taken his ivory gilt-topped cane, rather than in top hat and tails, as tradition dictated, since he *wanted* be noticed by the bride. But as he parked outside in his Rambler, his courage deserted him, and he pulled off his short white gloves. She would never forgive him if he ruined her wedding. Although ostensibly a relatively small affair, Eli noticed there were several press photographers waiting outside the church to capture the auspicious occasion.

Eli tried his best to remain calm, though his hands clutched the steering wheel so hard, his knuckles were white. After what seemed like a lifetime of waiting, the radiant bride and groom came out of the church. They were followed by the rest of the handsomely attired bridal party, who stood with them to be photographed, the guests flooding out from behind them, the ladies in their finest long dresses, large hats and carrying lacy parasols, the men in their long-tailed tuxedoes, black bowties and wearing top hats..

And with his eyes pinned on the bridal couple, Eli saw that Annabel made a truly beautiful bride, as he knew she would. An almost celestial vision, she glowed with loveliness. She wore a white lace dress, with muttonchop sleeves and ruffles up to her high neck – the white falsely signifying the virginity she had already given to him just three weeks ago – and a veil attached to a diamond tiara, set in her high pompadour, a single long black ringlet laying across her shoulder. A huge bouquet of cascading white dog roses, daisies, and lily of the valley further enhanced the image of a virginal bride, which was a considerable vexation to him, in the circumstances.

Watching her, the pain was so acute he thought his heart was being wrenched from his breast. She had been the one shining light in the darkness of his world, the lost, lonely, hellish world inside him that he inhabited when he was alone at night, when alcohol was often his only respite. Now his one chance at happiness was gone forever. For Annabel looked so happy and excited, not anything like a woman torn by conflicting emotions, as he hoped she would. He was utterly devastated, unable to credit that the woman he loved was now lost to him.

Whatever she had said about remaining his lover, she would never become his wife as he so desperately wanted and had dreamed of for so many years. He cursed Reverend Cotterell for his interference, and hatred for the pompous Alexander raged through him like a dose of poison. The high-and-mighty snot had robbed him of what was rightly his!

Alexander had won the ultimate prize and Eli loathed him with his 'old-money' blue-blood family and all the status that it had automatically gained him. For sure, it had won him the most beautiful young woman in all of Washington. *It wasn't fair!* After all, Eli had plotted so diligently towards his goal, seriously straining all his resources for it. More than that, he had completely reinvented himself for Annabel – changed himself from an illiterate hillbilly into a city sophisticate, with all the hard work, dedication and wits that it had taken. After all that effort on his part, the plotting and the planning and the infinite patience, *he had lost!*

It was a terrible, cruel blow to see her standing now with her new husband, looking as if Eli Buchanan didn't exist for her, as if he had never invaded her pale porcelain body with his own. He felt the crushing pain of heartache in his chest and suddenly wished that he had not come. He jumped out of the automobile, went to the front, cranked it furiously to start up the engine, leapt back up into the coach seat, and took off from the curb at a dangerous speed of at least five miles an hour, spooking a horse attached to a smart buggy parked next to the curb in front of him. He had to yank wildly at the steering wheel to miss it, but succeeded in catching the end of it, causing the horse to neigh, buck and jump around in its harness in fright. Eli was slightly mollified to see Annabel in the rearview mirror, staring in dismay after the elegant Rambler tearing away from the scene, causing the buggy's driver and some of the wedding guests to yell after him. He heard their howls of disapproval following him all the way down the street . . .

Falling Leaves and Mountain Ashes

Book VII

'The Eagles are Restless'

'Change is a'comin',
Not swiftly, like the
Pounce of a predator,
But slowly, like the first
Painful drops of spring thaw.
Aye, how insidiously it comes to
Wrench apart the very fabric of
Mountain sweet life.'

Brenda George

63

Mary could not believe it. Eli had made a sudden, totally unexpected departure from Claw Mountain shortly after returning from Skyland. He had left for Washington to start a distillery with a senator. How on earth had he managed to fool such an important man? she wondered. His presence on the mountain after his return from the summer resort had quickly become intolerable to her. She had felt an actual physical repulsion towards him. Even the mention of his name made her skin crawl. God, she was so thankful he was away. She despised him with all her being and had felt an immediate sense of relief and release the day he left on the buckboard. Though followed by most of the clan (she had watched the loud, jolly scene from the heights of Eagle Spur), Mary had a feeling that most of them would also be glad to see the back of him. She found it difficult to comprehend that she did not have to live in the deep constant fear that he had engendered in her, especially of late. What's more, her depression had lifted since he'd left and everything seemed bright and clear again, like rising mist lifting off a murky scene making the world beneath it seem bright and vibrant again.

With Eli gone, the fragile peace pact with the Galtreys was holding, with only two fairly minor, quickly sorted out incidents to mar it. The first time, a gormless Galtrey youth had crossed Devil's Creek, and Emma, appointed by Zachary Thomas to oversee the border between the two mountains and, ever vigilant, had swiftly escorted him back across at shotgun point before the rest of the Buckos had even realized the infraction. The second breach was when a Bucko had shot a cow belonging to the Galtreys, which had wandered near the creek. This was a much more serious infraction. A mountaineer's cows often mean survival to him. After Emma had reported this infraction to her uncle, Zachary Thomas had ordered the Buckos to hide the carcass. When the culprit wouldn't own up, Zachary Thomas had made each of the Buckos contribute a dollar, except Jake, whom Zachary Thomas strongly suspected was the guilty party, pointblank refused. Though the others had reportedly groaned and complained bitterly at having to hand over this sum, Mary was gratified that they had clearly considered the peace pact important enough to do so. Zachary Thomas had taken the money to Dean Galtrey, himself, as compensation.

Thankfully, although the Galtrey patriarch had been incensed by the senseless act, he had accepted the money and the peace had held though a little more precariously than before. Other than these two infractions, things were pretty calm between the two clans. Indeed, they had not even exchanged pot shots over Devil's Creek since Zachary Thomas and Dean Galtrey had shaken hands on it.

That had been a daily occurrence before then. Now, Eli's departure had given the peace pact a real chance of enduring. Had he not gone when he did, Mary was convinced he would have done everything in his power to wreck it, spurred on not only by his hatred for the Galtreys, but his hatred of Mary herself.

* * *

Mary avoided having any contact with Eli when he returned to oversee the stills. Though he never once came up to Eagle Spur to visit his brother, she continued to regard him as being a physical threat to her, especially now that she was with child again. His threat against her during the meeting to discuss the peace pact had not been an idle one. However, with his departure, it seemed as if her two biggest worries had been successfully dealt with by divine providence. There was another benefit, of course. Without Eli's evil agitation, there was a good chance that the peace pact would hold and there was no danger of him and his cronies ever taking up again the destroying of the brush arbors.

The monthly services should have been a joy to Mary, after that. But they weren't, mainly because the relationship between herself and Reverend Hubbly had failed to improve after their discussion regarding the "Beatific Vision", and indeed, had become decidedly strained. Though Mary continually strived for a measure of conciliation with him in the interests of unity, the reverend refused to give her any consideration.

The congregation at his brush arbor monthly service continued to grow, yet Reverend Hubbly was to regard Mary with ever-increasing suspicion, as if he truly believed that she had become a willing lackey of the devil. Even Eli's abrupt departure for Washington had not improved his humor. And whereas once the reverend had viewed Eli as the anti-Christ, he now seemed to view Mary in almost the same light. It was not an obvious thing. He did not ban her from the services, or publicly decry her from the stump-pulpit, though she suspected he would dearly love to. Perhaps the only thing that prevented him from doing just that was that he feared losing the support of the other congregants. But he generally treated her to the ignominy of ignoring her, or became tight-lipped and snappy whenever she addressed him. It was for this reason that she was surprised when he approached her after one service.

"Mary, I have good news," he declared in a loud voice, hailing her with a raised finger as she and her family turned to leave the brush arbor. She carried in her arms her second child, Caleb, a four-month-old baby boy, while Jed clung to her skirts. The reverend left the stump-pulpit and rushed over to her with a grim, satisfied smile on his face.

"What is it, Reverend?"

"The Church Board has agreed to build a church to serve this congregation at last."

Mary gave a little whoop of heartfelt joy. She had pestered Reverend Hubbly about this incessantly over the nearly eighteen months he had been servicing them and could hardly believe it was about to come to pass at last. "Oh, how wonderful, Reverend! I have prayed so hard fer it fer so long, I was beginnin' to believe it would never happen."

Reverend Hubbly gave an annoyed sniff, and said harshly, "Patience is a godly virtue, Mary, which you should practice to obtain. I told you right from the beginning that the community would have to prove itself worthy."

Mary was so happy she did not even mind this stern rebuke. "Yes you did, Reverend. Oh, it must be built right here, Reverend! It's the perfect spot and so centrally situated."

"Oh no," he declared pontifically, "It's not to be built on Claw Mountain at all. I informed the Board that a church would not be safe here, since it would likely be subject to rockings or arson."

There was a moment of terrible, stricken silence, during which time Mary could hear the light summer breeze soughing through the brush of the roof of the arbor. Unable to believe her ears, she stared at him in shocked dismay. "Why, Reverend, *how could you?* You know full well thar ain't no chance of sech a thing happenin' now. Th' folk of this mountain dearly love this tabernacle, brush, though it may be. It's thar church and has special meanin' for them. You must know that. They'll be devastated."

"Aah, the congregants may love it, but have you forgotten how many times it was pulled down in the past? Have you so easily forgotten the rockings, the insults to God's servant, the threats? Would you have me lie to my Board?"

"Of course not! But that's jest it. It were in th' *past.* All that stopped some time ago and, besides, th' main culprit no longer even resides here, and all th' others, bar one, have since been converted. Why must they be punished when they have repented and come into th' fold?"

"*Punished?* How odd that you should view it that way. I tell you a church is to be built and you call it punishment!"

The indictment was clear. The words '*Devil Woman*' blazed from his eyes.

"Reverend, you are deliberately twistin' my meanin'. I jest feel that th' inhabitants of this here mountain have raised th' arbors time and time agin and have been in faithful attendance, even during th' most tryin' times. They strongly deserve to have Claw Mountain considered a worthy site for th' new church."

"Oh, do you, indeed? Well, I happen to think differently. Who is to say that Eli Buchanan will not return to this mountain one day? We both know the man is devil-driven. He has made innumerable threats to rid this mountain of its church

483

and he repeatedly carried out those threats. He is doubtless just awaiting the opportunity to destroy it for good."

"That may have been so once, Reverend, but I doubt he will return. He has a home in Washington now and his business is there. He only pays Claw Mountain occasional visits and then never on Sundays. Thar ain't nuthin' fer him here no more."

"Aah, but can you *guarantee* that he will never return?"

"Of course not, but it's so unlikely as to be without any grounds fer consideration."

Zachary Thomas, standing beside her, cleared his throat and spoke for the first time. "I've got to agree with my wife, Reverend. Eli ain't comin' back here. He's a real city boy now. Even talks and dresses like one."

"Well, that may be so, but that is not the only reason I decided not to recommend Claw Mountain. Quite frankly, this mountain does not *deserve* the privilege of having a proper church serviced by a resident preacher."

"*Why not*, Reverend?" cried Mary indignantly. "I don't thunk thar's a community anywhar that deserves it more. They've stopped thar violent ways and most of them have stopped drinkin'. All but a few of them have turned to th' Lord!"

"Yes, that may well be, but I've heard strong rumors that there are several stills being operated on this mountain, so clearly they have not changed that much, after all. There is strong evidence that they are earning their living from making devil's potions."

Mary bit back a retort. She was on dangerous ground here. If she admitted to the existence of the stills, she would not put it past him to alert the Revenue Men. She tried using a more conciliatory tone. "Oh Reverend, you have to understand that makin' moonshine has been th' way of mountain folk fer centuries past. It's second nature to them."

"So it bothers you none that it has been the cause for much of the killing and violence that has beset these mountains over the years?"

"Well, yes, of course it bothers me. I don't condone it, but I do understand it."

"So as long as *you* understand it, it's okay, is it? It's okay for intemperance and violence to rock and destroy whole communities, just because it has some scant historical significance?"

Mary stared at him, at a loss for words. She gave a huge weary sigh. Too much of what he said about moonshining was true for her to argue the point. Indeed, it was what she herself had felt all along. Clearly, there was no use trying to change his mind about the church. It was made up and about as intractable as an eagle clutching its prey in its talons. *Nothing could shake it loose!*

She said helplessly, "Well, if'n not here, Reverend, whar exactly is it to be built?"

Knowing she was beaten, the Reverend smiled, a smirking supercilious smile, the light of triumph in his light-brown eyes. "*Beacon Mountain!* After all, many of the present congregants spring from there. I also wish to expand my congregation to include the communities from Fork Mountains, and others beyond. Beacon Mountain has not the sordid reputation of Claw Mountain. No matter what you say about the reformation of the inhabitants here on Claw Mountain, many folk from other mountains are still too afraid to venture forth onto its slopes.

"News of Eli's blatant endangerment of the congregation and his willful destruction of the arbors has spread like wildfire throughout more peace-abiding mountain communities and deterred those timid souls who might otherwise have received salvation from the Lord. Proof of this is that this congregation has not expanded to any great number. It would be sacrilege for me to deny God His rightful due any longer."

So that was it! Despite the growing numbers, he was greedy for more converts. But it went way beyond that. By the smug look his face, Mary knew that Reverend Hubbly's recommendation had sprung from pure spite rather than for any of the reasons he had just spouted. He refused to give her the satisfaction of realizing her dream to have a church built on this mountain, even after all she had done to promote it. She wondered if she should go and speak to the Board herself, try to persuade them that Claw Mountain was not the place it once was, that its community was now responsible and God-fearing, and deserving for that reason alone. But the reverend's next words quick sabotaged that plan of action.

"The Board was more than willing to confirm my strong recommendation that it be built elsewhere instead. All the plans have been approved. I, and the members of the Board, have already found a suitable site on Beacon Mountain. It'll take only a short while to arrange things. Once the building starts, it will go quickly. I imagine the new church will be up and running by fall."

Mary heard his words with a spurt of annoyance. It was already a done deed! Yet he had not bothered to tell her until now. Clearly, there was nothing she could do about it now, since a site on Beacon Mountain had already been approved. Without Reverend Hubbly's support, she knew changing the minds of those on the Board would be an impossible task.

"Have you forgotten that Jed and Caleb were to hace thar infant-sprinlin's at that time?" she asked peevishly.

Clearly he had, but he quickly covered it up. "Well, that's easy. We will simply combine the sanctification of the new chapel with the two christenings. Quite an honor, I fancy."

Beacon Mountain! The thought of the new church being built on another mountain, even a neighboring one, pained Mary deeply. And it wasn't just that they would have to walk five miles or more to go to the new church every month.

It was because her dream had become the dream of all the service-attending folk on this mountain. She herself felt a fondness for this brush tabernacle that she doubted any built church could provide. Worshipping God amidst the natural cathedral of trees right in the heart of the Claw Mountain forests, gave her a deep sense of reverence. Even so, it would be good for the community to have something more permanent, something not subject to the whims of the elements. Now that honor was going to *Beacon* Mountain!

Mary felt sad and bereft. To be sure, a number of the worshippers were indeed from that mountain, but they had not fought for the survival of the services like the Bucko clan had fought for them, helping to build a new structure each time the old one was torn down, flying in the face of Eli – *that evil, evil man!* Now, because of his misdeeds, Claw Mountain would not be getting its church. He had won in the end, after all! And so had Reverend Hubbly won! Well, maybe she could do nothing about the church, but she could not let the gloating reverend get away with such pettiness, such contemptuous disregard of the feelings of his faithful parishioners. She eyed him levelly with calm hazel eyes.

"Oh dear, Reverend, I guess the Board must have been *real* disappointed to hear that your faithful ministerin' has had so little impact on the Claw Mountain community after all this time."

Reverend Hubbly quailed, blinking his eyes rapidly, as the realization of her words hit him. So keen to destroy *her dream,* he clearly had not considered this angle. She could read his face like a book, his thoughts as loud as spoken words. His insistence on building the church elsewhere must surely reflect badly on him in the end. *He had shot himself in the foot!*

Mary clucked sympathetically. "It's sech a pity that all your fine efforts here have come to naught, after all. Th' Buchanans are still as godless and violent as they were that first terrible day you came to give service."

Considering how disastrous that first service had been and how peaceful the services had been for such a long time now, her words had the impact of a rude clout. The reverend stood looking shattered, his reputation with his Board, once so hallowed and fine, was clearly in tatters in his mind.

Mary, chin raised, turned and ushered her smart barefoot family along the row. But her victory was a hollow one. She had lost the fight to bring a proper church to Claw Mountain and, knowing how bitterly disappointed the others would be when they found out, the knowledge sat like a stone in the pit of her stomach.

64

That Sunday in late October, 1902, promised to be a memorable day for Doc Adams. Not only was the Presbyterian Church that had been recently built on Beacon Mountain, to be sanctified, but there were to be two further special sacraments. Both little Jed and Caleb, the infant second son of Zachary Thomas and Mary Buchanan, were to be christened. Doc had been invited along since Mary had asked him to be Jed's godfather and to attend the "infant sprinkling" ceremony – *for the second time.* Jed, along with several other children on Claw Mountain, was to have been christened in a joint ceremony in the brush tabernacle on Claw Mountain some time back and Doc had been asked by Mary to be Jed's godfather then too. To Doc, the honor of being godfather to such a child as Jed was something he treasured beyond words. The small adventurous boy was truly "the apple of his eye" and he loved him with a depths that confounded him. He had only to look upon the child to get a warm squishy feeling in his stomach.

Unfortunately, a medical emergency had stopped him from attending the joint christening the last time, and Mary, knowing how Doc felt about the child, had chosen to withdraw Jed from the ceremony, rather than have Doc miss the special event. Doc was touched by her consideration and was determined not to miss this one and disappoint her yet again. Fortunately, when the day of the double christening dawned, there were no calls to make, no one scheduled to have a baby, nobody fever-bound or in the final throes of some life-threatening disease and it was with a rare sense of freedom and anticipation that Doc found himself able to attend.

The fine new log chapel had been built about six miles from where the Buchanans lived, in the middle of a little bluegrass clearing, up on a sunny ridge about halfway up Beacon Mountain, to serve the little mountain communities of all the surrounding mountains. Up till the time Mary had persuaded the mountain people of these parts to erect the brush arbors so that the circuit-preacher could attend to their spiritual needs, Doc fancied that as steeped as they were in their colorful myths and superstitions, they had been far more concerned with survival, than with such lofty ecclesiastical matters as repentance and salvation. According to Mary, Reverend Hubbly had expressed the opinion that only *organized* religion (inside a proper built church, that is, would change all that. Considering the monthly brush arbor services had already had an amazing effect on the folk of Claw Mountain, this sentiment hardly seemed true.

Word had it that the Claw Mountain community had been dashed by the choice of Beacon Mountain as the site for the permanent structure and that some of the Buckos and their families had threatened to boycott today's proceedings because of it. Doc hoped they wouldn't – for Mary's sake! He knew how hard she had fought for the building of the church.

Doc decided to drive his fine horse-and-buggy for a change, having been assured that there was a traversable road all the way there, as he felt it more befitted the occasion than arriving on old Bessie. Though he loved his dear saddle nag fiercely, he fancied she was looking rather old and flea-bitten of late. He'd have to put her out to pasture one of these days. He had been looking forward to the drive immensely for the crisp colder weather had singed the greenness from the leaves and set the forests violently alight with flaming reds, oranges and golds. Indeed, it would be a truly awe-inspiring sight, especially from the loftiness of the mountain ridges.

However, he was soon to rue his rash decision. The steep, rocky road was bumpy and full of holes and several times he almost succeeded in overturning his more elaborate transport. Furthermore, he had to concentrate so hard that he had no time at all to gaze down at the wondrous sights. He had to pull so often and so hard on the reins, to negotiate the treacherous track, that it raised welts on the palms of his hands.

By the time Doc finally arrived, feeling quite exhausted, discomforted and over-wrought, there was a large crowd of mountain folk already assembled outside the log chapel. A huge wooden cross proudly hammered to the top of its pitched roof on the outside, directly above the double doors at its entrance, signified to all its holy portals. He climbed shakily out of his buggy, his smart dark-gray pin-striped suit, already creased at the knees and his fancy silver waist-coat, blackened with patches of anxious sweat. He tipped an acknowledging derby hat at the mountain folk, as they called out pleasant greetings to him. It was obvious that they were in fine humor today. Everybody was smiling. And Doc could scarcely blame them. This fine new church would link whole mountain communities together in a spirit of fellowship, such as never before. There were a few families Doc had not seen before – they would be from the more remote hollows, into which he had yet to venture – but most of them, he knew well, either from his mountain clinics or from the general store.

Besides a scattering of folk from Fork Mountain, like Chaucy Yates, Porky Brown, Will Pickens and Edgar Sharp and their families, there stood a goodly contingent from Bear Rock Mountain – Eliza and Elliot Jenkins and their brood, the good-looking Wilkens brothers, Josiah and Claude, Hepley Riley, Caleb and Effie Johnson, all with their large families. Ernest McGreedy, with his full-blown beard and patch over an eye some said he'd lost in a fight over a woman in his youth, looked like some disreputable pirate from the high seas, but it was said that his thin little wife, Myrtle, made his life a misery and ruled him with a rod of iron, though none of her rigidity or disagreeability showed in her frail, insipid appearance. He also caught sight of Dwayne Ealy, the ageing bachelor in the milling throng, the Taylors, the Calloways and the Dooleys, who were all there with their little attendant tribes. The members of the Ficks clan from Beacon Mountain stood in a proud host group, looking smug and superior, as if the church belonged to them alone and was only being shared at their largesse, while a large contingent of Claw Mountain folk, all dressed in the best finery they possessed, respectably swelled the numbers. Obviously, their threats to boycott the event had been forgotten in all the excitement.

Clearly, the prospect of attending the grand opening service and having a proper building in which to worship for the first time had ultimately proved irresistible to them. He noticed that the Buchanan clan stood a little apart from the others, looking a little like goldfish out of water now that they were out of their own environment, either uncomfortable to be here amongst the mountain folk they had previously preyed upon, or because it was the others who remembered their excesses in the past and did not care to chummy up to them as yet.

Forsaking their working dungarees for once, some of the men appeared in the regulation mountain duds of hickory shirt, denim jeans and broad straw hats, while a few wore black funeral suits and white shirts with detachable collars; some even sported the odd bow or string tie and they wore an assortment of battered hats. The women wore frilly bonnets, shawls and long gathered skirts. The children, their faces scrubbed with homemade soap, were dressed in their Sunday best. Little girls wore calf-length cotton dresses, with over-aprons, and had their heads braided or curled; the boys, with washbowl haircuts, wore over-large caps, overalls and sweaters. But despite their best efforts, it was obvious to Doc that poverty stalked amongst these remote highland people. It was reflected in the patches upon faded skirts and on threadbare knees; the holes at insistent elbows. All of the children were barefoot. Though most of the adults wore shoes, they were mainly worn out and splitting at the seams. Mary, in an elegant cream lacy gown with long muttonchop sleeves, wore the only forgotten or unheard of luxury amongst them; black button-up soft-kid boots, though they were dusty and scuffed from the long walk.

But it mattered not. What the others lacked in fine clothing and material possessions, they had gained in newfound dignity and pride. Though many of them had once shunned religion of any sort in the distant past, before the advent of the monthly brush arbor services, now they embraced it like a cape on a winter night. There was a murmuring among them, a great hushed excitement that rippled through their midst like a brush fire. *A fine church of their very own!* Imagine that!

489

Mary and Zachary Thomas Buchanan, with both of their children about to be christened and Mary's long fight to get the church built, were rightly the center of attention. They stood at the middle of the group, the giant hillbilly proudly holding Mary's elbow, while she held their four-month-old new baby swathed in a shawl in her arms. Clinging to her skirts was the two-year old toddler and Doc's pride and joy, little Jed. Doc's eyes had eagerly sought him out. He had grown some. A wiry barefoot little thing, he was dressed in neat blue dungarees with a short-sleeved white shirt beneath. His little moppet face, framed by unruly brown hair and ears that stuck out, was almost the color of mud. He looked solemn and bewildered by all the fuss, but when someone bent to tweak his ear and tickle him under the chin, he managed a half-hearted, uncertain smile . . .

* * *

As often happens with the distances people had to travel in the mountains, two people were late; Reverend Hubbly and the new graduate preacher. They leapt off their buggy and approached the milling group of mountain people at a fair trot. Introduced in a flurry of haste, the Reverend Benjamin Crawley looked, to Doc, like a nice clean-cut young fellow, with slicked-back brown hair and the youthful soft white skin of an adolescent who had escaped the agonies of acne. But before he could get properly acquainted with either of them, the novice preacher was whipped inside the new chapel by the frightfully stern and proper Reverend Hubbly, shortly before the double doors were flung open to admit the throng.

Inside the small chapel, which smelt of freshly cut chestnut logs, there were pews for the people to sit on. In the front was a small pulpit on a raised platform, where Reverend Hubbly and Preacher Crawley went to sit down on wooden chairs. Holding back to allow the mountain folk to go in before him as was their due, Doc, as proud godfather, walked straight down the aisle and sat on a pew right in the front, in a place saved for him next to Mary Buchanan and her small family, Edna Buchanan, who was to be Jed's godmother, and Toad and Ellie Mae Buchanan, who were to be the godparents of the new baby, Caleb. In a great surging tide, the mountaineers had poured into the pews, sitting squashed together, with children sitting on laps and a few of the adults being forced to stand at the back, all in a great, excited calamitous uproar.

"SSSSSSSH!" came a loud admonition from Reverend Hubbly, who leapt to his feet. "You have now entered the house of the Lord. Try to act like it!"

There was an immediate shocked silence as if they'd all been instantly struck by muteness, while the reverend eyed them with pointed disdain. Doc had heard that the stern circuit-preacher had been deeply offended by the appointment of a novice fresh out of the Presbyterian Union Theological Seminary in Richmond, to preside over the new church when he had been expecting to get the position himself. Apparently, he had accused Mary at his last service on Claw Mountain of having gone to the Board behind his back and spread vicious lies about him, when in actual fact she had done no such thing.

After everybody had been seated, Reverend Hubbly, a tall, thin fellow, with a balding head, stood up to pontifically inform the congregation that the beatification ceremony and service were to be conducted by himself, whereupon, he would introduce them to their new preacher, who would then perform the two separate christenings of Jed and Caleb Buchanan. He said the latter with some distaste and there was no doubt in Doc's mind that he had handed over this duty over to the new preacher because he had no desire to perform it himself, blaming Mary, as he did, for not getting the position he had so sorely coveted. Indeed, the words 'new full-time preacher' seemed to stick in his craw, as if he had a deal of trouble getting them out.

After saying a few disgruntled words of welcome, he ordered the cong-regation to stand up to open the service with the hymn "Lead Kindly Light". Led by the booming baritone of Zachary Thomas and the rich honey tones of Ellie Mae Buchanan, it was sung without hymn books (precious few of them could read) or musical accompaniment, their voices raised in hope and joy. Such was Doc's pride at being in their midst this blessed day that he was surprised to find his own voice booming out with untypical fervor. But he was soon to discover that Reverend Hubbly was a dreadfully ineffective and flagellate preacher with the tendency to drone.

Almost immediately, the black-suited minister, who seemed to use his white collar as a license to chastise, began to tell the eager, bright-eyed mountain folk what terrible sinners they were, listing their many trespasses like items on a shopping list. Moonshine headed the list and warranted a lengthy diatribe on its evils, but it included blaspheming, cussing, lust, slovenliness, tardiness, vanity, ignorance, non-church attendance, pride and laziness, to name his main concerns. He then proceeded to threaten them with eternal damnation for their wayward-ness, causing them to sag in dismay and squirm on their seats.

Doc glanced at Mary holding baby Caleb in her arms, to see her frowning with consternation and distress. She had told him that she had grave doubts about this man's ability to lead a flock and now he knew why. Though it was odd how such a man could have made the remarkable difference in the Buckos' behavior as had come about, Doc thought it was probably far more *in spite* of the man rather than because of him. He found him sadly lacking in the love and compassion which Jesus stood for. His anemic preaching was a mixture of dull hellfire and brimstone, fear and condemnation. It was sad to see how quickly he had removed the smiles from the faces of these simple mountain folk.

Some way into the service, the reverend stopped to have a drink of water, and in the ensuing quiet, a small boy blurted that he needed a pee. The congregation burst into amused guffaws, the guileless remark coming as something of a relief after the virulent attack from the pulpit. It broke through the tension like a knife slicing through butter.

But Reverend Hubbly was not amused. He rose up with a howl of effrontery, his face like a thundercloud. "IS THAT LAUGHTER THAT I HEAR AMONGST YOU?" he roared. "HOW DARE YOU MOCK THE SANCTUARY OF THE LORD WITH SUCH FRIVOLITY?"

The congregation froze as one, laughter dying instantly in their throats. The mother of the miscreant child fought her anxious way through the tangle of mountaineers' feet and fled outside with him, her face beet-red. The reverend had immediately scotched their moment of abandonment and joy like a buzzing bee caught and squashed in an iron fist. The elder preacher actually seemed to despise the people he served and Doc concluded that the Church Board had been wise to take this church away from the grasp of this mirthless, merciless creature, which stood hunched like a vulture behind the pulpit.

The reverend glared at the congregation for several minutes before he spoke again. Doc rather wished he hadn't. Watched by a bowed-and-gagged congregation, he rambled on with his service in such a mild, boring manner that despite the fact that Doc felt that such condemnation during a special service to bless the new church, highly inappropriate, he actually began to wish the fellow had a bit more life in him if he insisted on pursuing such a line. (He now pointedly brought in the mountain people's lack of discipline of their children.) Right now, a bit of rip-roaring hellfire and brimstone seemed an attractive alternative to his deathly dull delivery since it would at least keep the eyelids from closing. As it was, the interminable sermon, delivered in a dreary monotone, punctuated by the wracking coughs and trumpeting nose-blowing of the congregation, went on so long it had the children fidgeting and more than one adult, including himself, illicitly dozing on the wooden benches.

At long last, Reverend Hubbly ended the torture with a surprisingly brief prayer pronouncing elaborate blessing. He raised both his arms, threw his head heavenward, closed his eyes and in a deep, sonorous voice asked God to shower the new sanctuary with His love and glory, a complete mockery considering what had gone on before.

Doc seated right in the front felt irked and disgusted by this belated display of devotion to the cause. Nevertheless, he at last sensed the backbones straightening behind him and the once drooping heads being held high with pride and stirred faith. Doc just hoped they weren't fooled by it.

Thank heavens they'd soon be rid of this supposed servant of the Lord. After the prayer, Reverend Hubbly formally handed over the pulpit to its new presider,

Reverend Crawley, to conduct the first of the two christening ceremonies. But, alas, the young man was so nervous that Doc felt desperately sorry for him. Shaking from head to foot, the raw young preacher, yanking at his clerical collar, called upon the proud parents to bring forward the baby, Caleb, in a loud quavering voice that seemed to lose power before he had quite finished, Zachary Thomas and Mary, sitting on the front bench, obediently rose and walked forward with the babe, who had been remarkably good throughout the proceedings, his occasional niggles, barely audible. The baby's godparents also rose and joined them at the altar.

But Reverend Crawley's initiation turned into even more of a nightmare for him. He proceeded to stumble badly over his words, causing an embarrassed hush to descend on the congregation, and when the time came to sprinkle water over the baby's head, his hand shook so fiercely that the babe was instead splashed liberally in the face with a shock of water. Of course, little Caleb immediately started to cry. The new reverend began to lightly pat his tiny arm, in an effort to comfort and subdue, but unable to control the force of the "pats", they were more like slaps and the baby wailed even louder.

Lord knew what the young Reverend Crawley would have done next had there not been an interruption to the proceedings that drew immediate attention away from his blundering efforts. At first, it seemed Reverend Hubbly had read Doc's earlier thoughts, for he suddenly started acting like some wild-eyed lunatic evangelist. Leaping off the chair he was sitting on, he banged an adamant fist on the pulpit, and pointing down the aisle, yelled, "ALAS! HE BRINGS THE SERPENT AMONG US! SATAN IS HERE! CAST HIM OUT! CAST HIM OUT!"

This dramatic pronouncement caught the immediate attention of the congregation, and all heads turned to see what he was pointing at. As quizzical eyes lit upon the strange sight, they drew back in horror, wailing and screaming with fright. Doc felt riveted to his seat with like horror, unable to give credence to what he saw. For there – slowed in his uncertain walk up the aisle by the gasps and screams – was little Jed. He was wrapped from his waist to his neck, with only his arms free of encumbrance, by the coils of a live rattlesnake!

Now, like most human beings, the mountain people had an extreme dread and fear of snakes. They spoke about them in hushed whispers and stories and legends about them were legion – there were snakes that sang; snakes that bit people after their heads had been cut off; snakes that wrapped around unwary throats while a person slept, choking the life out of them; snakes that lay in wait for hunters in the forest at night, in order to trip them up, snakes that caught their tails in their mouths and traveled down the mountain slopes in hoops. Indeed, if one man were to curse another, he had only to mention the word "snake" to cause the other to tremble. Copperheads, rattlers, vipers, they were all guaranteed to spook mountaineer flesh, and cause the shudders.

And now here was little Jed, the very picture of innocence, calmly walking into their new place of worship solemnly bringing this loathsome reptilian creature – the powerful symbol of all that was evil – among them. How on earth had he managed to slip out of the church without anybody seeing him? His little hand was lightly stroking the patterned scaly skin of the two-inch thick viperine and he was talking to it with unintelligible noises, which sounded oddly like some strange incantation. As he was met with aghast cries and whimpers, his hand slowed and he went quiet, his brilliant blue eyes quickly filling with embarrassed tears, causing him to blink rapidly.

It was a chilling sight that raised the hairs on the back of Doc's neck before he was clouted with an acute awareness of the extreme danger the child was in. But though he was sitting at the end of the row, right next to the aisle, just six feet in front of the little boy, in his panic, he could not think of a single thing that he could do. He merely stared at the incongruous pair in fascinated, unmoving desperation.

The rattlesnake's raised broad head faced the pulpit and its black tongue darted in and out of its mouth sinisterly. If Doc was not mistaken, it was a young giant rattler since it had a string of rattles on its tail three inches long. The whole chapel was stunned into agonized watchful silence. Nobody moved, not even the children. In fact, it seemed that nobody even dared breathe. Even Reverend Hubbly suddenly seemed at a loss for words.

"Son . . ." It was Zachary Thomas who at last broke the silence. "Son," he croaked hoarsely.

Mary gave a little wounded cry and caught at her huge husband's arm as he left the little christening group and started to walk slowly down the aisle towards his first-born son. The snake obviously sensed his cautious approach and, in the deathly silence that followed, there was only the ominous sound of the rattles that started up in the hollow horny section of its tail as it slowly began to unwind itself from Jed's little body. The toddler's whole upper half and neck was a series of moving bands of snake-flesh as the snake moved itself up into a position to strike. It opened its mouth to reveal long curved fangs that seemed to drip with venom. Zachary Thomas stopped mid-stride. He looked helpless and aghast. Everybody else looked stunned, their eyes wild with anxiety and fear. The silence stretched. Doc tried desperately to find some sane solution. But there was nothing he could do that would not endanger the life of the boy.

Finally it was little Jed, himself, who saved the situation. There were gasps of horror and disbelief as he calmly grasped the head of the snake in his one hand, bringing it down to the level of his face. They all stared in breathbated amazement as he caressed the head along his cheek, murmuring as if to comfort the snake. The snake seemed to immediately calm. It slackened its body and closed its mouth. Then as if seeming totally unaware of the considerable stir he had caused, the toddler turned and wandered out of the church as idly as he had entered it. After a moment of stunned immobility, several of the men, including Doc and Zachary Thomas, rushed to the double doors of the church in time to see the snake sliding down the extended arm of the squatting child to the ground. It slithered into the grass and lay there without moving.

Suddenly, there was pandemonium! Harvey Taylor produced a shovel from somewhere. Others, emerging from the crowded chapel, hurriedly picked up sticks and rocks in the grassy yard outside, while the women and children gathered fearfully about the doorway. Zachary Thomas rushed up to little Jed, and hurriedly pulled him aside, as Harvey, approaching cautiously from the rear, raised the shovel, took careful aim and slammed it down on the snake's head with such force, it neatly chopped it off. The men bore down on it like an army given the signal to attack. They started viciously beating its writhing headless body with sticks, rocks, their feet and the bloodied shovel, until, at last, it stopped moving. But now as Doc stared down at the awful bloody mess of chopped and shredded skin and snake flesh at their feet he heard, amidst the loud grunts of glee and satisfaction around him, an awful choking crying. He turned to see little Jed standing about three feet away, his small face agonized and streaked with tears, one tiny fist ground into an eye, and Doc suddenly realized how it must have appeared to him.

Ten huge grown men, hacking, kicking, and butchering a creature even long after its death . . . a highly dangerous reptile that, somehow, this little innocent had been able to handle without any harm to himself. That little child had witnessed their barbarism – for suddenly that was how it appeared to Doc – and having added his own vicious kick to the hapless reptile in his anxiety over the little boy, Doc was suddenly smitten with a terrible gnawing shame . . .

65

A few days after the snake incident at the church, Doc called in at the general store at Graves Mill to collect his post and get few much-needed home supplies. The fly-pestered donkeys and pack-horses and mules of the mountain folk, who came to sell or trade pelts, chickens, eggs, chestnuts, mushrooms and berries, in exchange for seed, food or basic supplies, were hitched to the rails outside, while four-horse produce wagons bound for the overnight camp at Somerset paused beneath some shady trees to be watered and rested.

Old-timer regulars, Ernie Walts, Jediah Horner, Gillespie Smith and the ornery

Clarence Simpkins were sitting sunning themselves outside on the porch, chewing tobacco or smoking pipes and they raised hats or dipped pipes in greeting. These hardy grizzled old folk, with their long beards, wit and home-spun wisdom, knew everything that was going on, not only in the valley, but up in the mountains too. Oft'times, they would play their banjos and sing. Occasionally, one of them would get up and do the flat-foot dance just to show there was plenty of life in the old bones yet.

It always pleasured Doc to come to this crowded little community center, where he was able to pleasantly pass the time of day and a body could get anything from a can of beans to fruit jars, flatirons to castor oil, bales of cloth to a new pair of shoes, while breathing in the smell of leather saddlery and the rich aroma of fine chewing tobacco, roll-your-own tobacco and cigars. The goods were piled everywhere; on shelves, on the floor and on the counter. There were big glass jars for penny candies, gumballs and liquorice sticks next to the till, barrels of pickles and flour on the floor, gallon cans of kerosene and lye for making soap. Ladies bonnets and hats, dresses, shoes, slippers and bales of floral and gingham cloth and other female flippancies, were to the one side, while to the other were men's boots, trousers, shirts, dungarees, braces, garters and fair array of hats, from the floppy felt and straw types favored by the mountain men, banded with different furs, some bedecked with raccoon tails or plumaged with eagle or wild turkey feathers, to the western-style ten-gallons and stetsons. There was even the occasional more stylish bowler and straw boater.

But the mellow, congenial atmosphere that usually greeted Doc in the store was not apparent today. He found several of the mountain people gathered around the pot-bellied stove in the center of the room, and they were so riled up about something, they failed to even notice his entrance. All of them he had recently seen at the uniquely aborted Sunday church service on Beacon Mountain. Harvey Tayler, Ernest McGreedy, Porky Brown, Josiah Wilkens, Hepley Riley, Dwayne Ealy, Chaucy Yates and Edgar Sharp were all keenly engaged in an animated discussion, their faces harrowed and concerned-looking. It was some minutes before Doc realized they were talking about the incident of little Jed and the rattlesnake. Though he was not normally a man to butt into a conversation or to eavesdrop, upon hearing the name "Jed" mentioned in context with a snake, he felt constrained to find out what was being said about the dear child.

Dewey Stokes, the amiable elderly storekeeper, was busy serving Will Pickens' boy, at the counter and Doc, indicating to the man that he was in no great hurry with an airy wave of the hand, kind of sidled up to the group in order to hear better.

". . . why it were th' damndest thung I ever seen," said Harvey Taylor, sounding much awed, scratching the back of his head. "Lawd knows I ain't never seen nuthin' like th' way he handled that thar rattler. I swar it made my blood run clean cold. I'm inclined to thunk that thar young'un's got somethung real strange 'bout him."

Doc saw Myrtle McCreedy, who was enviously eyeing bales of gingham cloth in one corner, turn slowly around, her flat broad lace-up shoes, dusty with the miles she must have walked to get here. A woman totally lacking female grace, she had a narrow, pious-looking face that was harrowed and work-worn. It was said that she had been jilted by a rich lowlander once (Doc found it mighty hard to believe that anyone of that ilk might have wanted her in the first place), and bitterly resented her present life of comparative poverty and unending hard work, and spent her life blaming poor Ernest for it.

However, she liked to give the impression of being subservient to her husband in public, with primly clasped hands and meekly bowed head, never saying very much, though, of course, it was well-known what a tartar she was at home. But today, no doubt driven to it by the force of her feelings on the matter, she showed a little of her true colors. With her face tightened up in screwed-up fury within the frame of her sad-looking cloth hat, she abruptly left the able serving ministrations of Jessie Stokes who was hovering not too hopefully at her side, dramatically flounced up to the little group and announced flatly, "*Strange?* That child ain't jest *strange.* I say that little monster is a *demon child!* A tool of th' devil! You saw th' way he brought Satan amongst us – right into our newly blessed chapel and right at th' very time his own brother was receivin' his water sprinklin', too! Savin' hisself from bein' christened, he was. *Surely, you kin see th' signs? Ain't* you noticed th' color of his eyes a'fore?" she whispered darkly. "Them ain't natural eyes. I tell you that young'un's got th' 'evil eye!'"

"*The evil eye!*" echoed Earnest McCreedy weakly, squinting through his one good eye, looking painfully embarrassed at the presumptiousness of his wife to so butt into this all-male conversation.

"Why, Myrtle," said Chaucy Yates, fingering his stubbly chin thoughtfully. "I find it that mighty hard to believe. But it was mighty weird jest th' same. Why, th' way that little fella grabbed that snake's head, I swar I thought he was a dead'un fer sure. But th' snake behaved jest like it had bin . . . whacha call it? . . . *hyp-notized!* We-ell, could be somethung in what you're sayin', I s'pose."

"'Cos there is," Myrtle snorted. "And I say, we cain't have wicked demon young'uns in our house of worship. That ain't fittin' at all. What do you expect from th' son of a Bucko? *That wicked lot!* Took a chance lettin' a single one of 'em on th' mountain let alone inside that church! If'n you ain't careful that boy'll put th' evil eye on y'all! Yer crops will fail and all yer hogs will die fer sure."

There was a sudden chilled silence as the mountain men digested her dire warning words. Doc saw the panic flare in their eyes. At first even Doc felt an icy ripple run down his back. Then he swiftly shed himself of the sobering thought and felt his hackles rise. How dare these people talk about little Jed as if he were some ghastly lackey of the devil, instead of just a dear, adventurous, highly sensitive little boy, with an affinity for all of Nature, that he was. Why, Doc had delivered that little innocent himself, had followed his progress like a doting spinster aunt, and he, for one, was utterly convinced there was nothing satanical about him whatsoever.

"Now, hold on there, Myrtle." Doc was surprised to hear his own angry voice enter the conversation. Everybody turned to look at him in some surprise. "There's no need to get carried away. Zack and Mary Buchanan happen to be the finest couple I know. Indeed, without Mary Buchanan there wouldn't even be a church! And as for young Jed, why that dear little boy is no more a 'child of the devil' than I am . . . !"

But after Doc had climbed up into his buggy, his meager supplies already loaded up on the buffed leather seat beside him and lightly flicked his whip to send his chestnut buggy horse, Wishbone, homeward, he ruefully allowed that nothing he had said had made any impression on the gathering. Myrtle's words had really hit home, while his own, had merely stirred an unconvinced muttering among the men.

In a way, one could scarcely blame them. The incident itself had been as bizarre a thing as he'd ever seen. And the mountain folk had so little, naturally they would be concerned if anything remotely threatened their livelihood, no matter how fanciful. How could they risk not taking heed of Myrtle's malicious mouthings? Little Jed *had* brought a highly dangerous serpent into their holy place and handled it with ease. That had cast an air of evil about it and bespoke of strange mystical powers in their minds. But Doc had no doubt that their assumptions were quite ludicrous.

Why, he had noticed in the past how animals were drawn to the toddler. The two coon dogs rarely left his side and were constantly licking him all over his face. The chickens clucked around him as if he were their provider instead of Mary, and even the hogs contentedly grunted around him, nudging him with their long wet snouts. The goat was always gently butting its horns against him, as if to just let him know it was there. The child couldn't even talk, and already he was able to sit in the middle of an ant nest, according to Mary, and handle a dangerous reptile, with no harm to himself. What did it all mean? After pondering deeply upon it, Doc came to the conclusion that the only thing little Jed was guilty of was bearing a profound love for all living creatures, and having the unique ability to communicate with them on a level Doc had never seen before and yet vainly struggled to understand. But just because he and others didn't understand it, did not make it *evil!*

But, sadly, no amount of protest from Doc had held sway with that fearful little group. For against their deep superstitions, Myrtle's ghastly aspersions and the provocative power of the incident itself, his defense of the child had seemed horribly weak and unconvincing. After the aborted service had been summarily halted by an enraged Reverend Hubbly (though Doc suspected the reverend had been secretly pleased to end it on such a highly dramatic note), it seemed Myrtle had heard from one of the Ficks' wives (who in turn had heard it from one of the Bucko wives), of the little boy's strange nature and habits and how Mary could not keep him out of the forest. – this, added to the fact that he had seldom cried as a baby. Myrtle hinted at how unnatural this all was and said she was sure they had all noticed the boy's calm intensity for themselves. The mountain men discussed this new information at length and they all kept harking back at the extraordinary brilliance of Jed's blue eyes and, before too long, with Myrtle constantly feeding their fears with snide interjections, they had twisted the little toddler's willful visits into the forest from very early age, into dark unholy consorts with his evil Satanic master ...

* * *

Everywhere that Doc went to over the next few days, people were talking about the "Child of Darkness" and the rattlesnake. It had even reached beyond the mountains to Carlisle! When he started hearing veiled suggestions that the Buchanans should be banished from the church, Doc, in his concern, felt he should be present at the church services whenever he could, to act as a kind of staunch ally for them, even though up till now, on every Sunday he was able, he attended his own church in the valley community of Carlisle, where he had lived from nearly half-a-century now.

Sensibly negotiating the torturous road on Bessie the first few Sundays after the incident, he couldn't fail to notice how the assembled worshippers were walking wide circles around Zack Buchanan and his family, and how nobody sat anywhere near them in the church, except for a single brave soul. (Even Edna and her brood kept their distance, although Mary's best friend amongst the Bucko wives, did look shamed and worried.) Only young Emma, Mary's constant companion and Jed's oft'times careminder, was brave enough to flout the wall of hostility and sat primly next to Jed, tightly holding his hand. Dressed in dungarees and vest and barefoot, the mountain-thin child looked fierce as an eagle protecting its eaglet, her eyes mere slits, as if daring anybody to do her precious toddler harm! Once again, Doc was forced to acknowledge what a plucky child she was. After all, the incident with the rattlesnake had proved terrifying to the superstitious mountain folk. In addition to what they had witnessed for them-selves, Reverend Hubbly's and Myrtle's evil connotations had injected them with fear as never before. Thus Emma's display of devotion and solidarity to the beleaguered young family was quite heartwarming to Doc.

They sat perched on the hard front bench – that ostracized little family of four – in anguished aloofness, obviously keenly feeling the hurtful brunt of their isolation. Mary sat with her head raised high, but a wounded look on her face. *Poor Mary!* After all the trouble she had to contend with, first with Eli and his cronies pulling down the arbors, now this! Zachary Thomas looked straight ahead, head also held up high, but with his face set like granite. Naturally, the baby, Caleb, was totally oblivious to it all, but little Jed, the cause of all this bitter dissension, seemed to feel the antagonism towards them too.

Once, the little mite clambered up on the pew and turned around to peer perplexedly at those behind him, as if sensing their hostility ntowards him. Well, anyone would swear that the child could fire bullets from his eyes the way they all cringed and ducked, whispering loudly, fear – contagious as the measles – a terrible, tangible thing among them. The same people who had approached the family that first day with impunity, chucked little Jed under the chin and patted his head, and whose children had begged to play with him, were suddenly terrified when the same little boy merely looked at them, in case it should bring the glibly prophesied ill-fortune upon them.

Thankfully, it was young Reverend Crawley, who, in rather ingenious fashion, put a stop to the matter. Though the young man had started off so badly, without the critical assessing eye of Reverend Hubbly upon him, he had managed to overcome his nerves to a large extent. Once he got started, he seemed to be able to forget that they were all watching him and talked with increasing confidence. True, he sometimes blushed when he felt their eyes upon him and his hand tended to tremble slightly as he turned the pages of the Good Book, but he was bursting with fine Christian goodness and fervor, and whatever he said came straight from the heart; his direct, intense way of preaching was kind of soul-stirring and the mountain folks' early uncertainty about him, was clearly beginning to burgeon into cautious respect.

He could not have failed to notice what was going on in his congregation, however, but being a valley lad himself, probably did not quite know how to handle the situation amongst these deeply superstitious mountain folk. Had he failed to respect their feelings, Doc had no doubt he would lose them forever. Doc felt keenly for him. The bizarre rattlesnake incident and the resultant division among his congregation was a rough way to start his ministr and, though he gazed upon the ostracized family with a look of compassion, Doc had no doubt that if he chose to openly take sides with the Buchanans, it could easily result in outright rejection by the others.

As it turned out, his silence about the matter was about biding his time to allow the impact of the incident time to settle down, rather than his fear of losing favor among them. One Sunday morning, about a month after the incident with the snake, the Buchanan family and young Emma arrived at the chapel, on foot, Zachary Thomas carrying Jed in his strong arms, while Mary carried the babe. After the six-mile walk, they seemed tired and reluctant to venture forward into the usual wasp's nest of hostility and suspicion.

But to Doc's gladness and surprise, he wasn't the only one to make a great show of welcoming them. Reverend Crawley approached them with his arms opened wide, warm benevolence glowing forth from him, as he embraced them both. Big Zachary Thomas tensed rigidly with embarrassment, his face turning slightly purple, as he set little Jed down on the ground. This action sent the worshippers gathered about the log cabin chapel, cringing back. Reverend Crawley then knelt down beside the little boy and spoke to him for several minutes, while everyone stood around warily watching him, with a mingling of horror and avid curiosity. At last, the young preacher stood up and taking the child's hand in his, his back straight with steely determination, he led the toddler inside.

As the others trailed reluctantly into the chapel behind them, keeping a safe distance, he led the little boy to the front pew and lifting him up it, placed a light kiss upon his little puckered brow. But if they fully expected him to be struck down during this act of incredible folly, they were disappointed. His sermon that day had to do with the innocence of children and the abundant love that Jesus had for them all. He began with the words, "Suffer little children to come unto me . . ."

He carried on in this vein every Sunday, for several weeks, before the mountain folk were satisfied that the preacher had not been smote with any evil or ill-fortune and, gradually, their hostility towards Jed and his family, broke down. Now, as Doc stood staunchly beside the Buchanans, swaying on his heels, Will Jenkins came up and asked Zachary Thomas how his crops were faring. He kissed Mary on the cheek and then, hesitantly and most courageously, he took little Jed's hand in his, for which he was rewarded with a bright, sunny, dimpled smile. Will broke out laughing with pure relief. After that, Will was joined by Harvey Taylor, then Chaucy Yates and soon the ice was broken.

One by one, the mountain folk, giving way to their natural friendliness and caring, each seeming to take courage from the one before him or her, gathered around Zachary Thomas and Mary, laughing and exclaiming, some hugging them with tears running down their faces, until only Myrtle McCreedy stood alone, staunchly suspicious and unrelenting. They exclaimed on and admired the babe-in-arms and talked about the weather. They made frightened gestures of reconciliation to little Jed, with a trembling hand; a quick ruffling of his head, a

501

pinch on the cheek or the ear. But as time went by it was true to say that the child was ever after to be regarded with a certain amount of uneasy awe.

66

Much to Eli's disgust, the last Bucko to get "religion" was the brother he was closest to – Jake. It happened soon after Jake had returned to Claw Mountain from Washington, disillusioned with city life after having spent only a year there, unable to adapt himself to it as had Eli. But as much as he hated the idea of having lost Jake to religion, Eli had long ago lost his grip on Claw Mountain affairs, and there was little he could do about it. Apparently, when Jake, encouraged by family and curiosity to see what it was all about, finally ventured over the threshold of the church that had been built on Beacon Mountain, Mary had greeted him with great joy and warmth, escorting him to the front to sit with her and Zack, their two little boys, Jed and Caleb, Emma and Doc Adams.

That day, according to Jake's telling, he had been "saved" by the grace of Jesus Christ. Cleansed of all his sin. *Praise the Lord!* It sickened Eli to see such sloppy joy emanating from the man, the imbecilic grin on his brother's face whenever he spoke about it – which he did all the time. Jake had always been a true rogue like himself. Had even helped him to murder a child! How could *anyone* forgive such a ghastly crime, let alone some fool who had been dead for two thousand years? Peace could never be Eli's. *Praise the devil!* Yet, despite his many sins, Eli loved children, pitied them, and adored their feckless innocence. He saw in them Taggart, both Jamie's, himself, victims all! Only he was victim, turned villain. Tormented, turned tormentor. When had one ended and the other begun? *Now that was the easy one!*

And where once Jake had despised Mary almost as much as did Eli, now he had only praise for her. According to him, she even encouraged their former arch enemies, *the Galtreys*, to attend the Beacon Mountain church. The first time that the Galtreys had arrived there on horseback and by buckboard, there had been great tension among the congregants as old wounds and grievances were prominent in the minds of the two old warring clans but, gradually, as they became regular church-attendees, so the wounds were gradually healed and love and good neighborliness slowly replaced the hatred borne of many years of bitter enmity.

Jake told Eli that Mary had an endless capacity for compassion and forgiveness, worked ceaselessly to improve all their lives, mending them all as if they were broken dolls. Even Eli, who despised her, had to admit that her soul was not the empty vessel that was the soul of Annabel Cotterell – Annabel had kept him on a string for years – too afraid of her father and the opinions of society to embrace true love. She, too, did charity work, but only when it could be noted on the society pages and to impress Washington's social elite, not out of compassion or the love of a people, like Mary. Her beauty, stunning as it was, was only skin-deep. She was so self-absorbed she didn't spare a thought for others, let alone Eli.

After her marriage, she only managed to get away and come to "Rose Haven" once or twice a month. On those occasions, she often seemed cool and distracted and she endlessly complained about her dull husband, about the Washington hostesses who had failed to invite her to some affair or other that she desperately wanted to attend, about lazy and dishonest servants, and about how little allowance her husband gave her.

Oh, she was always passionate when she and Eli made love and constantly told him how much she adored him, but when her father died and Eli asked her to consider leaving Alexander, she pointblank refused, putting her hands on her curved hips and pouting luscious dark ruby lips, saying she could not possibly face the scandal. 'Besides,' she had said, 'Why ruin something that is perfect the way it is . . .?'

Though Eli still suffered a useless love for her and did not have the strength to tell her to never come back, five years down the line, he no longer liked her very much. He began seeing other women in an effort to overcome the countless humiliations she heaped on him, the only woman who ever could, except Mary, his brother's wife, that is. Society women found him attractive and were more than happy to warm his bed, even though he treated them abominably, never keeping his promises to call them later. He had sampled also plenty of quim on a regular basis at the high-class whore house, yet nothing satisfied him, and he despised the high-classed harlots there for their willingness to be debased in this way.

Washington had been good for him, though. It had put a stop to the killing habit to settle his disputes. He had soon found that the rough justice of the mountains had no place in civilized society. And he had been so concerned with becoming respectable that he had become just that. *Civilized!* Of course there was nothing he could do to erase his past, but at least nobody here in the nation's capital had learned about it, or seemed to suspect it. Even his reputation on the streets and his nickname of "The Whistle-Whip Kid", due to his unique skill with the whip, had been earned without loss of life. He had everything – a highly successful and lucrative business, money, fine possessions, prestige, as many women as he desired, yet happiness, even to a small degree, continued to elude him.

And he spent many sleepless nights tossing and turning or, if he did sleep, he was plagued by nightmares. Though he had done everything to change his life, to become "respectable", the long dark shadow of Claw Mountain reached him even here. It would not leave him alone, mentally torturing him so there was a great big empty hollow inside him that nothing and nobody – especially Annabel Cotterell – could fill.

67

It was the following September that another big change came about on Claw Mountain, this time involving young Emma. The mountain child was such a bright student, she had reached the zenith of the (by now attainable) sixth grade in the little school on Claw Mountain in just two years. Proudly following her amazing progress, Doc Adams and Mary discussed future plans for her.

"She's got to go further, Mary," said Doc on one of his regular visits to the mountain. "She needs to go to high school, maybe even college. She's the dangdest kid I ever came across and when I think of how far she's come since the day she came to fetch me to assist in Jed's birth. Well, it's quite remarkable! But you have got to take most of the credit, Mary. You had her reading and writing beautifully, before the school ever opened. I will never forget her reading the day we opened the school. *What a fine rendition!*

Mary beamed at Doc's words. "Oh, I were jest a steppin' stone, is all," she said modestly.

"Miss Prescott showed me her work the other day. Beside winning all the spelling bees and ciphering contests, she gets full marks in just about everything. And for a kid who isn't too prissy about her appearance, she sure writes as neat as can be. Puts my old doctor's scrawl to shame!"

Mary nodded firmly in agreement. "My thoughts exactly, Doc. I thunk she needs to further her education too. She has expressed th' desire to become a teacher – she said when I taught her to read and write, it changed her whole life and she wants to do that fer other young'uns. The trouble is th' nearest high school is miles away in Madison and it would mean she would have to board near there. She's only fourteen and too young to send away by herself. Whar would she stay?"

"What about your family in Richmond, Mary? The one whose deceased daughter is the one for whom the school is named? Perhaps they'd be willing to take Emma in and see she attends school. I'll pay for the child's board and tuition myself. It would be such a shame for her to languish in these hills when there's so much she can do to improve her circumstances."

Mary stared at Doc in a blaze of newfound hope. "Why, that's a right dandy idea, Doc! I don't know why I didn"t thunk of that m'self. I guess it's 'cuz I had no mind of sendin' her far away, but now that you mention it, it's th' perfect solution. Aunt Clara sure took to Emma when the Emily Tuttle School was open-ed, and even said she would likely go far. Reckon I'll write her and find out if'n they'd be willin' to do that . . ."

And so it came about. Mary's aunt, Clara Tuttle, wrote back immediately, saying they would be more than happy to accommodate the child at their own cost, and to enroll her in a good private high school in Richmond, as Doc Adams had requested and, what's more, they would be prepared to share the tuition costs with him. Emma was beside herself with excitement when Mary received the letter sent through the general store and read it at least a dozen times, as if trying to convince herself that it wasn't a hoax of sorts.

Proud that she had come so rapidly through a school named after their precious deceased daughter, the Tuttles welcomed Emma into their home with glad hearts and warm smiles when Doc and Mary traveled with her to Richmond by train to install her in the Tuttle household.

The tall, thin young mountain girl was wearing a calf-length flounced white organza dress, trimmed with frilly white lace, white blue-ribboned cotton petticoat, long white stockings, low-heeled white shoes with a gold buckle on top, and an extravagant blue hat made of mulland valenciennes lace. The tam crown was made of six fluted ruffles of mull, edged with lace, while the brim was made of double-fluted ruffles with lace edging. The whole outfit Doc had purchased for her, especially for the occasion.

He had left it with Mary to give to her, but the girl took one look at it, stuck out her tongue and stuck her finger down her throat, as if she was about to gag, and flatly refused to wear it. Indeed, it took all of Mary's powers of persuasion to encourage her to wear it to save Doc's feelings, reminding her that Doc was going to be paying for half of her expensive tuition and, furthermore, had been the one to suggest that she board with the Tuttles in the first place.

The girl capitulated in the end, but only after she had offered much strident argument against it. Mary knew it took all the girl's considerable courage to don the outfit that fateful morning at her cabin. She looked as if her flesh was crawling when she grumpily pulled first the petticoat then the dress over her head. The elaborate hat was placed on a head totally unsuited to its fussy splendor, the face beneath it, looking grim and thoroughly humiliated. Doc unwittingly made matters worse. When he came with his fringed horse-and-buggy to take them to the train station at Shenandoah Junction, he declared that she looked exactly like Alice in Wonderland. The poor child looked positively horrified to be compared to such a literary character. Mary had no doubt she would have much prefered to be compared to someone like Huck Finn, and attired like him too! And in truth, for all her fancy finery, with her surly, slit-eyed look, mountain-thin body and straight fair hair, Emma totally lacked the feminine grace needed to carry off such a pretty outfit. Indeed, to Mary's mind, she looked about as odd as a bear in human clothing in it!

Furthermore, she looked so out of place and forlorn in the luxurious Tuttle household that it had taken all of Mary's will to leave her behind. It had been Mary's own first venture into a big city and she had found the experience overwhelming, so she could well understand how alien it must feel to this spunky mountain-bred girl.

* * *

But Mary needn't have worried about Emma. The girl settled into suburbia well enough and, right from the start, did remarkably at her lessons in her new school, getting good marks in every subject. The Tuttles had given her Emily's old bedroom and found her forthright, sassy manner, mountain ways and high intelligence, greatly endearing, according to the letters Mary got from her Aunt Clara.

Of course, Emma wasn't nearly as forthcoming in her letters to Mary, though Mary sensed how much she missed Claw Mountain and mountain life. There was nothing about her new life in her letters. All she wanted to know was about how Jed was faring, what new words he had learned, if Mary had spotted any new eaglets, had the rhododendrons came out yet, had they let off Roman Candles at Christmas (a practice Mary had introduced to the mountain)? It was Emma's first Christmas away from the mountain. Since it had come so soon after they had dropped her off there, it was felt she would settle down better if she wasn't whisked away almost immediately to spend it with her family.

The departure of the tough little spitfire from Claw Mountain was much harder on Mary than she cared to admit and she fiercely missed the child, despite the fact that she had her own little family to keep her busy and she was with child again. The girl had wormed her way into her heart right from the start and she missed her stimulating company, her unique slant on things and the deep genuine friendship that had developed between them despite the difference in their ages.

And of course, little Jed keenly missed her too. Beside herself, Zack and Doc,

Emma was the only person he was close to. Why, she had practically raised him up, Mary thought ruefully. Jed had at last started to talk, thanks to Emma's perseverance with him, and he kept asking his mother where Emma was. He looked so sad when Mary told him that she had been sent away so she could become clever, that there were selfish moments when Mary wished that Emma would walk through the door and announce she'd left civilization and schooling behind for good.

Now with little Caleb to contend with – and he was a naughty little fellow given to tantrums – who took up much of Mary's time and energy, she realized how much she had valued Emma's help with Jed. Still, deep-down, and selfishness aside, she was enormously thankful that Emma was getting the education she needed and deserved.

68

It was the 11th July, 1904, and Zachary Thomas was beside himself with excitement. It was his wife's birthday in two days' time and he had ordered a perfect gift for her from the general store, having paid a hefty $32.89 for it. But she had been his wife for five years now and he felt she fully deserved something special. He kept badgering the proprietor about it, fearful that it would not arrive on time from the manufacturers in Newark, Ohio. Then just when he was about to despair of it ever happening, the proprietor had sent word through one of his brothers that it had at long last arrived and he could fetch it anytime.

The whole of the clan knew about his gift and were to become part of an elaborate plan to give it to her. This was going to present quite a problem, since the buckboard was broken and two of the mules were ill. Instead, Zachary Thomas rounded up all of his brothers to go with him to fetch it. They gladly braved the twenty-mile round journey to the store, leaving in the early hours of the morning, because they felt it was a fitting tribute to the young woman who had done so much for them.

* * *

A group of about thirty young men were busy playing tan-ball, a form of softball, outside the store when they arrived, hot and weary from the long walk. But as they entered the store's wooden stilted structure, the Buckos, dressed in their shirtless dungarees and slouch hats to combat the fierce mid-summer heat, burst into grins. They walked around the gleaming 555-lb cast iron Wehrle stove standing in the middle of the crowded store, whistling admiringly at its six-hole blue polished steel range and attractive brass ornamentation, which could burn any kind of fuel, including soft or hard coal, wood, coke or corn cobs, while the other customers formed an interested smiling circle around them. Once, Zachary Thomas knew, these valley folk and the folk from the surrounding mountains, would have feared such an *en-masse* visit by the Buckos, but the menfolk of their once-dreaded clan had been reformed through Mary's perseverance, and the fact that they no longer stirred up trouble everywhere they went – especially now that Eli had moved away and they were beyond his evil influence.

Zachary Thomas cast a critical eye over the huge monstrosity, and found, to his satisfaction, that it came up to expectation. How he had longed to give Mary this luxury to make her life a little easier. It had been the one thing that she had bemoaned not having when she first arrived at Claw Mountain and it had taken him five long years to save up enough money and credit from his trapping furs, chickens and eggs, to buy it for her. God knows she had cooked up wonders in the hearth with her three-legged pots, but it was hard work cooking big meals that way, since it took a good deal of time and planning.

The Buckos set to work, covering the stove with sacking before strapping the monstrosity to two long wooden poles they'd brought with them, with ropes. When it was secure and had been checked and rechecked by Zachary Thomas, they stood in two lines, and on Zachary Thomas's command, they hoisted the poles onto their bony shoulders like pall-bearers lifting a coffin, four Buckos on each side. There were only ten Buckos still living, but Eli was in Washington and Zachary Thomas was much too tall to act as one of the bearers, since his height would greatly offset the load and make it much harder to carry. Though the other Buckos were lean and slightly-built, this canny disbursement of the considerable weight of the handsome stove, proved sound. Even so, his lean brothers staggered under its weight as they moved out of the store and went down the steps, before setting off toward Claw Mountain once again. Zachary Thomas, anxious as a mother hen over wayward chicks, kept shouting all sorts of instructions at his brothers, much to their intense annoyance.

"Shuddup, Zack!" yelled Clem, "You sure is gittin' on m'nerves!"

"If'n you don't shuddup, Zack, you kin carry it on yer own," threatened Toad, as his nerves wore thin.

The others joined in from time to time with their annoyed quips. It was very hot and they were soon all drenched with sweat, but they kept doggedly walking, their hardened bare feet working in unison. They stopped only four times along the way for a rest and to drink water from streams, dropping their loaded litter to the ground. Then they would swop sides before hoisting their load onto their reddened and blistered shoulders once more. The miles disappeared under their disciplined cartage.

Once they had at last reached Claw Mountain, however, it proved even more tiring work to scale the steep slopes. There was much slipping and sliding and cussing going on while the air was positively blue around Zachary Thomas, who kept envisioning his wife's fine present tumbling headlong down the mountain, getting scratched and covered in mud. Once they got it up to just below Eagle Spur, the stove, still tied to the poles, had to be winched up over the ridge, like Dapple, the cow, had once been.

Fortunately, Zachary Thomas had liaised with Miss Prescott to get Mary to go to the school on some pretext, and the pretty young school teacher had promised to keep his wife there until she heard Zachary Thomas's two-shot rifle signal. They hid the stove under some sacking in a far stall on the barn, where Mary would not be able to see it even when she milked Dapple. Zachary Thomas thanked his brothers and asked them to come and help him move the stove inside the cabin the day after next. Though they moaned and groaned and rolled their eyes, Zachary Thomas knew that he could count on them.

On the morning of Mary's birthday, the 13th of July, Zachary Thomas pretended that he did not remember what day it was. He had arranged with Edna to fetch Mary to see her latest rag dolls, while he pretended to go tracking with his two coon dogs. When she was gone, he alerted his brothers, who came back like he knew they would, and they helped him move the thing from the barn into the kitchen, on shortened poles.

They removed the sacking covering the huge resplendent stove and shone the dusty thing up so it gleamed like it had when it was in the store. All the wives and children also came up to await Mary's return. The wives waited in the cabin while the children stayed outside to act as look-outs. When they heard Edna and Mary up over the ridge about an hour later, they dashed inside to alert their elders and were told to all hide in the bedroom.

Then the Buckos and their womenfolk stood in an excited huddle in front of the stove. When Mary pushed open the cabin door and entered in front of Edna, she looked astounded to see them all assembled there.

"HAPPY BIRTHDAY, MARY!" they cried out in unison.

Mary stood staring in surprise and amazement.

"Oh, my," said Mary, clasping a hand to her throat. "I cain't believe y'all remembered."

"Happy birthday, Mary," Zachary Thomas said gruffly, moving forward to take her hand. "I got me a surprise fer you."

"Fer me? Oh, Zack, you shouldn't have," she whispered, but her eyes were shining with anticipation. Then the wall of bodies broke away to give Mary an unimpeded view of the resplendent cast iron stove.

Mary's hands flew to her face, and she gave a startled little cry, before her eyes filled with tears of gratitude and wonder. Zachary Thomas swallowed over a lump in his throat to see her reaction.

"Oh my Lord, Zack, it sure is purty," she whispered, as tears of joy flowed down her cheeks.

69

In the years that followed, it seemed to Doc Adams he was never to see Mary Buchanan unless she had a roundly bulging stomach, but child-bearing suited her, bringing a pinch of pink to her cheek and a glowing maternal contentment that seemed to shine through her seeming plainness and make her almost pretty.

Caleb had come just over two years after Jed and was closely followed by Lottie, Harriet, Elsie, Lona and Louella-Sue. Doc delivered none of Mary's other children save little Harriet. Because of the distance involved in getting there in time, he had found it necessary to leave her deliveries to the capable ministrations of the local "granny-woman", Jenny Addis, an ancient old crone. Fortunately, mountain women were often skilled in midwifery, due to the isolation of their homes and the dearth of medical facilities, and Jenny, the mother of nine children herself, appeared handier at it than most.

Chubby little Caleb was a bright child, full of pure energy and sass, and four of the girls, their looks forged after their father's, were pretty, dark-haired little things. Harriet alone took after her mother, both in features and in ways. But, like her mother also, what she lacked in looks she gained in character – a straight back, a sure authority and a good deal of horse sense. Though Harriet was young--er than the eldest girl, Lottie, it was she who organized the other children, making sure they did their chores, taking much of the strain off her mother. But though Doc had grown fond of all the Buchanan children, it was to the first-born, Jed, that his strong unfailing allegiance remained.

In between the regular mountain clinics, Doc found himself returning to the Buchanan homesite more often than he had good reason to, and on the glibbest pretext, perhaps four or five times a year, becoming quite adept at scaling the steep heights that led up to it, always in the secret hopes that he could get to catch a glimpse of young Jed. Very often the "pretext" was that he was "inspecting the school" and had called upon them "to enquire as to their state of health". (Though in truth it was always his express intention to be there.) And indeed, he would dutifully examine each of the ragged barefoot children, checking them for lice, infected tonsils and other childhood ailments, all free of charge, of course.

Mountain children did not have an easy life and these ragamuffin Buchanans did their fair share of work around the place. They took it in turns to keep the ground squirrels and chipmunks from raiding the crops when the shoots were tender, fetched endless pails of water from the stream, worked in the fields and vegetable gardens, gathered berries and nuts in the forest to sell, and took care of the livestock. Doc had even seen the two youngest ones, Lona, the shy one, and Louella-Sue, a cute little imp with a mop of dark curls, dragging a half-full bucket between them up to the cabin.

But despite all this endless daily toil, it seemed Jed always managed to slip into the forest each day, no matter what. He was an intense boy, a habitual loner, and a dreamer, typically barefoot, with his coarse dungarees rolled up to his knees and his long legs covered in the dust of discovery.

Thankfully, by now, almost a decade had gone by since the incident of Jed and the rattlesnake. Nowadays, it was only ever mentioned when somebody began telling exaggerated hunting tales or ghost stories, a favorite pastime of the mountain folk. Then they might laughingly recall the day that the toddler, Jed Buchanan, had scared the pants off of them. Of course, each time the tale was told, it was embellished a little. But there was never any more mention of Jed being a consort of the devil. By now everybody recognized that he had an amazing rapport with all manner of creatures and his fierce love for them was undoubted.

Come butchering day, when Zack's kin came up to help slaughter hogs in the fall, Jed could never be found. He would promptly disappear into the forest the whole day and, for a week afterwards, he would go off his food, worrying his parents with the depth of his pining. But Doc thought he understood the boy's soft heart. After all, he would have known those razorback hogs by name since they were little shoats foraging chestnuts in the forest. To him they were pets, not indiscriminate chunks of meat for the pot!

According to Mary, he was always bringing animals and birds home, especially injured ones. He would make splints for broken legs, pet and cosset, heal and save, and then he would release them to the wilds once more. Once, after one of his little disappearing acts into the forest, which by that time were so commonplace, Zachary Thomas and Mary had long ago ceased to fuss about them, he brought home a skunk and kept it hidden for a whole week in the loft, where he slept with his brothers and sisters. But it got mad at a rooster strutting about in the straw, lifted its devilish tail and released a stinking squrt of liquid that had them all blocking their noses for well over a month.

It was the only time Jed had ever felt the angry sweep of his mother's yard broom on his backside, and the next animal he brought home was a lot more acceptable. This time it was a baby raccoon, a tiny little creature with its distinctive long bushy striped tail and black mask on its face, whose mother had became the devoured contents of some mountaineer's cooking pot when Jed rescued it. Rascal, as he so named it, became his much-loved pet. He carried it around on his shoulder all the time. It slept cuddled inside his nightshirt and was with him while he worked in the gardens and the fields. The only place he was not allowed to bring it was to the supper table.

But as much as Jed loved animals, so his brother, Caleb, despised them. He was the type of child to viciously kick a coon dog as he went past, just for the hang of it. Doc had witnessed him doing it more than once. He was big in build, like his father, not lean and wiry like Jed. He had a sunny disposition, and the sort of round cherubic face that homely matrons liked to pinch the cheeks of. He had an amazing aim with his sling-shot and would often kill birds and small animals with it. He was but eight years old when he went "coon-hunting" at night with his father and the two coon dogs.

They came back that first time with Caleb triumphantly holding up a pair of hapless blood-dripping raccoons by the tails that he had shot with his father's prized Kentucky rifle, though his father had helped him balance the long muzzle on the fork of a sapling. He had no qualms about cutting the coons' jugulars himself to bleed them, before skinning them under the skilled direction of his father, who was flushed with pride. *At least one of his sons had the makings of a man!*

Caleb loved to tease and he took great delight in ragging his elder brother, scoffing at his softness. After one butchering day, while the whole family sat eating around the table, Jed lifted his mug of milk and out plopped a hog's eyeball which landed right in the middle of his plate of broth. Caleb and his father hooted with laughter, as Jed quietly pushed aside his plate got up and left the room.

Much to Mary's unspoken distress and Doc's own, there was no doubt that Zachary Thomas viewed his second son in a favored light. He went down to the general store two or three times a year for their basic provisions of salt, flour, coffee, sugar, lye, vinegar, kerosene for the lamps, chewing tobacco and other staples, which he hauled back up on the strong backs of a couple of Obediah's ornery old mules.

Now none of the children had ever stepped off the mountain. After all they had their necessary chores to do and couldn't be spared for the day-long trip down to the Graves Mill general store. But Caleb regularly used to plead with his father to go with him and, one day, Zachary Thomas gave the boy permission to accompany him, sparing him from work in the fields. Caleb came back that night with sticks of liquorice and gumballs he refused to share with anyone and, furthermore, sported a brand-new western-style straw hat. But Mary only admonished her husband with her eyes.

For the next couple of weeks, Caleb was never to be seen without that darned hat. A disturbing incident followed shortly after that, relayed to Doc in great detail by Mary, who was very distressed by it all. One morning, Jed woke up to find Rascal was missing. He searched everywhere for his beloved pet and kept leaving his chores and his field-work to search for him in the forest, calling his name. By supper time, he came in tired and deeply dispirited. Rascal was gone and he could not understand why. No animal had ever run away from him before. He toyed with his food, while Caleb made a great show of eating his, slurping it up with a big spoon.

"Mmmm . . . this here 'possom stew is real good, Maw," he said, licking his lips exaggeratedly.

Mary laughed softly at her younger son. "You mean 'coon stew, don't you, son? You brung th' 'coon to me yerself first thung this mornin', all nicely cleaned and ready to cook. Just had to cut it up and toss it all in."

"*Coon* stew?"Jed stared down at the meat swimming in gravy and vegetables in his almost untouched plate. "What size th' 'coon he done brung you, Maw?"

"Size?" she said unsurely. "Well, 'bout the size of Rasc . . . No, it cain't be!" She turned slowly back to her younger son. "Cal? *No!*"

"Pardon, Maw?" Caleb's round face was the picture of innocence.

"You done that?"

"Done what, Maw?"

Mary looked at him severely. "Did you kill Jed's raccoon fer our supper?"

Caleb's eyes widened in mock-horror. "Maw! You surely don't thunk I would do somethung like that, do ya?"

All around the table spoons were slowly lowered and Mary's anguished eyes and those of the little dark-haired girls turned from Caleb to Jed. Harriet's little mouth fell open. Tears filled Jed eyes and he brokenly but, with astonishing dignity, asked permission to leave the table. They all listened as he went outside and threw up over the edge of the porch.

The next day, he announced that he was never going to eat meat again. And true to his word, he never did after that. He lived on berries, wild fruit, honey and the special vegetable dishes that his mother prepared for him – and for herself. For that was the day that Mary gave up eating meat too!

J ed took Caleb's nonsense and senseless cruelty without any form of retaliation whatsoever, but it could be that he had his own unique ways of dealing with the major provocations of the world. About a month after the incident of Rascal, the two boys went out to hoe the potato patch on an extremely hot and sunny day. Jed wore his oversized cap and Caleb, his new straw hat, which he liked to wear at a bit of a jaunty angle. They were barefoot and wore tough denim dungarees rolled up to the knees.

Jed was a hard and willing worker, stopping only to wipe the sweat from his brow with his bare arm, but Caleb was lazy and given to complaining. As usual, he alleviated his boredom by spurring his elder brother, calling him a sissy and taking great delight in telling him in gory detail of all the animals he had killed.

Well, this carried on for hours with Jed quietly gritting his teeth and saying very little, as the sun beat down on them. At lunchtime, their mother called them in for lunch, and, leaving their headgear on the rocker on the porch, they went inside to eat. Later, donning their headgear once more, they returned to the potato patch, Caleb giving a loud uncouth belch. For a while, neither of them said anything, as Jed worked steadily and Caleb half-heartedly chopped at the earth. Then, as the heat began to slick their flesh with sweat once more, Caleb suddenly took to sniffing.

"Pooh! What a stink!" he complained. "I swar I smell somethung real bad."

"Must be yer feet," said Jed philosophically.

"No, it ain't," scoffed Caleb loudly, sniffing the air like some blood-hound trying to catch whiff of an elusive scent.

"You ain't done nuthin', have ya?" asked Jed.

"You mean messed m'pants? 'Cos not!" Caleb sneered contemptuously.

"What then?"

Suddenly, after sniffing several more times, Caleb whipped his straw hat off his head.

"This is it! *Doggone it.* This damn thung stinks worse than that foul skunk you had hid that time. *Poooh . . ."*

Holding his nose between a disgusted finger and thumb, Caleb held the offending object away from him at arm's length. Jed crossed to the row he was in and sniffed at Caleb's hat.

"*Whew!* Sure stinks alright. That thar is cat pee. That's mountain lion pee, fer sure. A young'un hardly more 'n a year old."

Caleb's face was a picture of dismay. "You tellin' me th' some mountain lion came right to th' porch while we was eatin' an' whizzed in my hat? *You're lyin'.* Ev'rybody knows thar ain't bin no mountain lion in these here hills fer years."

"Oh, thar be plenty mountain lion around alright. They jest keep themselves hid real good." Already Jed was carefully examining the ground around the cabin. "I'm tellin' you it was mountain lion. Look, see, here's th' spoor."

Caleb looked down at the perfect paw-indentations in the dust and said with disgusted vehemence, "You mean some wild cat had th' whole danged mountain forest t'whizz in, and chose to go do it in *my new hat?*" He swung around at Jed accusingly, angry tears sparking his eyes. "You done it, ain't ya? You sent that danmed cat t'do it t'me!"

Jed stared at him unblinkingly. "Y'thunk I kin do that?"

"Yeah, sure do! Y'did, didn't ya?"

But Jed only smiled . . .

70

Ｏne day Jed came into the cabin while Mary was up to her elbows in flour, making corn bread in a big mixing bowl on the table. He seemed low in spirit and said disconsolately, "I wish I were more like Cal, Maw."

Mary looked at her tall, handsome, sun-browned fourteen-year-old son with long brown hair, with genuine perplexion. *Thank heavens the boy was nothing like Caleb!*

"Now why on earth would you wish for somethung like that, honey?"

He didn't answer her question immediately, instead looking at her with wounded eyes so like his father's, except his father's were a scintillating turquoise-green and his were brilliant blue, then he said, "Why am I so different, Maw?"

Mary knew exactly what he meant, but she enquired cautiously, "Different, how?"

"Different to everybody else. Seems nobody kin do th' thungs I kin, Maw. Nobody else understands what th' wind is telling 'em, or th' rain, or th' trees, or th' birds, or th' bugs. Maw, I'm real tired of bein' regarded as a freak of Nature."

Mary, her long black hair drawn back into a bun, wiped her flour-coated hands on her blue-and-white-striped apron and drew her son down beside her on the old puncheon bench. *Poor Jed!* He'd been different from other children his whole life and that couldn't be easy for anyone to bear, let alone for someone as young as he was. She wondered if he remembered once being ostracized because of his ability to handle a dangerous rattlesnake without harm to himself when he was still a toddler.

She sought the answer in his amazing blue eyes, plunging to the depths of his soul and finding an intuitive, quiet wisdom there, steady and sure as a rock. Yet, despite this, right now, he seemed as vulnerable as a sapling in the wind. She knew how badly his younger brother teased and bullied him, and, sometimes, the other children at school and at church called him "Oddball" and "Freak" and other hurtful names, too.

Although he always smiled indulgently and seemed to take it well enough, she knew how much it pained him inside. And it didn't stop at his peers either. She constantly worried about the fact that Zachary Thomas continued to favor their younger son so much. She knew it wasn't that her husband loved Cal more than he did Jed, but he did *understand* Caleb a whole lot more and thus was able to show him affection in a way he no longer could with Jed.

Her husband and Caleb were always fooling around and rough-housing, while Jed, a tall, solemn boy would stand apart from them, watching them with sad eyes, the benign expression on his face hiding the hurt he felt underneath at his exclusion from the affectionate horseplay.

Mary knew how her son felt, because she and Jed had always been so very close. She knew what a tender heart he had, of his deep sensitivity and how closely attuned to Nature he was, while her husband just did not know what to make of his firstborn son. While Caleb was a typical mountain child, high-spirited, and given to hunting and fishing and trapping like his father, Jed was quiet and withdrawn and always happy to be alone, and he had some habits and traits that puzzled and exasperated his father, who had once dreamed of teaching him all these things. Jed refused to hunt and would eat no meat. And he didn't even like to fish.

Caleb, on the other hand, loved fishing. He used red worm for bait and unsporting methods like sewing a hoop to the open end of a sack, then bending the hoop so it rested flat on the bottom, he would place it between the rocks of the river where the water ran swiftest, catching huge hauls of brook trout at a time. He even used explosives once to kill schools of fish, by taking a quart jar, filling two-thirds full of slaked lime and screwing the top back on. He only used that method once though, because it damn near blew his head off and there were dead fish lying all over the banks! When he relayed this to the family at supper while they were eating the spoils of his mischief, Zachary Thomas laughed so hard, he nearly rolled off his chair onto the floor, while Mary and Jed had exchanged concerned looks.

When Jed fished, he would refuse to use red worm for bait, because he didn't want to kill the worms. Instead, he would make lures out of feathers and twine and tiny hooks, because he couldn't bear the thought of hurting the fish. Caleb loudly reported to his father, in disgust, that Jed would sit on a big rock down in the stream in the hollow with his hickory stick and line, but if he ever chanced to catch anything, he promptly threw it back in again. Later, he stopped taking his homemade fishing rod with him at all and would just gaze down at the water, or wade in the stream, bending over and trailing a hand in it and, instead of darting away, the fish would swarm thickly around him.

516

Sometimes, when he learned things like this about his eldest son, Zachary Thomas would get mad and yell at the boy, telling him to be a man and not such a sissy. And though Mary berated her husband privately for saying such things, which she knew he didn't mean – he was simply frustrated by his own lack of understanding of his firstborn son. Still, the damage was done and she knew Jed must believe his father thought him silly, inept and weak. She knew the reason Jed longed be more like Caleb was because he desperately wanted to earn the love and respect of his father. *Poor misunderstood child!*

She raised a tender hand to Jed's cheek. "Oh son, you ain't no freak of Nature! You're jest real special, is all. God made you different to everybody else 'cuz you've got things to teach th' rest of us. *Important thungs.* Now, somethung like that ain't always easy to bear, but He wouldn't have given it to you if'n He didn't know that you could handle it. And don't you pay no mind to your paw. He's a good man, if'n a little dim sometimes. But he loves you so much, Jed. He always has. He loved you th' minute he set eyes on you on th' day you were born. Why, he came after us to bring us both back from Lewis Mountain, 'cuz he loved us both so much and he helped me take care of you, too. He was one tough Bucko back then, yet he didn't thunk it beneath him to change yer diapers. He never changed Caleb's diapers when he was a baby, not a'once. If he seems to favor Cal now, it's only 'cuz he don't quite know what to make of you, Jed.

"You see, Caleb has all the accepted makings of a mountain man, but he sure as heck don't love and understand th' mountains th' way you do. Your paw cain't understand yer need to protect and not to kill. How you cain't even bear to fell a tree. Such thinking ranks as bizarre to men like your paw, 'cuz killin' animals for th' pot, fur-trappin' an' tree-fellin' means survival in th' mountains. He fears you won't be able to fend fer yerself when he's gone, if'n you don't learn from him, is all.

"The winter a'fore you were born was one of th' worst ever in th' Blue Ridge. Th' mountain folk called it 'Th' Big Freeze'. It were brutal, alright! Many of them died of starvation or froze to death. Your paw saw it firsthand, with many of his kin and our neighbors succumbin', anh he sure wouldn't want it to ever happen to you. One day, when you git married and have young'uns of yer own, you'll understand his concerns."

"I guess I do already, Maw. I jest wish I could be a normal son to him instead of sech a trial. But even so, thar ain't no way I kin change. I am who I am."

"Oh honey, I sure wouldn't want you any other way. You're such a beautiful person, Jed! *Inside and out!* I reckon I must be th' luckiest woman in th' world to have a son as special as you! 0ne who is so caring. Who has sech a vast store of knowledge about God's kingdom on earth."

Jed shook his head and gave her a wan smile.

"Thanks, Maw I'm real lucky to have a maw like you too! Nobody understands me th' way you do. *Nobody.*" Then regarding her seriously, he added, "And tell Paw not to worry about me. God will always provide me with what I need. He's in everythung you know, Maw. It's Him who speaks to me thru' th' birds and th' animals and th' trees. But nobody will ever understand that. They all thunk that God kin only be found in church or sits on a throne up in heaven. Well, it ain't true. He's ev'rywhar. In everythung."

Mary sat in silent awe of her firstborn son, whispering, "I know, son. I know He is."

She saw the marvelous innocence and purity of the boy glowing on his handsome, sun-browned face, in his magnificent blue eyes. He was the lonely, bewildered bearer of Truth and there were times when he found the burden too great. But he had the qualities of an angel, a heart as large and pure as heaven itself, and she loved him with every fiber of her being, in a way she could never love Caleb or even her six daughters. She loved them all, of course, but Jed was her firstborn, and she was sure God would forgive her for such unseemly favoritism. In Jed, she saw the very best of humanity. But she worried about his place in the world. If he didn't fit in in the sheltered environment of the mountains, God knows how he would ever fare in life on the outside. Fortunately, she never had to worry about *that* ever happening. He would never leave the mountain. After all, the forests of the Blue Ridge were Jed's lungs, the sky, his brain, the earth, his feet, the streams, his life blood! He loved his natural world so. He worried over it and the fact that the birdlife and wildlife were getting less and less with every passing year. He was as immersed in the mountains as a shepherd with his sheep. *Her blessed angel child!* Oh, how she loved him. She reached out and hugged him tightly to her.

"Don't you ever wish to be nobody else but who you are, Jed, 'Cuz what you are, is a real blessing to me and to this here world."

Indeed, she had known that full well ever since the day they had experienced the "Beatific Vision" together, all those years ago. But the knowledge was both a privilege and a burden to her. Jed was right. Few, if any, would be able to understand such a thing – even Reverend Hubbly had warned that it was evil simply because he did not understand it – yet nothing could be further from the truth! Never had she experienced such powerful, all-encompassing, ineffable Love, as she had on that momentous day. But she discovered that when it came to religion, few had the capacity to understand anything beyond the narrow dictates of orthodoxy. They did not have the ability to seek or understand that which went so much deeper. Neither did they understand that some things were intangible.

Religion was fine, but right from an early age, she had witnessed how it created divisions amongst folk. How folks went to church and sang hymns and prayed, but failed to *live* in the manner that Jesus had taught them. And each felt so strongly that their religion was right and believed that those who followed other religions, even other Christian religions, would burn in hell for all eternity. *That God was the torturer of souls!* How very intolerant Reverend Hubbly had been of other religions, having reserved a special contempt for the Primitive Baptists, the "Hardshells", of the southern Blue Ridge.

Mary knew that a spark of God and a sacred universal Truth, lay deep within her, inside Jed, within *everybody,* without them even knowing it. But if this was true, it had to come out. What was a rare and precious secret now, was bound to be revealed at its right time. She was certain of it. Her Jed was a kind of John the Baptist, the harbinger of great things to come, hopefully ushering in a time when all would see with his clear, uncluttered vision . . .

71

Doc was mighty pleased with the way things had worked out on Claw Mountain over the years, what with his regular medical clinic and the school, where the teacher now worked for thirty dollars a month, and an abiding love of teaching. Though Eli Buchanan had long since moved to Washington and had established himself there as a businessman, he continued to pay her salary, coming out himself in his fancy Rambler automobile to bring it to her at the end of every month.

Once, the community was the most feared mountain in the northern Blue Ridge. Now, it was largely peaceable and law-abiding, thanks to the efforts of that remarkable young woman, Mary Buchanan. The school, especially, was a great success, with so many children attending that some had to sit on extra benches put in the front of the class, with their chalk and slates.

The school terms had been scheduled to satisfy the work requirements of the community. There were three terms of three months each, the summer term starting on 1st July to allow time for the crop to get laid by, and running till late September, when it was time for the harvesting. The second school term ran right through the winter months, (though there were days when it was impossible for the children to reach the schoolhouse, the weather conditions were so bad), while the third began in the spring. There were breaks of varying lengths between each term.

Doc took a keen interest in the school's development, having been instrumental in getting it started, and he always insisted in going across there with Mary during the lunch break of his intermittent clinic at Horseshoe Hollow, to inspect the health of the children. He rather enjoyed the fact that he had become something of a celebrity amongst them and they would surround him in a group when he arrived, tugging at his coat-tails to make themselves heard.

When Miss Prescott rang the school bell at eight o'clock in the morning, it was the signal for lessons to begin and children would come running into the school yard from all directions, splashing barefoot through the creek, except in the winter, of course, when they wore shoes and had to leap across it, to file into the classroom and sit quietly in desks on either side of the pot-bellied stove.

All Mary's children attended, including Doc's special favorite, Jed (though from what he'd heard, the dear child would either rock up at school hours late or forget to appear at all). As a result his education was doomed to be somewhat sketchy. This was not because he was a willfully disobedient child, however, but because the journey from Eagle Spur right across to the other side of the mountain was far too much of a temptation for the likes of him, since he'd get waylaid by the slightest wonder of Nature along the way.

His brother, Caleb, was most definitely a willfully disobedient child, however! He was also given to playing hookey, but not because he was enchanted at all by the wonders of Nature, but because he was a bad student, obnoxious, and thoroughly bored with lessons. According to the long-suffering Miss Prescott, he was a holy terror and a constant disruption in class, to the other pupils as well as to her, and she had been forced to box his ears and use her cane on countless occasions. Amongst many other indiscretions, he would hum loudly, belch, fart, flick chalk, put frogs in the teacher's table drawer or into the desks of the girls, and chew tobacco and spit it on the classroom floor, so it was all stained with his tobacco juice against his teacher's stern decree that the nasty habit was banned in class.

He was just as bad at the breaks, stealing lunch from the pails and lard buckets of the other children, putting tadpoles from the creek down the backs of their necks, disrupting their games of marbles and hopscotch, or disturbing the peace even more than the chatter and laughter of the other children by taking potshots at birds with his squirrel rifle, which he always brought with him even though Miss Prescott insisted he leave it out on the porch.

Given half a chance, he'd be out the window or the door, not to appear for the rest of the day. (If the truth be known, they'd all willed him to it!) Only the sweep of his mother's broom on his backside or her angry railing at him seemed to persuade him to show his face again. Hers was the lone voice he seemed to listen to, though it failed to improve his nasty disposition or his abominable behavior. And only Mary's countless pleas on her miscreant son's behalf stopped Miss Prescott from banning him permanently from the classroom. Nevertheless, when he left school, even Caleb, troublemaker though he was, had learned to read and write, count and do sums, a tribute to the extraordinary teaching capabilities of Miss Prescott.

Indeed, she had long proved that she was a fine teacher who encouraged healthy competition amongst the children, by organizing spelling bees and ciphering contests every Friday afternoon, giving the lower grades easy words and numbers, and the higher grades, real jawbreakers and more difficult cube roots and fractions to tackle. Right from the start, Emma had proved herself an outstanding student and was the star of every contest. She was presently enrolled in a teachers' training college in Richmond, her tutelage being paid for by himself and the Tuttles. Doc and all Emma's relatives, and Mary, especially, were immensely proud of her, and keenly followed her progress through the sporadic letters she and Aunt Clara sent them.

On the Sunday church meetings at the Presbyterian Church on Beacon Mountain that Doc managed to intermittently attend, he saw for himself that Jed's brother, Caleb, was as different from Jed as regular hog from a whistle pig! While Jed was a dreamer and an inveterate loner, who was always going off by himself into the forests, his younger brother was a rowdy, handsome, gregarious youth, who craved the company of others. A bully and a tease to weaker mountain boys than himself, he was a big, strapping lad, who was always after the girls, either pulling their pigtails, whispering sweet nothings in their ears, or stealing kisses, whereas poor Jed nearly fainted if a girl so much as looked at him, blushing the color of sumac fruit in the winter if one even ventured to greet him. And while Jed was totally enthralled with mountain life, Caleb, young, and restless as an alley cat, wasn't at all taken by it. He was always scoffing at it, sneering to anyone who cared to listen, that there had to be more to life than hand-hoeing rock-hard earth for corn, and hunting 'possums, 'coons and squirrels.

To the dismay of his parents, especially his bereft father, he ran away at the age of sixteen, so big and good-looking, he had mountain daughters weeping and wailing for months after he'd left. Despite his declaration that he was off to see the world, he only got as far as Front Royal, in the Shenandoah Valley, where he got a job in a mill owned by a wealthy landowner, Weenan Tanner, who was part of the cream of Front Royal society. (The size of Front Royal was no reflection on the quality of its more affluent residents who had chosen to settle in the charming little town, since Washington D.C. was a mere seventy miles away and many who worked there, were involved in politics, or had business interests in the capitol.) Though naturally lazy, Caleb was an inveigler and a schemer, who worked hard when it could be noticed, quickly working his way to foreman over men with far more experience and twice his age.

He met the owner's only daughter, Priscilla, and swept her off her pretty, dainty feet. Before too long, at the age of eighteen, he had got her pregnant, and to save a scandal, promptly married her. Some said her daddy was none too pleased at her having to marry a mountain boy, but he admired Caleb's drive and audacity, and he started to come around when his granddaughter was born.

Then Weenan Tanner suddenly died of a heart attack shortly after the birth of his grandchild, leaving all his residential and business properties and interests to his only daughter. After that, it was said that Caleb had his finger in every business pie in the town, and when he returned to show his parents their first grandchild, it was in a shiny black automobile. What's more, the mountain boy spoke like a lowlander, wore a dapper black cashmere coat, a dove-gray homburg hat and fine leather shoes, which all proved to Doc that even those mountain people who were largely unlettered, were highly resourceful and far from stupid.

72

One Sunday morning in the fall of 1917, only two people from Buck Knob Mountain came to the church on Bear Rock Mountain, instead of the usual sizable contingent. Gussie Galtrey and her cousin, Charles, arrived on a buckboard drawn by two horses, while Mary and her barefoot family were standing outside in the frail sunshine chatting to the crowd of spruced-up mountaineers who had made it to church from the surrounding mountains that day. Folk liked to arrive early to ensure they got a seat because there were always people who had to stand at the back, or outside, as the congregation had grown so handsomely with Reverend Crawley presiding over it.

Indeed, most were already inside. Mary and her family were privileged to have the two front pews reserved for her family on a permanent basis. How that had happened, Mary wasn't quite sure. It had been right from the beginning, though, and continued even after the other parishioners had wanted them banned after the rattlesnake incident with Jed.

Gussie, dressed in a long blue dress, flat black boots and a man's black felt hat on her head, with her long gray hair streaming from beneath it, caught at Mary's arm as they were about to enter the church and took her aside.

"Have you heerd th' news?" Gussie asked, her broad plain face ashen and grim. Mary knew that something terrible must have happened to make her look like this.

"What news, Gussie? What's wrong?" she asked, taking the older woman's rough, workworn hand in hers, as an ominous feeling washed over her.

"It's my paw, Dean Galtrey. He's dead! Him an' a great-grandson 'a his too."

Mary's hand flew to her chest. "Oh, my goodness, Gussie, what happened?"

"His cabin got burned down yesterday. Flames got him, an' th' boy. Thunk'd I ought'a let ye know, seein' as he thunk'd so highly of you."

"Oh, Gussie," crooned Mary sympathetically. "I'm so, so sorry! What a terrible way to die."

Mary was shocked by the news. Oh, how Obediah would have wished this final act of disaster upon his foe! Of course, the clan had been responsible for Obediah's murder, yet Mary couldn't help but feel sadness and a deep twinge of regret over his killer's demise. There was no doubt in her mind that even if he hadn't killed Obediah himself, Dean Galtrey had ordered it, just as he had set the women upon her that fateful day she had gone to Buck Knob Mountain to seek an end to the feud.

She knew that despite her husband's continued antipathy towards the clan, he would be saddened by the news too, for she suspected he had also come to respect the fierce old Galtrey patriarch as much as she had, though a lot more grudgingly. Gussie looked devastated by her father's ugly death, and Mary murmured, "When's th' funeral?"

"Tomorrer."

"Come inside, Gussie. Service is jest about to start. You kin sit with us. I'll ask Reverend Crawley to say a special prayer fer them."

But the older woman shook her head. "No, we're a'goin straight back to organize thungs. But ask th' reverend jest th' same. An' I know paw refused to come to church, but would you be kind enough to ask him if'n he'd be willin' to give service to bury him an' th' boy?"

"I will," Mary promised.

She watched Gussie climb awkwardly onto the buckboard and Charles set the pair of horses into motion with his whip. Mary stared after them in dismay. *Why did she suddenly have the awful feeling that these ill-tidings were an omen of bad things to follow?* Mary shook her head to rid herself of the ridiculous notion. She was just being silly and superstitious in the way mountain folk had always been. They looked for signs in everything and she ought to know better. But still the feeling persisted, bearing down on her chest throughout the entire service.

After the service had ended and the congregation had spilled out into the large clearing in front of the church, everybody was aflutter with the news of the death of Obediah Buchanan's old arch enemy. Unfortunately, memories were long on Claw Mountain. Though Samuel and Alvin were long moldy in their graves, their kin had never forgotten their ugly fate and despite the peace pact that had held for sixteen long years, most members of the Buchanan clan hailed the incident, saying it was no less than the old patriarch deserved after the grief he had caused them in the past.

And looking at all the frowning, belligerent faces, Mary was suddenly clouted with the possibility that one of them might have decided to take belated revenge

523

on their old enemies. Peace pact or no peace pact, she wouldn't put it past any of them actually. Perhaps Eli had got Jake to do his dirty work for him and at long last carried out the threat he'd made all those years before. Genuinely alarmed now that one of their clan might have started the fire, or be blamed for it even if they hadn't, Mary told the clan that she and Zachary Thomas would be attending the funeral and asked if any of the other parishioners would care to accompany them.

Despite the fact that the Galtreys now attended church and that the Buchanan clan were on civil if not over-friendly terms with them, this suggestion was met with a stony silence, a sea of shaking heads. All of the other members of the clan refused to go, including Edna, her best friend on the mountain since young Emma had left, many saying they did not want to step foot on Buck Knob Mountain, especially not for Dean Galtrey's funeral. Mary guessed she could understand her sister-in-law not wanting to. After all, her handsome young husband, Samuel, had been murdered by the Galtrey clan, and Lila's reluctance too, since her husband, Alvin, had been the other Bucko victim that terrible day. But even knowing and understanding this, Mary was disappointed that they could not put their personal feelings aside for once.

They had talked about burying the hatchet and pretended to have forgiven their enemies after Reverend Crawley had given a moving service all about forgiveness, the first time the Galtreys had attended the chapel. Now she realized they had only paid lip-service to forgiveness in order to impress their preacher. The enmity between the two clans had been too deep-seated, the acts committed against each other too foul, for them to perform as simple an act of Christian charity as attending a funeral. And here she was, saying that she and Zachary Thomas would be going when she hadn't even asked her husband yet! Could be he would not want to go either! Oh well, at least Reverend Crawley had promised to be there.

Mary had been right about her husband's reluctance to attend the funeral, but after she had told him of the many reasons why he should, not least of which was to ensure that the peace pact held, he capitulated without too much of an argument. Having started out well before sun-up the next morning, the two of them arrived at Buck Knob at midday, having taken two of Obediah's mules to get there in time leaving eighteen-year-old Jed to look after his six sisters, who ranged in ages from two to sixteen.

The funeral was to be held at the homestead of the deceased patriarch, and when they finally got there, Mary was sad to see the blackened remains of the cabin, standing as a stark and tragic reminder of how the old patriarch and his young great-grandson had died so recently.

A new generation of wild-looking, raggedly dressed Galtreys greeted her and Zachary Thomas with closed, furtive looks. The older ones, including those black-attired women, who had tried to kill Mary that awful day so long ago, stared at them with grief-stricken eyes and a certain proud aloofness, their faces beneath cloth bonnets, now deeply lined with the years.

The Galtrey clan was out in full force and stood to the side of the ruins of the old cabin, in front of the two mounted hand-hewn closed coffins. Two graves had already been dug a little way behind the coffins and a restrained sobbing could be heard, which filled the mid-afternoon air with a terrible bruising sadness. Such had been Dean Galtrey's formidable and strong presence that his sudden death seemed to have left a gaping hole in the atmosphere.

The old patriarch had proved to be a rigid disciplinarian who had abided by the peace pact strenuously. Minor incursions had been dealt with severely on both sides. Thankfully, Mary mused, the fear of Eli breaking that early fragile peace in a big way had not materialized, mainly because shortly afterwards, he left the mountain for good.

And just being on this mountain again evoked old bad memories about the day the women of the mountain had attacked her. They came back to Mary like a slap in the face and she suddenly felt slightly uneasy in such a large congregation of their former enemies, afraid that the peace pact might have died with its maker. What if they had suspected Bucko arson and Gussie coming to tell her the news had been nothing more than a trap? Mary shivered in apprehension. Thank goodness she had not brought her whole family as she had first considered. The time constraint had meant that they had to travel quickly and, with her whole family in tow, they would not have arrived on time.

Only Gussie came over to talk to them, drawing them to the front of the almost-silent throng. Mary could sense tension in the air and was hugely relieved when Reverend Crawley arrived. Although the good reverend had reached middle age, his looks were still open and boyish and his fine Christian goodness seemed to ooze from his pores, as he clasped a multitude of Galtrey hands and expressed deep sorrow for their loss. His arrival seemed to dissipate the tension in the air like sunshine does morning mist.

After a short while, the reverend moved behind the two coffins and began the service with an opening prayer. Then came some hymn-singing, before he gave a stirring service for the two victims of the fire, during which he spoke of Dean Galtrey's courage in accepting the peace pact with the Buchanan clan after three decades of violence and hostility and then ensuring that it was not broken thereafter. Pallbearers then carried the coffins the short way to the graves and lowered them in with ropes, while the mourners gathered around weeping and wailing.

It reminded Mary of the double Buchanan funeral she had attended all those years ago as a young bride. After the reverend had said a prayer over the double graves, Dean Galtrey's oldest son, Quaid Galtrey, moved to the front and stood beside him proceeding to give a short eulogy for the patriarch and the boy. He said that his father had been a hard, but fair, man and that his loss would be keenly felt by his devoted family. He broke down completely when he talked of the courage of his grandson, wiping his eyes on his shirt-sleeve, before thanking the reverend for making the journey to see that the pair went to their graves in a righteous manner. Earth was spaded over the grave, every thud a reminder to the mourners of their own mortality. After the graves were completely covered, the reverend gave a closing prayer and the service was over.

As soon as it ended, both Sloane and Quaid Galtrey, their hair still long but streaked with gray now, approached the Claw Mountain visitors. Unbelievably, Sloane was still wearing his old Confederate hat, which was battered and much the worse for long years of wear. Mary remembered the day that she had first met this wild and ornery-looking pair on Claw Mountain when their intension had been to murder her and Jed by slitting their throats. She felt a moment of inexplicable throat-tightening fear.

Then the two hardy mountain men soberly stuck out their hands to them. Zachary Thomas took hands with each of them in turn, expressing his sympathy for the loss of their father and the boy. Mary too took their proffered hands and, looking into their grief-tormented eyes, she felt ashamed of her earlier suspicions. When she asked them about the tragic incident, expressing her deep sorrow, they told her that it was thought that the old man had suffered a heart attack, for he had suddenly stood up and clutched at his chest, causing him to knock over a kerosene lantern on the bureau. It had broken and flames had spread over the rug, catching it alight, causing the inferno that had engulfed them in minutes.

They had been told this by twelve-year-old Hank, who was also in the cabin at the time. The boy had tried to save his great-grandfather by dragging him outside, but Dean Galtrey was already dead, and badly burned himself, the boy had died a few hours later. Numbly relieved that it hadn't been Buchanan arson that had caused their deaths, after all, Mary shook her head in mute sympathy.

Later, the family and Reverend Crawley were invited to join the Galtrey clan for food and refreshment at trestle tables that had been set up. They joined in the solemn feasting and Mary helped afterward with the washing up and cleaning. She and Zachary Thomas left with the reverend, feeling that what was left of the old antagonisms had died this sad day, and that a stronger friendship and a new solidarity had been spawned with the clan. Yet Mary could not help a vague but persistent feeling that Dean Galtrey's death was definitely an ominous omen of bad things still to come . . .

In the spring of 1918, Jed, by now a tall youth, who wore his sun-streaked brown hair down to his shoulders, brought disturbing news to Mary.

"Maw, th' big chestnut out in th' yard is dyin'."

Mary wheeled around to find that those arresting brilliant blue eyes in his lean, handsome, sun-browned face were filled with tears.

"Oh Jed, you cain't mean that! Look at all th' new honeydew. Why, thar be more bees buzzing' around it than ever. What makes you thunk sech a terrible thung, honey?"

"It done tole me."

"Oh Jed, don't be so fanciful, boy. Trees cain't talk."

"Naw," he admitted. "But you know I kin hear them jest them same! It's ailin', Maw. It an' all th' other chestnuts in th' forest. They're all ailin'. A'fore too long they'll all be dead."

Mary stared at her son in shocked dismay. Though her logic told her it couldn't be possible, she knew that her sensitive eldest son's affinity with Nature was nothing short of startling. Indeed, she had long witnessed how he seemed to silently commune with all of the natural world around him, right from the time he was a toddler. For a brief, wonderful while, she had even shared the mysterious "Beatific Vision" with him. Though she had never again witnessed Nature in the same scintillating way that she had the fortnight following that experience, she was convinced that Jed still did.

She knew that his understanding of the workings and intricacies of Nature was profound, extending even to plants and insects. She had also witnessed his devotion to animals and reptiles and the remarkable way they responded to him, remembering how he had handled the rattlesnake on the day both he and Caleb were to have their "infant-sprinkling" ceremonies.

Of course, Jed was not christened that day because Reverend Hubbly had refused to carry on with the service after the incident with the rattlesnake, and here he was, all of eighteen years old, and still not christened! All her other children had been christened in due course by Reverend Crawley, but on the three other Sundays, many months apart appointed for him to be christened, something always happened to prevent it. On the first Sunday, he, who hadn't had a sick day in his life, suddenly caught the measles. His face was full of spots that disappeared soon after Zachary Thomas had left to go to church carrying baby Caleb, and she had stayed behind to tend to him.

The next time, Jed had hurt his leg, so he couldn't walk the long miles to church. And the final Sunday, he had to stay behind to comfort a dying pet. It was left in abeyance for a long while after that, and then suddenly, he was much too old to be christened in an "*infant*-sprinkling" ceremony, and though she kept guiltily thinking she should put it to rights, it hadn't yet happened.

Even though she knew what she did about her son, he *had* to be wrong about the chestnut trees. Chestnuts had always been an integral part of mountain life. *Dear Lord*, Mary thought despairingly. Not only did the mountain folk depend heavily on the chestnuts for their very existence, they were the dominant tree of all the forest. Their loss would be utterly devastating for them all. Besides, she comforted herself, she went through the forests of Claw Mountain every day herself, usually with her son, and she had never seen a single sign that they might be diseased and dying as he claimed. Surely this time, Jed was mistaken.

But within weeks, her hopes were crushed. The abundant new growth on the spectacular giant chestnut in their yard, withered and died, and whole branches went black, the life gone out of them. Then the chestnut blight began spreading silent, insidious death throughout Claw Mountain, before spreading slowly south-ward over the Blue Ridge, giving testimony to her son's amazing and unfailing intuition. Mary had prayed that the disease would stop at a few dead limbs, but the following year, whole trees began dying, including the special giant one at the homesite on Eagle Spur.

Like all the others in the forests of Claw Mountain, the giant chestnut, which for so many years had given her and her family sustenance, shade and beauty, stood blackened and bare-limbed as if fire had swept over it. Mary felt she'd lost a member of her family. It was utterly heartbreaking and she couldn't bear to look at it. But she couldn't bear to cut it down like Zachary Thomas suggested, either. To do so would be to dishonor it somehow. No, it would remain part of their existence, even if it was no longer the magnificent specimen it once was. Instead, she would grow beautiful flowering creepers up it. Anything to hide its present bleak countenance!

A walk through the tableland forest of Claw Mountain, was equally as depressing. The chestnut trees had been hit with the devastating, exotic blight, which left them crippled and forlorn and forever stripped of their dignity. Within four years, thousands of dead trees gave grim testimony to the fact that the mighty American chestnut had once claimed half the forests, leaving pathetic whitened skeletons in their wake. The loss of each beloved tree affected Jed like the loss of a close friend. Chestnut saplings would sprout from the roots of dead trees but they seldom reached fifteen feet before the deadly Asian blight brought them down too.

The chestnuts had provided the mountaineers with a livelihood with their nuts, bark and wood, and had been used for everything from building their homes to feeding foraging razorback hogs. Their loss was a crippling blow to them. Now there were no nuts to feed the livestock and the mainstay of the mountains' commercial crop was wiped out. Farmers were robbed of a durable wood for posts, logs and rails. In the wake of the devastating blight, mountain men were forced to find new sources of revenue. In the autumn, many of them road freight trains to Winchester to pick apples, or hired out to valley farmers. Commercial logging also suffered greatly. Slowly, oak began to replace the chestnut as the dominant tree of the forests. All too soon, all the chestnuts were dead save the odd, lonely, living monument.

October, once a time of great, munificent bounty, when the thousands of spiky chestnut burrs burst open and showered their three nuts each onto the ground, became instead a bleak time of sorrow and sad nostalgia for the despairing mountain folk, as haunting memories of big chestnut harvests crowded in. To Mary, the most poignant one of all was of young'uns with brown-stained hands and feet! This painful loss was a terrible tragedy for those who had relied heavily on the chestnut bounty, seeming to echo the unforgiving harshness of mountain life. Indeed many were being forced to leave their mountain homes and seek work in the more prosperous lowlands. The remaining mountain people, most of whom fiercely loved the life, hung on grimly in increasing deprivation. Mountain life had become, in the wake of the accursed blight, even more tough and frugal than before.

As if the chestnut blight was not enough for the mountain folk to contend with, in the winter of 1918, another crippling blow hit the mountains on a scale that equaled "The Big Freeze" of 1899/1900. A terrible influenza epidemic swept though the mountains, causing many deaths among the mountain folk, who contracted it when they went to the general stores down in the valleys, or from the apple-pickers when they returned to the mountains. There was hardly a mountain family that it did not strike. It was during this catastrophic epidemic, which had swept through the entire country and the rest of the world like a tornado, causing the death of some twenty million people, that Mary fully appreciated the sheer dogged dedication of Doc Adams.

As an old man of nearly eighty, Doc regularly came out on horseback to tend to the sick, his black medical bag and pharmaceutical trunk strapped to the saddle. He would pack enough medicines for three days, climb on his horse, travel all the way from Carlisle to the mountains, then ride up and down each hollow, covering a route within a radius of some fifty miles. He did this in weather so foul, battling through sleet, snow and streams of slush that his feet would get stuck to the stirrups with ice and boiling water would have to be poured over them to unstick them by those not yet affected by the epidemic once he reached his destination.

Whenever he reached a cabin, he would treat the patients, cut wood, prepare food, fed his horse and then go on to the next cabin. Then, after three days, utterly exhausted, he would go home, he and his horse would rest up, he would get fed by Hilda and, after a single night's sleep, he would be off again for another three days on a fresh horse. Despite the fact that he hardly got any sleep, with a regimen that would cower many a much younger man, the old man was indefatigable in this time of great need.

Mary, too, did her best for the sick, sometimes accompanying Doc. She nursed struck-down folk on Claw and Bear Rock Mountains and even went into Buck Knob territory on her own to nurse their sick, chop firewood, cook and clean house for those affected, defying the danger to herself and further cementing friendship with the Buchanans' former enemies. Miraculously, she never suffered from anything more than sheer exhaustion.

But she and Zachary Thomas did not escape the sweep of the dreaded virus. They lost two of their little girls in quick succession, to the flu. Fever-bound, with bright-red cheeks, the two little cherubs succumbed one after the after, within the space of a week. Joannie was five years old and little Mattie, only three. Zachary Thomas's home remedies had proved ineffective against the scourge of this disease as had Doc's more expert ministrations.

They buried the doomed little pair under the skeleton of the chestnut tree. Mary, who blamed herself for infecting the girls, grieved deeply for them, the pain inside her, almost unbearable. She did her daily chores in a kind of daze and Zachary Thomas became moody and inconsolable. In the last throes of the epidemic, Doc, too, was struck down with the accursed flu. Fortunately, he survived, but was bedded for several months, while his body fought off the effects of the disease and the arduous trials to which he had subjected his aged body.

Mary and Zachary Thomas visited him in his house in Carlisle by buckboard and mules, because her husband said she needed a change of scenery to peak up her low spirits, and because he knew how worried she was about Doc. They were let into the handsome double-storied house by Jason Darwin, the pleasant young doctor, whom Doc had taken into his practice and who was now running it for him. His housekeeper, Hilda Gross, was away at market and fetching home supplies.

Mary was shocked at how much Doc had deteriorated. Always a portly fellow, he had lost so much weight, he was but a shadow of his former self. Though he was dressed and seated in the drawing room, which was dominated by a huge moldy mounted head of an old bear, his clothes hung on him, and he looked desperately pale and weak. Mary rushed over to him, taking both his cold white hands in hers, sinking at his feet and laying her head on his lap. "Oh, my dear, dear Doc . . ."

He stroked her loosened long black hair and said in a calm reassuring voice, "There, there, Mary, there's no need to fuss. I get enough of that from Hilda. I'm fine, just fine. Strong as an ox. Now tell me about Jed. How is the dear boy . . .?"

But that fine old man never fully recovered from his valiant efforts during the epidemic, or from his own bout of the deadly influenza, and he died the following year. Although not totally unexpected, Mary heard the news from young Dr. Darwin – who'd made the journey on horseback to Claw Mountain to tell her of his mentor's peaceful demise – with shock and a good deal of sadness. Grieving tears streamed down her face. She had loved that dear old man, who had responded so magnificently to the needs of the mountain folk he had come to love and admire so much. He had done so much for them, helping them by establishing regular mountain clinics and to acquire a school of their own, and paying towards young Emma's education. But it was his efforts during the epidemic that loomed largest in her estimation. That tireless old soul had truly shown his glowing worth during that awful time, battling sleet and snow, sacrificing his own health and, in the end, his life, to save so many others.

But he was not only a doctor who had served them magnificently well over the years, he was also her good friend and confidante and she knew that she would miss him greatly. With an aching lump in her throat, she imagined him tending the sick at his clinic on Claw Mountain, or coming on his horse to the church on Beacon Mountain, which in the end he had adopted as his own, as he admired Reverend Crawley so much, giving her a cheery wave. (He had never driven his buggy up after that first "rattlesnake" service and, though he told her he had acquired an automobile some years ago, he had never used it to come to the mountains, because of the bad, or non-existent, roads.)

She knew there had been two reasons for Doc attending the mountain church, though, the second one being that it gave him the regular opportunity to see Jed, who continued to be his special interest, though he was good to all her children, always bringing them candies and special treats. But he loved her eldest boy with all the warm, partial enthusiasm of a devoted grandfather and was ever anxious to see and hear about him. She knew that Jed would be devastated when he heard the news, as would Emma.

All the surviving mountain folk he had tended to during the deadly course of the flu epidemic, attended his funeral. These included the Ficks, Addis, Galtrey and Buchanan clans, (with the exception of Eli Buchanan), but also all those clans from the surrounding mountains. Even young Emma and the Tuttles came all the way from Richmond to attend his funeral, which was held at the chapel on Beacon Mountain, according to his wishes.

Emma had returned to Claw Mountain every Christmas and Mary had watched her blossom from a stick-thin, tough-as-nails, graceless, young mountain urchin, who dressed in dungarees and vests, into a tall, graceful, educated pretty young woman with bangs in her hair, who wore make-up and stylish dresses, with a sense of pride and amazement. Like Eli, she had lost her mountain speech and now talked with a cultured, lowlander voice. Though she was proud of Emma's remarkable achievements, Mary oh-so-missed that tough little spitfire of old!

Now a mature woman of thirty, Emma was a teacher at a secondary school in the city. She made a beeline for Jed, whom she had always adored, and the pair of them sat together on the pew with their arms about one another, silently sobbing for the old man who had meant so much to them both. While Mary's own tears flowed and even Zachary Thomas's eyes were wet, Mary felt keenly for the grieving pair sitting beside her. Doc had not only paid handsomely towards Emma's education, he remained staunchly supportive of her right up to the end, showing glowing pride at her achievements, especially when she graduated from the teaching college with top honors.

Mary and Doc had attended the graduation ceremony together, traveling by train to Richmond, as they had when they had delivered her to civilization years before. She knew how fond Emma was of the old man. And she well knew what a special place the old man had held in Jed's big heart and how much he would feel the loss of the old man who had doted on him for so long.

Reverend Crawley grated his throat to begin the funeral service, standing straight and tall on the pulpit in his black suit and white clerical collar, his face kindly and understanding, as he overlooked the fine oak casket covered in flowers below him and the overwrought congregation, who gazed at him for comfort and direction at this most sad of times.

"Every once in a while," his strong voice rang out, "someone comes along who restores your faith in the essential goodness of mankind. Doc Adams, as he was affectionately known to all those who knew and loved him – and indeed to know him *was* to love him – was just such a man . . ."

Reverend Crawley proceeded to give Doc Adams a fine sending-off, telling of his unfailing love of, and service to, the mountain folk, both in the educational and medical fields, and of his extraordinary efforts during the flu epidemic. He spoke, too, of his love for children and his special love for Jed Buchanan, whom he had delivered twenty years before and who he had told the reverend, had been the catalyst for his returning to the mountains time and time again. Mary turned to Jed when the reverend said that. Her elder son was sitting tightly holding Emma's hand, almost as if he were a child again, and she, his minder, his head upraised to the pulpit, his sad, upraised face filled with such a pure radiant beauty, it almost took Mary's breath away.

The reverend spoke too of Doc's love for Emma and his pride in her remarkable achievements, which he had partly made possible, listing them for everybody's benefit. Lastly, he spoke of Doc's special love for Mary Buchanan. Mary felt her heart leap at the sound of her name. "Indeed," Reverend Crawley said, smiling softly down at her, "he so often spoke of Mary to me, always with the utmost admiration, saying she was the finest woman it was his privilege to know and I know that he would want me to tell her this now."

The stirring sentiments expressed by her old friend through Reverend Crawley made Mary break down and openly weep. *Oh, that darling old man!* She knew he was here now, standing beside his coffin and telling her not to fuss so. That he would always be beside her and that she could talk to him and ask his advice and confide in him whenever something was troubling her. She could hear his voice inside her head, telling her these things. Then she raised her tear-filled eyes andS to her astonishment, she *did* see him standing beside his coffin, smiling at her. Then she blinked and he was gone. Had she really seen him or had grief made her start imagining things? He had looked so hale and hearty, not a bit like the wizened old man she had last seen. Then suddenly she knew for sure that she *had* seen him and that he was now in the care of the angels. She smiled to herself and a welling comfort filled her heart *Oh, Doc! Goodbye, dear, dear friend, till we meet again . . .*

After the moving service, as she and the others were leaving the church, Mary noticed an unfamiliar heavy-set woman, with gray hair and a bull-dog jaw sitting tearfully next to Dr. Darwin, on a pew right at the back. Thinking that the poor woman must be some distant relative of Doc's, Mary went over to her to offer her condolences and learned that she was in fact Hilda Gross, Doc Adams' German housekeeper he'd told her so much about. They never did get to meet her the day they went to visit Doc. It was clear to Mary, as the poor woman hung onto her proffered hand and sobbed like a child that the good doctor had meant a great deal to her too.

"He thought the verld of you, he did," she told Mary with a loud sniff.

"As indeed, he did you, dear Hilda," Mary assured the grieving old woman. "He often told me what a fine housekeeper you are. He said you cooked like a dream and always kept his house like a shiny new penny."

They agreed that that wonderful old man had been a credit to his profession, and a fine human being.

* * *

Several weeks after the funeral, a lawyer called Abel Augustine, wrote a letter to Mary, requesting her, Zachary Thomas and Jed to be present at a will-reading which was to be held at the late doctor's house in Carlisle. Emma and Reverend Crawley were each sent a similar letter. The five of them, Hilda Gross and Dr. Darwin gathered in Doc's living room at the appointed hour while the lawyer, a prosperous-looking fellow with a thin black mustache, opened the will and read from it in a monotone.

Doctor Adams had left $50,000 to set up a trust, the income of which was to be used for an annual bursary for further education for a suitable candidate, providing he or she was a graduate of The Emily Tuttle School on Claw Mountain. He appointed Mary Buchanan as the sole trustee of this trust as he knew she would choose students worthy of furthering their education. He bequeathed a further $10,000 to the school for its upkeep and new books. He left $5,000 and all his clothing to the Beacon Mountain Presbyterian Church, the fund to be used for special projects and the clothing for distribution amongst destitute mountain people.

Doc had left his housekeeper a sizable pension, which would allow her to retire on a comfortable income. His medical practice and the surgery adjoining the house, he had left to the young Dr. Darwin. He left the Carlisle house to Emma, with the option to sell, if she so wished, providing she gave the young Dr. Darwin first option to buy. Otherwise, if she did not wish to reside in it herself, she could lease it out to him at a fair rental. Much to her astonishment, he left a staggering sum of $10,000 and his automobile to Mary. *Ten thousand dollars!* She sat stunned. She had no idea that Doc had been worth so much. His horse and buggy, stethoscope, black bag and medical trunk he left to Zachary Thomas. Since her husband wasn't a doctor, Mary found this a little puzzling, thinking the medical paraphernalia should perhaps have gone to Dr. Darwin instead. He left a token sum of $100 to each of the Buchanan children. Finally, he left his saddle horse, a fine animal, and all of his books to Jed.

The horse Mary could understand, since Jed loved animals so much, but she was rather mystified by his bequest of the books, since Doc knew what an outdoor boy Jed was and what an indifferent scholar he had been. It would have made more sense if he had left the house to Jed, though he would never choose to live in it, of course, and the books to Emma, since she was a teacher, though, of course, she did not begrudge the young woman such a handsome gift. Indeed, she was thrilled for her. Perhaps dear Doc had become a little befuddled in his old age, though she was deeply touched and grateful for his kind and generous bequests to her and her family.

But she might have known that Doc would have had all his faculties right up to the end. In a letter which he said was to be read out to his heirs after the will-reading, he gave his reasoning behind each bequest and they showed what a wise and discerning old man he had been, after all.

Hilda, he said, had served him long and faithfully and had been an outstanding and diligent servant. He wished her a long and happy retirement. This caused poor Hilda, sitting in an upright chair next to the doctor, to collapse into broken sobs. Dr. Darwin, Doc said, deserved to have his practice and surgery, for he had proved an invaluable asset to it for many years now, always putting a patient's needs before his own.

He noted that Emma had been the first child to graduate from the Claw Mountain School and venture out into the world and said how she had so distinguished herself. He said that the day he met her had changed his entire life and that he had benefited much through knowing her. She had made him extremely proud, and he felt she deserved the house to set her up in life.

Doc then said he knew how much the Buchanan family struggled financially, so he was giving the money to Mary to use as she saw fit, knowing how sensible she was. The automobile was for her also because she was the one who visited the folk on other mountains, spreading her fine Christian goodness, and had done this, on foot, for many years. Now he wished to ease her burden somewhat.

He had left to his buggy and buggy horse, Wishbone, to Zachary Thomas to ease his passage to the general store. He had also left his medical paraphernalia to him despite the fact that he was not a registered doctor, to help him in ascertaining which of his old natural remedies needed to be used for those who sought his help. *Dear, dear Doc!* He must have known how much the deaths of his two little daughters had badly affected her husband and had dented his faith in the old remedies and, by giving him this special gift, Doc was acknowledging that there was still a use for the old-fashioned remedies, after all.

Doc said that his most difficult choice of bequest had been to Jed. He had pondered long and hard when considering what to leave the young man, at first considering the house as a possible bequest. He knew that his eventual choice of all his books must seem like a puzzling one to many, even inappropriate. But he knew material things did not interest Jed and, by leaving him something to enrich the mind, he hoped that it would cause him to grow mentally and spiritually, which was the greatest gift he could think of giving him. He knew the horse was meant for him, and that it would be well looked after by him. He spoke long about the joy Jed had given him from the moment of his birth on 6th April, 1900, and how blessed he had been to have watched him grow up into the fine young man that he was. He said he had always had a special and devoted love for the boy and would always watch over him, even after death.

They all cried after that, even the rather stern-looking lawyer wiping away a surreptitious tear. As they sat surrounded by the things that had surrounded the old man for so many years, Mary felt an aching nostalgia. *Oh, how she missed dear old Doc already!*

W hen Doc's estate was finally wound up and the bequests distributed, they were all delighted and grateful to dear old Doc Adams. Mary opened her first banking account at the Wells Fargo Bank in Madison, in which she deposited the personal funds Doc had left her. She used a small part of it to buy shoes for her entire family, including herself and Zachary Thomas. (Those belonging to Hedina Buchanan had long since become unwearable for her, and times had changed. Footwear was becoming more familiar among the mountain people, even during the summer months, their one small concession to a world on the outside in mainstream America.) A trust account was also opened for the bursaries and another for the school supplies. Reverend Crawley was given the $5,000 to administer and the clothes to distribute. The automobile, the black-fringed buggy and the buggy horse, Wishbone, were also all kept at Horseshoe Hollow, since it was impossible and impractical to take them up to Eagle Spur. Mary quickly learned to drive the Model-T Ford and would maneuver the contraption over rough mountain roads, often getting stuck in mud or snow, or stranded someplace after a flash flood.

She visited sick or lonely folk all over the surrounding mountains, did their chores for them, sat with them when they were grieving, washed and dressed the dead, and even persuaded the people to make rudimentary all-weather bridges and better roads. There was some resistance, of course, since easier access meant the law could get in much easier – and of course, the hated Revenue Men! – but they eventually did it, anyway.

Zachary Thomas, on the other hand, would not go near the auto and they rode the horse and buggy to church every Sunday. How proud Zachary Thomas was of his fine bequest!

The large book collection he had left Jed was fine and leather-bound, embracing the works of all the great philosophers, poets, and politicians. There were religious writings of all the world's religions, political, scientific and historical volumes, biographies of many great people, and classic novels.

Doc's words must have deeply affected Jed. Though he had never been much of a reader up till then, his father had made him a special roof-high bookcase for them, and he hardly ever had his nose out of a book, if he was at home. He loved the horse that had been left to him, an elegant brown saddle horse, called Prince, and rode him to explore further afield in the mountains than he had ever been before. He rode the horse bare-back and as if he had been born on it, and not surprisingly, the two seemed to have a deep intuitive understanding of one another. He was also stabled in the big barn at Horseshoe Hollow, with the buggy horse and four mules for his companions.

Oh, how wise old Doc had been, understanding each and every one of them so well.

* * *

In 1920, a storm of violence hit the Blue Ridge, which made front-page news all over America. On March 14th, twenty fierce, mud-splattered mountain men galloped in on horseback from the surrounding hills, leapt off their mounts and sped up the steps of a quaint old red-bricked courthouse in Hillsville, Virginia. They killed the judge, the prosecutor and the sheriff with blazing rifles. Several members of the jury were wounded, one fatally, and two civilian bystanders were also wounded. A short distance from town, a young female witness collapsed and died from a gunshot wound she'd received in the court.

Before the gun smoke had cleared, after firing at least two hundred bullets inside the courthouse, the Allen clan ran back outside, raced down the steps, leapt back onto their saddles, and charged through the shocked and immobilized village, like a bunch of wild horsemen at a horse race, taking with them, the prisoner, Floyd Allen, who'd been riddled with thirteen of their bullets. It seemd that the reason for this senseless carnage, was because Floyd Allen had beat up a deputy sheriff for arresting two members of the clan for church rocking, and it seemed likely that he would get sentenced to a year in jail for the assault. No Allen had ever done time before. The Allen clan had acquired a reputation for toughness and daring before the raid, but this naked audacity stunned and outraged the lawmakers.

Troops were held in readiness in Roanoke and Lynchburg and the Second Virginia Regimen was ordered to Hillsville. A 1000-strong posse with bloodhounds took up the trail of the Allen outlaws, pressing so close to a clan near Buzzard's Roost, which was their hideout, that they fled, scattering into surrounding hollows and coves. After weeks of hiding, one by one they were all captured . . .

Mary read the whole horrifying account in an old newspaper Zachary Thomas brought her from the general store. While her husband was amazed by the extent of the hullabaloo it caused throughout the land, muttering that it had always been the mountain way, Mary was deeply shocked and saddened by such an event. It proved that there were mountain clans who still believed they were above the law, as had once been the case with the Buchanan clan. Indeed, the callous and reprehensible actions by the Allen clan had brought disrepute down on the whole mountain community.

In the same year, the country was gripped in fake teetotalism, and bootlegging rose up in violent response, spawning speakeasies and gangsters on an unheard-of scale, pushing moonshine sales on Claw Mountain to an all-time high. Indeed, things for the Buchanan clan had improved steadily over the years. But even more importantly, and contrarily, their lives were meaningful in a much more positive way. The men worked hard at their crops, their wives kept their children and the homes clean, sewed their clothes and cooked them hot, nourishing meals, the children did their chores and proudly attended The Emily Tuttle School and they all went to church on Sundays.

Though Doc Adams was no longer around to hold mountain clinics, Dr. Darwin had taken up where he had left off and, every few months, he came to see to their medical needs, as had done the good late doctor. Hatred and violence had left the steep slopes of Claw Mountain at last, disappearing on the wings of widespread temperance and faith. Now, despite the alcohol that bubbled and thumped in the stills, which left the mountain in the hidden panels of cars, contentment and peace stole over the mountain like morning mist. It seemed to Mary that nothing could destroy what had been built up by the clan.

But in the mid-1920s, even more disturbing news reached Mary's ears via Zachary Thomas after he had heard about it at the general store. He said that rumors had spread throughout the mountains that a National Park was to be established in the Blue Ridge. When Mary questioned him about what a National Park was exactly, he said he wasn't sure, but he'd heard tell it was that the land would become "protected" from things like hunting and fishing and crop-planting and tree-felling and such, and set aside for visitors to come and view. Mary heard the news with a jangling of alarm.

"But how will th' mountain folk live if'n they cain't hunt and fish and grow their crops, Zack?"

"Beats me," replied Zack, with a deeply worried look on his face.

Mary prayed that it was just idle rumor.

73

*I*n 1917, *Temperance Societies had won the day in Virginia and the state enacted Prohibition, outlawing the production and sale of alcoholic beverages. This triumph was followed in 1920 by National Prohibition. It had been creeping over the whole country, county by county, state by state, for nearly a century before it was finally nationally upheld by the 18th amendment to the United States Constitution. Consequently, there had been "Dry" and "Wet" states long before this total clamp-down.*

That this had happened at all was due to the efforts of the great Temperance Movement, which started out trying to limit alcoholic intake, before fanatics pushed for outright abstinence. Most evangelical churches demanded complete abstinence of their parishioners and moral camp aigns spread the "truth" about "demon rum" and "Lucifer Liquids". Indeed, according to the clerics, Satan dwelled in every drop of alcohol consumed.

The Civil War had caused Prohibition to be put on hold for a while, as it was extensively used as an anesthetic and disinfectant, and was hard to keep away from the troops about to engage in battle, or suffering from its horrific after-effects, in any event. The Prohibition bandwagon was revived in the 1880s, when women became actively involved and political for the first time. Their target was the saloons, which they saw as hotbeds of vice and corruption. The Anti-Saloon League was formed in 1883 and it began to succeed in enacting prohibition laws, until eventually the campaign became a national effort. Their message of abstinence was cried out from pulpits everywhere and temperance pledges were signed by all those who feared hellfire and the eternal damnation of their immortal souls. By the 1890s, prohibitionists were prominent on school boards and flooded the schools with anti-booze material.

The Prohibitionists gained an unexpected ally in their fight to rid the country of booze. Disease! The preachers shamelessly blamed the major global disaster, the 1918 influenza epidemic on sin, saying that God was punishing them for their wicked indulgence in alcohol, and only a great moral crusade could save the nation. By 1920, thirty-three states had voted themselves "Dry"! On 29th January, 1920, Prohibition became the law of the land, pushed through Congress by the ultra-dry, ultra-religious congressman from Minnesota, Andrew Volstead.

Volstead, backed by triumphant clerics, defined 'intoxicating liquor' as any beverage containing more than one-half of one-percent alcoholic content. The crusading congressman succeeded in passing his National Prohibition Act over President Wilson's veto. The "Drys" celebrated this ultimate victory, saying that an enemy of God had been overthrown and that victory crowned the forces of righteousness.

The whole thing left a bad taste in the mouths of Eli and ex-Senator Huntington (Eli's mentor had retired from politics after his fourth term and had opted to remain in Washington). They were disgusted by this unexpected turn of events. Oh, the Prohibitionists were mighty vocal, but nobody expected them to be able to enforce such an outlandish law.

To Eli, nobody personified the Prohibitionists he despised more than Reverend Cotterell, though, to Eli's everlasting satisfaction he did not live long enough to see the fruits of his efforts enacted. The fiery, out-spoken Reverend Cotterell, with his loudly proclaimed aim to achieve a dry and crime-free America (in other words, National Prohibition), had become a shining symbol of hope to those in the Temperance Movement before his death. But Eli felt that the reverend's outright war against alcohol had been less matter of principle with him than a personal vendetta against himself, which had lasted several years until the reverend's death.

He had never forgiven Eli for his blatant pursuit of his engaged daughter and he considered his small disruption outside the church on her wedding day the ultimate insult, according to Annabel. After all, she had said, his tearing away at such a dangerous speed and spooking the horse attached to the buggy of one of their most influential guests, had provoked great agitation amongst the bridal party and guests alike and, furthermore, had been the talk of the reception that followed, totally ruining 'poor Father's day', to say nothing of her own.

A few months after the wedding, the man had actually led a delegation of pious-looking men and women into Eli's office at the distillery and demanded that he cease operations forthwith. The big bloated churchman had marched right in without knocking, while the rest hovered around his opened door in a censorious huddle. As if to reinforce his contention that he had been sent by God himself, the white-haired, contemptuous old "Bible-Thumper", complete with monocle and flourishing white mutton-chops sideburns, came dressed in a black suit and wore his white clerical collar, and was waving a firebrand hand that clutched a black leather Bible. One or two of the ladies were elaborately pinching their noses against the strong malodorous smells emanating from the mixing vats. At least one of them appeared to be overcome by the fumes and fainted, having to be revived with smelling salts, while yet another old marm kept a gloved hand across her eyes as if taking in the very sight of the sinful giant vats might cause God to strike her blind!

Eli stood up and stretched a hand across his desk, making a pretence of ignorance about why they were there, despite the fact that the reverend already had begun writing a barrage of letters and articles to the editors of the *Washington Post* and other national dailies, shortly after Annabel's wedding, decrying the moral decline of the country, the increase of rape statistics, and the increase of drunkenness and crime, all of which he attributed directly to the 'wholesale consumption of alcoholic beverages'. He would go on to say that the real culprits were the men who supplied the poison to the public, corrupting the youth, especially, turning them into 'drink-sodden wretches', drug addicts and sloths. Though he stopped short of mentioning Eli by name in these vitriolic and impassioned missives (published no doubt because of Eli's partnership with Senator Huntington though, in truth, the senator's influence and interest in the distillery besides reaping its profits, were minimal), he spoke of 'undesirables' coming from the Blue Ridge mountains with 'malevolent moonshine mentalities'.

Eli would have been a fool if he hadn't realized that the old fart was targeting him specifically. He was annoyed by the sheer gall of the man to challenge him so directly, yet strangely amused by it at the same time. Had this been the mountains, there would have been no contest, but here in the midst of civilization, the rules were different. Besides, Annabel stopped him from turning nasty. With her tears and her tantrums, her well-developed feminine wiles, she could make him jump through as many hoops as she so desired. *And her father was strictly off limits!* 'Oh, darling,' she would say, 'he's harmless. He may prove an irritation, but what could he possibly actually achieve? It's not as if you're doing anything illegal . . .'

So when the reverend blustered into his office that day, much as Eli wanted to send the man and his gawking group packing in a most unceremonious way, preferably with the aid of his bullwhip, he was forced to restraint by Annabel's pleas. But not to be completely outwitted, he said, with a great show of bonhomie, "Why, Reverend, what a delightful surprise. You're just in time to sample my latest batch of whiskey. I remember how much you enjoyed it at Skyland! Indeed, you purchased a whole barrel of the stuff from George Pollock back in 1901."

There was a chorus of shocked gasps and the reverend, all pent up to harangue him on the evils of alcohol, looked utterly startled at this unexpected disclosure within earshot of the present staid company. He flushed purple with guilt, looking ludicrously comical as he opened and closed his mouth without being able to utter a sound, before he finally recovered his wits, and roared, "What utter nonsense! You're such a scoundrel, you'd say anything to discredit me. I'm a teetotaler and always have been."

"Oh yes, I forgot," said Eli, coming around the desk and clamping a chummy hand on the reverend's fleshy shoulder. "Now that I think of it, I do recall your daughter, Annabel, telling me that you bought the *ten-gallon* barrel strictly for *medicinal purposes!* Silly me! By the way, how is your lovely daughter, Reverend?"

The reverend looked apoplectic, his one, monocled, pale-blue eye looming large as he shoved his face close to Eli's.

"My daughter's state of health has nothing, whatsoever, to do with you. She's a respectable married society lady now and you have no business enquiring after her. It's your devil's brew we're here about!" he snapped with such fury that spittle flew.

Elaborately wiping his face with a handkerchief, Eli gave him a boyish, mischievous grin. "Very well then. How many cases would you like to buy today, Reverend?"

Infuriated by Eli's irreverence and knowing he had been thoroughly outwitted, the reverend rose himself up to his full haughty height, before turning and storming his way out of his office, leading his temperance flock out the distillery and away.

But the fight was not over yet! The reverend held large placard-bearing protests with a brigade of mainly old women, in front of the distillery every day for a whole month thereafter. There were loud chants of "Alcohol is sinful!" "Satan is Drink!" "Save the Children!" "Lips that Touch Liquor Shall Not Touch Ours" (Eli felt that the sour, screwed-up face within a black bonnet of the bearer of that particular placard was enough to keep the most stouthearted man drinking!) and "We demand Prohibition!", and the weighty figure of the reverend in his black preacher's attire and white clerical collar was always there with his bullhorn to encourage them and give speeches against the 'wicked distillery owners' who had set America on such a moral decline.

The press was there in full force to record it all and photographs were splashed all over the front pages of every national newspaper in the land. Eli fancied that Cotterell had been given such a "loud" voice by the press, not so much for his message of prohibition and abstinence, but by virtue of his daughter's social position as the wife of a senator, who had once been the personal aide to the president of the United States, and the fact that his son-in-law's family happened to be one of the most prominent in the country.

To Eli's enormous chagrin, his own social standing began to suffer. Invitations to parties and dinners dropped off and he wasn't to recover fully socially until well after the reverend's sudden and most welcome death some two years later. Though he had longed to confront his old enemy when he was waving banners and holding forth outside the distillery, Eli, concerned that some prying reporter might find out about his shady past, had kept himself very much in the background, refusing interviews and not responding at all, while doing business as usual.

But during one such annoying protest led by the reverend, one old biddy chained herself to an outside lamppost and loudly declared to anybody who would listen that she was not going to unlock the chain until Eli closed the distillery. Eli couldn't resist the chance of getting a little even. It was in the middle of a heat wave and Eli had young Tossed Daniels, the open-faced youngster he had hired when he had first opened the distillery, who had climbed the ranks to become his right-hand man after Jake's return to Claw Mountain, rush up to her with a cup containing what she thought was water. She gulped it down in gratitude before realizing that it was pure gin. She went blue in the face and spluttered, grasping at her scrawny throat as if she had been poisoned. Gasping for air, she had somebody unlock the chain immediately and she ran away screaming as if the devil himself were after her, never to return . . .

But the upshot of it all was that Reverend Augustus Cotterell became the country's leading Prohibitionist. He had started the current final groundswell that was to lead directly to the United States constitutional amendment, making the manufacture, sale and transportation of alcoholic beverages illegal, except for medicinal and scientific purposes.

All the bonded distilleries were closed, causing a drastic shortage of whiskey and brandy, greatly increasing the demand for moonshine products. But with the banning, America's thirst grew as raw and uncontrollable as a rabid dog's. Bootleg booze quickly became a booming home industry for anyone after a quick buck. Home-cooked alcohol, known as "alky", was distilled in humble kitchens, basements and garages, and brewed from garbage, potato peelings and rotten vegetables, oft containing such alarming impurities as bedbugs, rodents, cockroaches and mouse-crap. As a result, whole city streets stank like putrid garbage dumps. Reeking fumes from these myriad bubbling concoctions hung over entire neighborhoods, causing eyes to water and noses to run. Gangsters were more sophisticated, but far more mercenary, having found numerous ways of poisoning pure alcohol with dangerous additives like pyridine, benzene, sulfuric ether and ammonium iodide. This often caused imbibers to go lame, blind, crazy or even die.

Some brews were so lethal that a tiny drop could dissolve enamel in a bathtub. But anything went as long as it turned a handsome profit! And there was no question that bootlegging was highly profitable. What had been called "The Noble Experiment" by Herbert Hoover became not the peace, happiness, prosperity and salvation predicted by the Prohibitionists, but the predatory province of the machine gun and the gangster, the bootlegger and the rum-runner, the speakeasy-owner and the racketeer!

Eli's distillery in Washington was closed down too, but this did not mean that production had come to a halt. It continued behind steel-reinforced doors and boarded up windows, with truck deliveries carried out in the dead of night. His biggest challenge was to obtain the alcohol needed as a base for his products. This was supplied to him by the Claw Mountain stills. To make access to them easier, he had a winding dirt road built by his brothers and nephews up to Horseshoe Hollow.

While Federal Prohibition agents prowled city streets smashing stills and apprehending trucks loaded with alcohol destined for cities in other states, the Revenue Men increased their assault on mountain stills, in an effort to stop the flow. As in the past, whenever strangers suspected of being Revenue Men, came to Claw Mountain, the Buchanan wives would fire signal shots to warn their men of the danger. The men, including a new generation of Buchanan young bloods, would come down from the stills to surround the strangers in a covey, escorting them off the mountain. Though they no longer were as fierce as they once were, their old bloodthirsty reputation lingered still and it would be many, many months before another stranger dared venture up its steep slopes.

Thus Eli became a wily and committed bootlegger, running raw alcohol and moonshine in hidden panels in his automobile from Claw Mountain to his distillery in Washington, where, protected from seizure by pay-offs to Prohibition agents, cops, judges and Feds, his fine liquor was destined for not only the top speakeasies and restaurants of the capitol and New York, but those throughout the country. And because it was illegal, they could charge top dollar for it. Of course other bootleggers also bought liquor from mountaineer moonshiners. They would dilute it by fifty-percent with water, adding cayenne pepper and wild ginger root to it to keep the taste strong, and then add a few drops of Red Devil's lye to it, to give a "bead".

What raw alcohol wasn't used specifically for the production of Obediah's old special, his traditional rye whiskey, Eli made into slightly lesser products for he had discovered that there were even greater profits to be made by cutting and rebottling his products. He hired a reputable pharmacist, Robert Gilfarf, a studious-looking man of about forty, to do the mixing.

The white-coated man set up a new assembly line to supervise the cutting, flavoring and bottling. He had to have a vast supply of stores to achieve this new cheap line, including ethyl, burnt sugar, prune juice, fusel oil, juniper flavoring, glycerin, iodine, oils of scotch, bourbon and rye, barrels of charred woodchips to assist with the 'ageing' process, which he used to achieve concoctions worthy of the Buchanan name. When he wasn't being supplied enough raw alcohol from the mountain stills to keep up with the demand, Eli hired men to steal grain alcohol from a bonded warehouse. Being much cheaper than his company's more superior brands, the new brands sold like ice cream in the middle of a heat wave.

The Buchanan clan had never been flush and Eli's old Rambler had long ago given way to a succession of automobiles, the latest being a sleek gray Oldsmobile, with plush soft black leather seats. And he now owned full title to "Rose Haven".

74

In 1929, the glare of national publicity was again on the Blue Ridge Mountains, although this time Mary fancied it was somewhat more favorable than that occasioned by the notorious Allen clan. President Herbert Hoover had bought 160 acres of land on Fork Mountain where Laurel Prong and Mill Prong came together to form the Rapidan River and built his "Summer White House" in a hemlock grove. An access road was constructed to the presidential retreat by one hundred marines, who also guarded the area. In order to build an observation tower for the president's guests on the summit of Fork Mountain, they blasted their way through the Wilderness Valley, using case upon case of dynamite. Zachary Thomas, especially, was deeply offended by this desecration of the previously untouched Wilderness, a place that had become as familiar to him over the years as his own back yard.

During the springs and summers, motorcades for up to a hundred presidential, weekend guests would tear through the mountain roads, and the invasion of these rich outsiders angered Zachary Thomas, who complained bitterly about them scaring the wildlife and disturbing the peace. Furthermore, to add insult to injury in her husband's eyes, Hoover's domestic staff gave kitchen garbage to Casey Spencer on Fork Mountain, who fed it to his pigs. The poor animals contracted hog cholera that spread to the wild hog population. At least one other farmer on Fork Mountain had to butcher his entire pen of domestic hogs to prevent the highly infectious disease from spreading.

There were two other national disasters that affected the mountain people – the drought of 1929 and the Great Depression of the early 1930s. Of the two, it was the drought that was tougher on them. Since the mountain folk were used to leading frugal lives and grew everything they ate, they had little use for money, and thus the great Depression, which saw mass unemployment in the rest of the country, made less of an impression on them than did the drought. Indeed, Prohibition had created such an increased demand for moonshine, the Depression era was about their most prosperous time. The Buchanan clan was no exception.

But with no rain falling from May, 1929, until the first frost, they had to carry water long distances from springs that hadn't gone dry, for use in their gardens and homes. The spring Mary used went dry and she and the children had to haul heavy pails of water from a mile away. The foliage grew dry and turned the land brown and desolate, as leaves shriveled and grass withered.

Since the drought had also damaged the apple orchards down in the valley, it meant fewer pickers would be able to find work in the fall. Every day, the mountaineers' eye turned anxiously to the sky to search for sign of rain. But day after day, the sun beat down, parching the thirsting mountain earth ever more, and still there was no relief. Some were even forced to sell their cattle. The mountain people were worn out and worried, but thankfully, resilience was their chief character trait. Still, by the time the rain finally came one blissful day, when dark clouds gathered on the horizon in a black toiling mass and released their watery load in a wild refreshing deluge over the mountains, it was the time for great rejoicing throughout the Blue Ridge.

To celebrate God's great blessing, Mary invited all the Buckos and their families to lunch the next day, cooking up a storm on her wood-fire stove, with the other families all contributing in the traditional mountain manner. (Oh, how far they had come!) Though she often had several clan families at a time to lunch or supper over the years, this was the first time since that first butchering day so very long ago that the whole lot of them had assembled to feast. It was a time of great fellowship and love and laughter, and watching them tucking in to the grand fare, Mary thought how much she had come to love this clan that was once the scourge of the Blue Ridge. And what's more, how, at last, she felt she truly belonged amongst them.

Falling Leaves and Mountain Ashes

Book VIII

'The End of an Era'

'Malevolent forces, irresistible,
Menace those who are mountain-born.
Loved lifestyles get swept away
As relentlessly as logs tossed,
like matchsticks, into
a flash flood.'

Brenda George

Prologue

*W*hile Blue Ridge mountain families went about their daily lives in blissful ignorance on the isolated hollows and slopes, events were slowly taking shape that would drastically alter their lives forever. George Foreman Pollock, owner of Skyland, and two of his frequent guests, a Washingtonian by the name of Harold Allen and a man called George Judd, became convinced that the Skyland area of the Blue Ridge was the perfect place for the proposed National Park being touted for the eastern United States. Indeed, such was their enthusiasm that they called themselves "Park Nuts". Meanwhile, an organization called Shenandoah Valley Inc. favored the Massanuttan Mountain range as their choice of location for the envisaged park. Pollock invited the members of this group to come to Skyland to convince them to switch their allegiance to the Blue Ridge, where he won the ardent support of L. Ferdinand Zerkel, a Luray businessman. The four then lobbied members of the Southern Appalachian National Park Committee, inviting them to Skyland, as well as members of Shenandoah Valley Inc., who hadn't come the first time around. The result was that both these organizations abandoned their support of their previously favored sites and threw their weight behind the Blue Ridge Mountain bid. To promote a wider interest in the location, a new organization called the Northern Virginia Park Association was formed, uniting the three original proponents, the leaders of Shenandoah Valley Inc. and a few interested Washingtonians in the cause. This led to support by the newspapers in Richmond and Washington, while the "Park Nuts" were so enthused they even spent personal funds to realize their dream. They scored a major victory in December, 1924, when the Southern Appalachian National Park Committee recommended the Blue Ridge Mountains of Virginia as the most logical place for the first National Park in the eastern United States.

During the next summer, yet another group was formed, calling themselves the Shenandoah National Park Association. This statewide group lobbied for the passage of the bill for the establishment of the park. In May, 1926, after sixteen months of working its way through Congress, the bill was finally passed, authorizing the establishment of the Shenandoah National Park, mandating that no federal monies were to be used to purchase the land, and that instead, state and private funds were needed, after which it was up to the State of Virginia to condemn the land and then present it to the Federal Government. The Shenan-

doah National Park Association then began to raise funds for this purpose, launching a highly successful "Buy an Acre" campaign amongst Virginians.

And so plans for the National Park moved slowly, but inexorably, forward. It was finally to be a hundred miles long and comprise approximately 175,000 acres, downscaled from an originally proposed and authorized 521,000 acres, due to a gross underestimation of the market land values by park backers. The proclamation of the Shenandoah National Park was unique in that it did not set aside wilderness area for public use; it actually reclaimed land that was already inhabited or owned by thousands of people. Once the boundaries of the Park had been determined, a large contingent of timber technicians, orchard specialists, grassland experts and building inspectors were dispatched to appraise all properties to ensure that people who lost their land would get a fair price for it. The land was universally condemned under a blanket condemnation law in 1928, to prevent lawsuits by 'stubborn, selfish and avaricious litigants from holding up the acquisition of the land'.

The building of a "Skyline Drive" along the crest of the Blue Ridge was the vision of the Southern Appalachian Mountains Commission in 1924, when it advocated the Blue Ridge for a National Park. After President Herbert Hoover bought 160 acres on Fork Mountain and built his summer "White House" in a hemlock grove, in 1929, the lofty idea of building a "skyline drive" was revived by William Carson, who suggested a paved road to carry President Hoover between his camp at Rapidan and the White House in Washington. He also felt it could be used to publicize the Park. He further argued that the building of it could help mountain families stricken by the devastation of the drought in 1930, by providing some work-relief for them. In 1930, President Hoover backed a bill to allocate drought-relief funds to be used to build the first segment of the envisaged drive, a twelve-mile stretch from Panorama to George Pollock's famous summer resort, Skyland. Construction began in 1931 and, by 1932, Congress had allocated more than $1,000,000 to extend the highway to Front Royal, in the north, and to Jarman's Gap, Waynesboro, in the south.

The Civilian Conservation Corps (or CCC as it became known) was one of Franklin D. Roosevelt's "New Deal" programs, which put unemployed young men, who had been unable to find work during the harsh years of the Depression to work in forests and parks across the nation. The first of the "CCC boys" (as they soon became known), arrived in the Shenandoah in May, 1933, and soon, approximately 1,000 of them, including a fair number of hardy young mountain men, were based within the soon-to-be-established Park. Much of their work was focused on Skyline Drive, the proposed 105-mile mountain parkway, on which they built overlooks and stone walls, and constructed guardrails. They blasted a tunnel through Great Pass Mountain, did sign work, cleared trails, built campgrounds and picnic areas and fought occasional forest fires.

The mountain people still living on proposed Park land began to hear dark whisperings about the creation of the Park and had no idea what was to become of them and, as a result, fear and insecurity ran deep in them. Indeed, the biggest challenge in establishing the Park had been what to do with the people who lived within its proposed borders. Although, initially, the position of Park supporters had been amenable to allowing the mountain folk to remain in their homes after the acquisition of their land or, at least, those who desired to do so, as time went on, nearly all the Park's backers, as well as the state officials in Richmond and the politicians in Washington, began to falsely categorize the mountain folk as backward, ignorant and shiftless.

Some saw them all as moonshining hillbillies of a violent disposition, with a lack of independence, resourcefulness, drive and ambition. The result of this was the generally hard-working, fiercely independent and fun-loving mountain people came to be seen as cultural curiosities, relics of an earlier age, and a problem – a major obstacle to the successful creation of the Park – and the mood suddenly changed towards favoring their complete removal. And because they came to be seen as the main problem, the mountain people were never consulted in any way, or given an opportunity to take part in any of the discussions that would so greatly affect their lives.

This unfair stereotypical view of the mountain people was perhaps first generated by the bad publicity that surrounded the Allen clan back in 1920, and had been perpetuated by further published accounts caricaturing them all as shiftless hillbillies living in squalid conditions. This highly negative view of them, unfortunately, came to be held as the general one. On February 1st, 1934, Arnold Cammarer, the director of the Park, whose own opinion of the mountain people was that there were 'none so canny as certain mountaineer folk and none so disreputable', announced that the Federal Government had declared that they would not accept land for the Park from the state until all the residents had departed the area. This announcement was the final death knell for the mountain folk and shattered their hopes and dreams that they would be allowed to remain on in their homes after the Park's creation.

The Federal Government also insisted that those people forced to leave their land must be relocated to areas suitable for farming and close to job opportunities, schools and medical facilities. Ferdinand Zerkel was chosen to head this relocation project. His first step was to survey the Park's human population and, in 1934, he sent out twenty-five enumerators to interview the remaining families still living in the Park area, to complete an extensive questionnaire on each of them.

After extensive field work, seven sites were finally chosen for resettlement by the displaced mountaineers. They were Ida Valley in Page County, Elton in Rockingham County, C.B.I School in Green County, Woolfton and Madison in

Madison County, and Washington and Flint Hill in Rappahannock County. Each family was to be provided with a homestead consisting of a house, a combination barn/poultry house, a vegetable storage/meat house, and a pig pen with a fenced pig lot. Some were to be provided with 56-acre farms, while most would receive 15-acre subsistence farms and have to hold outside jobs. Of those families interviews by Zerkel's enumerators, 64 had already made plans of their own, a few of the elderly were recommended for special permission to stay in their homes and 293 were selected as homesteader prospects in the federally funded programs especially set up to help them start new lives outside the Park. The remainder, many of whom were older, and therefore unlikely to be able to repay the government loans that would finance the homesteads, were turned over to the state welfare department.

The new removal policy caused great trauma, despair, dissatisfaction and heartache amongst the mountaineers and there was widespread resistance to it. They felt cheated and angry at not being consulted about the events that were to affect them so profoundly. Many had to be forcibly removed to dispossess them of their land. Some felt their land had been grossly undervalued during the evaluation process, especially since they had been forced to sell when the Depression had caused land values to plummet. Infuriated landowners threatened the authorities evicting them, with bodily harm and even death.

Some of the landowners banded together forming the Landowner Protective Association, in 1929, and filed suits against the state which, although to no avail, succeeded in holding up the acquisition process. While landowners at least received payment for their land, tenants and squatters were offered no compensation. As a result, they refused to leave their homes except by force, some of them stubbornly moving to other vacated homes nearby. Eleven years lapsed between the time the bill was passed and the relocation of the mountain people. This transition period was an agonizing one for them, leaving them in limbo, and causing them much heartache, depression and despair.

Before 1934, many mountain folk left the Park area of their own accord, unable to stand the insecurity anymore, or they had no wish to live inside a National Park, or rightly feared that in the end they would be forced to leave anyway. But the vast majority of them wanted to remain on their land and gen-uinely believed they would be allowed to do so, since many state officials, expecting this would indeed be the case, had actually encouraged them to remain in their homes after the state had purchased their land. Even after the state 'blanket condemnation' law was passed, they expected to be able to remain. But they were fighting an irresistible force . . .

It was not until late 1937 that some of the resettlement homes were finished and the resettlement process begun. Skyline Drive was opened at Big Meadows on 15th September, 1934, and within one year, 500,000 people in 150,000 auto-

mobiles had driven along the elevated parkway, and admired the spectacular views that had henceforth been solely for the edification of the mountain folk that lived there. More than $1,300,000 had been raised by 24.000 Virginians, for the acquisition costs plus another $1,000,000 had been added by the Legislature of Virginia, who had arranged for the blanket condemnation of the land in 1928. The mountain people had received very little of this, since most of the mountain land was owned by outsiders – valley farmers who owned large tracts of grazing land, the timber companies and those with mineral concerns. Indeed, more than half of the mountain people lived on land that did not belong to them. Some were tenants, while others were squatters. After eleven years had passed, all litigation was finally settled and the state owned clear title to 250 square miles of Blue Ridge Mountain splendor. The State of Virginia then presented the land to the Federal Government as a gift to the people of the United States.

On December the 26th, 1935, the Shenandoah National Park became a reality. On 3rd July, 1936, President Franklin Roosevelt formally dedicated the Park before a crowd of 5,000 people at Big Meadows. The Shenandoah National Park was now a harsh reality for those mountain people still living inside the Park's boundaries. Alas, for them, time was quickly running out ...

75

The talk about a National Park being created in the Blue Ridge had not been idle rumor, after all. Mary and Zachary Thomas's worries about it were well-founded; within a few years, in an unwelcome invasion, land specialists and surveyors came to lay out the boundaries of the proposed Park. To the horror of the whole Buchanan clan, they embraced half of Fork and Chapman Mountains and took in the whole of Claw and Buck Knob Mountains, Beacon Mountain and most of the hollows and ridges of Bear Rock Mountain and the whole of the Wilderness Valley. The Wilson Run watershed and most of the adjacent Rapidan Valley were also earmarked for Park acquisition. Even Lewis Mountain where Mary was born and raised and where her family still lived fell within Park boundaries.

Mary was devastated by the extent of the cruel sweep. Then disaster struck with the force of a sledge hammer! The fateful decree that would force the mountain people from their beloved mountain homes. This highly disturbing bit of information, heard during the anxious chatter after church one Sunday, struck terror in Mary's heart. She could not believe it! It was unthinkable for them all to lose their homes. It was unthinkable that the Harleys would have to leave Lewis Mountain, and the Buckos, Claw Mountain, let alone all their friends and neighbors scattered around the surrounding mountains.

Zachary Thomas was extremely angry that the Park boosters could have acted in such an arbitrary manner and went about in a thunderous mood, cursing the powers that be. So much so that when one of Zerkel's enumerators crested Eagle Spur to interview Mary and her husband, he sent him skittering hastily back down again followed by blasts from his old Kentucky rifle. Mary could well understand his frustration, however. Suddenly, it seemed that the highly independent Blue Ridge mountain folk no longer had a smidgeon of control over their own lives. They were now subject willy-nilly to both state and federal government intervention. The Buchanan clan's natural aversion to government, spawned in them by their flamboyant patriarch, Obediah, rose fulsomely in his eldest son. In deep despair, Zachary Thomas roared that Eagle Spur legally belonged to him now that his father was gone and nobody would ever drive him from his own land!

Then Louella-Sue, a pretty, winsome girl and their last remaining daughter, for the other five had married into other mountain families and moved away from the mountains, broke her father's heart when she, too, left home and ran off and married a CCC man. She broke much of his spirit too.

It was about this time that Mary was told by Reverend Crawley that he had heard that some of the older mountain folk were being recommended to be allowed to stay in their homes. She heard his words with a stirring of hope. Her family just *had* to be among those chosen to stay behind. And, of course, she had to also ensure that Jed got permission to stay on, despite the fact that he wasn't old, because she knew how it would clean break his heart to leave the mountains he knew and loved so well. She would make them understand that. But she didn't know how to go about it when Zachary Thomas had threatened that he would not allow anyone connected with the scheme to come anywhere near Eagle Spur ever again. After the last time, she could not fail to know he meant it.

As the deadline grew nearer, so the pressure on the mountain people increased. Insecurity was running rife amongst them. They felt as if a noose was slowly being tightened around their anxious necks. Indeed, life for them had changed radically from the time the idea of the National Park was first mooted in 1924. Since they first caught wind of the dark whisperings, they had been living on borrowed time, not knowing when or if they would be forced out of their homes. Increased killings and lawlessness, including a spate of murders, vandalism and fire-setting that followed the establishment of the Park, Mary knew, was their way of expressing their helplessness as these catastrophic events overtook them.

There were at least two fires that she knew of that she suspected were a result of arson. On Beacon Mountain, a forest fire raged out of control for twenty-seven days before they finally managed to extinguish it. Fortunately, it was nowhere near the chapel, which escaped being damaged or burned down. Not long afterwards, a fire started on Bear Rock Mountain, destroying much of the natural habitat, before being extinguished by frantic sack-thrashing members of the Addis, Ficks and Buchanan clans, who emerged from the ordeal, totally exhausted and covered in soot and grime.

When a contingent of specialists came to Claw Mountain, "to assess the land owned by Devon Ansley's heir, his son, Clement", it was a rude shock. Not least of all to Mary! So despite Obediah's loud claims that the mountain had belonged to him, the notches on the trees outlining "his" land, and his self-proclaimed regal title, the Buchanan clan were nothing more than common squatters, after all! The Buchanans had not only hoped, but *believed*, that the land had legally belonged to their father, although his dealings with the legal owner, Devon Ansley, all those years ago, had never been made clear. Now they knew that nothing more than pure unadulterated cheek had kept Obediah Buchanan as "King of Claw Mountain" for so long. It was too much for some of the remaining Buchanans, who, knowing that they would not get a cent of compensation, decided it was time to leave the mountain to get themselves established outside of the Park. They begged Mary and Zachary Thomas to join them, saying that sooner or later they would have to go too. But her husband stubbornly refused to budge, saying he'd rather die than move. Mary felt exactly the same way.

Once she had despised and feared those Buckos leaving the mountain, but now they were family and she was dreadfully sad to see Johnny, Willie and Toad and their families depart Claw Mountain, their humble goods piled up in the back of a borrowed truck, with chicken coops and animals perched precariously on top of a huge unwieldy mound. Clearly, their leaving marked the end of an era, causing a gnawing ache in Mary's heart. Later, they heard that their older sons had all joined the CCC, and were now receiving a welcome thirty dollars a month, of which the government sent twenty-five dollars home to their families. Fortunately, this helped immeasurably in their new lives outside the Park's boundaries.

Like these families, members of the Addis and Ficks families who were tenants, as well as other financially independent families in the Park, couldn't stand the uncertainty any longer and chose to leave the Park before being kicked out. The Galtreys, however, hung on grimly on Buck Knob Mountain, also deeply resenting this dastardly plan by Park officials to dispossess the mountain people of all they held dear.

The months wore on and still nobody came to interview Mary and Zachary Thomas, and they began to hope that they might have decided to simply let them be. But just knowing that they did not own the land they lived on as they had once believed, made Mary feel all the more vulnerable and afraid, as if something that God, Himself, had delivered unto them was now under serious threat . . .

Mary loved Eagle Spur with every fiber of her being, as did Zachary Thomas and Jed. Indeed, she had told Jed from the time he was a baby that one day it would belong to him and she knew that he, in turn, considered it a bequest of great magnitude. She was inconsolable and broke down one day.

Jed came upon her in the cabin weeping into her hands at the kitchen table. He gently touched her shoulder and said sadly, "Never mind, Maw. Please don't cry. I've bin thunkin' on it an' mebbe th' Park is a good thung, after all. It will sure help brung back all th' animals an' birds that have bin destroyed by us mountain folk."

Mary well knew that her eldest son had been long worried about the way the animal and birdlife had been vanishing from the forests over the years. He had often opined that unless the mountain men stopped hunting, there'd soon be nothing left. Mary had seen this for herself. The wildlife of today was nothing compared to the abundance there had been when she first came to the mountain. Maybe it *was* what was needed to save the forests and all that lived in it. But it didn't make things any easier to know that in order for this to happen, it must necessarily destroy their whole way of life.

"Don't you understand, son? We're going to have to leave. I know how much that will hurt you."

In fact, it was more than that. She worried terribly about how her sensitive son would fare in the world outside the mountains.

Jed stayed silent for a long, long time. Then he muttered "Nuthin' ever stays th' same, Maw. Sometimes, you jest gotta let thungs flow and see whar they take you."

The acceptance in his words and the wisdom she had come to expect from her elder son, calmed her a little, but in the days to come, they failed to give her comfort. For despite the ostensibly lofty intentions of those proposing the National Park, the clan had counted on living out their days here. *There must be something to be done!* They could not simply rob people of their birthright.

76

Mary, concerned about her elderly widowed mother and siblings on Lewis Mountain, got Zachary Thomas to take her to visit them in Doc's old buggy, leaving Jed behind to look after the livestock. It was a much more subdued reunion than all those many joyous ones over the years, with the marked exception of the time they had attended her father's funeral. He had died suddenly and unexpectedly in 1913, after a brief illness, and though it was so long ago now, Mary still felt she missed him more each passing year.

He had left the fiddle he had inherited from Grandpaw Meadows to Jed, having never learned to play the thing. Jed, on the other hand, loved singing, and had learned to play the fiddle well, having inherited his natural musical talent from his grandmother, Mary was sure. Indeed, Mary had started up having shindigs on Claw Mountain whenever there was cause for celebration, and Jed always played his fiddle and sang. At shindigs on Lewis Mountain, he used to join in with the other musicians and, overcoming his shyness with girls, even joined in the square dancing. To his mother's great surprise, Jed had the natural fun-loving spirit of most mountain people.

Now the same sense of grief and doom pervaded the air as on that sad occasion of her father's funeral sixteen years ago. Their common fate hung over them as if they were chickens whose necks were on a chopping block. Her mother was a vigorous seventy-eight-year-old now and, despite the fact that she was shrunken and her hair was white, she was still very beautiful.

Mary's sisters came with their husbands and children to visit her and Zachary Thomas, but the atmosphere was positively gloomy. Her sisters were also in their fifties, but they were still slim, golden-haired and very pretty, with delightful young'uns. Percy was not there. He had moved to Luray with his wife, Betty, and their family of five, where he had also joined the CCC. Joe was there, of course. He had lived on at the homestead with their mother after the death of their father, marrying the daughter of a neighbor, a petite brunette, named Mersia Rogers. They had two shy daughters in their late teens, Rose and Tamith, who also lived with them. Joe, now a handsome 61-year-old, especially, seemed very low in spirit. Mary knew how much this home and the mountain meant to him and how being forced to leave it would affect him.

Neighbors came to visit and the talk was angry and despairing, and very depressing. Why had none of the mountain folk whose lives would be most affected by this Park thing been consulted? It was the same as the talk at church, at the general stores, at everywhere the mountain folk gathered or visited. They could not understand this concept, devised by outsiders that would destroy their known and loved lives forever. Mary felt their pain and bewilderment, because it was echoed inside herself and her own family.

And then she learned of a new threat that outraged her. That even though they were to be removed from their former homes, it would not stop at that. The authorities would then *destroy* their homes by setting fire to them, so that the mountain people would not be tempted to return. *What an abomination! Had these people any idea what they were inflicting on her people? Had they not an ounce of compassion inside them? Because if they did, they wouldn't do this terrible thing to them.*

Her family home here at Harley Hollow to go up in flames! She couldn't bear the thought, let alone think of it happening to their beautiful beloved home on Eagle Spur. After hearing that, poor Zachary Thomas could not stand the morbid talk a moment longer and excused himself. Mary felt she couldn't suffer it any longer, either. It pressed down on her chest like a ton weight. Her grandparents had died years back now, but the thought of their cabin perched on the side of the mountain and set amongst trees at Meadows Hollow, with a magnificent view of countless hazy blue mountain ridges in front of it, being burned to the ground, brought fresh grief to Mary. She managed to persuade Joe to go with her to go see it for the last time, and excusing herself apologetically to the company, she exited the cabin with a sense of intense relief.

The old cabin at Meadows Hollow was empty and abandoned, but holding her brother's hand as if they were young children again, Mary could still see Grandmaw sitting on the porch in her rocking chair, smoking her long clay pipe, a wad of tobacco in her cheek, while Grandpaw played his harmonica or fiddle sitting on the bench beside her. They were images she knew she would carry with her to her grave.

She and Joe sat on the side of the mountain amongst the waving blue-grass, talking of their happy shared childhood on this beloved mountain. It was both painful and purging, and they both cried in-between peels of laughter at some funny things they remembered. Though it had been a terrible wrench of the heart to get away, Mary was glad they had come to see the old place.

Later, when she and Joe returned to Harley Hollow, her daintily thin frail little white-haired mother admitted to Mary that they would all be leaving the mountain very soon. The Tuttle family in Richmond had offered her a home and jobs for Joe and the others in their retail stores. They had never forgotten how their mountain kin had looked after their daughter, Emily, before she had succumbed to her illness, all those years ago, long before they had let young Emma stay with them during her schooling and teachers' training days.

Mary couldn't bear the thought of her family leaving so soon, but she realized that it was an offer the Harleys could not refuse, because sooner or later, they would have to leave anyway. Mary could not imagine Lewis Mountain without her family living there or without their beloved log-cabin home, draped in blossoms, standing on it. She and her mother wrapped their arms around one another and wept bitterly.

The next morning, as she and Zachary Thomas left in the old-fashioned fringed buggy, Mary looked back at the old homesite that she had loved so well for the last time, and felt as if her heart was being ripped out of her chest. Her family had gathered there in a silent grieving group to see them off and she took in the scene, willing it to memory, as well as the faces of each loved one, one by one, as if she was destined never to see any of them again.

She beheld the old cabin with fond, aching familiarity, taking in the pink climbing roses, the honeysuckle, the tub of petunias on the porch, the old crabapple tree, the sweet peas creeping up their wire structure at the side of the house. *Home of her happy childhood!* The place that had nurtured her youthful soul. She cried all the bumpy way home, silently cursing the Shenandoah National Park and all who had thought it up in the first place.

* * *

It seemed to Mary that saying goodbye to kin, old neighbors and friends became a regular occurrence from 1934. Every week brought fresh tears and heartbreak, and every Sunday saw the congregation at the Presbyterian Church on Beacon Mountain shrinking smaller and smaller, as people from the surrounding mountains either left the mountains of their own accord, or were systematically removed from their homes by the CCC boys, who would help each family load their furniture onto a dump truck and drive them to one of the resettlement areas to which they had been allocated. Like Sheridan's ruthless army during the Civil War, as each family left, they torched their homes and barns and sheds, so that Mary seldom looked down from Eagle Spur, without seeing plumes of black smoke pumping into the sky from all over the surrounding mountains. It was worse than "The Burning' in some ways, since Sheridan's soldiers were instructed to spare dwellings, which they had for the most part.

Then the folk of the neighboring Bear Rock and Beacon Mountains were struck. With so many of the mountain folk removed and his congregation reduced a trickle, the Presbyterian Church Board transferred Reverend Crawley to Roanoke. The last service proved a heartbreaking one for the small group of mountaineers who attended. Mary and her family bid the kindly reverend farewell with a sense of helpless futility. Did anybody out there understand what they were putting the mountain people through? Mary felt that they were under a devastating military attack without any means of repulsing it! Oh, how she dreaded seeing Claw Mountain go up in smoke. She had no idea of their personal fate either. *Nobody had ever been back to Eagle Spur to complete their question- naire!* Had they somehow been overlooked? Should she alert the authorities to their existence and risk losing everything? She stayed quiet and prayed. The months slipped uneasily by and still there were no further visits by the auth- orities.

I t was early in the spring of 1939 that it finally happened. Mary, in her usual early-morning ritual, went to look at the view from the ridge of Eagle Spur and was shocked and horrified to see black smoke billowing into the sky from Horseshoe Hollow.

"ZACK!" she cried. "JED! THEY'RE TORCHIN' TH' OLD HOMESTEAD! OH MY GOD, ZACK! COME QUICK!"

Zachary Thomas and Jed ran out of the barn at her shouting and, hurrying over to the edge of the ridge to stand beside her, looked to where she was pointing below. They stared sickly down at the billowing smoke escaping the slight indentation in the tall trees where the homestead was, stricken to silence. Zachary Thomas's eyes narrowed and he looked deadly grim. Mary squeezed his hand, wondering what was going on inside him in this awful moment. What did Horseshoe Hollow represent to him right now? *A brutalized childhood? His mother? His siblings? His cruel father?* She didn't know. But she did know that emotions were churning inside him despite his stoic face. Jed was shaking his head in disbelief. He put his arm around his mother's shoulders, drawing her close to him, as she choked back sobs.

"Reckon we'd best go see, Maw," he suggested softly.

The three of them scrambled down the steep slopes of the mountain to Horseshoe Hollow just in time to see a CCC dump truck disappearing down the narrow dirt road that Eli had had built for easier access to the now long-redundant stills. They stared at the licking flames devouring Obediah's cabin, barn and sheds in dumb dismay, emotions tearing at them. Other members of the clan, alerted by the smoke came rushing up to stand beside them in stunned silence, the smoke catching Mary in her throat and smarting her eyes as a frisky breeze whirled in their direction, Mary turned to Zachary Thomas standing at her side, and said accusingly, "Why didn't you tell me they'd received thar eviction orders, Zack?"

He shook his head, eyes narrowed, and grunted, "Were no point upsettin' you a'fore time."

Otis had removed the mules from the barn (they had replaced Obediah's old ones as they died off) and they were snorting and stamping, upset by the leaping flames and the general uproar, as he held them by their reins. Prince, Jed's horse, and the buggy horse, Wishbone, had died some years before, and the buggy and the Model-T Ford belonging to Mary, stood under a nearby tree. Otis, the last Bucko to marry, had been staying at the old homestead with his much younger wife, Irma, and he looked at them now with hot, haunted eyes that said it all.

He told Zachary Thomas that Irma had gone with the CCC boys to their new place at the resettlement area at Madison and that he would follow her the next day with the mules, when the CCC boys had promised to come back for them. The stuff inside the barn and the furniture from the cabin had already been removed by them and was on the dump truck on its way to Madison. The mountain people were not allowed to take any part of their buildings or fences from the homesites or farms, and bits and pieces lay around that the CCC boys had refused to let them take to their new home. It seemed the federal government meant to recycle these to help pay to relocate them.

As she watched the old Buchanan homestead being devoured by fire, Mary remembered how she had come here as an eloping bride, forty years ago almost to the day. How she'd been married here. How long ago that seemed. *A different lifetime.* She had been so horrified about what she had encountered on this mountain. Yet, she'd had since spent so many happy, rewarding years here since those dark days. Then she remembered the tangible terror that had once existed at this homestead. She remembered, with horror, being led like a cow on a rope, heavily pregnant, and tied to the porch post, to witness the most appalling scene of her entire life – twenty-five cruel lashes raining down on a frail young boy's back. She thought of Obediah that day, breathing heavily with exertion, his face and thickly-furred chest saturated with salt and sweat, his damp hair raised in devil's horns. Yet, contrarily, how utterly charming he had been when he had given her Hedina's oak chest. Then he had vanished without a trace! At first, it was as if he'd been swallowed up in quick-sand. She had not dared tell a single soul that the *Galtreys* had been responsible for his disappearance and subsequent demise.

Soon cries went up all over the mountain as other CCC boys in other dump trucks systematically torched and plundered lives on Claw Mountain. Although the inhabitants of the mountain had all received their eviction notices, they just hadn't known the exact day they would come.

Mary had no stomach to witness any more of it up close. Indeed, she felt weak and feverish. She returned to Eagle Spur sick at heart, leaving Zachary Thomas and Jed to assist and comfort his kin. She had always been the strong one in the past, the one who had comforted those on this great mountain in their times of need or trouble or grief. Yet she felt totally incapable of doing so this time. She could not look into their eyes and see the raw pain there that no words could take away. All her adult life she had fought for them, sometimes even against them, and now she felt she had no more fight left in her.

Against Zachary Thomas's pleas for her not to do so, she compulsively went to stand at the end of the ridge to watch as homesite after homesite on the massive mountain became consumed in flames and belching smoke. *Oh God, thar goes Emma's Maw's old place! Clem's! Toad's!* It was as if the whole world had gone mad. She could not bear what was happening. A great bruising hurting descended on her chest, tightening it in a vice-like grip. She felt stifled and unable to breathe, as tears streamed silently down her face. Even the animals in the barn seemed skittish and unsettled, if they sensed something real bad was happening down below.

* * *

The dreadful, calamitous day finally drew to an end. Zachary Thomas and Jed returned to Eagle Spur, with Otis in tow. They were all withdrawn and deeply depressed. Mary knew without asking that they were the last human beings left on the whole of Claw Mountain. She felt strange. Raw inside. Lonely. Sad. Deserted. Had the government representatives simply forgotten about her and Zack, or had they been left till last for a reason? Could she stand the uncertainty of not knowing? Of having the anguish of what had happened today to her close kin and neighbors happen to her tomorrow or the next day or the day after that.

That night she couldn't sleep. She tossed and turned on Obediah and Hedina's fine old brass bed, trying to find a solution, but feeling a deep sense of doom invading her being. She prayed long and deeply, begging God to help her save Eagle Spur. She felt flushed, feverish and slightly nauseous. But by the morning, although she felt considerably worse, her mind was made up. *She would not give up Eagle Spur without a fight!*

She refused to simply yield to the inevitable. None of them could abide the thought of leaving such a remarkably beautiful spot – a place that had fed her soul from the moment she had ascended to its heady heights, with its Sacred Forest, the Indian burial mound, and all that they had meant to her and Jed. Why, Jed had been born and raised here! *Had lived here nearly forty years.* He knew nothing of the world beyond this isolated mountain. He loved and hallowed it more than any person alive, even more than she and Zachary Thomas, and God knows how much they both loved their beloved home on Eagle Spur. *The place was his by divine right!* She knew she was thinking like Obediah once had, but it was true.

After Mary had given them breakfast, unable to eat a morsel herself, she and Zachary Thomas went with Otis back to Horseshoe Hollow, while Jed went for his daily sojourn into the tableland forest. Having no stomach for seeing the still-smoking ruins of his childhood home, or the departure of his brother when the CCC boys came to transport him and the mules down to Madison, Zachary Thomas embraced his brother in a brief bear hug, tears filling his eye before breaking off to go tracking in the Wilderness, taking his old-fashioned long-muzzled Kentucky rifle and his coon dogs with him.

Before he left, he sternly instructed Mary to go back up to Eagle Spur and get back into bed. He said she was looking very flushed and clearly had a temperature. Mary had nodded meekly but, as soon as he left, she'd descended the path to Horseshoe Hollow and jumped into her Model-T Ford with the intention of speeding down to the general store at Graves Mill in it, knowing if she left it any longer, it might be too late. *It was her last hope!*

As it was, Otis didn't want to let her go, because even he could see how ill she looked. But he must have seen the desperation in her eyes, because he finally relented with a huge sigh and let her drive off after she had sworn him to secrecy about the trip, telling him Zachary Thomas would be extremely angry with her if he ever found out she had disobeyed him. She did not tell her depressed brother-in-law the reason why she needed to go to the store so urgently.

When she finally arrived at the general store, set on stilts amongst big shady trees, she felt dizzy and weak, her skin burning and slicked with sweat, but she forced herself to go inside, heading straight for the public telephone. She lifted the receiver and asked the operator to connect her with the Washington Exchange. She dialed the number given to her by the operator with a shaking finger, praying he would be home. It was a call she dreaded making, but she knew she had no alternative. Then a man's voice answered. The moment she recognized who was speaking, Mary felt herself begin to shake from head to foot and a feeling of loathing entered her veins. It took all her will to stem the vomit that rose in her throat. She said breathlessly, "Eli, it's Mary. I need yer help ..."

77

Beset with the cruel rigors of typhoid fever, Mary lay in a sweat-drenched bed. She was in the throes of a high fever, her temperature so high, she felt as if her blood was being boiled from the inside. Her long loosened hair was wet and plastered to the sides of her head. Large rose-colored spots had spread over her chest and stomach in a sinister rash and she was suffering terrible cramps accompanied by severe abdominal bleeding. She wore that beautiful white nightgown that had once belonged to Hedina Buchanan, who had preceded her to the spirit world, and whom she had never met. The garment – and indeed, the dead woman – had played a significant part in Mary's life, one way or another, and it was fitting that it should now serve as her death garment. Mary wore it as a kind of tribute to her long-deceased mother-in-law, her husband's highborn mother, who she never had the honor of meeting.

To Mary, the woman had been an unsung heroine, who had suffered untold hardships and heartache in her arduous life in the mountains. Mary had called on her invisible strength any number of times over the years. Indeed, she felt her presence now as she had so often through her own years of struggle. It grieved Mary that the exquisite nightgown that she had so seldom worn was now soiled with her blood and sodden to the touch. In the soothing silence she could hear God's sweet voice calling her home and felt at peace.

Then a cramp hit her of such intensity that it caused her to convulse in her bed. She gasped and uttered a low crooning moan. This was far worse than any of her eight childbirths and tears spilled out of her eyes and rolled down the sides of her face in an unending stream. Like everything else in life, death was not easy. It was hard-won as were all worthwhile things, she had found. She was not afraid of death for she knew it was death unto life, and that she would see again her beloved father and the two precious babies she had buried under the dead chestnut tree.

She felt the anxious pressure of her husband's hand upon her own then he stood up and gently wiped the tears away with a thumb, his deeply wrinkled, gray-bearded face creased with worry. Thankfully, Zachary Thomas had at last accepted the inevitable and had ceased trying to persuade her to go to a valley hospital. She knew that it was her time to go and that nothing would change that. More than anything she wanted to die with those she loved, in a place she loved more than any other in this world rather than in the sterile confines of an unfamiliar hospital . . .

Zachary Thomas sat on a wooden chair beside Mary holding her hand as she lay with her eyes closed on the big brass double bed, periodically wiping her burning, damp forehead with a cold wet rag. The thermometer that Dr. Darwin had given him to monitor her fever had reached an alarming 104 degrees and had stayed there for days. He had loosened her thick long hair that he loved so much from its customary bun and it was lying on either side of her sallow-skinned sweat-glistening, sunken face in long, black, wet strands that were lightly strewn with gray. At fifty-nine years old, her face barely had a wrinkle.

Despite the fact that he had kept anxious vigil over her for many days now, and that she had taken the medication Dr. Darwin had given her, and that he, himself, had used the full range of his apothecary on her, there had been no improvement. She was dying, he knew, beyond the help of any hospital he might have taken her to. She had taken the "mountain fever" too bad.

He had warned her not to go and take care of Gussie Galtrey, who had apparently come down bad with it, according to Perda Galtrey, Gussie's great-niece, the scrawny young woman who'd summoned Mary to help tend to her. But Mary always rushed to wherever she was needed and immediately left with her. It mattered not to her that mountain fever, that dreaded foe, or typhoid fever, as Dr. Darwin called it, was as catching as the smallpox and generally fatal. She'd cleaned and fed and looked after the sick old woman for days, finally returning home to Eagle Spur from Buck Knob Mountain exhausted from lack of sleep. To those designated to look after Gussie after she had gone, she had preached the necessity for washing hands and keeping clean, and had further instructed them to bury Gussie's feces so that flies would not settle on them to ensure the disease did not spread. She had been taught these hygienic measures by Dr. Darwin, which she preached whenever she came across a case. But while Gussie's fever had broken and she had been on the road to recovery when Mary had left her, Mary had taken the fever bad herself.

As soon as Zachary Thomas had recognized, with a sinking heart, the first telltale symptoms, on the day that Otis left the mountain, he had sent Jed to fetch Dr. Darwin and tell him of his strong belief that she had caught mountain fever. Like the good doctor that he was, the doctor had come without hesitation, and found her already in the firm grip of the fever. While he examined her the doctor had told Mary that Emma had begged him to let her come and see her, but he had persuaded her not to. But it was not until he had told Emma the story of Mary Mallon, who became known as "Typhoid Mary", in 1906, that she had finally relented. "Typhoid Mary" had become an inadvertent carrier of the disease, infecting fifty-three people, three of whom had died. The doctor had pointed out to Emma that she could not risk infecting the children she was teaching at the school in Carlisle. Of course, Emma had been a regular visitor to Eagle Spur over the years since she and Mary had shared such a close relationship. Emma had always been a fearless one and Zachary Thomas could just imagine how much it must have cost her to heed her husband's wise words.

Zachary Thomas had doubted that Mary had heard a single word of what Dr. Darwin had said, though. Although she nodded as if she understood, her eyes were wild and darting about feverishly. Taking Zachary Thomas aside, a very worried-looking, graying Dr. Darwin had warned him that even if he had managed to persuade Mary to go to a hospital, which he had been unable to, there was very little he could do for her even there, beyond supportive measures, and he strongly doubted she would pull through. He said he'd never seen a case of typhoid fever this bad before. Zachary Thomas hadn't either.

The doctor stressed that in the event of her death, she must be washed down with disinfectant and there should be a closed coffin to prevent the risk of any mourners catching the disease. His words had struck terror in Zachary Thomas's heart. He had listened to the doctor with pain in his eyes and a heavy ache in his heart that was almost too great to bear. No, he told himself, the doctor did not know how tough Mary was. She could do anything she put a mind to. *She would pull through!* She had to pull through.

At first, despite the doctor's opinion that there was nothing more to be done for her, unable to let her go, and praying for a miracle, Zachary Thomas kept begging her to go to the hospital.

"No," she had whispered weakly the first time he had asked. "I want to die in peace in my own home, here at Eagle Spur, with my husband and son . . .," she had broken off then, her mouth dry, and he had wet her lips with sprinkles of water from a wet cloth.

He had finally been forced to accept the inevitable and he no longer pressured her. The journey alone would likely kill her, anyway. When she had returned from her mysterious mission to the general store that day, and he had insisted that she go straight to bed, Mary had been so worried that he and Jed would catch the fever, she had told them that they must wash their hands frequently, that they must not touch her and that they must be careful when getting rid of her waste matter. He and Jed had taken it in turns looking after her so each could snatch a few winks of sleep. While they were careful to obey the rules of hygiene as far as they could, they ignored her entreaties not to touch her, and they bathed her and changed her nightgowns and her bedclothes, and tried to feed her, but she was semi-conscious for most of the time and had no appetite when she surfaced at odd times.

Watching his beloved succumb to the terrible disease was a nightmare for Zachary Thomas. It seemed so cruel to him that Mary had contracted the fever after saving somebody else with it. *That darned Galtrey woman!* Those Galtreys had been a curse to his family one way or another, his whole life. If they had not sent Perda to fetch Mary, she wouldn't be lying here now on the brink of death. And the end was very near now, Zachary Thomas could tell. He had watched his sick young brother, Jamie, all those years ago and had sensed the imminence of his death back then too. Until a few minutes ago, Jed had shared this agonizing vigil with him, but he had left minutes ago, saying he needed to enter the sanctuary of his beloved forest to restore his soul. He had gently squeezed his mother's hand and kissed her forehead and Zachary Thomas knew he was

566

mentally saying his goodbyes to her. He was a gentle, sensitive man and Zachary Thomas was sure that his son had sensed his own need to be alone with the woman with whom he'd spent a good part of a lifetime.

As Zachary Thomas anxiously watched over her, she opened her eyes and slowly raising a hand, swept it lovingly over his anxious, weather-beaten face, smiling gently at him.

"It's time, my love," she said softly, without a trace of fear in her clear brown eyes. Indeed, she was facing death in the way she had faced life – *fearlessly!* And with the common sense and lack of self-pity that was typical of her. "You will join me when it's yer time, Zack. I don't know when that will be, of course, but I will be waitin' fer you. You mustn't grieve for me too much. Promise me you won't. I couldn't bear to cause you pain."

Zachary Thomas turned away, unable to promise such a thing, knowing that her death would tear his heart out. He could not bear to face the inevitable. Mary was as much a necessary part of him as were his heart and his lungs. Without her, he wouldn't be able to go on, he knew. She had borne him a fine family of eight children, two whom had died in early childhood, and theirs had been a strong and deep relationship that had survived much. It was unthinkable that she should leave him now.

"And you must marry agin, y'hear?" she whispered. "I won't mind. I won't have you gittin' lonesome. And, when you git off th' mountain, git Jed to git hisself a girl too. He won't have them critters of his to keep him company down in th' valley. He'll need somebody too. He's a handsome young man, but I worry so much fer him, Zack. Make real sure he chooses a real nice girl - somebody who'll appreciate him fer who he is. And bury me here, Zack. Under th' old dead chestnut tree. Next to my two little angels . . ."

Zachary Thomas nodded, tears rolling down his cheeks, a terrible ache in his throat, which stopped any words from coming – *marry again?* She did not know it, but he could never marry again, for he had not been married a first time! He had kept his lonely secret of their bogus wedding for so many years, yet now, with her on her deathbed, it seemed a terrible sin for him not to admit it to her and beg her forgiveness. Guilt had gnawed at him for years, even though he knew of many mountain folk who had never got married because of the remoteness of their hollows and the lack of access to genuine preachers. He'd heard tell it was common throughout the Blue Ridge for a preacher to come upon whole families from young couples to the grandparents, who'd never married for this reason, and he'd up and done the deed for the whole danged bunch of them. But Zachary Thomas was so afraid. What if she died cursing him to her grave?

He remembered the day he had "married" her now, in his father's cabin at Horseshoe Hollow. She had looked so beautiful dressed in his mother's finery, a spunky eighteen-year-old out to change the whole darned world, though he hadn't known it at the time and she didn't either, he fancied. Well, maybe not the whole world, but Claw Mountain, that's for sure. She was known throughout the Blue Ridge for the changes she had brought about in these parts. It'd been forty years now. *Forty years!* How they had flashed by. And yet in another way, they had stood still. *Timeless.* He was an old man now. Seventy-one years old and he'd been feeling every last one of them of late. The uncertainty of the last few years had been an unbearable strain on him.

Zachary Thomas finally found his voice. "Mary, thar's somethung I've got to tell you. Now you gonna be real mad and I sure as heck don't want to upset you none."

"What is it, Zack?" she whispered huskily. "Tell me. I won't be mad, I promise."

"Mary, I did a terrible thung to you . . . a long time ago."

She stirred in her bed. "What was that, Zack?"

It took all his courage to get the next words out. "D'you remember that thar preacher man, Horace Cleats?"

"Of course I do. He married us."

"Well, that's jest it, Mary. He did marry us, and he didn't."

Her eyes clouded over with puzzlement. "What do you mean, Zachary Thomas?"

Zachary Thomas shifted in his seat and sniffed hugely, feeling a wave of hot, awful shame overcome him. "'Fraid he weren't no preacher, Mary."

"What do you mean?" she repeated incredulously.

"I mean we ain't married. He weren't no preacher. He were a member of th' Addis clan."

"You mean . . . you mean you done *tricked* me?"

"Yeah, 'fraid I did. I jest knew you wouldn't agree to come to Claw Mountain with me less'n I promised to marry you, and I couldn't wait to do all that courtin' stuff. Thunk you were underage without yer parent's consent anyhow. Jest knew yer paw wouldn't stand fer it. Oh, Mary, I've wanted to tell you th' truth fer years, but I was too ashamed."

As stark realization visibly set in, Mary swallowed hard, her face such a mask of misery and shock that he bitterly regretted telling her.

She swallowed hard, her voice barely a whisper. "So why are you tellin' me now?"

"Guess I'm real skeer'd my sin will become yer sin and th' good Lord won't let you in whar you rightly b'long. I couldn't live with m'self, knowin' mebbe you wouldn't git into heaven 'cuz of me. Figger'd maybe we ought to pray together fer forgiveness, th' two of us."

There was a long drawn-out period of silence. Then she murmured, "If'n that's what you want . . . let's do it."

Zachary Thomas bowed his head, waiting for her to pray as she always had. But there was a terrible silence and, for an awful moment, Zachary Thomas thought that she must have gone. His eyes opened and flew to her face. But no, she was still with him, her chest rising and falling slightly, her eyes closed, a look of consternation on her face.

"Go on then," he urged.

"No," she whispered. "You pray this time, Zack. You need to rid yerself of this terrible sin."

Zachary Thomas swallowed hard. He had never prayed out loud before and he stumbled over his clumsy words, which hardly seem remotely adequate for the magnitude of the sin. He finished with, "Receive her into paradise, oh, Lord. Don't send her to them lickin' flames of hell 'cuz of me, I beg." He opened his eyes to find Mary staring at him strangely, and felt terribly afraid. "Mary, please say you forgive me. I couldn't bear hit if'n you didn't."

* * *

*T*o *think that all these years, she had been living a lie!* Zachary Thomas's words had shocked her beyond belief. How could this be? Her mind tiredly roved the distant decades seeking the final remedy of a life lived in such utter falsehood. Through burning hallucitory mists, she began to see with compelling clarity the events that had shaped her destiny. So much had happened in that time. So much . . .

She stirred in her reverie, gazing with dimming hazel eyes at the man who had caused her this belated suffering. His face was wracked with so much pain and torment that her heart twisted with anguish inside her. Did she have the right to blame him when she had kept her own dark secret for so long . . .?

The shadows in the room played strange tricks with Mary's mind. For a moment, Zachary Thomas seemed young and handsome still, not stooped and gray with age. His piercing turquoise-green eyes had scarcely faded and lost none of their power to unsettle. And seeing him as she'd known him back then, made love for him come flooding back into her heart. They had been through so much and been so happy together. He had been the solid rock that she had leaned on over the years. She could never turn her back on him, especially now. Mary smiled then, faintly.

"Oh, I do forgive you, Zack," she whispered, against a dry throat. "I guess I always knew deep down inside that Preacher Cleats weren't no real preacher. But even if he wasn't one, you were th' best darned husband any wimmin could ever ask fer. In my eyes, you were and *are* my husband in every respect and I feel no shame in it. *I love you*, Zachary Thomas. I always have an' I will fer all eternity. And Lord, how happy I've bin with you, Zack. It's bin so wonderful all these years, livin' with you and our family in this here paradise on earth. Why that's . . ." She lapsed into silence, suddenly much too tired to go on.

Zachary Thomas gave her a look of profound, indescribable relief at her words, and visibly fought back huge sobs.

"Oh, Mary," he said distraughtly, his cheeks wetted by an unending deluge of tears, "mebbe we weren't hitched up fer real, but I swar we were in spirit. I never thought of you as nuthin' but my wife. I've bin so proud to have you fer my wife. And I've loved you from th' moment my eyes laid themselves upon you in that thar general store when you gave my brother, Eli, sech a hard time."

"Me, too." She gave him a sweet, serene smile that she could see filled him with raw emotion and pain. "Oh, my love . . . ," she whispered weakly.

And then suddenly, to her surprise, she saw the huge Indian spirit who was the guardian of the burial site, standing slightly behind and to the side of her husband. He was smiling, his paint-encircled coal-black eyes glowing as he came forward and held out a hand to her.

"It's time," he said, without words.

It seemed like the most natural thing in the world to do as he said. With one last longing look at her beloved husband, Mary took the Indian's hand . . .

78

*T*he displaced mountain folk of Claw Mountain and all the surrounding mountains within a radius of fifty miles flocked to Mary Buchanan's funeral like wild birds to flung seed. Hundreds upon hundreds of them scaled the steep narrow pathway between giant craggy buttresses of gray granite rock to get to Eagle Spur where she was to be buried. After Jed had telephoned some family members and friends from the Graves Mill general store, news of her death had gone out to the mountain families who had left the Park area, like wild bees swarming through a valley. These folk dashed to other general stores to telephone other old neighbors and kin who had also left their old mountain homes, circulating the news through the resettlement areas of Ida Valley, Elkton, C.B.I. School, Wolftown, Madison, Washington and Flint Hill, and still further afield, to those financially independent mountain folk who had scattered in towns and cities throughout Virginia.

From across the state, displaced mountain folk boarded pick-up trucks and automobiles for the trip to Claw Mountain, taking old rocky logging trails and back roads that were now closed to Park visitors, to get there. But these mountains had once been home, after all! And such a special occasion demanded bending the rules some. After reaching Claw Mountain, they climbed the difficult, formidable heights to reach the old homesite at Eagle Spur, spreading out in a sea of bodies from the very edge of the ridge, wherefrom was the magnificent view that had enchanted the departed mountain woman her whole married life. The throng surrounded the cabin and outbuildings, and stretched right to the edge of the tableland forest on the other side.

It was a rare honor, this huge gathering of hardy displaced Blue Ridge mountain folk – but then they all knew what a rare and special person Mary Harley Buchanan had been. Many of them had only heard of her by reputation, rather than by acquaintanceship, friendship or kinship, for she had grown to be a legend in these parts – the woman who had single-handedly tamed the notorious Buckos of Claw Mountain! As a slim, innocent eighteen-year-old mountain lass, she had eloped to the most feared mountain of the entire Blue Ridge, and through love, compassion, tenaciousness and fearlessness, she had healed and transformed it. What's more she had been responsible for stopping one of the most famous and ugly feuds in the Blue Ridge – the thirty-year feud between the Buchanan and Galtrey clans. Once, Claw Mountain had rung to the sound of gunfire and drunken laughter, whereas until the dedication of the Shenandoah National Park five years ago, it had even boasted a school house and a full-time teacher. Many of the pupils from The Emily Tuttle School on Claw Mountain had gone on to attend high school in the valley. A few had even gone on to graduate college, because of Mary's determination to cut the curse of ignorance on this once-backward and fiercely hostile mountain. And not being satisfied with all that, she had brought religion to Claw Mountain, which had resulted in a church being built on the neighboring Beacon Mountain. Nothing had been too much trouble to her, nor was there a problem too big to surmoun, and, in recent years, she could be seen driving around in her Model-T Ford ministering to her friends and neighbors over all the surrounding mountains. So it was no surprise to anyone that this remarkable woman, who had brought love and compassion to all those souls she came into contact with, was being labeled, in death, a saint . . .

Zachary Thomas, dressed in his smartest clothes and wearing his seldom-used shoes as befitted the occasion, felt utterly devastated. He hadn't worn these clothes for a long time – since the church was abandoned, in fact, and they hung on him, such was the toll that the last decade or so had placed on him. He and Jed, who was similarly dressed in his Sunday best, stood together beside his wife's coffin with their heads bent, both tormented with grief. Zachary Thomas could barely contain his – he wanted to curse and holler and damn God. Anything to stop the cruel wracking pain that engulfed him like some horrible disease, making him feel raw and bleeding inside.

Beside him, Jed looked face-wracked and as inconsolable. Zachary Thomas alone knew how very close he had been to his mother. They had shared such a deep understanding that very often they seemed to know what the other was thinking, without words. All they needed was a slight nod, the touch of a hand, a meeting of the eyes. Such was their incredible closeness that he had often felt excluded by them. Perhaps that is why he had turned to his other son, Caleb, so long ago now. To Caleb, he had been king. Yet, Zachary Thomas had grown close to Jed himself these past ten years or so. His elder son had often accompanied him when he went to the Wilderness – though never when he was hunting – and they would be together for hours on end without saying a single word. He realized that Jed was very much like him in many ways. He loved the solitude and didn't need people around to stimulate him.

He was continually being amazed at his son's intimate knowledge of the natural world they inhabited. Zachary Thomas had always considered himself an expert on forest- and mountain-lore, but Jed seemed to add a whole new dimension to everything, till Zachary Thomas felt almost blind in comparison to him, thereby fast gaining his admiration and respect.

He knew that only Jed could fully appreciate what was going on inside him at that moment. The two of them, staunch loners both, would much rather have been on their own right now, instead of having this huge crowd witnessing their pain. Yet, despite this, he could not deny that this remarkable farewell was entirely fitting, for there was no doubt that Mary Harley Buchanan – the wife he had loved so deeply for forty years – was a woman who had made an indelible mark on these mountains. He hadn't seen a turn-out like this for a funeral since that of Doc Adams back in 1918! And then some.

Mary's family was well-represented and stood looking stunned by her unexpected death. Joe Harley, Mary's brother, stood on one side of him and Jed on the other. Joe, who had always been so close to Mary, was here with his family and seemed stricken with grief. And Mary's sisters, Lona, Laura and Nellie and their families, were here too, as well as Percy and his family. Even Ellie, Mary's frail seventy-eight-year-old mother had climbed the treacherous slopes to attend her daughter's funeral. They could not believe she was dead when they had seen her alive and well (if most unhappy about current events), just weeks ago.

Zachary Thomas's other son, Caleb, and his brood, who still lived in Front Royal, just outside the northern entrance to the Park, had come to attend the funeral too. But his second son's glad rags and cool aloofness – the cold, derisive eyes that mocked everything he held precious did nothing to comfort Zachary Thomas. Caleb, now a somewhat portly, middle-aged man, had barely shaken his hand. How could a man and his son have become such strangers to one another? Caleb seemed like a pompous fool to his father now. To think that he had once favored this cold snotty fellow over *Jed*. Never had Zachary Thomas appreciated Jed's quiet strength more.

Caleb's family, of whom only his dark-haired wife and first child he had met, all seemed timid and shy and barely raised their eyes to him. Mary had traveled to Front Royal to see them once and, over the years, had invited the family to come visit over and over again, but it had taken her death to get them here.

Zachary Thomas's daughters were there, too, with his grandchildren gathered around their skirts, along with their husbands. Of them all, he was closest to dark-haired Harriet, who was her mother all over again. Though his daughters hadn't visited Eagle Spur much since they left to get married, at least they had all been sweet and doting, hugging him and telling them how sorry they were and how much they had loved their mother.

But his thoughts soon shifted back to the woman he had lost. Life was unthinkable without Mary! Her strength and compassion and joy of life! Over the last few days, wild with grief, all he could think about was killing himself so that he could join her. But he knew she would strongly disapprove. Besides, what a terrible legacy to leave poor Jed with. What a wonderful wife Mary had turned out to be! The hatred and scorn and derision she had initially met with from his kin had soon vanished, and now the last few remaining Buckos and the families, the squatter and tenant folk of the Addis and the Ficks clans and those from mountains much further afield, already forced from their mountain homes, wept unashamedly. Even the Galtreys of Buck Knob Mountain, former arch enemies of the Buchanan clan, who had never before set foot on Claw Mountain except to commit an act of revenge, stood wet-eyed among the mourners to pay unique final tribute to her. They had been evicted from their homes at the same time as the Buchanans, yet they too had returned in numbers to mourn her death. That was the effect she had had on all who came into contact with her.

Despite the summer heat, on the heady heights of Eagle Spur, the air was much cooler. Mourners whose faces and bare arms that had been slick with sweat from the steep climb, now welcomed the freshness of the light breeze that rustled leaves and stirred the air currents, as they listened to the moving eulogy being given by Reverend Crawley, who was taking the service. Gray-haired and confident with the lofty sweep of his calling, he put into words what was written on every mourner's heart. The reverend's voice rang out in the hazy summer air, resonating with truth and harmony.

Above them, the wing-spread eagles of Eagle Spur were circling the sky in uncommon numbers, giving loud mournful cries that echoed all around, adding to the feeling of desolation and sorrow. The grave was already dug, every shovelful by Zachary Thomas's own hands. He had even spurned Jed's help. Besides insisting on stripping and washing down the corpse of his beloved wife with disinfectant as Dr. Darwin had instructed him, all by himself, and clothing her in his mother's dress Mary had worn to get "wed" in, he wanted to do this one last thing for her. But the hole, beside the graves of his two darling little girls, Mattie and Joannie, was filled with his tears. Behind the graves stood the once-mighty relic of mountain good times, the huge gray stump of the magnificent old chestnut tree that used to spread its glory over much of the yard.

The withered stump, still about thirty feet tall, was covered with Virginia creeper and, to the right of it, stood the beautiful paulownia or "Princess Tree" of Japanese origin with its heart-shaped leaves and clusters of purplish flowers, that Mary had planted as a special tribute to it. She had requested that she be buried at the foot of this special old dead chestnut tree, so that her dust and that of the doomed old tree would mingle and become entwined together throughout eternity. Thinking about the woman she was and her deep love of Nature, Zachary Thomas could not think of anything more fitting than that . . .

79

One man stood apart at the very edge of the ridge, dry-eyed and stoic. He was dressed in an expensive double-breasted tailor-made suit of dark gray, with a thin white stripe, matching Italian hand-stitched shoes made of finest leather, and was wearing a neat gray hat. He had driven his black Cadillac up the narrow rocky mountain road, now grassy, overgrown and barely discernable, up past his father's fire-destroyed homestead before parking it far off the beaten track under a large evergreen tree, climbing out and pressing the rest of the way up to Eagle Spur by foot, passing scores of mountain folk dressed in their Sunday best, doing the same thing.

Seeing their simple homemade outfits made him realize how good Washington, Prohibition and the Depression had been to him. The distillery, which had produced large quantities of the finest whiskey to come out of the Blue Ridge, had set him on the road to fortune. But boot-legging inferior brands had made him rich and powerful. Eli still lived in Washington, in a twilight world that ranged between associating with corrupt politicians, straight politicians, and the cream of Washington society, which included the president himself, the effects and rough edges of his mountain-cracker upbringing honed remarkably smooth, his speech as eloquent as his father's had once been. He had kept the strong, lean build of his mountain youth, but his once bright-yellow hair had turned slightly paler with the passing years and the whiteness of his facial scar blended in more with an otherwise handsome face turned pasty with city living. His pistol was now a Dillenger, tucked discreetly into a holster beneath his left armpit, though he had kept his two Iver Johnson .32 caliber nickel-plated pocket revolvers, with four-inch blue steel barrels and an Owl's head on the grips – each grooved with enough notches to move a genuine mountain man to considerable sentiment.

The Dillenger had never been fired. He had felt an odd aversion to killing ever since he had left this accursed mountain and the memories of such fighting successes of a wild heller mountain youth when killing was almost as natural to him as breathing, were as bitter as ashes on his tongue right now. Of these killings, he bitterly regretted only one. *The Galtrey boy!* He had lived with the painful guilt of that reprehensible act ever since. He often questioned himself about why he had done it, but it remained a mystery to him. Perhaps it was because the boy had reminded him so much of himself at that age? *A symbolic killing of himself?*

To this day, the child haunted him. The look of wide-eyed fright on his face when he recognized them. The look of terror when he saw the knife. But he'd been so brave. He had not even cried out when Eli forced his head under the water again and again and held it there, while he was struggling in Jake's firm grip. Then the bubbles and the struggles had ceased and it was the turn of his knife. It was over in a matter of seconds. The boy, already dead, was mutilated, the river running red with his innocent blood. It was only then that it had hit him what he'd done. It had sickened him to his stomach. *Child killer!* He'd wiped the blade of his knife against the leg of his dungarees and then, unable to look his brothers, Jake and Samuel, in the eye, he'd turned grimly away after swearing them to secrecy.

All the other killings he didn't even regard as murder and had felt no remorse for them. In the remote hollows and mountains of the Blue Ridge, mountain men had for centuries sought their own justice! The Buckos, in common with them, had cussed, raised hell and killed with no legal repercussions whatsoever, except that Sheriff Coley had been a constant thorn in Eli's side. The only people Eli cared about at all were kin. *The Buckos!* Once he had reveled in the notoriety of being the meanest one of them all, now he felt embarrassed at the thought of the total lack of sophistication that implied, especially amongst his more refined Washington politician and high society friends.

Suddenly, Eli was aware of a middle-aged woman standing beside him, neatly dressed in a black, tailored suit and black high-heeled pumps. She wore a black hat with a veil and her hair beneath it was bunched into fat fair curls. She lifted the veil and turned to glare at him with narrowed pale-blue eyes. He could feel the blast of her contempt. It was only then that he recognized his niece, Emma.

Without the solace of a family of his own, his loyalty had remained staunchly with the clan. He had kept up on all the members of the clan, mainly through Jake, rejoicing in their triumphs and ruing their failures, griefs and sorrows. He remembered the time Emma had come to him years ago, long before she left the mountain to go to high school in Richmond, and told him that she had witnessed him and Jake murdering the Galtrey child, with Samuel looking on. She said if he didn't stop pulling down the brush arbors, she would report the matter to Sheriff Coley and testify in court as an eye-witness against him. Eli had been angry and highly alarmed. The sheriff had been after his blood for years, after all, and he knew that the murder of a child could never be challenged as self-defense, the pretext that freed most mountain men from the jails on the rare occasions when they had been forced to appear in court over killings.

He'd even briefly considered killing Emma, too, but he didn't have it in him to kill another child. Besides, he'd always admired little fair-haired Emma with those fierce pale-blue eyes narrowed into slits. She had been full of sass and spunk and grit, yet, like it had for him, city-living had brought out an unexpected gentility. Maybe breeding had counted for something, after all. Both his parents had been of the old-Virginian "aristocracy". Well, he'd been forced to agree to stop pulling down the brush arbors on the one condition that she did not tell Mary the reason why. Especially, he did not want Mary to know that he had killed a defenseless child, or that a shrimp like Emma was blackmailing him in the manner that she was. Emma must have kept her promise, otherwise Mary would have challenged him about it for sure. That had been another good reason for him to leave the mountain and go to Washington.

Well, Emma had not only graduated high school but had trained as a teacher at college, returning to the mountains to teach mountain children at the school on Claw Mountain when it was offered to her after Miss Prescott had got married to a man she'd met in Winchester on a vacation, and moved away. When the school on Claw Mountain was closed after the opening of the Park, Emma had moved to Carlisle, and lived in Doc Adams' old house that he left her in his will, and he'd heard she now taught at a local school there. Word had it she had spurned several marriage proposals, to devote her life to the nurturing of young souls, but romance had blossomed between herself and Dr. Jason Darwin, who had rented the house from her at that time, and later rented a room from her, after she had taken occupation of the house herself. They had married a year later, so she was now Mrs. Jason Darwin.

Thinking of her dedication and achievements, Eli suddenly felt a spurt of deep admiration for her. She was one child who had not only escaped the dark shadow of Claw Mountain; she had survived its curse and had triumphed, just as he himself had as an adult. Though she had been ever a threat to him, he felt a strong strong bond with her now.

He noticed her face was anguished and awash with tears, and remembering how devoted she had been to Mary, he found himself reaching out a comforting arm to her. She hesitated a moment then, most surprisingly, she moved towards him. He put his arm around her shoulders, feeling her shake with deep, silent, grieving sobs. It took him back to the time long ago when he had placed his arm around the thin shoulders of his backward youngest brother, Jamie, during the double funeral of his two brothers, Alvin and Samuel, who'd been murdered by the Galtrey. He noticed that members of the despised clan had dared to show up here today. Even *Sloane Galtrey* who had disfigured his face! Years ago, he would have done something about it. But he was no longer the man he was then. And today, he felt too distracted, too . . . He swallowed against a curious ache in his throat as his mind roved back tiredly over the years . . .

M*ary!* She had been some woman. Impossible to overlook or forget. She had not been pretty – at least not in the conventional sense – yet somehow a man ended up thinking of her as quite extraordinary. *Beautiful* in her own unique way! With that long shiny black hair, high forehead and those clear brown eyes that feared nobody, she had a radiance and inner glow that made her far outshine much prettier women. He remembered the day she had stood up to him at the general store, while everybody else had been quaking with fear.

And the day she had married his brother, Zack, in a rigged-up wedding ceremony, and how even with her face all swollen where he had punched her, she had carried herself with such inherent dignity and grace in his mother's elegant city clothing that she had taken away the breath of every Bucko, including himself. He had felt intense attraction towards her deep in his loins and, used to getting his own way with women, and having been denied getting his way with her that very day, it had fermented inside him, growing in intensity over the years.

Though he was still loathe to admit it, even now while he was busy candidly examining the tempestuous relationship that had existed between them, he recognized that she had brought about many beneficial changes to the lives of the Buchanan clan. Changes he had bitterly resented and resisted at first. Without being embroiled in the emotion and tension of the times, he was able to fully appreciate the extent of her positive influence objectively for the first time. Besides getting medical clinics and a school on the mountain, she had single-handedly ended the long-standing feud between the Galtreys and the Buchanans.

Fearing for the safety of her precious child, she had gone to see the Galtrey patriarch on Buck Knob Mountain at great personal risk in a bid to bring to an end the hostilities between the two warring mountain clans – and had miraculously succeeded. That alone proved the guts she had possessed. It had effectively ceased the fierce, ugly feud. Her pact with Dean Galtrey had led to a peaceful existence for the inhabitants of both mountains. Though he still hated the Galtreys with a passion, especially Sloane Galtrey, the man who had caused his disfigurement, Eli found himself marveling now at her bravery and ingenuity. *What a remarkable achievement that had been!* Though, of course, he had not appreciated it at the time.

He remembered how when he and some of his brothers had gone to the first service at the brush arbor to disrupt it, she had stood firm, fearless and noble, when he had thrown a rock at her that had caused a deep gash in her temple, bludgeoning him with the depths her courage. *She had been a worthy opponent!* One that had both infuriated and beguiled him.

And standing on the high plateau of Claw Mountain, mourning its saint, made other memories rush to the fore for Eli. Memories that had caused the blackness deep within him. That haunted and terrified him. That he had been too afraid to face squarely before today, but that had long ago shaped his destiny. Memories of a single event that had changed him from innocent child to unspeakable monster . . .

*O*ne *night when Eli was ten years old, his father woke him up with a kerosene lantern turned down low, whispering to him that his dark-haired baby brother, Taggart, who slept on the straw tick beside him, had died during the night. The day before had been Taggart's sixth birthda, and, in best Buchanan tradition, the day of his 'initiation into manhood'! His father had lined all his sons up and then made the little boy drink nearly a jar of 100-proof mountain moonshine. Taggart was very small for his age and his reaction was immediate. He'd puked his little heart out, before promptly passing out. Since this was the usual reaction, however, his father had proudly swept his 'little man' into his strong arms and carried him to his straw tick to 'sleep it off'. He had remained there the rest of the day. Now, here was his father telling Eli that his baby brother was* dead*? Eli stared at the slumped, unmoving little form beside him with a sick feeling in his stomach. Hours earlier, when Eli had changed little Taggart into his nightgown, his body had been limp and his head rolling around, but he'd whimpered every now and then, so Eli knew that he must have been alive then. What had made his father check on him during the night? Had he known he'd gone too far this time? Eli was numb with shock.*

But it was what came next that made Eli rear up from his bedding. For his father insisted that Eli was to take his dead brother in a sack and throw him over the edge of the bluff. Appalled by such a heinous command, Eli refused. But his father insisted, saying it was necessary. Eli asked why he could not do it then and his father sternly told him he did not want his mother to find out about it. He said she would be very angry with him if she found out that he had fed too much moonshine to her youngest child and caused his death. He could not take the risk that she would wake up and find him gone. So he was commanding Eli to do it.

Eli did not want to do this terrible thing and begged his father not to make him, saying Taggart should get a proper funeral. But his father threatened him with a severe beating at the flogging post and a week without food, if he did not obey his command. And so Eli, fearing his father's retribution far more than he did the God his mother had told him of, was finally forced to obey.

His father lifted Taggart, Eli's angel-faced youngest brother off the straw tick, put him onto his shoulder and took him outside into the barn. He made Eli hold open a grain sack and placed the small corpse inside the sack, sealing the opening off by winding twine around it, and severely swearing Eli to secrecy. He gave Eli the kerosene lantern to light up the way, before leaving Eli alone in the barn with the bulging sack, and disappearing.

It was a hot summer's night, but Eli felt icy inside. He was shaking with the force of the wild emotions thrashing about inside him. He was slight of build and the bundle containing the tiny corpse of his six-year-old brother was yet heavy as he reluctantly took the top of the sack and dragged the sack along behind him into the forest of tall, towering, silent, accusing trees, while holding the lantern aloft. The sack bumped and lurched and pulled against his puny shoulder, till it ached unbearably. It was at least a five-mile walk. Clouds scudded across the moon, throwing eerie shadows and making him fearful of witches and haints. His breath was ragged and he was terrified, filled with the enormity of what he was being forced to do.

At last he came to the edge of the escarpment that was midway up on the south-facing side of the mountain, where the forest was thick and entangled with undergrowth and the rocky cliffs were sheer and spilled with creepers and vines, which overlooked a valley of tall trees. He knew it was terribly wrong to get rid of his brother as if he were a litter of unwanted puppies, yet he didn't know what else to do.

Tears flowed freely down his cheeks as he looked out across the dark valley of black shapeless shadows below, breathing heavily, and trying to gather the courage to commit his baby brother to such a merciless grave. In the end, after a long, tormented time spent railing against it, he finally did it. He pitched the pitifully bulging sack over the side, hearing a cry as it bumped against granite boulders on the way down, till it landed with a soft thud far below. Whether it was his brother's cry, or that of an owl, Eli couldn't be sure.

He wondered if his brother had actually been dead, or still just unconscious. He imagined him waking up inside the sack devoid of light and sucked of air, his slender limbs being battered and bruised as the sack bumped along the ground, then breaking as they hit against boulders and rocks on the treacherous way down and, alive and broken and bleeding, him suffering a slow and agonizing death, all alone. Sweet and tender Taggart!

Wracked with terrible guilt, he sat on the ground and sobbed and sobbed, cursing his father and God. Cursing this very mountain! It was then that the blackness entered his soul, an innocent who had become possessed by the demons that wandered through the forests that evil night. That night he swore that one day he would wreak equally terrible revenge on his father.

The next day, his father told his mother that Taggart had gone missing and organized search parties supposedly to try and find him. Eli had to pretend that he was looking too, when all along he knew the terrible truth, that his baby brother would never be found. After several weeks, it was accepted that Taggart must have walked in his sleep and that a rogue bear from the Wilderness area must have taken him, as his father so slyly mooted. Though his body was never found, his mother accepted that Taggart must be dead. Indeed, she said she knew it deep inside her, with a mother's keen intuition and, in a bizarre twist, she insisted that they hold a funeral service for him. They buried a child's empty coffin behind the homesite on the steep slopes of the mountain.

* * *

*I*t had all been too much for Eli to bear. His little brother's ghastly death, the bogus search parties and the bogus funeral were to fill him with a deep-seated rage, unleashing a wave of violence from him that had never been fully contained since. He had even taken up the whip at that time, one from his father's collection, practicing using it every day of his life, to become proficient at it so that he could one day use it on his father. (His father had even encouraged it, not knowing what his true intentions were.)

Taggart's death had remained an ugly secret between Eli and his father. However, later, badly tormented by it, he had spoken of it to Zack, swearing him to secrecy.

* * *

A nd standing high up on Eagle Spur, Eli, whose throat ached as the ghastly memories of that horrible night filled his being, believed and fervently hoped that Zack had kept the secret too, for it was too grim and terrible to divulge to anyone, let alone to those not connected to the clan. Especially, he was despairing of the fact that he may have told Mary.

God help me! he silently cried, closing his eyes, again feeling a pain so deep and wounding, so raw and uncompromising, that he wished desperately for the release of tears, or anything to cleanse him of it. *After all, nobody would think anything of tears at a funeral.* Indeed, he could hear the sounds of weeping and broken sobs all around him. But tears could not come from a heart that had long been dead as the chestnut tree. Still, there was so much in his past that was eating at him …

H e had loved his backward brother, Jamie, with a depths that confounded him, perhaps because Jamie had been the one human being who'd loved him with the generous, unconditional love of the dog for his master, whereas all his other brothers had grown to fear him – except for Zack, of course, and Jake, who was naturally bad. Guilt gnawed relentlessly inside him.

Mary had been right, after all! He had been young Jamie's fierce protector because of what had happened to Taggart, and yet, he had failed Jamie when he had needed him the most. He had allowed their father to flog him – a truly abominable act – which had eventually led to his death. Thus, Eli had lost two of his baby brothers to his father's evil excesses.

But he had finally got his revenge on his father. One night when his unmarried brothers were asleep in the loft, helped by a considerable intake of moonshine, he had woken his father up in his stinking sickbed, a wizened, white-haired bag of bones, with red rheumy eyes. When he saw Eli's face in the light of the kerosene lantern, he began trembling with fear. Eli forced him outside, making him climb into a sack and sit down in it, and then he had pulled the sack up and tightly tied twine around the mouth of it. He dragged his father, who was whining and crying piteously, in the bulging grain sack, bumping along the steep, endless treacherous mountain paths to the edge of the same escarpment, over which he'd thrown his baby brother.

Once he reached the escarpment, without the hesitation and repulsion that had come with him being forced to so rudely dispose of the sack containing Taggart, he committed his father to unending hell by tossing him off the edge of the mountain. There was another marked difference this time. This time, Eli knew for sure that the body inside the sack was definitely *alive when he did it. It was a terrible repeat of that terrible night years before.*

Eli had imagined that this ghastly act of patricide, this final act of justifiable retribution that had been so long plotted and planned and coddled over, would give him a sense of relief, the peace he so badly craved, but instead, it had only added to his torment, to his nightmares. He kept seeing the whites of his father's terrified eyes as he forced him inside the sack. He had looked so pale and pathetic. So defenseless! *The act had robbed Eli of his last shred of humanity, he knew, and it had inexplicably sickened and shamed him. And he knew why that was. He knew that by his father forcing him to throw his six-year-old brother over a cliff, dead or alive, he had been turned into an unfeeling monster, but by Eli doing the same thing to his father, he had become his father incarnate.* God forbid!

* * *

Eli's mind came back to the present, with the singing of the closing hymn, the one the reverend said was Mary's favorite, "The Old Ragged Cross". Several of his brothers moved forward and start piling shovelful after shovelful of the piled earth onto the lid of the lowered coffin. Then the coffin containing Mary's corpse was committed to the earth. Jed moved forward and placed a pink wildflower on the mound of earth and Zack hammered a wooden cross at its head. Reverend Crawley said his final prayer and at last the funeral service was over.

Emma abruptly moved away from him as if suddenly seared by the contact, and the last he saw of her was her threading her way through the mourners and throwing her arms around her gray-bearded, favorite uncle, Zack, who was weeping unashamedly, his huge shoulders shuddering. With his own heart burning with grief and sorrow and deep remorse, Eli considered that the depths of his eldest brother's pain must be unbearable. Zachary Thomas had lost the woman he had deeply loved and with whom he shared forty solid years of happy married life, and he looked distraught and inconsolable. Oh, how he envied him. To have had a good woman like Mary with which to share his life. Eli moved through the crowd towards the bereaved family to give them his condolences. When he reached them, he and Zack hugged with their eyes tightly closed, both overcome by terrible grief, before they broke apart, their eyes wet.

"I never told you this before, Zack, but I grew to admire her," said Eli earnestly, meaning it with all his heart. "I truly did. She was some fine woman. *Saintly.* What's more she was truly one of us."

Zachary Thomas nodded solemnly, his brother's startling turquoise-green eyes gazing at Eli with a look like love. "I sure appreciate that comin' from you, Eli."

You wouldn't if you knew!

"Did you ever tell her?" Eli whispered hoarsely.

Zack knew instantly what he meant, for he said quietly, "Naw, Eli, I never did. I promised you I wouldn't tell nobody and I kept me that promise. Sure, I used it to keep you in line every now and then, but I never would have told. You see, more than anyone, I saw what it did to you when Paw forced you to do that evil thung."

Eli nodded, feeling a terrible rawness in his throat. A wave of relief swept over him. He could have borne almost anything but to have his family find out that he had been forced to commit such an unforgivable act and had almost certainly unwittingly murdered his baby brother. *Taggart!* The shame of that would have been too terrible to bear. As it was, just the torment of living with that terrible secret for so many years had nearly destroyed him – always, the blackness inside him and the nightmares, night after night. *Taggart and then young Jamie Galtrey!*

Eli turned to his nephew, Jed, unable to meet his brilliant blue all-knowing eyes, wordlessly shaking his hand, before hugging each of his nieces in turn. There was no need for words. Suffering had found its mark in the Buchanan clan once more and was shared and understood by them all.

Then the next minute, he was shaking the hand of his blond-haired, dry-eyed, only child, his thirty-seven-year-old son, Caleb, finding it surprisingly soft. He had never set eyes on him before. He saw his bored expression, as if all this outpouring of grief for his mother irked and annoyed him and, as he gazed into his pale-yellow eyes, Eli saw himself reflected there – all the smirking insolence, the cocksure arrogance! By all accounts, this seed of his loins was a respectable citizen, a leader in the Front Royal community, with a paunch from good living, and a pretty dark-haired wife and five pretty daughters – Eli's grandchildren – but rumor had it that he would get drunk and then beat them for no reason, and when it came to business, he was a cunning and merciless opponent. *The sins of the father!*

He wanted to tell his son that he knew what devils tormented him, the pent-up rage that had nowhere to go but into violence, the devils with which he had cursed him. Violence was an inevitable part of his son's make-up, passed to him through his grandfather's and then his father's genes. He had been conceived in violence, after all, this innocent he had cursed with his evil. His flesh and blood. *My son! Mine! Mine and Mary's!* He wanted to say something to his only son, but he didn't know what. *Anything!*

"Your Maw was a fine woman," he croaked finally. "Caleb, I'm your . . . I'm your . . . Uncle Eli."

Caleb nodded, turning away impatiently, totally disinterested, his heart as hardened as that of his father's. And in that instant, Eli knew that Caleb was only here under duress, probably at his wife's, or Zack's, insistence, that instead of wanting to say his last farewell to a mother who had loved him unconditionally, in spite of the fact that she must have long ago guessed the awful truth, that Caleb was his son and not Zack's, he was impatient and thoroughly bored by the proceedings, by the fumbling condolences of friends and relatives.

Eli felt he wanted to slap him, to let him know that family – *clan!* – was everything. In the end, it was the only meaningful thing in this life beyond the mountain they stood on. This timeless mountain that had so rudely been proclaimed part of the Shenandoah National Park, thereby bringing about the end of an era, the end of the Buchanan clan's habitation on the Blue Ridge Mountains! But none of this meant anything to Caleb, he could tell. His son was eager to get away from this magnificent mountain, caring nothing for those he'd be leaving behind. *Was this then the child that he had spawned?* Eli had a sick, shamed feeling in his stomach . . .

80

A few days after Mary had made peace with the Galtreys, Eli dressed in his city duds, climbed the steep slopes to Eagle Spur, carrying his bullwhip. He had imbibed in a great deal of moonshine, tormented by the thought that his brother's wife had unilaterally brokered a peace pact with their arch enemies. Little Jed was playing in the yard. The mute boy regarded him silently with brilliant blue eyes, as Eli skipped up the steps of the porch and banged loudly on the door. The next minute, Mary stood in the doorway with that aloof dignity he had come to expect of her, her black hair in a bun, barefoot, in a simple blue cotton calf-length dress.

She looked shocked when she saw him, her brown eyes wary, but she said shortly, "Zack has gone trackin' in th' Wilderness, Eli. He won't be back fer hours yet."

"I didn't come to see him. I came to see you," he snarled.

There was a flare of alarm in her eye, and she swallowed hard, but her voice when it came, was surprisingly calm. Indeed, it was haughty. "Eli, you're not welcome here. I would like you to leave."

The uppity bitch! Infuriated, he hit her across her face with the back of his hand, sending her flying backwards across the room. She gave a little shocked scream at the unexpectedness of his blow, landing heavily on the floor, on her back, her legs sprawling as they tried to somehow gain purchase, her arms behind her in her effort to break her fall, her dress raised to expose slim, long legs, the breath knocked clean out of her. She sat up, hastily pulled her dress back over her knees. She looked up at him with a look of stunned bewilderment, her chest heaving.

"You kilt Jamie!" *cried Eli, barging into the cabin and pointing the bullwhip at her.* "And now you dare make peace with th' clan that kilt my two brothers, that caused my disfigurement! You gonna pay fer that, you bitch!"

Mary slowly got up from the floor, using the wall behind her for support. "I didn't kilt him!" *she said softly and vehemently, holding a hand to the flaming cheek he had struck.* "You did! You and Jake offered yer brother up to yer paw like he was th' sacrificial lamb! You tied his hands to that post and allowed your paw to lash his back* twenty-five *times without attemptin' to stop him! Now you've got th' almighty cheek t'say that I kilt him!"

The truth in her words hit Eli squarely in the chest, plunging deep inside him with the sharpness of a dagger. But the guilt that evoked only made him madder. Mary clearly saw the fury in him as he faced her with the whip in his hand for there was fear and recognition in her eyes. With a roar of outrage, he lashed the bullwhip onto the floor beside her. It sliced through the air with a high-pitched whistle and landed on the pine floor with a loud sizzling crack, making her jump.

"Now, Eli thar ain't no need fer all this," *she said nervously.* "If'n you got a problem with me, let's talk about hit."

"I'm done with talkin', bitch!" *To give his words added emphasis, he lashed the whip onto the floor on the other side of her. She tensed and there was a quick indrawing of her breath as she eyed him warily, looking like a caged animal. It gave Eli a feeling of tremendous power to be able to have her cower this way. He began a terrorizing series of whip lashes on either side of her like he had with Hannibal Hanford, and countless others, years ago. He had lost none of his expertise with the whip. It whistled and cracked, the long leather tongue of black leather slightly deviating at the last second so that it just missed her person each time. But whereas the wealthy landowner had flinched and whimpered and wept in the stricture of his attack, Mary somehow managed to gather her courage, for she stood before him now firm and unflinching, holding her head up high, only a slight flutter of her eyelashes giving clue to the fact that the whizzing leather kept missing her by a hair's breath.*

But gradually, his rage and the seminal look in his eyes must have conveyed itself to her, for she suddenly turned and bolted blindly into the bedroom like a spooked jack-rabbit. And when she did that, a new plan of action instantly rose up inside Eli. He had only come to scare the living daylights out of her with his whip. To make her understand who the boss was around here, once and for all! He knew that he dared risk no more than that with Zack around.

But suddenly, he felt a coursing desire for her. She was the one woman who had got away and, right now, the one woman he simply had to have. All thoughts of her being the wife of his brother left him then. He lunged after her as she was trying to close the door on him. He easily pushed it open and stood staring her with his scary pale-yellow eyes. She backed away from him, looking aghast and truly frightened, now, as if she knew what he was about to do.

"Take yer clothes off!" he commanded.

Mary fiercely shook her head. "I will not!"

He took her and slammed her back against the wall, pushing the tough handle of the bullwhip so cruelly against her throat that she struggled wildly for breath. She made a harsh gargling sound and the whites of her eyes showed.

He sneered, "You'd better do as I say, or I'll kill you here and now."

"Don't . . . do . . . this, Eli," she managed to gasp in a strangled voice. "Thunk . . . of yer brother. Yer . . . soul!"

"I don't got no soul!" he said, pushing even harder, this time threatening to cut off her windpipe completely and suffocate her.

"Do it!" he hissed.

And this time, struggling for breath and clawing frantically at the whip handle pressing harshly against her throat, she nodded. Eli immediately released his hold and gave her a smirk, his icy washed-yellow eyes gloating with triumph. He stepped away from her and watched. Seeming highly embarrassed and ashamed, she took off her dress to reveal she was wearing just a pair of ugly, voluminous, black bloomers underneath. She stood with her arms folded in front of her full enticing breasts, shuddering with fear.

She gave a yelp of fright when Eli reached behind her head to release her bun. Her thick straight black hair tumbled down, slick as oil. He arranged it so that it fell in front of her shoulders, loosely covering her breasts, almost reaching down to her slim waist. He forced her arms to her sides and leaned forward and sucked at one light-brown nipple peeping at him through strands of thick hair. Though she was clearly terrified, she shoved him awa, and, giving him a glare of utter contempt, she struck him forcefully across his face.

"You bitch!" he said scathingly, and spat in her face.

Mary quickly lowered her eyes and wiped his spittle off her cheek with a shaking hand.

"You've bin drinkin', Eli. Don't do this. When you're sober, ye'll be real sorry. Please," she begged. "It ain't right. He's yer brother and he loves you."

In answer to her pleas, he grabbed her by the shoulders and threw her back onto the big brass bed so hard that she bounced several times. Such was his bitterness and rage that, without the slightest hesitation, he disrobed, and fully naked, approached the bed and ripped off her pathetic bloomers, so that she lay fully naked and exposed before his greedy eyes.

He noticed for the first time that her torso was covered in black, purple, mauve and yellowish bruise,s and he frowned. Then he remembered how she had told the gathered clan about the beating she had endured at the hands of the Galtrey women. Now he could not doubt that she had been telling the truth. He noticed she had a black, white-tipped eagle feather tied onto a leather thong around her neck. He was about to rip it from her neck then decided against it. He'd heard that she considered it her good-luck charm, saying it had brought her back to Claw Mountain. Well, let her see how much good luck the charm had actually brought her. Let her see that her good-luck charm was no match for him!

He climbed on top of her with a snarling grunt, holding his forearm forcibly across her throat. He took her without pity, thrusting himself viciously inside her and sucking hard on the light-brown nipples of her ripe, pale breast. She was pinned beneath his forceful heaving, struggling feebly, screaming and crying, but he regarded her with cold, disinterested eyes. After mindlessly rutting for a long brutal time, he lifted himself off her and forced her over onto her stomach. Then came the final insult! Lifting her pale buttocks, he entered her from the back. She cried out in terrible agony and anguish, and thrashed about beneath him like a helpless pinned butterfly, but he viciously punched the back of her head with his bunched fist and, though she tried, she was too weak to buck him away. He held her down while he rammed his hips violently against her bottom like a bull at stud, making the wench pay for trying to take over the mountain, for usurping his power, for making a peace pact with their hated enemies, for daring to defy him! She screamed and cried and called out to God to help her.

He cackled at her keen distress. Then he heard a noise. Zack! Eli felt a moment of sheer utter panic. Then the door opened and he saw little Jed standing the doorway, grinding a fist into one eye and crying. The two-year-old stood and stared with a look of sheer bewilderment on his little earnest face. His brilliant-blue hurting gaze bothered him far more than had Mary's screams. Eli hastily removed himself from inside her, as Mary yelled at the child to go away. Jed turned and stumbled out of view, crying loudly. Eli hastily leapt up and closed the door behind him.

"Git dressed!" he ordered Mary, shaking with fright.

As they both quickly put their clothes back on, Mary, shaking, whimpering and weeping with rage and humiliation, said scathingly, "You may have taken my body, Eli Buchanan, but you ain't got my soul. And I'll tell Zachary Thomas about this," she threatened, her eyes narrowing with loathing. "I'll tell him and he'll git you fer this! He'll kill you! If'n I don't kill you first!"

Cold fear entered Eli then. He suddenly realized the enormity of what he had done. Zack would kill him if he ever found out.

"How dare you corrupt that little innocent!" she wept. "You cruel, wicked man! *You* monster . . . you . . ." *She collapsed on the bed in a heap of weeping.*

Eli turned around at the door and snarled, "You tell Zack and I swar I'll kill that young'un of your'n! And I kin assure you, I'd make a much better job of it than what them Galtreys did, the same ones you want to become sech bosom buddies with . . ."

* * *

Eli swallowed, highly disturbed by the memory of the evil that he had committed in a drunken, mindless rage so many years ago. *God, how Mary must have hated him all these years.* Thankfully, her threat to expose him to his brother had proved to be an idle one, though, of course, her silence had been to protect her child and Zachary Thomas, and not himself. She had obviously taken his threat to kill her son seriously, not knowing that he would never have touched the child.

Thankfully, she had never told his brother about the terrible, brutal act he had committed against her, for his behavior in no way changed towards him after that. Eli wondered how she had managed to explain away to Zack the bruises and welts she must have suffered as a result of his debauchery. No doubt Zack had attributed them to the beating she had taken from the Galtrey women, never suspecting she had been further assaulted and raped. But even though Eli had felt mounting guilt about what had done to his brother, he had left the mountain shortly afterwards in triumph, thinking what sweet revenge he had wreaked on Mary – revenge beyond his wildest expectations!

Then something happened to change all that. He heard through Jake that Mary had given birth to a son. He worked out that the boy had been born exactly nine months after he had raped her and he knew, with a certainty that defied logic, and with a sick feeling inside, that she had borne him his first and only child – a son that he could never claim. He realized too, with a gnawing sense of terrible shame that his son was *a child of rape!*

The knowledge of what he had done to Mary – and his son, Caleb – had stayed with Eli over the years, so that he was never able to forget her no matter how much he was under Annabel's bewitching spell. No matter how many city women he slaked his lust on.

On the rare occasions that he had unexpectedly bumped into Mary after his son had been born – once at the school when he was paying Miss Prescott her meager salary and a couple of times at different clan get-togethers – she was to treat Eli without a trace of fear and a fiery-eyed disgust, devoid of any of the

588

simpering weakness he had expected from her, considering the cruel and merciless way he had taken her.

So instead of earning his contempt, she had gradually earned, first his grudging respect, and finally, to his eternal perplexion, a deep and honest admiration, and in a strange, non-physical sense, his *love*. After all, she was the mother of his only child – his son! The deliverer of the one thing he had wanted in life above all else for so long – *his own child!* His need for a child of his own had grown so strong inside him that he could almost taste it. He knew that any child of his would not live in the thrall of terror and brutality that had been the mainstay of his own childhood, and those of his brothers and their sons. Yet he had been denied the role of fatherhood – and rightly so, in the circumstances. It pleased him, though, to know that whatever else, his son had a caring mother and father in his stead. He found he didn't like to analyse this love he felt for Mary too deeply. It bewildered and disturbed him. Perhaps because it was no longer a carnal thing with him – but of such sweet purity that it caused him almost to weep.

He was not sure whether he felt this way because she had born him the child he had yearned for so long, or because, through blinded eyes grown astonishingly clear with time and distance as a result of his removal from Claw Mountain, he so respected her for tearing down, one by one, the ruins of a collection of badly brutalized Buchanan childhoods, and slowly rebuilt these wretched souls into functioning human beings for the first time, through love and caring and courage, drawing them from the darkness of their tawdry and traumatic lives. The story of the Buchanan clan was one of mirthless tragedy, of horrors beyond imagination. She had successfully removed the aching burden of the sordid life on Claw Mountain that had so damaged himself and all his kin.

He had thought he loved Annabel once, and indeed, her lovely body was still like a drug to him, but he had quickly become disillusioned by her. By her inability – or unwillingness – to act in the face of her father's and society's disapproval! She was beautiful and very desirable, yes, but she lacked the dauntless spirit of Mary – *his brother's wife!* How strange that he should end up truly admiring Mary, the woman he had loathed so ardently for so long. *How goddamned ironic!* How odd that he, the epitome of evil, should come to admire goodness, courage and determination, above shallowness and intoxicating beauty. He found his thoughts returning to her often.

Thankfully, as the years passed, the memory of Mary gradually faded, fed only by reports of her doings from members of his clan, until the phone call just days ago had caused it to all come flooding back. He knew how much that phone call must have cost her! How much it must have galled her to have to make it. He had longed for the opportunity to make it up to her after his disgusting treatment of her, and her phone call had given him one. He had plunged into the task with an almost manic determination.

And yesterday, upon hearing about her death from his brother, Jake, he had felt a pain so raw and crushing that he could scarcely credit it. Leaving an important meeting to his right-hand man, Tosser Daniels, he had immediately driven back to Claw Mountain to attend her funeral. On his way here, he had spotted the old abandoned church on the slopes of Beacon Mountain that Mary had fought so valiantly to have erected on Claw Mountain – his repeated attacks on the brush arbors had put paid to that. *She had good reason to despise him!* Now he viewed those attacks as those of a destructive child. In those days, he saw the world in a much different light. It was one of torment and dark shadows.

Amazed that the church had not been torched like other structures in the Park area, an administrative oversight, no doubt, on impulse, he parked and climbed up to it, entering the empty chestnut-log chapel she had apparently attended so many times, feeling strange and hollow inside – a lost soul trying to make some sense of the life and death of the only woman he had ever loved for her soul rather than her flesh. The useless love he'd borne for the selfish and faithless Annabel seemed ridiculously meaningless in restrospect. And with the clarity of hindsight, he saw that his love for his Washington socialite was more lust and obsession than true love, for he despised her shallowness and self-absorption. And like Annabel, Mary, the mother of his only child, was a woman he could never have, could never call his own – who would not want him, even if she were not his brother's wife.

His heart had been so deadened over the years of violence done to him and by him that he had not expected to find the peace that stole over him as he sat, head bowed, in the worn, dusty pew, reflecting, without satisfaction, on his own life – a life often spent clouded in an alcoholic blur to stop the terrible images from the past from crowding into his mind, the bitter burning, the blackness. He closed his eyes, immersed in dark, pitiless thoughts. Then, suddenly, awareness returned and he felt a presence. It was so strong and profound that he opened his eyes fully, expecting to find somebody in the chapel with him. But the hot, dusty church was as empty as it had been before. He felt a rash of gooseflesh stipple his flesh . . .

81

Eli was thankful that his presence at Mary's funeral was appreciated by his eldest brother. Considering the caustic relationship between the dead woman and himself, he hadn't been sure about how he would be received. Others came forward now to give the family their condolences, and Eli stood awkwardly around, within the family circle, though not part of it. Caleb and his family had left straight after the service, with nods and a few stiff handshakes. Eli knew he would probably never see his son again, except perhaps at Zachary Thomas's funeral, but the thought of it did not bother him as much as he thought it would. Once, he had longed to forge some sort of relationship with his son. Now he knew that it was never to be. At least his curiosity about his son had been partially satisfied. And watching the subsequent warm interaction of his brothers and their families, with the bereaved family, Eli suddenly felt like an outsider – as if he was no longer an integral part of the clan whose roots had been shattered by their forced removal from this mighty mountain. He decided to leave. He had done what he had come for. To be a support to Zack and to pay his last respects to Mary, the mother of his son. Now he was feeling oddly disturbed and anxious to be away from here, the place where he had committed such an unspeakable crime as the brutal rape of his own brother's wife. *Where he had murdered an innocent child!* He went to tell Zachary Thomas he was leaving and his brother begged him to stay, his unfaded turquoise-green eyes narrowed in pleading, "Please stay till after th' others go, Eli. I sure would appreciate it."

But Eli found he couldn't bear the thought of entering Zack's home. He had lost the right to do so the day he had raped Mary and planted his accursed seed inside her. Instead, shaking his head regretfully and muttering excuses about needing to attend an important meeting in Washington, he left them all – all those grieving Buckos and their families, all those friends and neighbors, all those strangers and one-time enemies – and made his way through the thinning crowd of mourners, back down the steep mountain to where his automobile was parked.

He knew that he was leaving Claw Mountain for the last time. When Mary had telephoned him from the general store just ten days ago, begging his help in getting his influential politician friends to intercede urgently on their behalf and save Eagle Spur as their home, he had pursued the matter relentlessly. But to his great frustration and dismay, his efforts on Mary's behalf had been met with embarrassed shrugs and apologies. He had been told that it was impossible to do anything at this late stage, since L. Ferdinand Zerkel, who was in charge of the Relocation Project, had strongly advised against the couple being allowed to remain on in their home, citing the way Zachary Thomas had chased off his enumerator by firing on him when he had gone to interview them.

Eli motored all the way up to Skyland to see his if old friend, George Pollock, could influence Zerkel to change his mind. Eli knew that Pollock had done much to bring about the formation of the Shenandoah National Park and that Zerkel had supported him in advocating the Blue Ridge as the location for the national park rather than the Massanuttan area. Pollock had talked about wanting Skyland to be inside a national park for as long as Eli had known him. He said he wanted to protect the mountains from the mercy of barkers, lumberers and miners, but Eli knew it was more than that – he'd hope to save Skyland from the clutches of his many creditors, his ongoing financial troubles.

Always in debt, and just one step ahead of his infernal creditors, he had hoped that a national park would save him from losing the place that he loved so well. He had even sold Eli a lot on the mountain for $100, but Eli was always too busy to build a cabin on it. He had been paid out a nominal sum for it by the Commonwealth of Virginia after the blanket condemnation of land. Pollock had loaned money from Eli several times in the past, but had always fully repaid the loans, though always late, sometimes by years. But Eli had never pressured him in any way. The man had been directly responsible for his present status and prosperity, after all. Indeed, without the hand of friendship extended to him at Skyland all those decades past, he would probably have died an ignominious death in a mountain fracas, years ago.

Now he was shocked to discover that the man, who had once personified the mountain resort, was no longer running it. No longer the slight figure of his youth, Polly had gained quite a bit of weight with the years. At a robust seventy years, when other men had settled into staid retirement, his old friend had been keen to carry on running this place until his last breath. Though clearly happy to see Eli again after a good number of years, he had not a happy tale to tell for things had not turned out the way he had expected. Sadly, in 1935, he'd lost the concession to run Skyland for the rest of his life, though he and Mrs. Pollock had been give life-long use of Massanuttan Lodge and Annex Cottage. He had turned his beloved resort over to the new Concessionaires, the Virginia Skyline Company, in January, 1937. He told Eli, frankly, that he'd lost so much favor with those in the National Park Service and Virginia Commission for Conservation and Developement that perhaps Eli would do better to approach Zerkel directly without mentioning his name.

Despite his irrepressible optimism, Eli could see the light of disappointment in Pollock's eyes as he told Eli how different things were around here now. No longer did people come and spend a month, or even a whole summer here, and become close friends – now they roared up in their automobiles, stayed a night or two and left. There were no more Masquerade Balls, Wild West Shows, Pow-Wows, or Snake Shows.

His marriage to Addie had not been a success either. They'd married in 1911 and, after nine years, he'd left Massanuttan Lodge at the request of his wife, to reside in Annex Cottage, where Eli had once come across a bathtub full of scores of writhing snakes his first night in Skyland. Polly and Mrs. Pollock had rarely even eaten meals together thereafter. It had been a marriage of opposites, however, and Eli was not surprised to hear this. Pollock was open, fun-loving and gregarious, and something of a ladies' man, Eli fancied, while his wife, a raven-haired, middle-aged woman, when Eli had first met her, who must have been a Mediterrean-type beauty in her youth, was a quiet, cultured, intensely private person, who preferred to play cards with a few intimate friends in her cabin than attend the lavish affairs thrown by Polly at Skyland. It seemed the only thing they had in common was their love of the Blue Ridge Mountains.

Nowadays, Pollock revealed, with a wry smile, that he spent a lot of time down in Luray visiting his old Negro friend and former major-domo, Will Grigsby, when they would reminisce about the glory days of Skyland. And knowing that Skyland was no longer the province of George Freeman Pollock, killed it for Eli – he knew that he would never come here again. *The soul of Skyland was gone!* He felt a wrench of heartache as he looked in his rearview mirror to see the lonely figure of his friend standing there, watching him go, as he drove his handsome black Cadillac out of the grounds.

The memory of him striding up to meet him after he'd saved Annabel from the rattlesnake, jaunty and cocksure, wearing a sombrero and carrying a bugle, flashed into his mind. Seeing him now divested of all his authority it was as if all his dignity had been stripped from him. Yet Eli knew you could not keep a man like George Freeman Pollock down. His irrepressible spirit would rise to the fore as it so often had in the past. And the old Skyland would always be a part of him! *Of Eli, too!*

Despite Pollock's reservations about his standing with this man standing before him, Eli wasn't shy about dropping Pollock's name as his good friend upon introducing himself to Ferdinand Zerkel at his home in Luray. Zerkel was small dapper man, with keen, intelligent eyes and a small gray mustache. However, after giving the man the reason for his visit, Eli was crisply informed by Zerkel that as much as he sympathized with the situation, nothing would persuade him to accede to his request. Indeed, he said straight after his enumerators had been chased off by Eli's brother he had personally gone to see someone he felt might help him ascertain what to do about the head of the Buchanan clan – the retired sheriff of Madison County, Horace Coley. Eli blanched when he heard the name.

From Coley, Zerkel had learned of the Buckos' sordid reputation for violence and this had prompted him to turn down flatly, the last-minute plea on behalf of the last family left in the area of the Blue Ridge encompassed by the Park – other than those who had gained special permission to stay on, of course. After all, he could not take the risk of Eli's brother taking pot shots at innocent Park visitors, now could he? Eli groaned inwardly when he heard this. Of them all, Zachary Thomas was the one who least deserved to be punished for the early wrongdoings of the notorious Buckos, and one who loved the mountain with a passion lacking in the others, such was the desperate state of their lives. And he was able to do what the others lacked the courage to do. Leave the clan to go and live on his own on the top of the mountain. Away from the madness! Eli cursed Coley inwardly. *His old enemy had got his own back on him in the end!* El could just imagine what he had said to Zerkel.

Though Eli tried for a further hour to try to change Zerkel's mind, the man was intransigent. So the official – and final – verdict from him was that the Buchanan family would not be allowed to remain at Eagle Spur under any circumstances. With his confidence badly dented, but not destroyed, Eli's efforts did not stop there. He had managed to secure a meeting with President Roosevelt and he felt confident that he would be able to convince him to instruct Zerkel to change his verdict.

Eli had held the ear of every president since Huntington had introduced him to the present president's fifth cousin, Theodore Roosevelt, all those years ago, in 1904. Now Eli's influence was such he didn't need anyone to intercede on his behalf. Indeed, Eli had prospered greatly since then, pouring his energies into expanding his wealth through legitimate means, rather than the shady ones he had been party to with Senator Huntington. (The retired senator had passed on in 1925.) He had made vastly more money in oil and iron and property ventures, than he had in his ever-expanding distillery business. (By now, he owned a whole string of distilleries.)

Indeed, he had acquired enormous wealth and was an influential man, who made copious contributions to both the Democratic and Republican Parties, through whose leaders' influence, he had finally made the sought-after A-list. Although he had told himself it was to finally get Annabel Montgomery away from Alexander, in truth, it was more for his own burning need to conquer all that came before him. And while Annabel was impressed by his swift passage to the hallowed providence of the blue-bloods, she was too comfortable in her own social environment to undergo even a whiff of scandal by divorcing Alexander to marry him. Despite her advancing years, and the fact that she was as beautiful and desirable as ever, he wasn't sure if he even wanted her for his wife anymore. Still, it would have been satisfying to him to finally win that decades-long battle, after all the humiliation he had suffered through the status quo.

He had been invited to several functions in the White House since then, including several balls and formal dinners held in the State Dining Room. At one of them, Eli had gained an unexpected bonus. During Woodrow Wilson's tenure, shortly after the president had asked Congress for a declaration of war upon Germany, calling it a crusade to make the world "safe for democracy", a pall of gloom had been cast over the proceedings. Eli, who had expressed a wish to see the renovations undertaken by Theodore Roosevelt decades before, was given a brief tour of the magnificent state rooms of the White House by President Wilson himself, who seemed anxious to get away from his somber dinner guests.

* * *

Eli met with President Franklin Roosevelt at the Oval Office of the White House, at the southeast corner of the west wing, overlooking the Rose Garden. It was a different office to the one in which he had been introduced to President Theodore Roosevelt and the pompous Alexander Montgomery. That office had been next to the Cabinet Room and rectangular in shape. However, there were some familiar features. The Resolute Desk, for instance, made from the timbers of the *"HMS Resolute"*, still dominated the room as it had in Theodore Roosevelt's day, as did the white marble mantel.

FDR, as he was affectionately known, sat in his wheelchair, necessitated by a bout of polio at the advanced age of thirty-nine, a fact that was not widely known by the public. They puffed on long Cuban cigars and sipped from goblets of Buchanan's finest whiskey, speaking first of world affairs, especially of the war-clouds gathering over Europe. The president considered Adolf Hitler, the Nazi fascist in Germany, a great threat to world peace. He said Europe was poised on the brink of war and he was deeply concerned by the ravings of that madman. When Eli enquired if it was likely that the United States would go to the assistance of its European allies, the president said he wished to keep the country out of any war between Germany and Europe and would provide his Allies with material support, rather than military support. Eli knew that Roosevelt had pledged the United States to a "good neighbor" policy, but wondered how long the president could afford to remain neutral. Yet the man was up to any challenge, he knew.

He was a formidable warrior in spite of his handicap, which he fought hard to overcome, especially by swimming, having had a swimming pool built in the west wing to build up his wasted muscles. When he was first elected to the presidency in 1932, shortly after the Depression, there were thirteen million unemployed and nearly every bank on the country was closed. Unlike his cousin, Theodore, who was a Republican, Franklin was an ardent reform Democrat. Already nearing the end of his second term, he had embarked on a program of sweeping social and economic reform. A man of the people, he instituted reform to help the recovery of business and agriculture and brought much-needed relief to the unemployed. Eli felt that such a man would be amenable to a request such as the one he was about to ask. He had heard that the president had been a staunch supporter of the Park initiative right from the start. Indeed, his "New Deal" policies had made the construction of Skyline Drive possible, with the creation of the Civilian Conservation Corps. The CCC had been responsible for building the roads, conduits, buildings, trails and over-looks on the scenic drive. Furthermore, Roosevelt had dedicated the Park himself in 1936, so the chances were good that he was intimately familiar with the whole concept of the Park and the removal of the mountain people living in it, and Eli would not have to do too much explaining.

Eli was right. President Roosevelt knew the story of the Shenandoah National Park, like a man knows the story of his own life. Eli went on to describe the predicament of his brother, Zachary Thomas, and his wife and elder son. But after Eli's diatribe on the merits of allowing them to remain on in their mountain home as other elderly fortunates had been, the president shook his head firmly.

"Much as I sympathize with your brother's predicament, Eli, I simply cannot interfere in this matter. Ferdinand Zerkel has done a splendid job, in very difficult circumstances, and it would be wrong of me to override a decision he has made in all good faith. Furthermore, I happen to think Zerkel is right. We cannot afford for your brother to get angry at hikers invading what he considers to be his land and taking shots at them."

"Listen, Zachary Thomas would never do something like that!" blustered Eli, springing to his eldest brother's defense. "He would never hurt hikers."

"Yes, well, in view of the high emotions these removals have caused, you cannot be absolutely certain of that, and neither can we. I'm sorry, Eli, but this time, I must turn you down in the public interest."

"Mr. President," Eli coaxed, "surely, you can give the matter some thought?"

"I'm afraid not. Oh, and thank you for the bottle of Buchanan's. I shall greatly enjoy partaking more of it . . ."

So despite all Eli's efforts, nothing could be done to save Mary and Zack's home for them. Thus he had failed the woman who had been his adversary for so long. How good it would have been for him to be able to give the gift of Eagle Spur to her to compensate in some small way for the way that he had so cruelly wronged her – and his brother – all those years ago.

What's more, by pursuing this matter, Eli's own wild, unsavory, hillbilly roots had been exposed and, already, he sensed that attitudes were subtly changing towards him in Washington. Perhaps it was just his imagination, but it seemed to him that eyes that once held deference now held a modicum of contempt . . .

Remembering his father's old still site was situated not to far from where he had parked, Eli found himself plunging into the forest to track it down again. It had been at least five years since the stills had last operated – the coming of the Park had seen to that. But the end of Prohibition in 1933 had made them redundant as far as he was concerned, anyway.

He passed through thick underbrush and thorny brambles, which made the going difficult to traverse as well as to identify his whereabouts after so many years had passed. Eli noticed things that he had taken for granted in his youth. The white and deep-red trillium, pink columbine and purple and yellow wild iris, which carpeted the forest floor, lichens on the barks of oak trees, whole glades filled with ferns, or the elegant white-flowered spires of black cohosh, the whimsical white arching spears of crow poison. And the beauty had not touched him then as it did now. The barely discernable path was strewn with lilac petals. A white-tailed deer bounded out of his path. It was if he was suddenly seeing everything for the very first time and with amazing clarity.

After thrashing through the forest and undergrowth for what seemed like hours, Eli suddenly found that he had abruptly exited the forest and was standing on the edge of an escarpment. To his shocked dismay, he realized that it was the same escarpment from which he had dispatched two members of his own blood family. *Brother and father!* Had this been his subconscious destination all along? He stood at the edge of the bluff, staring dazedly down at the tangle of forest and undergrowth below, wondering if any wild animals had fought over the old bones in rotted grain sacks – human bones. Bones that had once propped up an angel-faced six-year-old, and that of his murderer! Eli's throat ached peculiarly, as heat slicked his skin in the sullen air.

The scene seemed to beckon him and he wondered if he should step off the edge of the bluff and add his bones to those below. Then he would feel himself buffeted against granite boulder after granite boulder on the way down and he would feel, for himself,, the pain and terror of it. The thought appealed to him like the exquisite need to aggravate a toothache, no matter the increase in pain. But no, though the plunge seemed to lure him with an irresistible compulsion, there was still too much unresolved stuff sulking inside him that he needed to explore.

He dragged himself back from the edge with a supreme effort and renewed his search for the elusive still site. There was not a breath of wind and the air was molten and heavy beneath the trees. At last he came to the clump of thick under-growth where his father had hidden the still, so overgrown, he was barely able to recognize it at such. He pulled aside the thick foliage with great difficulty since vines had entangled it as if it'd been sewn together with thick stitching thread. There was a huge wrenching sound as they finally gave way. He enter the large, dark, dripping glen with a deep sense of misgiving as he always had when he visited there with his father, for it was when the tongue of the mighty Obediah would become its tyrannical worst. He held a light to the kerosene lantern on the chestnut barrel and was surprised that despite the fact that many years had passed since the still site had last been used, it took readily, lighting up the place with its dull glow. He could hear the sound of the waterfall which spilled over in the pool below before being released into a lively rocky stream.

All the stilling equipment was still there, but it was surrounded by weeds, entangled in vines, while moss had crept over the ground like a green velvet carpet, and it smelled of dank humus, though his nostrils detected a faint whiff of sour corn-mash. There was still the row of chestnut barrels that Mary had hidden behind. And standing there in the gloom the memory of his father's vicious and humiliating tongue-lashings descended on him. They reverberated inside his head till he wanted to block his ears and scream. Remembering how it was Mary's stumbling over a half-buried glass jar that had led to Jamie being flogged, he felt a flash of outrage as the dark memories of that evil day swirled around him like vapor mist, filling him with deep, pitiless sorrow, which slowly turned into burning, terrible rage that his father could have used this slight, unlikely pretext to commit such a barbaric act against his innocent, backward young brother.

Both he and Mary had been wrong. *She* hadn't been responsible for Jamie's death and neither had *he!* That dubious distinction belonged strictly to his father. Grabbing a long funnel on one of the stills, Eli wrenched it off then, using it like a club, began to smash all ten of the stills to smithereens, as if he was some demented Revenue Man of old. But afterwards, as he viewed the shattered re-mains, panting with exertion, he was unable to feel any sense of satisfaction. Instead, he felt useless and empty and spent and tears were flowing freely down his cheeks – tears that had been kept in check for a lifetime!

He fled from the still site, a man being chased by the ghosts of his past, and found himself heading towards his father's old homestead with a grim compulsion that was frightening. He knew it had already been razed to the ground by the CCC boys. He remembered, as he made his way back to Horseshoe Hollow, how he had dragged Mary behind him on a rope that day, her hands tied together over a belly swollen with child. *How terrified she must have been!* He remembered the ice-cold slick of his own fear that had embraced him when his father ordered the "hearing" that was to have such a terrible climax.

At last, Eli came to the desolate, overgrown place of his persecuted childhood and stared at the blackened ruins of the cabin and barn, trying not to think, not to remember, yet knowing he had to face this now, or he would never be free of its cruel shackles. It had been years since he'd last been here and already much of the empty, desolate yard had been reclaimed by the forest and was full of saplings and weeds. In the middle of the untidy, overgrown yard, stood the flogging post in a stand of burdock weeds. Eli thought how ironic it was that it was the one and only thing that had been left standing, as if someone had known that this day must surely come.

As he stared at the monument to torture and despair, terrible memories rose up inside him. He closed his eyes and raised his face to the heavens. He could almost feel the pain of terrible stinging lashes unleashed across his own immature back and, with his mind's eye, he could see again those merciless lashes delivered to the thin back of his brother, Jamie, turning it bloody and raw. He could almost feel Jamie's pain as much as his own – the imagined pain, suddenly real. He felt the full thrust of so much pain, both physical and mental, so much hurt and humiliation. Utterly despairing . . . and so desperately tired. There was no place he could hide, anymore. No escape from this terrible torment that had sulked inside him for so long.

He slowly tramped back through the forest where his automobile was parked, feeling broody with mixed emotions – futile rage and heart-searing pain so raw, he felt bludgeoned by it – amazed that this day he was able to feel so much and so deeply after so many long unfeeling, emotionless years. He longed for the blessed numbness of them now.

He climbed into the front seat and, placing both hands on the steering wheel, he stared into the dense forest straight ahead. He could see the ash-white skeleton of a long-dead chestnut tree and could hear the once-familiar sound of a wild turkey gobbling inside a thicket. Steadily, the birds and wildlife on Claw Mountain had been decimated so that the sounds of his youth had all but ceased, but already in five years, protected and no longer hunted for the pot within the sanctuary of the Shenandoah National Park, they had returned in their droves. He listened for a short time, identifying different bird calls, thinking for the first time that perhaps the Park had been a good thing, after all.

After a long ruminating while, during which the pain refused to desist, he climbed out of the automobile and went to the trunk, opened it and removed a bunch of rags and a long length of hosepipe. He shoved one end of it up the exhaust as far as it would go, jamming a rag around it, and the other end of the hosepipe, he stuck in the back seat window, winding it up as high as he could, before stuffing rags along the rest of the window to effectively block it off. He climbed back into the driver's seat and sat there for what seemed like an eternity.

Returned whippoorwills were starting their call as twilight descended, bringing with it a drop in temperature, which made him shiver slightly. He pulled out a liquor flask of fine legally brewed Buchanan whiskey from his left inside pocket and took a deep draft, wiping his mouth on the back of his hand. He wondered if he should use his revolver instead. *No, too messy!* He had never been afraid to die, but there had been many times he had been afraid to live. Afraid of whom and what he had become in the dark shadow of Claw Mountain.

He suddenly remembered how Mary had led his family in prayer that long-distant day of his brothers' double funeral and tried to remember what words she had used then. 'Our Father who art in heaven . . .' *How did it go again?* It didn't matter. There was no God. No heaven – at least not for him. Only hell, and a devil – and his name was Obediah. *Or was it Eli?*

He switched on the engine and let it idle. After a while, he felt the same strange presence he had felt in the old chapel and, all at once, he was filled with a deep sense of peace. *Forgive me, Mary!*

Afterword

Beginning at first light, Jed was on a final lone, soul-stirring sojourn through the dark, brooding tableland forest of Claw Mountain, saying his silent farewells to all that was part of it: the ancient trees of the primeval forest, the shrubs, the bushes, the creepers and vines, the moss, the lichens, the wildflowers, the animals, the birds, the insects, the tadpoles, the fish, the salamanders, the snakes, the boulders, the waters, the earth and the elementals of the earth, feeling, as always, an amazing connectedness to them all. He asked God to protect and bless this place and all that was part of it, and to give him the strength to bear this excruciating loss. Though his heart was heavy and ached with the sudden loss of his beloved mother and the thought of losing this paradise, he knew that it was time to move on.

He had been greatly comforted when he had seen his mother what must have been just minutes after her death, in the forest. She had been with Spirit of an Eagle. She looked younger and more radiant than he had ever seen her. She moved forward and smiled at him. Then she untied the eagle feather on its leather thong from around her neck that she had worn for as long as Jed had known her, which had hardly seemed the worse for such long wear, and left it on a rock. Understanding her symbolic gesture, Jed had picked up the eagle feather, half-expecting it not to be solid, but it was, and he tied it around his own neck. His beautiful mother had smiled at him then with such a melting look of love that it caused a constant flow of Jed's tears. And then she and Spirit of an Eagle vanished. Jed rushed back to the cabin to find his father sobbing over the bed of his beloved wife, and his mother's body lying lifeless on her deathbed. He had the full expectation of finding the eagle feather still tied around her neck – but it was missing! It had somehow been de-materialized from his dead mother's neck and re-materialized on the rock. Was the one around her neck when he saw her spirit just an illusion then? *It mattered not!* It was definitely the same feather his mother had worn around her neck for decades and she had wanted him to have it. He felt humbled and deeply blessed to be the receiver of such a gift.

For days afterwards, he felt inconsolable and bereft. Yet, right now, he was comforted by the feel of the eagle feather against his chest, which despite its lightness, seemed to leave a burning impression on his skin, and the strong feeling of his mother's unseen presence, walking beside him as she so often used to before she took ill and died nearly a week ago. This forest was so sacred and special to them both, its remoteness and inaccessibility, ensuring that it had re-mained their private domain – and Spirit of an Eagle's – except for that one frightening occasion many years before when two of the Galtreys had invaded it with evil intent.

In this elevated place that touched the glory of the heavens, Jed could silently commune with all of Nature, with God, the Creator of all, the Great Mystery, the Great White Spirit. It was where his spirit was moved and could soar like the dozens of gathering eagles who were his friends. He knew this probably would be his last communication with the Indian spirit who was guardian of the burial site, Spirit of an Eagle, for he and his father would be leaving Claw Mountain soon. An eviction order had been left pinned to a tree outside the cabin two days ago. It worried Jed that his father was still so stubborn and defiant, saying that he would never leave Eagle Spur and that no one could force him off his land. *That he would die first!*

As Jed arrived at the pine grove where there was the huge ancient burial mound covered in growth, to say his farewell to Spirit of an Eagle, who'd been his friend and spiritual mentor for so long, he remembered what he had told him about himself so long ago …

Spirit of an Eagle had been the priest and medicine man of the small, ancient,t peaceful Senedo tribe, and had lived on the earth plane about two centuries ago. He had been so-named, since, from the time he was thirteen, so tall, he was already the size of a grown man, he was able to get the golden eagles of the mountains to do his bidding. It was thus considered natural by the rest of the tribe that he would become their priest and medicine man when their present one, Spirit of an Eagle's father, Great Buffalo, passed on to the Sky World. To them it was clear that the boy had been chosen in his calling by the Great Spirit Himself for displaying such extraordinary powers at such an early age.

Spirit of an Eagle lived with his tribe in the great Wilderness Valley below Claw Mountain, having moved there from their hunting grounds on the west bank of the north fork of the Sherando River further south, near Buffalo Mountain. They had moved because Spirit of an Eagle had dreamed that his dead father had come to him and told him that the tribe must move from the buffalo killing grounds, where the grass was sweet and tender, to "The Place of the Eagles".

Bear Claw did not hesitate to order his tribe to move to the Wilderness Valley, believing strongly in the medicine of Spirit of an Eagle, as he had his father before him. Also, Bear Claw feared the constant danger from other tribes with whm they shared their hunting grounds. Smaller tribes like the Senedoes were forced to give way to the greater tribes and, though this tree-shrouded Wilderness Valley did not have the grazing grass necessary for bison, there were plenty of deers and bears in the forest to feed the tribe, as well as smaller game and birds, like hares, raccoons and wild turkeys, and the river was full of trout and other fish, so his people would not starve.

The Senedoes had established a base camp of their shared longhouses next to the river. The long buildings, containing two levels of large platforms, had curved roofs of saplings and most were covered with the bark of birch and oak trees. The one belonging to the chief, Bear Claw, was covered with buffalo and bear hides, but it was also home to four other families. Here, the Senedoes lived a peaceful existence, fishing with bone hooks, hunting game, and foraging the mountains for grapes, berries, and herbs. They also planted tobacco, corn, pumpkins and beans. The Elders of his tribe, including the ageing chief, Bear Claw, had told Spirit of an Eagle tales about how, many moons ago, the mountains were covered with snow, all year round, and reindeer, buffalo, creatures with humps on their back and nine-foot mastodons and mammoths, with hairy coats and long curved tusks, had browsed in the meadows below.

It was nearing the time of the colored leaves and Spirit of an Eagle was at "The Place of the Eagle" as it was his daily habit to practice the secrets of his vocation and pray to the Great Spirit here. Today, however, he had decided to enter the large sweat lodge he had built deep in the forest of the tableland. He had built it like an oven in a high bank near a spring, strengthening it with saplings and clay so that there was no danger that it would collapse. Sometimes some of the Elders, or the young braves, joined him in the sweat lodge, but today he was on his own. He was glad of that for he had felt a strong sense of purpose, of destiny even, ever since setting out at dawn that morning.

He ducked his naked seven-foot frame into the entrance, symbolically stepping "into the womb of Mother Earth". Then he closed the sweat-lodge door and sat down, cross-legged. He had already heated stones from a fire he had built right outside the lodge, till they were red-hot then he carried them inside on elk horns to a central firepit. Now he poured water from a gourd into his buffalo-horn scoop at intervals onto the stones. The stones sizzled as the water hit them, sending up clouds of steam. Digging in his medicinal bundle, he withdrew and assembled, the two parts of his sacred pipe for the ceremony ahead, filling it with a knot of tobacco.

In the dim rosy glow of the red-hot stones, he set up a little stone altar and covered it with sage, sweetgrass, cleansing cedar and other ceremonial items. He also set out his eagle feathers with a prayer of offering to the Great Spirit. He smoked the pipe, sending gray puffs of smoke into the cloistered atmosphere. He took a pinch of sage and sprinkled it in his hair. Then he offered cedar to the stones, sprinkling it on them, to cleanse and purify the air and drive away bad thoughts. They hissed loudly as they filled the dense air inside the lodge with a sweet, fragrant scent. He blessed the water four times, and humbly offered up more prayers to the Great Mystery, the giver of all blessings.

By now, the heat was so intense, the steam scalded his bare flesh, the atmosphere so thick and cloying, it was almost more than he could stand. He sucked in his stomach and dug his fingers into the bare earth of the floor. He began beating his small ceremonial drum that he had placed between his crossed legs, and starting chanting, in an effort to overcome the pain and the fear of the pain, which was almost worse than the pain itself. He drummed and chanted till he entered a state of thoughtlessness.

He was sweating so profusely, it slicked his skin and dripped like raindrops from his naked body. Then, with his eyes closed and still softly chanting, there came a certain awareness and he entered into another realm, beyond suffering and pain, beyond the papable fear that had threatened to suffocate him, and he experienced a disturbing dream vision. In it, he was standing near the edge of the ridge of Eagle Spur. There was a great wind and the sky was black with clouds. Then it started raining, but this was no ordinary rain. It was raining blood. *Thick and hotly red, it was falling everywhere, as if giant gourds of paint had been dropped from the black, turbulent, overhead clouds. It splashed thickly over his sleek naked body that rippled with muscles and sinews, until he was drenched with blood, and it was getting into his eyes, almost blinding him, and splashing into his nose and his ears. He felt he was drowning in it, suffocating. He was filled with a sense of deep despair. Then through the deluge of blood, Bear Claw emerged in a cocoon of brilliant light. There was no blood on him. He was holding a naked white baby in his arms, which, without saying a word, he handed solemnly over to Spirit of an Eagle to hold in his arms. The howling wind and the red rain stopped suddenly, the sun came out and his body was instantly cleansed of the thick glutinous blood, as he stared down at the bald-headed baby in his arms.*

The dream vision ended abruptly then and, despite the cleansing, and the purifying effect of the baby and the emergence of the sun right at the end of it, Spirit of an Eagle was yet bludgeoned with a premonition of doom. He stayed in the lodge for as long as he could stand, before rushing out the sweat-lodge door and plunging into the icy cold water of the spring. He then sat on the bank and rubbed his naked body with a yellow ointment made of puccoon (bloodroot) and wild angelica, mixed with bear fat, before adorning the scant raiments and buckskin moccasins of a Senedo medicine man, the large golden circle around his neck and resting against his chest, signifying he'd led a life of honor.

He descended the mountain, all the time struggling to grasp the significance of his powerful dream vision: the horror of the blood and the white baby he'd been handed. Why the blood? Why a white baby? *He searched each moment of today's sweat-lodge ceremony and the dream vision to try to divine the instructions given to him by the Great Mystery, but could find none. He was forced to wait patiently for events to unfold that would reveal His wishes to him.*

When he approached his village, after several hours, he found the silence ominous. There was no sound coming from the village, no singing of the squaws or laughter of the children. He could smell the ripe smell of death, and he discovered in the longhouses of his people and scattered around on the river banks, the horrifying evidence of a bloody massacre of every Senedo man, woman and child of the tribe, their twisted, bloodied bullet-ridden corpses horribly mutilated, every one of them scalped. The bodies of the women in their deerkin skirts and bright linen blouses, which had been mutilated by innu-erable tomahawk blows, looked so vulnerable in death, the children, likewise mutilated by the blows of tomahawks, pitiful. Though Spirit of an Eagle had lived past twenty-four summers, he had not taken himself a woman and had no children, but this fact had little impact on him now. All of them were family to him. How had he not heard the sound of the muskets and their screams? He realized that he would have had he not been in his sweat lodge at the time. Now he understood the blood in his vision and the bad feelings he had experienced. His hopes that he might at least find Bear Claw alive because of his dream vision, were soon shattered. He found the wise old chief with a tomahawk sticking out of his forehead and many bullet wounds in his chest, which proved to Spirit of an Eagle tht he had been brave and hard to bring down.

There were also several bodies belonging to Catawba warriors, with their distinctive hair and feathers, which told Spirit of an Eagle that his people had been attacked by that particular tribe. The Senedoes had been caught up in the fighting that had been going on between the Catawbas and the Delawares for some time. Both tribes were friendly with the small tribe of Senedoes, who had refrained from telling either warring tribe of the other tribe's visits, as a matter of survival. So far it had worke, as neither side had captured Senedo braves to use as their warriors or their women to act as their slaves.

As he walked around the village in a daze of horror, Spirit of an Eagle was utterly devastated by the terrible carnage he witnessed. And mingled with the horror was guilt – instead of ensuring their safety, his dream had led his people to their deaths. He was angry and disturbed that his father, Great Buffalo, had chosen to deceive him. Had it been his father or some demon, posing as him? But it mattered not. He had been cruelly deceived and now his entire village of about one hundred Senedo Indians – men, women and children – had been massacred. Spirit of an Eagle was the sole survivor of his tribe. His torment was great. He was heartbroken to lose all his loved ones at once; he thought of the children, so pure, the young braves, so full of courage, the squaws, so full of fun and caring, the Elders, so wise, Bear Claw, so noble. How could he honor his murdered kin? He fell down on his knees and prayed to the Great Spirit for guidance. Then he opened his eyes and knew what he must do to honor his brothers and sisters of the tribe. He would carry the bodies of each and every tribe member up here to the sacred forest of the "Place of the Eagles".

He collected all the bodies of his slain tribe and stacked them on one of the elevated platforms in Bear Claw's longhouse to protect them from predators then, one by one, he took them to the top of the mountain and buried them in the manner used by his tribe, in an earth mound, which grew steadily higher and higher. He buried each one in a blanket, after covering them in wood ash, along with their scant personal possessions. It had taken him many months to complete the gruesome task, and was one that had been extremely physically arduous and mentally grueling. When, at last, all the decomposed, putrid-smelling corpses and skeletons were buried in the mound (he had left the corpses of the Catawba warriors to the scavenging of bears and buzzards), he suddenly felt terribly alone and depressed, as if life no longer had any purpose. Why had the Catawbas done this terrible thing? It was true the Delawares and Catawbas often raided each other and lifted scalps, but the Senedoes had maintained a peaceful relationship with both tribes. Spirit of an Eagle had suspected that the last Delaware delegation to visit the Senedo village was actually a small war party. Perhaps the Catawba had learned of this and suspected treachery on the part of the innocent, Senedoes, however.

For many months after that, Spirit of an Eagle stayed on his own on top of the mountain, contemplating the burial mound, while sitting on a massive boulder, suffering such excruciating loneliness that he began to rant and rave and fear that he was losing his mind. One day, when winter snows covered the mound and saw him wrapped in a thick buffalo hide as he sat on that same ice-slicked boulder, he could not stand the guilt and torment of having led his whole tribe to their deaths, or the excruciating loneliness, any longer. Because of him, the Senedoes, who had survived for thousands of summers, were no more. He was the last of the Senedoes. Furthermore, he had not been able to unravel the mystery of the second part of his dream vision. Swearing to protect this mass grave from plunderers for all eternity, he invoked the blessings and forgiveness of the Great Spirit and then killed himself with a dagger to his heart, causing the white snow to turn red with his blood . . .

The tragic tale had wrenched at Jed's heart and, even now, the thought of what this noble Indian had gone through made his heart burn with empathic suffering, for how deeply he was feeling that same sense of emptiness and desolation, in the face of terrible loss.

Spirit of an Eagle appeared to Jed almost at once. He greeted Jed by pulling his right fist to the middle of his bare chest where his gold honor-circle rested.

Jed responded in like manner. As usual, the giant Indian spirit wore only his otter-skin breech clout with his fringed leather bag for medicinal roots and herbs hanging from his right side and buckskin mocassins. His head was shaved at the sides and his long black hair was tied on the top in a knot. Jed noticed his top-knot tie was bound with more feathers than usual, those of the eagle and the hawk. One of his eyes was encircled with red, and the other, black. For the first time, however, his body was also painted – half-black and half-red, in the manner of a Senedo medicine man. Jed knew intuitively that this extra ornamentation was in honor of this solemn occasion. *The parting of their ways!*

He and Jed sat on the big boulder and talked telepathically to each other for a long while, the Senedo priest imparting to him many more things of wisdom of this world and the next. Jed knew that Spirit of an Eagle lived mainly in the Spirit World, and seemed not unhappy in his chosen task to protect the mass grave of those tribal loved ones he had chosen to bury at such effort and cost to him. But then the giant Indian revealed something to Jed for the first time. He told him his vow at his time of deepest despair when he had plunged the dagger in his heart, to guard the bones of those who had long ago departed to the Sky World, was not the real reason he chose to return to the mound so often. All that had happened so long ago had been necessary because Jed's birth had been long foretold and Spirit of an Eagle had been given a great mission by the Great Spirit to be his guide and spiritual mentor. Thus the second part of Spirit of an Eagle's dream mission had only been revealed to him *after* death. He told Jed that was the reason why Jed's mother had been given such a welcome by the eagles, for she was to bear this babe of such import to the world. Jed had long known he was very different to other mortal men, and had felt always a great sense of destiny, yet he was overwhelmed and deeply humbled by the magnitude of Spirit of an Eagle's revelation.

Now he understood why their communications, always silent mind communications, not verbal, had been so vast and of such great import. Through the Indian spirit, Jed had fully developed his natural and early ability to become at one with all of Nature. To become at one with the flowers, the trees, the birds and the animals, the stones and Mother Earth herself, so that he was able to communicate with them . . . *be* them.

How he would miss this huge fellow with his immense but sleek muscular build and nobleness of stance. As if reading his thoughts, Spirit of an Eagle assured Jed in his native Senedo tongue that Jed somehow understood, "We shall meet again, but not for a long while. Promise me, He Who Knows, that you will remember your dream vision, and all else you have been taught, and will go forth and tell others of what you have learned."

In the manner of the ancient tribe, Jed pointed to the sun peeping through the pines, clapped his right hand over his heart and said solemnly, "I promise."

The Senedo Indian smiled and said, "I shall miss you, He Who Knows."

"And I, you ..."

After a long period of silence between them, the majestic Indian spirit struck his head and his breast with a hand, doing the same to Jed, to indicate brotherhood. Jed did not feel him actually touching him, yet he felt a burning sensation on the spots just the same. Then Spirit of an Eagle dipped his head in silent farewell, his black eyes burning like coals. It was all so achingly sad.

Then, suddenly, Jed heard the familiar echoing sound of a shot from his father's old Kentucky rifle coming from the homesite. The sound struck terror in his heart! Fearful that his father had decided to end it all, cursing himself for leaving him alone when he knew he was so depressed, Jed left Spirit of an Eagle at the ancient burial site and ran all the way back to Eagle Spur, feeling branches and brambles tugging at him, as if they wanted to slow him down. Panting with exertion, Jed felt he would never get there, as he dodged wildly through the trees and foliage. He could not bear the thought of losing his father too.

At last, he burst from the forest behind the cabin. To his considerable alarm, he immediately spotted a man wearing a hat and carrying a rifle, behind a boulder, on the edge of the ridge, while other rifles ominously poked out from behind other boulders. Pulling up short, Jed ducked down and carefully edged around the other side of the cabin, taking cover behind great granite boulders, so he wouldn't be seen shinnying up a leafy oak tree to watch the impending drama, his heart thudding painfully.

From his raised position, he could clearly spy the sheriff and at least five deputies, hiding behind boulders, their rifles pointed towards the cabin. With a sinking heart, Jed realized that his father would indeed fiercely resist this last-ditched effort to get him off what he considered to be his land, as he had sworn to do. He feared that his father would die for his right to remain where he had lived so long with the woman he had loved so deeply, and who he had so recently buried.

After discovering the eviction notice, Jed had tried to get his father to accept the inevitable, but the gruff, grief-stricken old man would hear none of it. He had been inconsolable since the moving funeral and had not set foot outside the cabin, except to spend a short while each day at sunset on his knees before his wife's grave. Later, he would go to the edge of the ridge to view the magnificent sweeping scene below as his mother had done nearly every day of her married life. Jed knew his father could not bear the thought of leaving her remains – and all this splendor – behind. And how well Jed understood it. It broke his heart to think of leaving it all behind.

Using a loud-hailer, the sheriff yelled, "Zachary Thomas Buchanan, this here is Sheriff Wallace Peery. Acting in the interests of the Virginia Commission of Conservation and Development, Judge McGanter of Madison has ordered me to forcibly evict you. I'm ordering you to surrender yourself real peaceful-like. There ain't no need for anyone to get hurt ..."

There was a long period of silence – a silence that was filled with tension and uncertainty. Would it end in the bloody violence his mother would have so abhorred? Finally, the door of the cabin slowly opened and his father stumbled pitifully into view, his huge emaciated shoulders slumped, head bowed. Jed's eyes sought for his weapon, of which there was no sign, and then widened in shock. For the bearded old man, in a pathetic striving for some dignity, had parted his white hair down the middle and combed it flat, and was dressed in the fancy expensive suit that had once belonged to his father. Jed knew very little of his grandfather – his name had seldom passed his parent's lips. But even Jed knew that Obediah Buchanan had bought this old-fashioned, flamboyant suit with some of his moonshine profits. Indeed, his mother had told him once how his grandfather had worn the suit on the first occasion she had met him.

Navy-blue, with garish red stripes, it was double-breasted, with an enormous collar and, tucked into its top pocket was a flaming red kerchief. But, sadly, what had ostensibly looked handsome that day on the cavalier-like Obediah, according to his mother, looked wholly ludicrous on his eldest son. Although his father's frame had shrunk a good few inches with old age, the suit was much too small for him. The sleeves were several inches too short, the buttons strained across his chest and the trouser legs flared comically at half-mast. Over the years, his parent's one concession to "civilization" had made the wearing of shoes. Yet now, in almost palpable defiance, his father's big feet were bare ...

Jed could scarcely believe the sad spectacle. Pain rose so fiercely in his chest, he felt it was almost suffocating him. His proud father, fine and noble mountain man, *reduced to this!* But at least he had bowed to the inevitable and had found the will inside him to resist violence, knowing that his wife had resisted it her whole life. There was a moment of stunned silence when the only sound was the offended cries of soaring overhead eagles in the immense blue sky up above. Jed resisted the urge to call to them. Even his silent mind-beckoning might give away his hiding place.

When he saw Zachary Thomas was unarmed, the sheriff came out from behind his cover, though Jed saw that he was still covered by his deputies' rifles, and went reluctantly forward to arrest him. He was followed by an enthusiastic young man, with slicked-down black hair and pale pasty skin, clutching a camera, and wore a brown suit and a bowtie. The young man yelled to his father that his name was Dale Abernathy and that he was a reporter and press photographer from *The Washington Post* newspaper. He asked his father what his feelings were about being forced to leave his mountain home in this manner, but his father said nothing, staring at him with a dazed, bewildered expression on his face as the flashbulbs popped. But, as Sheriff Peery clamped the handcuffs onto his thick wrists, his father reared up like a spooked horse with a heart-rending keening animal wail of despair, his eyes glazed with raw pain, his teeth bared. With an apologetic clearing of his throat, the sheriff then read aloud the eviction order issued by the Virginia Commission of Conservation and Development.

Jed felt a wave of intense pain wash over him, akin to his father's. He wanted so badly to join his father, to stand beside him in staunch alliance. *To leave with him.* But something told him that his father would not want him to witness his pain and humiliation this way. And he would want him to remain behind to take care of the livestock. They took the aged mountain man down Claw Mountain for the last time, struggling like a wild man.

Jed sat in the tree, hugging its trunk as if he were welded it, feeling his throat tighten, and tears burning his eyes. He was stunned, unable to believe what he had just witnessed. The thing they had dreaded for so many years was finally happening, and there was nothing he could do about it. Though it deeply affected him personally, he had embraced the concept of the Park, with its necessary laws of protection to the wildlife and plant life that proliferated in its boundaries, but the forced removal from the place that he loved with every fiber of his being, was so heart-searing and painful, he knew he would never forget it for as long as he lived . . .

A short while later, eight young men, dressed in telltale blue denim work uniforms, and hats, swarmed up the mountain and over the ridge, yelling and laughing. The young men immediately moved into the cabin and started dragging the bits of homemade furniture, the furniture that had once belonged to his grandfather, and his parent's personal possessions, onto the little clearing of bluegrass outside, piling it into a huge untidy heap. He could spot the handsome talking machine with its huge flower horn amongst the pile, the fancy coal burner and one of his mother's most prized possessions, the parlor lamp that they had kept in their bedroom.

The hogs and chickens, sensing the coming desecration, sent up a squealing, squawking objecting racket. Watching from his leafy perch in numbed shock, Jed saw one of the CCC boys emerge with his mother's chamber pot on his head, doing a comical flat-foot dance on the wooden porch. This raised a howl of crude laughter from the others. Jed thought it was fortunate for him that the chamber pot had been scrubbed with disinfectant, as Dr. Darwin had said that one of the ways the highly contagious "fever" was spread was through infected waste matter.

Another, with a lunatic grin on his face waltzed out the door with a drape wrapped around him like a skirt, while yet another emerged wearing his mother's best Sunday dress. There was much frivolity, hooting and whinnying. One of them carried his father's much-beloved long-barreled, muzzle-loading old Kentucky rifle and added it to the haphazard pile. The last of his father's possessions to be added to the pile were his shoes!

After a while, the removal of possessions from inside the cabin was complete. Jed felt a moment of raw panic as one of the men sprinkled a tin of kerosene on the porch, lit a torch and moved forward to set fire to it, while the others watched him from a short distance away. The flames leapt on the dry wood, enveloping it, spreading quickly until the whole cabin was burning, sending thick, black smoke billowing into the clean, pure air of Eagle Spur. A terrible raw feeling suffused Jed's chest and hot scalding tears blinded him as he watched the hellish flames licking the ancient chestnut logs, destroying, forever, not only his home, with all its precious memories of his beloved mother, but a whole way of life . . .

S lowly, Jed climbed down the tree and walked numbly towards the raging inferno. When the tall, lean, but broad-shouldered, long-haired man approached the CCC boys, his smooth brown face and startling blue eyes greatly belying his thirty-nine years, his calm dignified bearing belying the tumult he felt inside him, they froze with horror, looking instantly foolish and ashamed.

One of them, red-haired, freckled and wholesome-looking, clamped a hand on his hat, cleared his throat and said hoarsely: "Oh, Lawdee be, tell me this here ain't yer place!"

Jed nodded dumbly, grieving tears streaming unashamedly down his cheeks as his anguish gained full expression.

"Say, we ain't meant nuthin' by it. We was jest funnin'. She-et! Sorry!" the same CCC fellow said, unable to look Jed in the eye.

Later, while the CCC boys began to clear the barn for torching, Jed reluctantly chased some of the hogs, hovering around the homesite, into the forest behind Eagle Spur and to freedom, knowing they would be able to survive on its plentiful mast. The lone handsome rooster and fifty-odd chickens that were so recently his mother's pride and joy and which had yielded her a great many eggs for sale at the general store, he gently coaxed one by one from the henhouse into crude portable coops brought by the CCC members for this purpose.

One CCC fellow remarked that he'd never seen such an orderly capture. Those other mountaineers they'd help on their way had all been forced to long chaotic chases characterized by wildly flapping arms and wings, yells and loud squawks. Jed merely nodded, not saying a word. Thankfully, they didn't own much livestock. Cedric, the billy goat, one beloved childhood pet amongst many, had died many years ago.

When they entered the barn, Jed expressed the opinion that they would have great difficulty leading their latest cow, a brown Jersey, still in its stall after early-morning milking, down the steep mountainside, as it had taken a winch to get her up. He immediately regretted his words. One of the CCC members promptly solved the problem by taking out a revolver and shooting sweet lovable old Mildred, with her long languid eyelashes and trusting brown eyes, in the middle of her forehead. She sunk to her knees with a surprised grunt before flopping heavily over onto her side. Blood spurted from the head of this precious beast, in a crimson fountain. Jed's shock was compounded by the fact that he knew that the CCC boys lived under strict, almost military, discipline, living in 100-foot-long barracks, and were not allowed to carry any weapons. He knelt down beside the dead animal and stroked her pale brown hide soothingly till her body finally stopped jerking and her eyes began to glaze.

Jed left the barn then and puked into the grass. Hastily calling to his side his father's two latest coon dogs, a black-and-tan tick and a redbone, named Spud and Moby respectively, before the same fate could befall them, Jed slipped leashes on them retrieved from the barn then he turned and watched as the barn, too, was torched. He watched as the smoke billowed blackly into the air, keenly feeling the excruciating anguish of the moment, silently begging God to forgive these young men, in their ignorance, and trying to keep uppermost in his mind, the need for this cruel and seeming senseless destruction – the urgent need for this Shenandoah Nation Park, which Nature, herself, had cried for so loudly ...

J ed left Eagle Spur holding the coon dogs by their leashes, feeling as if his heart had been ripped out of his chest. Awkwardly carting the furniture and personal possessions down the mountain and onto the waiting lumbering truck left at Horseshoe Hollow below, the CCC men then gave Jed a lift to the Madison jail to see his father. Leaving the coon dogs tied to the legs of chairs in the back of the truck, Jed alighted from the truck and went inside with some of the CCC boys, who seemed somewhat subdued by his somber mood, their former high spirits long ago vanished.

There was a time of awkwardness, for nobody knew where they were supposed to move the furniture and livestock to. A telephone call by the sheriff indicated that there had been some official bungling and no place had been allocated for the last remaining Buchanans in any of the seven relocation sites. They asked Jed where he wanted their possessions moved to, and the first kin Jed thought of was his Uncle Clem and his wife, Aunt Rosie, who he knew had moved recently to the resettlement camp of Ida Valley, with their children and grandchildren. A phone call from Sheriff Peery's office to the general store in Ida

Valley evoked a return call, after some delay, to say they were willing to take him and his father in until alternative arrangements could be made.

Jed was not surprised to hear this willingness to share their home, despite how crowded it must be already. After all, they were kin, and mountain kin always stuck together, especially Bucko kin. After Jed had retrieved his father's shoes, the CCC boys went ahead to Ida Valley to drop their furniture and livestock off, taking the coon dogs with them. Jed was allowed to spend the night in the jail cell with his father, as, with their aim achieved, no one had a mind to press further punishment or charges against his heartbroken father, beyond a single night of incarceration.

The next morning, Sheriff Peery let the somber unspeaking pair out of the cell and personally drove them out to Ida Valley, west of Hawksbill Mountain, in his sheriff's car, leaving them at the gate of the smallholding belonging to their kin. Before he left, the sheriff returned Jed's father's old Kentucky rifle to him, which must have been handed over to him by one of the CCC fellows. The two watched the sheriff's car as it drove away. It left behind an incongruous pair that belonged to another age.

Daunted by the flatness and relative austerity of the surroundings, they stood gazing around them dazedly. Then his father's two coon dogs and the household hounds came bounding up, barking a furious fanfare, and licking at the hands of both his rifle-toting father and himself. Alerted to their arrival, Uncle Clem and Aunt Rosie, with their grown children and noisy grandchildren, rushed out of the house to bid them welcome. They proceeded to proudly show them around the new showpiece, not seeming to notice how quiet they both were.

They were excitedly shown the large frame house, which was painted gleaming white, with a handsome red roof, a front porch across the width of it, supported by wooden beams and surrounded by a low, neat, wooden railing, all painted white. Then they were escorted to the combination barn and the large poultry house, which his mother's chickens and rooster had already claimed as their own. Clucking around contentedly, they, at least, seemed not to be traumatized by the ordeal of their forced removal from the mountains.

The group then moved on to the vegetable storage and meat houses, before going to the hog pen with its fenced hog lot, where a single hog rooted. They bragged that the general store was just down the road rather than half-a-day's walk away and that they were near schools and doctors, and that Clem had already landed a job as a maintenance man. But Zachary Thomas and Jed stood stonily unimpressed, their hearts heavy as mountain boulders. They had mountain dew, hominy and freedom running through their veins, after all. The ascetic value of the magnificent old mountain home could never be replaced by mere modern convenience.

Indeed, the move from Eagle Spur proved too much for his father. Heartbroken and recently bereaved, barely a week after moving into the crowded, noisy lowland home of his relatives, Jed's beloved father died during his sleep. Jed found him lying lifeless on a mattress on the porch. He thought that maybe the old man had caught the "fever" too. But his forehead was cool and his expression relaxed, as if he had just slipped away. Comforted only by the thought that Paw had joined the woman he had loved so deeply, it was a cruel blow to Jed, who, like his father, didn't set well in company. Though he knew his father had never been able to understand him; his profound love of Nature and his hatred of hunting, they had in recent years discovered they had much in common, after all. *Their deep love of the Blue Ridge Mountains – and his mother!*

Without any transport to take his body back to Eagle Spur to be buried next to his mother's, as would be his ardent wish, Jed's father was buried instead under a lone puny tree at his brother's new smallholding in Ida Valley, in distant sight of the Blue Ridge Mountains he loved so well. In sharp contrast to his wife's well-attended funeral, there were only a few family mourners to send him off to the afterlife. Jed had begged them to only tell the rest of his family and the clan of his death, after his burial, and they had obliged, knowing that his father, with his highly reclusive soul, would have wanted it that way. And so, Jed mused, the grand old mountain man from Claw Mountain, the eldest of the Buckos, and widower of the woman who had tamed the once fearsome and notorious mountain clan, had finally departed this earth from strange, unfamiliar lowland soil, leaving Jed to face an uncertain future in an untried modern world that had completely evaded him for the thirty-nine years of his former mountain life . . .

* * *

*T*he relocation of the Blue Ridge mountain people to make way for the Shenandoah National Park was considered by many to be a good thing for them, a public service, at last bringing them into the 20th century to join the rest of mainstream America. They were, after all, considered "backward hillbillies" by those tasked with the establishment of the Park. Miriam Sizer, a teacher hired by the Commonwealth of Virginia to study the mountain people, said of them: '. . . Steeped in ignorance, wrapped in self-satisfaction and complacency, possessed of little or no ambition, little sense of citizenship, little comprehension of law, or respect for the law, these people present a problem that demands and challenges the attention of thinking men and women . . .' When the Park was established there were still 432 families, about 2,250 individuals, living within its boundaries. Some of them had been unable to leave their farms before they were forced to,* *because they had no savings in a world where barter was the currency, no marketable skills, nothing to help them get started in the unknown world that lay beyond the mountains. Others clung fiercely onto their homes, hard times or not; because the mountains were home. But all of them had to leave and face the strange and frightening world on the outside. A few managed to do so without federal or state assistance. The Resettlement Administration of the Department of Agriculture set up seven resettlement communities close to the Park, where a displaced family could buy a house and land with no down payment, and a 30-year mortgage at very low interest. Many families moved to these communities. The rest were resettled by the Virginia State Welfare Department. Only 17 elderly souls were given special use permits to stay on in their homes within the Park, under strict conditions. One of the hardest things for these hardworking independent people to take was losing control over their own lives. They were told what to do, where to go, and had no say in anything that concerned them. Nobody seemed to understand what it cost the mountain people to lose their homes in such a harsh and relentless way. They didn't only lose their homes, they lost a cherished way of life. And more than anything, it robbed them of a priceless heritage that only Nature in all her glory can provide. After all, man needs bread for the soul as much as bread for the table, and they had plenty of both in the mountains, even though life was tough. Zachary Thomas Buchanan and his elder son, Jed, were amongst the last of those forced to leave their beloved mountain homes. Along with many other displaced mountain families, they left behind their hearts and their souls . . .*

The End

Author's Notes

The "Claw Mountain" of my book is not real, but a product of my imagination, although I have geographically "placed" it where the real Jones Mountain is situated in the Upper Staunton Valley of the Blue Ridge Mountains of Virginia, and have used other license, geographically speaking. For dramatic effect, I have named this valley the Wilderness Valley, to complement a real 1,122-acre unspoiled tract called the Wilderness positioned there and have made the whole valley totally uninhabited in my story, to increase the sense of isolation. The Staunton River was known as Wilson Run by the mountain folk at the time my story is set, and I have used this name in my story.

I have weaved into my story the major events that affected the lives of the Blue Ridge mountain people over the period 1899-1939. The winter of 1899/1900, I described in my book as the worst and coldest natural catastrophe to hit the northern Blue Ridge Mountains in living memory, becoming known as "The Big Freeze" amongst the mountain people. It must be said, however, that although I wrote this particular piece from my imagination many years ago, I was absolutely astounded when I recently came across a piece on the Internet, while hunting for something else, which described a great cold wave across the whole of America, in 1899, with record cold being set in Virginia, in February, 1899. According to that source, and many others I also found on the Internet, it was one of the most severe and longest in duration on record. It became known as "The Great Arctic Outbreak". *Such synchronicity!*

While there was definitely a culture of violence in some notorious hollows in the Blue Ridge Mountains and a kind of rough "frontier" justice existent in them, the fictional characters of Claw Mountain are not meant to represent the majority of mountain folk dwelling in the Blue Ridge at that time, most of whom were good, honorable, hard-working and highly independent people. However, I hope I have succeeded in realistically portraying mountain life and mountain people in general.

The former owner of Skyland, George Freeman Pollock, actually existed. No story about the famed summer resort could be written without including in it this colorful, larger-than-life character, now long-deceased. I hope and believe I have portrayed him realistically. I have also mentioned some of the other "characters" of Skyland, like Will Grigsby, the Negro head waiter and band leader, Sam Sours, the Mail Carrier, Augustus B. Heaton, who was known as the "Patriarch" of Skyland, and Dr. George W. Johnson, a physician who was resident at Sky even from land, to further lend the story a further ring of authenticity. I have also used poetic license by weaving into my story, actual events that took place at Skyland, while using my own characters and dialogues, to give it an added sense of depths and realism.

Little is known about the ancient primitive Indian tribe, the Senedoes. However, huge burial mounds such as the one described in my book have been found at sites in Virginia, some of which have been attributed to the Senedoes, who were known to bury their dead in this manner. They were known to be a small peaceable tribe that had little encampments next to rivers, and were hunters/gatherers. With a dearth of detailed data about their customs and ornamentation, even from the Smithsonian Institute of the American Indian, I have used mainly those similar to the Siouan Indian tribes that were settled in the Shenandoah Valley in the 17th century. After I had finished my book, however, in a last-gasp effort to discover more about the Senedo Indians, I came across a novel called *"Through Buffalo Gap"* by John Corns. Unbelievably, it was also about the the massacre of the Senedo Indians and the lone survivor, a female. I sent to America for the book and though our stories are very different, I was able to glean some important details from it, such as the gold honor circle for those of the tribe who had led an honourable life and details of how the Senedo lived. Thus, I owe a deep debt of gratitude to John Corns and take this opportunity to thank him. The eventual fate of the Senedo tribe is real, but the male Senedo Indian character – also the lone survivor of the massacre – in my book is a product of my imagination, as are all the events involving him.

Although based on actual historical events and an authentic background of mountain life, this is a work of fiction. In a very few instances, I have loosely based my own character and dialogues on some true-life character and situations, changing them to suit my story, as I did with Skyland characters and events. For instance, there was a real doctor, who heroically served the mountain people during the Flu' Epidemic of 1918, as does my fictional character, Doc Adams but, otherwise, he bears no known resemblance to my character. So, with the exception of these and the afore-mentioned characters at Skyland and some historical figures, all other characters are entirely products of my imagination and any resemblance to actual persons, living or dead, is entirely coincidental.

I began my five-book saga, of which *Falling Leaves and Mountain Ashes* is the first, way back in 1982, after visiting the Shenandoah National Park the year before, when the mountains of the Blue Ridge in early spring captured my soul. Then I learned the history of the displaced mountain people who had lived there before the formation of the Park and were finally forced out, their unique and tragic story captured my imagination. I sincerely hope that this book serves to honor them in some small way . . .

Acknowledgements

I started writing and researching my five-book saga way back in 1981 and, sadly, in that time many of the people that I have to thank have now passed on. Others may have since passed on without my knowledge.

I would like to extend my sincere and grateful thanks to all those persons who helped me with the research that went into this particular novel. They include my dear Front Royal, Virginia, friends: my old stalwart, **W. Briley Morrison**, who kept me well-supplied with great support and encouragement over many years, as well as information and many books about the mountain people, the Shenandoah National Park and Front Royal. He also took me for one of several drives I had into the Shenandoah National Park. The late **B Ney Scheu**er, who gave me information about the Shenandoah National Park and Front Royal. The late **Alvin Dohme**, author of many books and magazine articles, wrote the invaluable *Shenandoah, The Valley Story* and helped me with my research into the early Virginian Indians, the mountain people and the Shenandoah National Park. The late **John Stoneberger**, a genuine "hillbilly", author of the charming *Memories of a Lewis Mountain Man*, who many years ago, spawned in me a great love of the mountain people of the Blue Ridge with his warm letters and writing, and who also sent me many invaluable books about them and their lives. The late **Hugh "Spike" Naylor** and his wife, **Ann "Maud" Naylor** (late of Front Royal). Spike was involved in the saga of the formation of the Shenandoah National Park and helped me with my research on it. Maud helped me with my research into life in the White House at the time my story is set (her father was a presidential aide, who worked in the White House, her playground, the corridors of this famous residence). She also supplied me with books about Virginia and the Virginian Indians. And lastly, **John D. Weaver** (late of Front Royal), esteemed author of *The Brownsville Raid, The Senator and the Share-croppers Son*, the amusing *As I Live and Breathe,* and a collection of mountain tales entitled *Hear the Wing Blow and other Stories,* who helped me with my research into the mountain people and gave me much encouragement and publishing advice. There are many other people I would like to thank, such as the **staff of the Dickey Ridge Information Center** in the Shenandoah National Park, whose names I failed to record. In conclusion, I would like to point out that any mistakes that may have been made in the gathering and transposal of this research are mine and mine alone.

My very dear friend, **Krista-Jo Merget**, who I met in a very fateful way in New York in 1988, fought the good fight for this book, and introduced me, electronically, to Annette Handley-Chandler, once a Hollywood high-achiever, now of Sag Harbor, USA. (See below.) Krista-Jo is a warm, compassionate and highly intelligent human being, who fights hard for justice and her own special cause. I am privileged to be able to call her my friend.

My dear, dear friend and Soul Sister, **Annette Handley-Chandler**, who I have never met, but with whom I have developed such a warm, meaningful relationship, over the email waves, over years. This highly talented, accomplished, intelligent and compassionate lady is extremely modest about her astonishing achievements. She gave me much invaluable advice regarding my book when it was still in manuscript form, including advising me to change the title, for which I am so thankful. *Thank you for your invaluable input, and for having such unwavering belief in this book, dear Annette. Your unstinting support – and wonderful friendship – has meant so much to me!*

June Johnson and **Trish Boshoff** were good enough to read through my massive manuscript and give me many worthy suggestions, as well as pointing out errors I'd missed. They both have my deepest gratitude for their contributions to this book. *Many thanks for your observations and suggestions, gals!*

My kind and caring brother-in-law, **David Alexander**, gave me the data I needed about cameras in the nineteenth century. He's a gentle genius! *Thanks, Davy!*

Special thanks goes to my nephew, **Jason Oxley**, for his unbelievable patience in sorting out the many computer problems with my ancient Apple 11e computer, for his kindness and generosity in supplying me with an incredible updated computer system after struggling so long on such antiquated equipment, and for the many other favors he has done for me concerning this book. *Jase, you're terrific!*

Another nephew, **Bruce Johnson**, was also a star for sorting out many computer problems for me during the course of the book's evolvement. Always so willing! *Thanks, Bru!*

My dear, dear friend, **Felicity Keats-Morrison.** This wonderful extraordinary human being is a gifted right-brain specialist, publisher, and writer. *Thank you, Twin Star, for being such an inspiration to me, for your warmth, grand vision, unfailing faith and generosity – and for believing in my book!*

Where would I have been without **John Scotson Abbey**? I am so grateful to him for his long and valued friendship, his unfailing belief in my writing, his invaluable research assistance over the years – and for so many great memories! *Thanks, Jean Abbey!!!!*

On a personal note:

My wacky and wonderful brother-in-law, **John Oxley**, for replacing my old jalopy with "Silver Wings" and giving me so many other things out of his deep and generous pockets. *Thank you, darling John!*

My darling niece, **Michelle Haldane** – the Girl with Magic in her Soul – and her wonderful husband, **Bryan**. *Thanks for your warmth and unstinting generosity over many years!*

My witty and wonderful (fellow) Aquarian brother-in-law, **Michael Johnson**, for loving my book so much and being one of its most ardent supporters. *Here's to ya, Mike!!!*

I would like to thank *all* the members of my family, young and old, and my faithful friends (*you know who you are!*), simply for being as precious to me as they are, and for all the love and caring they have given me over the 30 years it has taken me to write this and other books in the 5-book series. *I have been truly blessed.*

My special and grateful thanks go to the wonderful and gifted physician, Dr K.M. Cassim, now a resident of Australia, who saved my life through his incredible medical skill. His smiling humility, the rare high quality of his care, and his dedication towards his patients know no bounds.

Lastly, I would like to thank the authors of the following books, which proved to be an invaluable source of information and inspiration to me in the writing of **Falling Leaves and Mountain Ashes,** and from which I extracted a few incidents and made them my own by using my own characters and dialogues:

A History of the Valley of Virginia by Samuel Kerchival
Blue Ridge Parkway - The Story Behind the Scenery by Margaret Rose Rives
Cold Mountain Tales by Maryon Wood Harper
Driftwood Valley by Theodora C. Stanwell-Fletcher; Rhonda M. Love; Windell Berry
Foxfire 2 various author contributions edited by Elliot Wigginton.
Great Smoky Mountains - The Story Behind the Scenery by Rita Cantu
Hear the Wind Blow and Other Stories by John D. Weaver
Herbert Hoover's Hideaway by Darwin Lambert
In the Light of the Moon by Reed L. Engle
Indians in Seventeenth-Century Virginia by Ben C. McCary
Lost Trails and Forgotten People - The Story of Jones Mountain by Tom Floyd
Ma's Cookin' - Mountain Recipes by "Sis and Jake"
Memories of a Lewis Mountain Man by the late John Stoneberger
Prohibition: A Lesson in the Futility (and Danger) of Prohibiting: Internet article by an unknown author.
Recollections - The People of the Blue Ridge Remember by Dorothy Noble Smith
Shenandoah Heritage - The Story of the People Before the Park by Carolyn and Jack Reed
Shenandoah National Forest Impressions by Pat and Chuck Blackley
Shenandoah - The Story Behind the Scenery by Hugh Crandall

Shenandoah - The Valley Story by Alvin Dohme
Shenandoah Vestiges - What the Mountain People Left Behind by Carolyn and Jack Reeder
Skyland - The Heart of the Shenandoah National Park by George Freeman Pollock
The Appalachian Trail by Ronald M Fisher
The Blue Ridge by William A. Bake
The Chisolms by Evan Hunter
The Dean Mountain Story by Gloria Dean
The Foxfire Book edited by Elliot Wigginton.
The Man Who Moved a Mountain by Richard C. Davids
The Ragged Trousered Philanthropists by Robert Tressel
Through Buffalo Gap by John Corns
Way Back in the Hills by James C. Hefley
Shenandoah National Park Website – the below-mentioned articles by unknown authors
{Chp. 1: SNP Boosters}
(Chp. 2: Commssion on Conservation and Development}
{Chp. 3: Blanket condemnation}
{Chp. 4: Skyline Drive and the CCC}
{Chp. 5: The Story of the removals}

Brenda George

Further Selected Praise for "Falling Leaves and Mountain Ashes"

'...I have a library of some 2000 books, of which only about 50 are fiction, because I'm not interested in fiction. But I am so enjoying this book, I am just loving it, and am so impressed with it – it is too beautiful! It is so beautifully descriptive, the leaves and the snow and the mountain that I feel as if I am right there... the characters are so real, they are alive. I have never been so excited about a book in my life. (Later.) It was fantastic, absolutely fantastic! Have you ever read a book where you want to read slowly because you know you are getting near the end? That was your book. I really and truly loved it! Your characters were real-live characters – magnificent.. And I could see everything and felt I was there.* **Colleen Ritchie**

'... absolutely loving the book – I'm right inside the main character's head, and can't put the book down, often reading paragraphs over and over again because of the words you have used... The book is so precious I will never lend it out to anybody. And I am going to start reading it again immediately after I am finished. You are so deep and understand human nature so well.' (Later). 'Falling Leaves and Mountain Ashes' was GREAT! ... I couldn't put it down. (The scene) ... about the barn was so evocatively descriptive I was in there with Mary. There are many such passages in the book. Mary and Zachary will forever be etched in my mind, and Eli and Obediah actually drew some sympathy from me, especially Eli who was so damaged emotionally. I knew nothing about the mountain folk and customs, but now I feel I could go and dwell with them, having learned so much about them from your hugely well-researched book...* **Lisa Sutherland**

'I have just finished reading it TWICE. I loved it so much. I began reading it again the moment I finished it the first time. It was magnificent and I loved the characters and lived with them. I couldn't believe the research that had been done on the book. I even wrote a detailed assessment on the book afterwards so she could see how the author had constructed it.' (Later.) '...I can't remember ever being transported in time and place as I was when I read your masterful descriptions of people, places and events in this book. Right from the first chapter, one feels one must get to know what's eating at Eli for him to behave in that fashion. I simply had to get to know these poor disturbed people better. Your portrayal of the characters was nothing short of superb. I felt as if I had met them myself, and that I had to know more about them, what made them tick. What an *absolute tragedy it all was, but through it all ran the wonderful character of Mary, and supported later by Zachary Thomas, not forgetting that Jediah made a very positive statement with his personality. I am waiting with bated breath to see how he, with his mission, is going to change things.'* **Heather Chorn**

'Started reading the book. Cannot put it down – fantastic!!!!!!!!!!!!!!!! My poor family is being neglected. Every spare moment my nose is in the book – went to sleep at four on Sunday morning!" (Later.) *'It was absolutely fantastic, stunning, stunning, stunning, with brilliant writing. I loved the characters and the story, which was very, very sad in the end. It haunted me and I haven't been so moved by a book since I read "A Man Cannot Cry" many years ago.* ("A Man Cannot Cry" was written by the author's sister, Gloria Keverne, and edited by Brenda George!)' **Debbie Khan**

'Oh, fantastic! She's a brilliant writer. Bloody good! She and Gloria are both brilliant writers." (He was referring to Gloria Keverne, the author of the international bestseller "A Man Cannot Cry", which Brenda George edited.) *Referring to Brenda's book, he said over and over how he felt like he was right there in that place, and that the characters were so real to him, he felt like that were living beings and that he knew them personally. Regarding the characters, he said how much he loved the main character, Mary, who did so much for the people who lived on Claw Mountain, and through her goodness, changed their lives. And he even fpund himself sympathizing with the main antagonist, Eli, especially when he understood why he became the man he did.'* **Michael Johnson**

'...brilliant, absolutely stunning, and I could not put it down. You are such an unbelievably talented writer I even found sympathy for the main antagonist, Eli. I love all the characters, especially Mary, Zachary Thomas, the spunky little mountain child, Emma, and Mary's little mystic son, Jed. I found the end very moving and sad, and I never wanted it to end. I want to read it again in a few months time, because I am so haunted by it.' **Jenni Riddell**

*'I loved every single word of the book...absolutely stunning..my .previous all-time favourite book was "Gone With the Wind" but the author has set a new standard in excellence with her brilliant writing. In fact I don't know what I can possibly read after this because she has set such a high standard...so involved with the characters that I could not put the book down and felt really heartsore when I finished it, because I just wanted it to carry on and on...so moving at times that I was reduced to tears. '***Norma Piquito**

'I enjoyed Brenda George''s book thoroughly, thoroughly, thoroughly!! You know how well read I am... Well, when I say a book has a future, believe me, it has a future! I wouldn't be in the least surprised if Brenda's book receives film rights! I found it fascinating, and a truly fine read. Oh, without question, I've really enjoyed 'Falling Leaves and Mountain Ashes'!'
Vivienne Grant

'I've just finished reading your book and I didn't want it to end – I wanted it to go on forever. It's divine! Absolutely divine! I loved it so much I didn't want it to end. It's so different. But I'm sure I'm only one in a long line of people to say how fantastic it is. You must have because it IS fantastic. Like Gloria, you describe everything so well, you feel as if you are right there. What is it about you two Keverne girls that you can both write so brilliantly? You write differently, but both so descriptively that it comes to life.'
Vio Cameron

*'...I felt as if I was living amongst the mountain people. I love the charact-ers, and think the story is amazing! I didn't want it to end! ...wonderful book. I'd dragged it out as best I could...savoured every word...I smiled. I cried. My heartbeat increased. My heart filled with love. Loved it. Loved it, Loved it!!'***Jan Kernan**

'I loved it. 'I loved the descriptions of the mountains and the eagles... the scene when the eagles attack Obediah mademe go cold. Was it something true or from your imagination? (Imagination.) *Because I had a similar experience with owls, and the whole thing in the book was utterly astonishing and believable. I felt as if I was there, and that the characters were all so believable, the story so compelling, I could not put it down.I gave it to my husband, PIERRE, a very recently retired banker, to read. He has been so busy he had not read a book in about four years. He is a very reticent man, but he raves about the book to everybody he meets about how fantastic it is. He says he has never read such a well-researched book in his life, and that he just HAS to meet the author.* (Later) *'This book has been an exciting experience worthy of being made into a top class film. You are so precise in your descriptions of the area (Blue Ridge Mountains) and the people (mountain men and women) that I could see the words I read like a movie in my mind. I especially enjoyed the part where the eagles surrounding the mountain, reacted to sinister intruders, as this brought back memories of my own, of a female Great Horned Owl when I was a young girl. I was very curious about a nest the owl had on the ledge of a cliff and, amazingly, she would allow*

me to climb up to the nest to observe the growth of her owlets. However, when my uncle tried to climb up the female owl attacked him, embedding her claws into the back of his jacket as she attempted to pull him off the cliff face. The owl's acceptance of me continued until she sent the last owlet into its first flight. Brenda, thank you, for bringing back memories of how sensitive nature is to our intentions. **Di Poupard - internationally known horse whisperer**

'I have never, ever read such magnificent descriptions in my whole life!...similes the author used are quite amazing...so evocative I could see it all. I adored the characters and actually cried a few times during the course of the book. I can't rave about it enough.' **Hazel Foster**

'...loved the story and the characters... excellent...couldn't put it down...my husband kept complaining I never talked to him anymore, but I got cross with him and said I simply couldn't put it down, especially as I was at a particularly exciting and dramatic part... it would make a wonderful movie. I would love to hold an Oprah-style dinner to discuss every facet of the book with the author.' **Geraldine Talbot**

'...magnificent book...characters really stand out... Eli is such an intriguing and believable character...I will remember Mary, the main character, for the rest of my life!' **Neville Hodgson**

'Absolutely loved it... the end deeply, deeply moving, and I cried.' **Dawn Darby**

'As for your book, it is wonderful! I got lost in it and this is what I love in a reading experience ... Your book deserves all the accolades it is getting! Amazing!' **Annette Handley-Chandler**

'... it was beautiful, absolutely beautiful...characters were amazing... descriptions of the mountains so magnificent and so real, I felt as if I was actually there. This book, this woman – It's so amazing... I HAVE to meet her.' **Karen Worth**

'It was divine, just divine! The book was absolutely brilliant.' **Joy Moodley**

'...Like everything else in life, death was not easy. It was hard-won as were all worthwhile things, she had found' – *is one of the greatest lines I've read in any story...It's been a long time, perhaps never, in my so-called adult life, that a book has made me cry. A truly fantastic book!'* **Shaun Ebelthite**

'... *so compelling, I couldn't wait to go to bed every night just to read it. I did not want it to end..I was .fascinated by the character of Eli... one the best books I have ever read, and I absolutely loved it.'* **Celia Vergari**

'I am *an avid reader, and have read many, many books, but I've never read anything like this book. I could not put it down, and would often read till late into the night. I found Eli an intriguing character who, despite his evil deeds, redeems himself. I could not help empathizing with him.'* **Peet Oelofse**

'This *is a fantastic book! Fantastic! Fantastic! It's a book I'll read five, six, seven, eight, nine, ten times!'* **Colin Cason**

'I *just could not put it down, to the extent that my husband commented that it must be some book, because he'd never seen me like that with any other book I've read... an excellent story about pioneer life... loved the characters.'* **Tessa Barnard.**

'What *an amazing book! ... definitely a film in the making... the best I've ever read.'* **Sharon Hartog**

'This *is a book that gets you into trouble, because you can't do anything but read it. You can't work!You can't cook! You can't sleep! It is a wonderful book. So different'* **Claudette Jackson**

'I *could not put this book down! It's spellbinding...descriptions are magnificent. In other books, I skip description and carry on with the story, but with this one I read every word, and felt as if I was right there. As for the twists in the end!!'* **Beverley Biggar**

'I *read it nonstop and it is a masterpiece. I could not put it down, and I felt I was right back in those times.'* **Ngoni Zenda**

'I *could not put it down, and kept getting annoyed at my wife, because she would borrow it to read, and I couldn't find it. We both read and absolutely loved it.'* **Luke Karamba**

'I *absolutely loved it...it's stunning ...The eagles and their greatness and sheer magnificence were a truly spiritual experience for me...beautifully descriptive with wonderful relationships and a diverse range of characters.'* **Shirley Brown**

'*What a book! A lot of the time I had tears running down my face. And that twist at the end....what can I say? A total surprise.*' **Ann Gardner**

'*...absolutely loved the book and the characters...the descriptions of the mountain and the mountain people were excellent and evocative. Mary was such a strong woman, that she is an inspiration to all women even today. The story gripped me right from the start. It had so many layers, and was so different and had such depths.*' **Neetha Singh**

'*Oh, Brenda, it's absolutely beautiful. Just amazing, and I'm loving it. I'm more than halfway through and I just can't put it down. I've told all my friends about it, and said they just have to read this amazing book. I loved your sister's book "A Man Cannot Cry" and read it at least five times. You can't compare the two books, as such, as they are so different, but both of them make you feel as if you are right there. I can just picture Eli with his scarred face. And Zack. I can't wait to go to bed to night, and my daughter makes sure that I have a drink and your book is put on my pillow, because she knows how much I am loving reading it. I sometimes read till all hours even though I have to get up early for work.*
Oh, it's absolutely beautiful!...This just has to be made into a movie...it would make an epic film...It is so authentic, it was like reading history.' **Lesley Robin-son**

'*It was .excellent, a remarkable piece of work. It was so descriptive and real, I felt I was right there. I loved the characters, Zachary Thomas and the antagonist, Eli, and the main character, Mary, was in a class of her own.. The parts at the end with Eli moved me so deeply I had to put the book aside for a while, before reading again. I am an avid reader, reading about twenty books a month.*'
Sewraj Ghurparsadh

'*...remarkable book. Wow! What a brilliant work of art! Stunning!...enthralled throughout*'! **Sally Bosch**

'*...out of 100, I give the book 100... Fantastic!..I .couldn't put it down.*' **Jenny Cairns**

'*...it was brilliant. 'It is beautiful, beautiful! I love the characters, and the writing is so descriptive, it felt like I was there! It is beautiful, beautiful...stunningly BRILLIANT! So warm and tender...characters so real...It is very moving... I was so enthralled all the way through...it moved me so much ...The disclosure at the* *end comes as a shock... thank you for the thrill reading it gave me...My goodness, I just couldn't put the damn thing down...I was completely enthralled by the style and presentation.Your attention to detail is absolutely stupendous... I felt the pain and anguish, joy and laughter of the "Blue Ridge Mountain" folk. The Buchanan stronghold on "Claw Mountain" while the crowning glory of "Eagles Claw" (Eagle Spur) is magnificent. Written with such warmth and candour about the things of nature and humanity that I am almost persuaded that Mary Harley is the epitome of Brenda George?.. And, my goodness, what a climax to this superb tale...an exceptional story.* **Joe Naicker**

'Absolutely love it! FANTASTIC! I've read many books but this is the best!'
Estelle Hinckley

'There is genius in this book. It's an exciting book, and uplifting. The author's love of nature is apparent – the love of nature comes through in the writing.' **Lynda Wyngaard**

'I am really, really enjoying the book. I can't put it down and I even sit in the bath to read, and till 1 o'clock in the morning. I have you to thank for introducing me to reading – I've never read a book from cover to cover before, always getting bored after a few pages/chapters. This book has now given me an appetite for reading.' **Shirley Freeman**

'I have just finished reading your novel "Falling Leaves and Mountain Ashes" twice...I found the characters to be so real. I was so moved at times that I teared and teared and teared. It is a wonderful book. How did you manage to write such a book?'In almost fifty years of reading many books I have never come across one that was so brilliantly written. It was very interesting to read about Mary who sacrificed many years of her unselfish life so others could live better under those harsh conditions. While reading, teardrops came from my eyes. I read the book twice because I couldn't help it! It is one of the best books I have read in my life.' **Cyril James**

'Your book is out of this world! It's breathtaking. I couldn't put it down! I just couldn't stop reading it! The characters are just wonderful.. This book...this book...is really something special!' **Maureen Webstock**

'...It's magnificent and marvellous!' **Richie Dickson**

'I LOVE your book! It's really good and I even cried in a few places. You really are a very good writer.' **Sandy Dixon**

'I loved it! It was excellent, and you are such a good writer I found myself reading until three o'clock in the morning.' **Liz Bruce**

'I read the novel and found it EXCELLENT, with fantastic characters and story, and the most beautiful cover – it's stunning.' **Ester Lee**

'It was excellent.' **Vanessa Talbot**

'I am three-quarters of the way through, and it is too beautiful for words.' **Deborah Edwards**

'My husband and I both thoroughly enjoyed your book Falling Leaves and Mountain Ashes. . . a really good book. . . Your research and dedication easily rivals Wilbur Smith. Please put me on your contact list for the rest of the series. Thanks for a really good read.' **Theresa Spuyt**

'I read your book in a week and it was a magnificent read. It was like "GONE WITH THE WIND", but even better.I loved Mary and Zachary Thomas and the way their love story developed. There were magnificent passages in it and the characters were very real. I loved all the parts with the Jed and the Red Indian. I'm going to read it for a second time...The characters I loved were, of course, the "good ones" – Mary and Zack, Jed, the Doc, and Emma. Eli, I hated, but at the end, I could understand why he turned out so evil after his father's terrible hold over him. The book had tremendous power and the graphic description made me feel part of it all, especially Claw Mountain and the Red Indian.' (Later) *'I did read it a second time, and reiterate how much I loved all the parts with Jed and the Red Indian. I hope that Jed appears in the next book of the series.* (The author assured him that Jed is, in fact, the main character of "Song of the Shenandoah", soon to be published.) *I'll write later to tell of the particular parts I enjoyed – there are so many of them.'* **Mervyn Askew – a retired English teacher**

'I'm writing to you regarding your book "Falling Leaves and Mountain Ashes". Throughout the week it took me to read the book I could barely put it down, I felt as though I was living with Mary and Zack on Claw mountain and that I could feel all of the emotions that they felt. I think that the story was very interesting and it definitely increased my knowledge of how mountain people lived in the

past and of all the difficulties and challenges they had to face...I thought that the book was very descriptive and well written and I look forward to reading more of your stories. Thank you for a lovely story.' **Jamie Black**

'I really loved it. It should be a movie. Beautiful scenery. Done so lovely.' **Jenny Foord**

'Stunning! I absolutely loved it! My sister is reading it now.' **Carol Beijer**

'Very impressed. I enjoyed it because the characters and setting were very good. I read it in a few days. I couldn't put it down!' **Andrea**

'I loved it, and that something beautiful came out of heartbreak (the Shenandoah National Park).' **Rob Hill**

'Characters very strong. Story very good. Mary was wonderful.' ***Judith Kirby***

'Absolutely loved it. So real. A masterpiece.' **Grechen Green**

'Loved it. It was excellent. It was a lovely, lovely story. The descriptions of the scenery were fantastic! I was right there in the story.' **Millie Russell**

'Loved it. Absolutely amazing. So real. Mary so determined. It was an eye-opener. Really, really inspiring.' **Michelle Gran**

'It was bought for me by my wife, Sharyn , and I told her I had find the author, because I've read the book and was so impressed by it. I wanted to meet and discuss it with her. What a very different story. Wonderful. Everyone so true to life. Fastastic – it's almost like Eli is the main character. So real, it seemed like a true story. Kerry Russell in "August Rush" might be a good actress to play Mary in the movie.' **Lance McNeil**

'A gem of a book. I simply could not put it down! Beautifully written. Can't wait for the second book, "Song of the Shenandoah"' **Di Sclanders**

'Both my wife and I read it. What an inspirational story! Very heart-warming! Very captivating and earthy. The characters were all believable, all had different characteristics. Mary is the best character, but Eli is a fantastic antagonist. It was incredible. What I found so amazing was how in the end the level of violence

in the clan had been calmed. It was so well done. Thank you for writing such a lovely story!' **Tom MacQuet**

'Excellent! Really loved it! I really enjoyed the characters, especially Zachary Thomas.' **Peter Rutsch**

'I'm telling all my friends about what fantastic book it is. It's the first time I've read in the toilet. Beautifully descriptive.. Can recommend it to anybody. I lived the book. Every character was perfect!' **Shirley Serra**

'This book is brilliant, absolutely brilliant. You are a star. It's excellent. Oh my, I'm nearly finished and where's my family going to go? Love it! I can't wait to read the next book in the series "Song of the Shenandoah". **Edith Sturgeon**

'I found "Falling Leaves and Mountain Ashes" rivitting. I couldn't put it down. It was lovely. A period of history come to life'. **Gilda de Freitas**

'Unputdownable! Absolutely! I was sad when I finished it. I loved Zachary Thomas. So real.' **Annie Junge**

'Fantastic! Phenomenal! I absolutely loved every word! I ignored my whole family while i was reading it.' **Jenny Green**

'You must have done so much research. Absolutely enthralling. The main character was very brave.' **Denise Upfold**

'You've got such an imagination! There were so many facts. Research superb!' **Billy Dicks**

'Absolutely brilliant. I couldn't put it down. Loved the characters and found Eli fascinating.' ***Anne Brennan***

'I loved your book. You made the mountains come alive.' **Karen Evans**

'It was a beautiful read and brought the mountain people to life. Loved it! I really, really loved it!' **Ingrid Markton**

'A very memorable book. Wonderful story. Really lovely.' **Tina Warby**

'It was absolutely fabulous! I lived it!' **Pat Webb**

'Read it in hospital, and couldn't put it down. Fascinating characters. Eli is brilliant. Mary very strong but humble. Very, very good!' **Liz du Plessis**

'Beautiful! Vivid! I felt like I was there.' **Cheryl Dormer**

'Amazing. Best book I've read in a long, long time! Another one, please!' **Danee Deocan**

'I absolutely loved it , you made me feel part of it and the descriptions of the scenery were magnificent - I can't wait to see the movie! I will recommend your book to as many people as I can! Good Luck!' **Monica Allanson**

'I read your book and it was wonderful. It lends itself to a movie. My husband bought it for me and I was very selfish because I couldn't stop reading it! It was fantastic, absolutely fantastic! Ever read a book you don't want to get to the end? Yours was such a book. I really and truly loved it. It had real live characters. All the characters were magnificent!' **Paige**

'It was brilliant. It had a lot and could hold you. Very real characters, some very dysfunctional. The characters were so real. Well done, well done! Very good! Very good!' **Carol Anderson**

'It was a beautiful read and brought the mountain people to life. Loved it! I really, really loved it' **Ingrid Markton!**

'Enthralling! I could not put it down! Read it in 36 hours straight!'
Darryl Tammadge

'Very good! Wonderful surprise to get a book from a craft market and discover how very impressed I was by it.' **Win Johnstone**

'Brilliant read...my fiancé read and loved it. Enjoyed the characters. Couldn't put it down. Fantastically put-together book! Highly recommended.' **Veronica Taylor**

'A very memorable book. Wonderful story. Really lovely **Tina Warby**

' It was absolutely fabulous! I lived it!' **Pat Webb**

'Beautiful! Vivid! I felt like I was living in the book. It transported me!' **Cheryl Dormer**

'I absolutely loved it...feel part of it and the descriptions of the scenery were magnificent - I can't wait to see the movie!' **Monica Allanson**

'Both my twin sister and myself LOVED IT! We hated to have to stop reading. You are indeed a very gifted writer. What a wonderful story – we felt we were right there. This was the best birthday present my hubby bought me ever. I did not at first understand the title, but now that I have finished it, could not have been anything else. The cover is beautiful **Gail van Staden**.

'Brilliant! Characters awesome. (The author's) mind is brilliant. Same level as Stephen King's – keeping me from sleep!' **Paddy Lottering**

'It's beautiful! Such command of the English language. I felt I could even empathize with Eli.' **Jeannette Dunn**

'The book is fantastic! I couldn't put it down...such a phenomenal author.' **Cyndi Naude**

'...It's too beautiful for words.' **Deborah Edwards**

'I was thoroughly enthralled. It was a very different background. The characters were very vivid. Excellent, heartwarming, with lots of suspense. Eli was horrible, but such a sad character. I loved it. Brilliant. Thanks very much.' **Laureen Grebe**

'I have just finished your book and it was so interesting. I couldn't put it down. I really enjoyed it. It's amazing how the main character coped with it all. I loved it and the characters. I really love your descriptions. As for Eli – I wouldn't want to meet him. The first reverend was so awful' **Wendy Pellewe**.

'I am really enjoying the book. Well done, it is lovely. My favourite character is the mountain child, Emma.' **Bernadette Buitendach**